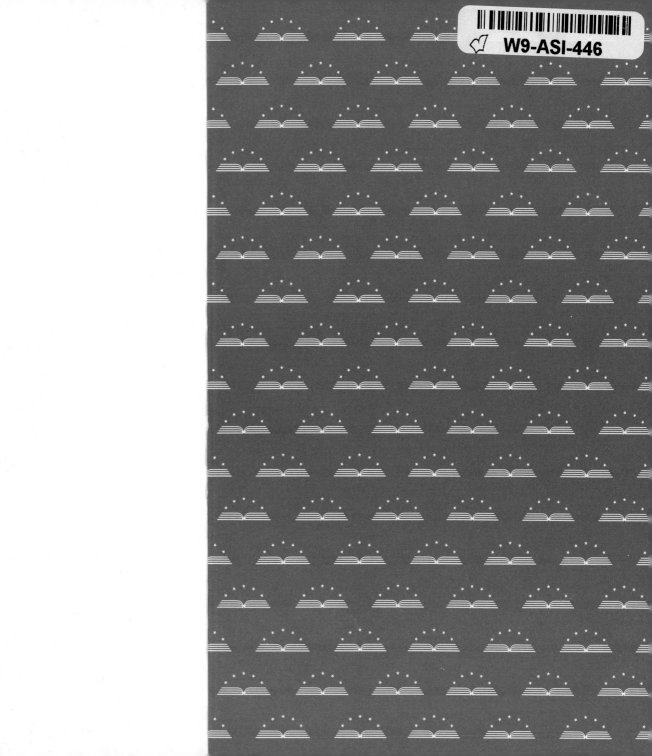

JAMES FENIMORE COOPER

# JAMES FENIMORE COOPER

## SEA TALES
*The Pilot*
*The Red Rover*

THE LIBRARY OF AMERICA

Manufactured in the United States of America

KAY SEYMOUR HOUSE AND THOMAS L. PHILBRICK
WROTE THE NOTES FOR THIS VOLUME

*The texts in this volume are from The Writings of James Fenimore Cooper, Kay Seymour House, Editor-in-Chief, and James P. Elliott, Chief Textual Editor, sponsored by Clark University and the American Antiquarian Society, assisted by the Program for Editions of the National Endowment for the Humanities, and published by the State University of New York Press. The text of The Pilot was edited by Kay Seymour House; the text of The Red Rover was edited by Thomas and Marianne Philbrick.*

*Grateful acknowledgment is made to the National Endowment for the Humanities, the Ford Foundation, and the Andrew W. Mellon Foundation for their generous support of this series.*

# Contents

# THE PILOT

## A TALE OF THE SEA

*"List! ye Landsmen, all to me."*
G. A. Stevens, "The Storm," l. 2.

TO
WILLIAM BRANFORD SHUBRICK,
ESQ.,
U.S. NAVY

MY DEAR SHUBRICK,

Each year brings some new and melancholy chasm in what is now the brief list of my naval friends and former associates. War, disease, and the casualties of a hazardous profession, have made fearful inroads in the limited number; while the places of the dead are supplied by names that to me are those of strangers. With the consequences of these sad changes before me, I cherish the recollection of those with whom I once lived in close familiarity with peculiar interest, and feel a triumph in their growing reputations, that is but little short of their own honest pride.

But neither time nor separation has shaken our intimacy: and I know that in dedicating to you this volume, I tell you nothing new, when I add, that it is a tribute paid to an enduring friendship, by

Your old messmate,
THE AUTHOR

# Preface.

[1823]

THE PRIVILEGES of the Historian and of the writer of
Romances are very different, and it behooves them
equally to respect each other's rights. The latter is permitted to
garnish a probable fiction, while he is sternly prohibited
from dwelling on improbable truths; but it is the duty of
the former to record facts as they have occurred, without a
reference to consequences, resting his reputation on a firm
foundation of realities, and vindicating his integrity by his
authorities. How far and how well the Author has adhered to
this distinction between the prerogatives of truth and fiction,
his readers must decide; but he cannot forbear desiring the
curious inquirers into our annals to persevere, until they shall
find good poetical authority for every material incident in this
veritable legend.

As to the Critics, he has the advantage of including them all
in that extensive class, which is known by the sweeping appellation of "Lubbers." If they have common discretion, they
will beware of exposing their ignorance.

If, however, some old seaman should happen to detect any
trifling anachronisms in marine usages, or mechanical improvements, the Author begs leave to say to him, with a
proper deference for his experience, that it was not so much
his intention to describe the customs of a particular age, as to
paint those scenes which belong only to the ocean, and to
exhibit, in his imperfect manner, a few traits of a people who,
from the nature of things, can never be much known.

He will probably be told, that Smollett has done all this,
before him, and in a much better manner. It will be seen,
however, that though he has navigated the same sea as Smollett, he has steered a different course; or, in other words, that
he has considered what Smollett has painted as a picture
which is finished, and which is not to be daubed over by
every one who may choose to handle a pencil on marine
subjects.

The Author wishes to express his regret, that the daring
and useful services of a great portion of our marine in the old

war should be suffered to remain in the obscurity under which it is now buried. Every one has heard of the victory of the Bon-Homme Richard, but how little is known of the rest of the life, and of the important services of the remarkable man who commanded, in our behalf, in that memorable combat. How little is known of his actions with the Milford, and the Solebay; of his captures of the Drake and Triumph; and of his repeated and desperate projects to carry the war into the 'island home' of our powerful enemy. Very many of the officers who served in that contest were to be found, afterwards, in the navy of the confederation; and it is fair to presume that it owes no small part of its present character to the spirit that descended from the heroes of the revolution.

One of the last officers reared in that school died, not long since, at the head of his profession; and now, that nothing but the recollection of their deeds remains, we should become more tenacious of their glory.

If his book has the least tendency to excite some attention to this interesting portion of our history, one of the objects of the writer will be accomplished.

The Author now takes his leave of his readers, wishing them all happiness.

# Preface.
## [1849]

IT IS PROBABLE a true history of human events would show that a far larger proportion of our acts are the results of sudden impulses and accidents, than of that reason of which we so much boast. However true, or false, this opinion may be in more important matters, it is certainly and strictly correct as relates to the conception and execution of this book.

The Pilot was published in 1823. This was not long after the appearance of "The Pirate," a work which it is hardly necessary to remind the reader, has a direct connection with the sea. In a conversation with a friend, a man of polished taste and extensive reading, the authorship of the Scottish novels came under discussion. The claims of Sir Walter were a little distrusted, on account of the peculiar and minute information that the romances were then very generally thought to display. The Pirate was cited as a very marked instance of this universal knowledge, and it was wondered where a man of Scott's habits and associations could have become so familiar with the sea. The writer had frequently observed that there was much looseness in this universal knowledge, and that the secret of its success was to be traced to the power of creating that *vraisemblance*, which is so remarkably exhibited in those world-renowned fictions, rather than to any very accurate information on the part of their author. It would have been hypercritical to object to the Pirate, that it was not strictly nautical, or true in its details; but, when the reverse was urged as a proof of what, considering the character of other portions of the work, would have been most extraordinary attainments, it was a sort of provocation to dispute the seamanship of the Pirate, a quality to which the book has certainly very little just pretension. The result of this conversation was a sudden determination to produce a work which, if it had no other merit, might present truer pictures of the ocean and ships than any that are to be found in the Pirate. To this unpremeditated decision, purely an impulse, is not only the Pilot due, but a tolerably numerous school of nautical romances that have succeeded it.

The author had many misgivings concerning the success of the undertaking, after he had made some progress in the work; the opinions of his different friends being anything but encouraging. One would declare that the sea could not be made interesting; that it was tame, monotonous, and without any other movement than unpleasant storms, and that, for his part, the less he got of it the better. The women very generally protested that such a book would have the odour of bilge-water, and that it would give them the *maladie de mer*. Not a single individual among all those who discussed the merits of the project, within the range of the author's knowledge, either spoke, or looked, encouragingly. It is probable that all these persons anticipated a signal failure.

So very discouraging did these ominous opinions get to be, that the writer was, once or twice, tempted to throw his manuscript aside, and turn to something new. A favourable opinion, however, coming from a very unexpected quarter, put a new face on the matter, and raised new hopes. Among the intimate friends of the writer, was an Englishman, who possessed most of the peculiar qualities of the educated of his country. He was learned even, had a taste that was so just as always to command respect, but was prejudiced, and particularly so in all that related to this country and its literature. He could never be persuaded to admire Bryant's Water-Fowl, and this mainly because if it were accepted as good poetry, it must be placed at once amongst the finest fugitive pieces of the language. Of the Thanatopsis he thought better, though inclined to suspect it of being a plagiarism. To the tender mercies of this one-sided critic, who had never affected to compliment the previous works of the author, the sheets of a volume of The Pilot were committed, with scarce an expectation of his liking them. The reverse proved to be the case; — he expressed himself highly gratified, and predicted a success for the book which it probably never attained.

Thus encouraged, one more experiment was made, a seaman being selected for the critic. A kinsman, a namesake, and an old messmate of the author, one now in command on a foreign station, was chosen, and a considerable portion of the first volume was read to him. There is no wish to conceal the satisfaction with which the effect on this listener was observed. He treated the whole matter as fact, and his criticisms were strictly professional, and perfectly just. But the interest he betrayed could not be mistaken. It gave a perfect and most gratifying assurance that the work would be more likely to find favour with nautical men, than with any other class of readers.

The Pilot could scarcely be a favourite with females. The story has little interest for them, nor was it much heeded by the author of the book, in the progress of his labours. His aim was to illustrate vessels and the ocean, rather than to draw any pictures of sentiment and love. In this last respect, the book has small claims on the reader's attention, though it is hoped that the story has sufficient interest to relieve the more strictly nautical features of the work.

It would be affectation to deny that the Pilot met with a most unlooked-for success. The novelty of the design probably contributed a large share of this result. Sea-tales came into vogue, as a consequence; and, as every practical part of knowledge has its uses, something has been gained by letting the landsman into the secrets of the seaman's manner of life. Perhaps, in some small degree, an interest has been awakened in behalf of a very numerous, and what has hitherto been a sort of proscribed class of men, that may directly tend to a melioration of their condition.

It is not easy to make the public comprehend all the necessities of a service afloat. With several hundred rude beings confined within the narrow limits of a vessel, men of all nations and of the lowest habits, it would be to the last degree indiscreet, to commence their reformation by relaxing the bonds of discipline, under the mistaken impulses of a false philanthropy. It has a lofty sound, to be sure, to talk about American citizens being too good to be brought under the lash, upon the high seas; but he must have a very mistaken notion who does not see that tens of thousands of these pretending persons on shore, even, would be greatly benefited by a little judicious flogging. It is the judgment in administering, and not the mode of punishment, that requires to be looked into; and, in this respect, there has certainly been a great improvement of late years. It is seldom, indeed, that any institution, practice, or system, is improved by the blind interference of those who know nothing about it. Better would it be to trust to the experience of those who have long governed turbulent men, than to the impulsive experiments of those who rarely regard more than one side of a question, and that the most showy and glittering; having, quite half of the time, some selfish personal end to answer.

There is an uneasy desire among a vast many well-disposed persons to get the fruits of the Christian Faith, without troubling themselves about the Faith itself. This is done under the sanction of Peace Societies, Temperance and Moral Reform societies, in which the end is too often mistaken for the means. When the Almighty sent his Son on earth, it was to point out the way in which all this was to be brought about, by means of the Church; but men have so frittered away that body of divine organisation, through their divisions and subdivisions, all arising from human conceit, that it is no longer regarded as the agency it was obviously intended to be, and various contrivances are to be employed as substitutes for that which proceeded directly from the Son of God!

Among the efforts of the day, however, there is one connected with the moral improvement of the sailor that commands our profound respect. Cut off from most of the charities of life, for so large a portion of his time, deprived altogether of association with the gentler and better portions of the other sex, and living a man in a degree proscribed, amid the many signs of advancement that distinguish the age, it was time that he should be remembered and singled out, and become the subject of combined and Christian philanthropy. There is much reason to believe that the effort, now making in the right direction and under proper auspices, will be successful; and that it will cause the lash to be laid aside in the best and most rational manner,—by rendering its use unnecessary.

Cooperstown, August 10, 1849.

# Chapter I.

"Sullen waves, incessant rolling,
    Rudely dash against her sides."
"Fresh and Strong," *Dibdin's Charms of Melody*, ll. 3–4.

A SINGLE GLANCE at the map will make the reader acquainted with the position of the eastern coast of the island of Great Britain, as connected with the shores of the opposite continent. Together they form the boundaries of the small sea, that has for ages been known to the world as the scene of maritime exploits, and as the great avenue through which commerce and war have conducted the fleets of the northern nations of Europe. Over this sea the islanders long asserted a jurisdiction, exceeding that which reason concedes to any power on the highway of nations, and which frequently led to conflicts that caused an expenditure of blood and treasure, utterly disproportioned to the advantages that can ever arise from the maintenance of a useless and abstract right. It is across the waters of this disputed ocean that we shall attempt to conduct our readers, selecting a period for our incidents that has a peculiar interest for every American, not only because it was the birth-day of his nation, but because it was also the era when reason and common sense began to take the place of custom and feudal practices in the management of the affairs of nations.

Soon after the events of the revolution had involved the kingdoms of France and Spain, and the republics of Holland, in our quarrel, a group of labourers was collected in a field that lay exposed to the winds of the ocean, on the northeastern coast of England. These men were lightening their toil, and cheering the gloom of a day in December, by uttering their crude opinions on the political aspects of the times. The fact that England was engaged in a war with some of her dependencies on the other side of the Atlantic, had long been known to them, after the manner that faint rumours of distant and uninteresting events gain on the ear; but now that nations, with whom she had been used to battle, were armed against her in the quarrel, the din of war had disturbed the quiet even of these secluded and illiterate rustics. The principal speakers, on the occasion, were a Scotch drover, who was waiting the leisure of the occupant of the fields, and an Irish labourer, who had found his way across the channel, and thus far over the island, in quest of employment.

"The Nagurs wouldn't have been a job at all for ould England, letting alone Ireland," said the latter, "if these French and Spanishers hadn't been troubling themselves in the matter. I'm sure it's but little rason I have for thanking them, if a man is to kape as sober as a praist at mass, for fear he should find himself a souldier, and he knowing nothing about the same."

"Hoot! mon! ye ken but little of raising an airmy in Ireland, if ye mak' a drum o' a whiskey keg," said the drover, winking to the listeners. "Noo, in the north, they ca' a gathering of the folk, and follow the pipes as graciously as ye wad journey kirkward o' a Sabbeth morn. I've seen a' the names o' a Heeland raj'ment on a sma' bit paper, that ye might cover wi' a leddy's hand. They war' a' Camerons and M'Donalds, though they paraded sax hundred men! But what ha' ye gotten here! That chield has an ow'r liking to the land for a seafaring body; an' if the bottom o' the sea be ony thing like the top o't, he's in gr'at danger o' a shipwrack!"

This unexpected change in the discourse, drew all eyes on the object towards which the staff of the observant drover was pointed. To the utter amazement of every individual present, a small vessel was seen moving slowly round a point of land that formed one of the sides of the little bay, to which the field the labourers were in composed the other. There was something very peculiar in the externals of this unusual visiter, which added in no small degree to the surprise created by her appearance in that retired place. None but the smallest vessels, and those rarely, or, at long intervals, a desperate smuggler, were ever known to venture so close to the land, amid the sand-bars and sunken rocks with which that immediate coast abounded. The adventurous mariners who now attempted this dangerous navigation in so wanton, and, apparently, so heedless a manner, were in a low, black schooner, whose hull seemed utterly disproportioned to the raking masts it upheld, which, in their turn, supported a lighter set of spars, that tapered away until their upper extremities appeared no larger than the lazy pennant, that in vain endeavoured to display its length in the light breeze.

The short day of that high northern latitude was already drawing to a close, and the sun was throwing his parting rays obliquely across the waters, touching the gloomy waves here and there with streaks of pale light. The stormy winds of the German ocean were apparently lulled to rest; and, though the incessant rolling of the surge on the shore, heightened the gloomy character of the hour and the view, the light ripple that ruffled the sleeping billows was produced by a gentle air, that blew directly from the land. Notwithstanding this favourable circumstance, there was something threatening in the aspect of the ocean, which was speaking in hollow, but deep murmurs, like a volcano on the eve of an eruption, that greatly heightened the feelings of amazement and dread with which the peasants beheld this extraordinary interruption to the quiet of their little bay. With no other sails spread to the action of the air, than her heavy mainsail, and one of those light jibs that projected far beyond her bows, the vessel glided over the water with a grace and facility that seemed magical to the beholders, who turned their wondering looks from the schooner to each other, in silent amazement. At length the drover spoke in a low, solemn voice—

"He's a bold chield that steers her! and if that bit craft has wood in her bottom, like the brigantines that ply between Lon'on and the Frith at Leith, he's in mair danger than a prudent mon could wish. Ay! he's by the big rock that shows his head when the tide runs low, but it's no mortal man who can steer along in the road he's journeying, and not speedily find land wi' water a top o't."

The little schooner, however, still held her way among the rocks and sand-spits, making such slight deviations in her course, as proved her to be under the direction of one who knew his danger, until she had entered as far into the bay as prudence could at all justify, when her canvass was gathered into folds, seemingly without the agency of hands, and the vessel, after rolling for a few minutes on the long billows that hove in from the ocean, swung round in the currents of the tide, and was held by her anchor.

The peasants, now, began to make their conjectures more freely, concerning the character and object of their visiter; some intimating that she was engaged in contraband trade, and others that her views were hostile, and her business war. A few dark hints were hazarded on the materiality of her construction, for nothing of artificial formation, it was urged, would be ventured by men in such a dangerous place, at a time when even the most inexperienced landsman was enabled to foretell the certain gale. The Scotchman, who, to all the sagacity of his countrymen, added no small portion of their superstition, leaned greatly to the latter conclusion, and had begun to express this sentiment warily and with reverence, when the child of Erin, who appeared not to possess any very definite ideas on the subject, interrupted him, by exclaiming—

"Faith! there's two of them! a big and a little! sure the bogles of the saa likes good company the same as any other christians!"

"Twa!" echoed the drover; "twa! ill luck bides o' some o' ye. Twa craft a sailing without hand to guide them, in sic a place as this, whar' eyesight is na guid enough to show the dangers, bodes evil to a' that luik thereon. Hoot! she's na yearling the tither! Luik, mon! luik! she's a gallant boat, and a gr'at;" he paused, raised his pack from the ground, and first giving one searching look at the objects of his suspicions, he nodded with great sagacity to the listeners, and continued, as he moved slowly towards the interior of the country, "I should na wonder if she carried King George's commission aboot her; 'weel 'weel, I wull journey upward to the town, and ha' a crack wi' the guid mon, for they craft have a suspeecious aspect, and the sma' bit thing wu'ld nab a mon quite easy and the big ane wu'ld hold us a' and no feel we war' in her."

This sagacious warning caused a general movement in the party, for the intelligence of a hot press was among the rumours of the times. The husbandmen collected their implements of labour, and retired homewards; and though many a curious eye was bent on the movements of the vessels from the distant hills, but very few of those not immediately interested in the mysterious visiters, ventured to approach the little rocky cliffs that lined the bay.

The vessel that occasioned these cautious movements, was a gallant ship, whose huge hull, lofty masts, and square yards, loomed in the evening's haze, above the sea, like a distant mountain rising from the deep. She carried but little sail, and though she warily avoided the near approach to the land that the schooner had attempted, the similarity of their movements was sufficiently apparent to warrant the conjecture that they were employed on the same duty. The frigate, for the ship belonged to this class of vessels, floated across the entrance of the little bay, majestically in the tide, with barely enough motion through the water to govern her movements, until she arrived opposite to the place where her consort lay, when she hove up heavily into the wind, squared the enormous yards on her mainmast, and attempted, in counteracting the power of her sails by each other, to remain stationary; but the light air that had at no time swelled her heavy canvass to the utmost, began to fail, and the long waves that rolled in from the ocean, ceased to be ruffled with the breeze from the land. The currents, and the billows, were fast sweeping the frigate towards one of the points of the estuary, where the black heads of the rocks could be seen running far into the sea, and, in their turn, the mariners of the ship dropped an anchor to the bottom, and drew her sails in festoons to the yards. As the vessel swung round to the tide, a heavy ensign was raised to her peak, and a current of air opening, for a moment, its folds, the white field, and red cross, that distinguish the flag of England, were displayed to view. So much, even the wary drover had loitered at a distance to behold; but when a boat was launched from either vessel, he quickened his steps, observing to his wondering and amused companions, that "they craft were a' thegither, mair bonny to luik on than to abide wi'."

A numerous crew manned the barge that was lowered from the frigate, which, after receiving an officer, with an attendant youth, left the ship, and moved with a measured stroke of its oars, directly towards the head of the bay. As it passed at a short distance from the schooner, a light whale-boat, pulled by four athletic men, shot from her side, and rather dancing over, than cutting through the waves, crossed her course with a wonderful velocity. As the boats approached each other, the men, in obedience to signals from their officers, suspended their efforts, and for a few minutes they floated at rest, during which time, there was the following dialogue:

"Is the old man mad!" exclaimed the young officer in the whale-boat, when his men had ceased rowing; "does he think that the bottom of the Ariel is made of iron, and that a rock can't knock a hole in it! or does he think she is mann'd with alligators, who can't be drown'd!"

A languid smile played for a moment round the handsome features of the young man, who was rather reclining than sitting in the stern-sheets of the barge, as he replied,

"He knows your prudence too well, Captain Barnstable, to fear either the wreck of your vessel, or the drowning of her crew. How near the bottom does your keel lie?"

"I am afraid to sound," returned Barnstable. "I have never the heart to touch a lead-line when I see the rocks coming up to breathe like so many porpoises."

"You are afloat!" exclaimed the other, with a vehemence that denoted an abundance of latent fire.

"Afloat!" echoed his friend; "ay! the little Ariel would float in air!" As he spoke, he rose in the boat, and lifting his leathern sea-cap from his head, stroked back the thick clusters of black locks which shadowed his sun-burnt countenance, while he viewed his little vessel with the complacency of a seaman who was proud of her qualities. "But it's close work, Mr. Griffith, when a man rides to a single anchor in a place like this, and at such a nightfall. What are the orders?"

"I shall pull into the surf and let go a grapnel; you will take Mr. Merry into your whale-boat, and try to drive her through the breakers on the beach."

"Beach!" retorted Barnstable; "do you call a perpendicular rock of a hundred feet in height, a beach!"

"We shall not dispute about terms," said Griffith, smiling; "but you must manage to get on the shore; we have seen the signal from the land, and know that the pilot, whom we have so long expected, is ready to come off."

Barnstable shook his head with a grave air, as he muttered to himself, "this is droll navigation; first we run into an unfrequented bay that is full of rocks, and sand-spits, and shoals, and then we get off our pilot. But how am I to know him?"

"Merry will give you the pass-word, and tell you where to look for him. I would land myself, but my orders forbid it. If you meet with difficulties, show three oar-blades in a row, and I will pull in to your assistance. Three oars on end, and a pistol, will bring the fire of my muskets, and the signal repeated from the barge will draw a shot from the ship."

"I thank you, I thank you," said Barnstable, carelessly; "I believe I can fight my own battles against all the enemies we are likely to fall in with on this coast. But the old man is surely mad. I would—"

"You would obey his orders if he were here, and you will now please to obey mine," said Griffith, in a tone that the friendly expression of his eye contradicted. "Pull in, and keep a look out for a small man in a drab pea-jacket; Merry will give you the word; if he answer it bring him off to the barge."

The young men now nodded familiarly and kindly to each other, and the boy, who was called Mr. Merry, having changed his place from the barge to the whale-boat, Barnstable threw himself into his seat, and making a signal with his hand, his men again bent to their oars. The light vessel shot away from her companion, and dashed in boldly towards the rocks; after skirting the shore for some distance in quest of a favourable place, she was suddenly turned, and, dashing over the broken waves, was run upon a spot where a landing could be effected in safety.

In the mean time the barge followed these movements, at some distance, with a more measured progress, and when the whale-boat was observed to be drawn up along side of a rock, the promised grapnel was cast into the water, and her crew deliberately proceeded to get their firearms in a state for immediate service. Every thing appeared to be done in obedience to strict orders that must have been previously communicated; for the young man, who has been introduced to the reader by the name of Griffith, seldom spoke, and then only in the pithy expressions that are apt to fall from those who are sure of obedience. When the boat had brought up to her grapnel, he sunk back at his length on the cushioned seats of the barge, and drawing his hat over his eyes in a listless manner, he continued for many minutes apparently absorbed in thoughts altogether foreign to his present situation. Occasionally he rose, and would first bend his looks in quest of his companions on the shore, and then, turning his expressive eyes towards the ocean, the abstracted and vacant air that so often usurped the place of animation and intelligence in his countenance, would give place to the anxious and intelligent look of a seaman gifted with an experience beyond his years. His weather-beaten and hardy crew, having made their dispositions for offence, sat in profound silence, with their hands thrust into the bosoms of their jackets, but with their eyes earnestly regarding every cloud that was gathering in the threatening atmosphere, and exchanging looks of deep care, whenever the boat rose higher than usual on one of those long, heavy ground-swells that were heaving in from the ocean with increasing rapidity and magnitude.

# Chapter II.

—"A horseman's coat shall hide
Thy taper shape and comeliness of side;
And with a bolder stride and looser air,
Mingled with men, a man thou must appear."
    Prior, "Henry and Emma," ll. 437–438, 441–442.

W HEN THE WHALE-BOAT obtained the position we have
described, the young lieutenant, who, in consequence
of commanding a schooner, was usually addressed by the title
of captain, stepped on the rocks, followed by the youthful
midshipman, who had quitted the barge, to aid in the hazardous duty of their expedition.

"This is, at best, but a Jacob's ladder we have to climb," said
Barnstable, casting his eyes upwards at the difficult ascent,
"and it's by no means certain that we shall be well received,
when we get up, even though we should reach the top."

"We are under the guns of the frigate," returned the boy;
"and you remember, sir, three oar blades and a pistol, repeated from the barge, will draw her fire."

"Yes, on our own heads. Boy, never be so foolish as to trust
a long shot. It makes a great smoke and some noise, but it's a
terrible uncertain manner of throwing old iron about. In such
a business as this, I would sooner trust Tom Coffin and his
harpoon to back me, than the best broadside that ever rattled
out of the three decks of a ninety-gun ship. Come, gather
your limbs together, and try if you can walk on terra firma,
Master Coffin."

The seaman who was addressed by this dire appellation,
arose slowly from the place where he was stationed as cockswain of the boat, and seemed to ascend high in air by the
gradual evolution of numberless folds in his body. When
erect, he stood nearly six feet and as many inches in his shoes,
though, when elevated in his most perpendicular attitude,
there was a forward inclination about his head and shoulders,
that appeared to be the consequence of habitual confinement
in limited lodgings. His whole frame was destitute of the
rounded outlines of a well-formed man, though his enormous
hands furnished a display of bones and sinews which gave

indication of gigantic strength. On his head he wore a little, low, brown hat of wool, with an arched top, that threw an expression of peculiar solemnity and hardness over his harsh visage, the sharp prominent features of which were completely encircled by a set of black whiskers, that began to be grizzled a little with age. One of his hands grasped, with a sort of instinct, the staff of a bright harpoon, the lower end of which he placed firmly on the rock, as, in obedience to the order of his commander, he left the place, where, considering his vast dimentions, he had been established in an incredibly small space.

As soon as Captain Barnstable received this addition to his strength, he gave a few precautionary orders to the men in the boat, and proceeded to the difficult task of ascending the rocks. Notwithstanding the great daring and personal agility of Barnstable, he would have been completely baffled in this attempt, but for the assistance he occasionally received from his cockswain, whose prodigious strength, and great length of limbs, enabled him to make exertions which it would have been useless for most men to attempt. When within a few feet of the summit, they availed themselves of a projecting rock, to pause for consultation and breath; both of which seemed necessary for their further movements.

"This will be but a bad place for a retreat, if we should happen to fall in with enemies," said Barnstable. "Where are we to look for this pilot, Mr. Merry, or how are we to know him; and what certainty have you that he will not betray us?"

"The question you are to put to him is written on this bit of paper," returned the boy, as he handed the other the word of recognition; "we made the signal on the point of the rock at yon headland, but as he must have seen our boat, he will follow us to this place. As to his betraying us, he seems to have the confidence of Captain Munson, who has kept a bright look-out for him ever since we made the land."

"Ay," muttered the lieutenant, "and I shall have a bright look-out kept on him, now we are *on* the land. I like not this business of hugging the shore so closely, nor have I much faith in any traitor. What think you of it, Master Coffin?"

The hardy old seaman, thus addressed, turned his grave visage on his commander, and replied with a becoming gravity —

"Give me a plenty of sea-room, and good canvass, where there is no 'casion for pilots at all, sir. For my part, I was born on board a chebacco-man, and never could see the use of more land than now and then a small island, to raise a few vegetables, and to dry your fish—I'm sure the sight of it always makes me feel oncomfortable, unless we have the wind dead off shore."

"Ah! Tom, you are a sensible fellow," said Barnstable, with an air half comic, half serious. "But we must be moving; the sun is just touching those clouds to sea-ward, and God keep us from riding out this night at anchor in such a place as this."

Laying his hand on a projection of the rock above him, Barnstable swung himself forward, and following this movement with a desperate leap or two, he stood at once on the brow of the cliff. His cockswain very deliberately raised the midshipman after his officer, and proceeding with more caution, but less exertion, he soon placed himself by his side.

When they reached the level land, that lay above the cliffs, and began to inquire, with curious and wary eyes, into the surrounding scenery, the adventurers discovered a cultivated country, divided, in the usual manner, by hedges and walls. Only one habitation for man, however, and that a small dilapidated cottage, stood within a mile of them, most of the dwellings being placed as far as convenience would permit, from the frogs and damps of the ocean.

"Here seems to be neither any thing to apprehend, nor the object of our search," said Barnstable, when he had taken the whole view in his survey; "I fear we have landed to no purpose, Mr. Merry. What say you, long Tom; see you what we want?"

"I see no pilot, sir," returned the cockswain; "but it's an ill wind that blows luck to nobody; there is a mouthful of fresh meat stowed away under that row of bushes, that would make a double ration to all hands in the Ariel."

The midshipman laughed, as he pointed out to Barnstable the object of the cockswain's solicitude, which proved to be a fat ox, quietly ruminating under a hedge near them.

"There's many a hungry fellow aboard of us," said the boy merrily, "who would be glad to second long Tom's motion, if the time and business would permit us to slay the animal."

"It is but a lubber's blow, Mr. Merry," returned the cockswain, without a muscle of his hard face yielding, as he struck the end of his harpoon violently against the earth, and then made a motion towards poising the weapon; "let Captain Barnstable but say the word, and I'll drive the iron through him to the quick; I've sent it to the seizing in many a whale, that hadn't a jacket of such blubber as that fellow wears."

"Pshaw! you are not on a whaling voyage, where every thing that offers is game," said Barnstable, turning himself pettishly away from the beast, as if he distrusted his own forbearance; "but stand fast! I see some one approaching behind the hedge. Look to your arms, Mr. Merry—the first thing we hear may be a shot."

"Not from that cruiser," cried the thoughtless lad; "he is a younker, like myself, and would hardly dare run down upon such a formidable force as we muster."

"You say true, boy," returned Barnstable, relinquishing the grasp he held on his pistol. "He comes on with caution, as if afraid. He is small, and is in drab, though I should hardly call it a pea-jacket—and yet he may be our man. Stand you both here, while I go and hail him."

As Barnstable walked rapidly towards the hedge, that in part concealed the stranger, the latter stopped suddenly, and seemed to be in doubt whether to advance or to retreat. Before he had decided on either, the active sailor was within a few feet of him.

"Pray, sir," said Barnstable, "what water have we in this bay?"

The slight form of the stranger started, with an extraordinary emotion, at this question, and he shrunk aside involuntarily, as if to conceal his features, before he answered, in a voice that was barely audible—

"I should think it would be the water of the German ocean."

"Indeed! you must have passed no small part of your short life in the study of geography, to be so well informed," returned the lieutenant; "perhaps, sir, your cunning is also equal to telling me how long we shall sojourn together, if I make you a prisoner, in order to enjoy the benefit of your wit?"

To this alarming intimation, the youth who was addressed made no reply; but, as he averted his face, and concealed it with both his hands, the offended seaman, believing that a salutary impression had been made upon the fears of his auditor, was about to proceed with his interrogatories. The singular agitation of the stranger's frame, however, caused the lieutenant to continue silent a few moments longer, when, to his utter amazement, he discovered that what he had mistaken for alarm, was produced by an endeavour, on the part of the youth, to suppress a violent fit of laughter.

"Now, by all the whales in the sea," cried Barnstable, "but you are merry out of season, young gentleman. It's quite bad enough to be ordered to anchor in such a bay as this, with a storm brewing before my eyes, without landing to be laughed at, by a stripling who has not strength to carry a beard if he had one, when I ought to be getting an offing for the safety of both body and soul. But I'll know more of you and your jokes, if I take you into my own mess, and am giggled out of my sleep for the rest of the cruise."

As the commander of the schooner concluded, he approached the stranger, with an air of offering some violence, but the other shrunk back from his extended arm, and exclaimed, with a voice in which real terror had gotten the better of mirth—

"Barnstable! dear Barnstable! would you harm me?"

The sailor recoiled several feet, at this unexpected appeal, and rubbing his eyes, he threw the cap from his head, before he cried—

"What do I hear! and what do I see! There lies the Ariel— and yonder is the frigate. Can this be Katherine Plowden!"

His doubts, if any doubts remained, were soon removed, for the stranger sunk on the bank at her side, in an attitude in which female bashfulness was beautifully contrasted to her attire, and gave vent to her mirth in an uncontrollable burst of merriment.

From that moment, all thought of his duty, and the pilot, or even of the Ariel, appeared to be banished from the mind of the seaman, who sprang to her side, and joined in her mirth, though he hardly knew why or wherefore.

When the diverted girl had in some degree recovered her

composure, she turned to her companion, who had sat good-naturedly by her side, content to be laughed at, and said—

"But this is not only silly, but cruel to others. I owe you an explanation of my unexpected appearance, and perhaps, also, of my extraordinary attire."

"I can anticipate every thing," cried Barnstable; "you heard that we were on the coast, and have flown to redeem the promises you made me in America. But I ask no more; the chaplain of the frigate—"

"May preach as usual, and to as little purpose," interrupted the disguised female; "but no nuptial benediction shall be pronounced over me, until I have effected the object of this hazardous experiment. You are not usually selfish, Barnstable; would you have me forgetful of the happiness of others?"

"Of whom do you speak?"

"My poor, my devoted cousin. I heard that two vessels, answering the description of the frigate and the Ariel, were seen hovering on the coast, and I determined at once to have a communication with you. I have followed your movements for a week, in this dress, but have been unsuccessful till now. To-day I observed you to approach nearer to the shore than usual, and happily, by being adventurous, I have been successful."

"Ay, God knows we are near enough to the land! But does Captain Munson know of your wish to get on board his ship?"

"Certainly not—none know of it but yourself. I thought that if Griffith and you could learn our situation, you might be tempted to hazard a little to redeem us from our thraldom. In this paper I have prepared such an account as will, I trust, excite all your chivalry, and by which you may govern your movements."

"Our movements!" interrupted Barnstable, "you will pilot us in person."

"Then there's two of them," said a hoarse voice near them.

The alarmed female shrieked as she recovered her feet, but she still adhered, with instinctive dependence, to the side of her lover. Barnstable, who recognised the tones of his cockswain, bent an angry brow on the sober visage that was peering at them above the hedge, and demanded the meaning of the interruption.

"Seeing you were hull-down, sir, and not knowing but the chase might lead you ashore, Mr. Merry thought it best to have a look-out kept. I told him that you were overhauling the mail bags of the messenger for the news, but as he was an officer, sir, and I nothing but a common hand, I did as he ordered."

"Return, sir, where I commanded you to remain," said Barnstable, "and desire Mr. Merry to wait my pleasure."

The cockswain gave the usual reply of an obedient seaman, but before he left the hedge, he stretched out one of his brawny arms towards the ocean, and said, in tones of solemnity suited to his apprehensions and character—

"I showed you how to knot a reef-point, and pass a gasket, Captain Barnstable, nor do I believe you could even take two half hitches when you first came aboard of the Spalmacitty. These be things that a man is soon expart in, but it takes the time of his nat'ral life to larn to know the weather. There be streaked wind-galls in the offing, that speak as plainly, to all that see them, and know God's language in the clouds, as ever you spoke through a trumpet, to shorten sail; besides, sir, don't you hear the sea moaning, as if it knew the hour was at hand when it was to wake up from its sleep!"

"Ay, Tom," returned his officer, walking to the edge of the cliffs, and throwing a seaman's glance at the gloomy ocean, " 'tis a threatening night indeed: but this pilot must be had—and—"

"Is that the man?" interrupted the cockswain, pointing towards a man who was standing not far from them, an attentive observer of their proceedings, at the same time that he was narrowly watched himself by the young midshipman. "God send that he knows his trade well, for the bottom of a ship will need eyes to find its road out of this wild anchorage."

"That must indeed be the man!" exclaimed Barnstable, at once recalled to his duty. He then held a short dialogue with his female companion, whom he left concealed by the hedge, and proceeded to address the stranger. When near enough to be heard, the commander of the schooner demanded—

"What water have you in this bay?"

The stranger, who seemed to expect this question, answered, without the least hesitation—

"Enough to take all out in safety, who have entered with confidence."

"You are the man I seek," cried Barnstable; "are you ready to go off?"

"Both ready and willing," returned the pilot, "and there is need of haste. I would give the best hundred guineas that ever were coined for two hours more use of that sun which has left us, or for even half the time of this fading twilight."

"Think you our situation so bad?" said the lieutenant. "Follow this gentleman to the boat then; I will join you by the time you can descend the cliffs. I believe I can prevail on another hand to go off with us."

"Time is more precious now than any number of hands," said the pilot, throwing a glance of impatience from under his lowering brows, "and the consequences of delay must be visited on those who occasion it."

"And, sir, I will meet the consequences with those who have a right to inquire into my conduct," said Barnstable, haughtily.

With this warning and retort, they separated; the young officer retracing his steps impatiently towards his mistress, muttering his indignation in suppressed execrations, and the pilot, drawing the leathern belt of his pea-jacket mechanically around his body, as he followed the midshipman and cockswain to their boat, in moody silence.

Barnstable found the disguised female who had announced herself as Katherine Plowden, awaiting his return, with intense anxiety depicted on every feature of her intelligent countenance. As he felt all the responsibility of his situation, notwithstanding his cool reply to the pilot, the young man hastily drew an arm of the apparent boy, forgetful of her disguise, through his own, and led her forward.

"Come, Katherine," he said, "the time urges to be prompt."

"What pressing necessity is there for immediate departure?" she inquired, checking his movements by withdrawing herself from his side.

"You heard the ominous prognostic of my cockswain, on the weather, and I am forced to add my own testimony to his opinion. 'Tis a crazy night that threatens us, though I cannot repent of coming into the bay, since it has led to this interview."

"God forbid that we should either of us have cause to repent of it," said Katherine, the paleness of anxiety chasing away the rich bloom that had mantled the animated face of the brunette. "But you have the paper—follow its directions, and come to our rescue; you will find us willing captives, if Griffith and yourself are our conquerors."

"What mean you, Katherine!" exclaimed her lover; "you at least are now in safety—'twould be madness to tempt your fate again. My vessel can and shall protect you, until your cousin is redeemed; and then, remember, I have a claim on you for life."

"And how would you dispose of me in the interval," said the young maiden, retreating slowly from his advances.

"In the Ariel—by heaven, you shall be her commander; I will bear that rank only in name."

"I thank you, thank you, Barnstable, but distrust my abilities to fill such a station," she said, laughing, though the colour that again crossed her youthful features was like the glow of a summer's sunset, and even her mirthful eyes seemed to reflect their tints. "Do not mistake me, saucy-one. If I have done more than my sex will warrant, remember it was through a holy motive, and if I have more than a woman's enterprise, it must be—"

"To lift you above the weakness of your sex," he cried, "and to enable you to show your noble confidence in me."

"To fit me for, and to keep me worthy of being one day your wife." As she uttered these words, she turned, and disappeared, with a rapidity that eluded his attempt to detain her, behind an angle of the hedge, that was near them. For a moment, Barnstable remained motionless through surprise, and when he sprang forward in pursuit, he was able only to catch a glimpse of her light form, in the gloom of the evening, as she again vanished in a little thicket at some distance.

Barnstable was about to pursue, when the air lighted with a sudden flash, and the bellowing report of a cannon rolled along the cliffs, and was echoed among the hills far inland.

"Ay, grumble away, old dotard!" the disappointed young

sailor muttered to himself, while he reluctantly obeyed the signal; "you are in as great a hurry to get out of your danger as you were to run into it."

The quick reports of three muskets from the barge beneath where he stood, urged him to quicken his pace, and as he threw himself carelessly down the rugged and dangerous passes of the cliffs, his experienced eye beheld the well-known lights displayed from the frigate, which commanded the recall of all her boats.

# Chapter III.

"In such a time as this it is not meet
That every nice offence should bear its comment."
*Julius Caesar*, IV.iii.7–8.

T HE CLIFFS threw their dark shadows wide on the waters, and the gloom of the evening had so far advanced, as to conceal the discontent that brooded over the ordinary open brow of Barnstable, as he sprang from the rocks into the boat, and took his seat by the side of the silent pilot.

"Shove off," cried the lieutenant, in tones that his men knew must be obeyed. "A seaman's curse light on the folly that exposes planks and lives to such navigation, and all to burn some old timber-man, or catch a Norway trader asleep! give way, men, give way."

Notwithstanding the heavy and dangerous surf that was beginning to tumble in upon the rocks, in an alarming manner, the startled seamen succeeded in urging their light boat over the waves, and in a few seconds were without the point where danger was most to be apprehended. Barnstable had seemingly disregarded the breakers as they passed, but sat sternly eyeing the foam that rolled by them in successive surges, until the boat rose regularly on the long seas, when he turned his looks around the bay, in quest of the barge.

"Ay, Griffith has tired of rocking in his pillowed cradle," he muttered, "and will give us a pull to the frigate, when we ought to be getting the schooner out of this hard-featured landscape. This is just a place as one of your sighing lovers would doat on: a little land, a little water, and a good deal of rock. Damme, long Tom, but I am more than half of your mind, that an island, now and then, is all the terra firma that a seaman needs."

"It's reason and philosophy, sir," returned the sedate cockswain; "and what land there is, should always be a soft mud, or a sandy ooze, in order that an anchor might hold, and to make soundings sartin. I have lost many a deep-sea, besides hand-leads by the dozens, on rocky bottoms; but give me the roadsted where a lead comes up light, and an anchor heavy.

There's a boat pulling athwart our fore-foot, Captain Barnstable; shall I run her aboard, or give her a birth, sir?"

"'Tis the barge!" cried the officer; "Ned has not deserted
me after all!"

A loud hail from the approaching boat confirmed this opinion, and, in a few seconds, the barge and whale-boat were
again rolling by each other's side. Griffith was no longer reclining on the cushions of his seats, but spoke earnestly, and
with a slight tone of reproach in his manner.

"Why have you wasted so many precious moments, when
every minute threatens us with new dangers? I was obeying
the signal, but I heard your oars, and pulled back, to take out
the pilot. Have you been successful?"

"There he is, and if he finds his way out, through the
shoals, he will earn a right to his name. This bids fair to be a
night when a man will need a spy-glass to find the moon. But
when you hear what I have seen on those rascally cliffs, you
will be more ready to excuse my delay, Mr. Griffith."

"You have seen the true man, I trust, or we incur this hazard to an evil purpose."

"Ay, I have seen him that is a true man, and him that is
not," replied Barnstable, bitterly; "you have the boy with you,
Griffith—ask him what his young eyes have seen."

"Shall I!" cried the young midshipman, laughing; "then I
have seen a little clipper, in disguise, outsail an old man-of-
war's-man in a hard chase, and I have seen a straggling rover
in long-togs as much like my cousin—"

"Peace, gabbler!" exclaimed Barnstable, in a voice of thunder; "would you detain the boats with your silly nonsense, at
a time like this? Away into the barge, sir, and if you find him
willing to hear, tell Mr. Griffith what your foolish conjectures
amount to, at your leisure."

The boy stepped lightly from the whale-boat to the barge,
whither the pilot had already preceded him, and as he sunk,
with a mortified air, by the side of Griffith, he said, in a low
voice—

"And that won't be long, I know, if Mr. Griffith thinks
and feels on the coast of England as he thought and felt at
home."

A silent pressure of his hand, was the only reply that the

young lieutenant made, before he paid the parting compliments to Barnstable, and directed his men to pull for their ship.

The boats were separating, and the plash of the oars was already heard, when the voice of the pilot was for the first time raised in earnest.

"Hold!" he cried; "hold water, I bid ye!"

The men ceased their efforts, at the commanding tones of his voice, and turning towards the whale-boat, he continued—

"You will get your schooner under-way immediately, Captain Barnstable, and sweep into the offing, with as little delay as possible. Keep the ship well open from the northern headland, and as you pass us, come within hail."

"This is a clean chart and plain sailing, Mr. Pilot," returned Barnstable; "but who is to justify my moving without orders, to Captain Munson? I have it in black and white, to run the Ariel into this feather-bed sort of a place, and I must at least have it by signal or word of mouth from my betters, before my cut-water curls another wave. The road may be as hard to find going out as it was coming in—and then I had daylight, as well as your written directions to steer by."

"Would you lie there to perish on such a night!" said the pilot, sternly. "Two hours hence, this heavy swell will break where your vessel now rides so quietly."

"There we think exactly alike; but if I get drowned now, I am drowned according to orders; whereas, if I knock a plank out of the schooner's bottom, by following your directions, 'twill be a hole to let in mutiny, as well as sea-water. How do I know but the old man wants another pilot or two?"

"That's philosophy," muttered the cockswain of the whale-boat, in a voice that was audible: "but it's a hard strain on a man's conscience to hold on in such an anchorage."

"Then keep your anchor down, and follow it to the bottom," said the pilot to himself; "it's worse to contend with a fool than a gale of wind; but if—"

"No, no, sir—no fool neither," interrupted Griffith. "Barnstable does not deserve that epithet, though he certainly carries the point of duty to the extreme. Heave up at once, Mr. Barnstable, and get out of this bay as fast as possible."

"Ah! you don't give the order with half the pleasure with which I shall execute it; pull away, boys—the Ariel shall never lay her bones in such a hard bed, if I can help it."

As the commander of the schooner uttered these words with a cheering voice, his men spontaneously shouted, and the whale-boat darted away from her companion, and was soon lost in the gloomy shadows cast from the cliffs.

In the mean time, the oarsmen of the barge were not idle, but by strenuous efforts they forced the heavy boat rapidly through the water, and in a few minutes she ran alongside of the frigate. During this period the pilot, in a voice which had lost all the startling fierceness and authority it had manifested in his short dialogue with Barnstable, requested Griffith to repeat to him, slowly, the names of the officers that belonged to his ship. When the young lieutenant had complied with this request, he observed to his companion—

"All good men and true, Mr. Pilot; and though this business in which you are just now engaged may be hazardous to an Englishman, there are none with us who will betray you. We need your services, and as we expect good faith from you, so shall we offer it to you in exchange."

"And how know you that I need its exercise?" asked the pilot, in a manner that denoted a cold indifference to the subject.

"Why, though you talk pretty good English, for a native," returned Griffith, "yet you have a small bur-r-r in your mouth that would prick the tongue of a man who was born on the other side of the Atlantic."

"It is but of little moment where a man is born, or how he speaks," returned the pilot, coldly, "so that he does his duty bravely, and in good faith."

It was perhaps fortunate for the harmony of this dialogue, that the gloom, which had now increased to positive darkness, completely concealed the look of scornful irony that crossed the handsome features of the young sailor, as he replied—

"True, true, so that he does his duty, as you say, in good faith. But, as Barnstable observed, you must know your road well to travel among these shoals on such a night as this. Know you what water we draw?"

" 'Tis a frigate's draught, and I shall endeavour to keep you in four fathoms; less than that would be dangerous."

"She's a sweet boat!" said Griffith; "and minds her helm as a marine watches the eye of his sergeant at a drill; but you must give her room in stays, for she fore-reaches, as if she would put out the wind's eye."

The pilot attended, with a practised ear, to this description of the qualities of the ship that he was about to attempt extricating from an extremely dangerous situation. Not a syllable was lost on him; and when Griffith had ended, he remarked, with the singular coldness that pervaded his manner—

"That is both a good and a bad quality in a narrow channel. I fear it will be the latter, to-night, when we shall require to have the ship in leading strings."

"I suppose we must feel our way with the lead?" said Griffith.

"We shall need both eyes and leads," returned the pilot, recurring insensibly to his soliloquizing tone of voice. "I have been both in and out in darker nights than this, though never with a heavier draught than a half-two."

"Then, by heaven, you are not fit to handle that ship, among these rocks and breakers!" exclaimed Griffith; "your men of a light draught never know their water; 'tis the deep keel only, that finds a channel—pilot! pilot! beware how you trifle with us ignorantly; for 'tis a dangerous experiment to play at hazards with an enemy."

"Young man, you know not what you threaten, nor whom," said the pilot, sternly, though his quiet manner still remained undisturbed; "you forget that you have a superior here, and that I have none."

"That shall be as you discharge your duty," cried Griffith; "for if—"

"Peace," interrupted the pilot, "we approach the ship; let us enter in harmony."

He threw himself back on the cushions, when he had said this, and Griffith, though filled with the apprehensions of suffering, either by great ignorance, or treachery, on the part of his companion, smothered his feelings so far as to be silent, and they ascended the side of the vessel in apparent cordiality.

The frigate was already riding on lengthened seas, that

rolled in from the ocean, at each successive moment, with increasing violence, though her topsails still hung supinely from her yards; the air, which continued to breathe, occasionally, from the land, being unable to shake the heavy canvass of which they were composed.

The only sounds that were audible, when Griffith and the pilot had ascended to the gangway of the frigate, were produced by the sullen dashing of the sea against the massive bows of the ship, and the shrill whistle of the boatswain's mate, as he recalled the side-boys, who were placed on either side of the gangway, to do honour to the entrance of the first lieutenant and his companion.

But though such a profound silence reigned among the hundreds who inhabited the huge fabric, the light produced by a dozen battle lanterns, that were arranged in different parts of the decks, served not only to exhibit, faintly, the persons of the crew, but the mingled feeling of curiosity and care that dwelt on most of their countenances.

Large groups of men were collected in the gangways, around the mainmast, and on the booms of the vessel, whose faces were distinctly visible, while numerous figures, lying along the lower yards, or bending out of the tops, might be dimly traced in the back ground, all of whom expressed, by their attitudes, the interest they took in the arrival of the boat.

Though such crowds were collected in other parts of the vessel, the quarter deck was occupied only by the officers, who were disposed according to their several ranks, and were equally silent and attentive as the remainder of the crew. In front stood a small collection of young men, who, by their similarity of dress, were the equals and companions of Griffith, though his juniors in rank. On the opposite side of the vessel was a larger assemblage of youths, who claimed Mr. Merry as their fellow. Around the capstern, three or four figures were standing, one of whom wore a coat of blue, with the scarlet facings of a soldier, and another the black vestments of the ship's chaplain. Behind these, and nearer the passage to the cabin, from which he had just ascended, stood the tall, erect form of the commander of the vessel.

After a brief salutation between Griffith and the junior officers, the former advanced, followed slowly by the pilot, to the place where he was expected by his veteran commander. The young man removed his hat entirely, as he bowed with a little more than his usual ceremony, and said—

"We have succeeded, sir, though not without more difficulty and delay than were anticipated."

"But you have not brought off the pilot," said the captain, "and without him, all our risk and trouble have been in vain."

"He is here," said Griffith, stepping aside, and extending his arm towards the man that stood behind him, wrapped to the chin in his coarse pea-jacket, and with his face shadowed by the falling rims of a large hat, that had seen much and hard service.

"This!" exclaimed the captain; "then there is a sad mistake—this is not the man I would have seen, nor can another supply his place."

"I know not whom you expected, Captain Munson," said the stranger, in a low, quiet voice; "but if you have not forgotten the day when a very different flag from that emblem of tyranny that now hangs over yon tafferel was first spread to the wind, you may remember the hand that raised it."

"Bring here the light!" exclaimed the commander, hastily.

When the lantern was extended towards the pilot, and the glare fell strong on his features, Captain Munson started, as he beheld the calm blue eye that met his gaze, and the composed, but pallid countenance of the other. Involuntarily raising his hat, and baring his silver locks, the veteran cried—

"It is he! though so changed—"

"That his enemies did not know him," interrupted the pilot, quickly; then touching the other by the arm as he led him aside, he continued, in a lower tone, "neither must his friends, until the proper hour shall arrive."

Griffith had fallen back, to answer the eager questions of his messmates, and no part of this short dialogue was overheard by the officers, though it was soon perceived that their commander had discovered his error, and was satisfied that the proper man had been brought on board his vessel. For many minutes the two continued to pace a part of the quarter-deck, by themselves, engaged in deep and earnest discourse.

As Griffith had but little to communicate, the curiosity of

his listeners was soon appeased, and all eyes were directed towards that mysterious guide, who was to conduct them from a situation already surrounded by perils, which each moment not only magnified in appearance, but increased in reality.

# Chapter IV.

——"behold the threaden sails,
Borne with the invisible and creeping winds,
Draw the huge bottoms through the furrowed sea,
Breasting the lofty surge."
*Henry V*, III.i.10—13.

---

IT HAS BEEN already explained to the reader, that there were threatening symptoms in the appearance of the weather to create serious forebodings of evil in the breast of a seaman. When removed from the shadows of the cliffs, the night was not so dark but objects could be discerned at some little distance, and in the eastern horizon there was a streak of fearful light impending over the gloomy waters, in which the swelling outline formed by the rising waves, was becoming each moment more distinct, and consequently more alarming. Several dark clouds overhung the vessel, whose towering masts apparently propped the black vapour, while a few stars were seen twinkling, with a sickly flame, in the streak of clear sky that skirted the ocean. Still, light currents of air, occasionally, swept across the bay, bringing with them the fresh odour from the shore, but their flitting irregularity too surely foretold them to be the expiring breath of the land breeze. The roaring of the surf, as it rolled on the margin of the bay, produced a dull, monotonous sound, that was only interrupted, at times, by a hollow bellowing, as a larger wave than usual broke violently against some cavity in the rocks. Every thing, in short, united to render the scene gloomy and portentous, without creating instant terror, for the ship rose easily on the long billows, without even straightening the heavy cable that held her to her anchor.

The higher officers were collected around the capstern, engaged in earnest discourse about their situation and prospects, while some of the oldest and most favoured seamen would extend their short walk to the hallowed precincts of the quarter-deck, to catch, with greedy ears, the opinions that fell from their superiors. Numberless were the uneasy glances that were thrown from both officers and men at their commander and the pilot, who still continued their secret communion in a distant part of the vessel. Once, an ungovernable curiosity, or the heedlessness of his years, led one of the youthful midshipmen near them, but a stern rebuke from his captain sent the boy, abashed and cowering, to hide his mortification among his fellows. This reprimand was received by the elder officers as an intimation that the consultation which they beheld, was to be strictly inviolate; and, though it by no means suppressed the repeated expressions of their impatience, it effectually prevented an interruption to the communications, which all, however, thought were unreasonably protracted for the occasion.

"This is no time to be talking over bearings and distances," observed the officer next in rank to Griffith. "But we should call the hands up, and try to kedge her off while the sea will suffer a boat to live."

" 'Twould be a tedious and bootless job to attempt warping a ship for miles against a head-beating sea," returned the first lieutenant; "but the land-breeze yet flutters aloft, and if our light sails would draw, with the aid of this ebb tide we might be able to shove her from the shore."

"Hail the tops, Griffith," said the other, "and ask if they feel the air above; 'twill be a hint at least to set the old man and that lubberly pilot in motion."

Griffith laughed, as he complied with the request, and when he received the customary reply to his call, he demanded, in a loud voice—

"Which way have you the wind, aloft?"

"We feel a light cat's-paw, now and then, from the land, sir," returned the sturdy captain of the top; "but our topsail hangs in the clewlines, sir, without winking."

Captain Munson and his companion suspended their discourse, while this question and answer were exchanged, and then resumed their dialogue as earnestly as if it had received no interruption.

"If it did wink, the hint would be lost on our betters," said the officer of the marines, whose ignorance of seamanship added greatly to his perception of the danger, but who, from pure idleness, made more jokes than any other man in the ship. "That pilot would not receive a delicate intimation through his ears, Mr. Griffith; suppose you try him by the nose."

"Faith, there was a flash of gunpowder between us in the barge," returned the first lieutenant, "and he does not seem a man to stomach such hints as you advise. Although he looks so meek and quiet, I doubt whether he has paid much attention to the book of Job."

"Why should he!" exclaimed the chaplain, whose apprehensions at least equalled those of the marine, and with a much more disheartening effect; "I'm sure it would have been a great waste of time; there are so many charts of the coast, and books on the navigation of these seas, for him to study, that I sincerely hope he has been much better employed."

A loud laugh was created at this speech, among the listeners, and it apparently produced the effect that was so long anxiously desired, by putting an end to the mysterious conference between their captain and the pilot. As the former came forward towards his expecting crew, he said, in the composed, steady manner, that formed the principal trait in his character —

"Get the anchor, Mr. Griffith, and make sail on the ship; the hour has arrived when we must be moving."

The cheerful "ay! ay! sir!" of the young lieutenant was hardly uttered, before the cries of half a dozen midshipmen were heard summoning the boatswain and his mates to their duty.

There was a general movement in the living masses that clustered around the mainmast, on the booms, and in the gangways, though their habits of discipline held the crew a moment longer in suspense. The silence was first broken by the sounds of the boatswain's whistle, followed by the hoarse cry of "all hands, up anchor, ahoy!" — the former rising on the night air, from its first low, mellow notes, to a piercing shrillness, that gradually died away on the waters; and the latter, bellowing through every cranny of the ship, like the hollow murmurs of distant thunder.

The change produced by this customary summons was magical. Human beings sprung out from between the guns, rushed up the hatches, threw themselves with careless activity from the booms, and gathered from every quarter so rapidly, that, in an instant, the deck of the frigate was alive with men. The profound silence, that had hitherto been only interrupted by the low dialogue of the officers, was now exchanged for the stern orders of the lieutenants, mingled with the shriller cries of the midshipmen, and the hoarse bawling of the boat-swain's crew, rising above the tumult of preparation and general bustle.

The captain and the pilot alone remained passive, in this scene of general exertion; for apprehension had even stimulated that class of officers which is called "idlers," to unusual activity, though frequently reminded by their more experienced messmates, that instead of aiding, they retarded, the duty of the vessel. The bustle, however, gradually ceased, and in a few minutes the same silence pervaded the ship as before.

"We are brought-to, sir," said Griffith, who stood over-looking the scene, holding in one hand a short speaking trumpet, and grasping, with the other, one of the shrouds of the ship, to steady himself in the position he had taken on a gun.

"Heave round, sir," was the calm reply.

"Heave round!" repeated Griffith, aloud.

"Heave round!" echoed a dozen eager voices at once, and the lively strains of a fife struck up a brisk air, to enliven the labour. The capstern was instantly set in motion, and the measured tread of the seamen was heard, as they stamped the deck in the circle of their march. For a few minutes, no other sounds were heard, if we except the voice of an officer, occasionally, cheering the sailors, when it was announced that they "were short," or, in other words, that the ship was nearly over her anchor.

"Heave and pall," cried Griffith; when the quivering notes of the whistle were again succeeded by a general stillness in the vessel.

"What is to be done now, sir?" continued the lieutenant; "shall we trip the anchor? There seems not a breath of air, and as the tide runs slack, I doubt whether the sea do not heave the ship ashore."

There was so much obvious truth in this conjecture, that all eyes turned from the light and animation afforded by the decks of the frigate, to look abroad on the waters, in a vain desire to pierce the darkness, as if to read the fate of their apparently devoted ship, from the aspect of nature.

"I leave all to the pilot," said the captain, after he had stood a short time by the side of Griffith, anxiously studying the heavens and the ocean. "What say you, Mr. Gray?"

The man who was, thus, first addressed by name, was leaning over the bulwarks, with his eyes bent in the same direction as the others; but as he answered, he turned his face towards the speaker, and the light from the deck fell full upon his quiet features, which exhibited a calmness bordering on the supernatural, considering his station and responsibility.

"There is much to fear from this heavy ground-swell," he said, in the same unmoved tones as before; "but there is certain destruction to us, if the gale that is brewing in the east, finds us waiting its fury in this wild anchorage. All the hemp that was ever spun into cordage would not hold a ship an hour, chafing on these rocks, with a north-easter pouring its fury on her. If the powers of man can compass it, gentlemen, we must get an offing, and that speedily."

"You say no more, sir, than the youngest boy in the ship can see for himself," said Griffith—"ha! here comes the schooner!"

The dashing of the long sweeps in the water, was now plainly audible, and the little Ariel was seen through the gloom, moving heavily under their feeble impulse. As she passed slowly under the stern of the frigate, the cheerful voice of Barnstable was first heard, opening the communications between them.

"Here's a night for spectacles, Captain Munson!" he cried; "but I thought I heard your fife, sir; I trust in God, you do not mean to ride it out here till morning?"

"I like the birth as little as yourself, Mr. Barnstable," returned the veteran seaman, in his calm manner, in which anxiety was however beginning to grow evident. "We are short, but are afraid to let go our hold of the bottom, lest the sea cast us ashore. How make you out the wind?"

"Wind!" echoed the other; "there is not enough to blow a lady's curl aside. If you wait, sir, till the land breeze fills your sails, you will wait another moon, I believe. I've got my egg-shell out of that nest of gray-caps, but how it has been done in the dark, a better man than myself must explain."

"Take your directions from the pilot, Mr. Barnstable," re-

turned his commanding officer, "and follow them strictly and
to the letter."

A death-like silence, in both vessels, succeeded this order,
for all seemed to listen eagerly to catch the words that fell
from the man, on whom, even the boys now felt, depended
their only hopes for safety. A short time was suffered to
elapse, before his voice was heard, in the same low, but distinct tones as before—

"Your sweeps will soon be of no service to you," he said,
"against the sea that begins to heave in; but your light sails
will help them to get you out. So long as you can head east-
and-by-north, you are doing well, and you can stand on till
you open the light from that northern headland, when you
can heave to, and fire a gun; but if, as I dread, you are struck
aback, before you open the light, you may trust to your lead
on the larboard tack, but beware, with your head to the
southward, for no lead will serve you there."

"I can walk over the same ground on one tack as on the
other," said Barnstable, "and make both legs of a length."

"It will not do," returned the pilot. "If you fall off a point
to starboard from east-and-by-north, in going large, you will
find both rocks and points of shoals to bring you up; and
beware, as I tell you, of the starboard tack."

"And how shall I find my way; you will let me trust to
neither time, lead, nor log."

"You must trust to a quick eye and a ready hand. The
breakers only will show you the dangers, when you are not
able to make out the bearings of the land. Tack in season, sir,
and don't spare the lead, when you head to port."

"Ay, ay," returned Barnstable, in a low, muttering voice.
"This is a sort of blind navigation with a vengeance, and all
for no purpose that I can see—see! damme, eyesight is of
about as much use now, as a man's nose would be in reading
the bible."

"Softly, softly, Mr. Barnstable," interrupted his commander, for such was the anxious stillness in both vessels, that
even the rattling of the schooner's rigging was heard, as she
rolled in the trough of the sea—"the duty on which Congress
has sent us must be performed at the hazard of our lives."

"I don't mind my life, Captain Munson," said Barnstable;

"but there is a great want of conscience in trusting a vessel in such a place as this. However, it is a time to do, and not to talk. But if there be such danger to an easy draught of water, what will become of the frigate? had I not better play jackall, and try and feel the way for you."

"I thank you," said the pilot; "the offer is generous, but would avail us nothing. I have the advantage of knowing the ground well, and must trust to my memory and God's good favour. Make sail, make sail, sir, and if you succeed, we will venture to break ground."

The order was promptly obeyed, and in a very short time, the Ariel was covered with canvass. Though no air was perceptible on the decks of the frigate, the little schooner was so light, that she succeeded in stemming her way over the rising waves, aided a little by the tide, and in a few minutes, her low hull was just discernible in the streak of light along the horizon, with the dark outline of her sails rising above the sea, until their fanciful summits were lost in the shadows of the clouds.

Griffith had listened to the foregoing dialogue, like the rest of the junior officers, in profound silence; but when the Ariel began to grow indistinct to the eye, he jumped lightly from the gun to the deck, and cried—

"She slips off, like a vessel from the stocks! shall I trip the anchor, sir, and follow?"

"We have no choice," replied his captain. "You hear the question, Mr. Gray? shall we let go the bottom?"

"It must be done, Captain Munson; we may want more drift than the rest of this tide to get us to a place of safety," said the pilot; "I would give five years from a life, that I know will be short, if the ship lay one mile further seaward."

This remark was unheard by all, except the commander of the frigate, who again walked aside with the pilot, where they resumed their mysterious communications. The words of assent were no sooner uttered, however, than Griffith gave forth from his trumpet the command to "heave away!" Again the strains of the fife were followed by the tread of the men at the capstern. At the same time that the anchor was heaving up, the sails were loosened from the yards, and opened to invite the breeze. In effecting this duty, orders were thun-

dered through the trumpet of the first lieutenant, and executed with the rapidity of thought. Men were to be seen, like
spots in the dim light from the heavens, lying on every yard,
or hanging as in air, while strange cries were heard issuing
from every part of the rigging, and each spar of the vessel.
"Ready the fore-royal," cried a shrill voice, as if from the
clouds; "ready the fore yard," uttered the hoarser tones of a
seaman beneath him; "all ready aft, sir," cried a third, from
another quarter; and in a few moments, the order was given
to "let fall."

The little light which fell from the sky, was now excluded
by the falling canvass, and a deeper gloom was cast athwart
the decks of the ship, that served to render the brilliancy of
the lanterns even vivid, while it gave to objects outboard a
more appalling and dreary appearance than before.

Every individual, excepting the commander and his associate, was now earnestly engaged in getting the ship under
way. The sounds of "we're away," were repeated by a burst
from fifty voices, and the rapid evolutions of the capstern
announced that nothing but the weight of the anchor was to
be lifted. The hauling of cordage, the rattling of blocks,
blended with the shrill calls of the boatswain and his mates,
succeeded; and though to a landsman all would have appeared confusion and hurry, long practice and strict discipline
enabled the crew to exhibit their ship under a cloud of canvass, from her deck to the trucks, in less time than we have
consumed in relating it.

For a few minutes, the officers were not disappointed by
the result, for though the heavy sails flapped lazily against the
masts, the light duck on the loftier spars swelled outwardly,
and the ship began sensibly to yield to their influence.

"She travels! she travels!" exclaimed Griffith, joyously; "ah!
the hussy! she has as much antipathy to the land as any fish
that swims! it blows a little gale aloft, yet!"

"We feel its dying breath," said the pilot, in low, soothing
tones, but in a manner so sudden as to startle Griffith, at
whose elbow they were unexpectedly uttered. "Let us forget,
young man, every thing but the number of lives that depend,
this night, on your exertions and my knowledge."

"If you be but half as able to exhibit the one, as I am

willing to make the other, we shall do well," returned the lieutenant, in the same tone. "Remember, whatever may be your feelings, that *we* are on an enemy's coast, and love it not enough to wish to lay our bones there."

With this brief explanation, they separated, the vessel requiring the constant and close attention of the officer to her movements.

The exultation produced in the crew by the progress of their ship through the water, was of short duration; for the breeze that had seemed to await their motions, after forcing the vessel for a quarter of a mile, fluttered for a few minutes amid their light canvass, and then left them entirely. The quarter-master, whose duty it was to superintend the helm, soon announced that he was losing the command of the vessel, as she was no longer obedient to her rudder. This ungrateful intelligence was promptly communicated to his commander, by Griffith, who suggested the propriety of again dropping an anchor.

"I refer you to Mr. Gray," returned the captain; "he is the pilot, sir, and with him rests the safety of the vessel."

"Pilots sometimes lose ships, as well as save them," said Griffith; "know you the man well, Captain Munson, who holds all our lives in his keeping, and so coolly as if he cared but little for the venture?"

"Mr. Griffith, I do know him; he is, in my opinion, both competent and faithful. Thus much I tell you, to relieve your anxiety; more you must not ask;—but is there not a shift of wind?"

"God forbid!" exclaimed his lieutenant; "if that north-easter catches us within the shoals, our case will be desperate indeed!"

The heavy rolling of the vessel caused an occasional expansion, and as sudden a re-action, in their sails, which left the oldest seamen in the ship in doubt which way the currents of air were passing, or whether there existed any that were not created by the flapping of their own canvass. The head of the ship, however, began to fall off from the sea, and notwithstanding the darkness, it soon became apparent that she was driving in, bodily, towards the shore.

During these few minutes of gloomy doubt, Griffith, by

one of those sudden revulsions of the mind, that connect the opposite extremes of feeling, lost his animated anxiety, and relapsed into the listless apathy that so often came over him, even in the most critical moments of trial and danger. He was standing, with one elbow resting on the capstern, shading his eyes from the light of the battle-lantern that stood near him, with one hand, when he felt a gentle pressure of the other, that recalled his recollection. Looking affectionately, though still recklessly, at the boy who stood at his side, he said—

"Dull music, Mr. Merry."

"So dull, sir, that I can't dance to it," returned the midshipman. "Nor do I believe there is a man in the ship who would not rather hear 'The girl I left behind me,' than those execrable sounds."

"What sounds, boy! The ship is as quiet as the quaker meeting in the Jerseys, before your good old grandfather used to break the charm of silence with his sonorous voice."

"Ah! laugh at my peaceable blood, if thou wilt, Mr. Griffith," said the arch youngster; "but remember, there is a mixture of it in all sorts of veins. I wish I could hear one of the old gentleman's chants now, sir; I could always sleep to them, like a gull in a surf. But he that sleeps to-night, with that lullaby, will make a nap of it."

"Sounds! I hear no sounds, boy, but the flapping aloft; even that pilot, who struts the quarter-deck like an admiral, has nothing to say."

"Is not that a sound to open a seaman's ear?"

"It is in truth a heavy roll of the surf, lad, but the night air carries it heavily to our ears. Know you not the sounds of the surf yet, younker?"

"I know it too well, Mr. Griffith, and do not wish to know it better. How fast are we tumbling in towards that surf, sir?"

"I think we hold our own," said Griffith, rousing again; "though we had better anchor. Luff, fellow, luff, you are broadside to the sea!"

The man at the wheel repeated his former intelligence, adding a suggestion that he thought the ship "was gathering stern-way."

"Haul up your courses, Mr. Griffith," said Captain Munson, "and let us feel the wind."

The rattling of the blocks was soon heard, and the enormous sheets of canvass that hung from the lower yards were instantly suspended "in the brails." When this change was effected, all on board stood silent and breathless, as if expecting to learn their fate by the result. Several contradictory opinions were, at length, hazarded among the officers, when Griffith seized the candle from the lantern, and springing on one of the guns, held it on high, exposed to the action of the air. The little flame waved, with uncertain glimmering, for a moment, and then burned steadily, in a line with the masts. Griffith was about to lower his extended arm, when, feeling a slight sensation of coolness on his hand, he paused, and the light turned slowly towards the land, flared, flickered, and finally deserted the wick.

"Lose not a moment, Mr. Griffith," cried the pilot, aloud; "clew up and furl every thing but your three topsails, and let them be double-reefed. Now is the time to fulfil your promise."

The young man paused one moment, in astonishment, as the clear, distinct tones of the stranger struck his ears so unexpectedly; but turning his eyes to seaward, he sprang on the deck, and proceeded to obey the order, as if life and death depended on his despatch.

# Chapter V.

"She rights, she rights, boys! ware off shore!"
G. A. Stevens, "The Storm." l. 64.

THE EXTRAORDINARY ACTIVITY of Griffith, which communicated itself with promptitude to the crew, was produced by a sudden alteration in the weather. In place of the well-defined streak along the horizon, that has been already described, an immense body of misty light appeared to be moving in, with rapidity, from the ocean, while a distinct but distant roaring announced the sure approach of the tempest, that had so long troubled the waters. Even Griffith, while thundering his orders through the trumpet, and urging the men, by his cries, to expedition, would pause, for instants, to cast anxious glances in the direction of the coming storm, and the faces of the sailors who lay on the yards were turned, instinctively, towards the same quarter of the heavens, while they knotted the reef-points, or passed the gaskets, that were to confine the unruly canvass to the prescribed limits.

The pilot alone, in that confused and busy throng, where voice rose above voice, and cry echoed cry, in quick succession, appeared as if he held no interest in the important stake. With his eyes steadily fixed on the approaching mist, and his arms folded together, in composure, he stood calmly waiting the result.

The ship had fallen off, with her broadside to the sea, and was become unmanageable, and the sails were already brought into the folds necessary to her security, when the quick and heavy fluttering of canvass was thrown across the water, with all the gloomy and chilling sensations that such sounds produce, where darkness and danger unite to appal the seaman.

"The schooner has it!" cried Griffith; "Barnstable has held on, like himself, to the last moment—God send that the squall leave him cloth enough to keep him from the shore!"

"His sails are easily handled," the commander observed, "and she must be over the principal danger. We are falling off before it, Mr. Gray; shall we try a cast of the lead?"

The pilot turned from his contemplative posture, and

moved slowly across the deck, before he returned any reply to this question—like a man who not only felt that every thing depended on himself, but that he was equal to the emergency.

" 'Tis unnecessary," he at length said; " 'twould be certain destruction to be taken aback, and it is difficult to say, within several points, how the wind may strike us."

" 'Tis difficult no longer," cried Griffith; "for here it comes, and in right earnest!"

The rushing sounds of the wind were now, indeed, heard at hand, and the words were hardly past the lips of the young lieutenant, before the vessel bowed down heavily to one side, and then, as she began to move through the water, rose again majestically to her upright position, as if saluting, like a courteous champion, the powerful antagonist with which she was about to contend. Not another minute elapsed, before the ship was throwing the waters aside, with a lively progress, and, obedient to her helm, was brought as near to the desired course, as the direction of the wind would allow. The hurry and bustle on the yards gradually subsided, and the men slowly descended to the deck, all straining their eyes to pierce the gloom in which they were enveloped, and some shaking their heads, in melancholy doubt, afraid to express the apprehensions they really entertained. All on board anxiously waited for the fury of the gale; for there were none so ignorant or inexperienced in that gallant frigate, as not to know, that as yet, they only felt the infant efforts of the wind. Each moment, however, it increased in power, though so gradual was the alteration, that the relieved mariners began to believe that all their gloomy forebodings were not to be realized. During this short interval of uncertainty, no other sounds were heard than the whistling of the breeze, as it passed quickly through the mass of rigging that belonged to the vessel, and the dashing of the spray, that began to fly from her bows, like the foam of a cataract.

"It blows fresh," cried Griffith, who was the first to speak in that moment of doubt and anxiety; "but it is no more than a cap-full of wind, after all. Give us elbow-room, and the right canvass, Mr. Pilot, and I'll handle the ship like a gentleman's yacht, in this breeze."

"Will she stay, think ye, under this sail?" said the low voice of the stranger.

"She will do all that man, in reason, can ask of wood and iron," returned the lieutenant; "but the vessel don't float the ocean that will tack under double-reefed topsails alone, against a heavy sea. Help her with the courses, pilot, and you shall see her come round like a dancing-master."

"Let us feel the strength of the gale first," returned the man who was called Mr. Gray, moving from the side of Griffith to the weather gangway of the vessel, where he stood in silence, looking ahead of the ship, with an air of singular coolness and abstraction.

All the lanterns had been extinguished on the deck of the frigate, when her anchor was secured, and as the first mist of the gale had passed over, it was succeeded by a faint light that was a good deal aided by the glittering foam of the waters, which now broke in white curls around the vessel, in every direction. The land could be faintly discerned, rising like a heavy bank of black fog, above the margin of the waters, and was only distinguishable from the heavens, by its deeper gloom and obscurity. The last rope was coiled, and deposited in its proper place, by the seamen, and for several minutes the stillness of death pervaded the crowded decks. It was evident to every one, that their ship was dashing at a prodigious rate through the waves; and as she was approaching, with such velocity, the quarter of the bay where the shoals and dangers were known to be situated, nothing but the habits of the most exact discipline could suppress the uneasiness of the officers and men within their own bosoms. At length the voice of Captain Munson was heard, calling to the pilot.

"Shall I send a hand into the chains, Mr. Gray," he said, "and try our water?"

Although this question was asked aloud, and the interest it excited drew many of the officers and men around him, in eager impatience for his answer, it was unheeded by the man to whom it was addressed. His head rested on his hand, as he leaned over the hammock-cloths of the vessel, and his whole air was that of one whose thoughts wandered from the pressing necessity of their situation. Griffith was among those who had approached the pilot, and after waiting a moment, from respect, to hear the answer to his commander's question, he presumed on his own rank, and leaving the circle that stood at a little distance, stepped to the side of the mysterious guardian of their lives.

"Captain Munson desires to know whether you wish a cast of the lead?" said the young officer, with a little impatience of manner. No immediate answer was made to this repetition of the question, and Griffith laid his hand, unceremoniously, on the shoulder of the other, with an intent to rouse him, before he made another application for a reply, but the convulsive start of the pilot held him silent in amazement.

"Fall back there," said the lieutenant, sternly, to the men who were closing around them in a compact circle; "away with you to your stations, and see all clear for stays." The dense mass of heads dissolved, at this order, like the water of one of the waves commingling with the ocean, and the lieutenant and his companion were left by themselves.

"This is not a time for musing, Mr. Gray," continued Griffith; "remember our compact, and look to your charge —is it not time to put the vessel in stays? of what are you dreaming?"

The pilot laid his hand on the extended arm of the lieutenant, and grasped it with a convulsive pressure, as he answered—

" 'Tis a dream of reality. You are young, Mr. Griffith, nor am I past the noon of life; but should you live fifty years longer, you never can see and experience what I have encountered in my little period of three-and-thirty years!"

A good deal astonished at this burst of feeling, so singular at such a moment, the young sailor was at a loss for a reply; but as his duty was uppermost in his thoughts, he still dwelt on the theme that most interested him.

"I hope much of your experience has been on this coast, for the ship travels lively," he said, "and the daylight showed us so much to dread, that we do not feel over-valiant in the dark. How much longer shall we stand on, upon this tack?"

The pilot turned slowly from the side of the vessel, and walked towards the commander of the frigate, as he replied, in a tone that seemed deeply agitated by his melancholy reflections—

"You have your wish, then; much, very much of my early life was passed on this dreaded coast. What to you is all darkness and gloom, to me is as light as if a noon-day sun shone upon it. But tack your ship, sir, tack your ship; I would see how she works, before we reach the point, where she *must* behave well, or we perish."

Griffith gazed after him in wonder, while the pilot slowly paced the quarter-deck, and then, rousing from his trance, gave forth the cheering order that called each man to his station, to perform the desired evolution. The confident assurances which the young officer had given to the pilot, respecting the qualities of his vessel, and his own ability to manage her, were fully realized by the result. The helm was no sooner put a-lee, than the huge ship bore up gallantly against the wind, and dashing directly through the waves, threw the foam high into the air, as she looked boldly into the very eye of the wind, and then, yielding gracefully to its power, she fell off on the other tack, with her head pointed from those dangerous shoals that she had so recently approached with such terrifying velocity. The heavy yards swung round, as if they had been vanes to indicate the currents of the air, and in a few moments the frigate again moved, with stately progress, through the water, leaving the rocks and shoals behind her on one side of the bay, but advancing towards those that offered equal danger on the other.

During this time, the sea was becoming more agitated, and the violence of the wind was gradually increasing. The latter no longer whistled amid the cordage of the vessel, but it seemed to howl, surlily, as it passed the complicated machinery that the frigate obtruded on its path. An endless succession of white surges rose above the heavy billows, and the very air was glittering with the light that was disengaged from the ocean. The ship yielded, each moment, more and more before the storm, and in less than half an hour from the time that she had lifted her anchor, she was driven along, with tremendous fury, by the full power of a gale of wind. Still, the hardy and experienced mariners who directed her movements, held her to the course that was necessary to their preservation, and still Griffith gave forth, when directed by their unknown pilot, those orders that turned her in the narrow channel where alone safety was to be found.

So far, the performance of his duty appeared easy to the stranger, and he gave the required directions in those still, calm tones, that formed so remarkable a contrast to the responsibility of his situation. But when the land was becoming dim, in distance as well as darkness, and the agitated sea alone was to be discovered as it swept by them in foam, he broke in upon the monotonous roaring of the tempest, with the sounds of his voice, seeming to shake off his apathy, and rouse himself to the occasion.

"Now is the time to watch her closely, Mr. Griffith," he cried; "here we get the true tide and the real danger. Place the best quarter-master of your ship in those chains, and let an officer stand by him, and see that he gives us the right water."

"I will take that office on myself," said the captain; "pass a light into the weather mainchains."

"Stand by your braces!" exclaimed the pilot, with startling quickness. "Heave away that lead!"

These preparations taught the crew to expect the crisis, and every officer and man stood in fearful silence, at his assigned station, awaiting the issue of the trial. Even the quarter-master at the cun gave out his orders to the men at the wheel, in deeper and hoarser tones than usual, as if anxious not to disturb the quiet and order of the vessel.

While this deep expectation pervaded the frigate, the piercing cry of the leadsman, as he called, "by the mark seven," rose above the tempest, crossed over the decks, and appeared to pass away to leeward, borne on the blast, like the warnings of some water spirit.

" 'Tis well," returned the pilot, calmly; "try it again."

The short pause was succeeded by another cry, "and a half-five!"

"She shoals! she shoals!" exclaimed Griffith; "keep her a good full."

"Ay! you must hold the vessel in command, now," said the pilot, with those cool tones that are most appalling in critical moments, because they seem to denote most preparation and care.

The third call "by the deep four!" was followed by a prompt direction from the stranger to tack.

Griffith seemed to emulate the coolness of the pilot, in issuing the necessary orders to execute this manœuvre.

The vessel rose slowly from the inclined position into which she had been forced by the tempest, and the sails were shaking violently, as if to release themselves from their confinement, while the ship stemmed the billows, when the well-known voice of the sailing-master was heard shouting from the forecastle—

"Breakers! breakers, dead ahead!"

This appalling sound seemed yet to be lingering about the ship, when a second voice cried—

"Breakers on our lee-bow!"

"We are in a bight of the shoals, Mr. Gray," cried the commander. "She loses her way; perhaps an anchor might hold her."

"Clear away that best-bower," shouted Griffith through his trumpet.

"Hold on!" cried the pilot, in a voice that reached the very hearts of all who heard him; "hold on every thing."

The young man turned fiercely to the daring stranger, who thus defied the discipline of his vessel, and at once demanded—

"Who is it that dares to countermand my orders?—is it not enough that you run the ship into danger, but you must interfere to keep her there! If another word—"

"Peace, Mr. Griffith," interrupted the captain, bending from the rigging, his gray locks blowing about in the wind, and adding a look of wildness to the haggard care that he exhibited by the light of his lantern; "yield the trumpet to Mr. Gray; he alone can save us."

Griffith threw his speaking trumpet on the deck, and as he walked proudly away, muttered, in bitterness of feeling—

"Then all is lost, indeed, and among the rest, the foolish hopes with which I visited this coast."

There was, however, no time for reply; the ship had been rapidly running into the wind, and as the efforts of the crew were paralyzed by the contradictory orders they had heard, she gradually lost her way, and in a few seconds, all her sails were taken aback.

Before the crew understood their situation, the pilot had

applied the trumpet to his mouth and in a voice that rose above the tempest, he thundered forth his orders. Each command was given distinctly, and with a precision that showed him to be master of his profession. The helm was kept fast, the head yards swung up heavily against the wind, and the vessel was soon whirling around on her heel, with a retrograde movement.

Griffith was too much of a seaman, not to perceive that the pilot had seized, with a perception almost intuitive, the only method that promised to extricate the vessel from her situation. He was young, impetuous, and proud—but he was also generous. Forgetting his resentment and his mortification, he rushed forward among the men, and, by his presence and example, added certainty to the experiment. The ship fell off slowly before the gale, and bowed her yards nearly to the water, as she felt the blast pouring its fury on her broadside, while the surly waves beat violently against her stern, as if in reproach at departing from her usual manner of moving.

The voice of the pilot, however, was still heard, steady and calm, and yet so clear and high as to reach every ear; and the obedient seamen whirled the yards at his bidding, in despite of the tempest, as if they handled the toys of their childhood. When the ship had fallen off dead before the wind, her head sails were shaken, her after yards trimmed, and her helm shifted, before she had time to run upon the danger that had threatened, as well to leeward as to windward. The beautiful fabric, obedient to her government, threw her bows up gracefully towards the wind again, and as her sails were trimmed, moved out from amongst the dangerous shoals, in which she had been embayed, as steadily and swiftly as she had approached them.

A moment of breathless astonishment succeeded the accomplishment of this nice manœuvre, but there was no time for the usual expressions of surprise. The stranger still held the trumpet, and continued to lift his voice amid the howlings of the blast, whenever prudence or skill required any change in the management of the ship. For an hour longer, there was a fearful struggle for their preservation, the channel becoming, at each step, more complicated, and the shoals thickening around the mariners, on every side. The lead was cast rapidly, and the quick eye of the pilot seemed to pierce the darkness, with a keenness of vision that exceeded human power. It was apparent to all in the vessel, that they were under the guidance of one who understood the navigation thoroughly, and their exertions kept pace with their reviving confidence. Again and again, the frigate appeared to be rushing blindly on shoals, where the sea was covered with foam, and where destruction would have been as sudden as it was certain, when the clear voice of the stranger was heard warning them of the danger, and inciting them to their duty. The vessel was implicitly yielded to his government, and during those anxious moments when she was dashing the waters aside, throwing the spray over her enormous yards, each ear would listen eagerly for those sounds that had obtained a command over the crew, that can only be acquired, under such circumstances, by great steadiness and consummate skill. The ship was recovering from the inaction of changing her course, in one of those critical tacks that she had made so often, when the pilot, for the first time, addressed the commander of the frigate, who still continued to superintend the all-important duty of the leadsman.

"Now is the pinch," he said, "and if the ship behaves well, we are safe—but if otherwise, all we have yet done will be useless."

The veteran seaman whom he addressed left the chains, at this portentous notice, and calling to his first lieutenant, required of the stranger an explanation of his warning.

"See you yon light on the southern headland?" returned the pilot; "you may know it from the star near it—by its sinking, at times, in the ocean. Now observe the hom-moc, a little north of it, looking like a shadow in the horizon—'tis a hill far inland. If we keep that light open from the hill, we shall do well—but if not, we surely go to pieces."

"Let us tack again!" exclaimed the lieutenant.

The pilot shook his head, as he replied—

"There is no more tacking or box-hauling to be done to-night. We have barely room to pass out of the shoals on this course, and if we can weather the 'Devil's-Grip,' we clear their outermost point—but if not, as I said before, there is but an alternative."

"If we had beaten out the way we entered!" exclaimed Griffith, "we should have done well."

"Say, also, if the tide would have let us do so," returned the pilot, calmly. "Gentlemen, we must be prompt; we have but a mile to go, and the ship appears to fly. That topsail is not enough to keep her up to the wind; we want both jib and mainsail."

" 'Tis a perilous thing, to loosen canvass in such a tempest!" observed the doubtful captain.

"It must be done," returned the collected stranger; "we perish, without it—see! the light already touches the edge of the hom-moc; the sea casts us to leeward!"

"It shall be done!" cried Griffith, seizing the trumpet from the hand of the pilot.

The orders of the lieutenant were executed almost as soon as issued, and every thing being ready, the enormous folds of the mainsail were trusted, loose, to the blast. There was an instant when the result was doubtful; the tremendous threshing of the heavy sail, seeming to bid defiance to all restraint, shaking the ship to her centre; but art and strength prevailed, and gradually the canvass was distended, and bellying as it filled, was drawn down to its usual place, by the power of a hundred men. The vessel yielded to this immense addition of force, and bowed before it, like a reed bending to a breeze. But the success of the measure was announced by a joyful cry from the stranger, that seemed to burst from his inmost soul.

"She feels it! she springs her luff! observe," he said, "the light opens from the hom-moc already; if she will only bear her canvass, we shall go clear!"

A report, like that of a cannon, interrupted his exclamation, and something resembling a white cloud was seen drifting before the wind from the head of the ship, till it was driven into the gloom far to leeward.

" 'Tis the jib, blown from the bolt-ropes," said the commander of the frigate. "This is no time to spread light duck—but the mainsail may stand it yet."

"The sail would laugh at a tornado," returned the lieutenant; "but that mast springs like a piece of steel."

"Silence all!" cried the pilot. "Now, gentlemen, we shall soon know our fate. Let her luff—luff you can!"

This warning effectually closed all discourse, and the hardy mariners, knowing that they had already done all in the power of man, to ensure their safety, stood in breathless anxiety, awaiting the result. At a short distance ahead of them, the whole ocean was white with foam, and the waves, instead of rolling on, in regular succession, appeared to be tossing about in mad gambols. A single streak of dark billows, not half a cable's length in width, could be discerned running into this chaos of water; but it was soon lost to the eye, amid the confusion of the disturbed element. Along this narrow path the vessel moved more heavily than before, being brought so near the wind as to keep her sails touching. The pilot, silently, proceeded to the wheel, and, with his own hands, he undertook the steerage of the ship. No noise proceeded from the frigate to interrupt the horrid tumult of the ocean, and she entered the channel among the breakers, with the silence of a desperate calmness. Twenty times, as the foam rolled away to leeward, the crew were on the eve of uttering their joy, as they supposed the vessel past the danger; but breaker after breaker would still heave up before them, following each other into the general mass, to check their exultation. Occasionally, the fluttering of the sails would be heard; and when the looks of the startled seamen were turned to the wheel, they beheld the stranger grasping its spokes, with his quick eye glancing from the water to the canvass. At length the ship reached a point, where she appeared to be rushing directly into the jaws of destruction, when, suddenly, her course was changed, and her head receded rapidly from the wind. At the same instant, the voice of the pilot was heard, shouting—

"Square away the yards!—in mainsail!"

A general burst from the crew echoed, "square away the yards!" and, quick as thought, the frigate was seen gliding along the channel, before the wind. The eye had hardly time to dwell on the foam, which seemed like clouds driving in the heavens, and directly the gallant vessel issued from her perils, and rose and fell on the heavy waves of the sea.

The seamen were yet drawing long breaths, and gazing about them like men recovered from a trance, when Griffith approached the man who had so successfully conducted them through their perils. The lieutenant grasped the hand of the other, as he said—

"You have this night proved yourself a faithful pilot, and such a seaman as the world cannot equal."

The pressure of the hand was warmly returned by the unknown mariner, who replied—

"I am no stranger to the seas, and I may yet find my grave in them. But you, too, have deceived me; you have acted nobly, young man, and Congress—"

"What of Congress?" asked Griffith, observing him to pause.

"Why, Congress is fortunate, if it has many such ships as this," said the stranger, coldly, walking away towards the commander.

Griffith gazed after him, a moment, in surprise; but as his duty required his attention, other thoughts soon engaged his mind.

The vessel was pronounced to be in safety. The gale was heavy and increasing, but there was a clear sea before them, and, as she slowly stretched out into the bosom of the ocean, preparations were made for her security during its continuance. Before midnight, every thing was in order. A gun from the Ariel soon announced the safety of the schooner also, which had gone out by another and an easier channel, that the frigate had not dared to attempt; when the commander directed the usual watch to be set, and the remainder of the crew to seek their necessary repose.

The captain withdrew with the mysterious pilot to his own cabin. Griffith gave his last order, and renewing his charge to the officer intrusted with the care of the vessel, he wished him a pleasant watch, and sought the refreshment of his own cot. For an hour, the young lieutenant lay musing on the events of the day. The remark of Barnstable would occur to him, in connexion with the singular comment of the boy; and then his thoughts would recur to the pilot, who, taken from the hostile shores of Britain, and with her accent on his tongue, had served them so faithfully and so well. He remembered the anxiety of Captain Munson to procure this stranger, at the very hazard from which they had just been relieved, and puzzled himself with conjecturing why a pilot was to be sought at such a risk. His more private feelings would then resume their sway, and the recollection of America, his mistress, and his home, mingled with the confused images of the drowsy youth. The dashing of the billows against the side of the ship, the creaking of guns and bulk-heads, with the roaring of the tempest, however, became gradually less and less distinct, until nature yielded to necessity, and the young man forgot even the romantic images of his love, in the deep sleep of a seaman.

# Chapter VI.

"The letter! ay! the letter!
'Tis there a woman loves to speak her wishes;
It spares the blushes of the love-sick maiden,
And every word's a smile, each line a tongue."
                                        *Duo.*

THE SLUMBERS of Griffith continued till late on the following morning, when he was awakened by the report of a cannon, issuing from the deck above him. He threw himself, listlessly, from his cot, and perceiving the officer of marines near him, as his servant opened the door of his stateroom, he inquired, with some little interest in his manner, if "the ship was in chase of any thing, that a gun was fired?"

" 'Tis no more than a hint to the Ariel," the soldier replied, "that there is bunting abroad for them to read. It seems as if all hands were asleep on board her, for we have shown her signal, these ten minutes, and she takes us for a collier, I believe, by the respect she pays it."

"Say, rather, that she takes us for an enemy, and is wary," returned Griffith. "Brown Dick has played the English so many tricks himself, that he is tender of his faith."

"Why, they have shown him a yellow flag over a blue one, with a cornet, and that spells Ariel, in every signal-book we have; surely he can't suspect the English of knowing how to read Yankee."

"I have known Yankees read more difficult English," said Griffith, smiling; "but, in truth, I suppose that Barnstable has been, like myself, keeping a dead reckoning of his time, and his men have profited by the occasion. She is lying-to, I trust."

"Ay! like a cork in a mill-pond, and I dare say you are right. Give Barnstable plenty of sea-room, a heavy wind, and but little sail, and he will send his men below, put that fellow he calls long Tom at the tiller, and follow himself, and sleep as quietly as I ever could at church."

"Ah! yours is a somniferous orthodoxy, Captain Manual," said the young sailor, laughing, while he slipped his arms into the sleeves of a morning round-about, covered with the gilded trappings of his profession; "sleep appears to come most naturally to all you idlers. But give me a passage, and I will go up, and call the schooner down to us, in the turning of an hour-glass."

The indolent soldier raised himself from the leaning posture he had taken against the door of the state-room, and Griffith proceeded through the dark ward-room, up the narrow stairs, that led him to the principal battery of the ship, and thence, by another and broader flight of steps, to the open deck.

The gale still blew strong, but steadily; the blue water of the ocean was rising in mimic mountains, that were crowned with white foam, which the wind, at times, lifted from its kindred element, to propel, in mist, through the air, from summit to summit. But the ship rode on these agitated billows, with an easy and regular movement, that denoted the skill with which her mechanical powers were directed. The day was bright and clear, and the lazy sun, who seemed unwilling to meet the toil of ascending to the meridian, was crossing the heavens with a southern inclination, that hardly allowed him to temper the moist air of the ocean with his genial heat. At the distance of a mile, directly in the wind's eye, the Ariel was seen, obeying the signal, which had caused the dialogue we have related. Her low, black hull was barely discernible, at moments, when she rose to the crest of a larger wave than common; but the spot of canvass that she exposed to the wind, was to be seen, seeming to touch the water on either hand, as the little vessel rolled amid the seas. At times, she was entirely hid from view, when the faint lines of her raking masts would be again discovered, issuing, as it were, from the ocean, and continuing to ascend, until the hull itself would appear, thrusting its bows into the air, surrounded by foam, and apparently ready to take its flight into another element.

After dwelling a moment on the beautiful sight we have attempted to describe, Griffith cast his eyes upward, to examine, with the keenness of a seaman, the disposition of things aloft, and then turned his attention to those who were on the deck of the frigate.

His commander stood, in his composed manner, patiently awaiting the execution of his order by the Ariel, and at his side was placed the stranger, who had so recently acted such a conspicuous part in the management of the ship. Griffith availed himself of daylight and his situation, to examine the appearance of this singular being more closely than the darkness and confusion of the preceding night had allowed. He was a trifle below the middle size in stature, but his form was muscular and athletic, exhibiting the finest proportions of manly beauty. His face appeared rather characterized by melancholy and thought, than by that determined decision which he had so powerfully displayed in the moments of their most extreme danger; but Griffith well knew, that it could also exhibit looks of the fiercest impatience. At present, it appeared, to the curious youth, when compared to the glimpses he had caught by the lights of their lanterns, like the ocean at rest, contrasted with the waters around him. The eyes of the pilot rested on the deck, or when they did wander, it was with uneasy and rapid glances. The large pea-jacket, that concealed most of his other attire, was as roughly made, and of materials as coarse, as that worn by the meanest seaman in the vessel; and yet, it did not escape the inquisitive gaze of the young lieutenant, that it was worn with an air of neatness and care, that was altogether unusual in men of his profession. The examination of Griffith ended here, for the near approach of the Ariel attracted the attention of all on the deck of the frigate, to the conversation that was about to pass between their respective commanders.

As the little schooner rolled along under their stern, Captain Munson directed his subordinate to leave his vessel, and repair on board the ship. As soon as the order was received, the Ariel rounded-to, and drawing ahead into the smooth water occasioned by the huge fabric that protected her from the gale, the whale-boat was again launched from her decks, and manned by the same crew that had landed on those shores which were now faintly discerned far to leeward, looking like blue clouds on the skirts of the ocean.

When Barnstable had entered his boat, a few strokes of the oars sent it, dancing over the waves, to the side of the ship. The little vessel was then veered off, to a distance, where it rode in safety, under the care of a boat-keeper, and the officer and his men ascended the side of the lofty frigate.

The usual ceremonials of reception were rigidly observed by Griffith and his juniors, when Barnstable touched the deck; and though every hand was ready to be extended towards the reckless seaman, none presumed to exceed the salutations of official decorum, until a short and private dialogue had taken place between him and their captain.

In the mean time, the crew of the whale-boat passed forward, and mingled with the seamen of the frigate, with the exception of the cockswain, who established himself in one of the gangways, where he stood in the utmost composure, fixing his eyes aloft, and shaking his head, in evident dissatisfaction, as he studied the complicated mass of rigging above him. This spectacle soon attracted to his side some half-dozen youths, with Mr. Merry at their head, who endeavoured to entertain their guest in a manner that should most conduce to the indulgence of their own waggish propensities.

The conversation between Barnstable and his superior soon ended; when the former, beckoning to Griffith, passed the wondering group who had collected around the capstern, awaiting his leisure to greet him more cordially, and led the way to the ward-room, with the freedom of one who felt himself no stranger. As this unsocial manner formed no part of the natural temper or ordinary deportment of the man, the remainder of the officers suffered their first lieutenant to follow him alone, believing that duty required that their interview should be private. Barnstable was determined that it should be so, at all events; for he seized the lamp from the mess-table, and entered the state-room of his friend, closing the door behind them, and turning the key. When they were both within its narrow limits—pointing to the only chair the little apartment contained, with a sort of instinctive deference to his companion's rank—the commander of the schooner threw himself carelessly on a sea-chest, and, placing the lamp on the table, he opened the discourse as follows:

"What a night we had of it! twenty times I thought I could see the sea breaking over you, and I had given you over as drowned men, or, what is worse, as men driven ashore, to be led to the prison-ships of these islanders, when I saw your lights in answer to my gun. Had you hoisted the conscience out of a murderer, you wouldn't have relieved him more than you did me, by showing that bit of tallow and cotton, tip'd with flint and steel.—But, Griffith, I have a tale to tell of a different kind—"

"Of how you slept, when you found yourself in deep water, and how your crew strove to outdo their commander, and how all succeeded so well, that there was a gray-head on board here, that began to shake with displeasure," interrupted Griffith; "truly, Dick, you will get into lubberly habits on board that bubble in which you float about, where all hands go to sleep as regularly as the inhabitants of a poultry yard go to roost."

"Not so bad, not half so bad, Ned," returned the other, laughing; "I keep as sharp a discipline as if we wore a flag. To be sure, forty men can't make as much parade as three or four hundred; but as for making or taking in sail, I am your better, any day."

"Ay, because a pocket handkerchief is sooner opened and shut than a table-cloth. But I hold it to be unseamanlike, to leave any vessel without human eyes, and those open, to watch whether she goes east or west, north or south."

"And who is guilty of such a dead-man's watch?"

"Why, they say on board here, that when it blows hard, you seat the man you call long Tom by the side of the tiller, tell him to keep her head-to-sea, and then pipe all hands to their night-caps, where you all remain, comfortably stowed in your hammocks, until you are awakened by the snoring of your helmsman."

" 'Tis a damned scandalous insinuation," cried Barnstable, with an indignation that he in vain attempted to conceal. "Who gives currency to such a libel, Mr. Griffith?"

"I had it of the marine," said his friend, losing the archness that had instigated him to worry his companion, in the vacant air of one who was careless of every thing; "but I don't believe half of it myself—I have no doubt you all had your eyes open, last night, whatever you might have been about this morning."

"Ah! this morning! there was an oversight, indeed! But I was studying a new signal-book, Griffith, that has a thousand times more interest for me, than all the bunting you can show, from the head to the heel of your masts."

"What! have you found out the Englishman's private talk?"

"No, no," said the other, stretching forth his hand, and grasping the arm of his friend. "I met, last night, one, on those cliffs, who has proved herself what I always believed her to be and loved her for, a girl of quick thought and bold spirit."

"Of whom do you speak?"

"Of Katherine—"

Griffith started from his chair involuntarily, at the sound of this name, and the blood passed quickly through the shades of his countenance, leaving it now pale as death, and then burning as if oppressed by a torrent from his heart. Struggling to overcome an emotion, which he appeared ashamed to betray even to the friend he most loved, the young man soon recovered himself so far as to resume his seat, when he asked, gloomily—

"Was she alone?"

"She was; but she left with me this paper, and this invaluable book, which is worth a library of all other works."

The eye of Griffith rested vacantly on the treasure that the other valued so highly, but his hand seized, eagerly, the open letter which was laid on the table for his perusal. The reader will at once understand, that it was in the handwriting of a female, and that it was the communication Barnstable had received from his betrothed, on the cliffs. Its contents were as follows:

"Believing that Providence may conduct me where we shall meet, or whence I may be able to transmit to you this account, I have prepared a short statement of the situation of Cecilia Howard and myself; not, however, to urge you and Griffith to any rash or foolish hazards, but that you may both sit down, and, after due consultation, determine what is proper for our relief.

"By this time, you must understand the character of Colonel Howard too well to expect he will ever consent to give his niece to a rebel. He has already sacrificed to his loyalty, as he calls it, (but I whisper to Cecilia, 'tis his treason,) not only his native country, but no small part of his fortune also. In the frankness of my disposition, (you know my frankness, Barnstable, but too well!) I confessed to him, after the defeat of the mad attempt Griffith made to carry off Cecilia, in Carolina, that I had been foolish enough to enter into some weak promise to the brother officer who had accompanied the young sailor in his traitorous visits to the plantation. Heigho! I sometimes think it would have been better for us all, if your ship had never been chased into the river, or after she was there, if Griffith had made no attempt to renew his acquaintance with my cousin. The colonel received the intelligence as such a guardian would hear that his ward was about to throw away thirty thousand dollars and herself on a traitor to his king and country. I defended you stoutly; said that you had no king, as the tie was dissolved; that America was your country, and that your profession was honourable; but it would not all do. He called you rebel; that I was used to. He said you were a traitor; that, in his vocabulary, amounts to the same thing. He even hinted that you were a coward; and that I knew to be false, and did not hesitate to tell him so. He used fifty opprobrious terms that I cannot remember, but among others were the beautiful epithets of 'disorganizer,' 'leveller,' 'democrat,' and 'jacobin.' (I hope he did not mean a monk!) In short, he acted Colonel Howard in a rage. But as his dominion does not, like that of his favourite kings, continue from generation to generation, and one short year will release me from his power, and leave me mistress of my own actions, that is, if your fine promises are to be believed, I bore it all very well, being resolved to suffer any thing but martyrdom, rather than abandon Cecilia. She, dear girl, has much more to distress her than I can have; she is not only the ward of Colonel Howard, but his niece, and his sole heir. I am persuaded this last circumstance makes no difference in either her conduct or her feelings, but he appears to think it gives him a right to tyrannize over her on all occasions. After all, Colonel Howard is a gentleman when you do not put him in a passion, and, I believe, a thoroughly honest man, and Cecilia even loves him. But a man who is driven from his country, in his sixtieth year, with the loss of near half his fortune, is not apt to canonize those who compel the change.

"It seems that when the Howards lived on this island, a

hundred years ago, they dwelt in the county of Northumberland. Hither, then, he brought us, when political events, and his dread of becoming the uncle to a rebel, induced him to abandon America, as he says, for ever. We have been here now three months, and for two thirds of that time we lived in tolerable comfort; but latterly, the papers have announced the arrival of the ship and your schooner in France, and from that moment as strict a watch has been kept over us, as if we had meditated a renewal of the Carolina flight. The colonel, on his arrival here, hired an old building, that is part house, part abbey, part castle, and all prison, because it is said to have once belonged to an ancestor of his. In this delightful dwelling there are many cages, that will secure more uneasy birds than we are. About a fortnight ago an alarm was given in a neighbouring village, which is situated on the shore, that two American vessels, answering your description, had been seen hovering along the coast; and, as people in this quarter dream of nothing but that terrible fellow, Paul Jones, it was said that he was on board one of them. But I believe that Colonel Howard suspects who you really are. He was very minute in his inquiries, I hear; and since then, has established a sort of garrison in the house, under the pretence of defending it against marauders, like those who are said to have laid my Lady Selkirk under contribution.

"Now, understand me, Barnstable; on no account would I have you risk yourself on shore; neither must there be blood spilt, if you love me; but that you may know what sort of a place we are confined in, and by whom surrounded, I will describe both our prison and the garrison. The whole building is of stone, and not to be attempted with slight means. It has windings and turnings, both internally and externally, that would require more skill than I possess to make intelligible; but the rooms we inhabit are in the upper or third floor of a wing, that you may call a tower, if you are in a romantic mood, but which, in truth, is nothing but a wing. Would to God I could fly with it! If any accident should bring you in sight of the dwelling, you will know our rooms, by the three smoky vanes that whiffle about its pointed roof, and, also, by the windows in that story being occasionally open. Opposite to our windows, at the distance of half a mile, is a retired, unfrequented ruin, concealed, in a great measure, from observation by a wood, and affording none of the best accommodations, it is true, but shelter in some of its vaults or apartments. I have prepared, according to the explanations you once gave me on this subject, a set of small signals, of differently coloured silks, and a little dictionary of all the phrases that I could imagine as useful, to refer to, properly numbered to correspond with the key and the flags, all of which I shall send you with this letter. You must prepare your own flags, and of course I retain mine, as well as a copy of the key and book. If opportunity should ever offer, we can have, at least, a pleasant discourse together; you from the top of the old tower in the ruins, and I from the east window of my dressing-room! But now for the garrison. In addition to the commandant, Colonel Howard, who retains all the fierceness of his former military profession, there is, as his second in authority, that bane of Cecilia's happiness, Kit Dillon, with his long Savannah face, scornful eyes of black, and skin of the same colour. This gentleman, you know, is a distant relative of the Howards, and wishes to be more nearly allied. He is poor, it is true, but then, as the colonel daily remarks, he is a good and loyal subject, and no rebel. When I asked why he was not in arms in these stirring times, contending for the prince he loves so much, the colonel answers, that it is not his profession, that he has been educated for the law, and was destined to fill one of the highest judicial stations in the colonies, and that he hoped he should yet live to see him sentence certain nameless gentlemen to condign punishment. This was consoling, to be sure, but I bore it. However, he left Carolina with us, and here he is, and here he is likely to continue, unless you can catch him, and anticipate his judgment on himself. The colonel has long desired to see this gentleman the husband of Cecilia, and since the news of your being on the coast, the siege has nearly amounted to a storm. The consequences are, that my cousin at first kept her room, and then the colonel kept her there, and even now she is precluded from leaving the wing we inhabit. In addition to these two principal gaolers, we have four men servants, two black and two white; and an officer and twenty soldiers from the neighbouring town are billeted on us, by particular desire, until the coast is declared free from pirates! yes, that is the musical name they give you—and when their own people land, and plunder, and rob, and murder the men and insult the women, they are called heroes! It's a fine thing to be able to invent names and make dictionaries—and it must be your fault, if mine has been framed for no purpose. I declare, when I recollect all the insulting and cruel things I hear in this country, of my own and her people, it makes me lose my temper, and forget my sex; but do not let my ill humour urge you to any thing rash; remember your life, remember their prisons, remember your reputation, but do not, do not forget your

KATHERINE PLOWDEN.

"P. S. I had almost forgotten to tell you, that in the signalbook you will find a more particular description of our prison, where it stands, and a drawing of the grounds, &c."

When Griffith concluded this epistle, he returned it to the man to whom it was addressed, and fell back in his chair, in an attitude that denoted deep reflection.

"I knew she was here, or I should have accepted the command offered to me by our commissioners in Paris," he at length uttered; "and I thought that some lucky chance might throw her in my way; but this is bringing us close, indeed! This intelligence must be acted on, and that promptly. Poor girl, what does she not suffer, in such a situation!"

"What a beautiful hand she writes!" exclaimed Barnstable; " 'tis as clear, and as pretty, and as small, as her own delicate fingers. Griff. what a log-book she would keep!"

"Cecilia Howard touch the coarse leaves of a log-book!" cried the other, in amazement; but perceiving Barnstable to be poring over the contents of his mistress's letter, he smiled at their mutual folly, and continued silent. After a short time spent in cool reflection, Griffith inquired of his friend the nature and circumstances of his interview with Katherine Plowden. Barnstable related it, briefly, as it occurred, in the manner already known to the reader.

"Then," said Griffith, "Merry is the only one, besides ourselves, who knows of this meeting, and he will be too chary of the reputation of his kinswoman to mention it."

"Her reputation needs no shield, Mr. Griffith," cried her lover; " 'tis as spotless as the canvass above your head, and—"

"Peace, dear Richard; I entreat your pardon; my words may have conveyed more than I intended; but it is important that our measures should be secret, as well as prudently concerted."

"We must get them both off," returned Barnstable, forgetting his displeasure the moment it was exhibited, "and that too before the old man takes it into his wise head to leave the coast. Did you ever get a sight of his instructions, or does he keep silent?"

"As the grave. This is the first time we have left port, that he has not conversed freely with me on the nature of the cruise; but not a syllable has been exchanged between us on the subject, since we sailed from Brest."

"Ah! that is your Jersey bashfulness," said Barnstable; "wait till I come alongside him, with my eastern curiosity, and I pledge myself to get it out of him in an hour."

" 'Twill be diamond cut diamond, I doubt," said Griffith, laughing; "you will find him as acute at evasion, as you can possibly be at a cross-examination."

"At any rate, he gives me a chance to-day; you know, I suppose, that he sent for me to attend a consultation of his officers, on important matters."

"I did not," returned Griffith, fixing his eyes intently on the speaker; "what has he to offer?"

"Nay, that you must ask your pilot; for while talking to me, the old man would turn and look at the stranger, every minute, as if watching for signals how to steer."

"There is a mystery about that man, and our connexion with him, that I cannot fathom," said Griffith. "But I hear the voice of Manual, calling for me; we are wanted in the cabin. Remember, you do not leave the ship without seeing me again."

"No, no, my dear fellow, from the public, we must retire to another private consultation."

The young men arose, and Griffith, throwing off the roundabout in which he had appeared on deck, drew on a coat of more formal appearance, and taking a sword carelessly in his hand, they proceeded together, along the passage already described, to the gun-deck, where they entered, with the proper ceremonials, into the principal cabin of the frigate.

# Chapter VII.

"Sempronius, speak."
Addison, *Cato*, II.i.23.

THE ARRANGEMENTS for the consultation were brief and simple. The veteran commander of the frigate received his officers with punctilious respect, and pointing to the chairs that were placed around the table, which was a fixture in the centre of his cabin, he silently seated himself, and his example was followed by all, without further ceremony. In taking their stations, however, a quiet, but rigid observance was paid to the rights of seniority and rank. On the right of the captain was placed Griffith, as next in authority; and opposite to him, was seated the commander of the schooner. The officer of marines, who was included in the number, held the next situation in point of precedence, the same order being observed to the bottom of the table, which was occupied by a hard-featured, square-built, athletic man, who held the office of sailing-master. When order was restored, after the short interruption of taking their places, the officer who had required the advice of his inferiors, opened the business on which he demanded their opinions.

"My instructions direct me, gentlemen," he said, "after making the coast of England, to run the land down—"

The hand of Griffith was elevated respectfully for silence, and the veteran paused, with a look that inquired the reason of his interruption.

"We are not alone," said the lieutenant, glancing his eye towards the part of the cabin where the pilot stood, leaning on one of the guns, in an attitude of easy indulgence.

The stranger moved not at this direct hint; neither did his eye change from its close survey of a chart that lay near him on the deck. The captain dropped his voice to tones of cautious respect, as he replied—

" 'Tis only Mr. Gray. His services will be necessary on the occasion, and, therefore, nothing need be concealed from him."

Glances of surprise were exchanged among the young men,

but Griffith bowing his silent acquiescence in the decision of his superior, the latter proceeded—

"I was ordered to watch for certain signals from the head-lands that we made, and was furnished with the best of charts, and such directions as enabled us to stand into the bay we entered last night. We have now obtained a pilot, and one who has proved himself a skilful man; such a one, gentlemen, as no officer need hesitate to rely on, in any emergency, either on account of his integrity or his knowledge."

The veteran paused, and turned his looks on the counte-nances of the listeners, as if to collect their sentiments on this important point. Receiving no other reply than the one con-veyed by the silent inclinations of the heads of his hearers, the commander resumed his explanations, referring to an open paper in his hand—

"It is known to you all, gentlemen, that the unfortunate question of retaliation has been much agitated between the two governments, our own and that of the enemy. For this reason, and for certain political purposes, it has become an object of solicitude with our commissioners in Paris, to obtain a few individuals of character from the enemy, who may be held as a check on their proceedings, while at the same time it brings the evils of war, from our own shores, home to those who have caused it. An opportunity now offers to put this plan in execution, and I have collected you, in order to con-sult on the means."

A profound silence succeeded this unexpected communica-tion of the object of their cruise. After a short pause, their captain added, addressing himself to the sailing-master—

"What course would you advise me to pursue, Mr. Bolt-rope?"

The weather-beaten seaman who was thus called on to break through the difficulties of a knotty point, with his opin-ion, laid one of his short, bony hands on the table, and began to twirl an inkstand with great industry, while with the other he conveyed a pen to his mouth, which was apparently masti-cated with all the relish that he could possibly have felt had it been a leaf from the famous Virginian weed. But perceiving that he was expected to answer, after looking first to his right hand, and then to his left, he spoke as follows, in a hoarse, thick voice, in which the fogs of the ocean seemed to have united with sea-damps and colds, to destroy every thing like melody—

"If this matter is ordered, it is to be done, I suppose," he said; "for the old rule runs, 'obey orders, if you break own-ers;' though the maxim, which says, 'one hand for the owner, and t'other for yourself,' is quite as good, and has saved many a hearty fellow from a fall that would have balanced the purs-er's books. Not that I mean a purser's books are not as good as any other man's, but that when a man is dead, his account must be closed, or there will be a false muster. Well, if the thing is to be done, the next question is, how is it to be done? There is many a man that knows there is too much canvass on a ship, who can't tell how to shorten sail. Well, then, if the thing is really to be done, we must either land a gang to seize them or we must show false lights, and sham colours, to lead them off to the ship. As for landing, Captain Munson, I can only speak for one man, and that is myself, which is to say, that if you run the ship with her jib-boom into the king of England's parlour windows, why, I'm consenting, nor do I care how much of his crockery is cracked in so doing; but as to putting the print of my foot on one of his sandy beaches, if I do, that is always speaking for only one man, and saving your presence, may I hope to be d——d."

The young men smiled as the tough old seaman uttered his sentiments so frankly, rising with his subject, to that which with him was the climax of all discussion; but his commander, who was but a more improved scholar from the same rough school, appeared to understand his arguments entirely, and without altering a muscle of his rigid countenance, he re-quired the opinion of the junior lieutenant.

The young man spoke firmly, but modestly, though the amount of what he said was not much more distinct than that uttered by the master, and was very much to the same pur-pose, with the exception, that he appeared to entertain no personal reluctance to trusting himself on dry ground.

The opinions of the others grew gradually more explicit and clear, as they ascended in the scale of rank, until it came to the turn of the captain of marines to speak. There was a trifling exhibition of professional pride about the soldier, in delivering his sentiments on a subject that embraced a good deal more of his peculiar sort of duty than ordinarily occurred in the usual operations of the frigate.

"It appears to me, sir, that the success of this expedition depends altogether upon the manner in which it is conducted." After this lucid opening, the soldier hesitated a moment, as if to collect his ideas for a charge that should look down all opposition, and proceeded. "The landing, of course, will be effected on a fair beach, under cover of the frigate's guns, and could it be possibly done, the schooner should be anchored in such a manner as to throw in a flanking fire on the point of debarkation. The arrangements for the order of march must a good deal depend on the distance to go over; though I should think, sir, an advanced party of seamen, to act as pioneers for the column of marines, should be pushed a short distance in front, while the baggage and baggage-guard might rest upon the frigate, until the enemy was driven into the interior, when it could advance without danger. There should be flank-guards, under the orders of two of the oldest midshipmen; and a light corps might be formed of the top-men, to co-operate with the marines. Of course, sir, Mr. Griffith will lead, in person, the musket-men and boarders, armed with their long pikes, whom I presume he will hold in reserve, as I trust my military claims and experience entitle me to the command of the main body."

"Well done, field marshal!" cried Barnstable, with a glee that seldom regarded time or place; "you should never let salt-water mould your buttons, but in Washington's camp, ay! and in Washington's tent, you should swing your hammock in future. Why, sir, do you think we are about to invade England?"

"I know that every military movement should be executed with precision, Captain Barnstable," returned the marine. "I am too much accustomed to hear the sneers of the sea-officers, to regard what I know proceeds from ignorance. If Captain Munson is disposed to employ me and my command in this expedition, I trust he will discover that marines are good for something more than to mount guard and pay salutes." Then, turning haughtily from his antagonist, he continued to address himself to their common superior, as if disdaining further intercourse with one who, from the nature of the case, must be unable to comprehend the force of what he said. "It will be prudent, Captain Munson, to send out a party to reconnoitre, before we march; and as it may be necessary to defend ourselves, in case of a repulse, I would beg leave to recommend that a corps be provided with entrenching tools, to accompany the expedition. They would be extremely useful, sir, in assisting to throw up field-works; though, I doubt not, tools might be found in abundance in this country, and labourers impressed for the service, on an emergency.—"

This was too much for the risibility of Barnstable, who broke forth in a fit of scornful laughter, which no one saw proper to interrupt; though Griffith, on turning his head, to conceal the smile that was gathering on his own face, perceived the fierce glance which the pilot threw at the merry seaman, and wondered at its significance and impatience. When Captain Munson thought that the mirth of the lieutenant was concluded, he mildly desired his reasons for amusing himself so exceedingly with the plans of the marine.

" 'Tis a chart for a campaign!" cried Barnstable, "and should be sent off express to Congress, before the Frenchmen are brought into the field!"

"Have you any better plan to propose, Mr. Barnstable?" inquired the patient commander.

"Better! ay, one that will take no time, and cause no trouble, to execute it," cried the other; " 'tis a seaman's job, sir, and must be done with a seaman's means."

"Pardon me, Captain Barnstable," interrupted the marine, whose jocular vein was entirely absorbed in his military pride; "if there be service to be done on shore, I claim it as my right to be employed."

"Claim what you will, soldier, but how will you carry on the war, with a parcel of fellows who don't know one end of a boat from the other," returned the reckless sailor. "Do you think, that a barge or a cutter is to be beached in the same manner you ground firelock, by word of command? No, no, Captain Manual—I honour your courage, for I have seen it tried, but d——e if—"

"You forget we wait for your project, Mr. Barnstable," said the veteran.

"I crave your patience, sir; but no project is necessary. Point out the bearings and distance of the place where the men you want are to be found, and I will take the heel of the gale, and run into the land, always speaking for good water and no rocks. Mr. Pilot, you will accompany me, for you carry as true a map of the bottom of these seas, in your head, as ever was made of dry ground. I will look out for good anchorage, or, if the wind should blow off shore, let the schooner stand off and on, till we should be ready to take the broad sea again. I would land, out of my whale-boat, with long Tom and a boat's crew, and finding out the place you will describe, we shall go up, and take the men you want, and bring them aboard. It's all plain-sailing; though, as it is a well-peopled country, it may be necessary to do our shore work in the dark."

"Mr. Griffith, we only wait for your sentiments," proceeded the captain, "when, by comparing opinions, we may decide on the most prudent course."

The first lieutenant had been much absorbed in thought, during the discussion of the subject, and might have been, on that account, better prepared to give his opinion with effect. Pointing to the man who yet stood behind him, leaning on a gun, he commenced by asking—

"Is it your intention that man shall accompany the party?"

"It is."

"And from him you expect the necessary information, sir, to guide our movements?"

"You are altogether right."

"If, sir, he has but a moiety of the skill on the land that he possesses on the water, I will answer for his success," returned the lieutenant, bowing slightly to the stranger, who received the compliment by a cold inclination of his head. "I must desire the indulgence of both Mr. Barnstable and Captain Manual," he continued, "and claim the command as of right belonging to my rank."

"It belongs naturally to the schooner," exclaimed the impatient Barnstable.

"There may be enough for us all to do," said Griffith, elevating a finger to the other, in a manner, and with an impressive look, that was instantly comprehended. "I neither agree wholly with the one nor the other of these gentlemen. 'Tis said, that since our appearance on the coast, the dwellings of many of the gentry are guarded by small detachments of soldiers from the neighbouring towns."

"Who says it?" asked the pilot, advancing among them, with a suddenness that caused a general silence.

"I say it, sir," returned the lieutenant, when the momentary surprise had passed away.

"Can you vouch for it?"

"I can."

"Name a house, or an individual, that is thus protected."

Griffith gazed at the man who thus forgot himself in the midst of a consultation like the present, and yielding to his native pride, hesitated to reply. But mindful of the declarations of his captain, and the recent services of the pilot, he at length said, with a little embarrassment of manner—

"I know it to be the fact, in the dwelling of a Colonel Howard, who resides but a few leagues to the north of us."

The stranger started at the name, and then raising his eye keenly to the face of the young man, appeared to study his thoughts in his varying countenance. But the action, and the pause that followed, were of short continuance. His lip slightly curled, whether in scorn or with a concealed smile, would have been difficult to say, so closely did it resemble both, and as he dropped quietly back to his place at the gun, he said—

" 'Tis more than probable you are right, sir; and if I might presume to advise Captain Munson, it would be to lay great weight on your opinion."

Griffith turned, to see if he could comprehend more meaning in the manner of the stranger than his words expressed, but his face was again shaded by his hand, and his eyes were once more fixed on the chart with the same vacant abstraction as before.

"I have said, sir, that I agree wholly neither with Mr. Barnstable nor Captain Manual," continued the lieutenant, after a short pause. "The command of this party is mine, as the senior officer, and I must beg leave to claim it. I certainly do not think the preparation that Captain Manual advises necessary; neither would I undertake the duty with as little caution as Mr. Barnstable proposes. If there are soldiers to be encountered, we should have soldiers to oppose to them; but as it must be sudden boat-work, and regular evolutions must give place to a seaman's bustle, a sea-officer should command. Is my request granted, Captain Munson?"

The veteran replied, without hesitation —

"It is, sir; it was my intention to offer you the service, and I rejoice to see you accept it so cheerfully."

Griffith with difficulty concealed the satisfaction with which he listened to his commander, and a radiant smile illumined his pale features, when he observed —

"With me, then, sir, let the responsibility rest. I request that Captain Manual, with twenty men, may be put under my orders, if that gentleman does not dislike the duty." The marine bowed, and cast a glance of triumph at Barnstable. "I will take my own cutter, with her tried crew, go on board the schooner, and when the wind lulls, we will run in to the land, and then be governed by circumstances."

The commander of the schooner threw back the triumphant look of the marine, and exclaimed, in his joyous manner —

" 'Tis a good plan, and done like a seaman, Mr. Griffith. Ay, ay, let the schooner be employed, and if it be necessary, you shall see her anchored in one of their duck-ponds, with her broadside to bear on the parlour-windows of the best house in the island! But twenty marines! they will cause a jam in my little craft."

"Not a man less than twenty would be prudent," returned Griffith. "More service may offer than that we seek."

Barnstable well understood his allusion, but still he replied —

"Make it all seamen, and I will give you room for thirty. But these soldiers never know how to stow away their arms and legs, unless at a drill. One will take the room of two sailors; they swing their hammocks athwart-ships, heads to leeward, and then turn-out wrong end uppermost at the call. Why, damn it, sir, the chalk and rotten-stone of twenty soldiers will chock my hatches!"

"Give me the launch, Captain Munson!" exclaimed the indignant marine, "and we will follow Mr. Griffith in an open boat, rather than put Captain Barnstable to so much inconvenience."

"No, no, Manual," cried the other, extending his muscular arm across the table, with an open palm, to the soldier; "you would all become so many Jonahs in uniform, and I doubt whether the fish could digest your cartridge-boxes and bayonet-belts. You shall go with me, and learn, with your own eyes, whether we keep the cat's-watch aboard the Ariel, that you joke about."

The laugh was general, at the expense of the soldier, if we except the pilot and the commander of the frigate. The former was a silent, and apparently an abstracted, but in reality a deeply interested listener to the discourse; and there were moments when he bent his looks on the speakers, as if he sought more in their characters than was exhibited by the gay trifling of the moment. Captain Munson seldom allowed a muscle of his wrinkled features to disturb their repose; and if he had not the real dignity to repress the untimely mirth of his officers, he had too much good nature to wish to disturb their harmless enjoyments. He expressed himself satisfied with the proposed arrangements, and beckoned to his steward, to place before them the usual beverage, with which all their consultations concluded.

The sailing-master appeared to think that the same order was to be observed in their potations as in council, and helping himself to an allowance which retained its hue even in its diluted state, he first raised it to the light, and then observed—

"This ship's-water is nearly the colour of rum itself; if it only had its flavour, what a set of hearty dogs we should be. Mr. Griffith, I find you are willing to haul your land-tacks aboard. Well, it's natural for youth to love the earth; but there is one man, and he is sailing-master of this ship, who saw land enough, last night, to last him a twelve-month. But if you will go, here's a good land-fall and a better offing to you. Captain Munson, my respects to you. I say, sir, if we should keep the ship more to the south'ard, it's my opinion, and that's but one man's, we should fall in with some of the enemy's homeward-bound West-Indiamen, and find where-withal to keep the life in us when we see fit to go ashore ourselves."

As the tough old sailor made frequent application of the glass to his mouth, with one hand, and kept a firm hold of the decanter with the other, during this speech, his companions were compelled to listen to his eloquence, or depart with their thirst unassuaged. Barnstable, however, quite coolly dispossessed the tar of the bottle, and mixing for himself a more equal potation, observed, in the act—

"That is the most remarkable glass of grog you have, Bolt-rope, that I ever sailed with; it draws as little water as the Ariel, and is as hard to find the bottom. If your spirit-room enjoys the same sort of engine to replenish it, as you pump out your rum, Congress will sail this frigate cheaply."

The other officers helped themselves with still greater moderation, Griffith barely moistening his lips, and the pilot rejecting the offered glass altogether. Captain Munson continued standing, and his officers, perceiving that their presence was no longer necessary, bowed, and took their leave. As Griffith was retiring last, he felt a hand laid lightly on his shoulder, and turning, perceived that he was detained by the pilot.

"Mr. Griffith," he said, when they were quite alone with the commander of the frigate, "the occurrences of the last night should teach us confidence in each other; without it, we go on a dangerous and fruitless errand."

"Is the hazard equal?" returned the youth. "I am known to all to be the man I seem—am in the service of my country—belong to a family, and enjoy a name, that is a pledge for my loyalty to the cause of America—and yet I trust myself on hostile ground, in the midst of enemies, with a weak arm, and under circumstances where treachery would prove my ruin. Who and what is the man who thus enjoys your confidence, Captain Munson? I ask the question less for myself than for the gallant men who will fearlessly follow wherever I lead."

A shade of dark displeasure crossed the features of the stranger, at one part of this speech, and at its close he sunk into deep thought. The commander, however, replied—

"There is a show of reason in your question, Mr. Griffith

—and yet you are not the man to be told that implicit obedience is what I have a right to expect. I have not your pretensions, sir, by birth or education, and yet Congress have not seen proper to overlook my years and services. I command this frigate—"

"Say no more," interrupted the pilot. "There is reason in his doubts, and they shall be appeased. I like the proud and fearless eye of the young man, and while he dreads a gibbet from my hands, I will show him how to repose a noble confidence. Read this, sir, and tell me if you distrust me now?"

While the stranger spoke, he thrust his hand into the bosom of his dress, and drew forth a parchment, decorated with ribbands and bearing a massive seal, which he opened, and laid on the table before the youth. As he pointed with his finger, impressively, to different parts of the writing, his eye kindled with a look of unusual fire, and there was a faint tinge discernible on his pallid features, when he spoke.

"See!" he said. "Royalty itself does not hesitate to bear witness in my favour, and that is not a name to occasion dread to an American."

Griffith gazed with wonder at the fair signature of the unfortunate Louis, which graced the bottom of the parchment; but when his eye obeyed the signal of the stranger, and rested on the body of the instrument, he started back from the table, and fixing his animated eyes on the pilot, he cried, while a glow of fiery courage flitted across his countenance—

"Lead on! I'll follow you to death!"

A smile of gratified exultation struggled around the lips of the stranger, who took the arm of the young man, and led him into a state-room, leaving the commander of the frigate, standing in his unmoved and quiet manner, a spectator of, but hardly an actor in the scene.

# Chapter VIII.

"Fierce bounding, forward sprung the ship,
Like grayhound starting from the slip,
To seize his flying prey."
Scott, *The Lord of the Isles*, Canto First, XXI.4–6.

ALTHOUGH the subject of the consultation remained a
secret with those whose opinions were required, yet
enough of the result leaked out among the subordinate officers, to throw the whole crew into a state of eager excitement. The rumour spread itself along the decks of the frigate,
with the rapidity of an alarm, that an expedition was to attempt the shore on some hidden service, dictated by the Congress itself; and conjectures were made respecting its force
and destination, with all that interest which might be imagined would exist among the men whose lives or liberties were
to abide the issue. A gallant and reckless daring, mingled with
the desire of novelty, however, was the prevailing sentiment
among the crew, who would have received with cheers the
intelligence that their vessel was commanded to force the passage of the united British fleet. A few of the older and more
prudent of the sailors were exceptions to this thoughtless hardihood, and one or two, among whom the cockswain of the
whale-boat was the most conspicuous, ventured to speak
doubtingly of all sorts of land service, as being of a nature
never to be attempted by seamen.

Captain Manual had his men paraded in the weather-
gangway, and after a short address, calculated to inflame their
military ardour and patriotism, acquainted them, that he required twenty volunteers, which was in truth half their number, for a dangerous service. After a short pause, the company
stepped forward, like one man, and announced themselves as
ready to follow him to the end of the world. The marine cast
a look over his shoulder, at this gratifying declaration, in
quest of Barnstable; but observing that the sailor was occupied with some papers, on a distant part of the quarter-deck,
he proceeded to make a most impartial division among the
candidates for glory; taking care, at the same time, to cull his

company in such a manner as to give himself the flower of his
men, and, consequently, to leave the ship the refuse.

While this arrangement was taking place, and the crew of
the frigate was in this state of excitement, Griffith ascended to
the deck, his countenance flushed with unusual enthusiasm,
and his eyes beaming with a look of animation and gayety
that had long been strangers to the face of the young man.
He was giving forth the few necessary orders to the seamen
he was to take with him from the ship, when Barnstable again
motioned him to follow, and led the way once more to the
state-room.

"Let the wind blow its pipe out," said the commander of
the Ariel, when they were seated; "there will be no landing on
the eastern coast of England, till the sea goes down. But this
Kate was made for a sailor's wife! see, Griffith, what a set of
signals she has formed, out of her own cunning head."

"I hope your opinion may prove true, and that you may be
the happy sailor who is to wed her," returned the other. "The
girl has indeed discovered surprising art in this business!
where could she have learnt the method and system so well?"

"Where! why, where she learnt better things; how to prize
a whole-hearted seaman, for instance. Do you think that my
tongue was jammed in my mouth, all the time we used to sit
by the side of the river in Carolina, and that we found nothing to talk about!"

"Did you amuse your mistress with treatises on the art of
navigation, and the science of signals?" said Griffith, smiling.

"I answered her questions, Mr. Griffith, as any civil man
would to a woman he loved. The girl has as much curiosity as
one of my own townswomen who has weathered cape forty
without a husband, and her tongue goes like a dog-vane in a
calm, first one way and then another. But here is her dictionary. Now own, Griff., in spite of your college learning and
sentimentals, that a woman of ingenuity and cleverness is a
very good sort of a helpmate."

"I never doubted the merits of Miss Plowden," said the
other, with a droll gravity that often mingled with his deeper
feelings, the result of a sailor's habits, blended with native
character. "But this indeed surpasses all my expectations!
Why, she has, in truth, made a most judicious selection of

phrases. 'No. 168. **** indelible;' '169. **** end only with life;' '170. **** I fear yours misleads me;' '171. —— ' "

"Pshaw!" exclaimed Barnstable, snatching the book from before the laughing eyes of Griffith; "what folly, to throw away our time now on such nonsense. What think you of this expedition to the land?"

"That it may be the means of rescuing the ladies, though it fail in making the prisoners we anticipate."

"But this pilot! you remember that he holds us by our necks, and can run us all up to the yard-arm of some English ship, whenever he chooses to open his throat, at their threats or bribes."

"It would have been better that he should have cast the ship ashore, when he had her entangled in the shoals; it would have been our last thought to suspect him of treachery then," returned Griffith. "I follow him with confidence, and must believe that we are safer with him than we should be without him."

"Let him lead to the dwelling of his fox-hunting ministers of state," cried Barnstable, thrusting his book of signals into his bosom; "but here is a chart that will show us the way to the port we wish to find. Let my foot once more touch terra firma, and you may write craven against my name, if that laughing vixen slips her cable before my eyes, and shoots into the wind's eye again, like a flying-fish chased by a dolphin. Mr. Griffith, we must have the chaplain with us to the shore."

"The madness of love is driving you into the errors of the soldier. Would you lie-by to hear sermons, with a flying party like ours?"

"Nay, nay, we must lay-to for nothing that is not unavoidable; but there are so many tacks in such a chase, when one has time to breathe, that we might as well spend our leisure in getting that fellow to splice us together. He has a handy way with a prayer-book, and could do the job as well as a bishop, and I should like to be able to say, that this is the last time these two saucy names, which are written at the bottom of this letter, should ever be seen sailing in the company of each other."

"It will not do," said his friend, shaking his head, and endeavouring to force a smile which his feelings suppressed; "it

will not do, Richard; we must yield our own inclinations to
the service of our country; nor is this pilot a man who will
consent to be led from his purpose."

"Then let him follow his purpose alone," cried Barnstable.
"There is no human power, always saving my superior officer,
that shall keep me from throwing abroad these tiny signals,
and having a private talk with my dark-eyed Kate. But for a
paltry pilot! he may luff and bear away as he pleases, while I
shall steer as true as a magnet for that old ruin, where I can
bring my eyes to bear on that romantic wing and three smoky
vanes. Not that I'll forget my duty; no, I'll help you catch the
Englishmen, but when that is done, hey! for Katherine Plowden and my true love!"

"Hush, madcap! the ward-room holds long ears, and our
bulkheads grow thin by wear. I must keep you and myself to
our duty. This is no children's game that we play; it seems the
commissioners at Paris have thought proper to employ a frigate in the sport."

Barnstable's gayety was a little repressed by the grave
manner of his companion; but after reflecting a moment, he
started on his feet, and made the usual movements for departure.

"Whither?" asked Griffith, gently detaining his impatient
friend.

"To old Moderate; I have a proposal to make, that may
remove every difficulty."

"Name it to me, then; I am in his council, and may save
you the trouble and mortification of a refusal."

"How many of those gentry does he wish to line his cabin
with?"

"The pilot has named no less than six, all men of rank and
consideration with the enemy. Two of them are peers, two
more belong to the commons' house of parliament, one is a
general, and the sixth, like ourselves, is a sailor, and holds the
rank of captain. They muster at a hunting seat, near the coast,
and believe me, the scheme is not without its plausibility."

"Well, then, there are two a-piece for us. You follow the
pilot, if you will; but let me sheer off for this dwelling of
Colonel Howard, with my cockswain and boat's-crew. I will
surprise his house, release the ladies, and on my way back, lay

my hands on two of the first lords I fall in with. I suppose, for our business, one is as good as another."

Griffith could not repress a faint laugh, while he replied—

"Though they are said to be each other's peers, there is, I believe some difference even in the quality of lords. England might thank us for ridding her of some among them. Neither are they to be found, like beggars, under every hedge. No, no, the men we seek must have something better than their nobility to recommend them to our favour. But let us examine more closely into this plan and map of Miss Plowden; something may occur, that shall yet bring the place within our circuit, like a contingent duty of the cruise."

Barnstable reluctantly relinquished his own wild plan, to the more sober judgment of his friend, and they passed an hour together, inquiring into the practicability, and consulting on the means, of making their public duty subserve the purposes of their private feelings.

The gale continued to blow heavily, during the whole of that morning; but towards noon, the usual indications of better weather became apparent. During these few hours of inaction in the frigate, the marines, who were drafted for service on the land, moved through the vessel with a busy and stirring air, as if they were about to participate in the glory and danger of the campaign their officer had planned, while the few seamen who were to accompany the expedition steadily paced the deck, with their hands thrust into the bosoms of their neat blue jackets, or, occasionally, stretched towards the horizon, as their fingers traced, for their less experienced shipmates, the signs of an abatement in the gale among the driving clouds. The last lagger among the soldiers had appeared with his knapsack on his back in the lee-gangway, where his comrades were collected, armed and accoutred for the strife, when Captain Munson ascended to the quarter-deck, accompanied by the stranger and his first lieutenant. A word was spoken by the latter in a low voice to a midshipman, who skipped gayly along the deck, and presently the shrill call of the boatswain was heard, preceding the hoarse cry of—

"Away there, you Tigers, away!"

A smart roll of the drum followed, and the marines paraded, while the six seamen who belonged to the cutter that owned so fierce a name, made their preparations for lowering their little bark from the quarter of the frigate into the troubled sea. Every thing was conducted in the most exact order, and with a coolness and skill that bade defiance to the turbulence of the angry elements. The marines were safely transported from the ship to the schooner, under the favouring shelter of the former, though the boat appeared, at times, to be seeking the cavities of the ocean, and again, to be riding in the clouds, as she passed from one vessel to the other.

At length, it was announced that the cutter was ready to receive the officers of the party. The pilot walked aside, and held private discourse, for a few moments, with the commander, who listened to his sentences with marked and singular attention. When their conference was ended, the veteran bared his gray head to the blasts, and offered his hand to the other, with a seaman's frankness, mingled with the deference of an inferior. The compliment was courteously returned by the stranger, who turned quickly on his heel, and directed the attention of those who awaited his movements, by a significant gesture, to the gangway.

"Come gentlemen, let us go," said Griffith, starting from a reverie, and bowing his hasty compliments to his brethren in arms.

When it appeared that his superiors were ready to enter the boat, the boy, who, by nautical courtesy, was styled Mr. Merry, and who had been ordered to be in readiness, sprang over the side of the frigate, and glided into the cutter, with the activity of a squirrel. But the captain of marines paused, and cast a meaning glance at the pilot, whose place it was to precede him. The stranger, as he lingered on the deck, was examining the aspect of the heavens, and seemed unconscious of the expectations of the soldier, who gave vent to his impatience, after a moment's detention, by saying—

"We wait for you, Mr. Gray."

Aroused by the sound of his name, the pilot glanced his quick eye on the speaker, but instead of advancing, he gently bent his body, as he again signed towards the gangway with his hand. To the astonishment not only of the soldier, but of all who witnessed this breach of naval etiquette, Griffith bowed low, and entered the boat with the same promptitude as if he were preceding an admiral. Whether the stranger became conscious of his want of courtesy, or was too indifferent to surrounding objects to note occurrences, he immediately followed himself, leaving to the marine the post of honour. The latter, who was distinguished for his skill in all matters of naval or military etiquette, thought proper to apologize, at a fitting time, to the first lieutenant, for suffering his senior officer to precede him into a boat, but never failed to show a becoming exultation, when he recounted the circumstance, by dwelling on the manner in which he had brought down the pride of the haughty pilot.

Barnstable had been several hours on board his little vessel, which was every way prepared for their reception; and as soon as the heavy cutter of the frigate was hoisted on her deck, he announced that the schooner was ready to sail. It has been already intimated, that the Ariel belonged to the smallest class of sea-vessels, and as the symmetry of her construction reduced even that size in appearance, she was peculiarly well adapted to the sort of service in which she was about to be employed. Notwithstanding her lightness rendered her nearly as buoyant as a cork, and at times she actually seemed to ride on the foam, her low decks were perpetually washed by the heavy seas that dashed against her frail sides, and she tossed and rolled in the hollows of the waves, in a manner that compelled even the practised seamen who trod her decks to move with guarded steps. Still she was trimmed and cleared with an air of nautical neatness and attention that afforded the utmost possible room for her dimensions; and though in miniature, she wore the trappings of war as proudly as if the metal she bore was of a more fatal and dangerous character. The murderous gun which, since the period of which we are writing, has been universally adopted in all vessels of inferior size, was then in the infancy of its invention, and was known to the American mariner only by reputation, under the appalling name of a "smasher." Of a vast caliber, though short, and easily managed, its advantages were even in that early day beginning to be appreciated, and the largest ships were thought to be unusually well provided with the means of offence, when they carried two or three cannon of this formidable invention among their armament. At a later day this weapon has been improved and altered, until its use has become general in vessels of a certain size, taking its appellation from the Carron, on the banks of which river it was first moulded. In place of these carronades, six light brass cannon were firmly lashed to the bulwarks of the Ariel, their brazen throats blackened by the sea-water, which so often broke harmlessly over these engines of destruction. In the center of the vessel, between her two masts, a gun of the same metal, but of nearly twice the length of the others, was mounted on a carriage of a new and singular construction, which admitted of its being turned in any direction, so as to be of service in most of the emergencies that occur in naval warfare.

The eye of the pilot examined this armament closely, and then turned to the well-ordered decks, the neat and compact rigging, and the hardy faces of the fine young crew, with manifest satisfaction. Contrary to what had been his practice during the short time he had been with them, he uttered his gratification freely and aloud.

"You have a tight boat, Mr. Barnstable," he said, "and a gallant looking crew. You promise good service, sir, in time of need, and that hour may not be far distant."

"The sooner the better," returned the reckless sailor; "I have not had an opportunity of scaling my guns since we quitted Brest, though we passed several of the enemy's cutters coming up channel, with whom our bull-dogs longed for a conversation. Mr. Griffith will tell you, pilot, that my little sixes can speak, on occasion, with a voice nearly as loud as the frigate's eighteens."

"But not to as much purpose," observed Griffith; "'vox et preterea nihil,' as we said at the school."

"I know nothing of your Greek and Latin, Mr. Griffith," retorted the commander of the Ariel; "but if you mean that those seven brass playthings won't throw a round shot as far as any gun of their size and height above the water, or won't scatter grape and cannister with any blunderbuss in your ship, you may possibly find an opportunity that will convince you to the contrary, before we part company."

"They promise well," said the pilot, who was evidently ignorant of the good understanding that existed between the two officers, and wished to conciliate all under his directions, "and I doubt not they will argue the leading points of a combat with good discretion. I see that you have christened them—I suppose for their respective merits. They are indeed expressive names!"

" 'Tis the freak of an idle moment," said Barnstable, laughing, as he glanced his eyes to the cannon, above which were painted the several quaint names of "boxer," "plumper," "grinder," "scatterer," "exterminator," and "nail-driver."

"Why have you thrown the midship-gun without the pale of your baptism?" asked the pilot; "or do you know it by the usual title of the 'old woman?' "

"No, no, I have no such petticoat terms on board me," cried the other; "but move more to starboard, and you will see its style painted on the cheeks of the carriage; it's a name that need not cause them to blush either."

" 'Tis a singular epithet, though not without some meaning!"

"It has more than you, perhaps, dream of, sir. That worthy seaman whom you see leaning against the foremast, and who would serve, on occasion, for a spare spar himself, is the captain of that gun, and more than once has decided some warm disputes with John Bull, by the manner in which he has wielded it. No marine can trail his musket more easily than my cockswain can train his nine-pounder on an object; and thus from their connexion, and some resemblance there is between them in length, it has got the name which you perceive it carries; that of 'long Tom.' "

The pilot smiled as he listened, but turning away from the speaker, the deep reflection that crossed his brow but too plainly showed that he trifled only from momentary indulgence; and Griffith intimated to Barnstable, that as the gale was sensibly abating, they would pursue the object of their destination.

Thus recalled to his duty, the commander of the schooner forgot the delightful theme of expatiating on the merits of his vessel, and issued the necessary orders to direct their movements. The little schooner slowly obeyed the impulse of her helm, and fell off before the wind, when the folds of her squaresail, though limited by a prudent reef, were opened to the blasts, and she shot away from her consort, like a meteor dancing across the waves. The black mass of the frigate's hull soon sunk in distance, and long before the sun had fallen below the hills of England, her tall masts were barely distinguishable by the small cloud of sail that held the vessel to her station. As the ship disappeared, the land seemed to issue out of the bosom of the deep, and so rapid was their progress, that the dwellings of the gentry, the humbler cottages, and even the dim lines of the hedges, became gradually more distinct to the eyes of the bold mariners, until they were beset with the gloom of the evening, when the whole scene faded from their view in the darkness of the hour, leaving only the faint outline of the land visible in the tract before them, and the sullen billows of the ocean raging with appalling violence in their rear.

Still the little Ariel held on her way, skimming the ocean like a water-fowl seeking its place of nightly rest, and shooting in towards the land as fearlessly as if the dangers of the preceding night were already forgotten. No shoals or rocks appeared to arrest her course, and we must leave her gliding into the dark streak that was thrown from the high and rocky cliffs, that lined a basin of bold entrance, where the mariners often sought and found a refuge from the dangers of the German ocean.

# Chapter IX.

"Sirrah! how dare you leave your barley broth,
To come in armour thus, against your king!"
*Drama.*

THE LARGE, irregular building, inhabited by Colonel Howard, well deserved the name it had received from the pen of Katherine Plowden. Notwithstanding the confusion in its orders, owing to the different ages in which its several parts had been erected, the interior was not wanting in that appearance of comfort which forms the great characteristic of English domestic life. Its dark and intricate mazes of halls, galleries, and apartments, were all well provided with good and substantial furniture, and whatever might have been the purposes of their original construction, they were now peacefully appropriated to the service of a quiet and well-ordered family.

There were divers portentous traditions, of cruel separations and blighted loves, which always linger, like cobwebs, around the walls of old houses, to be heard here also, and which, doubtless, in abler hands, might easily have been wrought up into scenes of high interest and delectable pathos. But our humbler efforts must be limited by an attempt to describe man as God has made him, vulgar and unseemly as he may appear to sublimated faculties, to the possessors of which enviable qualifications we desire to say, at once, that we are determined to eschew all things supernaturally refined, as we would the devil. To all those, then, who are tired of the company of their species, we would bluntly insinuate, that the sooner they throw aside our pages, and seize upon those of some more highly gifted bard, the sooner will they be in the way of quitting earth, if not of attaining heaven. Our business is solely to treat of man, and this fair scene on which he acts, and that not in his subtleties and metaphysical contradictions, but in his palpable nature, that all may understand our meaning as well as ourselves—whereby we manifestly reject the prodigious advantage of being thought a genius, by perhaps foolishly refusing the mighty aid of incomprehensibility to establish such a character.

Leaving the gloomy shadows of the cliffs, under which the little Ariel has been seen to steer, and the sullen roaring of the surf along the margin of the ocean, we shall endeavour to transport the reader to the dining parlour of St. Ruth's Abbey, taking the evening of the same day as the time for introducing another collection of those personages, whose acts and characters it has become our duty to describe.

The room was not of very large dimensions, and every part was glittering with the collected light of half a dozen candles, aided by the fierce rays that glanced from the grate, which held a most cheerful fire of seacoal. The mouldings of the dark oak wainscoting threw back upon the massive table of mahogany, streaks of strong light, which played among the rich fluids, that were sparkling on the board, in mimic haloes. The outline of this picture of comfort was formed by damask curtains of a deep red, and enormous oak chairs with leather backs and cushioned seats, as if the apartment were hermetically sealed against the world and its chilling cares.

Around the table, which still stood in the center of the floor, were seated three gentlemen, in the easy enjoyment of their daily repast. The cloth had been drawn, and the bottle was slowly passing among them, as if those who partook of its bounty well knew that neither the time nor the opportunity would be wanting for their deliberate indulgence in its pleasures.

At one end of the table an elderly man was seated, who performed whatever little acts of courtesy the duties of a host would appear to render necessary, in a company where all seemed to be equally at their ease and at home. This gentleman was in the decline of life, though his erect carriage, quick movements, and steady hand, equally denoted that it was an old age free from the usual infirmities. In his dress, he belonged to that class whose members always follow the fashions of the age anterior to the one in which they live, whether from disinclination to sudden changes of any kind, or from the recollections of a period which, with them, has been hallowed by scenes and feelings that the chilling evening of life can neither revive nor equal. Age might possibly have thrown its blighting frosts on his thin locks, but art had laboured to conceal the ravages with the nicest care. An accurate outline of powder covered not only the parts where the hair actually remained, but wherever nature had prescribed that hair should grow. His countenance was strongly marked in features, if not in expression, exhibiting, on the whole, a look of noble integrity and high honour, which was a good deal aided in its effect, by the lofty receding forehead, that rose like a monument, above the whole, to record the character of the aged veteran. A few streaks of branching red mingled with a swarthiness of complexion that was rendered more conspicuous by the outline of unsullied white which nearly surrounded his prominent features.

Opposite to the host, who it will at once be understood was Colonel Howard, was the thin, yellow visage of Mr. Christopher Dillon, that bane to the happiness of her cousin, already mentioned by Miss Plowden.

Between these two gentlemen was a middle-aged, hard-featured man, attired in the livery of King George, whose countenance emulated the scarlet of his coat, and whose principal employment, at the moment, appeared to consist in doing honour to the cheer of his entertainer.

Occasionally, a servant entered or left the room in silence, giving admission, however, through the opened door, to the rushing sounds of the gale, as the wind murmured amid the angles and high chimneys of the edifice.

A man, in the dress of a rustic, was standing near the chair of Colonel Howard, between whom and the master of the mansion a dialogue had been maintained, which closed as follows. The colonel was the first to speak, after the curtain is drawn from between the eyes of the reader and the scene.

"Said you, farmer, that the Scotchman beheld the vessels with his own eyes?"

The answer was a simple negative.

"Well, well," continued the colonel, "you can withdraw."

The man made a rude attempt at a bow, which being returned by the old soldier with formal grace, he left the room. The host, turning to his companions, resumed the subject.

"If those rash boys have really persuaded the silly dotard who commands the frigate, to trust himself within the shoals, on the eve of such a gale as this, their case must have been hopeless indeed! Thus may rebellion and disaffection ever

meet with the just indignation of Providence! It would not
surprise me, gentlemen, to hear that my native land has been
engulphed by earthquakes, or swallowed by the ocean, so awful and inexcusable has been the weight of her transgressions!
And yet it was a proud and daring boy who held the second
station in that ship! I knew his father well, and a gallant
gentleman he was, who, like my own brother, the parent of
Cecilia, preferred to serve his master on the ocean rather than
on the land. His son inherited the bravery of his high spirit,
without its loyalty. One would not wish to have such a youth
drowned either."

This speech, which partook much of the nature of a soliloquy, especially towards its close, called for no immediate
reply; but the soldier, having held his glass to the candle, to
admire the rosy hue of its contents, and then sipped of the
fluid so often that nothing but a clear light remained to gaze
at, quietly replaced the empty vessel on the table, and, as he
extended an arm towards the blushing bottle, he spoke, in the
careless tones of one whose thoughts were dwelling on another theme—

"Ay, true enough, sir; good men are scarce, and, as you say,
one cannot but mourn his fate, though his death be glorious;
quite a loss to his majesty's service, I dare say, it will prove."

"A loss to the service of his majesty!" echoed the host—
"his death glorious! no, Captain Borroughcliffe, the death of
no rebel can be glorious; and how he can be a loss to his
majesty's service, I am myself quite at a loss to understand."

The soldier, whose ideas were in that happy state of confusion that renders it difficult to command the one most
needed, but who still, from long discipline, had them under a
wonderful control for the disorder of his brain, answered,
with great promptitude—

"I mean the loss of his example, sir. It would have been so
appalling to others, to have seen the young man executed instead of shot in battle."

"He is drowned, sir."

"Ah! that is the next thing to being hanged; that circumstance had escaped me."

"It is by no means certain, sir, that the ship and schooner
that the drover saw are the vessels you take them to have

been," said Mr. Dillon, in a harsh, drawling tone of voice. "I should doubt their daring to venture so openly on the coast, and in the direct track of our vessels of war."

"These people are our countrymen, Christopher, though they are rebels," exclaimed the colonel. "They are a hardy and brave nation. When I had the honour to serve his majesty, some twenty years since, it was my fortune to face the enemies of my king in a few small affairs, Captain Borroughcliffe; such as the siege of Quebec, and the battle before its gates, a trifling occasion at Ticonderoga, and that unfortunate catastrophe of General Braddock—with a few others. I must say, sir, in favour of the colonists, that they played a manful game on the latter day; and this gentleman who now heads the rebels sustained a gallant name among us for his conduct in that disastrous business. He was a discreet, well-behaved young man, and quite a gentleman. I have never denied that Mr. Washington was very much of a gentleman."

"Yes," said the soldier, yawning, "he was educated among his majesty's troops, and he could hardly be otherwise. But I am quite melancholy about this unfortunate drowning, Colonel Howard. Here will be an end of my vocation, I suppose, and I am far from denying that your hospitality has made these quarters most agreeable to me."

"Then, sir, the obligation is only mutual," returned the host, with a polite inclination of his head; "but gentlemen, who, like ourselves, have been made free of the camp, need not bandy idle compliments about such trifles. If it were my kinsman Dillon, now, whose thoughts run more on Coke upon Littleton than on the gayeties of a mess-table, and a soldier's life, he might think such formalities as necessary as his hard words are to a deed. Come, Borroughcliffe, my dear fellow, I believe we have given an honest glass to each of the royal family, (God bless them all!) let us swallow a bumper to the memory of the immortal Wolfe."

"An honest proposal, my gallant host, and such a one as a soldier will never decline," returned the captain, who roused himself with the occasion. "God bless them all, say I, in echo, and if this gracious queen of ours ends as famously as she has begun, 'twill be such a family of princes as no other army in Europe can brag of around a mess-table."

"Ay, ay, there is some consolation in that thought, in the midst of this dire rebellion of my countrymen. But I'll vex myself no more with the unpleasant recollections; the arms of my sovereign will soon purge that wicked land of the foul stain."

"Of that there can be no doubt," said Borroughcliffe, whose thoughts still continued a little obscured by the sparkling Madeira that had long lain ripening under a Carolinian sun; "these Yankees fly before his majesty's regulars, like so many dirty clowns in a London mob before a charge of the horse-guards."

"Pardon me, Captain Borroughcliffe," said his host, elevating his person to more than its usually erect attitude; "they may be misguided, deluded, and betrayed, but the comparison is unjust. Give them arms and give them discipline, and he who gets an inch of their land from them, plentiful as it is, will find a bloody day on which to take possession."

"The veriest coward in Christendom would fight in a country where wine brews itself into such a cordial as this," returned the cool soldier; "I am a living proof that you mistook my meaning; for had not those loose-flapped gentlemen they call Vermontese and Hampshire-granters (God grant them his blessing for the deed!) finished two thirds of my company, I should not have been at this day under your roof, a recruiting instead of a marching officer; neither should I have been bound up in a covenant, like the law of Moses, could Burgoyne have made head against their long-legged marchings and counter-marchings. Sir, I drink their healths, with all my heart; and, with such a bottle of golden sunshine before me, rather than displease so good a friend, I will go through Gates's whole army, regiment by regiment, company by company, or, if you insist on the same, even man by man, in a bumper."

"On no account would I tax your politeness so far," returned the Colonel, abundantly mollified by this ample concession; "I stand too much your debtor, Captain Borroughcliffe, for so freely volunteering to defend my house against the attacks of my piratical, rebellious, and misguided countrymen, to think of requiring such a concession."

"Harder duty might be performed, and no favours asked,

my respectable host," returned the soldier. "Country quarters are apt to be dull, and the liquor is commonly execrable; but in such a dwelling as this a man can rock himself in the very cradle of contentment. And yet there is one subject of complaint, that I should disgrace my regiment did I not speak of, for it is incumbent on me, both as a man and a soldier, to be no longer silent."

"Name it, sir, freely, and its cause shall be as freely redressed," said the host, in some amazement.

"Here we three sit, from morning to night," continued the soldier, "bachelors all, well provisioned and better liquored, I grant you, but like so many well fed anchorites, while two of the loveliest damsels in the island pine in solitude within a hundred feet of us, without tasting the homage of our sighs. This I will maintain is a reproach both to your character, Colonel Howard, as an old soldier, and to mine as a young one. As to our friend Coke on top of Littleton here, I leave him to the quiddities of the law to plead his own cause."

The brow of the host contracted for a moment, and the sallow cheek of Dillon, who had sat during the dialogue in a sullen silence, appeared to grow even livid; but gradually the open brow of the veteran resumed its frank expression, and the lips of the other relaxed into a jesuitical sort of a smile, that was totally disregarded by the captain, who amused himself with sipping his wine, while he waited for an answer, as if he analyzed each drop that crossed his palate.

After an embarrassing pause of a moment, Colonel Howard broke the silence.

"There is reason in Borroughcliffe's hint, for such I take it to be—"

"I meant it for a plain, matter-of-fact complaint," interrupted the soldier.

"And you have cause for it," continued the colonel. "It is unreasonable, Christopher, that the ladies should allow their dread of these piratical countrymen of ours to exclude us from their society, though prudence may require that they remain secluded in their apartments. We owe the respect to Captain Borroughcliffe, that at least we admit him to the sight of the coffee-urn in an evening."

"That is precisely my meaning," said the captain; "as for

dining with them, why, I am well provided for here, but there is no one knows how to set hot water a hissing in so professional a manner as a woman. So forward, my dear and honoured colonel, and lay your injunctions on them, that they command your humble servant and Mr. Coke unto Littleton to advance and give the countersign of gallantry."

Dillon contracted his disagreeable features into something that was intended for a satirical smile, before he spoke as follows:

"Both the veteran Colonel Howard and the gallant Captain Borroughcliffe may find it easier to overcome the enemies of his majesty in the field than to shake a woman's caprice. Not a day has passed, these three weeks, that I have not sent my inquiries to the door of Miss Howard, as became her father's kinsman, with a wish to appease her apprehensions of the pirates; but little has she deigned me in reply, more than such thanks as her sex and breeding could not well dispense with."

"Well, you have been as fortunate as myself, and why you should be more so, I see no reason," cried the soldier, throwing a glance of cool contempt at the other; "fear whitens the cheek, and ladies best love to be seen when the roses flourish rather than the lilies."

"A woman is never so interesting, Captain Borroughcliffe," said the gallant host, "as when she appears to lean on man for support; and he who does not feel himself honoured by the trust is a disgrace to his species."

"Bravo! my honoured sir, a worthy sentiment, and spoken like a true soldier; but I have heard much of the loveliness of the ladies of the Abbey, since I have been in my present quarters, and I feel a strong desire to witness beauty encircled by such loyalty as could induce them to flee their native country, rather than to devote their charms to the rude keeping of the rebels."

The colonel looked grave, and for a moment fierce; but the expression of his displeasure soon passed away in a smile of forced gayety, and, as he cheerfully rose from his seat, he cried—

"You shall be admitted this very night, and this instant, Captain Borroughcliffe. We owe it, sir, to your services here, as well as in the field, and those froward girls shall be humoured no longer. Nay, it is nearly two weeks since I have seen my ward myself, nor have I laid my eyes on my niece but twice in all that time. Christopher, I leave the captain under your good care, while I go seek admission into the cloisters; we call that part of the building the cloisters, because it holds our nuns, sir! You will pardon my early absence from the table, Captain Borroughcliffe."

"I beg it may not be mentioned; you leave an excellent representative behind you, sir," cried the soldier, taking in the lank figure of Mr. Dillon in a sweeping glance, that terminated with a settled gaze on his decanter. "Make my devoirs to the recluses, and say all that your own excellent wit shall suggest as an apology for my impatience. Mr. Dillon, I meet you in a bumper to their healths and in their honour."

The challenge was coldly accepted, and while these gentlemen still held their glasses to their lips, Colonel Howard left the apartment, bowing low, and uttering a thousand excuses to his guest, as he proceeded, and even offering a very unnecessary apology of the same effect to his habitual inmate, Mr. Dillon.

"Is fear so very powerful within these old walls," said the soldier, when the door closed behind their host, "that your ladies deem it necessary to conceal themselves before even an enemy is known to have landed?"

Dillon coldly replied—

"The name of Paul Jones is terrific to all on this coast, I believe, nor are the ladies of St. Ruth singular in their apprehensions."

"Ah! the pirate has bought himself a desperate name, since the affair of Flamborough Head. But let him look to't, if he trusts himself in another Whitehaven expedition, while there is a detachment of the ——th in the neighbourhood, though the men should be nothing better than recruits."

"Our last accounts leave him safe in the court of Louis," returned his companion; "but there are men as desperate as himself, who sail the ocean under the rebel flag, and from one or two of them we have had much reason to apprehend the vengeance of disappointed men. It is they that we hope are lost in this gale."

"Hum! I hope they were dastards, then, or your hopes are a little unchristian, and —"

He would have proceeded, but the door opened, and his orderly entered, and announced, that a sentinel had detained three men, who were passing along the highway, near the Abbey, and who, by their dress, appeared to be seamen.

"Well, let them pass," cried the captain; "what, have we nothing to do better than to stop passengers, like footpads, on the king's highway! give them of your canteens, and let the rascals pass. Your orders were to give the alarm, if any hostile party landed on the coast, not to detain peaceable subjects on their lawful business."

"I beg your honour's pardon," returned the sergeant; "but these men seemed lurking about the grounds for no good, and as they kept carefully aloof from the place where our sentinel was posted, until to-night, Downing thought it looked suspiciously, and detained them."

"Downing is a fool, and it may go hard with him for his officiousness. What have you done with the men?"

"I took them to the guard-room in the east wing, your honour."

"Then feed them; and harkye, sirrah! liquor them well, that we hear no complaints, and let them go."

"Yes, sir, yes, your honour shall be obeyed; but there is a straight, soldierly looking fellow among them, that I think might be persuaded to enlist, if he were detained till morning. I doubt, sir, by his walk, but he has served already."

"Ha! what say you!" cried the captain, pricking up his ears, like a hound who hears a well-known cry, "served, think ye, already?"

"There are signs about him, your honour, to that effect. An old soldier is seldom deceived in such a thing, and considering his disguise, for it can be no other, and the place where we took him, there is no danger of a have-us corpses, until he is tied to us by the laws of the kingdom."

"Peace, you knave!" said Borroughcliffe, rising, and making a devious route towards the door; "you speak in the presence of my lord chief justice that is to be, and should not talk lightly of the laws. But still you say reason; give me your arm, sergeant, and lead the way to the east wing; my eyesight is good for nothing in such a dark night. A soldier should always visit his guard before the tattoo beats."

After emulating the courtesy of their host, Captain Borroughcliffe retired on this patriotic errand, leaning on his subordinate in a style of most familiar condescension. Dillon continued at the table, endeavouring to express the rancorous feelings of his breast by a satirical smile of contempt, that was necessarily lost on all but himself, as a large mirror threw back the image of his morose and unpleasant features.

But we must precede the veteran colonel in his visit to the "cloisters."

# Chapter X.

"—And kindness like their own
Inspired those eyes affectionate and glad,
That seemed to love whate'er they looked upon;
Whether with Hebe's mirth her features shone,
Or if a shade more pleasing them o'ercast—
Yet so becomingly th' expression past,
That each succeeding look was lovelier than the last."
Campbell, *Gertrude of Wyoming*, II.iv.2–6, 8–9.

THE WESTERN WING of St. Ruth house, or abbey, as the
building was indiscriminately called, retained but few
vestiges of the uses to which it had been originally devoted.
The upper apartments were small and numerous, extending
on either side of a long, low, and dark gallery, and might have
been the dormitories of the sisterhood who were said to have
once inhabited that portion of the edifice; but the ground-
floor had been modernized, as it was then called, about a century before, and retained just enough of its ancient character
to blend the venerable with what was thought comfortable in
the commencement of the reign of the third George. As this
wing had been appropriated to the mistress of the mansion,
ever since the building had changed its spiritual character for
one of a more carnal nature, Colonel Howard continued the
arrangement, when he became the temporary possessor of St.
Ruth's, until, in the course of events, the apartments which
had been appropriated for the accommodation and convenience of his niece, were eventually converted into her prison.
But as the severity of the old veteran was as often marked by
an exhibition of his virtues as of his foibles, the confinement
and his displeasure constituted the sole subjects of complaint
that were given to the young lady. That our readers may be
better qualified to judge of the nature of their imprisonment,
we shall transport them, without further circumlocution, into
the presence of the two females, whom they must be already
prepared to receive.

The withdrawing-room of St. Ruth's was an apartment
which, tradition said, had formerly been the refectory of the
little bevy of fair sinners who sought a refuge within its walls

from the temptations of the world. Their number was not large, nor their entertainments very splendid, or this limited space could not have contained them. The room, however, was of fair dimensions, and an air of peculiar comfort, mingled with chastened luxury, was thrown around it, by the voluminous folds of the blue damask curtains that nearly concealed the sides where the deep windows were placed, and by the dark leathern hangings, richly stamped with cunning devices in gold, that ornamented the two others. Massive couches in carved mahogany, with chairs of a similar material and fashion, all covered by the same rich fabric that composed the curtains, together with a Turkey carpet, over the shaggy surface of which all the colours of the rainbow were scattered in bright confusion, united to relieve the gloomy splendour of the enormous mantel, deep, heavy cornices, and the complicated carvings of the massive wood-work which cumbered the walls. A brisk fire of wood was burning on the hearth, in compliment to the wilful prejudice of Miss Plowden, who had maintained, in her most vivacious manner, that seacoal was "only tolerable for blacksmiths and Englishmen." In addition to the cheerful blaze from the hearth, two waxen lights, in candlesticks of massive silver, were lending their aid to enliven the apartment. One of these was casting its rays brightly along the confused colours of the carpet on which it stood, flickering before the active movements of the form that played around it with light and animated inflexions. The posture of this young lady was infantile in grace, and, with one ignorant of her motives, her employment would have been obnoxious to the same construction. Divers small, square pieces of silk, strongly contrasted to each other in colour, lay on every side of her, and were changed, as she kneeled on the floor, by her nimble hands, into as many different combinations, as if she were humouring the fancies of her sex, or consulting the shades of her own dark, but rich complexion, in the shop of a mercer. The close satin dress of this young female served to display her small figure in its true proportions, while her dancing eyes of jet-black shamed the dies of the Italian manufacturer by their superior radiancy. A few ribands of pink, disposed about her person with an air partly studied, and yet carelessly coquettish, seemed rather to reflect than lend the rich bloom that mantled around her laughing countenance, leaving to the eye no cause to regret that she was not fairer.

Another female figure, clad in virgin white, was reclining on the end of a distant couch. The seclusion in which they lived might have rendered this female a little careless of her appearance, or, what was more probable, the comb had been found unequal to its burthen, for her tresses, which rivalled the hue and gloss of the raven, had burst from their confinement, and, dropping over her shoulders, fell along her dress in rich profusion, finally resting on the damask of the couch, in dark folds, like glittering silk. A small hand, which seemed to blush at its own naked beauties, supported her head, imbedded in the volumes of her hair, like the fairest alabaster set in the deepest ebony. Beneath the dark profusion of her curls, which, notwithstanding the sweeping train that fell about her person, covered the summit of her head, lay a low, spotless forehead of dazzling whiteness, that was relieved by two arches so slightly and truly drawn that they appeared to have been produced by the nicest touches of art. The fallen lids and long silken lashes concealed the eyes, that rested on the floor, as if their mistress mused in melancholy. The remainder of the features of this maiden were of a kind that is most difficult to describe, being neither regular nor perfect in their several parts, yet harmonizing and composing a whole, that formed an exquisite picture of female delicacy and loveliness. There might or there might not have been a tinge of slight red in her cheeks, but it varied with each emotion of her bosom, even as she mused in quiet, now seeming to steal insidiously over her glowing temples, and then leaving on her face an almost startling paleness. Her stature, as she reclined, seemed above the medium height of womanhood, and her figure was rather delicate than full, though the little foot that rested on the damask cushion before her, displayed a rounded outline that any of her sex might envy.

"Oh! I'm as expert as if I were signal officer to the lord high admiral of this realm!" exclaimed the laughing female on the floor, clapping her hands together in girlish exultation. "I do long, Cecilia, for an opportunity to exhibit my skill."

While her cousin was speaking, Miss Howard raised her head, with a faint smile, and as she turned her eyes towards the other, a spectator might have been disappointed, but could not have been displeased, by the unexpected change the action produced in the expression of her countenance. Instead of the piercing black eyes that the deep colour of her tresses would lead him to expect, he would have beheld two large, mild, blue orbs, that seemed to float in a liquid so pure as to be nearly invisible, and which were more remarkable for their tenderness and persuasion, than for the vivid flashes that darted from the quick glances of her companion.

"The success of your mad excursion to the seaside, my cousin, has bewildered your brain," returned Cecilia; "but I know not how to conquer your disease, unless we prescribe salt-water for the remedy, as in some other cases of madness."

"Ah! I am afraid your nostrum would be useless," cried Katherine; "it has failed to wash out the disorder from the sedate Mr. Richard Barnstable, who has had the regimen administered to him through many a hard gale, but who continues as fair a candidate for bedlam as ever. Would you think it, Cicely, the crazy-one urged me, in the ten minutes' conversation we held together on the cliffs, to accept of his schooner as a shower-bath!"

"I can think that your hardihood might encourage him to expect much, but surely he could not have been serious in such a proposal!"

"Oh! to do the wretch justice, he did say something of a chaplain to consecrate the measure, but there was boundless impudence in the thought. I have not, nor shall I forget it, or forgive him for it, these six and twenty years. What a fine time he must have had of it, in his little Ariel, among the monstrous waves we saw tumbling in upon the shore to-day, coz! I hope they will wash his impudence out of him! I do think the man cannot have had a dry thread about him, from sun to sun. I must believe it is a punishment for his boldness, and, be certain, I shall tell him of it. I will form half a dozen signals, this instant, to joke at his moist condition, in very revenge."

Pleased with her own thoughts, and buoyant with the secret hope that her adventurous undertaking would be finally crowned with complete success, the gay girl shook her black locks, in infinite mirth, and tossed the mimic flags gayly around her person, as she was busied in forming new combinations, in order to amuse herself with her lover's disastrous situation. But the features of her cousin clouded with the thoughts that were excited by her remarks, and she replied, in a tone that bore some little of the accents of reproach—

"Katherine! Katherine! can you jest when there is so much to apprehend! Forget you what Alice Dunscombe told us of the gale, this morning! and that she spoke of two vessels, a ship and a schooner, that had been seen venturing with fearful temerity within the shoals, only six miles from the Abbey, and that unless God in his gracious providence had been kind to them, there was but little doubt that their fate would be a sad one! Can you, that know so well who and what these daring mariners are, be merry about the selfsame winds that cause their danger?"

The thoughtless, laughing girl, was recalled to her recollection by this remonstrance, and every trace of mirth vanished from her countenance, leaving a momentary death-like paleness crossing her face, as she clasped her hands before her, and fastened her keen eyes vacantly on the splendid pieces of silk that now lay unheeded around her. At this critical moment the door of the room slowly opened, and Colonel Howard entered the apartment with an air that displayed a droll mixture of stern indignation, with a chivalric and habitual respect to the sex.

"I solicit your pardon, young ladies, for the interruption," he said; "I trust, however, that an old man's presence can never be entirely unexpected in the drawing-room of his wards."

As he bowed, the colonel seated himself on the end of the couch, opposite to the place where his niece had been reclining, for Miss Howard had risen at his entrance, and continued standing until her uncle had comfortably disposed of himself. Throwing a glance, which was not entirely free from self-commendation, around the comfortable apartment, the veteran proceeded, in the same tone as before—

"You are not without the means of making any guest welcome, nor do I see the necessity of such constant seclusion from the eyes of the world as you thus rigidly practise."

Cecilia looked timidly at her uncle, with surprise, before she returned an answer to his remark.

"We certainly owe much to your kind attention, dear sir," she at length uttered; "but is our retirement altogether voluntary?"

"How can it be otherwise! are you not mistress of this mansion, madam! In selecting the residence where your, and, permit me to add, my ancestors, so long dwelt, in credit and honour, I have surely been less governed by any natural pride that I might have entertained on such a subject, than by a desire to consult your comfort and happiness. Every thing appears to my aged eyes as if we ought not to be ashamed to receive our friends within these walls. The cloisters of St. Ruth, Miss Howard, are not entirely bare, neither are their tenants wholly unworthy to be seen."

"Open, then, the portals of the Abbey, sir, and your niece will endeavour to do proper credit to the hospitality of its master."

"That was spoken like Harry Howard's daughter, frankly and generously!" cried the old soldier, insensibly edging himself nearer to his niece. "If my brother had devoted himself to the camp, instead of the sea, Cecilia, he would have made one of the bravest and ablest generals in his majesty's service — poor Harry! he might have been living at this very day, and at this moment leading the victorious troops of his sovereign through the revolted colonies in triumph. But he is gone, Cicely, and has left you behind him, as his dear representative, to perpetuate our family, and to possess what little has been left to us from the ravages of the times."

"Surely, dear sir," said Cecilia, taking his hand, which had unconsciously approached her person, and pressing it to her lips, "we have no cause to complain of our lot in respect to fortune, though it may cause us bitter regret that so few of us are left to enjoy it."

"No, no, no," said Katherine, in a low, hurried voice; "Alice Dunscombe is and must be wrong; providence would never abandon brave men to so cruel a fate!"

"Alice Dunscombe is here to atone for her error, if she has fallen into one," said a quiet, subdued voice, in which the accents of a provincial dialect, however, were slightly perceptible, and which, in its low tones, wanted that silvery clearness that gave so much feminine sweetness to the words of Miss

Howard, and which even rung melodiously in the ordinarily vivacious strains of her cousin.

The surprise created by these sudden interruptions caused a total suspension of the discourse. Katherine Plowden, who had continued kneeling, in the attitude before described, arose, and as she looked about her in momentary confusion, the blood again mantled her face with the fresh and joyous springs of life. The other speaker advanced steadily into the middle of the room, and after returning, with studied civility, the low bow of Colonel Howard, seated herself in silence on the opposite couch. The manner of her entrance, her reception, and her attire, sufficiently denoted that the presence of this female was neither unusual nor unwelcome. She was dressed with marked simplicity, though with a studied neatness, that more than compensated for the absence of ornaments. Her age might not have much exceeded thirty, but there was an adoption of customs in her attire that indicated she was not unwilling to be thought older. Her fair flaxen hair was closely confined by a dark bandeau, such as was worn in a nation further north by virgins only, over which a few curls strayed, in a manner that showed the will of their mistress alone restrained their luxuriance. Her light complexion had lost much of its brilliancy, but enough still remained to assert its original beauty and clearness. To this description might be added, fine, mellow blue eyes, beautifully white, though large teeth, a regular set of features, and a person that was clad in a dark lead-coloured silk, which fitted her full, but gracefully moulded form, with the closest exactness.

Colonel Howard paused a moment, after this lady was seated, and then turning himself to Katherine with an air that became stiff and constrained by attempting to seem extremely easy, he said—

"You no sooner summon Miss Alice, but she appears, Miss Plowden—ready and (I am bold to say, Miss Alice) able to defend herself against all charges that her worst enemies can allege against her."

"I have no charges to make against Miss Dunscombe," said Katherine, pettishly, "nor do I wish to have dissensions created between me and my friends, even by Colonel Howard."

"Colonel Howard will studiously avoid such offences in

future," said the veteran, bowing; and turning stiffly to the others, he continued—"I was just conversing with my niece, as you entered, Miss Alice, on the subject of her immuring herself like one of the veriest nuns who ever inhabited these cloisters. I tell her, madam, that neither her years, nor my fortune, nor, indeed, her own, for the child of Harry Howard was not left pennyless, require that we should live as if the doors of the world were closed against us, or there was no other entrance to St. Ruth's but through those antiquated windows. Miss Plowden, I feel it to be my duty to inquire why those pieces of silk are provided in such an unusual abundance, and in so extraordinary a shape?"

"To make a gala dress for the ball you are about to give, sir," said Katherine, with a saucy smile, that was only checked by the reproachful glance of her cousin. "You have taste in a lady's attire, Colonel Howard; will not this bright yellow form a charming relief to my brown face, while this white and black relieve one another, and this pink contrasts so sweetly with black eyes. Will not the whole form a turban fit for an empress to wear?"

As the arch maiden prattled on in this unmeaning manner, her rapid fingers entwined the flags in a confused maze, which she threw over her head in a form not unlike the ornament for which she intimated it was intended. The veteran was by far too polite to dispute a lady's taste, and he renewed the dialogue, with his slightly awakened suspicions completely quieted by her dexterity and artifice. But although it was not difficult to deceive Colonel Howard in matters of female dress, the case was very different with Alice Dunscombe. This lady gazed, with a steady eye and reproving countenance, on the fantastical turban, until Katherine threw herself by her side, and endeavoured to lead her attention to other subjects, by her playful motions and whispered questions.

"I was observing, Miss Alice," continued the colonel, "that although the times had certainly inflicted some loss on my estate, yet we were not so much reduced, as to be unable to receive our friends in a manner that would not disgrace the descendants of the ancient possessors of St. Ruth. Cecilia, here, my brother Harry's daughter, is a young lady that any uncle might be proud to exhibit, and I would have her, madam, show your English dames, that we rear no unworthy specimens of the parent stock on the other side of the Atlantic."

"You have only to declare your pleasure, my good uncle," said Miss Howard, "and it shall be executed."

"Tell us how we can oblige you, sir," continued Katherine, "and if it be in any manner that will relieve the tedium of this dull residence, I promise you at least one cheerful assistant to your scheme."

"You speak fair," cried the colonel, "and like two discreet and worthy girls! Well, then, our first step shall be to send a message to Dillon and the captain, and invite them to attend your coffee. I see the hour approaches."

Cecilia made no reply, but looked distressed, and dropped her mild eyes to the carpet; but Miss Plowden took it upon herself to answer.

"Nay, sir, that would be for them to proceed in the matter; as your proposal was that the first step should be ours, suppose we all adjourn to your part of the house, and do the honours of the tea-table in your drawing-room, instead of our own. I understand, sir, that you have had an apartment fitted up for that purpose, in some style; a woman's taste might aid your designs, however."

"Miss Plowden, I believe I intimated to you, some time since," said the displeased colonel, "that so long as certain suspicious vessels were known to hover on this coast, I should desire that you and Miss Howard would confine yourselves to this wing."

"Do not say that we confine ourselves," said Katherine, "but let it be spoken in plain English, that you confine us here."

"Am I a gaoler, madam, that you apply such epithets to my conduct! Miss Alice must form strange conclusions of our manners, if she receive her impressions from your very singular remarks. I—"

"All measures adopted from a dread of the ship and schooner that ran within the Devil's Grip, yester-eve, may be dispensed with now," interrupted Miss Dunscombe, in a melancholy, reflecting tone. "There are few living, who know the dangerous paths that can conduct even the smallest craft in safety from the land, with daylight and fair winds; but when darkness and adverse gales oppose them, the chance for safety lies wholly in God's kindness."

"There is truly much reason to believe they are lost," returned the veteran, in a voice in which no exultation was apparent.

"They are not lost!" exclaimed Katherine, with startling energy, leaving her seat, and walking across the room to join Cecilia, with an air that seemed to elevate her little figure to the height of her cousin. "They are skilful and they are brave, and what gallant sailors can do, will they do, and successfully; besides, in whose behalf would a just Providence sooner exercise its merciful power, than to protect the daring children of an oppressed country, while contending against tyranny and countless wrongs?"

The conciliating disposition of the colonel deserted him, as he listened. His own black eyes sparkled with a vividness unusual for his years, and his courtesy barely permitted the lady to conclude, ere he broke forth.

"What sin, madam, what damning crime, would sooner call down the just wrath of Heaven on the transgressors, than the act of foul rebellion? It was this crime, madam, that deluged England in blood in the reign of the first Charles; it is this crime that has dyed more fields red than all the rest of man's offences united; it has been visited on our race, as a condign punishment, from the days of the deservedly devoted Absalom, down to the present time; in short, it lost heaven for ever to some of the most glorious of its angels, and there is much reason to believe that it is the one unpardonable sin, named in the holy gospels."

"I know not that you have authority for believing it to be the heavy enormity that you mention, Colonel Howard," said Miss Dunscombe, anticipating the spirited reply of Katherine, and willing to avert it; she hesitated an instant, and then drawing a heavy, shivering sigh, she continued, in a voice that grew softer as she spoke—" 'tis indeed a crime of magnitude, and one that throws the common backslidings of our lives, speaking by comparison, into the sunshine of his favour. Many there are, who sever the dearest ties of this life, by madly rushing into its sinful vortex, for I fain think the heart grows hard with the sight of human calamity, and becomes callous to the miseries its owner inflicts; especially where we act the wrongs on our own kith and kin, regardless who or how many that are dear to us suffer by our evil deeds. It is, besides, Colonel Howard, a dangerous temptation, to one little practised in the great world, to find himself suddenly elevated into the seat of power; and if it do not lead to the commission of great crimes, it surely prepares the way to it, by hardening the heart."

"I hear you patiently, Miss Alice," said Katherine, dancing her little foot, in affected coolness, "for you neither know of whom nor to whom you speak. But Colonel Howard has not that apology. Peace, Cecilia, for I must speak! Believe them not, dear girl; there is not a wet hair on their heads. For you, Colonel Howard, who must recollect that the sister's son of the mothers of both your niece and myself is on board that frigate, there is an appearance of cruelty in using such language."

"I pity the boy! from my soul I pity him!" exclaimed the veteran; "he is a child, and has followed the current that is sweeping our unhappy colonies down the tide of destruction. But there are others in that vessel, who have no excuse of ignorance to offer. There is a son of my old acquaintance, and the bosom friend of my brother Harry, Cecilia's father, dashing Hugh Griffith, as we called him. The urchins left home together, and were rated on board one of his majesty's vessels on the same day. Poor Harry lived to carry a broad pennant in the service, and Hugh died in command of a frigate. This boy, too! he was nurtured on board his father's vessel, and learned, from his majesty's discipline, how to turn his arms against his king. There is something shockingly unnatural in that circumstance, Miss Alice; 'tis like the child inflicting a blow on the parent. 'Tis such men as these, with Washington at their head, who maintain the bold front this rebellion wears."

"There are men, who have never worn the servile livery of Britain, sir, whose names are as fondly cherished in America as any that she boasts of," said Katherine, proudly; "ay, sir, and those who would gladly oppose the bravest officers in the British fleet."

"I contend not against your misguided reason," said Colonel Howard, rising with cool respect. "A young lady who ventures to compare rebels with gallant gentlemen engaged in their duty to their prince, cannot escape the imputation of possessing a misguided reason. No man—I speak not of women, who cannot be supposed so well versed in human nature—but no man, who has reached the time of life that entitles him to be called by that name, can consort with these disorganizers, who would destroy every thing that is sacred—these levellers, who would pull down the great, to exalt the little—these jacobins, who—who—"

"Nay, sir, if you are at a loss for opprobrious epithets," said Katherine, with provoking coolness, "call on Mr. Christopher Dillon for assistance; he waits your pleasure at the door."

Colonel Howard turned in amazement, forgetting his angry declamations at this unexpected intelligence, and beheld in reality the sombre visage of his kinsman, who stood holding the door in his hand, apparently as much surprised at finding himself in the presence of the ladies, as they themselves could be at his unusual visit.

# Chapter XI.

"Prithee, Kate, let's stand aside, and see
the end of this controversy."
*The Taming of the Shrew*, V.i.61—62.

DURING THE WARM discussions of the preceding chapter, Miss Howard had bowed her pale face to the arm of the couch, and sate an unwilling and distressed listener to the controversy; but now that another, and one whom she thought an unauthorized intruder on her privacy, was announced, she asserted the dignity of her sex as proudly, though with something more of discretion, than her cousin could possibly have done. Rising from her seat, she inquired—

"To what are we indebted for so unexpected a visit from Mr. Dillon? Surely he must know that we are prohibited going to the part of the dwelling where he resides, and I trust Colonel Howard will tell him that common justice requires we should be permitted to be private."

The gentleman replied, in a manner in which malignant anger was sufficiently mingled with calculating humility—

"Miss Howard will think better of my intrusion, when she knows that I come on business of importance to her uncle."

"Ah! that may alter the case, Kit; but the ladies must have the respect that is due to their sex. I forgot, somehow, to have myself announced; but that Borroughcliffe leads me deeper into my Madeira than I have been accustomed to go, since the time when my poor brother Harry, with his worthy friend, Hugh Griffith—the devil seize Hugh Griffith, and all his race—your pardon, Miss Alice—what is your business with me, Mr. Dillon?"

"I bear a message from Captain Borroughcliffe. You may remember that, according to your suggestions, the sentinels were to be changed every night, sir."

"Ay! ay! we practised that in our campaign against Montcalm; 'twas necessary to avoid the murders of their Indians, who were sure, Miss Alice, to shoot down a man at his post, if he were placed two nights running in the same place."

"Well, sir, your prudent precautions have not been thrown away," continued Dillon, moving farther into the apartment, as if he felt himself becoming a more welcome guest as he proceeded; "the consequences are, that we have already made three prisoners."

"Truly it has been a most politic scheme!" exclaimed Katherine Plowden, with infinite contempt. "I suppose, as Mr. Christopher Dillon applauds it so highly, that it has some communion with the law! and that the redoubtable garrison of St. Ruth are about to reap the high glory of being most successful thief-takers!"

The sallow face of Dillon actually became livid as he replied, and his whole frame shook with the rage that he vainly endeavoured to suppress.

"There may be a closer communion with the law, and its ministers, perhaps, than Miss Plowden can desire," he said; "for rebellion seldom finds favour in any Christian code."

"Rebellion!" exclaimed the colonel; "and what has this detention of three vagabonds to do with rebellion, Kit? Has the damnable poison found its way across the Atlantic?—your pardon, Miss Alice—but this is a subject on which you can feel with me; I know your sentiments on the allegiance that is due to our anointed sovereign. Speak, Mr. Dillon, are we surrounded by another set of demons! if so, we must give ourselves to the work, and rally round our prince; for this island is the main pillar of his throne."

"I cannot say that there is any appearance, at present, of an intention to rise in this island," said Dillon, with demure gravity; "though the riots in London warrant any precautionary measures on the part of his majesty's ministers, even to a suspension of the habeas corpus. But you have had your suspicions concerning two certain vessels that have been threatening the coast, for several days past, in a most piratical manner?"

The little foot of Katherine played rapidly on the splendid carpet, but she contented herself with bestowing a glance of the most sovereign contempt on the speaker, as if she disdained any further reply. With the colonel, however, this was touching a theme that lay nearest his heart, and he answered, in a manner worthy of the importance of the subject—

"You speak like a sensible man, and a loyal subject, Mr. Dillon. The habeas corpus, Miss Alice, was obtained in the reign of King John, along with magna charta, for the security of the throne, by his majesty's barons; some of my own blood were of the number, which alone would be a pledge that the dignity of the crown was properly consulted. As to our piratical countrymen, Christopher, there is much reason to think that the vengeance of an offended Providence has already reached them. Those who know the coast well, tell me that without a better pilot than an enemy would be likely to procure, it would be impossible for any vessel to escape the shoals among which they entered, on a dark night, and with an adverse gale; the morning has arrived, and they are not to be seen!"

"But be they friends or be they enemies, sir," continued Dillon, respectfully, "there is much reason to think that we have now in the Abbey those who can tell us something of their true character; for the men we have detained carry with them the appearance of having just landed, and wear not only the dress but the air of seamen."

"Of seamen!" echoed Katherine, a deadly paleness chasing from her cheeks the bloom which indignation had heightened.

"Of seamen, Miss Plowden," repeated Dillon, with malignant satisfaction, but concealing it under an air of submissive respect.

"I thank you, sir, for so gentle a term," replied the young lady, recollecting herself, and recovering her presence of mind in the same instant; "the imagination of Mr. Dillon is so apt to conjure the worst, that he is entitled to our praise for so far humouring our weakness, as not to alarm us with the apprehensions of their being pirates."

"Nay, madam, they may yet deserve that name," returned the other, coolly; "but my education has instructed me to hear the testimony before I pronounce sentence."

"Ah! that the boy has found in his Coke upon Littleton," cried the colonel; "the law is a salutary corrective to human infirmities, Miss Alice, and, among other things, it teaches patience to a hasty temperament. But for this cursed, unnatural rebellion, madam, the young man would, at this moment, have been diffusing its blessings from a judicial chair, in one of the colonies, ay! and I pledge myself, to all alike, black and white, red and yellow, with such proper distinctions as nature has made between the officer and the private. Keep a good heart, kinsman; we shall yet find a time! the royal arms have many hands, and things look better at the last advices. But, come, we will proceed to the guard-room, and put these stragglers to the question; runaways, I'll venture to predict, from one of his majesty's cruisers, or, perhaps, honest subjects engaged in supplying the service with men. Come, Kit, come, let us go, and—"

"Are we, then, to lose the company of Colonel Howard so soon?" said Katherine, advancing to her guardian, with an air of blandishment and pleasantry. "I know that he too soon forgets the hasty language of our little disputes, to part in anger, if, indeed, he will even quit us till he has tasted of our coffee."

The veteran turned to the speaker of this unexpected address, and listened with profound attention. When she had done, he replied, with a good deal of softness in his tones—

"Ah! provoking one! you know me too well to doubt my forgiveness; but duty must be attended to, though even a young lady's smiles tempt me to remain. Yes, yes, child, you, too, are the daughter of a very brave and worthy seaman; but you carry your attachment to that profession too far, Miss Plowden—you do, indeed you do."

Katherine might have faintly blushed, but the slight smile which mingled with the expression of her shame gave to her countenance a look of additional archness, and she laid her hand lightly on the sleeve of her guardian, to detain him, as she replied—

"Yet why leave us, Colonel Howard? It is long since we have seen you in the cloisters, and you know you come as a father; tarry, and you may yet add confessor to the title."

"I know thy sins already, girl," said the worthy colonel, unconsciously yielding to her gentle efforts to lead him back to his seat; "they are, deadly rebellion in your heart to your prince, a most inveterate propensity to salt-water, and a great disrespect to the advice and wishes of an old fellow whom your father's will and the laws of the realm have made the guardian of your person and fortune."

"Nay, say not the last, dear sir," cried Katherine; "for there is not a syllable you have ever said to me, on that foolish subject, that I have forgotten. Will you resume your seat again? Cecilia, Colonel Howard consents to take his coffee with us."

"But you forget the three men, honest Kit, there, and our respectable guest, Captain Borroughcliffe."

"Let honest Kit stay there, if he please; you may send a request to Captain Borroughcliffe to join our party; I have a woman's curiosity to see the soldier; and as for the three men—" she paused, and affected to muse a moment, when she continued, as if struck by an obvious thought—"Yes, and the men can be brought in, and examined here; who knows but they may have been wrecked in the gale, and need our pity and assistance, rather than deserve your suspicions."

"There is a solemn warning in Miss Plowden's conjecture, that should come home to the breasts of all who live on this wild coast," said Alice Dunscombe; "I have known many a sad wreck among the hidden shoals, and when the wind has blown but a gentle gale, compared to last night's tempest. The wars, and the uncertainties of the times, together with man's own wicked passions, have made great havoc with those who knew well the windings of the channels among the "Ripples." Some there were who could pass, as I have often heard, within a fearful distance of the "Devil's-Grip," the darkest night that ever shadowed England; but all are now gone, of that daring set, either by the hand of death, or, what is even as mournful, by unnatural banishment from the land of their fathers."

"This war has then probably drawn off most of them, for your recollections must be quite recent, Miss Alice," said the veteran; "as many of them were engaged in the business of robbing his majesty's revenue, the country is in some measure requited for their former depredations, by their present services, and at the same time it is happily rid of their presence. Ah! madam, ours is a glorious constitution, where things are so nicely balanced, that, as in the physical organization of a healthy, vigorous man, the baser parts are purified in the course of things, by its own wholesome struggles."

The pale features of Alice Dunscombe became slightly

tinged with red, as the colonel proceeded, nor did the faint glow entirely leave her pallid face, until she had said —

"There might have been some who knew not how to respect the laws of the land, for such are never wanting; but there were others, who, however guilty they might be in many respects, need not charge themselves, with that mean crime, and yet who could find the passages that lie hid from common eyes, beneath the rude waves, as well as you could find the way through the halls and galleries of the Abbey, with a noonday sun shining upon its vanes and high chimneys."

"It is your pleasure, Colonel Howard, that we examine the three men, and ascertain whether they belong to the number of these gifted pilots?" said Christopher Dillon, who was growing uneasy at his awkward situation, and who hardly deemed it necessary to conceal the look of contempt which he cast at the mild Alice, while he spoke; "perhaps we may gather information enough from them, to draw a chart of the coast, that may gain us credit with my lords of the Admiralty."

This unprovoked attack on their unresisting and unoffending guest, brought the rich blood to the very temples of Miss Howard, who rose, and addressed herself to her kinsman, with a manner that could not easily be mistaken, any more than it could be condemned —

"If Mr. Dillon will comply with the wishes of Colonel Howard, as my cousin has expressed them, we shall not, at least, have to accuse ourselves of unnecessarily detaining men who probably are more unfortunate than guilty."

When she concluded, Cecilia walked across the apartment, and took a seat by the side of Alice Dunscombe, with whom she began to converse, in a low, soothing tone of voice. Mr. Dillon bowed with a deprecating humility, and having ascertained that Colonel Howard chose to give an audience, where he sate, to the prisoners, he withdrew to execute his mission, secretly exulting at any change that promised to lead to a renewal of an intercourse that might terminate more to his advantage, than the lofty beauty whose favour he courted, was, at present, disposed to concede.

"Christopher is a worthy, serviceable, good fellow," said

the colonel, when the door closed, "and I hope to live, yet, to see him clad in ermine; I would not be understood literally, but figuratively, for furs would but ill comport with the climate of the Carolinas. I trust I am to be consulted by his majesty's ministers when the new appointments shall be made for the subdued colonies, and he may safely rely on my good word being spoken in his favour. Would he not make an excellent and independent ornament of the bench, Miss Plowden?"

Katherine compressed her lips a little, as she replied—

"I must profit by his own discreet rules, and see testimony to that effect, before I decide, sir. But listen!" The young lady's colour changed rapidly, and her eyes became fixed in a sort of feverish gaze on the door. "He has at least been active; I hear the heavy tread of men already approaching."

"Ah! it is he certainly; justice ought always to be prompt as well as certain, to make it perfect; like a drum-head court-martial, which, by the way, is as summary a sort of government as heart could wish to live under. If his majesty's ministers could be persuaded to introduce into the revolted colonies—"

"Listen!" interrupted Katherine, in a voice which bespoke her deep anxiety; "they draw near!"

The sound of footsteps was in fact now so audible as to induce the colonel to suspend the delivery of his plan for governing the recovered provinces. The long, low gallery, which was paved with a stone flagging, soon brought the footsteps of the approaching party more distinctly to their ears, and presently a low tap at the door announced their arrival. Colonel Howard arose, with the air of one who was to sustain the principal character in the ensuing interview, and bade them enter. Cecilia and Alice Dunscombe merely cast careless looks at the opening door, indifferent to the scene; but the quick eye of Katherine embraced, at a glance, every figure in the group. Drawing a long, quivering breath, she fell back on the couch, and her eyes again lighted with their playful expression, as she hummed a low, rapid air, with a voice in which even the suppressed tones were liquid melody.

Dillon entered, preceding the soldier, whose gait had become more steady, and in whose rigid eye a thoughtful expression had taken the place of its former vacant gaze. In short, something had manifestly restored to him a more complete command of his mental powers, although he might not have been absolutely sobered. The rest of the party continued in the gallery, while Mr. Dillon presented the renovated captain to the colonel, when the latter did him the same kind office with the ladies.

"Miss Plowden," said the veteran, for she offered first in the circle, "this is my friend, Captain Borroughcliffe; he has long been ambitious of this honour, and I have no doubt his reception will be such as to leave him no cause to repent he has been at last successful."

Katherine smiled, and answered, with ambiguous emphasis—

"I know not how to thank him, sufficiently, for the care he has bestowed on our poor persons."

The soldier looked steadily at her, for a moment, with an eye that seemed to threaten a retaliation in kind, ere he replied—

"One of those smiles, madam, would be an ample compensation for services that are more real than such as exist only in intention."

Katherine bowed with more complacency than she usually bestowed on those who wore the British uniform, and they proceeded to the next.

"This is Miss Alice Dunscombe, Captain Borroughcliffe, daughter of a very worthy clergyman who was formerly the curate of this parish, and a lady who does us the pleasure of giving us a good deal of her society, though far less than we all wish for."

The captain returned the civil inclination of Alice, and the colonel proceeded.

"Miss Howard, allow me to present Captain Borroughcliffe, a gentleman who, having volunteered to defend St. Ruth in these critical times, merits all the favour of its mistress."

Cecilia gracefully rose, and received her guest with sweet complacency. The soldier made no reply to the customary compliments that she uttered, but stood an instant gazing at her speaking countenance, and then, laying his hand involuntarily on his breast, bowed nearly to his sword-hilt.

These formalities duly observed, the colonel declared his

readiness to receive the prisoners. As the door was opened by Dillon, Katherine cast a cool and steady look at the strangers, and beheld the light glancing along the arms of the soldiers who guarded them. But the seamen entered alone; while the rattling of arms, and the heavy dash of the muskets on the stone pavement, announced that it was thought prudent to retain a force at hand, to watch these secret intruders on the grounds of the abbey.

# Chapter XII.

"Food for powder; they'll fill a pit as well as better."
*1 Henry IV*, IV.ii.66–67.

THE THREE MEN, who now entered the apartment, appeared to be nothing daunted by the presence into which they were ushered, though clad in the coarse and weather-beaten vestments of seamen who had been exposed to recent and severe duty. They silently obeyed the direction of the soldier's finger, and took their stations in a distant corner of the room, like men who knew the deference due to rank, at the same time that the habits of their lives had long accustomed them to encounter the vicissitudes of the world. With this slight preparation, Colonel Howard began the business of examination.

"I trust ye are all good and loyal subjects," the veteran commenced, with a considerate respect for innocence, "but the times are such that even the most worthy characters become liable to suspicion; and, consequently, if our apprehensions should prove erroneous, you must overlook the mistake, and attribute it to the awful condition into which rebellion has plunged this empire. We have much reason to fear that some project is about to be undertaken on the coast by the enemy, who has appeared, we know, with a frigate and schooner; and the audacity of the rebels is only equalled by their shameless and wicked disrespect for the rights of the sovereign."

While Colonel Howard was uttering his apologetic preamble, the prisoners fastened their eyes on him with much interest; but when he alluded to the apprehended attack, the gaze of two of them became more keenly attentive, and, before he concluded, they exchanged furtive glances of deep meaning. No reply was made, however, and after a short pause, as if to allow time for his words to make a proper impression, the veteran continued—

"We have no evidence, I understand, that you are in the smallest degree connected with the enemies of this country; but as you have been found out of the king's highway, or, rather, on a by-path, which I must confess is frequently used

by the people of the neighbourhood, but which is nevertheless nothing but a by-path, it becomes no more than what
self-preservation requires of us, to ask you a few such questions as I trust will be satisfactorily answered. To use your
own nautical phrases, 'from whence came ye, pray?' and
'whither are ye bound?' "

A low, deep voice replied—"From Sunderland, last, and
bound, over-land, to Whitehaven."

This simple and direct answer was hardly given, before the
attention of the listeners was called to Alice Dunscombe, who
uttered a faint shriek, and rose from her seat involuntarily,
while her eyes seemed to roll fearfully, and perhaps a little
wildly, round the room.

"Are you ill, Miss Alice?" said the sweet, soothing tones of
Cecilia Howard; "you are, indeed you are; lean on me, that I
may lead you to your apartment."

"Did you hear it, or was it only fancy!" she answered, her
cheek blanched to the whiteness of death, and her whole
frame shuddering as if in convulsions; "say, did you hear it
too?"

"I have heard nothing but the voice of my uncle, who is
standing near you, anxious, as we all are, for your recovery
from this dreadful agitation."

Alice still gazed wildly from face to face. Her eye did not
rest satisfied with dwelling on those who surrounded her, but
surveyed, with a sort of frantic eagerness, the figures and appearance of the three men, who stood in humble patience, the
silent and unmoved witnesses of this extraordinary scene. At
length she veiled her eyes with both her hands, as if to shut
out some horrid vision, and then removing them, she smiled
languidly, as she signed for Cecilia to assist her from the
room. To the polite and assiduous offers of the gentlemen,
she returned no other thanks than those conveyed in her
looks and gestures; but when the sentinels who paced the gallery were passed, and the ladies were alone, she breathed a
long, shivering sigh, and found an utterance.

" 'Twas like a voice from the silent grave!" she said, "but it
could be no more than mockery. No, no, 'tis a just punishment for letting the image of the creature fill the place that
should be occupied only with the Creator. Ah! Miss Howard,

Miss Plowden, ye are both young—in the pride of your beauty and loveliness—but little do ye know, and less do ye dread, the temptations and errors of a sinful world."

"Her thoughts wander!" whispered Katherine, with anxious tenderness; "some awful calamity has affected her intellects!"

"Yes, it must be; my sinful thoughts have wandered, and conjured sounds that it would have been dreadful to have heard in truth, and within these walls," said Alice, more composedly, smiling with a ghastly expression, as she gazed on the two beautiful solicitous maidens who supported her yielding person. "But the moment of weakness is passed, and I am better; aid me to my room, and return, that you may not interrupt the reviving harmony between yourselves and Colonel Howard. I am now better, nay, I am quite restored."

"Say not so, dear Miss Alice," returned Cecilia; "your face denies what your kindness to us induces you to utter; ill, very ill, you are, nor shall even your own commands induce me to leave you."

"Remain, then," said Miss Dunscombe, bestowing a look of grateful affection on her lovely supporter; "and while our Katherine returns to the drawing-room, to give the gentlemen their coffee, you shall continue with me, as my gentle nurse."

By this time they had gained the apartment, and Katherine, after assisting her cousin to place Alice on her bed, returned to do the honours of the drawing-room.

Colonel Howard ceased his examination of the prisoners at her entrance, to inquire, with courtly solicitude, after the invalid; and, when his questions were answered, he again proceeded, as follows—

"This is what the lads would call plain-sailing, Boroughcliffe; they are out of employment in Sunderland, and have acquaintances and relatives in Whitehaven, to whom they are going for assistance and labour. All very probable, and perfectly harmless."

"Nothing more so, my respectable host," returned the jocund soldier; "but it seemeth a grievous misfortune that a trio of such flesh and blood should need work wherewithal to exercise their thews and sinews, while so many of the vessels of his majesty's fleet navigate the ocean in quest of the enemies of old England."

"There is truth in that; much truth in your remark," cried the colonel. "What say you, my lads, will you fight the French-man and the Don, ay! and even my own rebellious and infat-uated countrymen? Nay, by heaven, it is not a trifle that shall prevent his majesty from possessing the services of three such heroes. Here are five guineas a-piece for you the moment that you put foot on board the Alacrity cutter; and that can easily be done, as she lies at anchor this very night, only two short leagues to the south of this, in a small port, where she is riding out the gale as snugly as if she were in a corner of this room."

One of the men affected to gaze at the money with longing eyes, while he asked, as if weighing the terms of the engage-ment—

"Whether the Alacrity was called a good sea-boat, and was thought to give a comfortable birth to her crew?"

"Comfortable!" echoed Borroughcliffe; "for that matter, she is called the bravest cutter in the navy. You have seen much of the world, I dare say; did you ever see such a place as the marine arsenal at Carthagena, in old Spain?"

"Indeed I have, sir," returned the seaman, in a cool, col-lected tone.

"Ah! you have! well, did you ever meet with a house in Paris that they call the Thuilleries? because it's a dog-kennel to the Alacrity."

"I have even fallen in with the place you mention, sir," re-turned the sailor; "and must own the birth quite good enough for such as I am, if it tallies with your description."

"The deuce take these blue-jackets," muttered Borrough-cliffe, addressing himself unconsciously to Miss Plowden, near whom he happened to be at the time; "they run their tarry countenances into all the corners of the earth, and abridge a man most lamentably in his comparisons. Now, who the devil would have thought that fellow had ever put his sea-green eyes on the palace of King Louis!"

Katherine heeded not his speech, but sat eyeing the pris-oners with a confused and wavering expression of counte-nance, while Colonel Howard renewed the discourse, by exclaiming—

"Come, come, Borroughcliffe, let us give the lads no tales

for a recruit, but good, plain, honest English—God bless the language, and the land for which it was first made, too. There is no necessity to tell these men, if they are, what they seem to be, practical seamen, that a cutter of ten guns contains all the room and accommodation of a palace."

"Do you allow nothing for English oak and English comfort, mine host," said the immovable captain; "do you think, good sir, that I measure fitness and propriety by square and compass, as if I were planning Solomon's temple anew! All I mean to say is, that the Alacrity is a vessel of singular compactness and magical arrangement of room. Like the tent of that handsome brother of the fairy, in the Arabian Nights, she is big or she is little, as occasion needeth; and now, hang me, if I don't think I have uttered more in her favour than her commander would say to help me to a recruit, though no lad in the three kingdoms should appear willing to try how a scarlet coat would suit his boorish figure."

"That time has not yet arrived, and God forbid that it ever should, while the monarch needs a soldier in the field to protect his rights. But what say ye, my men? you have heard the recommendation that Captain Borroughcliffe has given of the Alacrity, which is altogether true—after making some allowances for language. Will ye serve? shall I order you a cheering glass a man, and lay by the gold, till I hear from the cutter that you are enrolled under the banners of the best of kings?"

Katherine Plowden, who hardly seemed to breathe, so close and intent was the interest with which she regarded the seamen, fancied she observed lurking smiles on their faces; but if her conjectures were true, their disposition to be merry went no farther, and the one who had spoken hitherto, replied, in the same calm manner as before—

"You will excuse us, if we decline shipping in the cutter, sir; we are used to distant voyages and large vessels, whereas the Alacrity is kept at coast duty, and is not of a size to lay herself alongside of a Don or a Frenchman with a double row of teeth."

"If you prefer that sort of sport, you must to the right-about for Yarmouth; there you will find ships that will meet any thing that swims," said the colonel.

"Perhaps the gentlemen would prefer abandoning the cares

and dangers of the ocean for a life of ease and gayety," said the captain. "The hand that has long dallied with a marlin-spike may be easily made to feel a trigger, as gracefully as a lady touches the keys of her piano. In short, there is and there is not a great resemblance between the life of a sailor and that of a soldier. There are no gales of wind, nor short-allowances, nor reefing topsails, nor shipwrecks, among soldiers—and at the same time, there is just as much, or even more grog-drinking, jollifying, care-killing fun around a canteen and an open knapsack, than there is on the end of a mess-chest, with a full can and a Saturday night's breeze. I have crossed the ocean several times, and I must own that a ship, in good weather, is very much the same as a camp or comfortable barracks; mind, I say only in very good weather."

"We have no doubt that all you say is true, sir," observed the spokesman of the three; "but what to you may seem a hardship, to us is pleasure. We have faced too many a gale to mind a cap-full of wind, and should think ourselves always in the calm latitudes, in one of your barracks, where there is nothing to do but to eat our grub, and to march a little fore and aft a small piece of green earth. We hardly know one end of a musket from the other."

"No!" said Borroughcliffe, musing; and then advancing with a quick step towards them, he cried, in a spirited manner—"attention! right dress!"

The speaker, and the seaman next him, gazed at the captain in silent wonder; but the third individual of the party, who had drawn himself a little aside, as if willing to be unnoticed, or perhaps pondering on his condition, involuntarily started at this unexpected order, and erecting himself, threw his head to the right, as promptly as if he had been on a parade ground.

"Oho! ye are apt scholars, gentlemen, and ye can learn, I see," continued Borroughcliffe. "I feel it to be proper that I detain these men till to-morrow morning, Colonel Howard, and yet I would give them better quarters than the hard benches of the guard-room."

"Act your pleasure, Captain Borroughcliffe," returned the host, "so you do but your duty to our royal master. They shall not want for cheer, and they can have a room over the servants' offices in the south side of the Abbey."

"Three rooms, my colonel, three rooms must be provided, though I give up my own."

"There are several small empty apartments there, where blankets might be taken, and the men placed for safe keeping, if you deem it necessary; though, to me, they seem like good, loyal tars, whose greatest glory it would be to serve their prince, and whose chief pleasure would consist in getting alongside of a Don or a Monsieur."

"We shall discuss these matters anon," said Borroughcliffe, dryly. "I see Miss Plowden begins to look grave at our abusing her patience so long, and I know that cold coffee is, like withered love, but a tasteless sort of a beverage. Come, gentlemen, en avant! you have seen the Thuilleries, and must have heard a little French. Mr. Christopher Dillon, know you where these three small apartments are 'situate, lying, and being,' as your parchments read?"

"I do, sir," said the complying lawyer, "and shall take much pleasure in guiding you to them. I think your decision that of a prudent and sagacious officer, and much doubt whether Durham Castle, or some other fortress, will be thought too big to hold them, ere long."

As this speech was uttered while the men were passing from the room, its effect on them was unnoticed; but Katherine Plowden, who was left for a few moments by herself, sat and pondered over what she had seen and heard, with a thoughtfulness of manner that was not usual to her gay and buoyant spirits. The sounds of the retiring footsteps, however, gradually grew fainter, and the return of her guardian alone, recalled the recollection of the young lady to the duties of her situation.

While engaged in the little offices of the tea-table, Katherine threw many furtive glances at the veteran; but, although he seemed to be musing, there was nothing austere or suspicious in his frank, open countenance.

"There is much useless trouble taken with these wandering seamen, sir," said Katherine, at length; "it seems to be the particular province of Mr. Christopher Dillon, to make all that come in contact with him excessively uncomfortable."

"And what has Kit to do with the detention of the men?"

"What! why, has he not undertaken to stand godfather to

their prisons?—by a woman's patience, I think, Colonel Howard, this business will gain a pretty addition to the names of St. Ruth. It is already called a house, an abbey, a place, and by some a castle; let Mr. Dillon have his way for a month, and it will add gaol to the number."

"Kit is not so happy as to possess the favour of Miss Plowden; but still Kit is a worthy fellow, and a good fellow, and a sensible fellow, ay! and what is of more value than all these put together, Miss Katherine, Mr. Christopher Dillon is a faithful and loyal subject to his prince. His mother was my cousin-german, madam, and I cannot say how soon I may call him my nephew. The Dillons are of good Irish extraction, and I believe that even Miss Plowden will admit that the Howards have some pretensions to a name."

"Ah! it is those very things called names that I most allude to," said Katherine, quickly. "But an hour since, you were indignant, my dear guardian, because you suspected that I insinuated you ought to write gaoler behind the name of Howard, and even now you submit to have the office palmed upon you."

"You forget, Miss Katherine Plowden, that it is the pleasure of one of his majesty's officers to detain these men."

"But I thought that the glorious British constitution, which you so often mention," interrupted the young lady, spiritedly, "gives liberty to all who touch these blessed shores; you know, sir, that out of twenty blacks that you brought with you, how few remain; the rest having fled on the wings of the spirit of British liberty!"

This was touching a festering sore in the colonel's feelings, and his provoking ward well knew the effects her observation was likely to produce. Her guardian did not break forth in a violent burst of rage, or furnish those manifestations of his ire that he was wont to do on less important subjects, but he arose, with all his dignity concentred in a look, and, after making a violent effort to restrain his feelings within the bounds necessary to preserve the decorum of his exit, he ventured a reply.

"That the British constitution is glorious, madam, is most true. That this island is the sole refuge where liberty has been able to find a home, is also true. The tyranny and oppression of the Congress, which are grinding down the colonies to the powder of desolation and poverty, are not worthy of the sacred name. Rebellion pollutes all that it touches, madam. Although it often commences under the sanction of holy liberty, it ever terminates in despotism. The annals of the world, from the time of the Greeks and Romans down to the present day, abundantly prove it. There was that Julius Caesar—he was one of your people's men, and he ended a tyrant. Oliver Cromwell was another—a rebel, a demagogue, and a tyrant. The gradations, madam, are as inevitable as from childhood to youth, and from youth to age. As for the little affair that you have been pleased to mention, of the—of the—of my private concerns, I can only say that the affairs of nations are not to be judged of by domestic incidents, any more than domestic occurrences are to be judged of by national politics." The colonel, like many a better logician, mistook his antithesis for argument, and paused a moment to admire his own eloquence; but the current of his thoughts, which always flowed in torrents on this subject, swept him along in its course, and he continued—"Yes, madam, here, and here alone is true liberty to be found. With this solemn asseveration, which is not lightly made, but which is the result of sixty years' experience, I leave you, Miss Plowden; let it be a subject of deep reflection with you, for I too well understand your treacherous feelings not to know that your political errors encourage your personal foibles; reflect, for your own sake, if you love not only your own happiness, but your respectability and standing in the world. As for the black hounds that you spoke of, they are a set of rebellious, mutinous, ungrateful rascals; and if ever I meet one of the damned—"

The colonel had so far controlled his feelings, as to leave the presence of the lady before he broke out into the bitter invectives we have recorded, and Katherine stood a minute, pressing her forefinger on her lips, listening to his voice as it grumbled along the gallery, until the sounds were finally excluded by the closing of a distant door. The wilful girl then shook her dark locks, and a smile of arch mischief, blended with an expression of regret, in her countenance, as she spoke to herself, while with hurried hands she threw her tea-equipage aside in a confused pile—

"It was perhaps a cruel experiment, but it has succeeded. Though prisoners ourselves, we are at least left free for the remainder of this night. These mysterious sailors must be examined more closely. If the proud eye of Edward Griffith was not glaring under the black wig of one of them, I am no judge of features; and where has Master Barnstable concealed his charming visage! for neither of the others could be he. But now for Cecilia."

Her light form glided from the room, while she was yet speaking, and flitting along the dimly lighted passages, it disappeared in one of those turnings that led to the more secret apartments of the abbey.

# Chapter XIII.

"How! Lucia, would'st thou have me sink away
In pleasing dreams, and lose myself in love—"
Addison, *Cato*, I.vi.447−448.

THE READER must not imagine that the world stood still
during the occurrence of the scenes we have related. By
the time the three seamen were placed in as many different
rooms, and a sentinel was stationed in the gallery common to
them all, in such a manner as to keep an eye on his whole
charge at once, the hour had run deep into the night. Captain
Borroughcliffe obeyed a summons from the colonel, who
made him an evasive apology for the change in their evening's
amusement, and challenged his guest to a renewal of the attack on the Madeira. This was too grateful a theme to be
lightly discussed by the captain, and the abbey clock had
given forth as many of its mournful remonstrances as the
division of the hours would permit, before they separated.
In the mean time, Mr. Dillon became invisible; though a servant, when questioned by the host on the subject, announced,
that "he believed Mr. Christopher had chosen to ride over
to ——, to be in readiness to join the hunt, on the morning,
with the dawn." While the gentlemen were thus indulging
themselves in the dining parlour, and laughing over the tales
of other times and hard campaigns, two very different scenes
occurred in other parts of the building.

When the quiet of the abbey was only interrupted by the
howling of the wind, or by the loud and prolonged laughs
which echoed through the passages from the joyous pair, who
were thus comfortably established by the side of the bottle, a
door was gently opened on one of the galleries of the "cloisters," and Katherine Plowden issued from it, wrapped in a
close mantle, and holding in her hand a chamber lamp, which
threw its dim light faintly along the gloomy walls in front,
leaving all behind her obscured in darkness. She was, however, soon followed by two other female figures, clad in the
same manner, and provided with similar lights. When all were

133

in the gallery, Katherine drew the door softly to, and proceeded in front to lead the way.

"Hist!" said the low, tremulous voice of Cecilia, "they are yet up in the other parts of the house; and if it be as you suspect, our visit would betray them, and prove the means of their certain destruction."

"Is the laugh of Colonel Howard in his cups so singular and unknown to your ear, Cecilia, that you know it not?" said Katherine with a little spirit; "or do you forget that on such occasions he seldom leaves himself ears to hear, or eyes to see with. But follow me; it is as I suspect—it must be as I suspect; and unless we do something to rescue them, they are lost, without they have laid a deeper scheme than is apparent."

"It is a dangerous road ye both journey," added the placid tones of Alice Dunscombe; "but ye are young, and ye are credulous."

"If you disapprove of our visit," said Cecilia, "it cannot be right, and we had better return."

"No, no, I have said naught to disapprove of your present errand. If God has put the lives of those in your custody whom ye have taught yourselves to look up to with love and reverence, such as woman is bound to yield to one man, he has done it for no idle purpose. Lead us to their doors, Katherine; let us relieve our doubts, at least."

The ardent girl did not wait for a second bidding, but she led them, with light and quick steps, along the gallery, until they reached its termination, where they descended to the basement floor, by a flight of narrow steps, and carefully opening a small door, emerged into the open air. They now stood on a small plat of grass, which lay between the building and the ornamental garden, across which they moved rapidly, concealing their lights, and bending their shrinking forms before the shivering blasts that poured their fury upon them from the ocean. They soon reached a large but rough addition to the buildings, that concealed its plain architecture behind the more laboured and highly finished parts of the edifice, into which they entered through a massive door, that stood ajar, as if to admit them.

"Chloe has been true to my orders," whispered Katherine,

as they passed out of the chilling air; "now, if all the servants are asleep, our chance to escape unnoticed amounts to certainty."

It became necessary to go through the servants' hall, which they effected unobserved, as it had but one occupant, an aged black man, who, being posted with his ear within two feet of a bell, in this attitude had committed himself to a deep sleep. Gliding through this hall, they entered divers long and intricate passages, all of which seemed as familiar to Katherine as they were unknown to her companions, until they reached another flight of steps, which they ascended. They were now near their goal, and stopped to examine whether any or what difficulties were likely to be opposed to their further progress.

"Now, indeed, our case seems hopeless," whispered Katherine, as they stood, concealed by the darkness, in one end of an extremely long, narrow passage; "here is the sentinel in the building, instead of being, as I had supposed, under the windows; what is to be done now?"

"Let us return," said Cecilia, in the same manner; "my influence with my uncle is great, even though he seems unkind to us at times. In the morning I will use it to persuade him to free them, on receiving their promise to abandon all such attempts in future."

"In the morning it will be too late," returned Katherine; "I saw that demon, Kit Dillon, mount his horse, under the pretence of riding to the great hunt of to-morrow, but I know his malicious eye too well to be deceived in his errand. He is silent that he may be sure, and if to-morrow comes, and finds Griffith within these walls, he will be condemned to a scaffold."

"Say no more," said Alice Dunscombe, with singular emotion; "some lucky circumstance may aid us with this sentinel."

As she spoke, she advanced; they had not proceeded far, before the stern voice of the soldier challenged the party.

" 'Tis no time to hesitate," whispered Katherine; "we are the ladies of the abbey, looking to our domestic affairs," she continued, aloud, "and think it a little remarkable that we are to encounter armed men, while going through our own dwelling."

The soldier respectfully presented his musket, and replied—

"My orders are to guard the doors of these three rooms, ladies; we have prisoners in them, and as for any thing else, my duty will be to serve you all in my power."

"Prisoners!" exclaimed Katherine, in affected surprise; "does Captain Borroughcliffe make St. Ruth's Abbey a gaol! Of what offences are the poor men guilty?"

"I know not, my lady; but as they are sailors, I suppose they have run from his majesty's service."

"This is singular, truly! and why are they not sent to the county prison?"

"This must be examined into," said Cecilia, dropping the mantle from before her face. "As mistress of this house, I claim a right to know whom its walls contain; you will oblige me by opening the doors, for I see you have the keys suspended from your belt."

The sentinel hesitated. He was greatly awed by the presence and beauty of the speakers, but a still voice reminded him of his duty. A lucky thought, however, interposed to relieve him from his dilemma, and at the same time to comply with the request, or, rather, order of the lady. As he handed her the keys, he said—

"Here they are, my lady; my orders are to keep the prisoners in, not to keep any one out. When you are done with them, you will please to return them to me, if it be only to save a poor fellow's eyes, for unless the door is kept locked, I shall not dare to look about me for a moment."

Cecilia promised to return the keys, and she had applied one of them to a lock, with a trembling hand, when Alice Dunscombe arrested her arm, and addressed the soldier.

"Say you there are three? are they men in years?"

"No, my lady, all good, serviceable lads, who couldn't do better than to serve his majesty, or, as it may prove, worse than to run from their colours."

"But are their years and appearance similar? I ask, for I have a friend who has been guilty of some boyish tricks, and has tried the seas, I hear, among other foolish hazards."

"There is no boy here. In the far room on the left is a smart, soldier-looking chap, of about thirty, who the captain thinks has carried a musket before now; on him I am charged to keep a particular eye. Next to him is as pretty a looking youth as eyes could wish to see, and it makes one feel mournful to think what he must come to, if he has really deserted his ship. In the room near you, is a smaller, quiet little body, who might make a better preacher than a sailor or a soldier either, he has such a gentle way with him."

Alice covered her eyes with her hand a moment, and then recovering herself, proceeded—

"Gentleness may do more with the unfortunate men than fear; here is a guinea; withdraw to the far end of the passage, where you can watch them as well as here, while we enter, and endeavour to make them confess who and what they really are."

The soldier took the money, and after looking about him in a little uncertainty, he at length complied, as it was obviously true they could only escape by passing him, near the flight of steps. When he was beyond hearing, Alice Dunscombe turned to her companions, and a slight glow appeared in feverish spots on her cheeks, as she addressed them.

"It would be idle to attempt to hide from you, that I expect to meet the individual whose voice I must have heard in reality to-night, instead of only imaginary sounds, as I vainly, if not wickedly supposed. I have many reasons for changing my opinion, the chief of which is that he is leagued with the rebellious Americans in this unnatural war. Nay, chide me not, Miss Plowden; you will remember that I found my being on this island. I come here on no vain or weak errand, Miss Howard, but to spare human blood." She paused, as if struggling to speak calmly. "But no one can witness the interview except our God."

"Go, then," said Katherine, secretly rejoicing at her determination, "while we inquire into the characters of the others."

Alice Dunscombe turned the key, and gently opening the door, she desired her companions to tap for her, as they returned, and then instantly disappeared in the apartment.

Cecilia and her cousin proceeded to the next door, which they opened in silence, and entered cautiously into the room.

Katherine Plowden had so far examined into the arrangements of Colonel Howard, as to know that at the same time he had ordered blankets to be provided for the prisoners, he had not thought it necessary to administer any further to the accommodations of men who had apparently made their beds and pillows of planks for the greater part of their lives.

The ladies accordingly found the youthful sailor whom they sought, with his body rolled in the shaggy covering, extended at his length along the naked boards, and buried in a deep sleep. So timid were the steps of his visiters, and so noiseless was their entrance, that they approached even to his side, without disturbing his slumbers. The head of the prisoner lay rudely pillowed on a billet of wood, one hand protecting his face from its rough surface, and the other thrust into his bosom, where it rested, with a relaxed grasp, on the handle of a dirk. Although he slept, and that heavily, yet his rest was unnatural and perturbed. His breathing was hard and quick, and something like the low, rapid murmurings of a confused utterance mingled with his respiration. The moment had now arrived when the character of Cecilia Howard appeared to undergo an entire change. Hitherto she had been led by her cousin, whose activity and enterprise seemed to qualify her so well for the office of guide; but now she advanced before Katherine, and, extending her lamp in such a manner as to throw the light across the face of the sleeper, she bent to examine his countenance, with keen and anxious eyes.

"Am I right?" whispered her cousin.

"May God, in his infinite compassion, pity and protect him!" murmured Cecilia, her whole frame involuntarily shuddering, as the conviction that she beheld Griffith flashed across her mind. "Yes, Katherine, it is he, and presumptuous madness has driven him here. But time presses; he must be awakened, and his escape effected at every hazard."

"Nay, then, delay no longer, but rouse him from his sleep."

"Griffith! Edward Griffith!" said the soft tones of Cecilia, "Griffith, awake!"

"Your call is useless, for they sleep nightly among tempests and boisterous sounds," said Katherine; "but I have heard it said that the smallest touch will generally cause one of them to stir."

"Griffith!" repeated Cecilia, laying her fair hand timidly on his own.

The flash of the lightning is not more nimble than the leap that the young man made to his feet, which he no sooner gained, than his dirk gleamed in the light of the lamps, as he brandished it fiercely with one hand, while with the other he extended a pistol, in a menacing attitude, towards his disturbers.

"Stand back!" he exclaimed; "I am your prisoner only as a corpse!"

The fierceness of his front, and the glaring eyeballs, that rolled wildly around him, appalled Cecilia, who shrunk back in fear, dropping her mantle from her person, but still keeping her mild eyes fastened on his countenance with a confiding gaze, that contradicted her shrinking attitude, as she replied—

"Edward, it is I; Cecilia Howard, come to save you from destruction; you are known even through your ingenious disguise."

The pistol and the dirk fell together on the blanket of the young sailor, whose looks instantly lost their disturbed expression in a glow of pleasure.

"Fortune at length favours me!" he cried. "This is kind, Cecilia; more than I deserve, and much more than I expected. But you are not alone."

" 'Tis my cousin Kate; to her piercing eyes you owe your detection, and she has kindly consented to accompany me, that we might urge you to—nay, that we might, if necessary, assist you to fly. For 'tis cruel folly, Griffith, thus to tempt your fate."

"Have I tempted it, then, in vain! Miss Plowden, to you I must appeal for an answer and a justification."

Katherine looked displeased, but after a moment's hesitation, she replied—

"Your servant, Mr. Griffith. I perceive that the erudite Captain Barnstable has not only succeeded in spelling through my scrawl, but he has also given it to all hands for perusal."

"Now you do both him and me injustice," said Griffith; "it surely was not treachery to show me a plan, in which I was to be a principal actor."

"Ah! doubtless your excuses are as obedient to your calls, as your men," returned the young lady; "but how comes it that the hero of the Ariel sends a deputy to perform a duty that is so peculiarly his own? is he wont to be second in rescues?"

"Heaven forbid that you should think so meanly of him, for a moment! We owe you much, Miss Plowden, but we may have other duties. You know that we serve our common country, and have a superior with us, whose beck is our law."

"Return, then, Mr. Griffith, while you may, to the service of our bleeding country," said Cecilia, "and, after the joint efforts of her brave children have expelled the intruders from her soil, let us hope there shall come a time when Katherine and myself may be restored to our native homes."

"Think you, Miss Howard, to how long a period the mighty arm of the British king may extend that time? We shall prevail; a nation fighting for its dearest rights must ever prevail; but 'tis not the work of a day, for a people, poor, scattered, and impoverished as we have been, to beat down a power like that of England; surely you forget that in bidding me to leave you with such expectations, Miss Howard, you doom me to an almost hopeless banishment!"

"We must trust to the will of God," said Cecilia; "if he ordain that America is to be free only after protracted sufferings, I can aid her but with my prayers; but you have an arm and an experience, Griffith, that might do her better service; waste not your usefulness, then, in visionary schemes for private happiness, but seize the moments as they offer, and return to your ship, if, indeed, it is yet in safety, and endeavour to forget this mad undertaking, and, for a time, the being who has led you to the adventure."

"This is a reception that I had not anticipated," returned Griffith; "for though accident, and not intention, has thrown me into your presence this evening, I did hope that when I again saw the frigate, it would be in your company, Cecilia."

"You cannot justly reproach me, Mr. Griffith, with your disappointment, for I have not uttered or authorized a syllable that could induce you or any one to believe that I would consent to quit my uncle."

"Miss Howard will not think me presumptuous, if I remind

her that there was a time when she did not think me unworthy to be intrusted with her person and her happiness."

A rich bloom mantled on the face of Cecilia, as she replied—

"Nor do I now, Mr. Griffith; but you do well to remind me of my former weakness, for the recollection of its folly and imprudence only adds to my present strength."

"Nay," interrupted her eager lover, "if I intended a reproach, or harboured a boastful thought, spurn me from you for ever, as unworthy of your favour."

"I acquit you of both, much easier than I can acquit myself of the charge of weakness and folly," continued Cecilia; "but there are many things that have occurred, since we last met, to prevent a repetition of such inconsiderate rashness on my part. One of them is," she added, smiling sweetly, "that I have numbered twelve additional months to my age, and a hundred to my experience. Another, and perhaps a more important one, is, that my uncle then continued among the friends of his youth, surrounded by those whose blood mingles with his own; but here he lives a stranger, and, though he finds some consolation in dwelling in a building where his ancestors have dwelt before him, yet he walks as an alien through its gloomy passages, and would find the empty honour but a miserable compensation for the kindness and affection of one whom he has loved and cherished from her infancy."

"And yet he is opposed to you in your private wishes, Cecilia, unless my besotted vanity has led me to believe what it would now be madness to learn was false; and in your opinions of public things, you are quite as widely separated. I should think there could be but little happiness dependant on a connexion where there is no one feeling entertained in common."

"There is, and an all-important one," said Miss Howard; " 'tis our love. He is my kind, my affectionate, and, unless thwarted by some evil cause, my indulgent uncle and guardian—and I am his brother Harry's child. This tie is not easily to be severed, Mr. Griffith, though, as I do not wish to see you crazed, I shall not add that your besotted vanity has played you false; but, surely, Edward, it is possible to feel a double tie, and so to act as to discharge our duties to both. I never, never can or will consent to desert my uncle, a stranger as he is in the land whose rule he upholds so blindly. You know not this England, Griffith; she receives her children from the colonies with cold and haughty distrust, like a jealous stepmother, who is wary of the favours that she bestows on her fictitious offspring."

"I know her in peace, and I know her in war," said the young sailor, proudly, "and can add, that she is a haughty friend, and a stubborn foe; but she grapples now with those who ask no more of her, than an open sea, and an enemy's favours. But this determination will be melancholy tidings for me to convey to Barnstable."

"Nay," said Cecilia, smiling, "I cannot vouch for others, who have no uncles, and who have an extra quantity of ill humour and spleen against this country, its people, and its laws, although profoundly ignorant of them all."

"Is Miss Howard tired of seeing me under the tiles of St. Ruth?" asked Katherine. "But hark! are there not footsteps approaching along the gallery?"

They listened, in breathless silence, and soon heard distinctly the approaching tread of more than one person. Voices were quite audible, and before they had time to consult on what was best to be done, the words of the speakers were distinctly heard at the door of their own apartment.

"Ay! he has a military air about him, Peters, that will make him a prize; come, open the door."

"This is not his room, your honour," said the alarmed soldier; "he quarters in the last room in the gallery."

"How know you that, fellow? come, produce the key, and open the way for me; I care not who sleeps here; there is no saying but I may enlist them all three."

A single moment of dreadful incertitude succeeded, when the sentinel was heard saying, in reply to this peremptory order—

"I thought your honour wanted to see the one with the black stock, and so left the rest of the keys at the other end of the passage; but—"

"But nothing, you loon; a sentinel should always carry his keys about him, like a gaoler; follow, then, and let me see the lad who dresses so well to the right."

As the heart of Katherine began to beat less vehemently, she said—

" 'Tis Borroughcliffe, and too drunk to see that we have left the key in the door; but what is to be done? we have but a moment for consultation."

"As the day dawns," said Cecilia, quickly, "I shall send here, under the pretence of conveying you food, my own woman—"

"There is no need of risking any thing for my safety," interrupted Griffith; "I hardly think we shall be detained, and if we are, Barnstable is at hand, with a force that would scatter these recruits to the four winds of heaven."

"Ah! that would lead to bloodshed, and scenes of horror!" exclaimed Cecilia.

"Listen!" cried Katherine, "they approach again!"

A man now stopped, once more, at their door, which was opened softly, and the face of the sentinel was thrust into the apartment.

"Captain Borroughcliffe is on his rounds, and for fifty of your guineas, I would not leave you here another minute."

"But one word more," said Cecilia.

"Not a syllable, my lady, for my life," returned the man; "the lady from the next room waits for you, and, in mercy to a poor fellow, go back where you came from."

The appeal was unanswerable, and they complied, Cecilia saying, as they left the room—

"I shall send you food in the morning, young man, and directions how to take the remedy necessary to your safety."

In the passage they found Alice Dunscombe, with her face concealed in her mantle, and it would seem by the heavy sighs that escaped from her, deeply agitated by the interview which she had just encountered.

But as the reader may have some curiosity to know what occurred to distress this unoffending lady so sensibly, we shall detain the narrative, to relate the substance of that which passed between her and the individual whom she sought.

# Chapter XIV.

"As when a lion in his den
Hath heard the hunters' cries,
And rushes forth to meet his foes,
So did the Douglass rise—"
    Percy, "The Hermit of Warkworth," Canto II, ll. 209–212.

---

ALICE DUNSCOMBE did not find the second of the prisoners buried, like Griffith, in sleep, but he was seated on one of the old chairs that were in the apartment, with his back to the door, and apparently looking through the small window, on the dark and dreary scenery, over which the tempest was yet sweeping in its fury. Her approach was unheeded, until the light from her lamp glared across his eyes, when he started from his musing posture, and advanced to meet her. He was the first to speak.

"I expected this visit," he said, "when I found that you recognised my voice, and I felt a deep assurance in my breast, that Alice Dunscombe would never betray me."

His listener, though expecting this confirmation of her conjectures, was unable to make an immediate reply, but she sunk into the seat he had abandoned, and waited a few moments, as if to recover her powers.

"It was, then, no mysterious warning! no airy voice that mocked my ear; but a dread reality!" she at length said. "Why have you thus braved the indignation of the laws of your country? on what errand of fell mischief has your ruthless temper again urged you to embark?"

"This is strong and cruel language, coming from you to me, Alice Dunscombe," returned the stranger, with cool asperity; "and the time has been, when I should have been greeted, after a shorter absence, with milder terms."

"I deny it not; I cannot, if I would, conceal my infirmity from myself or you; I hardly wish it to continue unknown to the world. If I have once esteemed you—if I have plighted to you my troth, and, in my confiding folly, forgot my higher duties, God has amply punished me for the weakness, in your own evil deeds."

"Nay, let not our meeting be embittered with useless and provoking recriminations," said the other; "for we have much to say before you communicate the errand of mercy on which you have come hither. I know you too well, Alice, not to see that you perceive the peril in which I am placed, and are willing to venture something for my safety. Your mother—does she yet live?"

"She is gone in quest of my blessed father," said Alice, covering her pale face with her hands; "they have left me alone, truly, for he who was to have been all to me, was first false to his faith, and has since become unworthy of my confidence."

The stranger became singularly agitated, his usually quiet eye glancing hastily from the floor to the countenance of his companion, as he paced the room with hurried steps; at length he replied—

"There is much, perhaps, to be said in explanation, that you do not know. I left the country, because I found in it nothing but oppression and injustice, and I could not invite you to become the bride of a wanderer, without either name or fortune. But I have now the opportunity of proving my truth. You say you are alone; be so no longer, and try how far you were mistaken in believing that I should one day supply the place to you of both father and mother."

There is something soothing to a female ear in the offer of even protracted justice, and Alice spoke with less of acrimony in her tones, during the remainder of their conference, if not with less of severity in her language.

"You talk not like a man whose very life hangs but on a thread that the next minute may snap asunder. Whither would you lead me? is it to the tower at London?"

"Think not I have weakly exposed my person without a sufficient protection," returned the stranger, with cool indifference; "there are many gallant men who only wait my signal, to crush the paltry force of this officer like a worm beneath my feet."

"Then has the conjecture of Colonel Howard been true! and the manner in which the enemy's vessels have passed the shoals, is no longer a mystery! you have been their pilot!"

"I have."

"What! would ye pervert the knowledge gained in the

spring-time of your guileless youth to the foul purpose of bringing desolation to the doors of those you once knew and respected! John! John! is the image of the maiden whom in her morning of beauty and simplicity I believe you did love, so faintly impressed, that it cannot soften your hard heart to the misery of those among whom she has been born, and who compose her little world."

"Not a hair of theirs shall be touched, not a thatch shall blaze, nor shall a sleepless night befall the vilest among them—and all for your sake, Alice! England comes to this contest with a seared conscience, and bloody hands, but all shall be forgotten for the present, when both opportunity and power offer, to make her feel our vengeance, even in her vitals. I came on no such errand."

"What, then, has led you blindly into snares, where all your boasted aid would avail you nothing; for, should I call aloud your name, even here, in the dark and dreary passages of this obscure edifice, the cry would echo through the country, ere the morning, and a whole people would be found in arms to punish your audacity."

"My name has been sounded, and that in no gentle strains," returned the pilot, scornfully, "when a whole people have quailed at it; the craven, cowardly wretches, flying before the man they had wronged. I have lived to bear the banners of the new republic, proudly, in sight of the three kingdoms, when practised skill and equal arms have in vain struggled to pluck it down. Ay! Alice, the echoes of my guns are still roaring among your eastern hills, and would render my name more appalling than inviting to your sleeping yeomen."

"Boast not of the momentary success that the arm of God has yielded to your unhallowed efforts," said Alice; "for a day of severe and heavy retribution must follow; nor flatter yourself with the idle hope, that your name, terrible as ye have rendered it to the virtuous, is sufficient, of itself, to drive the thoughts of home, and country, and kin, from all who hear it. Nay, I know not that even now, in listening to you, I am not forgetting a solemn duty, which would teach me to proclaim your presence, that the land might know that her unnatural son is a dangerous burthen in her bosom."

The pilot turned quickly in his short walk; and, after reading her countenance, with the expression of one who felt his security, he said, in gentler tones—

"Would that be Alice Dunscombe! would that be like the mild, generous girl whom I knew in my youth? But, I repeat, the threat would fail to intimidate, even if you were capable of executing it. I have said that it is only to make the signal, to draw around me a force sufficient to scatter these dogs of soldiers to the four winds of heaven."

"Have you calculated your power justly, John?" said Alice, unconsciously betraying her deep interest in his safety. "Have you reckoned the probability of Mr. Dillon's arriving, accompanied by an armed band of horsemen, with the morning's sun? for it's no secret in the Abbey, that he is gone in quest of such assistance."

"Dillon!" exclaimed the pilot, starting; "who is he! and on what suspicion does he seek this addition to your guard?"

"Nay, John, look not at me, as if you would know the secrets of my heart. It was not I who prompted him to such a step; you cannot, for a moment, think that I would betray you! But too surely he has gone, and, as the night wears rapidly away, you should be using the hour of grace to effect your own security."

"Fear not for me, Alice," returned the pilot, proudly, while a faint smile struggled around his compressed lip; "and yet, I like not this movement, either. How call you his name? Dillon! is he a minion of King George?"

"He is, John, what you are not, a loyal subject of his sovereign lord the King, and, though a native of the revolted colonies, he has preserved his virtue uncontaminated amid the corruptions and temptations of the times."

"An American! and disloyal to the liberties of the human race! By Heaven, he had better not cross me; for if my arm reach him, it shall hold him forth as a spectacle of treason to the world."

"And has not the world enough of such a spectacle in yourself? Are ye not, even now, breathing your native air, though lurking through the mists of the island, with desperate intent against its peace and happiness?"

A dark and fierce expression of angry resentment flashed

from the eyes of the pilot, and even his iron frame seemed to shake with emotion, as he answered—

"Call you his dastardly and selfish treason, aiming, as it does, to aggrandize a few, at the expense of millions, a parallel case to the generous ardour that impels a man to fight in the defence of sacred liberty? I might tell you that I am armed in the common cause of my fellow subjects and countrymen; that though an ocean divided us in distance, yet are we a people of the same blood, and children of the same parents, and that the hand which oppresses one, inflicts an injury on the other. But I disdain all such narrow apologies. I was born on this orb, and I claim to be a citizen of it. A man with a soul, not to be limited by the arbitrary boundaries of tyrants and hirelings, but one who has the right as well as the inclination to grapple with oppression, in whose name soever it is exercised, or in whatever hollow and specious shape it founds its claim to abuse our race."

"Ah! John, John, though this may sound like reason to rebellious ears, to mine it seemeth only as the ravings of insanity. It is in vain ye build up your new and disorganizing systems of rule, or rather misrule, which are opposed to all that the world has ever yet done, or ever will see done in peace and happiness. What avail your subtleties and false reasonings against the heart! It is the heart which tells us where our home is, and how to love it."

"You talk like a weak and prejudiced woman, Alice," said the pilot, more composedly; "and one who would shackle nations with the ties that bind the young and feeble of your own sex together."

"And by what holier or better bond can they be united!" said Alice. "Are not the relations of domestic life of God's establishing, and have not the nations grown from families, as branches spread from the stem, till the tree overshadows the land! 'Tis an ancient and sacred tie that binds man to his nation, neither can it be severed without infamy."

The pilot smiled disdainfully, and throwing open the rough exterior of his dress, he drew forth, in succession, several articles, while a glowing pride lighted his countenance, as he offered them singly to her notice.

"See, Alice!" he said, "call you this infamy! This broad

sheet of parchment is stamped with a seal of no mean importance, and it bears the royal name of the princely Louis also!
And view this cross! decorated as it is with jewels, the gift of
the same illustrious hand; it is not apt to be given to the
children of infamy, neither is it wise or decorous to stigmatize
a man who has not been thought unworthy to consort with
princes and nobles, by the opprobrious name of the 'Scotch
pirate.' "

"And have ye not earned the title, John, by ruthless deeds
and bitter animosity! I could kiss the baubles ye show me, if
they were a thousand times less splendid, had they been laid
upon your breast by the hands of your lawful prince; but now
they appear to my eyes as indelible blots upon your attainted
name. As for your associates, I have heard of them! and it
seemeth that a queen might be better employed than encouraging by her smiles the disloyal subjects of other monarchs,
though even her enemies. God only knows when his pleasure
may suffer a spirit of disaffection to rise up among the people
of her own nation, and then the thought that she has encouraged rebellion may prove both bitter and unwelcome."

"That the royal and lovely Antoinette has deigned to repay
my services with a small portion of her gracious approbation,
is not among the least of my boasts," returned the pilot, in
affected humility, while secret pride was manifested even in
his lofty attitude. "But venture not a syllable in her dispraise,
for you know not whom you censure. She is less distinguished by her illustrious birth and elevated station, than by
her virtues and loveliness. She lives the first of her sex in Europe—the daughter of an emperor, the consort of the most
powerful king, and the smiling and beloved patroness of a
nation who worship at her feet. Her life is above all reproach,
as it is above all earthly punishment, were she so lost as to
merit it, and it has been the will of Providence to place her far
beyond the reach of all human misfortunes."

"Has it placed her above human errors, John! punishment
is the natural and inevitable consequence of sin, and unless
she can say more than has ever fallen to the lot of humanity to
say truly, she may yet be made to feel the chastening arm of
One, to whose eyes all her pageantry and power are as vacant
as the air she breathes—so insignificant must it seem when

compared to his own just rule! But if you vaunt that you have been permitted to kiss the hem of the robes of the French queen, and have been the companion of high-born and flaunting ladies, clad in their richest array, can ye yet say to yourself, that amid them all ye have found one whose tongue has been bold to tell you the truth, or whose heart has sincerely joined in her false professions!"

"Certainly none have met me with the reproaches that I have this night received from Alice Dunscombe, after a separation of six long years," returned the Pilot.

"If I have spoken to you the words of holy truth, John, let them not be the less welcome, because they are strangers to your ears. Oh! think that she who has thus dared to use the language of reproach to one whose name is terrible to all who live on the border of this island, is led to the rash act by no other motive than interest in your eternal welfare."

"Alice! Alice, you madden me with these foolish speeches! Am I a monster to frighten unprotected women and helpless children? What mean these epithets, as coupled with my name? Have you too lent a credulous ear to the vile calumnies with which the policy of your rulers has ever attempted to destroy the fair fame of those who oppose them, and those chiefly who oppose them with success. My name may be terrible to the officers of the royal fleet, but where and how have I earned a claim to be considered formidable to the helpless and unoffending?"

Alice Dunscombe cast a furtive and timid glance at the pilot, which spoke even stronger than her words, as she replied—

"I know not that all which is said of you and your deeds is true. I have often prayed, in bitterness and sorrow, that a tenth part of that which is laid to your charge may not be heaped on your devoted head at the great and final account. But, John, I have known you long and well, and Heaven forbid, that, on this solemn occasion, which may be the last of our earthly interviews, I should be found wanting in christian duty, through a woman's weakness. I have often thought, when I have heard the gall of bitter reproach and envenomed language hurled against your name, that they who spoke so rashly, little understood the man they vituperated. But, though ye are at times, and I may say almost always, as mild and even as the smoothest sea over which ye have ever sailed, yet God has mingled in your nature a fearful mixture of fierce passions, which, roused, are more like the southern waters when troubled with the tornado. It is difficult for me to say, how far this evil spirit may lead a man, who has been goaded by fancied wrongs, to forget his country and home, and who is suddenly clothed with power to show his resentments."

The pilot listened with rooted attention, and his piercing eye seemed to reach the seat of those thoughts which she but half expressed; still, he retained the entire command of himself, and answered more in sorrow than in anger—

"If any thing could convert me to your own peaceful and unresisting opinions, Alice, it would be the reflections that offer themselves at this conviction, that even you have been led, by the base tongues of my dastardly enemies, to doubt my honour and conduct. What is fame, when a man can be thus traduced to his nearest friends! But no more of these childish reflections! They are unworthy of myself, my office, and the sacred cause in which I have enlisted!"

"Nay, John, shake them not off," said Alice, unconsciously laying her hand on his arm; "they are as the dew to the parched herbage, and may freshen the feelings of your youth, and soften the heart that has grown hard, if hard it be, more by unnatural indulgence, than its own base inclinations."

"Alice Dunscombe," said the pilot, approaching her with solemn earnestness, "I have learnt much this night, though I came not in quest of such knowledge. You have taught me how powerful is the breath of the slanderer, and how frail is the tenure by which we hold our good names. Full twenty times have I met the hirelings of your prince in open battle, fighting ever manfully under that flag which was first raised to the breeze by my own hands, and which, I thank my God, I have never yet seen lowered an inch; but with no one act of cowardice or private wrong, in all that service, can I reproach myself; and yet, how am I rewarded! The tongue of the vile calumniator is keener than the sword of the warrior, and leaves a more indelible scar!"

"Never have ye uttered a truer sentiment, John, and God send that ye may encourage such thoughts to your own eternal advantage," said Alice, with engaging interest. "You say that you have risked your precious life in twenty combats, and observe how little of Heaven's favour is bestowed on the abettors of rebellion! They tell me that the world has never witnessed a more desperate and bloody struggle than this last, for which your name has been made to sound to the furthermost ends of the isle."

" 'Twill be known wherever naval combats are spoken of," interrupted the pilot, the melancholy which had begun to lower in his countenance, giving place to a look of proud exultation.

"And yet, its fancied glory cannot shield your name from wrong, nor are the rewards of the victor equal, in a temporal sense, to those which the vanquished has received. Know you that our gracious monarch, deeming your adversary's cause so sacred, has extended to him his royal favour?"

"Ay! he has dubbed him knight!" exclaimed the pilot, with a scornful and bitter laugh; "let him be again furnished with a ship, and me with another opportunity, and I promise him an earldom, if being again vanquished can constitute a claim!"

"Speak not so rashly, nor vaunt yourself of possessing a protecting power, that may desert you, John, when you most need it, and least expect the change," returned his companion; "the battle is not always to the strong, neither is the race to the swift."

"Forget you, my good Alice, that your words will admit of a double meaning? Has the battle been to the strong! Though you say not well in denying the race to the swift. Yes, yes, often and again have the dastards escaped me by their prudent speed! Alice Dunscombe, you know not a thousandth part of the torture that I have been made to feel, by high born miscreants, who envy the merit they cannot equal, and detract from the glory of deeds that they dare not attempt to emulate. How have I been cast upon the ocean like some unworthy vessel that is commissioned to do a desperate deed, and then to bury itself in the ruin it has made! How many malignant hearts have triumphed, as they beheld my canvass open, thinking that it was spread to hasten me to a gibbet, or to a tomb in the bosom of the ocean; but I have disappointed them!"

The eyes of the pilot no longer gazed with their piercing and settled meaning, but they flashed with a fierce and wild pleasure, as he continued, in a louder voice—

"Yes, bitterly have I disappointed them! Oh! the triumph over my fallen enemies has been tame, to this heartfelt exultation which places me immeasurably above those false and craven hypocrites! I begged, I implored, the Frenchmen, for the meanest of their craft, which possessed but the common qualities of a ship of war; I urged the policy and necessity of giving me such a force, for even then I promised to be found in harm's way; but, envy and jealousy robbed me of my just dues, and of more than half my glory. They call me pirate! If I have a claim to the name, it was furnished more by the paltry outfit of my friends, than by any act towards my enemies!"

"And do not these recollections prompt you to return to your allegiance to your prince and native land, John?" said Alice, in a subdued voice.

"Away with the silly thought," interrupted the pilot, recalled to himself as if by a sudden conviction of the weakness he had betrayed; "it is ever thus where men are made conspicuous by their works—but to your visit—I have the power to rescue myself and companions from this paltry confinement, and yet I would not have it done with violence, for your sake.—Bring you the means of doing it in quiet?"

"When the morning arrives, you will all be conducted to the apartment where we first met. This will be done at the solicitation of Miss Howard, under the plea of compassion and justice, and with the professed object of inquiring into your situations. Her request will not be refused, and while your guard is stationed at the door, you will be shown, by another entrance through the private apartments of the wing, to a window, whence you can easily leap to the ground, where a thicket is at hand; afterwards we shall trust your safety to your own discretion."

"And if this Dillon, of whom you have spoken, should suspect the truth, how will you answer to the law for aiding our escape?"

"I believe he little dreams who is among the prisoners," said Alice, musing, "though he may have detected the character of one of your companions. But it is private feeling, rather than public spirit, that urges him on."

"I have suspected something of this," returned the pilot, with a smile, that crossed those features where ungovernable passions had so lately been exhibited, with an effect, that might be likened to the last glimmering of an expiring conflagration, serving to render the surrounding ruin more obvious. "This young Griffith has led me from my direct path, with his idle imprudence, and it is right that his mistress should incur some risk. But with you, Alice, the case is different; here you are only a guest, and it is unnecessary that you should be known in the unfortunate affair. Should my name get abroad, this recreant American, this Col. Howard, will find all the favour he has purchased by advocating the cause of tyranny, necessary to protect him from the displeasure of the ministry."

"I fear to trust so delicate a measure to the young discretion of my amiable friend," said Alice, shaking her head.

"Remember, that she has her attachment to plead in her excuse; but dare you say to the world that you still remember, with gentle feelings, the man whom you stigmatize with such opprobrious epithets!"

A slight colour gleamed over the brow of Alice Dunscombe, as she uttered in a voice that was barely audible—

"There is no longer a reason why the world should know of such a weakness, though it did exist." And, as the faint glow passed away, leaving her face pale, nearly as the hue of death, her eyes kindled with unusual fire, and she added, "They can but take my life, John, and that I am ready to lay down in your service!"

"Alice!" exclaimed the softened pilot, "my kind, my gentle Alice!"—

The knock of the sentinel at the door, was heard at this critical moment. Without waiting for a reply to his summons, the man entered the apartment, and, in hurried language, declared the urgent necessity that existed for the lady to retire. A few brief remonstrances were uttered by both Alice and the pilot, who wished to comprehend more clearly each other's intentions relative to the intended escape; but the fear of personal punishment rendered the soldier obdurate, and a dread of exposure at length induced the lady to comply. She arose, and was leaving the apartment with lingering steps, when the pilot, touching her hand, whispered to her impressively—

"Alice, we meet again before I leave this island for ever."

"We meet in the morning, John," she returned, in the same tone of voice, "in the apartments of Miss Howard."

He dropped her hand, and she glided from the room, when the impatient sentinel closed the door, and silently turned the key on his prisoner. The pilot remained in a listening attitude, until the light footsteps of the retiring pair were no longer audible, when he paced his confined apartment with per-turbed steps, occasionally pausing to look out at the driving clouds, and the groaning oaks that were trembling and rock-ing their broad arms in the fitful gusts of the gale. In a few minutes the tempest in his own passions had gradually sub-sided to the desperate and still calmness that made him the man he was; when he again seated himself where Alice had found him, and began to muse on the events of the times, from which, the transition to projecting schemes of daring enterprise and mighty consequences, was but the usual em-ployment of his active and restless mind.

# Chapter XV.

*"Sir And.* I have no exquisite reason for't,
but I've reason good enough."
*Twelfth Night,* II.iii.145–146.

THE COUNTENANCE of Captain Borroughcliffe, when the
sentinel admitted him to the apartment he had selected,
was in that state of doubtful illumination, when looks of peculiar cunning blend so nicely with the stare of vacancy, that
the human face is rendered not unlike an April day, now smiling and inviting, and at the next moment clouded and dreary.
It was quite apparent that the soldier had an object for his
unexpected visit, by the importance of his air, and the solemnity of the manner with which he entered on the business. He
waved his hand for the sentinel to retire, with lofty dignity,
and continued balancing his body, during the closing of the
door, and while a sound continued audible to his confused
faculties, with his eyes fixed in the direction of the noise, with
that certain sort of wise look, that in many men supplies the
place of something better. When the captain felt himself secure from interruption, he moved round with quick military
precision, in order to face the man of whom he was in quest.
Griffith had been sleeping, though uneasily, and with watchfulness; and the pilot had been calmly awaiting the visit which
it seemed he had anticipated; but their associate, who was no
other than Captain Manual, of the marines, was discovered in
a very different condition from either. Though the weather
was cool, and the night tempestuous, he had thrown aside his
pea-jacket, with most of his disguise, and was sitting ruefully
on his blanket, wiping, with one hand, the large drops of
sweat from his forehead, and occasionally grasping his throat
with the other, with a kind of convulsed, mechanical movement. He stared wildly at his visiter, though his entrance
produced no other alteration in these pursuits, than a more
diligent application of his handkerchief, and a more frequent
grasping of his naked neck, as if he were willing to ascertain
by actual experiment, what degree of pressure the part was
able to sustain, without exceeding a given quantity of inconvenience.

"Comrade, I greet ye!" said Borroughcliffe, staggering to the side of his prisoner, where he seated himself with an entire absence of ceremony; "Comrade, I greet ye! Is the kingdom in danger, that gentlemen traverse the island in the uniform of the regiment of incognitus, incognitii, 'torum—dammee, how I forget my Latin! Say, my fine fellow, are you one of these 'torums?"

Manual breathed a little hard, which, considering the manner he had been using his throat, was a thing to be expected; but, swallowing his apprehensions, he answered with more spirit than his situation rendered prudent, or the occasion demanded.

"Say what you will of me, and treat me as you please, I defy any man to call me tory with truth."

"You are no 'torum! Well, then, the war office has got up a new dress! Your regiment must have earned their facings in storming some water battery, or perhaps it has done duty as marines. Am I right?"

"I'll not deny it," said Manual, more stoutly; "I have served as a marine for two years, though taken from the line of"—

"The army," said Borroughcliffe, interrupting a most damning confession of which "state line" the other had belonged to. "I kept a dog watch myself, once, on board the fleet of my Lord Howe; but it is a service that I do not envy any man. Our afternoon parades were dreadfully unsteady, for it's a time, you know, when a man wants solid ground to stand on. However, I purchased my company with some prize money that fell in my way, and I always remember the marine service with gratitude. But this is dry work. I have put a bottle of sparkling Madeira in my pocket, with a couple of glasses, which we will discuss, while we talk over more important matters. Thrust your hand into my right pocket; I have been used to dress to the front so long, that it comes mighty awkward to me to make this backward motion, as if it were into a cartridge box."

Manual, who had been at a loss how to construe the manner of the other, perceived at once a good deal of plain English in this request, and he dislodged one of Colonel Howard's dusty bottles, with a dexterity that denoted the earnestness of his purpose. Borroughcliffe had made a suitable provision of glasses, and extracting the cork in a certain scientific manner, he tendered to his companion a bumper of the liquor, before another syllable was uttered by either of the expectants. The gentlemen concluded their draughts with a couple of smacks, that sounded not unlike the pistols of two practised duellists, though certainly a much less alarming noise; when the entertainer renewed the discourse.

"I like one of your musty-looking bottles, that is covered with dust and cobwebs, with a good southern tan on it," he said. "Such liquor does not abide in the stomach, but it gets into the heart at once, and becomes blood in the beating of a pulse. But how soon I knew you! That sort of knowledge is the freemasonry of our craft. I knew you to be the man you are, the moment I laid eyes on you in what we call our guard-room; but I thought I would humour the old soldier who lives here, by letting him have the formula of an examination, as a sort of deference to his age and former rank. But I knew you the instant I saw you. I have seen you before!"

The theory of Borroughcliffe, in relation to the incorporation of wine with the blood, might have been true in the case of the marine, whose whole frame appeared to undergo a kind of magical change by the experiment of drinking, which, the reader will understand, was diligently persevered in, while a drop remained in the bottle. The perspiration no longer rolled from his brow, neither did his throat manifest that uneasiness which had rendered such constant external applications necessary; but he settled down into an air of cool, but curious interest, which, in some measure, was the necessary concomitant of his situation.

"We may have met before, as I have been much in service, and yet I know not where you could have seen me," said Manual. "Were you ever a prisoner of war?"

"Hum! not exactly such an unfortunate devil; but a sort of conventional non-combatant. I shared the hardships, the glory, the equivocal victories, (where we killed and drove countless numbers of rebels—who were not,) and, wo is me! the capitulation of Burgoyne. But let that pass—which was more than the Yankees would allow us to do. You know not where I could have seen you? I have seen you on parade, in the field, in battle and out of battle, in camp, in barracks, in short, every where but in a drawing-room. No, no; I have never seen you before this night in a drawing-room!"

Manual stared in a good deal of wonder, and some uneasiness, at these confident assertions, which promised to put his life in no little jeopardy; and it is to be supposed that the peculiar sensation about the throat was revived, as he made a heavy draught before he said—

"You will swear to this—Can you call me by name?"

"I will swear to it in any court in Christendom," said the dogmatical soldier; "and your name is—is—Fugleman."

"If it is, I'll be damn'd!" exclaimed the other, with exulting precipitation.

"Swear not!" said Borroughcliffe, with a solemn air; "for what mattereth an empty name! Call thyself by what appellation thou wilt, I know thee. Soldier is written on thy martial front; thy knee bendeth not; nay, I even doubt if the rebellious member bow in prayer."—

"Come, sir," interrupted Manual, a little sternly; "no more of this trifling, but declare your will at once. Rebellious member, indeed! These fellows will call the skies of America rebellious heavens shortly!"

"I like thy spirit, lad," returned the undisturbed Borroughcliffe; "it sits as gracefully on a soldier, as his sash and gorget; but it is lost on an old campaigner. I marvel, however, that thou takest such umbrage at my slight attack on thy orthodoxy. I fear the fortress must be weak, where the outworks are defended with such a waste of unnecessary courage."

"I know not why or wherefore you have paid me this visit, Captain Borroughcliffe," said Manual, with a laudable discretion, which prompted him to reconnoitre the other's views a little, before he laid himself more open; "if captain be your rank, and Borroughcliffe be your name. But this I do know, that if it be only to mock me in my present situation, it is neither soldier-like nor manly; and it is what, in other circumstances, might be attended by some hazard."

"Hum!" said the other, with his immovable coolness; "I see you set the wine down as nothing, though the king drinks not as good; for the plain reason that the sun of England cannot find its way through the walls of Windsor Castle, as easily as the sun of Carolina can warm a garret covered with cedar shingles. But I like your spirit more and more. So draw yourself up in battle array, and let us have another charge at this black bottle, when I shall lay before your military eyes a plan of the whole campaign."

Manual first bestowed an inquiring glance on his companion, when, discovering no other expression than foolish cunning, which was fast yielding before the encroaching footsteps of stupid inebriety, he quietly placed himself in the desired position. The wine was drunk, when Borrough-cliffe proceeded to open his communications more unreservedly.

"You are a soldier, and I am a soldier. That you are a soldier, my orderly could tell; for the dog has both seen a campaign, and smelt villanous salt-petre, when compounded according to a wicked invention; but it required the officer to detect the officer. Privates do not wear such linen as this, which seemeth to me an unreasonably cool attire for the season; nor velvet stocks, with silver buckles; nor is there often the odorous flavour of sweet-scented pomatum to be discovered around their greasy locks. In short, thou art both soldier and officer."

"I confess it," said Manual; "I hold the rank of captain, and shall expect the treatment of one."

"I think I have furnished you with wine fit for a general," returned Borroughcliffe; "but have your own way. Now, it would be apparent to men, whose faculties had not been rendered clear by such cordials as this dwelling aboundeth with, that when you officers journey through the island, clad in the uniform incognitorum, which, in your case, means the marine corps, that something is in the wind of more than usual moment. Soldiers owe their allegiance to their prince, and next to him, to war, women, and wine. Of war, there is none in the realm; of women, plenty; but wine, I regret to say, that is, good wine, grows both scarce and dear. Do I speak to the purpose, comrade?"

"Proceed," said Manual, whose eyes were not less attentive than his ears, in a hope to discover whether his true character were understood.

"En avant! in plain English, forward march! Well then, the difficulty lies between women and wine; which, when the former are pretty, and the latter rich, is a very agreeable sort of an alternative. That it is not wine of which you are in quest, I must believe, my comrade captain, or you would not go on the adventure in such shabby attire. You will excuse me, but who would think of putting any thing better than their port before a man in a pair of tarred trowsers. No! no! Hollands, green-and-yellow Hollands, is a potation good enough to set before one of thy present bearing."

"And yet I have met with him who has treated me to the choicest of the south-side Madeira?"

"Know you the very side from which the precious fluid comes! That looks more in favour of the wine. But, after all, woman, dear, capricious woman, who one moment fancies she sees a hero in regimentals, and the next, a saint in a cassock; and who always sees something admirable in a suitor, whether he be clad in tow or velvet—woman is at the bottom of this mysterious masquerading. Am I right, comrade?"

By this time, Manual had discovered that he was safe, and he returned to the conversation with a revival of all his ready wits, which had been strangely paralyzed by his previous disorder in the region of the throat. First bestowing a wicked wink on his companion, and a look that would have outdone the wisest aspect of Solomon, he replied—

"Ah! woman has much to answer for!"

"I knew it," exclaimed Borroughcliffe; "and this confession only confirms me in the good opinion I have always entertained of myself. If his majesty has any particular wish to close this American business, let him have a certain convention burnt, and a nameless person promoted, and we shall see! But, answer as you love truth; is it a business of holy matrimony, or a mere dalliance with the sweets of Cupid?"

"Of honest wedlock," said Manual, with an air as serious as if Hymen already held him in his fetters.

" 'Tis honest! Is there money?"

"Is there money?" repeated Manual, with a sort of contemptuous echo. "Would a soldier part with his liberty, but with his life, unless the chains were made of gold?"

"That's the true military doctrine!" cried the other; "faith, you have some discretion in your amphibious corps, I find!

But why this disguise, are the 'seniors grave,' as well as 'potent and reverend?' Why this disguise, I again ask?"

"Why this disguise!" repeated Manual, coolly; "Is there any such thing as love in your regiment without disguise? With us it is a regular symptom of the disease."

"A most just and discreet description of the passion, my amphibious comrade!" said the English officer; "and yet the symptoms in your case are attended by some very malignant tokens. Does your mistress love tar?"

"No; but she loveth me; and, of course, whatever attire I choose to appear in."

"Still discreet and sagacious! and yet only a most palpable feint to avoid my direct attack. You have heard of such a place as Gretna Green, a little to the north of this, I dare say, my aquatic comrade. Am I right?"

"Gretna Green!" said Manual, a little embarrassed by his ignorance; "some parade ground, I suppose?"

"Ay, for those who suffer under the fire of Master Cupid. A parade ground! well, there is some artful simplicity in that! But all will not do with an old campaigner. It is a difficult thing to impose on an old soldier, my water battery. Now listen and answer; and you shall see what it is to possess a discernment—therefore deny nothing. You are in love?"

"I deny nothing," said Manual, comprehending at once that this was his safest course.

"Your mistress is willing, and the money is ready, but the old people say, halt!"

"I am still mute."

"'Tis prudent. You say march—Gretna Green is the object; and your flight is to be by water?"

"Unless I can make my escape by water, I shall never make it," said Manual, with another sympathetic movement with his hand to his throat.

"Keep mute; you need tell me nothing. I can see into a mystery that is as deep as a well, to-night. Your companions are hirelings; perhaps your shipmates; or men to pilot you on this expedition?"

"One is my shipmate, and the other is our pilot," said Manual, with more truth than usual.

"You are well provided. One thing more, and I shall become mute in my turn. Does she whom you seek lie in this house?"

"She does not; she lies but a short distance from this place; and I should be a happy fellow, could I but once more put foot—"

"Eyes on her. Now listen, and you shall have your wish. You possess the ability to march yet, which, considering the lateness of the hour, is no trifling privilege; open that window—is it possible to descend from it?"

Manual eagerly complied, but he turned from the place in disappointment.

"It would be certain death to attempt the leap. The devil only could escape from it."

"So I should think," returned Borroughcliffe dryly. "You must be content to pass for that respectable gentleman for the rest of your days, in St. Ruth's Abbey. For through that identical hole must you wing your flight on the pinions of love."

"But how! The thing is impossible."

"In imagination only. There is some stir; a good deal of foolish apprehension; and a great excess of idle curiosity, among certain of the tenants of this house on your account. They fear the rebels, who, we all know, have not soldiers enough to do their work neatly at home, and who of course would never think of sending any here. You wish to be snug—I wish to serve a brother in distress. Through that window you must be supposed to fly—no matter how; while by following me you can pass the sentinel, and retire peaceably, like any other mortal, on your own two stout legs."

This was a result that exceeded all that Manual had anticipated from their amicable but droll dialogue; and the hint was hardly given, before he threw on the garments that agitation had before rendered such encumbrances, and in less time than we have taken to relate it, the marine was completely equipped for his departure. In the mean time, Captain Borroughcliffe raised himself to an extremely erect posture, which he maintained, with the inflexibility of a rigid martinet. When he found himself established on his feet, the soldier intimated to his prisoner that he was ready to proceed. The door was instantly opened by Manual, and together they entered the gallery.

"Who comes there?" cried the sentinel, with a vigilance and vigour that he intended should compensate for his previous neglect of duty.

"Walk straight, that he may see you," said Borroughcliffe, with much philosophy.

"Who goes there!" repeated the sentinel, throwing his musket to a poise, with a rattling sound that echoed along the naked walls.

"Walk crooked," added Borroughcliffe, "that if he fire he may miss."

"We shall be shot at, with this folly," muttered Manual. "We are friends, and your officer is one of us."

"Stand friends—advance officer and give the countersign," cried the sentinel.

"That is much easier said than done," returned his captain; "forward! Mr. Amphibious, you can walk like a postman—move to the front, and proclaim the magical word, 'loyalty;' 'tis a standing countersign, ready furnished to my hands by mine host, the colonel; your road is then clear before you—but hark—"

Manual made an eager step forward, when, recollecting himself, he turned, and added—

"My assistants, the seamen! I can do nothing without them."

"Lo! the keys are in the doors, ready for my admission," said the Englishman; "turn them and bring out your forces."

Quick as thought, Manual was in the room of Griffith, to whom he briefly communicated the situation of things, when he re-appeared in the passage, and then proceeded on a similar errand to the room of the pilot.

"Follow, and behave as usual," he whispered; "say not a word, but trust all to me."

The pilot arose, and obeyed these instructions without asking a question, with the most admirable coolness.

"I am now ready to proceed," said Manual, when they had joined Borroughcliffe.

During the short time occupied in these arrangements, the sentinel and his captain had stood looking at each other, with great military exactitude. The former ambitious of manifesting his watchfulness; the latter awaiting the return of the marine. The captain now beckoned to Manual to advance and give the countersign.

"Loyalty," whispered Manual, when he approached the sentinel. But the soldier had been allowed time to reflect; and as he well understood the situation of his officer, he hesitated to allow the prisoner to pass. After a moment's pause, he said—

"Advance friends." At this summons, the whole party moved to the point of his bayonet; when the man continued, "The prisoners have the countersign, Captain Borroughcliffe, but I dare not let them pass."

"Why not?" asked the captain; "am I not here, sirrah; do you not know me?"

"Yes, sir, I know your honour, and respect your honour; but I was posted here by my sergeant, and ordered not to let these men pass out on any account."

"That's what I call good discipline," said Borroughcliffe, with an exulting laugh; "I knew the lad would not mind me any more than that he would obey the orders of that lamp. Here are no slaves of the lamp, my amphibious comrade; drill ye your marines in this consummate style to niceties?"

"What means this trifling?" said the pilot, sternly.

"Ah! I thought I should turn the laugh on you," cried Manual, affecting to join in the mirth; "we know all these things well, and we practise them in our corps; but though the sentinel cannot know you, the sergeant will; so let him be called, and orders be given through him to the man on post, that we may pass out."

"Your throat grows uneasy, I see," said Borroughcliffe; "you crave another bottle of the generous fluid. Well, it shall be done. Sentinel, you can throw up yon window, and give a call to the sergeant."

"The outcry will ruin us," said the pilot, in a whisper to Griffith.

"Follow me," said the young sailor. The sentinel was turning to execute the orders of his captain, as Griffith spoke; when springing forward, in an instant he wrenched the musket from his hands; a heavy blow with its butt, felled the astonished soldier to the floor; then, poising his weapon, Griffith exclaimed—

"Forward! we can clear our own way now!"

"On!" said the pilot, leaping lightly over the prostrate soldier, a dagger gleaming in one hand, and a pistol presented in the other.

Manual was by his side in an instant, armed in a similar manner; and the three rushed together from the building, without meeting any one to oppose their flight.

Borroughcliffe was utterly unable to follow; and so astounded was he by this sudden violence, that several minutes passed before he was restored to the use of his speech, a faculty which seldom deserted him. The man had recovered his senses and his feet, however; and the two stood gazing at each other in mute condolence. At length the sentinel broke the silence—

"Shall I give the alarm, your honour?"

"I rather think not, Peters. I wonder if there be any such thing as gratitude or good breeding in the marine corps!"

"I hope your honour will remember that I did my duty, and that I was disarmed while executing your orders."

"I can remember nothing about it, Peters, except that it is rascally treatment, and such as I shall yet make this amphibious, aquatic gentleman answer for. But, lock the door—look as if nothing had happened, and—"

"Ah! your honour, that is not so easily done as your honour may please to think. I have not any doubt but there is the print of the breech of a musket stamped on my back and shoulders, as plainly to be seen as that light."

"Then look as you please; but hold your peace, sirrah. Here is a crown to buy a plaster. I heard the dog throw away your musket on the stairs—go seek it, and return to your post; and when you are relieved, act as if nothing had happened. I take the responsibility on myself."

The man obeyed, and when he was once more armed, Borroughcliffe, a good deal sobered by the surprise, made the best of his way to his own apartment, muttering threats and execrations against the "corps of marines, and the whole race," as he called them, "of aquatic amphibii."

# Chapter XVI.

"Away! away! the covey's fled the cover;
   Put forth the dogs, and let the falcon fly—
   I'll spend some leisure in the keen pursuit,
   Nor longer waste my hours in sluggish quiet."

T HE SOLDIER passed the remainder of the night in the heavy sleep of a bacchanalian, and awoke late on the following morning, only when aroused by the entrance of his servant. When the customary summons had induced the captain to unclose his eye-lids, he arose in his bed, and after performing the usual operation of a diligent friction on his organs of vision, he turned sternly to his man, and remarked, with an ill-humour that seemed to implicate the innocent servant in the fault which his master condemned—

"I thought, sirrah, that I ordered Sergeant Drill not to let a drum-stick touch a sheep-skin while we quartered in the dwelling of this hospitable old colonel! Does the fellow despise my commands; or does he think the roll of a drum, echoing through the crooked passages of St. Ruth, a melody that is fit to disturb the slumbers of its inmates!"

"I believe, sir," returned the man, "it was the wish of Colonel Howard himself, that on this occasion the sergeant should turn out the guard by the roll of the drum."

"The devil it was! I see the old fellow loves to tickle the drum of his own ear now and then, with familiar sounds; but have you had a muster of the cattle from the farm-yard too, as well as a parade of the guard? I hear the trampling of feet, as if the old abbey were a second ark, and all the beasts of the field were coming aboard of us!"

" 'Tis nothing but the party of dragoons from —— who are wheeling into the court-yard, sir, where the colonel has gone out to receive them."

"Court-yard! light dragoons!" repeated Borroughcliffe, in amazement; "and has it come to this, that twenty stout fellows of the ——th are not enough to guard such a rookery as this old abbey, against the ghosts and north-east storms, but we must have horse to reinforce us. Hum! I suppose some of these booted gentlemen have heard of this South-Carolina Madeira."

"Oh, no, Sir!" cried his man, "it is only the party that Mr. Dillon went to seek last evening, after you saw fit, sir, to put the three pirates in irons."

"Pirates in irons!" said Borroughcliffe, again passing his hands over his eyes, though in a more reflecting manner than before; "ha! oh! I remember to have put three suspicious looking rascals in the black-hole, or some such place; but what can Mr. Dillon, or the light dragoons, have to do with these fellows?"

"That we do not know, sir; but it is said below, sir, as some suspicions had fallen on their being conspirators and rebels from the colonies, and that they were great officers and tories in disguise; some said that one was General Washington, and others, that it was only three members of the Yankee parliament, come over to get our good old English fashions, to set themselves up with."

"Washington! Members of Congress! Go—go, simpleton, and learn how many these troopers muster, and what halt they make; but stay, place my clothes near me. Now, do as I bid you; and if the dragoon officer inquire for me, make my respects, and tell him I shall be with him soon. Go, fellow; go."

When the man left the room, the captain, while he proceeded with the business of the toilet, occasionally gave utterance to the thoughts that crowded on his recollection, after the manner of a soliloquy.

"Ay! my commission to a half-pay ensigncy, that some of these lazy fellows, who must have a four-legged beast to carry them to the wars, have heard of the 'south side.' South side! I believe I must put an advertisement in the London Gazette, calling that amphibious soldier to an account. If he be a true man, he will not hide himself under his incognito, but will give me a meeting. If that should fail, damme, I'll ride across to Yarmouth, and call out the first of the mongrel breed that I fall in with. 'Sdeath! was ever such an insult practised on a gentleman, and a soldier, before! Would that I only knew his name! Why, if the tale should get abroad, I shall be the standing joke of the mess-table, until some greater fool than myself can be found. It would cost me at least six duels to get rid of it. No, no; not a trigger will I pull in my own regiment about the silly affair; but I'll have a crack at some marine in very revenge; for that is no more than reasonable. That Peters! if the scoundrel should dare whisper any thing of the manner in which he was stamped with the breech of the musket! I can't flog him for it, but if I don't make it up to him, the first time he gives me a chance, I am ignorant of the true art of balancing regimental accounts."

By the time the recruiting officer had concluded this soliloquy, which affords a very fair exposition of the current of his thoughts, he was prepared to meet the new comers, and he accordingly descended to the court-yard, as in duty bound, to receive them in his proper person. Borroughcliffe encountered his host, in earnest conversation with a young man in a cavalry uniform, in the principal entrance of the abbey, and was greeted by the former with—

"A good morning to you, my worthy guard and protector! here is rare news for your loyal ears. It seems that our prisoners are enemies to the king in disguise; and Cornet Fitzgerald—Captain Borroughcliffe, of the ——th, permit me to make you acquainted with Mr. Fitzgerald, of the ——th Light Dragoons." While the soldiers exchanged their salutations, the old man continued—"The cornet has been kind enough to lead down a detachment of his troop, to escort the rogues up to London, or some other place, where they will find enough good and loyal officers to form a court martial, that can authorize their execution as spies. Christopher Dillon, my worthy kinsman, Kit, saw into their real characters, at a glance, while you and I, like two unsuspecting boys, thought the rascals would have made fit men to serve the king. But Kit has an eye and a head that few enjoy like him, and I would that he might receive his dues at the English bar."

"It is to be desired, sir," said Borroughcliffe, with a grave aspect, that was produced chiefly by his effort to give effect to his sarcasm, but a little, also, by the recollection of the occurrences that were yet to be explained; "but what reason has Mr. Christopher Dillon to believe that the three seamen are more or less than they seem?"

"I know not what; but a good and sufficient reason, I will

venture my life," cried the colonel; "Kit is a lad for reasons, which you know is the foundation of his profession, and knows how to deliver them manfully in the proper place; but you know, gentlemen, that the members of the bar cannot assume the open and bold front that becomes a soldier, without often endangering the cause in which they are concerned. No, no, trust me, Kit has his reasons, and in good time will he deliver them."

"I hope, then," said the captain, carelessly, "that it may be found that we have had a proper watch on our charge, Colonel Howard; I think you told me the windows were too high for an escape in that direction, for I had no sentinel outside of the building."

"Fear nothing, my worthy friend," cried his host; "unless your men have slept, instead of watching, we have them safe; but, as it will be necessary to convey them away before any of the civil authority can lay hands on them, let us proceed to the rear, and unkennel the dogs. A party of the horse might proceed at once with them to ——, while we are breaking our fasts. It would be no very wise thing to allow the civilians to deal with them, for they seldom have a true idea of the nature of the crime."

"Pardon me, sir," said the young officer of horse; "I was led to believe, by Mr. Dillon, that we might meet with a party of the enemy in some little force, and that I should find a pleasanter duty than that of a constable; besides, sir, the laws of the realm guaranty to the subject a trial by his peers, and it is more than I dare do to carry the men to the barracks, without first taking them before a magistrate."

"Ay! you speak of loyal and dutiful subjects," said the colonel; "and, as respects them, doubtless, you are right; but such privileges are withheld from enemies and traitors."

"It must be first proved that they are such, before they can receive the treatment or the punishment that they merit," returned the young man, a little positively, who felt the more confidence, because he had only left the Temple the year before. "If I take charge of the men at all, it will be only to transfer them safely to the civil authority."

"Let us go, and see the prisoners," cried Borroughcliffe, with a view to terminate a discussion that was likely to wax warm, and which he knew to be useless; "perhaps they may quietly enrol themselves under the banners of our sovereign, when all other interference, save that of wholesome discipline, will become unnecessary."

"Nay, if they are of a rank in life to render such a step probable," returned the cornet, "I am well content that the matter should be thus settled. I trust, however, that Captain Borroughcliffe will consider that the ——th light dragoons has some merit in this affair, and that we are far short of our numbers in the second squadron."

"We shall not be difficult at a compromise," returned the captain; "there is one a piece for us, and a toss of a guinea shall determine who has the third man. Sergeant! follow, to deliver over your prisoners, and relieve your sentry."

As they proceeded, in compliance with this arrangement, to the building in the rear, Colonel Howard, who made one of the party, observed—

"I dispute not the penetration of Captain Borroughcliffe, but I understand Mr. Christopher Dillon that there is reason to believe one of these men, at least, to be of a class altogether above that of a common soldier, in which case your plans may fall to the ground."

"And who does he deem the gentleman to be?" asked Borroughcliffe—"A Bourbon in disguise, or a secret representative of the rebel congress?"

"Nay, nay; he said nothing more; my kinsman Kit keeps a close mouth, whenever Dame Justice is about to balance her scales. There are men who may be said to have been born to be soldiers; of which number I should call the Earl Cornwallis, who makes such head against the rebels in the two Carolinas; others seem to be intended by nature for divines, and saints on earth, such as their Graces of York and Canterbury; while another class appear as if it were impossible for them to behold things, unless with discriminating, impartial, and disinterested eyes; to which, I should say, belong my Lord Chief Justice Mansfield, and my kinsman, Mr. Christopher Dillon. I trust, gentlemen, that when the royal arms have crushed this rebellion, that his majesty's ministers will see the propriety of extending the dignity of the peerage to the colonies, as a means of reward to the loyal, and a measure of policy, to prevent future disaffection; in which case, I hope to see my kinsman decorated with the ermine of justice, bordering the mantle of a peer."

"Your expectations, my excellent sir, are right reasonable, as I doubt not your kinsman will become, at some future day, that which he is not at present, unhappily for his deserts, right honourable," said Borroughcliffe. "But be of good heart, sir, from what I have seen of his merits, I doubt not that the law will yet have its revenge in due season, and that we shall be properly edified and instructed how to attain elevation in life, by the future exaltation of Mr. Christopher Dillon; though by what title he is to be then known, I am at a loss to say."

Colonel Howard was too much occupied with his own ex parte views of the war and things in general, to observe the shrewd looks that were exchanged between the soldiers; but he answered with perfect simplicity—

"I have reflected much on that point, and have come to the opinion, that as he has a small estate on that river, he should cause his first barony to be known by the title of 'Pedee.'"

"Barony!" echoed Borroughcliffe; "I trust the new nobles of a new world will disdain the old worn out distinctions of a hackneyed universe—eschew all baronies, mine host, and cast earldoms and dukedoms to the shades. The immortal Locke has unlocked his fertile mind to furnish you with appellations suited to the originality of your condition, and the nature of your country. Ah! here comes the Cacique of Pedee, in his proper person!"

As Borroughcliffe spoke, they were ascending the flight of stone steps which led to the upper apartments, where the prisoners were still supposed to be confined; and, at the same moment, the sullen, gloomy features of Dillon were seen as he advanced along the lower passage, with an expression of malicious exultation hovering above his dark brow, that denoted his secret satisfaction. As the hours had passed away, the period had come round when the man who had been present at the escape of Griffith and his friends, was again posted to perform the duty of sentinel. As this soldier well knew the situation of his trust, he was very coolly adjusted, with his back against the wall, endeavouring to compensate himself for his disturbed slumbers during the night, when the sounds of the approaching footsteps warned him to assume the appearance of watchfulness.

"How now, fellow!" cried Borroughcliffe; "what have you to say of your charge?"

"I believe the men sleep, your honour; for I have heard no noises from the rooms since I relieved the last sentinel."

"The lads are weary, and are right to catch what sleep they can in their comfortable quarters," returned the captain. "Stand to your arms, sirrah! and throw back your shoulders; and do not move like a crab, or a train-band corporal; do you not see an officer of horse coming up? Would you disgrace your regiment!"

"Ah! your honour, Heaven only knows whether I shall ever get my shoulders even again."

"Buy another plaster," said Borroughcliffe, slipping a shilling into his hand; "observe, you know nothing but your duty."

"Which is, your honour—"

"To mind me and be silent. But here comes the sergeant with his guard, he will relieve you."

The rest of the party had stopped at the other end of the gallery, to allow the few files of soldiers, who were led by the orderly, to pass them, when they all moved toward the prisons in a body. The sentinel was relieved in due military style; when Dillon placed his hand on one of the doors, and said, with a malicious sneer,

"Open here first, Mr. Sergeant; this cage holds the man we most want."

"Softly, softly, my Lord Chief Justice, and most puissant Cacique," said the captain; "the hour has not yet come to empannel a jury of fat yeomen, and no man must interfere with my boys but myself."

"The rebuke is harsh, I must observe, Captain Borroughcliffe," said the colonel; "but I pardon it because it is military. No, no, Kit; these nice points must be left to martial usages. Be not impatient, my cousin; I doubt not the hour will come, when you shall hold the scales of justice, and satisfy your loyal longings on many a traitor. Zounds! I could almost turn executioner myself in such a cause!"

"I can curb my impatience, sir," returned Dillon, with hypocritical meekness, and great self-command, though his eyes were gleaming with savage exultation. "I beg pardon of Captain Borroughcliffe, if, in my desire to render the civil authority superior to the military, I have trespassed on your customs."

"You see, Borroughcliffe!" exclaimed the colonel, exultingly, "the lad is ruled by an instinct in all matters of law and justice. I hold it to be impossible that a man thus endowed can ever become a disloyal subject. But our breakfast waits, and Mr. Fitzgerald has breathed his horse this cool morning; let us proceed at once to the examination."

Borroughcliffe motioned to the sergeant to open the door, when the whole party entered the vacant room.

"Your prisoner has escaped!" cried the cornet, after a single moment employed in making sure of the fact.

"Never! it must not, shall not be," cried Dillon, quivering with rage, as he glanced his eyes furiously around the apartment; "here has been treachery! and foul treason to the king!"

"By whom committed, Mr. Christopher Dillon?" said Borroughcliffe, knitting his brow, and speaking in a suppressed tone; "dare you, or any man living, charge treason to the ——th?"

A very different feeling from rage appeared now to increase the shivering propensities of the future judge, who at once perceived it was necessary to moderate his passion, and he returned, as it were by magic, to his former plausible and insinuating manner, as he replied—

"Colonel Howard will understand the cause of my warm feelings, when I tell him, that this very room contained, last night, that disgrace to his name and country, as well as traitor to his king, Edward Griffith, of the rebel navy."

"What!" exclaimed the colonel, starting, "has that recreant youth dared to pollute the threshold of St. Ruth with his footstep! but you dream, Kit; there would be too much hardihood in the act."

"It appears not, sir," returned the other; "for though in this very apartment he most certainly was, he is here no longer. And yet from this window, though open, escape would seem to be impossible, even with much assistance."

"If I thought that the contumelious boy had dared to be guilty of such an act of gross impudence," cried the colonel, "I should be tempted to resume my arms, in my old age, to punish his effrontery. What! it is not enough that he entered my dwelling in the colony, availing himself of the distraction of the times, with an intent to rob me of my choicest jewel, ay! gentlemen, even of my brother Harry's daughter—but that he must also invade this hallowed island, with a like purpose, thus thrusting his treason, as it were, into the presence of his abused prince! No, no, Kit, thy loyalty misleads thee; he has never dared to do the deed!"

"Listen, sir, and you shall be convinced," returned the pliant Christopher. "I do not wonder at your unbelief; but as good testimony is the soul of justice, I cannot resist its influence. You know, that two vessels, corresponding in appearance to the two rebel cruisers that annoyed us so much in the Carolinas, have been seen on the coast for several days, which induced us to beg the protection of Captain Borroughcliffe. Three men are found, the day succeeding that on which we hear that these vessels came within the shoals, stealing through the grounds of St. Ruth, in sailors' attire. They are arrested, and in the voice of one of them, sir, I immediately detected that of the traitor Griffith. He was disguised, it is true, and cunningly so; but when a man has devoted his whole life to the business of investigating truth," he added, with an air of much modesty, "it is difficult to palm any disguise on his senses."

Colonel Howard was strongly impressed with the probability of these conjectures, and the closing appeal confirmed him immediately in his kinsman's opinion, while Borroughcliffe listened, with deep interest, to the speakers, and more than once bit his lip with vexation. When Dillon concluded, the soldier exclaimed—

"I'll swear there was a man among them, who has been used to the drill."

"Nothing more probable, my worthy friend," said Dillon; "for as the landing was never made without some evil purpose, rely on it, he came not unguarded or unprotected. I dare say, the three were all officers, and one of them might have been of the marines. That they had assistance is certain, and it was because I felt assured they had a force secreted at hand, that I went in quest of the reinforcement."

There was so much plausibility, and, in fact, so much truth, in all this, that conviction was unwillingly admitted by Borroughcliffe, who walked aside, a moment, to conceal the confusion which, in spite of his ordinary inflexibility of countenance, he felt was manifesting itself in his rubric visage, while he muttered—

"The amphibious dog! he was a soldier, but a traitor and an enemy. No doubt he will have a marvellous satisfaction in delighting the rebellious ears of his messmates, by rehearsing the manner in which he poured cold water down the back of one Borroughcliffe, of the ——th, who was amusing him, at the same time, by pouring good, rich south-side Madeira down his own rebellious throat. I have a good mind to exchange my scarlet coat for a blue jacket, on purpose to meet the sly rascal on the other element, where we can discuss the matter over again. Well, sergeant, do you find the other two?"

"They are gone together, your honour," returned the orderly, who just then re-entered from an examination of the other apartments; "and unless the evil one helped them off, it's a mysterious business to me."

"Colonel Howard," said Borroughcliffe, gravely, "your precious south-side cordial must be banished from the board, regularly with the cloth, until I have my revenge; for satisfaction of this insult is mine to claim, and I seek it this instant. Go, Drill; detail a guard for the protection of the house, and feed the rest of your command, then beat the general, and we will take the field. Ay! my worthy veteran host, for the first time since the days of the unlucky Charles Stuart, there shall be a campaign in the heart of England."

"Ah! rebellion, rebellion! accursed, unnatural, unholy rebellion, caused the calamity then and now!" exclaimed the colonel.

"Had I not better take a hasty refreshment for my men and their horses?" asked the cornet; "and then make a sweep for a few miles along the coast? It may be my luck to encounter the fugitives, or some part of their force."

"You have anticipated my very thoughts," returned Borroughcliffe. "The Cacique of Pedee may close the gates of St.

Ruth, and, by barring the windows, and arming the servants, he can make a very good defence against an attack, should they think proper to assail our fortress; after he has repulsed them, leave it to me to cut off their retreat."

Dillon but little relished this proposal; for he thought an attempt to storm the abbey would be the most probable course adopted by Griffith, in order to rescue his mistress; and the jurist had none of the spirit of a soldier in his composition. In truth, it was this deficiency that had induced him to depart in person, the preceding night, in quest of the reinforcement, instead of sending an express on the errand. But the necessity of devising an excuse for a change in this dangerous arrangement, was obviated by Colonel Howard, who exclaimed, as soon as Borroughcliffe concluded his plan—

"To me, Captain Borroughcliffe, belongs of right, the duty of defending St. Ruth, and it shall be no boy's play to force my works; but Kit would rather try his chance in the open field, I know. Come, let us to our breakfast, and then he shall mount, and act as a guide to the horse, along the difficult passes of the seashore."

"To breakfast then let it be," cried the captain; "I distrust not my new commander of the fortress; and in the field the Cacique for ever! We follow you, my worthy host."

This arrangement was hastily executed in all its parts. The gentlemen swallowed their meal in the manner of men who ate only to sustain nature, and as a duty; after which the whole house became a scene of bustling activity. The troops were mustered and paraded; Borroughcliffe, setting apart a guard for the building, placed himself at the head of the remainder of his little party, and they moved out of the courtyard in open order, and at quick time. Dillon joyfully beheld himself mounted on one of the best of Colonel Howard's hunters, where he knew that he had the control, in a great measure, of his own destiny; his bosom throbbing with a powerful desire to destroy Griffith, while he entertained a lively wish to effect his object without incurring any personal risk. At his side was the young cornet, seated with practised grace in his saddle, who, after giving time for the party of foot soldiers to clear the premises, glanced his eye along the few files he led, and then gave the word to move. The little division of horse wheeled briskly into open column, and, the officer touching his cap to Colonel Howard, they dashed through the gateway together, and pursued their route towards the seaside, at a hand gallop.

The veteran lingered a few minutes, while the clattering of hoofs was to be heard, or the gleam of arms was visible, to hear and gaze at sounds and sights that he still loved; after which, he proceeded, in person, and not without a secret enjoyment of the excitement, to barricade the doors and windows, with an undaunted determination of making, in case of need, a stout defence.

St. Ruth lay but a short two miles from the ocean; to which numerous roads led, through the grounds of the abbey, which extended to the shore. Along one of these paths, Dillon conducted his party, until, after a few minutes of hard riding, they approached the cliffs, when, posting his troopers under cover of a little copse, the cornet rode in advance, with his guide, to the verge of the perpendicular rocks, whose bases were washed by the foam that still whitened the waters from the surges of the subsiding sea.

The gale had broken, before the escape of the prisoners, and as the power of the eastern tempest had gradually diminished, a light current from the south, that blew directly along the land, prevailed; and, though the ocean still rolled in fearful billows, their surfaces were smooth, and they were becoming, at each moment, less precipitous, and more regular. The eyes of the horsemen were cast in vain over the immense expanse of water, that was glistening brightly under the rays of the sun, which had just risen from its bosom, in quest of some object or distant sail, that might confirm their suspicions, or relieve their doubts. But every thing of that description appeared to have avoided the dangerous navigation, during the violence of the late tempest, and Dillon was withdrawing his eyes in disappointment, from the vacant view, when, as they fell towards the shore, he beheld that which caused him to exclaim—

"There they go! and, by Heaven, they will escape!"

The cornet looked in the direction of the other's finger, when he beheld, at a short distance from the land, and apparently immediately under his feet, a little boat, that looked like a dark shell upon the water, rising and sinking amid the waves, as if the men it obviously contained, were resting on their oars in idle expectation.

" 'Tis they!" continued Dillon; "or, what is more probable, it is their boat waiting to convey them to their vessel; no common business would induce seamen to lie in this careless manner, within such a narrow distance of the surf."

"And what is to be done? They cannot be made to feel horse where they are; nor would the muskets of the foot be of any use. A light three pounder would do its work handsomely on them!"

The strong desire which Dillon entertained to intercept, or rather to destroy the party, rendered him prompt at expedients. After a moment of musing, he replied—

"The runaways must yet be on the land; and by scouring the coast, and posting men at proper intervals, their retreat can easily be prevented; in the mean time I will ride under the spur to —— bay, where one of his majesty's cutters now lies at anchor—It is but half an hour of hard riding, and I can be on board of her. The wind blows directly in her favour, and if we can once bring her down behind that headland, we shall infallibly cut off or sink these midnight depredators."

"Off, then!" cried the cornet, whose young blood was boiling for a skirmish; "you will at least drive them to the shore, where I can deal with them."

The words were hardly uttered, before Dillon, after galloping furiously along the cliffs, and turning short into a thick wood, that lay in his route, was out of sight. The loyalty of this gentleman was altogether of a calculating nature, and was intimately connected with what he considered his fealty to himself. He believed that the possession of Miss Howard's person and fortune were advantages that would much more than counterbalance any elevation that he was likely to obtain by the revolution of affairs in his native colony. He considered Griffith as the only natural obstacle to his success, and he urged his horse forward with a desperate determination to work the ruin of the young sailor, before another sun had set. When a man labours in an evil cause, with such feelings, and with such incentives, he seldom slights or neglects his work; and Mr. Dillon, accordingly, was on board the Alacrity, several minutes short of the time in which he had promised to perform the distance.

The plain old seaman, who commanded the cutter, listened to his tale with cautious ears; and examined into the state of the weather, and other matters, connected with his duty, with the slow and deliberate decision of one who had never done much to acquire a confidence in himself, and who had been but niggardly rewarded for the little he had actually performed.

As Dillon was urgent, however, and the day seemed propitious, he at length decided to act as he was desired, and the cutter was accordingly gotten under way.

A crew of something less than fifty men, moved with no little of their commander's deliberation; but as the little vessel rounded the point behind which she had been anchored, her guns were cleared, and the usual preparations were completed for immediate and actual service.

Dillon, sorely against his will, was compelled to continue on board, in order to point out the place where the unsuspecting boatmen were expected to be entrapped. Every thing being ready, when they had gained a safe distance from the land, the Alacrity was kept away before the wind, and glided along the shore, with a swift and easy progress, that promised a speedy execution of the business in which her commander had embarked.

# Chapter XVII.

*"Pol.* Very like a whale."
*Hamlet*, III.ii.382.

NOTWITHSTANDING the object of their expedition was of
a public nature, the feelings which had induced both
Griffith and Barnstable to accompany the pilot, with so much
willingness, it will easily be seen, were entirely personal. The
short intercourse that he had maintained with his associates,
enabled the mysterious leader of their party to understand the
characters of his two principal officers so thoroughly, as to
induce him, when he landed, with the purpose of reconnoitring to ascertain whether the objects of his pursuit still held
their determination to assemble at the appointed hour, to
choose Griffith and Manual as his only associates, leaving
Barnstable in command of his own vessel, to await their return, and to cover their retreat. A good deal of argument, and
some little of the authority of his superior officer, was necessary to make Barnstable quietly acquiesce in this arrangement;
but as his good sense told him that nothing should be unnecessarily hazarded, until the moment to strike the final blow
had arrived, he became gradually more resigned, taking care,
however, to caution Griffith to reconnoitre the abbey while
his companion was reconnoitring —— house. It was the
strong desire of Griffith to comply with this injunction, which
carried them a little out of their proper path, and led to the
consequences that we have partly related. The evening of that
day was the time when the pilot intended to complete his
enterprise, thinking to entrap his game while enjoying the festivities that usually succeeded their sports, and an early hour
in the morning was appointed when Barnstable should appear
at the nearest point to the abbey, to take off his countrymen,
in order that they might be as little as possible subjected to
the gaze of their enemies, by daylight. If they failed to arrive
at the appointed time, his instructions were, to return to his
schooner, which lay snugly embayed in a secret and retired
haven, that but few ever approached, either by land or water.

While the young cornet still continued gazing at the whale-boat (for it was the party from the schooner that he saw,) the hour expired for the appearance of Griffith and his companions, and Barnstable reluctantly determined to comply with the letter of his instructions, and leave them to their own sagacity and skill to regain the Ariel. The boat had been suffered to ride in the edge of the surf, since the appearance of the sun, and the eyes of her crew were kept anxiously fixed on the cliffs, though in vain, to discover the signal that was to call them to the place of landing. After looking at his watch for the twentieth time, and as often casting glances of uneasy dissatisfaction towards the shore, the lieutenant exclaimed—

"A charming prospect, this, Master Coffin, but rather too much poetry in it for your taste; I believe you relish no land that is of a harder consistency than mud!"

"I was born on the waters, sir," returned the cockswain, from his snug abode, where he was bestowed with his usual economy of room, "and it's according to all things for a man to love his natyve soil. I'll not deny, Captain Barnstable, but I would rather drop my anchor on a bottom that won't broom a keel, though at the same time, I harbour no great malice against dry land."

"I shall never forgive it, myself, if any accident has befallen Griffith, in this excursion," rejoined the lieutenant; "his pilot may be a better man on the water than on terra firma, long Tom."

The cockswain turned his solemn visage, with an extraordinary meaning, towards his commander, before he replied—

"For as long a time as I have followed the waters, sir, and that has been ever since I've drawn my rations, seeing that I was born while the boat was crossing Nantucket shoals, I've never known a pilot come off in greater need, than the one we fell in with, when we made that stretch or two on the land, in the dog-watch of yesterday."

"Ay! the fellow has played his part like a man; the occasion was great, and it seems that he was quite equal to his work."

"The frigate's people tell me, sir, that he handled the ship like a top," continued the cockswain; "but she is a ship that is a natural inimy of the bottom!"

"Can you say as much for this boat, Master Coffin?" cried Barnstable; "keep her out of the surf, or you'll have us rolling in upon the beach, presently, like an empty water-cask; you must remember that we cannot all wade, like yourself, in two-fathom-water."

The cockswain cast a cool glance at the crests of foam that were breaking over the tops of the billows, within a few yards of where their boat was riding, and called aloud to his men—

"Pull a stroke or two; away with her into dark water."

The drop of the oars resembled the movements of a nice machine, and the light boat skimmed along the water like a duck, that approaches to the very brink of some imminent danger, and then avoids it, at the most critical moment, apparently without an effort. While this necessary movement was making, Barnstable arose, and surveyed the cliffs, with keen eyes, and then turning once more in disappointment from his search, he said—

"Pull more from the land, and let her run down, at an easy stroke, to the schooner. Keep a look-out at the cliffs, boys; it is possible that they are stowed in some of the holes in the rocks, for it's no daylight business they are on."

The order was promptly obeyed, and they had glided along for nearly a mile, in this manner, in the most profound silence, when suddenly the stillness was broken by a heavy rush of air, and a dash of the water, seemingly at no great distance from them.

"By heaven, Tom," cried Barnstable, starting, "there is the blow of a whale."

"Ay, ay, sir," returned the cockswain, with undisturbed composure; "here is his spout, not half a mile to seaward; the easterly gale has driven the creater to leeward, and he begins to find himself in shoal water. He's been sleeping, while he should have been working to windward!"

"The fellow takes it coolly, too! he's in no hurry to get an offing!"

"I rather conclude, sir," said the cockswain rolling over his tobacco in his mouth, very composedly, while his little sunken eyes began to twinkle with pleasure at the sight, "the gentleman has lost his reckoning, and don't know which way to head, to take himself back into blue water."

"'Tis a fin-back!" exclaimed the lieutenant; "he will soon make head-way, and be off."

"No, sir, 'tis a right whale," answered Tom; "I saw his spout; he threw up a pair of as pretty rainbows as a Christian would wish to look at. He's a raal oil-butt, that fellow!"

Barnstable laughed, turned himself away from the tempting sight, and tried to look at the cliffs; and then unconsciously bent his longing eyes again on the sluggish animal, who was throwing his huge carcass, at times, for many feet from the water, in idle gambols. The temptation for sport, and the recollection of his early habits, at length prevailed over his anxiety in behalf of his friends, and the young officer inquired of his cockswain—

"Is there any whale-line in the boat, to make fast to that harpoon which you bear about with you in fair weather or foul?"

"I never trust the boat from the schooner without part of a shot, sir," returned the cockswain; "there is something nateral in the sight of a tub to my old eyes."

Barnstable looked at his watch, and again at the cliffs, when he exclaimed, in joyous tones—

"Give strong way, my hearties! There seems nothing better to be done; let us have a stroke of a harpoon at that impudent rascal."

The men shouted spontaneously, and the old cockswain suffered his solemn visage to relax into a small laugh, while the whale-boat sprung forward like a courser for the goal. During the few minutes they were pulling towards their game, long Tom arose from his crouching attitude in the stern-sheets, and transferred his huge frame to the bows of the boat, where he made such preparations to strike the whale as the occasion required. The tub, containing about half of a whale-line, was placed at the feet of Barnstable, who had been preparing an oar to steer with, in place of the rudder, which was unshipped, in order that, if necessary, the boat might be whirled round, when not advancing.

Their approach was utterly unnoticed by the monster of the deep, who continued to amuse himself with throwing the water, in two circular spouts, high into the air, occasionally flourishing the broad flukes of his tail with a graceful but terrific force, until the hardy seamen were within a few hundred feet of him, when he suddenly cast his head downward, and, without an apparent effort, reared his immense body for many feet above the water, waving his tail violently, and producing a whizzing noise, that sounded like the rushing of winds.

The cockswain stood erect, poising his harpoon, ready for the blow; but when he beheld the creature assume this formidable attitude, he waved his hand to his commander, who instantly signed to his men to cease rowing. In this situation the sportsmen rested a few moments, while the whale struck several blows on the water, in rapid succession, the noise of which re-echoed along the cliffs, like the hollow reports of so many cannon. After this wanton exhibition of his terrible strength, the monster sunk again into his native element, and slowly disappeared from the eyes of his pursuers.

"Which way did he head, Tom?" cried Barnstable, the moment the whale was out of sight.

"Pretty much up and down, sir," returned the cockswain, whose eye was gradually brightening with the excitement of the sport; "he'll soon run his nose against the bottom, if he stands long on that course, and will be glad to get another snuff of pure air; send her a few fathoms to starboard, sir, and I promise we shall not be out of his track."

The conjecture of the experienced old seaman proved true, for, in a few minutes, the water broke near them, and another spout was cast into the air, when the huge animal rushed, for half his length, in the same direction, and fell on the sea, with a turbulence and foam equal to that which is produced by the launching of a vessel, for the first time, into its proper element. After this evolution, the whale rolled heavily, and seemed to rest from further efforts.

His slightest movements were closely watched by Barnstable and his cockswain, and when he was in a state of comparative rest, the former gave a signal to his crew, to ply their oars once more. A few long and vigorous strokes sent the boat directly up to the broadside of the whale, with its bows pointing towards one of the fins, which was, at times, as the animal yielded sluggishly to the action of the waves, exposed to view. The cockswain poised his harpoon, with much precision, and then darted it from him with a violence that buried the iron in the blubber of their foe. The instant the blow was made, long Tom shouted, with singular earnestness—

"Starn all!"

"Stern all!" echoed Barnstable; when the obedient seamen, by united efforts, forced the boat in a backward direction, beyond the reach of any blow from their formidable
antagonist. The alarmed animal, however, meditated no such
resistance; ignorant of his own power, and of the insignificance of his enemies, he sought refuge in flight. One moment
of stupid surprise succeeded the entrance of the iron, when he
cast his huge tail into the air, with a violence that threw the
sea around him into increased commotion, and then disappeared, with the quickness of lightning, amid a cloud of
foam.

"Snub him!" shouted Barnstable; "hold on, Tom; he rises
already."

"Ay, ay, sir," replied the composed cockswain, seizing the
line, which was running out of the boat with a velocity that
rendered such a manœuvre rather hazardous, and causing it
to yield more gradually round the large loggerhead that was
placed in the bows of the boat for that purpose. Presently the
line stretched forward, and, rising to the surface, with tremulous vibrations, it indicated the direction in which the animal
might be expected to re-appear. Barnstable had cast the bows
of the boat towards that point, before the terrified and
wounded victim rose once more to the surface, whose time
was, however, no longer wasted in his sports, but who cast
the waters aside, as he forced his way, with prodigious velocity, along their surface. The boat was dragged violently in his
wake, and cut through the billows with a terrific rapidity,
that, at moments, appeared to bury the slight fabric in the
ocean. When long Tom beheld his victim throwing his spouts
on high again, he pointed with exultation to the jetting fluid,
which was streaked with the deep red of blood, and cried—

"Ay! I've touched the fellow's life! it must be more than
two foot of blubber that stops my iron from reaching the life
of any whale that ever sculled the ocean!"

"I believe you have saved yourself the trouble of using the
bayonet you have rigged for a lance," said his commander,
who entered into the sport with all the ardour of one whose
youth had been chiefly passed in such pursuits; "feel your
line, Master Coffin; can we haul alongside of our enemy? I

like not the course he is steering, as he tows us from the schooner."

"'Tis the creater's way, sir," said the cockswain; "you know they need the air in their nostrils, when they run, the same as a man; but lay hold, boys, and let's haul up to him."

The seamen now seized the whale-line, and slowly drew their boat to within a few feet of the tail of the fish, whose progress became sensibly less rapid, as he grew weak with the loss of blood. In a few minutes he stopped running, and appeared to roll uneasily on the water, as if suffering the agony of death.

"Shall we pull in, and finish him, Tom?" cried Barnstable; "a few sets from your bayonet would do it."

The cockswain stood examining his game, with cool discretion, and replied to this interrogatory—

"No, sir, no—he's going into his flurry; there's no occasion for disgracing ourselves by using a soldier's weapon in taking a whale. Starn off, sir, starn off! the creater's in his flurry!"

The warning of the prudent cockswain was promptly obeyed, and the boat cautiously drew off to a distance, leaving to the animal a clear space, while under its dying agonies. From a state of perfect rest, the terrible monster threw its tail on high, as when in sport, but its blows were trebled in rapidity and violence, till all was hid from view by a pyramid of foam, that was deeply died with blood. The roarings of the fish were like the bellowings of a herd of bulls, and to one who was ignorant of the fact, it would have appeared as if a thousand monsters were engaged in deadly combat, behind the bloody mist that obstructed the view. Gradually, these effects subsided, and when the discoloured water again settled down to the long and regular swell of the ocean, the fish was seen, exhausted, and yielding passively to its fate. As life departed, the enormous black mass rolled to one side, and when the white and glistening skin of the belly became apparent, the seamen well knew that their victory was achieved.

"What's to be done now," said Barnstable, as he stood and gazed with a diminished excitement at their victim; "he will yield no food, and his carcass will probably drift to land, and furnish our enemies with the oil."

"If I had but that creater in Boston Bay," said the cock-swain, "it would prove the making of me; but such is my luck for ever! Pull up, at any rate, and let me get my harpoon and line—the English shall never get them while old Tom Coffin can blow."

"Don't speak too fast," said the strokesman of the boat; "whether he gets your iron or not, here he comes in chase!"

"What mean you, fellow?" cried Barnstable.

"Captain Barnstable can look for himself," returned the seaman, "and tell whether I speak truth."

The young sailor turned, and saw the Alacrity, bearing down before the wind, with all her sails set, as she rounded a headland, but a short half league to windward of the place where the boat lay.

"Pass that glass to me," said the captain with steady composure. "This promises us work in one of two ways; if she be armed, it has become our turn to run; if not, we are strong enough to carry her."

A very brief survey made the experienced officer acquainted with the true character of the vessel in sight; and, replacing the glass with much coolness, he said,

"That fellow shows long arms, and ten teeth, beside King George's pennant from his top-mast-head. Now, my lads, you are to pull for your lives; for whatever may be the notions of Master Coffin on the subject of his harpoon, I have no inclination to have my arms pinioned by John Bull, though his majesty himself put on the irons."

The men well understood the manner and meaning of their commander; and, throwing aside their coats, they applied themselves in earnest to their task. For half an hour a profound silence reigned in the boat, which made an amazing progress. But many circumstances conspired to aid the cutter; she had a fine breeze, with smooth water, and a strong tide in her favour; and, at the expiration of the time we have mentioned, it was but too apparent that the distance between the pursued and pursuers was lessened nearly half. Barnstable preserved his steady countenance, but there was an expression of care gathering around his dark brow, which indicated that he saw the increasing danger of their situation.

"That fellow has long legs, Master Coffin," he said, in a

cheerful tone; "your whale-line must go overboard, and the fifth oar must be handled by your delicate hands."

Tom arose from his seat, and proceeding forward, he cast the tub and its contents together into the sea, when he seated himself at the bow oar, and bent his athletic frame with amazing vigour to the task.

"Ah! there is much of your philosophy in that stroke, long Tom," cried his commander; "keep it up, boys, and if we gain nothing else, we shall at least gain time for deliberation. Come, Master Coffin, what think you; we have three resources before us, let us hear which is your choice: first, we can turn and fight and be sunk; secondly, we can pull to the land, and endeavour to make good our retreat to the schooner in that manner; and, thirdly, we can head to the shore, and possibly by running under the guns of that fellow, get the wind of him, and keep the air in our nostrils, after the manner of the whale. Damn the whale! but for the tow the black rascal gave us, we should have been out of sight of this rover!"

"If we fight," said Tom, with quite as much composure as his commander manifested, "we shall be taken or sunk; if we land, sir, I shall be taken for one man, as I never could make any headway on dry ground; and if we try to get the wind of him by pulling under the cliffs, we shall be cut off by a parcel of lubbers that I can see running along their edges, hoping, I dare say, that they shall be able to get a skulking shot at a boat's crew of honest seafaring men."

"You speak with as much truth as philosophy, Tom," said Barnstable, who saw his slender hopes of success curtailed, by the open appearance of the horse and foot on the cliffs. "These Englishmen have not slept the last night, and I fear Griffith and Manual will fare but badly. That fellow brings a cap full of wind down with him—'tis just his play, and he walks like a race-horse. Ha! he begins to be in earnest!"

While Barnstable was speaking, a column of white smoke was seen issuing from the bows of the cutter, and as the report of a cannon was wafted to their ears, the shot was seen skipping from wave to wave, tossing the water in spray, and flying to a considerable distance beyond them. The seamen cast cursory glances in the direction of the passing ball, but it produced no manifest effect in either their conduct or appearance. The cockswain, who scanned its range with an eye of more practice than the rest, observed, "That's a lively piece for its metal, and it speaks with a good clear voice; but if they hear it aboard the Ariel, the man who fired it will be sorry it wasn't born dumb."

"You are the prince of philosophers, Master Coffin!" cried Barnstable; "there is some hope in that; let the Englishman talk away, and my life on it, the Ariels don't believe it is thunder; hand me a musket—I'll draw another shot."

The piece was given to Barnstable, who discharged it several times, as if to taunt their enemies, and the scheme was completely successful. Goaded by the insults, the cutter discharged gun after gun at the little boat, throwing the shot frequently so near as to wet her crew with the spray, but without injuring them in the least. The failure of these attempts of the enemy, excited the mirth of the reckless seamen, instead of creating any alarm; and whenever a shot came nearer than common, the cockswain would utter some such expression as—

"A ground swell, a long shot, and a small object, make a clean target;" or, "A man must squint straight to hit a boat."

As, notwithstanding their unsuccessful gunnery, the cutter was constantly gaining on the whale-boat, there was a prospect of a speedy termination of the chase, when the report of a cannon was thrown back like an echo from one of the Englishman's discharges, and Barnstable and his companions had the pleasure of seeing the Ariel stretching slowly out of the little bay where she had passed the night, with the smoke of the gun of defiance curling above her taper masts.

A loud and simultaneous shout of rapture was given by the lieutenant and all his boat's-crew, at this cheering sight, while the cutter took in all her light sails, and, as she hauled up on a wind, she fired a whole broadside at the successful fugitives. Many stands of grape, with several round shot, flew by the boat, and fell upon the water, near them, raising a cloud of foam, but without doing any injury.

"She dies in a flurry," said Tom, casting his eyes at the little vortex into which the boat was then entering.

"If her commander be a true man," cried Barnstable, "he'll

not leave us on so short an acquaintance. Give way, my souls! give way! I would see more of this loquacious cruiser."

The temptation for exertion was great, and it was not disregarded by the men; in a few minutes the whale-boat reached the schooner, when the crew of the latter received their commander and his companions with shouts and cheers that rung across the waters, and reached the ears of the disappointed spectators on the verge of the cliffs.

# Chapter XVIII.

"Thus guided, on their course they bore,
   Until they near'd the mainland shore;
When frequent on the hollow blast
Wild shouts of merriment were cast."
   Scott, *The Lord of the Isles*, Canto First, XXIII.1—4.

T HE JOYFUL SHOUTS and hearty cheers of the Ariel's crew
   continued for some time after her commander had
reached her deck. Barnstable answered the congratulations of
his officers by cordial shakes of the hand, and after waiting for
the ebullition of delight among the seamen to subside a little,
he beckoned with an air of authority for silence.

"I thank you, my lads, for your good will," he said, when
all were gathered around him in deep attention: "they have
given us a tough chase, and if you had left us another mile to
go, we had been lost. That fellow is a King's cutter, and
though his disposition to run to leeward is a good deal mollified, yet he shows signs of fight. At any rate, he is stripping
off some of his clothes, which looks as if he were game. Luckily for us, Captain Manual has taken all the marines ashore
with him, (though what he has done with them or himself, is
a mystery,) or we should have had our decks lumbered with
live cattle; but, as it is, we have a good working breeze, tolerably smooth water, and a dead match! There is a sort of
national obligation on us to whip that fellow, and, therefore,
without more words about the matter, let us turn to and do
it, that we may get our breakfasts."

To this specimen of marine eloquence, the crew cheered as
usual; the young men burning for the combat, and the few
old sailors who belonged to the schooner, shaking their heads
with infinite satisfaction, and swearing by sundry strange
oaths, that their captain "could talk, when there was need of
such thing, like the best Dictionary that ever was launched."

During this short harangue, and the subsequent comments,
the Ariel had been kept, under a cloud of canvass, as near to
the wind as she could lie, and as this was her best sailing, she
had stretched swiftly out from the land, to a distance whence

the cliffs, and the soldiers who were spread along their summits, became plainly visible. Barnstable turned his glass
repeatedly, from the cutter to the shore, as different feelings
predominated in his breast, before he again spoke.

"If Mr. Griffith is stowed away among those rocks," he at
length said, "he shall see as pretty an argument discussed, in
as few words, as he ever listened to, provided the gentlemen
in yonder cutter have not changed their minds as to the road
they intend to journey—what think you, Mr. Merry?"

"I wish with all my heart and soul, sir," returned the fearless boy, "that Mr. Griffith was safe aboard us; it seems the
country is alarmed, and God knows what will happen if he is
taken! As to the fellow to windward, he'll find it easier to deal
with the Ariel's boat, than with her mother; but he carries a
broad sail; I question if he means to show play."

"Never doubt him, boy," said Barnstable, "he is working off
the shore, like a man of sense, and besides, he has his spectacles on, trying to make out what tribe of Yankee Indians we belong to. You'll see him come to the wind presently, and send a
few pieces of iron down this way, by way of letting us know
where to find him. Much as I like your first lieutenant, Mr.
Merry, I would rather leave him on the land this day, than see
him on my decks. I want no fighting captain to work this
boat for me! but tell the drummer, sir, to beat to quarters."

The boy, who was staggering under the weight of his melodious instrument, had been expecting this command, and,
without waiting for the midshipman to communicate the order, he commenced that short rub-a-dub air, that will at any
time rouse a thousand men from the deepest sleep, and cause
them to fly to their means of offence, with a common soul.
The crew of the Ariel had been collected in groups, studying
the appearance of the enemy, cracking their jokes, and waiting only for this usual order to repair to the guns; and at the
first tap of the drum, they spread with steadiness to the different parts of the little vessel, where their various duties called
them. The cannon were surrounded by small parties of vigorous and athletic young men; the few marines were drawn up
in array with muskets; the officers appeared in their boarding
caps, with pistols stuck in their belts and naked sabres in their
hands. Barnstable paced his little quarter-deck with a firm

tread, dangling a speaking trumpet, by its lanyard, on his fore-finger, or occasionally applying the glass to his eye, which, when not in use, was placed under one arm, while his sword was resting against the foot of the mainmast; a pair of heavy ship's pistols were thrust in his belt also; and piles of muskets, boarding-pikes, and naked sabres, were placed on different parts of the deck. The laugh of the seamen was heard no longer; and those who spoke, uttered their thoughts only in low and indistinct whispers.

The English cutter held her way from the land, until she got an offing of more than two miles, when she reduced her sails to a yet smaller number, and heaving into the wind, she fired a gun in a direction opposite to that which pointed to the Ariel.

"Now I would wager a quintal of codfish, Master Coffin," said Barnstable, "against the best cask of porter that was ever brewed in England, that fellow believes a Yankee schooner can fly in the wind's eye! If he wishes to speak to us, why don't he give his cutter a little sheet, and come down."

The cockswain had made his arrangements for the combat, with much more method and philosophy than any other man in the vessel. When the drum beat to quarters, he threw aside his jacket, vest, and shirt, with as little hesitation as if he stood under an American sun, and with all the discretion of a man who had engaged in an undertaking that required the free use of his utmost powers. As he was known to be a priv- ileged individual in the Ariel, and one whose opinions, in all matters of seamanship, were regarded as oracles by the crew, and were listened to by his commander with no little demon- stration of respect, the question excited no surprise. He was standing at the breech of his long gun, with his brawny arms folded on a breast that had been turned to the colour of blood by long exposure, his grizzled locks fluttering in the breeze, and his tall form towering far above the heads of all near him.

"He hugs the wind, sir, as if it was his sweetheart," was his answer; "but he'll let go his hold, soon; and if he don't, we can find a way to make him fall to leeward."

"Keep a good full!" cried the commander, in a stern voice, "and let the vessel go through the water. That fellow walks well, long Tom; but we are too much for him on a bowline; though, if he continue to draw ahead in this manner, it will be night before we can get alongside him."

"Ay, ay, sir," returned the cockswain; "them cutters carries a press of canvass, when they seem to have but little; their gaffs are all the same as young booms, and spread a broad head to their mainsails. But it's no hard matter to knock a few cloths out of their bolt-ropes, when she will both drop astern and to leeward."

"I believe there is good sense in your scheme, this time," said Barnstable; "for I am anxious about the frigate's people —though I hate a noisy chase; speak to him, Tom, and let us see if he will answer."

"Ay, ay, sir," cried the cockswain, sinking his body in such a manner as to let his head fall to a level with the cannon that he controlled, when, after divers orders, and sundry movements, to govern the direction of the piece, he applied a match, with a rapid motion, to the priming. An immense body of white smoke rushed from the muzzle of the cannon, followed by a sheet of vivid fire, until, losing its power, it yielded to the wind, and, as it rose from the water, spread like a cloud, and, passing through the masts of the schooner, was driven far to leeward, and soon blended in the mists which were swiftly scudding before the fresh breezes of the ocean.

Although many curious eyes were watching this beautiful sight from the cliffs, there was too little of novelty in the exhibition to attract a single look, of the crew of the schooner, from the more important examination of the effect of the shot on their enemy. Barnstable sprang lightly on a gun, and watched the instant when the ball would strike, with keen interest, while long Tom threw himself aside from the line of the smoke, with a similar intention; holding one of his long arms extended towards his namesake, with a finger on the vent, and supporting his frame by placing the hand of the other on the deck, as his eyes glanced through an opposite port-hole, in an attitude that most men might have despaired of imitating with success.

"There go the chips!" cried Barnstable. "Bravo! Master Coffin, you never planted iron in the ribs of an Englishman with more judgment; let him have another piece of it, and if he like the sport, we'll play a game of long bowls with him!"

"Ay, ay, sir," returned the cockswain, who, the instant he witnessed the effects of his shot, had returned to superintend the reloading of his guns; "if he holds on half an hour longer, I'll dub him down to our own size, when we can close, and make an even fight of it."

The drum of the Englishman was now, for the first time, heard, rattling across the waters, and echoing the call to quarters, that had already proceeded from the Ariel.

"Ah! you have sent him to his guns!" said Barnstable; "we shall now hear more of it; wake him up, Tom—wake him up."

"We shall start him an end, or put him to sleep altogether, shortly," said the deliberate cockswain, who never allowed himself to be at all hurried, even by his commander. "My shot are pretty much like a shoal of porpoises, and commonly sail in each others' wake. Stand by—heave her breech forward—so; get out of that, you damned young reprobate, and let my harpoon alone."

"What are you at, there, Master Coffin?" cried Barnstable; "are you tongue-tied?"

"Here's one of the boys skylarking with my harpoon in the lee scuppers, and by-and-by, when I shall want it most, there'll be a no-man's-land to hunt for it in."

"Never mind the boy, Tom; send him aft here, to me, and I'll polish his behaviour; give the Englishman some more iron."

"I want the little villain to pass up my cartridges," returned the angry old seaman; "but if you'll be so good, sir, as to hit him a crack or two, now and then, as he goes by you to the magazine, the monkey will learn his manners, and the schooner's work will be all the better done for it. A young herring-faced monkey! to meddle with a tool ye don't know the use of. If your parents had spent more of their money on your edication, and less on your outfit, you'd ha' been a gentleman to what ye are now."

"Hurrah! Tom, hurrah!" cried Barnstable, a little impatiently; "is your namesake never to open his throat again!"

"Ay, ay, sir; all ready," grumbled the cockswain, "depress a little; so—so; a damn'd young baboon-behav'd curmudgeon; overhaul that forward fall more; stand by with your match— but I'll pay him! fire." This was the actual commencement of the fight; for as the shot of Tom Coffin travelled, as he had intimated, very much in the same direction, their enemy found the sport becoming too hot to be endured in silence; and the report of the second gun from the Ariel, was instantly followed by that of the whole broadside of the Alacrity. The shot of the cutter flew in a very good direction, but her guns were too light to give them efficiency at that distance, and as one or two were heard to strike against the bends of the schooner, and fall back, innocuously, into the water, the cock- swain, whose good humour became gradually restored, as the combat thickened, remarked, with his customary apathy—

"Them count for no more than love taps—does the En- glishman think that we are firing salutes!"

"Stir him up, Tom! every blow you give him will help to open his eyes," cried Barnstable, rubbing his hands with glee, as he witnessed the success of his efforts to close.

Thus far the cockswain and his crew had the fight, on the part of the Ariel, altogether to themselves, the men who were stationed at the smaller and shorter guns, standing in perfect idleness by their sides; but in ten or fifteen minutes the commander of the Alacrity, who had been staggered by the weight of the shot that had struck him, found that it was no longer in his power to retreat, if he wished it; when he decided on the only course that was left for a brave man to pursue, and steered, boldly, in such a direction as would soonest bring him in contact with his enemy, without expos- ing his vessel to be raked by his fire. Barnstable watched each movement of his foe with eagle eyes, and when the vessels had got within a lessened distance, he gave the order for a general fire to be opened. The action now grew warm and spirited on both sides. The power of the wind was counter- acted by the constant explosion of the cannon; and instead of driving rapidly to leeward, a white canopy of curling smoke hung above the Ariel, or rested on the water, lingering in her wake, so as to mark the path by which she was approaching to a closer and still deadlier struggle. The shouts of the young sailors, as they handled their instruments of death, became

more animated and fierce, while the cockswain pursued his
occupation with the silence and skill of one who laboured in a
regular vocation. Barnstable was unusually composed and
quiet, maintaining the grave deportment of a commander
on whom rested the fortunes of the contest, at the same time
that his dark eyes were dancing with the fire of suppressed
animation.

"Give it them!" he occasionally cried, in a voice that might
be heard amid the bellowing of the cannon; "never mind their
cordage, my lads; drive home their bolts, and make your
marks below their ridge ropes."

In the mean time, the Englishman played a manful game.
He had suffered a heavy loss by the distant cannonade, which
no metal he possessed could retort upon his enemy; but he
struggled nobly to repair the error in judgment with which he
had begun the contest. The two vessels gradually drew nigher
to each other, until they both entered into the common
cloud, created by their fire, which thickened and spread
around them in such a manner as to conceal their dark hulls
from the gaze of the curious and interested spectators on the
cliffs. The heavy reports of the cannon were now mingled
with the rattling of muskets and pistols, and, streaks of fire
might be seen, glancing like flashes of lightning through the
white cloud, which enshrouded the combatants, and many
minutes of painful uncertainty followed, before the deeply interested soldiers, who were gazing at the scene, discovered on
whose banners victory had alighted.

We shall follow the combatants into their misty wreath, and
display to the reader the events as they occurred.

The fire of the Ariel was much the most quick and deadly,
both because she had suffered less, and her men were less
exhausted; and the cutter stood desperately on to decide the
combat, after grappling, hand to hand. Barnstable anticipated
her intention, and well understood her commander's reason
for adopting this course, but he was not a man to calculate
coolly his advantages, when pride and daring invited him to a
more severe trial. Accordingly, he met the enemy half-way,
and, as the vessels rushed together, the stern of the schooner
was secured to the bows of the cutter, by the joint efforts of
both parties. The voice of the English commander was now

plainly to be heard, in the uproar, calling to his men to follow him.

"Away there, boarders! repel boarders on the starboard quarter!" shouted Barnstable through his trumpet.

This was the last order that the gallant young sailor gave with this instrument, for, as he spoke, he cast it from him, and seizing his sabre, flew to the spot where the enemy was about to make his most desperate effort. The shouts, execrations, and tauntings of the combatants, now succeeded to the roar of the cannon, which could be used no longer with effect, though the fight was still maintained with spirited discharges of the small arms.

"Sweep him from his decks!" cried the English commander, as he appeared on his own bulwarks, surrounded by a dozen of his bravest men; "drive the rebellious dogs into the sea!"

"Away there, marines!" retorted Barnstable, firing his pistol at the advancing enemy; "leave not a man of them to sup his grog again."

The tremendous and close volley that succeeded this order, nearly accomplished the command of Barnstable to the letter, and the commander of the Alacrity, perceiving that he stood alone, reluctantly fell back on the deck of his own vessel, in order to bring on his men once more.

"Board her! gray beards and boys, idlers and all!" shouted Barnstable, springing in advance of his crew—a powerful arm arrested the movement of the dauntless seaman, and before he had time to recover himself, he was drawn violently back to his own vessel, by the irresistible grasp of his cockswain.

"The fellow's in his flurry," said Tom, "and it wouldn't be wise to go within reach of his flukes; but I'll just step ahead and give him a set with my harpoon."

Without waiting for a reply, the cockswain reared his tall frame on the bulwarks, and was in the attitude of stepping on board of his enemy, when a sea separated the vessels, and he fell with a heavy dash of the waters into the ocean. As twenty muskets and pistols were discharged at the instant he appeared, the crew of the Ariel supposed his fall to be occasioned by his wounds, and were rendered doubly fierce by the sight, and the cry of their commander to—

"Revenge long Tom! board her; long Tom or death!"

They threw themselves forward in irresistible numbers, and forced a passage, with much bloodshed, to the forecastle of the Alacrity. The Englishman was overpowered, but still remained undaunted—he rallied his crew, and bore up most gallantly to the fray. Thrusts of pikes, and blows of sabres were becoming close and deadly, while muskets and pistols were constantly discharged by those who were kept at a distance by the pressure of the throng of closer combatants.

Barnstable led his men, in advance, and became a mark of peculiar vengeance to his enemies, as they slowly yielded before his vigorous assaults. Chance had placed the two commanders on opposite sides of the cutter's deck, and the victory seemed to incline towards either party, wherever these daring officers directed the struggle in person. But the Englishman, perceiving that the ground he maintained in person was lost elsewhere, made an effort to restore the battle by changing his position, followed by one or two of his best men. A marine, who preceded him, levelled his musket within a few feet of the head of the American commander, and was about to fire, when Merry glided among the combatants, and passed his dirk into the body of the man, who fell at the blow; shaking his piece, with horrid imprecations, the wounded soldier prepared to deal his vengeance on his youthful assailant, when the fearless boy leaped within its muzzle, and buried his own keen weapon in his heart.

"Hurrah!" shouted the unconscious Barnstable, from the edge of the quarter-deck, where, attended by a few men, he was driving all before him. "Revenge—long Tom and victory!"

"We have them!" exclaimed the Englishman; "handle your pikes! we have them between two fires."

The battle would probably have terminated very differently from what previous circumstances had indicated, had not a wild-looking figure appeared in the cutter's channels at that moment, issuing from the sea, and gaining the deck at the same instant. It was long Tom, with his iron visage rendered fierce by his previous discomfiture, and his grizzled locks drenched with the briny element, from which he had risen, looking like Neptune with his trident. Without speaking, he poised his harpoon, and with a powerful effort, pinned the unfortunate Englishman to the mast of his own vessel.

"Starn all!" cried Tom, by a sort of instinct, when the blow was struck; and catching up the musket of the fallen marine, he dealt out terrible and fatal blows with its butt, on all who approached him, utterly disregarding the use of the bayonet on its muzzle. The unfortunate commander of the Alacrity brandished his sword with frantic gestures, while his eyes rolled in horrid wildness, when he writhed for an instant in his passing agonies, and then, as his head dropped lifeless upon his gored breast, he hung against the spar, a spectacle of dismay to his crew. A few of the Englishmen stood, chained to the spot in silent horror at the sight, but most of them fled to their lower deck, or hastened to conceal themselves in the secret parts of the vessel, leaving to the Americans the undisputed possession of the Alacrity.

Two thirds of the cutter's crew suffered either in life or limbs, by this short struggle; nor was the victory obtained by Barnstable without paying the price of several valuable lives. The first burst of conquest was not, however, the moment to appreciate the sacrifice, and loud and reiterated shouts, proclaimed the exultation of the conquerors. As the flush of victory subsided, however, recollection returned, and Barnstable issued such orders as humanity and his duty rendered necessary. While the vessels were separating, and the bodies of the dead and wounded were removing, the conqueror paced the deck of his prize, as if lost in deep reflection. He passed his hand, frequently, across his blackened and blood-stained brow, while his eyes would rise to examine the vast canopy of smoke that was hovering above the vessels, like a dense fog exhaling from the ocean. The result of his deliberations was soon announced to the crew.

"Haul down all your flags," he cried; "set the Englishman's colours again, and show the enemy's jack above our ensign in the Ariel."

The appearance of the whole channel-fleet within half gun shot, would not have occasioned more astonishment among the victors, than this extraordinary mandate. The wondering seamen suspended their several employments, to gaze at the singular change that was making in the flags, those symbols that were viewed with a sort of reverence, but none presumed to comment openly on the procedure, except long Tom, who stood on the quarter-deck of the prize, straightening the pliable iron of the harpoon which he had recovered, with as much care and diligence as if it were necessary to the maintenance of their conquest. Like the others, however, he suspended his employment, when he heard this order, and manifested no reluctance to express his dissatisfaction at the measure.

"If the Englishmen grumble at the fight, and think it not fair play," muttered the old cockswain, "let us try it over again, sir; as they are somewhat short of hands, they can send a boat to the land, and get off a gang of them lazy riptyles, the soldiers, who stand looking at us, like so many red lizzards crawling on a beach, and we'll give them another chance; but damme, if I see the use of whipping them, if this is to be the better-end of the matter."

"What's that you're grumbling there, like a dead northeaster, you horse mackerel!" said Barnstable; "where are our friends and countrymen who are on the land! are we to leave them to swing on gibbets or rot in dungeons!"

The cockswain listened with great earnestness, and when his commander had spoken, he struck the palm of his broad hand against his brawny thigh, with a report like a pistol, and answered,

"I see how it is, sir; you reckon the red coats have Mr. Griffith in tow. Just run the schooner into shoal water, Captain Barnstable, and drop an anchor, where we can get the long gun to bear on them, and give me the whale-boat and five or six men to back me—they must have long legs if they get an offing before I run them aboard!"

"Fool! do you think a boat's crew could contend with fifty armed soldiers!"

"Soldiers!" echoed Tom, whose spirits had been strongly excited by the conflict, snapping his fingers with ineffable disdain, "that for all the soldiers that were ever rigged: one whale could kill a thousand of them! and here stands the man that has kill'd his round hundred of whales!"

"Pshaw, you grampus, do you turn braggart in your old age!"

"It's no bragging, sir, to speak a log-book truth! but if Captain Barnstable thinks that old Tom Coffin carries a speaking trumpet for a figure head, let him pass the word forrard to man the boats."

"No, no, my old master at the marlingspike," said Barnstable, kindly, "I know thee too well, thou brother of Neptune! but, shall we not throw the bread-room dust in those Englishmen's eyes, by wearing their bunting awhile, till something may offer to help our captured countrymen."

The cockswain shook his head, and cogitated a moment, as if struck with sundry new ideas, when he answered—

"Ay, ay, sir; that's blue-water-philosophy: as deep as the sea! Let the riptyles clew up the corners of their mouths to their eye-brows, now! when they come to hear the ra'al yankee truth of the matter, they will sheet them down to their leather neckcloths!"

With this reflection the cockswain was much consoled, and the business of repairing damages and securing the prize, proceeded without further interruption on his part. The few prisoners who were unhurt, were rapidly transferred to the Ariel. While Barnstable was attending to this duty, an unusual bustle drew his eyes to one of the hatchways, where he beheld a couple of his marines dragging forward a gentleman, whose demeanour and appearance indicated the most abject terror. After examining the extraordinary appearance of this individual, for a moment, in silent amazement, the lieutenant exclaimed—

"Who have we here! some amateur in fights! an inquisitive, wonder-seeking non-combatant, who has volunteered to serve his king, and perhaps draw a picture, or write a book, to serve himself! Pray, sir, in what capacity did you serve in this vessel?"

The captive ventured a sidelong glance at his interrogator, in whom he expected to encounter Griffith, but perceiving that it was a face he did not know, he felt a revival of confidence that enabled him to reply—

"I came here by accident; being on board the cutter at the time her late commander determined to engage you. It was not in his power to land me, as I trust you will not hesitate to do; your conjecture of my being a non-combatant—"

"Is perfectly true," interrupted Barnstable; "it requires no spy-glass to read that name written on you from stem to stern; but for certain weighty reasons—"

He paused to turn at a signal given him by young Merry, who whispered eagerly in his ear—

"'Tis Mr. Dillon, kinsman of Colonel Howard; I've seen him often, sailing in the wake of my cousin Cicily."

"Dillon!" exclaimed Barnstable, rubbing his hands with pleasure; "what, Kit of that name! he with 'the Savannah face, eyes of black, and skin of the same colour;' he's grown a little whiter with fear; but he's a prize, at this moment, worth twenty Alacritys!"

These exclamations were made in a low voice, and at some little distance from the prisoner, whom he now approached, and addressed—

"Policy, and consequently duty, require that I should detain you for a short time, sir; but you shall have a sailor's welcome to whatever we possess, to lessen the weight of captivity."

Barnstable precluded any reply, by bowing to his captive, and turning away, to superintend the management of his vessels. In a short time it was announced that they were ready to make sail, when the Ariel and her prize were brought close to the wind, and commenced beating slowly along the land, as if intending to return to the bay whence the latter had sailed that morning. As they stretched into the shore, on the first tack, the soldiers on the cliffs rent the air with their shouts and acclamations, to which Barnstable, pointing to the assumed symbols that were fluttering in the breeze from his masts, directed his crew to respond in the most cordial manner. As the distance, and the want of boats, prevented any further communication, the soldiers, after gazing at the receding vessels for a time, disappeared from the cliffs, and were soon lost from the sight of the adventurous mariners. Hour after hour was consumed in the tedious navigation, against an adverse tide, and the short day was drawing to a close, before they approached the mouth of their destined haven. While making one of their numerous stretches, to and from the land, the cutter, in which Barnstable continued, passed the victim of their morning's sport, riding on the water, the waves curling over his huge carcass as on some rounded rock, and already surrounded by the sharks, who were preying on his defenceless body.

"See! Master Coffin," cried the lieutenant, pointing out the object to his cockswain, as they glided by it, "the shovel-nosed gentlemen are regaling daintily; you have neglected the christian's duty of burying your dead."

The old seaman cast a melancholy look at the dead whale, and replied,

"If I had the creatur in Boston Bay, or on the Sandy Point of Munny-Moy, 'twould be the making of me! But riches and honour are for the great and the larned, and there's nothing left for poor Tom Coffin to do, but to veer and haul on his own rolling-tackle, that he may ride out the rest of the gale of life, without springing any of his old spars."

"How now, long Tom!" cried his officer, "these rocks and cliffs will shipwreck you on the shoals of poetry yet; you grow sentimental!"

"Them rocks might wrack any vessel that struck them," said the literal cockswain; "and as for poetry, I wants none better than the good old song of Captain Kidd; but it's enough to raise solemn thoughts in a Cape Poge Indian, to see an eighty barrel whale devoured by shirks—'tis an awful waste of property! I've seen the death of two hundred of the creaturs, though it seems to keep the rations of poor old long Tom as short as ever."

The cockswain walked aft, while the vessel was passing the whale, and seating himself on the taffrail, with his face resting gloomily on his bony hand, he fastened his eyes on the object of his solicitude, and continued to gaze at it with melancholy regret, while it was to be seen glistening in the sunbeams, as it rolled its glittering side of white into the air, or the rays fell unreflected on the black and rougher coat of the back of the monster. In the mean time, the navigators diligently pursued their way for the haven we have mentioned, into which they steered with every appearance of the fearlessness of friends, and the exultation of conquerors.

A few eager and gratified spectators lined the edges of the small bay, and Barnstable concluded his arrangement for deceiving the enemy, by admonishing his crew, that they were now about to enter on a service that would require their utmost intrepidity and sagacity.

# Chapter XIX.

"Our trumpet called you to this gentle parle."
*King John*, II.i.205.

As GRIFFITH and his companions rushed from the offices of St. Ruth, into the open air, they encountered no one to intercept their flight, or communicate the alarm. Warned by the experience of the earlier part of the same night, they avoided the points where they knew the sentinels were posted, though fully prepared to bear down all resistance, and were soon beyond the probability of immediate detection. They proceeded, for the distance of half a mile, with rapid strides, and with the stern and sullen silence of men who, expecting to encounter immediate danger, were resolved to breast it with desperate resolution; but, as they plunged into a copse, that clustered around the ruin which has been already mentioned, they lessened their exertions to a more deliberate pace, and a short but guarded dialogue ensued.

"We have had a timely escape," said Griffith; "I would much rather have endured captivity, than have been the cause of introducing confusion and bloodshed into the peaceful residence of Colonel Howard."

"I would, sir, that you had been of this opinion some hours earlier," returned the pilot, with a severity in his tones that even conveyed more meaning than his words.

"I may have forgotten my duty, sir, in my anxiety to inquire into the condition of a family in whom I feel a particular interest," returned Griffith, in a manner in which pride evidently struggled with respect; "but this is not a time for regrets; I apprehend that we follow you on an errand of some moment, where actions would be more acceptable than any words of apology. What is your pleasure now?"

"I much fear that our project will be defeated," said the pilot, gloomily; "the alarm will spread with the morning fogs, and there will be musterings of the yeomen, and consultations of the gentry, that will drive all thoughts of amusement from their minds. The rumour of a descent will, at any time, force sleep from the shores of this island, to at least ten leagues inland."

"Ay, you have probably passed some pleasant nights, with your eyes open, among them, yourself, Master Pilot," said Manual; "they may thank the Frenchman, Thurot, in the old business of '56, and our own dare-devil, the bloody Scotchman, as the causes of their quarters being so often beaten up. After all, Thurot, with his fleet, did no more than bully them a little, and the poor fellow was finally extinguished by a few small cruisers, like a drummer's boy under a grenadier's cap; but honest Paul sung a different tune for his countrymen to dance to, and—"

"I believe you will shortly dance yourself, Manual," interrupted Griffith, quickly, "and in very pleasure that you have escaped an English prison."

"Say, rather, an English gibbet," continued the elated marine; "for had a court-martial or a court-civil discussed the manner of our entrance into this island, I doubt whether we should have fared better than the dare-devil himself, honest—"

"Pshaw!" exclaimed the impatient Griffith, "enough of this nonsense, Captain Manual; we have other matters to discuss now;—what course have you determined to pursue, Mr. Gray?"

The pilot started, like a man aroused from a deep musing at this question, and after a pause of a moment, he spoke in a low tone of voice, as if still under the influence of deep and melancholy feeling—

"The night has already run into the morning watch, but the sun is backward to show himself in this latitude in the heart of winter—I must depart, my friends, to rejoin you some ten hours hence; it will be necessary to look deeper into our scheme before we hazard any thing, and no one can do the service but myself—where shall we meet again?"

"I have reason to think that there is an unfrequented ruin, at no great distance from us," said Griffith; "perhaps we might find both shelter and privacy among its deserted walls."

"The thought is good," returned the pilot, "and 'twill answer a double purpose. Could you find the place where you put the marines in ambush, Captain Manual?"

"Has a dog a nose! and can he follow a clean scent!" exclaimed the marine; "do you think, Signior Pilota, that a general ever puts his forces in an ambuscade where he can't find them himself? 'Fore God! I knew well enough where the rascals lay snoring on their knapsacks, some half-an-hour ago, and I would have given the oldest majority in Washington's army to have had them where a small intimation from myself could have brought them in line ready dressed for a charge. I know not how you fared, gentlemen, but with me, the sight of twenty such vagabonds would have been a joyous spectacle; we would have tossed that Captain Borroughcliffe and his recruits on the points of our bayonets, as the devil would pitch—"

"Come, come, Manual," said Griffith, a little angrily, "you constantly forget our situation and our errand; can you lead your men hither without discovery, before the day dawns?"

"I want but the shortest half-hour that a bad watch ever travelled over to do it in."

"Then follow, and I will appoint a place of secret rendezvous," rejoined Griffith; "Mr. Gray can learn our situation at the same time."

The pilot was seen to beckon, through the gloom of the night, for his companions to move forward, when they proceeded, with cautious steps, in quest of the desired shelter. A short search brought them in contact with a part of the ruinous walls that spread over a large surface, and which, in places, reared their black fragments against the sky, casting a deeper obscurity across the secret recesses of the wood.

"This will do," said Griffith, when they had skirted for some distance the outline of the crumbling fabric; "bring up your men to this point, where I will meet you, and conduct them to some more secret place, for which I shall search during your absence."

"A perfect paradise, after the cable-tiers of the Ariel!" exclaimed Manual; "I doubt not but a good spot might be selected among these trees for a steady drill; a thing my soul has pined after for six long months."

"Away, away!" cried Griffith; "here is no place for idle parades; if we find shelter from discovery and capture until you shall be needed in a deadly struggle, 'twill be well."

Manual was slowly retracing his steps to the skirts of the wood, when he suddenly turned, and asked—

"Shall I post a small picquet, a mere corporal's guard, in the open ground in front, and make a chain of sentinels to our works?"

"We have no works—we want no sentinels," returned his impatient commander; "our security is only to be found in secrecy. Lead up your men under the cover of the trees, and let those three bright stars be your landmarks—bring them in a range with the northern corner of the wood—"

"Enough, Mr. Griffith," interrupted Manual; "a column of troops is not to be steered like a ship, by compass, and bearings, and distances;—trust me, sir, the march shall be conducted with proper discretion, though in a military manner."

Any reply or expostulation was prevented by the sudden disappearance of the marine, whose retreating footsteps were heard, for several moments, as he moved at a deliberate pace through the underwood. During this short interval, the pilot stood reclining against a corner of the ruins in profound silence, but when the sounds of Manual's march were no longer audible, he advanced from under the deeper shadows of the wall, and approached his youthful companion.

"We are indebted to the marine for our escape," he said; "I hope we are not to suffer by his folly."

"He is what Barnstable calls a rectangular man," returned Griffith; "and will have his way in matters of his profession, though a daring companion in a hazardous expedition. If we can keep him from exposing us by his silly parade, we shall find him a man who will do his work like a soldier, sir, when need happens."

" 'Tis all I ask; until the last moment he and his command must be torpid; for if we are discovered, any attempt of ours, with some twenty bayonets and a half-pike or two, would be useless against the force that would be brought to crush us."

"The truth of your opinion is too obvious," returned Griffith; "these fellows will sleep a week at a time in a gale at sea, but the smell of the land wakes them up, and I fear 'twill be hard to keep them close during the day."

"It must be done, sir, by the strong hand of force," said the pilot sternly, "if it cannot be done by admonition; if we had no more than the recruits of that drunken martinet to cope with, it would be no hard task to drive them into the sea; but I learned in my prison that horse are expected on the shore with the dawn; there is one they call Dillon who is on the alert to do us mischief."

"The miscreant!" muttered Griffith; "then you also have had communion, sir, with some of the inmates of St. Ruth?"

"It behooves a man who is embarked in a perilous enterprise to seize all opportunities to learn his hazard," said the pilot, evasively; "if the report be true, I fear we have but little hopes of succeeding in our plans."

"Nay, then, let us take the advantage of the darkness to regain the schooner; the coasts of England swarm with hostile cruisers, and a rich trade is flowing into the bosom of this island from the four quarters of the world; we shall not seek long for a foe worthy to contend with, nor for the opportunities to cut up the Englishman in his sinews of war—his wealth."

"Griffith," returned the pilot in his still, low tones, that seemed to belong to a man who never knew ambition, nor felt human passion, "I grow sick of this struggle between merit and privileged rank. It is in vain that I scour the waters which the King of England boastingly calls his own, and capture his vessels in the very mouths of his harbours, if my reward is to consist only of violated promises, and hollow professions;—but your proposition is useless to me; I have at length obtained a ship of a size sufficient to convey my person to the shores of honest, plain-dealing America, and I would enter the hall of congress, on my return, attended by a few of the legislators of this learned isle, who think they possess the exclusive privilege to be wise, and virtuous, and great."

"Such a retinue might doubtless be grateful both to your own feelings and those who would receive you," said Griffith, modestly; "but would it affect the great purposes of our struggle, or is it an exploit, when achieved, worth the hazard you incur?"

Griffith felt the hand of the pilot on his own, pressing it with a convulsive grasp, as he replied, in a voice, if possible, even more desperately calm than his former tones—

"There is glory in it, young man; if it be purchased with danger, it shall be rewarded by fame! It is true, I wear your republican livery, and call the Americans my brothers, but it is because you combat in behalf of human nature. Were your cause less holy, I would not shed the meanest drop that flows in English veins to serve it; but now, it hallows every exploit that is undertaken in its favour, and the names of all who contend for it shall belong to posterity. Is there no merit in teaching these proud islanders that the arm of liberty can pluck them from the very empire of their corruption and oppression?"

"Then let me go and ascertain what we most wish to know; you have been seen there, and might attract—"

"You little know me," interrupted the pilot; "the deed is my own. If I succeed, I shall claim the honour, and it is proper that I incur the hazard; if I fail, it will be buried in oblivion, like fifty others of my schemes, which, had I power to back me, would have thrown this kingdom in consternation, from the look-outs on the boldest of its head-lands, to those on the turrets of Windsor-Castle. But I was born without the nobility of twenty generations to corrupt my blood and deaden my soul, and am not trusted by the degenerate wretches who rule the French marine."

" 'Tis said that ships of two decks are building from our own oak," said Griffith; "and you have only to present yourself in America, to be employed most honourably."

"Ay! the republics cannot doubt the man who has supported their flag, without lowering it an inch, in so many bloody conflicts! I do go there, Griffith, but my way lies on this path; my pretended friends have bound my hands often, but my enemies, never—neither shall they now. Ten hours will determine all I wish to know, and with you I trust the safety of the party till my return; be vigilant, but be prudent."

"If you should not appear at the appointed hour," exclaimed Griffith, as he beheld the pilot turning to depart, "where am I to seek, and how serve you?"

"Seek me not, but return to your vessel; my earliest years were passed on this coast, and I can leave the island, should it be necessary, as I entered it, aided by this disguise and my own knowledge; in such an event, look to your charge, and forget me entirely."

Griffith could distinguish the silent wave of his hand when

the pilot concluded, and the next instant he was left alone. For several minutes the young man continued where he had been standing, musing on the singular endowments and restless enterprise of the being with whom chance had thus unexpectedly brought him in contact, and with whose fate and fortune his own prospects had, by the intervention of unlooked-for circumstances, become intimately connected. When the reflections excited by recent occurrences had passed away, he entered within the sweeping circle of the ruinous walls, and after a very cursory survey of the state of the dilapidated building, he was satisfied that it contained enough secret places to conceal his men, until the return of the pilot should warn them that the hour had come when they must attempt the seizure of the devoted sportsmen, or darkness should again facilitate their return to the Ariel. It was now about the commencement of that period of deep night which seamen distinguish as the morning watch, and Griffith ventured to the edge of the little wood, to listen if any sounds or tumult indicated that they were pursued. On reaching a point where his eye could faintly distinguish distant objects, the young man paused, and bestowed a close and wary investigation on the surrounding scene.

The fury of the gale had sensibly abated, but a steady current of sea air was rushing through the naked branches of the oaks, lending a dreary and mournful sound to the gloom of the dim prospect. At the distance of a short half mile, the confused outline of the pile of St. Ruth rose proudly against the streak of light which was gradually increasing above the ocean, and there were moments when the young seaman even fancied he could discern the bright caps that topped the waves of his own disturbed element. The long, dull roar of the surf, as it tumbled heavily on the beach, or dashed with unbroken violence against the hard boundary of rocks, was borne along by the blasts distinctly to his ears. It was a time and a situation to cause the young seaman to ponder deeply on the changes and chances of his hazardous profession. Only a few short hours had passed since he was striving with his utmost skill, and with all his collected energy, to guide the enormous fabric, in which so many of his comrades were now quietly sleeping on the broad ocean, from that very shore on which

he now stood in cool indifference to the danger. The recollection of home, America, his youthful and enduring passion,
and the character and charms of his mistress, blended in a sort
of wild and feverish confusion, which was not, however,
without its pleasures, in the ardent fancy of the young man,
and he was slowly approaching, step by step, towards the abbey, when the sound of footsteps, proceeding evidently from
the measured tread of disciplined men, reached his ears. He
was instantly recalled to his recollection by this noise, which
increased as the party deliberately approached, and in a few
moments he was able to distinguish a line of men, marching
in order towards the edge of the wood from which he had
himself so recently issued. Retiring rapidly under the deeper
shadow of the trees, he waited until it was apparent the party
intended also to enter under its cover, when he ventured to
speak—

"Who comes, and on what errand?" he cried.

"A skulker, and to burrow like a rabbit, or jump from hole
to hole, like a wharf-rat!" said Manual, sulkily; "here have I
been marching, within half-musket shot of the enemy, without daring to pull a trigger even, on their out-posts, because
our muzzles are plugged with that universal extinguisher of
gun-powder, called prudence. 'Fore God! Mr. Griffith, I hope
you may never feel the temptation to do an evil deed which I
felt just now to throw a volley of small shot into that dog-
kennel of a place, if it were only to break its windows and let
in the night air upon the sleeping sot who is dozing away the
fumes of some as good, old, south-side—harkye, Mr. Griffith, one word in your ear."

A short conference took place between the two officers,
apart from the men, at the close of which, as they rejoined the
party, Manual might be heard urging his plans on the reluctant ears of Griffith, in the following words: —

"I could carry the old dungeon without waking one of the
snorers; and, consider, sir, we might get a stock of as rich cordial from its cellars as ever oiled the throat of a gentleman!"

" 'Tis idle, 'tis idle," said Griffith, impatiently; "we are not
robbers of hen-roosts, nor wine-gaugers, to be prying into
the vaults of the English gentry, Captain Manual, but honourable men, employed in the sacred cause of liberty and our

country. Lead your party into the ruin, and let them seek their rest; we may have work for them with the dawn."

"Evil was the hour when I quitted the line of the army, to place a soldier under the orders of an awkward squad of tarry jackets!" muttered Manual, as he proceeded to execute an order that was delivered with an air of authority that he knew must be obeyed. "As pretty an opportunity for a surprise and a forage thrown away, as ever crossed the path of a partisan! but, by all the rights of man! I'll have an encampment in some order. Here, you sergeant, detail a corporal and three men for a picket, and station them in the skirts of this wood. We shall have a sentinel in advance of our position, and things shall be conducted with some air of discipline."

Griffith heard this order with great inward disgust; but as he anticipated the return of the pilot before the light could arrive to render this weak exposure of their situation apparent, he forbore exercising his power to alter the arrangement. Manual had, therefore, the satisfaction of seeing his little party quartered as he thought in a military manner, before he retired with Griffith and his men into one of the vaulted apartments of the ruin, which, by its open and broken doors invited their entrance. Here the marines disposed themselves to rest, while the two officers succeeded in passing the tedious hours, without losing their characters for watchfulness, by conversing with each other, or, at whiles, suffering their thoughts to roam in the very different fields which fancy would exhibit to men of such differing characters. In this manner, hour after hour passed, in listless quiet, or sullen expectation, until the day had gradually advanced, and it became dangerous to keep the sentinels and picket in a situation, where they were liable to be seen by any straggler who might be passing near the wood. Manual remonstrated against any alteration, as being entirely unmilitary, for he was apt to carry his notions of tactics to extremes whenever he came in collision with a sea-officer, but in this instance his superior was firm, and the only concession the captain could obtain was the permission to place a solitary sentinel within a few feet of the vault, though under the cover of the crumbling walls of the building itself. With this slight deviation in their arrangements, the uneasy party remained for several hours longer, impatiently awaiting the period when they should be required to move.

The guns first fired from the Alacrity had been distinctly audible, and were pronounced by Griffith, whose practised ear detected the metal of the piece that was used, as not proceeding from the schooner. When the rapid though distant rumbling of the spirited cannonade became audible, it was with difficulty that Griffith could restrain either his own feelings or the conduct of his companions within those bounds that prudence and their situation required. The last gun was, however, fired, and not a man had left the vault, and conjectures as to the result of the fight, succeeded to those which had been made on the character of the combatants during the action. Some of the marines would raise their heads from the fragments which served them as the pillows on which they were seeking disturbed and stolen slumbers, and after listening to the cannon, would again compose themselves to sleep, like men who felt no concern in a contest in which they did not participate. Others, more alive to events, and less drowsy, lavishly expended their rude jokes on those who were engaged in the struggle, or listened with a curious interest to mark the progress of the battle, by the uncertain index of its noise. When the fight had been some time concluded, Manual indulged his ill-humour more at length—

"There has been a party of pleasure, within a league of us, Mr. Griffith," he said, "at which, but for our present subterraneous quarters, we might have been guests, and thus laid some claim to the honour of sharing in the victory. But it is not too late to push the party on as far as the cliffs, where we shall be in sight of the vessels, and we may possibly establish a claim to our share of the prize-money."

"There is but little wealth to be gleaned from the capture of a king's cutter," returned Griffith, "and there would be less honour were Barnstable encumbered with our additional and useless numbers."

"Useless!" repeated Manual; "there is much good service to be got out of twenty-three well-drilled and well-chosen marines; look at those fellows, Mr. Griffith, and then tell me if you would think them an encumbrance in the hour of need?"

Griffith smiled, and glanced his eye over the sleeping

group, for when the firing had ceased the whole party had again sought their repose, and he could not help admiring the athletic and sinewy limbs that lay scattered around the gloomy vault, in every posture that ease or whim dictated. From the stout frames of the men, his glance was directed to the stack of fire-arms, along whose glittering tubes and polished bayonets, strong rays of light were dancing, even in that dark apartment. Manual followed the direction of his eyes, and watched the expression of his countenance, with inward exultation, but he had the forbearance to await his reply before he manifested his feelings more openly.

"I know them to be true men," said Griffith, "when needed, but—hark! what says he?"

"Who goes there? what noise is that?" repeated the sentinel who was placed at the entrance of the vault.

Manual and Griffith sprang at the same instant from their places of rest, and stood, unwilling to create the slightest sounds, listening with the most intense anxiety to catch the next indications of the cause of their watchman's alarm. A short stillness, like that of death, succeeded, during which Griffith whispered—

" 'Tis the pilot; his hour has been long passed."

The words were hardly spoken, when the clashing of steel in fierce and sudden contact was heard, and at the next instant the body of the sentinel fell heavily along the stone steps that led to the open air, and rolled lifelessly to their feet, with the bayonet that had caused his death projecting from a deep wound in his breast.

"Away, away! sleepers away!" shouted Griffith.

"To arms!" cried Manual, in a voice of thunder.

The alarmed marines, suddenly aroused from their slumbers at these thrilling cries, sprang on their feet in a confused cluster, and at that fatal moment a body of living fire darted into the vault, which re-echoed with the reports of twenty muskets. The uproar, the smoke, and the groans which escaped from many of his party, could not restrain Griffith another instant; his pistol was fired through the cloud which concealed the entrance of the vault, and he followed the leaden messenger, trailing a half-pike, and shouting to his men—

"Come on! follow, my lads; they are nothing but soldiers."

Even while he spoke, the ardent young seaman was rushing up the narrow passage, but as he gained the open space, his foot struck the writhing body of the victim of his shot, and he was precipitated headlong into a group of armed men.

"Fire! Manual, fire!" shouted the infuriated prisoner; "fire, while you have them in a cluster."

"Ay, fire, Mr. Manual," said Borroughcliffe, with great coolness, "and shoot your own officer; hold him up, boys! hold him up in front; the safest place is nighest to him."

"Fire!" repeated Griffith, making desperate efforts to release himself from the grasp of five or six men; "fire, and disregard me."

"If he do, he deserves to be hung," said Borroughcliffe; "such fine fellows are not sufficiently plenty to be shot at like wild beasts in chains. Take him from before the mouth of the vault, boys, and spread yourselves to your duty."

At the time Griffith issued from the cover, Manual was mechanically employed in placing his men in order, and the marines, accustomed to do every thing in concert and array, lost the moment to advance. The soldiers of Borroughcliffe reloaded their muskets, and fell back behind different portions of the wall, where they could command the entrance to the vault with their fire, without much exposure to themselves. This disposition was very coolly reconnoitred by Manual in person, through some of the crevices in the wall, and he hesitated to advance against the force he beheld, while so advantageously posted. In this situation several shots were fired by either party, without effect, until Borroughcliffe, perceiving the inefficacy of that mode of attack, summoned the garrison of the vault to a parly.

"Surrender to the forces of his majesty, King George the Third," he cried, "and I promise you quarter."

"Will you release your prisoner, and give us free passage to our vessels?" asked Manual; "the garrison to march out with all the honours of war, and officers to retain their side-arms?"

"Inadmissible," returned Borroughcliffe, with great gravity; "the honour of his majesty's arms, and the welfare of the realm, forbid such a treaty; but I offer you safe quarter, and honourable treatment."

"Officers to retain their side-arms, your prisoner to be released, and the whole party to return to America, on parole, not to serve until exchanged?"

"Not granted," said Borroughcliffe. "The most that I can yield, is a good potation of the generous south-side, and if you are the man I take you for, you will know how to prize such an offer."

"In what capacity do you summon us to yield? as men entitled to the benefit of the laws of arms, or as rebels to your king?"

"Ye are rebels all, gentlemen," returned the deliberate Borroughcliffe, "and as such ye must yield; though so far as good treatment and good fare goes, you are sure of it while in my power; in all other respects you lie at the mercy of his most gracious majesty."

"Then let his majesty show his gracious face, and come and take us, for I'll be—"

The asseveration of the marine was interrupted by Griffith, whose blood had sensibly cooled, and whose generous feelings were awakened in behalf of his comrades, now that his own fate seemed decided.

"Hold, Manual," he cried, "make no rash oaths; Captain Borroughcliffe, I am Edward Griffith, a lieutenant in the navy of the United American States, and I pledge you my honour, to a parole—"

"Release him," said Borroughcliffe.

Griffith advanced between the two parties, and spoke so loud as to be heard by both—

"I propose to descend to the vault and ascertain the loss and present strength of Captain Manual's party; if the latter be not greater than I apprehend, I shall advise him to a surrender on the usual conditions of civilized nations."

"Go," said the soldier; "but stay; is he a half-and-half—an amphibious—pshaw! I mean a marine?"

"He is, sir, a captain in that corps—"

"The very man," interrupted Borroughcliffe; "I thought I recollected the liquid sounds of his voice. It will be well to speak to him of the good fare of St. Ruth; and you may add, that I know my man; I shall besiege instead of storming him, with the certainty of a surrender when his canteen is empty.

The vault he is in holds no such beverage as the cellars of the abbey."

Griffith smiled, in spite of the occasion and his vexation, and making a slight inclination of his head, he passed into the vault, giving notice to his friends, by his voice, in order to apprize them who approached.

He found six of the marines, including the sentinel, lying dead on the ragged pavement, and four others wounded, but stifling their groans, by the order of their commander, that they might not inform the enemy of his weakness. With the remainder of his command Manual had intrenched himself behind the fragment of a wall that intersected the vault, and regardless of the dismaying objects before him, maintained as bold a front, and as momentous an air, as if the fate of a walled town depended on his resolution and ingenuity.

"You see, Mr. Griffith," he cried, when the young sailor approached this gloomy but really formidable arrangement, "that nothing short of artillery can dislodge me; as for that drinking Englishman above, let him send down his men by platoons of eight or ten, and I'll pile them up on those steps, four and five deep."

"But artillery can and will be brought, if it should be necessary," said Griffith, "and there is not the least chance of your eventual escape; it may be possible for you to destroy a few of the enemy, but you are too humane to wish to do it unnecessarily."

"No doubt," returned Manual, with a grim smile; "and yet methinks I could find present pleasure in shooting seven of them—yes, just seven, which is one more than they have struck off my roster."

"Remember your own wounded," added Griffith; "they suffer for want of aid, while you protract a useless defence."

A few smothered groans, from the sufferers, seconded this appeal, and Manual yielded, though with a very ill grace, to the necessity of the case.

"Go, then, and tell him that we will surrender as prisoners of war," he said, "on the conditions that he grants me my side-arms, and that suitable care shall be taken of the sick—be particular to call them sick—for some lucky accident may yet occur before the compact is ratified, and I would not have him learn our loss."

Griffith, without waiting for a second bidding, hastened to Borroughcliffe with his intelligence.

"His side-arms!" repeated the soldier, when the other had done; "what are they, I pray thee, a marlingspike! for if his equipments be no better than thine own, my worthy prisoner, there is little need to quarrel about their ownership."

"Had I but ten of my meanest men, armed with such half-pikes, and Captain Borroughcliffe with his party were put at deadly strife with us," retorted Griffith, "he might find occasion to value our weapons more highly."

"Four such fiery gentlemen as yourself would have routed my command," returned Borroughcliffe, with undisturbed composure; "I trembled for my ranks when I saw you coming out of the smoke like a blazing comet from behind a cloud, and I shall never think of somersets without returning inward thanks to their inventor. But our treaty is made; let your comrades come forth and pile their arms."

Griffith communicated the result to the captain of marines, when the latter led the remnant of his party out of his sunken fortress into the open air.

The men, who had manifested throughout the whole business that cool subordination and unyielding front, mixed with the dauntless spirit that to this day distinguishes the corps of which they were members, followed their commander in sullen silence, and stacked their arms, with as much regularity and precision as if they had been ordered to relieve themselves after a march. When this necessary preliminary had been observed, Borroughcliffe unmasked his forces, and our adventurers found themselves once more in the power of the enemy, and under circumstances which rendered the prospects of a speedy release from their captivity nearly hopeless.

# Chapter XX.

"If your Father will do me any honour, so;
If not, let him kill the next Percy himself;
I look to be either Earl or Duke, I can assure you."
*1 Henry IV*, V.iv.140−143.

MANUAL CAST sundry discontented and sullen looks from his captors to the remnant of his own command, while the process of pinioning the latter was conducted, with much discretion, under the directions of Sergeant Drill, but meeting, in one of his dissatisfied glances, with the pale and disturbed features of Griffith, he gave vent to his ill-humour, as follows:

"This results from neglecting the precautions of military discipline. Had the command been with me, who, I may say, without boasting, have been accustomed to the duties of the field, proper picquets would have been posted, and instead of being caught like so many rabbits in a burrow, to be smoked out with brimstone, we should have had an open field for the struggle, or we might have possessed ourselves of these walls, which I could have made good for two hours at least, against the best regiment that ever wore King George's facings."

"Defend the outworks before retreating to the citadel!" cried Borroughcliffe; " 'tis the game of war, and shows science; but had you kept closer to your burrow, the rabbits might now have all been frisking about in that pleasant abode. The eyes of a timid hind were greeted this morning, while journeying near this wood, with a passing sight of armed men, in strange attire, and as he fled, with an intent of casting himself into the sea, as fear will sometimes urge one of his kind to do, he luckily encountered me on the cliffs, who humanely saved his life, by compelling him to conduct us hither. There is often wisdom in science, my worthy contemporary in arms, but there is sometimes safety in ignorance."

"You have succeeded, sir, and have a right to be pleasant," said Manual, seating himself gloomily on a fragment of the ruin, and fastening his looks on the melancholy spectacle of the lifeless bodies, as they were successively brought from the vault and placed at his feet; "but these men have been my own children, and you will excuse me if I cannot retort your pleasantries. Ah! Captain Borroughcliffe, you are a soldier, and know how to value merit. I took those very fellows, who sleep on these stones so quietly, from the hands of nature, and made them the pride of our art. They were no longer men, but brave lads, who ate and drank, wheeled and marched, loaded and fired, laughed or were sorrowful, spoke or were silent, only at my will. As for soul, there was but one among them all, and that was in my keeping! Groan, my children, groan freely now; there is no longer a reason to be silent. I have known a single musket-bullet cut the buttons from the coats of five of them in a row, without raising the skin of a man. I could ever calculate, with certainty, how many it would be necessary to expend in all regular service, but this accursed banditti business has robbed me of the choicest of my treasures. You 'stand at ease' now, my children; groan, it will soften your anguish."

Borroughcliffe appeared to participate, in some degree, in the feelings of his captive, and he made a few appropriate remarks in the way of condolence, while he watched the preparations that were making by his own men to move. At length his orderly announced that substitutes for barrows were provided to sustain the wounded, and inquired if it were his pleasure to return to their quarters.

"Who has seen the horse?" demanded the captain; "which way did they march? Have they gained any tidings of the discovery of this party of the enemy?"

"Not from us, your honour," returned the sergeant; "they had ridden along the coast before we left the cliffs, and it was said their officer intended to scour the shore for several miles, and spread the alarm."

"Let him; it is all such gay gallants are good for. Drill, honour is almost as scarce an article with our arms just now, as promotion. We seem but the degenerate children of the heroes of Poictiers;—you understand me, sergeant?"

"Some battle fou't by his majesty's troops against the French, your honour," returned the orderly, a little at a loss to comprehend the expression of his officer's eye.

"Fellow, you grow dull on victory," exclaimed Borroughcliffe; "come hither, I would give you orders. Do you think,

Mister Drill, there is more honour, or likely to be more profit, in this little morning's amusement than you and I can stand under?"

"I should not, your honour; we have both pretty broad shoulders—"

"That are not weakened by undue burthens of this nature," interrupted his captain, significantly; "if we let the news of this affair reach the ears of those hungry dragoons, they would charge upon us, open mouthed, like a pack of famished beagles, and claim at least half the credit, and certainly all the profit."

"But, your honour, there was not a man of them even—"

"No matter, Drill; I've known troops that have been engaged, and have suffered, cheated out of their share of victory by a well-worded despatch. You know, fellow, that in the smoke and confusion of a battle, a man can only see what passes near him, and common prudence requires that he only mention in his official letters what he knows can't be easily contradicted. Thus your Indians, and, indeed, all allies, are not entitled to the right of a general order, any more than to the right of a parade. Now, I dare say, you have heard of a certain battle of Blenheim?"

"Lord! your honour, 'tis the pride of the British army, that and the Culloden! 'Twas when the great Corporal John beat the French king, and all his lords and nobility, with half his nation in arms to back him!"

"Ay! there is a little of the barrack readings in the account, but it is substantially true; know you how many French were in the field, that day, Mister Drill?"

"I have never seen the totals of their muster, sir, in print, but judging by the difference betwixt the nations, I should suppose some hundreds of thousands."

"And yet, to oppose this vast army, the duke had only some ten or twelve thousand well-fed Englishmen! You look astounded, sergeant!"

"Why, your honour, that does seem rather an over-match for an old soldier to swallow; the random shot would sweep away so small a force."

"And yet the battle was fought, and the victory won! but the Duke of Marlborough had a certain Mr. Eugene, with some fifty or sixty thousand High-Dutchers, to back him. You never heard of Mr. Eugene?"

"Not a syllable, your honour; I always thought that Corporal John—"

"Was a gallant and great general; you thought right, Mister Drill. So would a certain nameless gentleman be also, if his majesty would sign a commission to that effect. However, a majority is on the high road to a regiment, and with even a regiment a man is comfortable! In plain English, Mister Drill, we must get our prisoners into the abbey with as little noise as possible, in order that the horse may continue their gambols along the coast, without coming to devour our meal. All the fuss must be made at the war-office. For that trifle you may trust me; I think I know who holds a quill that is as good in its way as the sword he wears. Drill is a short name, and can easily be written within the folds of a letter."

"Lord, your honour!" said the gratified halberdier, "I'm sure such an honour is more—but your honour can ever command me."

"I do; and it is, to be close, and to make your men keep close, until it shall be time to speak, when, I pledge myself, there shall be noise enough." Borroughcliffe shook his head, with a grave air, as he continued—"It has been a devil of a bloody fight, sergeant! look at the dead and wounded; a wood on each flank—supported by a ruin in the centre. Oh! ink! ink! can be spilt on the details with great effect. Go, fellow, and prepare to march."

Thus enlightened on the subject of his commander's ulterior views, the non-commissioned agent of the captain's wishes proceeded to give suitable instructions to the rest of the party, and to make the more immediate preparations for a march. The arrangements were soon completed. The bodies of the slain were left unsheltered, the seclusion of the ruin being deemed a sufficient security against the danger of any discovery, until darkness should favour their removal, in conformity with Borroughcliffe's plan, to monopolize the glory. The wounded were placed on rude litters, composed of the muskets and blankets of the prisoners, when the conquerors and vanquished moved together in a compact body from the ruin, in such a manner as to make the former serve as a mask to conceal the latter from the curious gaze of any casual passenger. There was but little, however, to apprehend on this head, for the alarm and the terror consequent on the exaggerated reports that flew through the country, effectually prevented any intruders on the usually quiet and retired domains of St. Ruth.

The party was emerging from the wood, when the cracking of branches, and rustling of dried leaves, announced, however, that an interruption of some sort was about to occur.

"If it should be one of their rascally patroles!" exclaimed Borroughcliffe, with very obvious displeasure; "they trample like a regiment of cavalry! but, gentlemen, you will acknowledge yourselves, that we were retiring from the field of battle when we met the reinforcement, if it should prove to be such."

"We are not disposed, sir, to deny you the glory of having achieved your victory single handed," said Griffith, glancing his eyes uneasily in the direction of the approaching sounds, expecting to see the pilot issue from the thicket in which he seemed to be entangled, instead of any detachment of his enemies.

"Clear the way, Caesar!" cried a voice at no great distance from them; "break through the accursed vines, on my right, Pompey!—press forward, my fine fellows, or we may be too late to smell even the smoke of the fight."

"Hum!" ejaculated the captain with his philosophic indifference of manner entirely re-established, "this must be a Roman legion just awoke from a trance of some seventeen centuries, and that the voice of a Centurion. We will halt, Mister Drill, and view the manner of an ancient march!"

While the captain was yet speaking, a violent effort disengaged the advancing party from the thicket of brambles in which they had been entangled, when two blacks, each bending under a load of fire-arms, preceded Colonel Howard into the clear space where Borroughcliffe had halted his detachment. Some little time was necessary to enable the veteran to arrange his disordered dress, and to remove the perspiring effects of the unusual toil from his features, before he could observe the addition to the captain's numbers.

"We heard you fire," cried the old soldier, making, at the same time, the most diligent application of his bandanna, "and I determined to aid you with a sortie, which, when judiciously timed, has been the means of raising many a siege; though, had Montcalm rested quietly within his walls, the plains of Abr'am might never have drunk his blood."

"Oh! his decision was soldierly, and according to all rules of war," exclaimed Manual, "and had I followed his example, this day might have produced a different tale!"

"Why, who have we here!" cried the colonel in astonishment; "who is it that pretends to criticise battles and sieges, dressed in such a garb!"

"'Tis a dux incognitorum, my worthy host," said Borroughcliffe, "which means, in our English language, a captain of marines in the service of the American Congress."

"What! have you then met the enemy! ay! and by the fame of the immortal Wolfe you have captured them!" cried the delighted veteran; "I was pressing on with a part of my garrison to your assistance, for I had seen that you were marching in this direction, and even the report of a few muskets was heard."

"A few!" interrupted the conqueror; "I know not what you call a few, my gallant and ancient friend; you may possibly have shot at each other by the week in the days of Wolfe, and Abercrombie, and Braddock, but I too have seen smart firing, and can hazard an opinion in such matters. There was as pretty a roll made by fire-arms at the battles on the Hudson, as ever rattled from a drum; it is all over, and many live to talk of it; but this has been the most desperate affair, for the numbers, I ever was engaged in! I speak always with a reference to the numbers. The wood is pretty well sprinkled with dead, and we have contrived to bring off a few of the desperately wounded with us, as you may perceive."

"Bless me!" exclaimed the surprised veteran, "that such an engagement should happen within musket shot of the Abbey, and I know so little of it! My faculties are on the wane, I fear, for the time has been when a single discharge would rouse me from the deepest sleep."

"The bayonet is a silent weapon," returned the composed captain, with a significant wave of his hand; "'tis the Englishman's pride, and every experienced officer knows, that one thrust from it is worth the fire of a whole platoon."

"What, did ye come to the charge!" cried the Colonel; "by the Lord, Borroughcliffe, my gallant young friend, I would have given twenty tierces of rice, and two able-bodied negroes, to have seen the fray!"

"It would have been a pleasant spectacle to witness sans disputation," returned the captain; "but victory is ours without the presence of Achilles, this time. I have them, all that survive the affair; at least, all that have put foot on English soil."

"Ay! and the king's cutter has brought in the schooner!" added Colonel Howard.—"Thus perish all rebellion for evermore! Where's Kit? my kinsman Mr. Christopher Dillon? I would ask him what the laws of the realm next prescribe to loyal subjects. Here will be work for the jurors of Middlesex, Captain Borroughcliffe, if not for a secretary of state's warrant. Where is Kit, my kinsman; the ductile, the sagacious, the loyal Christopher?"

"The Cacique 'non est,' as more than one bailiff has said of sundry clever fellows in our regiment, when there has been a pressing occasion for their appearance," said the soldier; "but the cornet of horse has given me reason to believe that his provincial lordship, who repaired on board the cutter to give intelligence of the position of the enemy, continued there to share the dangers and honours of naval combat."

"Ay, 'tis like him!" cried the colonel, rubbing his hands with glee; " 'tis like him! he has forgotten the law and his peaceful occupations, at the sounds of military preparation, and has carried the head of a statesman into the fight, with the ardour and thoughtlessness of a boy."

"The Cacique is a man of discretion," observed the captain, with all his usual dryness of manner, "and will doubtless recollect his obligations to posterity and himself, though he be found entangled in the mazes of a combat. But I marvel that he does not return, for some time has now elapsed since the schooner struck her flag, as my own eyes have witnessed."

"You will pardon me, gentlemen," said Griffith, advancing towards them with uncontrollable interest; "but I have unavoidably heard part of your discourse, and cannot think you will find it necessary to withhold the whole truth from a disarmed captive; say you that a schooner has been captured this morning?"

"It is assuredly true," said Borroughcliffe, with a display of nature and delicacy in his manner that did his heart infinite credit; "but I forbore to tell you, because I thought your own misfortunes would be enough for one time. Mr. Griffith, this gentleman is Colonel Howard, to whose hospitality you will be indebted for some favours before we separate."

"Griffith!" echoed the colonel, in quick reply, "Griffith! what a sight for my old eyes to witness!—the child of worthy, gallant, loyal Hugh Griffith a captive, and taken in arms against his prince! Young man, young man, what would thy honest father, what would his bosom friend, my own poor brother Harry, have said, had it pleased God that they had survived to witness this burning shame and lasting stigma on thy respectable name?"

"Had my father lived, he would now have been upholding the independence of his native land," said the young man, proudly; "I wish to respect even the prejudices of Colonel Howard, and beg he will forbear urging a subject on which I fear we never shall agree."

"Never, while thou art to be found in the ranks of rebellion!" cried the Colonel. "Oh! boy, boy! how I could have loved and cherished thee, if the skill and knowledge obtained in the service of thy Prince, were now devoted to the maintenance of his unalienable rights! I loved thy father, worthy Hugh, even as I loved my own brother Harry."

"And his son should still be dear to you," interrupted Griffith, taking the reluctant hand of the Colonel into both his own.

"Ah! Edward, Edward!" continued the softened veteran, "how many of my day-dreams have been destroyed by thy perversity! nay, I know not that Kit, discreet and loyal as he is, could have found such favour in my eyes as thyself; there is a cast of thy father, in that face and smile, Ned, that might have won me to any thing short of treason—and then Cicily, provoking, tender, mutinous, kind, affectionate, good Cicily, would have been a link to unite us for ever."

The youth cast a hasty glance at the deliberate Borroughcliffe, who, if he had obeyed the impatient expression of his eye, would have followed the party that was slowly bearing the wounded towards the Abbey, before he yielded to his feelings, and answered—

"Nay, sir; let this then be the termination of our misunderstanding—your lovely niece shall be that link, and you shall be to me as your friend Hugh would have been had he lived, and to Cecilia twice a parent."

"Boy, boy," said the veteran, averting his face to conceal the working of his muscles, "you talk idly; my word is now plighted to my kinsman, Kit, and thy scheme is impracticable."

"Nothing is impracticable, sir, to youth and enterprise, when aided by age and experience like yours," returned Griffith; "this war must soon terminate."

"This war!" echoed the Colonel, shaking loose the grasp which Griffith held on his arm; "ay! what of this war, young man? Is it not an accursed attempt to deny the rights of our gracious sovereign, and to place tyrants, reared in kennels, on the throne of princes! a scheme to elevate the wicked at the expense of the good! a project to aid unrighteous ambition, under the mask of sacred liberty and the popular cry of equality! as if there could be liberty without order! or equality of rights, where the privileges of the sovereign are not as sacred as those of the people!"

"You judge us harshly, Colonel Howard," said Griffith—

"I judge you!" interrupted the old soldier, who, by this time, thought the youth resembled any one rather than his friend Hugh; "it is not my province to judge you at all; if it were! but the time will come, the time will come. I am a patient man, and can wait the course of things; yes, yes, age cools the blood, and we learn to suppress the passions and impatience of youth; but if the ministry would issue a commission of justice for the colonies, and put the name of old George Howard in it, I am a dog, if there should be a rebel alive in twelve months. Sir," turning sternly to Borroughcliffe, "in such a cause, I could prove a Roman, and hang—hang! yes, I do think, sir, I could hang my kinsman, Mister Christopher Dillon!"

"Spare the Cacique such an unnatural elevation, before his time," returned the captain, with a grave wave of the hand; "behold," pointing towards the wood, "there is a more befitting subject for the gallows! Mr. Griffith, yonder man calls himself your comrade?"

The eyes of Colonel Howard and Griffith followed the direction of his finger, and the latter instantly recognized the Pilot, standing in the skirts of the wood, with his arms folded, apparently surveying the condition of his friends.

"That man," said Griffith, in confusion, and hesitating to utter even the equivocal truth that suggested itself, "that man does not belong to our ship's company."

"And yet he has been seen in *your* company," returned the incredulous Borroughcliffe; "he was the spokesman in last night's examination, Col. Howard, and, doubtless, commands the rear guard of the rebels."

"You say true," cried the veteran; "Pompey! Caesar! present! fire!"

The blacks started at the sudden orders of their master, of whom they stood in the deepest awe, and, presenting their muskets, they averted their faces, and shutting their eyes, obeyed the bloody mandate.

"Charge!" shouted the Colonel, flourishing the ancient sword, with which he had armed himself, and pressing forward with all the activity that a recent fit of the gout would allow; "charge, and exterminate the dogs with the bayonet! push on, Pompey—dress, boys, dress."

"If your friend stand this charge," said Borroughcliffe to Griffith, with unmoved composure, "his nerves are made of iron; such a charge would break the Coldstreams, with Pompey in the ranks!"

"I trust in God," cried Griffith, "he will have forbearance enough to respect the weakness of Colonel Howard!—he presents a pistol!"

"But he will not fire; the Romans deem it prudent to halt; nay, by heaven, they counter-march to the rear. Holla! Colonel Howard, my worthy host, fall back on your reinforcements; the wood is full of armed men; they cannot escape us; I only wait for the horse to cut off the retreat."

The veteran, who had advanced within a short distance of the single man, who thus deliberately awaited the attack, halted at this summons, and, by a glance of his eye, ascertained that he stood alone. Believing the words of Borroughcliffe to be true, he slowly retired, keeping his face manfully towards his enemy, until he gained the support of the captain.

"Recall the troops, Borroughcliffe!" he cried, "and let us charge into the wood; they will fly before his majesty's arms like guilty scoundrels, as they are. As for the negroes, I'll teach the black rascals to desert their master at such a moment. They say Fear is pale, but d——e, Borroughcliffe, if I do not believe his skin is black."

"I have seen him of all colours; blue, white, black, and party-coloured," said the captain; "I must take the command of matters on myself, however, my excellent host; let us retire into the Abbey, and trust me to cut off the remainder of the rebels."

In this arrangement, the colonel reluctantly acquiesced, and the three followed the soldier to the dwelling, at a pace that was adapted to the infirmities of its master. The excitement of the onset, and the current of his ideas, had united, however, to banish every amicable thought from the breast of the Colonel, and he entered the Abbey with a resolute determination of seeing justice dealt to Griffith and his companions, even though it should push them to the foot of the gallows.

As the gentlemen disappeared from his view, among the shrubbery of the grounds, the Pilot replaced the weapon that was hanging from his hand, in his bosom, and, turning with a saddened and thoughtful brow, he slowly re-entered the wood.

# Chapter XXI.

—"When these prodigies
Do so conjointly meet, let not men say,
These are their reasons,—They are natural;
For, I believe they are portentous things
Unto the climate that they point upon."
*Julius Caesar*, I.iii.28–32.

THE READER will discover, by referring to the time consumed in the foregoing events, that the Ariel, with her prize, did not anchor in the bay, already mentioned, until Griffith and his party, had been for several hours in the custody of their enemies. The supposed capture of the rebel schooner, was an incident that excited but little interest, and no surprise, among a people who were accustomed to consider their seamen as invincible; and Barnstable had not found it a difficult task to practise his deception on the few rustics whom curiosity induced to venture alongside the vessels during the short continuance of daylight. When, however, the fogs of evening began to rise along the narrow basin, and the curvatures of its margin were lost in the single outline of its dark and gloomy border, the young seaman thought it time to apply himself in earnest to his duty. The Alacrity, containing all his own crew, together with the Ariel's wounded, was gotten silently under way, and driving easily before the heavy air that swept from the land, she drifted from the harbour, until the open sea lay before her, when her sails were spread, and she continued to make the best of her way in quest of the frigate. Barnstable had watched this movement with breathless anxiety, for on an eminence that completely commanded the waters to some distance, a small but rude battery had been erected for the purpose of protecting the harbour against the depredations and insults of the smaller vessels of the enemy; and a guard of sufficient force to manage the two heavy guns it contained, was maintained in the work, at all times. He was ignorant how far his stratagem had been successful, and it was only when he heard the fluttering of the Alacrity's canvass, as she opened it to the breeze, that he felt he was, yet, secure.

"'Twill reach the Englishmen's ears," said the boy Merry, who stood on the forecastle of the schooner, by the side of his commander, listening with breathless interest to the sounds; "they set a sentinel on the point, as the sun went down, and if he is a trifle better than a dead man, or a marine asleep, he will suspect something is wrong."

"Never!" returned Barnstable, with a long breath, that announced all his apprehensions were removed; "he will be more likely to believe it a mermaid, fanning herself this cool evening, than to suspect the real fact. What say you, Master Coffin? will the soldier smell the truth?"

"They're a dumb race," said the cockswain, casting his eyes over his shoulders, to ascertain that none of their own marine guard was near him; "now, there was our sargeant, who ought to know something, seeing that he has been afloat these four years, maintained, dead in the face and eyes of what every man, who has ever doubled Good Hope, knows to be true, that there was no such vessel to be fallen in with in them seas, as the Flying Dutchman! and then, again, when I told him that he was a 'know-nothing,' and asked him if the Dutchman was a more unlikely thing, than that there should be places where the inhabitants split the year into two watches, and had day for six months, and night the rest of the time, the green-horn laughed in my face, and I do believe he would have told me I lied, but for one thing."

"And what might that be?" asked Barnstable, gravely.

"Why, sir," returned Tom, stretching his bony fingers, as he surveyed his broad palm, by the little light that remained, "though I am a peaceable man, I can be roused."

"And you have seen the Flying Dutchman?"

"I never doubled the east cape; though I can find my way through Le Maire in the darkest night that ever fell from the heavens; but I have seen them that have seen her, and spoken her too."

"Well, be it so; you must turn flying Yankee, yourself, to-night, Master Coffin. Man your boat at once, sir, and arm your crew."

The cockswain paused a moment, before he proceeded to obey this unexpected order, and, pointing towards the battery, he inquired, with infinite phlegm—

"For shore-work, sir? Shall we take the cutlashes and pistols? or shall we want the pikes?"

"There may be soldiers in our way, with their bayonets," said Barnstable, musing; "arm as usual, but throw a few long pikes into the boat, and harkye, Master Coffin, out with your tub and whale-line; for I see you have rigged yourself anew in that way."

The cockswain, who was moving from the forecastle, turned short at this new mandate, and, with an air of remonstrance, ventured to say—

"Trust an old whaler, Captain Barnstable, who has been used to these craft all his life. A whale-boat is made to pull with a tub and line in it, as naturally as a ship is made to sail with ballast, and—"

"Out with it, out with it," interrupted the other, with an impatient gesture, that his cockswain knew signified a positive determination. Heaving a sigh at what he deemed his commander's prejudice, Tom applied himself, without farther delay, to the execution of the orders. Barnstable laid his hand familiarly on the shoulder of the boy, and led him to the stern of his little vessel, in profound silence. The canvass hood that covered the entrance to the cabin was thrown partly aside, and by the light of the lamp that was burning in the small apartment, it was easy to overlook, from the deck, what was passing beneath them. Dillon sat supporting his head with his two hands, in a manner that shaded his face, but in an attitude that denoted deep and abstracted musing.

"I would that I could see the face of my prisoner," said Barnstable, in an under tone, that was audible only to his companion. "The eye of a man is a sort of light-house, to tell one how to steer into the haven of his confidence, boy."

"And sometimes a beacon, sir, to warn you, there is no safe anchorage near him," returned the ready boy.

"Rogue!" muttered Barnstable, "your cousin Kate spoke there."

"If my cousin Plowden were here, Mr. Barnstable, I know that her opinion of yon gentleman would not be at all more favourable."

"And yet, I have determined to trust him! Listen, boy, and tell me if I am wrong; you have a quick wit, like some others of your family, and may suggest something advantageous." The gratified midshipman swelled with the conscious pleasure of possessing his commander's confidence, and followed to the taffrail, over which Barnstable leaned, while he delivered the remainder of his communication. "I have gathered from the 'long-shore-men who have come off, this evening, to stare at the vessel which the rebels have been able to build, that a party of seamen and marines have been captured in an old ruin near the Abbey of St. Ruth, this very day."

"'Tis Mr. Griffith!" exclaimed the boy.

"Ay! the wit of your cousin Katherine was not necessary to discover that. Now, I have proposed to this gentleman with the Savannah face, that he should go into the Abbey, and negotiate an exchange. I will give him for Griffith, and the crew of the Alacrity for Manual's command and the Tigers."

"The Tigers!" cried the lad, with emotion; "have they got my Tigers, too! would to God that Mr. Griffith had permitted me to land!"

"It was no boy's work they were about, and room was scarcer in their boat than live-lumber. But this Mr. Dillon has accepted my proposition, and has pledged himself that Griffith shall return within an hour after he is permitted to enter the Abbey: will he redeem his honour from the pledge?"

"He may," said Merry, musing a moment, "for I believe he thinks the presence of Mr. Griffith under the same roof with Miss Howard, a thing to be prevented, if possible; he may be true in this instance, though he has a hollow look."

"He has bad-looking light-houses, I will own," said Barnstable; "and yet he is a gentleman, and promises fair; 'tis unmanly to suspect him in such a matter, and I will have faith! Now listen, sir. The absence of older heads must throw great responsibility on your young shoulders; watch that battery as closely as if you were at the mast-head of your frigate, on the look-out for an enemy; the instant you see lights moving in it, cut, and run into the offing; you will find me somewhere under the cliffs, and you will stand off and on, keeping the Abbey in sight, until you fall in with us."

Merry gave an attentive ear to these and divers other solemn injunctions that he received from his commander, who, having sent the officer next to himself in authority in charge

of the prize, (the third in command being included in the list
of the wounded,) was compelled to intrust his beloved schooner to the vigilance of a lad whose years gave no promise of
the experience and skill that he actually possessed.

When his admonitory instructions were ended, Barnstable
stepped again to the opening in the cabin-hood, and for a
single moment before he spoke, once more examined the
countenance of his prisoner, with a keen eye. Dillon had removed his hands from before his sallow features, and, as if
conscious of the scrutiny his looks were to undergo, had concentrated the whole expression of his forbidding aspect in a
settled gaze of hopeless submission to his fate. At least, so
thought his captor, and the idea touched some of the finer
feelings in the bosom of the generous young seaman. Dis-
carding, instantly, every suspicion of his prisoner's honour, as
alike unworthy of them both, Barnstable summoned him, in a
cheerful voice, to the boat. There was a flashing of the features of Dillon, at this call, which gave an indefinable expression to his countenance, that again startled the sailor; but it
was so very transient, and could so easily be mistaken for a
smile of pleasure at his promised liberation, that the doubts it
engendered passed away almost as speedily as the equivocal
expression itself. Barnstable was in the act of following his
companion into the boat, when he felt himself detained by a
slight hold of his arm.

"What would you have?" he asked of the midshipman, who
had given him the signal.

"Do not trust too much to that Dillon, sir," returned the
anxious boy, in a whisper; "if you had seen his face, as I did,
when the binnacle light fell upon it, as he came up the cabin
ladder, you would put no faith in him."

"I should have seen no beauty," said the generous lieutenant, laughing; "but, there is long-Tom, as hard-featured a
youth of two score and ten as ever washed in brine, who has a
heart as big, ay, bigger than that of a kraaken. A bright watch
to you, boy, and remember, a keen eye on the battery." As he
was yet speaking, Barnstable crossed the gunwale of his little
vessel, and it was not until he was seated by the side of his
prisoner, that he continued, aloud—"Cast the stops off your
sails, Mr. Merry, and see all clear, to make a run of every

thing; recollect, you are short-handed, sir. God bless ye! and d'ye hear? if there is a man among you who shuts more than one eye at a time, I'll make him, when I get back, open both wider than if Tom Coffin's friend, the Flying Dutchman, was booming down upon him. God bless ye, Merry, my boy; give 'em the square-sail, if this breeze off-shore holds on till morning; shove off."

As Barnstable gave the last order, he fell back on his seat, and, drawing his boat-cloak around him, maintained a profound silence, until they had passed the two small headlands that formed the mouth of the harbour. The men pulled, with muffled oars, their long, vigorous strokes, and the boat glided, with amazing rapidity, past the objects that could be yet indistinctly seen along the dim shore. When, however, they had gained the open ocean, and the direction of their little bark was changed to one that led them in a line with the coast, and within the shadows of the cliffs, the cockswain, deeming that the silence was no longer necessary to their safety, ventured to break it, as follows—

"A square-sail is a good sail to carry on a craft, dead afore it, and in a heavy sea; but if fifty years can teach a man to know the weather, it's my judgment that should the Ariel break ground after the night turns at eight bells, she'll need her main-sail to hold her up to her course."

The lieutenant started at this sudden interruption, and casting his cloak from his shoulders, he looked abroad on the waters, as if seeking those portentous omens which disturbed the imagination of his cockswain.

"How now, Tom," he said, sharply, "have ye turned croaker in your old age? what see you, to cause such an old woman's ditty!"

" 'Tis no song of an old woman," returned the cockswain, with solemn earnestness, "but the warning of an old man; and one who has spent his days where there were no hills to prevent the winds of heaven from blowing on him, unless they were hills of salt water and foam. I judge, sir, there'll be a heavy north-easter setting in upon us afore the morning watch is called."

Barnstable knew the experience of his old messmate too well, not to feel uneasiness at such an opinion, delivered in so confident a manner; but after again surveying the horizon, the heavens, and the ocean, he said, with a continued severity of manner—

"Your prophecy is idle, this time, Master Coffin; every thing looks like a dead calm. This swell is what is left from the last blow; the mist over-head is nothing but the nightly fog, and you can see, with your own eyes, that it is driving sea-ward; even this land-breeze is nothing but the air of the ground mixing with that of the ocean; it is heavy with dew and fog, but it's as sluggish as a Dutch galliot."

"Ay, sir, it is damp, and there is little of it," rejoined Tom; "but as it comes only from the shore, so it never goes far on the water. It is hard to learn the true signs of the weather, Captain Barnstable, and none get to know them well, but such as study little else, or feel but little else. There is only One who can see the winds of heaven, or who can tell when a hurricane is to begin, or where it will end. Still, a man isn't like a whale or a porpoise, that takes the air in his nostrils, but never knows whether it is a south-easter or a north-wester that he feeds upon. Look, broad-off to leeward, sir; see the streak of clear sky shining under the mists; take an old sea-faring man's word for it, Captain Barnstable, that whenever the light shines out of the heavens in that fashion, 'tis never done for nothing; besides, the sun set in a dark bank of clouds, and the little moon we had was dry and windy."

Barnstable listened attentively, and with increasing concern, for he well knew that his cockswain possessed a quick and almost unerring judgment of the weather, notwithstanding the confused medley of superstitious omens and signs with which it was blended; but, again throwing himself back in his boat, he muttered—

"Then let it blow; Griffith is worth a heavier risk, and if the battery can't be cheated, it can be carried."

Nothing further passed on the state of the weather. Dillon had not ventured a single remark since he entered the boat, and the cockswain had the discretion to understand that his officer was willing to be left to his own thoughts. For near an hour they pursued their way with diligence, the sinewy sea-men, who wielded the oars, urging their light boat along the edge of the surf with unabated velocity, and, apparently, with

untired exertions. Occasionally, Barnstable would cast an inquiring glance at the little inlets that they passed, or would
note, with a seaman's eye, the small portions of sandy beach
that were scattered here and there along the rocky boundaries
of the coast. One, in particular, a deeper inlet than common,
where a run of fresh water was heard gurgling as it met the
tide, he pointed out to his cockswain, by significant, but silent
gestures, as a place to be especially noted. Tom, who understood the signal as intended for his own eye alone, made his
observations on the spot, with equal taciturnity, but with all
the minuteness that would distinguish one long accustomed
to find his way, whether by land or water, by land-marks, and
the bearings of different objects. Soon after this silent communication between the lieutenant and his cockswain, the
boat was suddenly turned, and was in the act of dashing upon
the spit of sand before it, when Barnstable checked the movement by his voice—

"Hold water!" he said; " 'tis the sound of oars!"

The seamen held their boat at rest, while a deep attention
was given to the noise that had alarmed the ears of their
commander.

"See, sir," said the cockswain, pointing towards the eastern
horizon; "it is just rising into the streak of light to seaward of
us—now it settles in the trough—ah! here you have it
again!"

"By heavens!" cried Barnstable, " 'tis a man-of-war's stroke
it pulls; I saw the oar-blades as they fell! and, listen to the
sound! neither your fisherman nor your smuggler pulls such a
regular oar."

Tom had bowed his head nearly to the water, in the act
of listening, and now, raising himself, he spoke with confidence—

"That is the Tiger; I know the stroke of her crew as well as
I do of my own. Mr. Merry has made them learn the new-
fashioned jerk, as they dip their blades, and they feather with
such a roll in their rullocks! I could swear to the stroke."

"Hand me the night-glass," said his commander, impatiently; "I can catch them, as they are lifted into the streak.
You are right, by every star in our flag, Tom!—but there is
only one man in her stern-sheets. By my good eyes, I believe

it is that accursed Pilot, sneaking from the land, and leaving Griffith and Manual to die in English prisons. To shore with you—beach her at once."

The order was no sooner given, than it was obeyed, and in less than two minutes, the impatient Barnstable, Dillon, and the cockswain, were standing together on the sands.

The impression he had received, that his friends were abandoned to their fate by the Pilot, urged the generous young seaman to hasten the departure of his prisoner, as he was fearful every moment might interpose some new obstacle to the success of his plans.

"Mr. Dillon," he said, the instant they were landed, "I exact no new promise—your honour is already plighted"—

"If oaths can make it stronger," interrupted Dillon, "I will take them."

"Oaths cannot—the honour of a gentleman is, at all times, enough. I shall send my cockswain with you to the Abbey, and you will either return with him, in person, within two hours, or give Mr. Griffith and Captain Manual to his guidance. Proceed, sir; you are conditionally free; there is an easy opening by which to ascend the cliffs."

Dillon, once more, thanked his generous captor, and then proceeded to force his way up the rough eminence.

"Follow, and obey his instructions," said Barnstable to his cockswain, aloud.

Tom, long accustomed to implicit obedience, handled his harpoon, and was quietly following in the footsteps of his new leader, when he felt the hand of the lieutenant on his shoulder.

"You saw where the brook emptied over the hillock of sand?" said Barnstable, in an under tone.

Tom nodded assent.

"You will find us there, riding without the surf—'twill not do to trust too much to an enemy."

The cockswain made a gesture of great significance with his weapon, that was intended to indicate the danger their prisoner would incur, should he prove false; when, applying the wooden end of the harpoon to the rocks, he ascended the ravine at a rate that soon brought him to the side of his companion.

# Chapter XXII.

"Ay, marry, let me have him to sit under
He's like to be a cold soldier."
*2 Henry IV*, III.ii.122−123.

BARNSTABLE LINGERED on the sands for a few minutes, until the footsteps of Dillon and the cockswain were no longer audible, when he ordered his men to launch their boat once more into the surf. While the seamen pulled leisurely towards the place he had designated, as the point where he would await the return of Tom, the lieutenant first began to entertain serious apprehensions concerning the good faith of his prisoner. Now, that Dillon was beyond his control, his imagination presented, in very vivid colours, several little circumstances in the other's conduct, which might readily excuse some doubts of his good faith, and, by the time they had reached the place of rendezvous, and had cast a light grapnel into the sea, his fears had rendered him excessively uncomfortable. Leaving the lieutenant to his reflections, on this unpleasant subject, we shall follow Dillon and his fearless and unsuspecting companion, in their progress towards St. Ruth.

The mists, to which Tom had alluded, in his discussion with his commander, on the state of the weather, appeared to be settling nearer to the earth, and assuming, more decidedly, the appearance of a fog, hanging above them, in sluggish volumes, but little agitated by the air. The consequent obscurity added deeply to the gloom of the night, and it would have been difficult for one, less acquainted than Dillon with the surrounding localities, to find the path which led to the dwelling of Colonel Howard. After some little search, this desirable object was effected, and the civilian led the way, with rapid strides, towards the Abbey.

"Ay, ay!" said Tom, who followed his steps, and equalled his paces, without any apparent effort, "you shore-people have an easy way to find your course and distance, when you get into the track. I was once left by the craft I belonged to, in Boston, to find my way to Plymouth, which is a matter of fifteen leagues, or thereaway; and, so finding nothing was bound up the bay, after lying-by for a week, I concluded to haul aboard my land-tacks. I spent the better part of another week in a search for some hooker, on board which I might work my passage across the country, for money was as scarce then with old Tom Coffin as it is now, and is likely to be, unless the fisheries get a good luff soon; but it seems that nothing but your horse-flesh, and horned cattle, and jack-asses, are privileged to do the pulling and hauling in your shore-hookers; and I was forced to pay a week's wages for a birth, besides keeping a banyan on a mouthful of bread and cheese, from the time we hove-up in Boston, 'till we came-to in Plymouth town."

"It was certainly an unreasonable exaction, on the part of the waggoners, from a man in your situation," said Dillon, in a friendly, soothing tone of voice, that denoted a willingness to pursue the conversation.

"My situation was that of a cabin passenger," returned the cockswain; "for there was but one hand forward, beside the cattle I mentioned—that was he who steered—and an easy birth he had of it; for there his course lay a-tween walls of stone, and fences; and, as for his reckoning, why, they had stuck up bits of stone on-end, with his day's work footed up, ready to his hand, every half league or so. Besides, the land-marks were so plenty, that a man, with half-an-eye, might steer her, and no fear of getting to leeward."

"You must have found yourself, as it were, in a new world," observed Dillon.

"Why, to me, it was pretty much the same as if I had been set afloat in a strange country, though I may be said to be a native of those parts, being born on the coast. I had often heard shore-men say, that there was as much 'arth as water in the world, which I always set down as a rank lie, for I've sailed with a flowing sheet months an-end, without falling in with as much land or rock as would answer a gull to lay its eggs on; but I will own, that a-tween Boston and Plymouth, we were out-of-sight of water for as much as two full watches."

Dillon pursued this interesting subject with great diligence, and, by the time they reached the wall, which enclosed the large paddock that surrounded the Abbey, the cockswain was deeply involved in a discussion of the comparative magnitude of the Atlantic Ocean and the Continent of America.

Avoiding the principal entrance to the building, through the great gates which communicated with the court in front, Dillon followed the windings of the wall until it led them to a wicket, which he knew was seldom closed for the night, until the hour for general rest had arrived. Their way now lay in the rear of the principal edifice, and soon conducted them to the confused pile which contained the offices. The cockswain followed his companion, with a confiding reliance on his knowledge and good faith, that was somewhat increased by the freedom of communication that had been maintained during their walk from the cliffs. He did not perceive any thing extraordinary in the other's stopping at the room, which had been provided as a sort of barracks for the soldiers of Captain Borroughcliffe. A conference which took place between Dillon and the sergeant, was soon ended, when the former beckoned to the cockswain to follow, and, taking a circuit round the whole of the offices, they entered the Abbey together, by the door through which the ladies had issued, when in quest of the three prisoners, as has been already related. After a turn or two among the narrow passages of that part of the edifice, Tom, whose faith in the facilities of land navigation began to be a little shaken, found himself following his guide through a long, dark gallery, that was terminated at the end toward which they were approaching, by a half-open door, that admitted a glimpse into a well-lighted and comfortable apartment. To this door, Dillon hastily advanced, and, throwing it open, the cockswain enjoyed a full view of the very scene that we described, in introducing Col. Howard to the acquaintance of the reader, and under circumstances of great similitude. The cheerful fire of coal, the strong and glaring lights, the tables of polished mahogany, and the blushing fluids, were still the same in appearance, while the only perceptible change was in the number of those, who partook of the cheer. The master of the mansion, and Borroughcliffe, were seated opposite to each other, employed in discussing the events of the day, and diligently pushing to and fro the glittering vessel, that contained a portion of the generous liquor they both loved so well; a task which each moment rendered lighter.

"If Kit would but return," exclaimed the veteran, whose back was to the opening door, "bringing with him his honest brows encircled, as they will be, or ought to be, with laurel, I should be the happiest old fool, Borroughcliffe, in his majesty's realm of Great Britain!"

The captain, who felt the necessity for the unnatural restraint he had imposed on his thirst, to be removed by the capture of his enemies, pointed towards the door with one hand, while he grasped the sparkling reservoir of the "south side" with the other, and answered—

"Lo! the Cacique himself! his brow inviting the diadem— ha! who have we in his highness' train? By the Lord, sir Cacique, if you travel with a body guard of such grenadiers, old Frederic of Prussia himself will have occasion to envy you the corps! a clear six-footer in nature's stockings! and the arms as unique as the armed!"

The colonel did not, however, attend to half of his companion's exclamations, but turning, he beheld the individual he had so much desired, and received him with a delight proportioned to the unexpectedness of the pleasure. For several minutes, Dillon was compelled to listen to the rapid questions of his venerable relative, to all of which he answered with a prudent reserve, that might, in some measure, have been governed by the presence of the cockswain. Tom stood with infinite composure, leaning on his harpoon, and surveying, with a countenance where wonder was singularly blended with contempt, the furniture and arrangements of an apartment that was far more splendid than any he had before seen. In the mean time, Borroughcliffe entirely disregarded the private communications that passed between his host and Dillon, which gradually became more deeply interesting, and finally drew them to a distant corner of the apartment, but taking a most undue advantage of the absence of the gentleman, who had so lately been his boon companion, he swallowed one potation after another, as if a double duty had devolved on him, in consequence of the desertion of the veteran. Whenever his eye did wander from the ruby tints of his glass, it was to survey, with unrepressed admiration, the inches of the cockswain, about whose stature and frame there were numberless excellent points to attract the gaze of a recruiting officer. From this double pleasure, the captain was, however, at last summoned, to participate in the councils of his friends.

Dillon was spared the disgreeable duty of repeating the artful tale he had found it necessary to palm on the colonel, by the ardour of the veteran himself, who executed the task in a manner that gave to the treachery of his kinsman every appearance of a justifiable artifice and of unshaken zeal in the cause of his prince. In substance, Tom was to be detained as a prisoner, and the party of Barnstable were to be entrapped, and of course to share a similar fate. The sunken eye of Dillon cowered before the steady gaze which Borroughcliffe fastened on him, as the latter listened to the plaudits the colonel lavished on his cousin's ingenuity; but the hesitation that lingered in the soldier's manner vanished, when he turned to examine their unsuspecting prisoner, who was continuing his survey of the apartment, while he innocently imagined the consultations he witnessed were merely the proper and preparatory steps to his admission into the presence of Mr. Griffith.

"Drill," said Borroughcliffe, aloud, "advance and receive your orders." The cockswain turned quickly, at this sudden mandate, and, for the first time, perceived that he had been followed into the gallery by the orderly, and two files of the recruits, armed. "Take this man to the guard-room, and feed him; and see that he dies not of thirst."

There was nothing alarming in this order, and Tom was following the soldiers, in obedience to a gesture from the captain, when their steps were arrested in the gallery, by the cry of "Halt."

"On recollection, Drill," said Borroughcliffe, in a tone from which all dictatorial sounds were banished, "show the gentleman into my own room, and see him properly supplied."

The orderly gave such an intimation of his comprehending the meaning of his officer, as the latter was accustomed to receive, when Borroughcliffe returned to his bottle, and the cockswain followed his guide, with an alacrity and good will that were not a little increased by the repeated mention of the cheer that awaited him.

Luckily for the impatience of Tom, the quarters of the captain were at hand, and the promised entertainment by no means slow in making its appearance. The former was an apartment that opened from a lesser gallery, which communicated with the principal passage already mentioned; and the latter was a bountiful but ungarnished supply of that staple of the British isles, called roast beef; of which the kitchen of Colonel Howard was never without a due and loyal provision. The sergeant, who certainly understood one of the signs of his captain to imply an attack on the citadel of the cockswain's brain, mingled, with his own hands, a potation, that he styled a rummer of grog, and which he thought would have felled the animal itself that Tom was so diligently masticating, had it been alive, and in its vigour. Every calculation that was made on the infirmity of the cockswain's intellect, under the stimulus of Jamaica, was, however, futile. He swallowed glass after glass, with prodigious relish, but, at the same time, with immoveable steadiness; and the eyes of the sergeant, who felt it incumbent to do honour to his own cheer, were already glistening in his head, when, happily for the credit of his art, a tap at the door announced the presence of his captain, and relieved him from the impending disgrace of being drunk blind by a recruit.

As Borroughcliffe entered the apartment, he commanded his orderly to retire, adding—

"Mr. Dillon will give you instructions, which you are implicitly to obey."

Drill, who had sense enough remaining to apprehend the displeasure of his officer, should the latter discover his condition, quickened his departure, and the cockswain soon found himself alone with the captain. The vigour of Tom's attacks on the remnant of the sirloin was now much abated, leaving in its stead that placid quiet which is apt to linger about the palate, long after the cravings of the appetite have been appeased. He had seated himself on one of the trunks of Borroughcliffe, utterly disdaining the use of a chair, and, with the trencher in his lap, was using his own jack-knife on the dilapidated fragment of the ox, with something of that nicety with which the female goule, of the Arabian Tales, might be supposed to pick her rice with the point of her bodkin. The captain drew a seat nigh the cockswain, and, with a familiarity and kindness infinitely condescending, when the difference in their several conditions is considered, he commenced the following dialogue:

"I hope you have found your entertainment to your liking, Mr. a—a—I must own my ignorance of your name."

"Tom," said the cockswain, keeping his eyes roaming over the contents of the trencher; "commonly called long-Tom, by my shipmates."

"You have sailed with discreet men, and able navigators, it would seem, as they understand longitude so well," rejoined the captain; "but you have a patronymick—I would say, another name?"

"Coffin," returned the cockswain; "I'm called Tom, when there is any hurry, such as letting go the haulyards, or a sheet; long-Tom, when they want to get to windward of an old seaman, by fair weather; and long-Tom Coffin, when they wish to hail me, so that none of my cousins of the same name, about the islands, shall answer; for I believe the best man among them can't measure much over a fathom, taking him from his head-works to his heel."

"You are a most deserving fellow," cried Borroughcliffe, "and it is painful to think to what a fate the treachery of Mr. Dillon has consigned you."

The suspicions of Tom, if he ever entertained any, were lulled to rest too effectually by the kindness he had received, to be awakened by this equivocal lament; he, therefore, after renewing his intimacy with the rummer, contented himself by saying, with a satisfied simplicity—

"I am consigned to no one, carrying no cargo but this Mr. Dillon, who is to give me Mr. Griffith in exchange, or go back to the Ariel himself, as my prisoner."

"Ah! my good friend, I fear you will find, when the time comes to make this exchange, that he will refuse to do either."

"But I'll be d——d if he don't do one of them; my orders are to see it done, and back he goes; or Mr. Griffith, who is as good a seaman, for his years, as ever trod a deck, slips his cable from this here anchorage."

Borroughcliffe affected to eye his companion with great commiseration; an exhibition of compassion that was, however, completely lost on the cockswain, whose nerves were strung to their happiest tension, by his repeated libations, while his wit was, if any thing, quickened by the same cause, though his own want of guile rendered him slow to comprehend its existence in others. Perceiving it necessary to speak plainly, the captain renewed the attack in a more direct manner—

"I am sorry to say that you will not be permitted to return to the Ariel, and that your commander, Mr. Barnstable, will be a prisoner within the hour; and in fact, that your schooner will be taken, before the morning breaks."

"Who'll take her?" asked the cockswain, with a grim smile, on whose feelings, however, this combination of threatened calamities was beginning to make some impression.

"You must remember, that she lies immediately under the heavy guns of a battery that can sink her in a few minutes; an express has already been sent to acquaint the commander of the work with the Ariel's true character; and as the wind has already begun to blow from the ocean, her escape is impossible."

The truth, together with its portentous consequences, now began to glare across the faculties of the cockswain. He remembered his own prognostics on the weather, and the helpless situation of the schooner, deprived of more than half her crew, and left to the keeping of a boy, while her commander himself was on the eve of captivity. The trencher fell from his lap to the floor, his head sunk on his knees, his face was concealed between his broad palms, and in spite of every effort the old seaman could make to conceal his emotion, he fairly groaned aloud.

For a moment, the better feelings of Borroughcliffe prevailed, and he paused, as he witnessed this exhibition of suffering in one whose head was already sprinkled with the marks of time; but his habits, and the impressions left by many years passed in collecting victims for the wars, soon resumed their ascendancy, and the recruiting officer diligently addressed himself to an improvement of his advantage.

"I pity, from my heart, the poor lads whom artifice or mistaken notions of duty may have led astray, and who will thus be taken in arms against their sovereign; but, as they are found in the very island of Britain, they must be made examples to deter others. I fear, that unless they can make their peace with government, they will all be condemned to death."

"Let them make their peace with God, then; your government can do but little to clear the log-account of a man whose watch is up for this world."

"But, by making their peace with those who have the power, their lives may be spared," said the captain, watching, with keen eyes, the effect his words produced on the cockswain.

"It matters but little when a man hears the messenger pipe his hammock down for the last time; he keeps his watch in another world, though he goes below in this. But to see wood and iron, that has been put together after such moulds as the Ariel's, go into strange hands, is a blow that a man may remember long after the purser's books have been squared against his name for ever. I would rather that twenty shot should strike my old carcass, than one should hull the schooner that didn't pass out above her water-line."

Borroughcliffe replied, somewhat carelessly, "I may be mistaken, after all; and, instead of putting any of you to death, they may place you all on board the prison-ships, where you may yet have a merry time of it, these ten or fifteen years to come."

"How's that, shipmate!" cried the cockswain, with a start; "a prison-ship, d'ye say? you may tell them they can save the expense of one man's rations, by hanging him, if they please, and that is old Tom Coffin."

"There is no answering for their caprice; to-day, they may order a dozen of you shot for rebels; to-morrow they may choose to consider you as prisoners of war, and send you to the hulks for a dozen years."

"Tell them, brother, that I'm a rebel, will ye? and ye'll tell 'em no lie—one that has fou't them since Manly's time, in Boston bay, to this hour. I hope the boy will blow her up! it would be the death of poor Richard Barnstable, to see her in the hands of the English!"

"I know of one way," said Borroughcliffe, affecting to muse, "and but one, that will certainly avert the prison-ship; for, on second thoughts, they will hardly put you to death."

"Name it, friend," cried the cockswain, rising from his seat in evident perturbation, "and if it lies in the power of man, it shall be done."

"Nay," said the captain, dropping his hand familiarly on the shoulder of the other, who listened with the most eager attention, " 'tis easily done, and no dreadful thing in itself; you are used to gun-powder, and know its smell from otto of roses?"

"Ay, ay," cried the impatient old seaman; "I have had it flashing under my nose by the hour; what then?"

"Why, then, what I have to propose will be nothing to a man like you—you found the beef wholesome, and the grog mellow?"

"Ay, ay, all well enough; but what is that to an old sailor?" asked the cockswain, unconsciously grasping the collar of Borroughcliffe's coat, in his agitation; "what then?"

The captain manifested no displeasure at this unexpected familiarity, but smiled, with suavity, as he unmasked the battery, from behind which he had hitherto carried on his attacks.

"Why, then, you have only to serve your King, as you have before served the Congress—and let me be the man to show you your colours."

The cockswain stared at the speaker intently, but it was evident he did not clearly comprehend the nature of the proposition, and the captain pursued the subject—

"In plain English, enlist in my company, my fine fellow, and your life and liberty are both safe."

Tom did not laugh aloud, for that was a burst of feeling in which he was seldom known to indulge, but every feature of his weather-beaten visage contracted into an expression of bitter, ironical contempt. Borroughcliffe felt the iron fingers, that still grasped his collar, gradually tightening about his throat, like a vice, and, as the arm slowly contracted, his body was drawn, by a power that it was in vain to resist, close to that of the cockswain, who, when their faces were within a foot of each other, gave vent to his emotions in words:—

"A messmate, before a shipmate; a shipmate, before a stranger; a stranger, before a dog; but a dog before a soldier!"

As Tom concluded, his nervous arm was suddenly extended to the utmost, the fingers relinquishing their grasp at the same time, and, when Borroughcliffe recovered his disordered faculties, he found himself in a distant corner of the apartment, prostrate among a confused pile of chairs, tables, and wearing apparel. In endeavouring to rise from this humble posture, the hand of the captain fell on the hilt of his sword, which had been included in the confused assemblage of articles produced by his overthrow.

"How now, scoundrel!" he cried, baring the glittering weapon, and springing on his feet; "you must be taught your distance, I perceive."

The cockswain seized the harpoon which leaned against the wall, and dropped its barbed extremity within a foot of the breast of his assailant, with an expression of the eye that denoted the danger of a nearer approach. The captain, however, wanted not for courage, and, stung to the quick by the insult he had received, he made a desperate parry, and attempted to pass within the point of the novel weapon of his adversary. The slight shock was followed by a sweeping whirl of the harpoon, and Borroughcliffe found himself without arms, completely at the mercy of his foe. The bloody intentions of Tom vanished with his success; for, laying aside his weapon, he advanced upon his antagonist, and seized him with an open palm. One more struggle, in which the captain discovered his incompetency to make any defence against the strength of a man who managed him as if he had been a child, decided the matter. When the captain was passive in the hands of his foe, the cockswain produced sundry pieces of sennit, marline, and ratlin-stuff, from his pockets, which appeared to contain as great a variety of small cordage as a boatswain's store-room, and proceeded to lash the arms of the conquered soldier to the posts of his bed, with a coolness that had not been disturbed since the commencement of hostilities, a silence that seemed inflexible, and a dexterity that none but a seaman could equal. When this part of his plan was executed, Tom paused a moment, and gazed around him as if in quest of something. The naked sword caught his eye, and, with this weapon in his hand, he deliberately approached his captive, whose alarm prevented his observing, that the cockswain had snapped the blade asunder from the handle, and that he had already encircled the latter with marline.

"For God's sake," exclaimed Borroughcliffe, "murder me not in cold blood!"

The silver hilt entered his mouth as the words issued from

it, and the captain found, while the line was passed and re-
passed, in repeated involutions across the back of his neck,
that he was in a condition to which he often subjected his
own men, when unruly, and which is universally called, being
'gagged.' The cockswain now appeared to think himself entitled to all the privileges of a conqueror; for, taking the light
in his hand, he commenced a scrutiny into the nature and
quality of the worldly effects that lay at his mercy. Sundry
articles, that belonged to the equipments of a soldier, were
examined, and cast aside, with great contempt, and divers garments of plainer exterior, were rejected as unsuited to the
frame of the victor. He, however, soon encountered two articles, of a metal that is universally understood. But uncertainty
as to their use appeared greatly to embarrass him. The circular
prongs of these curiosities were applied to either hand, to the
wrists, and even to the nose, and the little wheels, at their
opposite extremity, were turned and examined with as much
curiosity and care, as a savage would expend on a watch, until
the idea seemed to cross the mind of the honest seaman, that
they formed part of the useless trappings of a military man,
and he cast them aside, also, as utterly worthless. Borroughcliffe, who watched every movement of his conqueror, with a
good humour that would have restored perfect harmony between them, could he but have expressed half what he felt,
witnessed the safety of a favourite pair of spurs, with much
pleasure, though nearly suffocated, by the mirth that was unnaturally repressed. At length, the cockswain found a pair of
handsomely mounted pistols, a sort of weapon, with which
he seemed quite familiar. They were loaded, and the knowledge of that fact appeared to remind Tom of the necessity of
departing, by bringing to his recollection the danger of his
commander and the Ariel. He thrust the weapons into the
canvass belt that encircled his body, and, grasping his harpoon, approached the bed, where Borroughcliffe was seated
in duresse.

  "Harkye, friend," said the cockswain, "may the Lord forgive you, as I do, for wishing to make a soldier of a sea-faring
man, and one who has followed the waters since he was an
hour old, and one who hopes to die off soundings, and to be
buried in brine. I wish you no harm, friend, but you'll have to

keep a stopper on your conversation 'till such time as some of your messmates call in this way, which I hope will be as soon after I get an offing as may be."

With these amicable wishes, the cockswain departed, leaving Borroughcliffe the light, and the undisturbed possession of his apartment, though not in the most easy or the most enviable situation imaginable. The captain heard the bolt of his lock turn, and the key rattle as the cockswain withdrew it from the door—two precautionary steps, which clearly indicated that the vanquisher deemed it prudent to secure his retreat, by insuring the detention of the vanquished, for at least a time.

# Chapter XXIII.

"Whilst Vengeance, in the lurid air,
   Lifts her red arm, expos'd and bare:—
Who, Fear, this ghastly train can see,
And look not madly wild, like thee?"
        Collins, "Ode to Fear," ll. 20–21, 24–25.

IT IS CERTAIN that Tom Coffin had devised no settled plan of operations, when he issued from the apartment of Borroughcliffe, if we except a most resolute determination to make the best of his way to the Ariel, and to share her fate, let it be either to sink or swim. But this was a resolution much easier formed by the honest seaman, than executed, in his present situation. He would have found it less difficult to extricate a vessel from the dangerous shoals of the "Devil's-Grip," than to thread the mazes of the labyrinth of passages, galleries, and apartments, in which he found himself involved. He remembered, as he expressed it to himself, in a low soliloquy, "to have run into a narrow passage from the main channel, but whether he had sheered to the starboard or larboard hand," was a material fact, that had entirely escaped his memory. Tom was in that part of the building that Colonel Howard had designated as the "cloisters," and in which, luckily for him, he was but little liable to encounter any foe; the room occupied by Borroughcliffe being the only one in the entire wing, that was not exclusively devoted to the service of the ladies. The circumstance of the soldier's being permitted to invade this sanctuary, was owing to the necessity, on the part of Colonel Howard, of placing either Griffith, Manual, or the recruiting officer, in the vicinity of his wards, or of subjecting his prisoners to a treatment that the veteran would have thought unworthy of his name and character. This recent change in the quarters of Borroughcliffe operated doubly to the advantage of Tom, by lessening the chance of the speedy release of his uneasy captive, as well as by diminishing his own danger. Of the former circumstance he was, however, not aware, and the consideration of the latter was a sort of reflection to which the cockswain was, in no degree, addicted.

Following, necessarily, the line of the wall, he soon emerged from the dark and narrow passage in which he had first found himself, and entered the principal gallery, that communicated with all the lower apartments of that wing, as well as with the main body of the edifice. An open door, through which a strong light was glaring, at a distant end of this gallery, instantly caught his eye, and the old seaman had not advanced many steps towards it, before he discovered that he was approaching the very room which had so much excited his curiosity, and by the identical passage through which he had entered the Abbey. To turn, and retrace his steps, was the most obvious course, for any man to take, who felt anxious to escape; but the sounds of high conviviality, bursting from the cheerful apartment, among which the cockswain thought he distinguished the name of Griffith, determined Tom to advance and reconnoitre the scene more closely. The reader will anticipate that when he paused in the shadow, the doubting old seaman stood once more near the threshold which he had so lately crossed, when conducted to the room of Borroughcliffe. The seat of that gentleman was now occupied by Dillon, and Colonel Howard had resumed his wonted station at the foot of the table. The noise was chiefly made by the latter, who had evidently been enjoying a more minute relation of the means by which his kinsman had entrapped his unwary enemy.

"A noble ruse!" cried the veteran, as Tom assumed his post, in ambush; "a most noble and ingenious ruse, and such a one as would have baffled Caesar! he must have been a cunning dog, that Caesar; but I do think, Kit, you would have been too much for him; hang me, if I don't think you would have puzzled Wolfe himself, had you held Quebec, instead of Montcalm! Ah! boy, we want you in the colonies, with the ermine over your shoulders; such men as you, cousin Christopher, are sadly, sadly wanted there to defend his majesty's rights."

"Indeed, dear sir, your partiality gives me credit for qualities I do not possess," said Dillon, dropping his eyes, perhaps with a feeling of conscious unworthiness, but with an air of much humility; "the little justifiable artifice—"

"Ay! there lies the beauty of the transaction," interrupted

the colonel, shoving the bottle from him, with the free, open air of a man who never harboured disguise; "you told no lie; no mean deception, that any dog, however base and unworthy, might invent; but you practised a neat, a military, a—a—yes, a classical deception on your enemy; a classical deception, that is the very term for it! such a deception as Pompey, or Mark Antony, or—or—you know those old fellows' names better than I do, Kit; but name the cleverest fellow that ever lived in Greece or Rome, and I shall say he is a dunce, compared to you. 'Twas a real Spartan trick, both simple and honest."

It was extremely fortunate for Dillon, that the animation of his aged kinsman kept his head and body in such constant motion, during this apostrophe, as to intercept the aim that the cockswain was deliberately taking at his head, with one of Borroughcliffe's pistols; and perhaps the sense of shame, which induced him to sink his face on his hands, was another means of saving his life, by giving the indignant old seaman time for reflection.

"But you have not spoken of the ladies," said Dillon, after a moment's pause; "I should hope, they have borne the alarm of the day like kinswomen of the family of Howard."

The colonel glanced his eyes around him, as if to assure himself they were alone, and dropped his voice, as he answered—

"Ah! Kit, they have come to, since this rebel scoundrel, Griffith, has been brought into the Abbey; we were favoured with the company of even Miss Howard, in the dining-room, to-day. There was a good deal of 'dear uncleing,' and 'fears that my life might be exposed by the quarrels and skirmishes of these desperadoes who have landed;' as if an old fellow, who served through the whole war, from '56 to '63, was afraid to let his nose smell gunpowder, any more than if it were snuff! But it will be a hard matter to wheedle an old soldier out of his allegiance! This Griffith goes to the Tower, at least, Mr. Dillon."

"It would be advisable to commit his person to the civil authority, without delay."

"To the constable of the Tower, the Earl Cornwallis, a good and loyal nobleman, who is, at this moment, fighting the rebels in my own native province, Christopher," interrupted the colonel; "that will be what I call retributive justice; but," continued the veteran, rising with an air of gentlemanly dignity, "it will not do to permit even the constable of the Tower of London, to surpass the master of St. Ruth, in hospitality and kindness to his prisoners. I have ordered suitable refreshments to their apartments, and it is incumbent on me to see that my commands have been properly obeyed. Arrangements must also be made for the reception of this Captain Barnstable, who will, doubtless, soon be here."

"Within the hour, at farthest," said Dillon, looking uneasily at his watch.

"We must be stirring, boy," continued the colonel, moving towards the door that led to the apartments of his prisoners; "but there is a courtesy due to the ladies, as well as to those unfortunate violators of the laws—go, Christopher, convey my kindest wishes to Cecilia; she don't deserve them, the obstinate vixen, but then she is my brother Harry's child! and while there, you arch dog, plead your own cause. Mark Antony was a fool to you at a 'ruse,' and yet Mark was one of your successful suitors, too; there was that Queen of the Pyramids—"

The door closed on the excited veteran, at these words, and Dillon was left standing by himself, at the side of the table, musing, as if in doubt, whether to venture on the step that his kinsman had proposed, or not.

The greater part of the preceding discourse was unintelligible to the cockswain, who had waited its termination with extraordinary patience, in hopes he might obtain some information that he could render of service to the captives. Before he had time to decide on what was now best for him to do, Dillon, suddenly, determined to venture himself in the cloisters; and, swallowing a couple of glasses of wine in a breath, he passed the hesitating cockswain, who was concealed by the opening door, so closely as to brush his person, and moved down the gallery with those rapid strides, which men, who act under the impulse of forced resolutions, are very apt to assume, as if to conceal their weakness from themselves. Tom hesitated no longer, but, aiding the impulse given to the door by Dillon as he passed, so as to darken the passage, he followed the sounds of the other's footsteps, while he trod, in the manner already described, the stone pavement of the gallery. Dillon paused an instant at the turning that led to the room of Borroughcliffe, but whether irresolute which way to urge his steps, or listening to the incautious and heavy tread of the cockswain, is not known; if the latter, he mistook them for the echoes of his own footsteps, and moved forward again, without making any discovery.

The light tap which Dillon gave on the door of the withdrawing-room of the cloisters, was answered by the soft voice of Cecilia Howard herself, who bid the applicant enter. There was a slight confusion evident in the manner of the gentleman as he complied with the bidding, and in its hesitancy, the door was, for an instant, neglected.

"I come, Miss Howard," said Dillon, "by the commands of your uncle, and, permit me to add, by my own—"

"May heaven shield us!" exclaimed Cecilia, clasping her hands in affright, and rising involuntarily from her couch; "are we, too, to be imprisoned and murdered?"

"Surely Miss Howard will not impute to me"—Dillon paused, observing that the wild looks, not only of Cecilia, but of Katherine and Alice Dunscombe, also, were directed at some other object, and turning, to his manifest terror, he beheld the gigantic frame of the cockswain, surmounted by an iron visage fixed in settled hostility, in possession of the only passage from the apartment.

"If there's murder to be done," said Tom, after surveying the astonished group with a stern eye, "it's as likely this here liar will be the one to do it, as another; but you have nothing to fear from a man who has followed the seas too long, and has grappled with too many monsters, both fish and flesh, not to know how to treat a helpless woman. None, who know him, will say, that Thomas Coffin ever used uncivil language, or unseaman-like conduct, to any of his mother's kind."

"Coffin!" exclaimed Katherine, advancing with a more confident air, from the corner, into which terror had driven her with her companions.

"Ay, Coffin," continued the old sailor, his grim features gradually relaxing, as he gazed on her bright looks; " 'tis a solemn word, but it's a name that passes over the shoals, among the islands, and along the cape, oftener than any other. My father was a Coffin, and my mother was a Joy; and the two names can count more flukes than all the rest in the island together; though the Worths, and the Gar'ners, and the Swaines, dart better harpoons, and set truer lances, than any men who come from the weather-side of the Atlantic."

Katherine listened to this digression in honour of the whalers of Nantucket, with marked complacency, and, when he concluded, she repeated, slowly—

"Coffin! this, then, is long-Tom!"

"Ay, ay, long-Tom, and no sham in the name either," returned the cockswain, suffering the stern indignation that had lowered around his hard visage, to relax into a low laugh, as he gazed on her animated features; "the Lord bless your smiling face and bright black eyes, young madam; you have heard of old long-Tom, then? most likely, 'twas something about the blow he strikes at the fish—ah! I'm old and I'm stiff, now, young madam, but, afore I was nineteen, I stood at the head of the dance, at a ball on the cape, and that with a partner almost as handsome as yourself—ay! and this was after I had three broad flukes logg'd against my name."

"No," said Katherine, advancing in her eagerness a step or two nigher to the old tar, her cheeks flushing while she spoke, "I had heard of you as an instructor in a seaman's duty, as the faithful cockswain, nay, I may say, as the devoted companion and friend of Mr. Richard Barnstable—but, perhaps, you come now as the bearer of some message or letter from that gentleman."

The sound of his commander's name suddenly revived the recollection of Coffin, and with it, all the fierce sternness of his manner returned. Bending his eyes keenly on the cowering form of Dillon, he said, in those deep, harsh tones, that seem peculiar to men, who have braved the elements, until they appear to have imbibed some of their roughest qualities—

"Liar! how now? what brought old Tom Coffin into these shoals and narrow channels? was it a letter? ha! but by the Lord that maketh the winds to blow, and teacheth the lost mariner how to steer over the wide waters, you shall sleep this night, villain, on the planks of the Ariel; and if it be the will of God, that beautiful piece of handicraft is to sink at her moorings, like a worthless hulk, ye shall still sleep in her; ay, and a sleep that shall not end, 'till they call all hands, to foot up the days'-work of this life, at the close of man's longest voyage."

The extraordinary vehemence, the language, the attitude of the old seaman, commanding in its energy, and the honest indignation that shone in every look of his keen eyes, together with the nature of the address, and its paralyzing effect on Dillon, who quailed before it like the stricken deer, united to keep the female listeners, for many moments, silent, through amazement. During this brief period, Tom advanced upon his nerveless victim, and lashing his arms together behind his back, he fastened him, by a strong cord, to the broad canvass belt that he constantly wore around his own body, leaving to himself, by this arrangement, the free use of his arms and weapons of offence, while he secured his captive.

"Surely," said Cecilia, recovering her recollection the first of the astonished group, "Mr. Barnstable has not commissioned you to offer this violence to my uncle's kinsman, under the roof of Colonel Howard?—Miss Plowden, your friend has strangely forgotten himself, in this transaction, if this man acts in obedience to his orders!"

"My friend, my cousin Howard," returned Katherine, "would never commission his cockswain, or any one, to do an unworthy deed. Speak, honest sailor; why do you commit this outrage on the worthy Mr. Dillon, Colonel Howard's kinsman, and a cupboard cousin of St. Ruth's Abbey?"

"Nay, Katherine—"

"Nay, Cecilia, be patient, and let the stranger have utterance; he may solve the difficulty altogether."

The cockswain, understanding that an explanation was expected from his lips, addressed himself to the task, with an energy suitable both to the subject and to his own feelings. In a very few words, though a little obscured by his peculiar diction, he made his listeners understand the confidence that Barnstable had reposed in Dillon, and the treachery of the latter. They heard him with increased astonishment, and Cecilia hardly allowed him time to conclude, before she exclaimed—

"And did Colonel Howard, could Colonel Howard listen to this treacherous project?"

"Ay, they spliced it together among them," returned Tom; "though one part of this cruise will turn out but badly."

"Even Borroughcliffe, cold and hardened as he appears to be by habit, would spurn at such dishonour," added Miss Howard.

"But, Mr. Barnstable?" at length Katherine succeeded in saying, when her feelings permitted her utterance, "said you not, that soldiers were in quest of him?"

"Ay, ay, young madam," the cockswain replied, smiling with grim ferocity, "they are in chase, but he has shifted his anchorage; and even if they should find him, his long pikes would make short work of a dozen red-coats. The Lord of tempests and calms have mercy though, on the schooner! Ah! young madam, she is as lovely to the eyes of an old sea-faring man, as any of your kind can be to human nature."

"But why this delay?—away then, honest Tom, and reveal the treachery to your commander; you may not yet be too late—why delay a moment?"

"The ship tarries for want of a pilot—I could carry three fathom over the shoals of Nantucket, the darkest night that ever shut the windows of heaven, but I should be likely to run upon breakers in this navigation. As it was, I was near getting into company that I should have had to fight my way out of."

"If that be all, follow me," cried the ardent Katherine; "I will conduct you to a path that leads to the ocean, without approaching the sentinels."

Until this moment, Dillon had entertained a secret expectation of a rescue, but when he heard this proposal, he felt his blood retreating to his heart, from every part of his agitated frame, and his last hope seemed wrested from him. Raising himself from the abject, shrinking attitude, in which both shame and dread had conspired to keep him, as though he had been fettered to the spot, he approached Cecilia, and cried, in tones of horror—

"Do not, do not consent, Miss Howard, to abandon me to the fury of this man! your uncle, your honourable uncle, even now, applauded and united with me in my enterprise, which is no more than a common artifice in war."

"My uncle would unite, Mr. Dillon, in no project of deliberate treachery, like this," said Cecilia, coldly.

"He did, I swear by—"

"Liar!" interrupted the deep tones of the cockswain.

Dillon shivered with agony and terror, while the sounds of this appalling voice sunk into his inmost soul; but as the gloom of the night, the secret ravines of the cliffs, and the turbulence of the ocean, flashed across his imagination, he again yielded to a dread of the horrors to which he should be exposed, in encountering them at the mercy of his powerful enemy, and he continued his solicitations—

"Hear me, once more hear me—Miss Howard, I beseech you, hear me; am I not of your own blood and country! will you see me abandoned to the wild, merciless, malignant fury of this man, who will transfix me with that—oh! God! if you had but seen the sight I beheld in the Alacrity!—hear me, Miss Howard, for the love you bear your Maker, intercede for me. Mr. Griffith shall be released—"

"Liar!" again interrupted the cockswain.

"What promises he?" asked Cecilia, turning her averted face once more at the miserable captive.

"Nothing at all that will be fulfilled," said Katherine; "follow, honest Tom, and I, at least, will conduct you in good faith."

"Cruel, obdurate Miss Plowden; gentle, kind Miss Alice, you will not refuse to raise your voice in my favour; your heart is not hardened by any imaginary dangers to those you love."

"Nay, address not me," said Alice, bending her meek eyes to the floor; "I trust your life is in no danger, and I pray that he who has the power, will have the mercy, to see you unharmed."

"Away," said Tom, grasping the collar of the helpless Dillon, and rather carrying than leading him into the gallery; "if a sound, one quarter as loud as a young porpoise makes, when he draws his first breath, comes from you, villain, you shall see the sight of the Alacrity over again. My harpoon keeps its edge well, and the old arm can yet drive it to the seizing."

This menace effectually silenced even the hard, perturbed breathings of the captive, who, with his conductor, followed the light steps of Katherine, through some of the secret mazes of the building, until, in a few minutes, they issued through a small door, into the open air. Without pausing to deliberate, Miss Plowden led the cockswain through the grounds, to a different wicket from the one by which he had entered the paddock, and pointing to the path, which might be dimly traced along the faded herbage, she bad God bless him, in a voice that discovered her interest in his safety, and vanished from his sight, like an aerial being.

Tom needed no incentive to his speed, now that his course lay so plainly before him, but, loosening his pistols in his belt, and poising his harpoon, he crossed the fields at a gait that compelled his companion to exert his utmost powers, in the way of walking, to equal. Once or twice, Dillon ventured to utter a word or two, but a stern "silence," from the cockswain, warned him to cease, until, perceiving that they were approaching the cliffs, he made a final effort to obtain his liberty, by hurriedly promising a large bribe. The cockswain made no reply, and the captive was secretly hoping that his scheme was producing its wonted effects, when he unexpectedly felt the keen, cold edge of the barbed iron of the harpoon pressing against his breast, through the opening of his ruffles, and even raising the skin.

"Liar," said Tom, "another word, and I'll drive it through your heart."

From that moment, Dillon was as silent as the grave. They reached the edge of the cliffs, without encountering the party that had been sent in quest of Barnstable, and at a point near where they had landed. The old seaman paused an instant on the verge of the precipice, and cast his experienced eyes along the wide expanse of water that lay before him. The sea was no longer sleeping, but already in heavy motion, and rolling its surly waves against the base of the rocks on which he stood, scattering their white crests high in foam. The cockswain, after bending his looks along the whole line of the eastern horizon, gave utterance to a low and stifled groan, and then striking the staff of his harpoon violently against the earth, he pursued his way along the very edge of the cliffs, muttering certain dreadful denunciations, which the conscience of his appalled listener did not fail to apply to himself. It appeared to the latter, that his angry and excited leader sought the

giddy verge of the precipice with a sort of wanton recklessness, so daring were the steps that he took along its brow,
notwithstanding the darkness of the hour, and the violence of
the blasts that occasionally rushed by them, leaving behind a
kind of reaction, that more than once brought the life of the
manacled captive in imminent jeopardy. But it would seem,
the wary cockswain had a motive for this, apparently, inconsiderate desperation. When they had made good quite half the
distance between the point where Barnstable had landed, and
that where he had appointed to meet his cockswain, the
sounds of voices were brought indistinctly to their ears, in
one of the momentary pauses of the rushing winds, and
caused the cockswain to make a dead stand in his progress.
He listened intently, for a single minute, when his resolution
appeared to be taken. He turned to Dillon, and spoke; though
his voice was suppressed and low, it was deep and resolute.

"One word, and you die; over the cliffs. You must take a
seaman's ladder; there is footing on the rocks, and crags for
your hands. Over the cliff, I bid ye, or I'll cast ye into the sea,
as I would a dead enemy."

"Mercy, mercy," implored Dillon; "I could not do it in the
day; by this light I shall surely perish."

"Over with ye," said Tom, "or—"

Dillon waited for no more, but descended, with trembling
steps, the dangerous precipice that lay before him. He was
followed by the cockswain, with a haste that unavoidably dislodged his captive from the trembling stand he had taken on
the shelf of a rock, who, to his increased horror, found himself dangling in the air, his body impending over the sullen
surf, that was tumbling in, with violence, upon the rocks beneath him. An involuntary shriek burst from Dillon, as he felt
his person thrust from the narrow shelf, and his cry sounded
amidst the tempest, like the screechings of the spirit of the
storm.

"Another such call, and I cut your tow-line, villain," said
the determined seaman, "when nothing short of eternity will
bring you up."

The sounds of footsteps and voices were now distinctly audible, and presently a party of armed men appeared on the
edges of the rocks, directly above them.

"It was a human voice," said one of them, "and like a man in distress."

"It cannot be the men we are sent in search of," returned Sergeant Drill; "for no watch-word that I ever heard sounded like that cry."

"They say, that such cries are often heard, in storms, along this coast," said a voice, that was uttered with less of military confidence than the two others; "and they are thought to come from drowned seamen."

A feeble laugh arose among the listeners, and one or two forced jokes were made, at the expense of their superstitious comrade; but the scene did not fail to produce its effect on even the most sturdy among the unbelievers in the marvellous; for, after a few more similar remarks, the whole party retired from the cliffs, at a pace that might have been accelerated by the nature of their discourse. The cockswain, who had stood, all this time, firm as the rock which supported him, bearing up not only his own weight, but the person of Dillon also, raised his head above the brow of the precipice, as they withdrew, to reconnoitre, and then drawing up the nearly insensible captive, and placing him in safety on the bank, he followed himself. Not a moment was wasted in unnecessary explanations, but Dillon found himself again urged forward, with the same velocity as before. In a few minutes they gained the desired ravine, down which Tom plunged, with a seaman's nerve, dragging his prisoner after him, and directly they stood where the waves rose to their feet, as they flowed far and foaming across the sands. The cockswain stooped so low as to bring the crests of the billows in a line with the horizon, when he discovered the dark boat playing in the outer edge of the surf.

"What hoa! Ariels there!" shouted Tom, in a voice that the growing tempest carried to the ears of the retreating soldiers, who quickened their footsteps, as they listened to sounds which their fears taught them to believe supernatural.

"Who hails?" cried the well-known voice of Barnstable.

"Once your master, now your servant," answered the cockswain, with a watch-word of his own invention.

" 'Tis he," returned the lieutenant; "veer away, boys, veer away. You must wade into the surf."

Tom caught Dillon in his arms, and throwing him, like a cork, across his shoulder, he dashed into the streak of foam that was bearing the boat on its crest, and before his companion had time for remonstrance or entreaty, he found himself once more by the side of Barnstable.

"Who have we here?" asked the lieutenant; "this is not Griffith!"

"Haul out, and weigh your grapnel," said the excited cockswain; "and then, boys, if you love the Ariel, pull while the life and the will is left in you."

Barnstable knew his man, and not another question was asked, until the boat was without the breakers; now skimming the rounded summits of the waves, or settling into the hollows of the seas, but always cutting the waters asunder, as she urged her course, with amazing velocity, towards the haven where the schooner had been left at anchor. Then, in a few, but bitter sentences, the cockswain explained to his commander the treachery of Dillon, and the danger of the schooner.

"The soldiers are slow at a night muster," Tom concluded, "and from what I overheard, the express will have to make a crooked course, to double the head of the bay; so, that but for this north-easter, we might weather upon them yet; but it's a matter that lies altogether in the will of Providence. Pull, my hearties, pull—every thing depends on your oars to-night."

Barnstable listened, in deep silence, to this unexpected narration, which sounded in the ears of Dillon like his funeral knell. At length, the suppressed voice of the lieutenant was heard, also, uttering—

"Wretch! if I should cast you into the sea, as food for the fishes, who could blame me? But if my schooner goes to the bottom, she shall prove your coffin."

# Chapter XXIV.

"Had I been any God of power, I would
Have sunk the sea within the earth, ere
It should the good ship so have swallowed."
*The Tempest*, I.i.10−12.

THE ARMS of Dillon were released from their confinement, by the cockswain, as a measure of humane caution against accidents, when they entered the surf, and the captive now availed himself of the circumstance, to bury his features in the folds of his attire, where he brooded over the events of the last few hours with that mixture of malignant passion and pusillanimous dread of the future, that formed the chief ingredients in his character. From this state of apparent quietude, neither Barnstable nor Tom seemed disposed to rouse him by their remarks, for both were too much engaged with their own gloomy forebodings, to indulge in any unnecessary words. An occasional ejaculation from the former, as if to propitiate the spirit of the storm, as he gazed on the troubled appearance of the elements, or a cheering cry from the latter, to animate his crew, were alone heard amid the sullen roaring of the waters, and the mournful whistling of the winds, that swept heavily across the broad waste of the German ocean. There might have been an hour consumed thus, in a vigorous struggle between the seamen and the growing billows, when the boat doubled the northern headland of the desired haven, and shot, at once, from its boisterous passage along the margin of the breakers, into the placid waters of the sequestered bay. The passing blasts were still heard rushing above the high-lands that surrounded, and, in fact, formed the estuary, but the profound stillness of deep night, pervaded the secret recesses, along the unruffled surface of its waters. The shadows of the hills seemed to have accumulated, like a mass of gloom, in the centre of the basin, and though every eye involuntarily turned to search, it was in vain that the anxious seamen endeavoured to discover their little vessel, through its density. While the boat glided into this quiet scene, Barnstable anxiously observed—

267

"Every thing is as still as death."

"God send it is not the stillness of death!" ejaculated the cockswain; "here, here," he continued, speaking in a lower tone, as if fearful of being overheard, "here she lies, sir, more to-port; look into the streak of clear sky above the marsh, on the starboard hand of the wood, there; that long black line is her main-top-mast; I know it by the rake; and there is her night-pennant fluttering about that bright star; ay, ay, sir, there go our own stars aloft yet, dancing among the stars in the heavens! God bless her! God bless her! she rides as easy and as quiet as a gull asleep!"

"I believe all in her sleep too," returned his commander; "ha! by heaven, we have arrived in good time; the soldiers are moving!"

The quick eye of Barnstable had detected the glimmering of passing lanterns, as they flitted across the embrasures of the battery, and, at the next moment, the guarded but distinct sounds of an active bustle, on the decks of the schooner, were plainly audible. The lieutenant was rubbing his hands together, with a sort of ecstacy, that probably will not be understood by the great majority of our readers, while long-Tom was actually indulging in a paroxysm of his low, spiritless laughter, as these certain intimations of the safety of the Ariel, and of the vigilance of her crew, were conveyed to their ears; when the whole hull and taper spars of their floating home, became unexpectedly visible, and the sky, the placid basin, and the adjacent hills, were illuminated by a flash as sudden and as vivid as the keenest lightning. Both Barnstable and his cockswain, seemed instinctively to strain their eyes towards the schooner, with an effort to surpass human vision, but ere the rolling reverberations of the report of a heavy piece of ordnance, from the heights, had commenced, the dull, whistling rush of the shot swept over their heads, like the moaning of a hurricane, and was succeeded by the plash of the waters, which was followed, in a breath, by the rattling of the mass of iron, as it bounded with violent fury from rock to rock, shivering and tearing the fragments that lined the margin of the bay.

"A bad aim with the first gun, generally leaves your enemy clean decks," said the cockswain, with his deliberate sort of philosophy; "smoke makes but dim spectacles; besides, the night always grows darkest, as you call off the morning watch."

"That boy is a miracle for his years!" rejoined the delighted lieutenant; "see, Tom, the younker has shifted his birth in the dark, and the Englishmen have fired by the day-range they must have taken, for we left him in a direct line between the battery and yon hommoc! what would have become of us, if that heavy fellow had plunged upon our decks, and gone out below the water-line!"

"We should have sunk into English mud, for eternity, as sure as our metal and kentledge would have taken us down," responded Tom; "such a point-blanker would have torn off a streak of our wales, outboard, and not even left the marines time to say a prayer! tend bow there!"

It is not to be supposed that the crew of the whale-boat continued idle, during this interchange of opinions between the lieutenant and his cockswain; on the contrary, the sight of their vessel acted on them like a charm, and, believing that all necessity for caution was now over, they had expended their utmost strength in efforts, that had already brought them, as the last words of Tom indicated, to the side of the Ariel. Though every nerve of Barnstable was thrilling with the excitement produced, by his feelings passing from a state of the most doubtful apprehension, to that of a revived and almost confident hope of effecting his escape, he assumed the command of his vessel, with all that stern but calm authority, that seamen find it most necessary to exert, in the moments of extremest danger. Any one of the heavy shot that their enemies continued to hurl from their heights into the darkness of the haven, he well knew must prove fatal to them, as it would, unavoidably, pass through the slight fabric of the Ariel, and open a passage to the water, that no means he possessed could remedy. His mandates were, therefore, issued, with a full perception of the critical nature of the emergency, but with that collectedness of manner, and intonation of voice, that were best adapted to enforce a ready and animated obedience. Under this impulse, the crew of the schooner soon got their anchor freed from the bottom, and, seizing their sweeps, they forced her, by their united efforts, directly in the face of the battery, under that shore, whose summit was now crowned with a canopy of smoke, that every discharge of the ordnance tinged with dim colours, like the faintest tints that are reflected from the clouds toward a setting sun. So long as the seamen were enabled to keep their little bark under the cover of the hill, they were, of course, safe; but Barnstable perceived, as they emerged from its shadow, and were drawing nigh the passage which led into the ocean, that the action of his sweeps would no longer avail them, against the currents of air they encountered, neither would the darkness conceal their movements from his enemy, who had already employed men on the shore to discern the position of the schooner. Throwing off at once, therefore, all appearance of disguise, he gave forth the word to spread the canvass of his vessel, in his ordinary cheerful manner.

"Let them do their worst now, Merry," he added; "we have brought them to a distance that I think will keep their iron above water, and we have no dodge about us, younker!"

"It must be keener marksmen than the militia, or volunteers, or fencibles, or whatever they call themselves, behind yon grass-bank, to frighten the saucy Ariel from the wind," returned the reckless boy; "but why have you brought Jonah aboard us again, sir? look at him, by the light of the cabin lamp; he winks at every gun, as if he expected the shot would hull his own ugly, yellow physiognomy. And what tidings have we, sir, from Mr. Griffith, and the marine?"

"Name him not," said Barnstable, pressing the shoulder on which he lightly leaned, with a convulsive grasp, that caused the boy to yield with pain; "name him not, Merry; I want my temper and my faculties at this moment undisturbed, and thinking of the wretch unfits me for my duty. But, there will come a time! go forward, sir; we feel the wind, and have a narrow passage to work through."

The boy obeyed a mandate which was given in the usual prompt manner of their profession, and which, he well understood, was intended to intimate, that the distance which years and rank had created between them, but which Barnstable often chose to forget while communing with Merry, was now to be resumed. The sails had been loosened and set; and, as the vessel approached the throat of the passage, the gale, which was blowing with increasing violence, began to make a very sensible impression on the light bark. The cockswain, who, in the absence of most of the inferior officers, had been acting, on the forecastle, the part of one who felt, from his years and experience, that he had some right to advise, if not to command, at such a juncture, now walked to the station which his commander had taken, near the helmsman, as if willing to place himself in the way of being seen.

"Well, Master Coffin," said Barnstable, who well understood the propensity his old shipmate had to commune with him, on all important occasions, "what think you of the cruise, now? Those gentlemen on the hill make a great noise, but I have lost even the whistling of their shot; one would think they could see our sails against the broad band of light which is opening to seaward."

"Ay, ay, sir, they see us, and mean to hit us, too, but we are running across their fire, and that with a ten-knot breeze; but when we heave in stays, and get in a line with their guns, we shall see, and, it may be, feel, more of their work than we do now; a thirty-two an't trained as easily as a fowling-piece or a ducking gun."

Barnstable was struck with the truth of this observation, but as there existed an immediate necessity for placing the schooner in the very situation to which the other alluded, he gave his orders at once, and the vessel came about, and ran with her head pointing towards the sea, in as short a time as we have taken to record it.

"There, they have us now, or never," cried the lieutenant, when the evolution was completed; "if we fetch to windward of the northern point, we shall lay out into the offing, and in ten minutes we might laugh at Queen Anne's pocket-piece; which, you know, old boy, sent a ball from Dover to Calais."

"Ay, sir, I've heard of the gun," returned the grave seaman, "and a lively piece it must have been, if the streights were always of the same width they are now. But I see that, Captain Barnstable, which is more dangerous than a dozen of the heaviest cannon that were ever cast, can be at half a league's distance. The water is bubbling through our lee-scuppers, already, sir."

"And what of that? haven't I buried her guns often, and yet kept every spar in her without crack or splinter?"

"Ay, ay, sir, you have done it, and can do it again, where there is sea-room, which is all that a man wants for comfort in this life. But when we are out of these chops, we shall be embayed, with a heavy north-easter setting dead into the bight; it is that which I fear, Captain Barnstable, more than all the powder and ball in the whole island."

"And yet, Tom, the balls are not to be despised, either; those fellows have found out their range, and send their iron within hail, again; we walk pretty fast, Master Coffin, but a thirty-two can out-travel us, with the best wind that ever blew."

Tom threw a cursory glance towards the battery, which had renewed its fire with a spirit that denoted they saw their object, as he answered—

"It is never worth a man's while to strive to dodge a shot, for they are all commissioned to do their work, the same as a ship is commissioned to cruise in certain latitudes; but for the winds and the weather, they are given for a seafaring man to guard against, by making or shortening sail, as the case may be. Now, the headland to the southward stretches full three leagues to windward, and the shoals lie to the north; among which God keep us from ever running this craft again!"

"We will beat her out of the bight, old fellow," cried the lieutenant; "we shall have a leg of three leagues in length to do it in."

"I have known longer legs too short," returned the cockswain, shaking his head; "a tumbling sea, with a lee-tide, on a lee-shore, make a sad lee-way."

The lieutenant was in the act of replying to this saying, with a cheerful laugh, when the whistling of a passing shot was instantly succeeded by the crash of splintered wood, and at the next moment the head of the main-mast, after tottering for an instant in the gale, fell toward the deck, bringing with it the main-sail, and the long line of top-mast, that had been bearing the emblems of America, as the cockswain had expressed it, among the stars of the heavens.

"That was a most unlucky hit!" Barnstable suffered to escape him, in the concern of the moment; but, instantly resuming all his collectedness of manner and voice, he gave his orders to clear the wreck, and secure the fluttering canvass.

The mournful forebodings of Tom seemed to vanish with the appearance of a necessity for his exertions, and he was foremost among the crew in executing the orders of their commander. The loss of all the sail on the main-mast forced the Ariel so much from her course, as to render it difficult to weather the point, that jutted, under her lee, for some distance into the ocean. This desirable object was, however, effected, by the skill of Barnstable, aided by the excellent properties of his vessel; and the schooner, borne down by the power of the gale, from whose fury she had now no protection, passed heavily along the land, heading, as far as possible, from the breakers, while the seamen were engaged in making their preparations to display as much of their main-sail, as the stump of the mast would allow them to spread. The firing from the battery ceased, as the Ariel rounded the little promontory; but Barnstable, whose gaze was now bent intently on the ocean, soon perceived that, as his cockswain had predicted, he had a much more threatening danger to encounter, in the elements. When their damages were repaired, so far as circumstances would permit, the cockswain returned to his wonted station near the lieutenant, and after a momentary pause, during which his eyes roved over the rigging, with a seaman's scrutiny, he resumed the discourse.

"It would have been better for us that the best man in the schooner should have been dubb'd of a limb, by that shot, than that the Ariel should have lost her best leg; a main-sail, close-reefed, may be prudent canvass, as the wind blows, but it holds a poor luff to keep a craft to windward."

"What would you have, Tom Coffin!" retorted his commander; "you see she draws ahead, and off-shore; do you expect a vessel to fly in the very teeth of the gale, or would you have me ware and beach her, at once?"

"I would have nothing, nothing, Captain Barnstable," returned the old seaman, sensibly touched at his commander's displeasure; "you are as able as any man who ever trod a plank to work her into an offing; but, sir, when that soldier-officer told me of the scheme to sink the Ariel at her anchor, there were such feelings come athwart my philosophy as never crossed it afore. I thought I saw her a wrack, as plainly, ay, as plainly as you may see the stump of that mast; and, I will own it, for it's as natural to love the craft you sail in, as it is to love one's self, I will own that my manhood fetched a heavy lee-lurch at the sight."

"Away with ye, ye old sea-croaker! forward with ye, and see that the head-sheets are trimmed flat. But hold! come hither, Tom; if you have sights of wrecks, and sharks, and other beautiful objects, keep them stowed in your own silly brain; don't make a ghost-parlour of my forecastle. The lads begin to look to leeward, now, oftener than I would have them. Go, sirrah, go, and take example from Mr. Merry, who is seated on your namesake there, and is singing as if he were a chorister in his father's church."

"Ah! Captain Barnstable, Mr. Merry is a boy, and knows nothing, so fears nothing. But I shall obey your orders, sir; and if the men fall astern, this gale, it shan't be for any thing they'll hear from old Tom Coffin."

The cockswain lingered a moment, notwithstanding his promised obedience, and then ventured to request, that—

"Captain Barnstable would please to call Mr. Merry from the gun; for I know, from having followed the seas my natural life, that singing in a gale is sure to bring the wind down upon a vessel the heavier; for He who rules the tempests is displeased that man's voice shall be heard, when He chooses to send His own breath on the water."

Barnstable was at a loss, whether to laugh at his cockswain's infirmity, or to yield to the impression which his earnest and solemn manner had a powerful tendency to produce, amid such a scene. But, making an effort to shake off the superstitious awe that he felt creeping around his own heart, the lieutenant relieved the mind of the worthy old seaman so far as to call the careless boy from his perch, to his own side; where respect for the sacred character of the quarter-deck, instantly put an end to the lively air he had been humming. Tom walked slowly forward, apparently much relieved by the reflection that he had effected so important an object.

The Ariel continued to struggle against the winds and ocean for several hours longer, before the day broke on the tempestuous scene, and the anxious mariners were enabled to form a more accurate estimate of their real danger. As the violence of the gale increased, the canvass of the schooner had been gradually reduced, until she was unable to show more than was absolutely necessary to prevent her driving, help-lessly, on the land. Barnstable watched the appearance of the weather, as the light slowly opened upon them, with an in-tense anxiety, which denoted, that the presentiments of the cockswain were no longer deemed idle. On looking to wind-ward, he beheld the green masses of water that were rolling in towards the land, with a violence that seemed irresistible, crowned with ridges of foam; and there were moments when the air appeared filled with sparkling gems, as the rays of the rising sun fell upon the spray that was swept from wave to wave. Towards the land, the view was still more appalling. The cliffs, but a short half-league under the lee of the schoo-ner, were, at times, nearly hid from the eye by the pyramids of water, which the furious element, so suddenly restrained in its violence, cast high into the air, as if seeking to overleap the boundaries that nature had fixed to its dominion. The whole coast, from the distant head-land at the south, to the well-known shoals that stretched far beyond their course, in the opposite direction, displayed a broad belt of foam, into which, it would have been certain destruction, for the proud-est ship that ever swam, to have entered. Still the Ariel floated on the billows, lightly and in safety, though yielding to the impulses of the waters, and, at times, appearing to be en-gulphed in the yawning chasms, which, apparently, opened beneath her to receive the little fabric. The low rumour of acknowledged danger, had found its way through the schoo-ner, and the seamen, after fastening their hopeless looks on the small spot of canvass that they were still able to show to the tempest, would turn to view the dreary line of coast, that seemed to offer so gloomy an alternative. Even Dillon, to whom the report of their danger had found its way, crept from his place of concealment in the cabin, and moved about the decks, unheeded, devouring, with greedy ears, such opin-ions as fell from the lips of the sullen mariners.

At this moment of appalling apprehension, the cockswain exhibited the calmest resignation. He knew all had been done, that lay in the power of man, to urge their little vessel from the land, and it was now too evident to his experienced eyes, that it had been done in vain; but, considering himself as a sort of fixture in the schooner, he was quite prepared to abide her fate, be it for better or for worse. The settled look of gloom that gathered around the frank brow of Barnstable, was, in no degree, connected with any considerations of himself, but proceeded from that sort of parental responsibility, from which the sea-commander is never exempt. The discipline of the crew, however, still continued perfect and unyielding. There had, it is true, been a slight movement made by one or two of the older seamen, which indicated an intention to drown the apprehensions of death in ebriety; but Barnstable had called for his pistols, in a tone that checked the procedure instantly, and, although the fatal weapons were, untouched by him, left to lie exposed on the capstern, where they had been placed by his servant, not another symptom of insubordination appeared among the devoted crew. There was even, what to a landsman might seem an appalling affectation of attention to the most trifling duties of the vessel; and the men, who, it should seem, ought to be devoting the brief moments of their existence to the mighty business of the hour, were constantly called to attend to the most trivial details of their profession. Ropes were coiled, and the slightest damages occasioned by the waves, which at short intervals, swept across the low decks of the Ariel, were repaired, with the same precision and order, as if she yet lay embayed in the haven from which she had just been driven. In this manner, the arm of authority was kept extended over the silent crew, not with the vain desire to preserve a lingering, though useless exercise of power, but with a view to maintain that unity of action, that now could alone afford them even a ray of hope.

"She can make no head against this sea, under that rag of canvass," said Barnstable, gloomily; addressing the cockswain, who, with folded arms, and an air of cool resignation, was balancing his body on the verge of the quarter-deck, while the schooner was plunging madly into waves that nearly buried her in their bosom; "the poor little thing trembles like a frightened child, as she meets the water."

Tom sighed heavily, and shook his head, before he answered—

"If we could have kept the head of the main-mast an hour longer, we might have got an offing, and fetched to windward of the shoals; but, as it is, sir, mortal man can't drive a craft to windward—she sets bodily in to land, and will be in the breakers in less than an hour, unless God wills that the wind shall cease to blow."

"We have no hope left us, but to anchor; our ground tackle may yet bring her up."

Tom turned to his commander, and replied, solemnly, and with that assurance of manner, that long experience only can give a man in moments of great danger—

"If our sheet-cable was bent to our heaviest anchor, this sea would bring it home, though nothing but her launch was riding by it. A north-easter in the German ocean must and will blow itself out; nor shall we get the crown of the gale until the sun falls over the land. Then, indeed, it may lull; for the winds do often seem to reverence the glory of the heavens, too much to blow their might in its very face!"

"We must do our duty to ourselves and the country," returned Barnstable; "go, get the two bowers spliced, and have a kedge bent to a hawser; we'll back our two anchors together, and veer to the better end of two hundred and forty fathoms; it may yet bring her up. See all clear there for anchoring, and cutting away the masts—we'll leave the wind nothing but a naked hull to whistle over."

"Ay, if there was nothing but the wind, we might yet live to see the sun sink behind them hills," said the cockswain; "but what hemp can stand the strain of a craft that is buried, half the time, to her foremast in the water!"

The order was, however, executed by the crew, with a sort of desperate submission to the will of their commander; and when the preparations were completed, the anchors and kedge were dropped to the bottom, and the instant that the Ariel tended to the wind, the axe was applied to the little that was left of her long, raking masts. The crash of the falling spars, as they came, in succession, across the decks of the vessel, appeared to produce no sensation amid that scene of complicated danger, but the seamen proceeded in silence to their hopeless duty, of clearing the wrecks. Every eye followed the floating timbers, as the waves swept them away from the vessel, with a sort of feverish curiosity, to witness the effect produced by their collision with those rocks that lay so fearfully near them; but long before the spars entered the wide border of foam, they were hid from view by the furious element in which they floated. It was, now, felt by the whole crew of the Ariel, that their last means of safety had been adopted, and, at each desperate and headlong plunge the vessel took, into the bosom of the seas that rolled upon her forecastle, the anxious seamen thought they could perceive the yielding of the iron that yet clung to the bottom, or could hear the violent surge of the parting strands of the cable, that still held them to their anchors. While the minds of the sailors were agitated with the faint hopes that had been excited, by the movements of their schooner, Dillon had been permitted to wander about the deck unnoticed; his rolling eyes, hard breathing, and clenched hands, excited no observation among the men, whose thoughts were yet dwelling on the means of safety. But, now, when, with a sort of frenzied desperation, he would follow the retiring waters along the decks, and venture his person nigh the group that had collected around and on the gun of the cockswain, glances of fierce or of sullen vengeance were cast at him, that conveyed threats of a nature that he was too much agitated to understand.

"If ye are tired of this world, though your time, like my own, is probably but short in it," said Tom to him, as he passed the cockswain in one of his turns, "you can go forward among the men; but if ye have need of the moments to foot up the reck'ning of your doings among men, afore ye're brought to face your maker, and hear the log-book of heaven, I would advise you to keep as nigh as possible to Captain Barnstable or myself."

"Will you promise to save me, if the vessel is wrecked!" exclaimed Dillon, catching at the first sounds of friendly interest that had reached his ears, since he had been recaptured; "Oh! if you will, I can secure you future ease; yes, wealth, for the remainder of your days!"

"Your promises have been too ill kept, afore this, for the peace of your soul," returned the cockswain, without bitterness, though sternly; "but it is not in me to strike even a whale, that is already spouting blood."

The intercessions of Dillon were interrupted by a dreadful cry, that arose among the men forward, and which sounded with increased horror, amid the roarings of the tempest. The schooner rose on the breast of a wave at the same instant, and, falling off with her broadside to the sea, she drove in towards the cliffs, like a bubble on the rapids of a cataract.

"Our ground tackle has parted," said Tom, with his resigned patience of manner undisturbed; "she shall die as easy as man can make her!" While he yet spoke, he seized the tiller, and gave to the vessel such a direction, as would be most likely to cause her to strike the rocks with her bows foremost.

There was, for one moment, an expression of exquisite anguish, betrayed in the dark countenance of Barnstable; but at the next, it passed away, and he spoke cheerfully to his men—

"Be steady, my lads, be calm; there is yet a hope of life for *you*—our light draught will let us run in close to the cliffs, and it is still falling water—see your boats clear, and be steady."

The crew of the whale-boat, aroused, by this speech, from a sort of stupor, sprang into their light vessel, which was quickly lowered into the sea, and kept riding on the foam, free from the sides of the schooner, by the powerful exertions of the men. The cry for the cockswain was earnest and repeated, but Tom shook his head, without replying, still grasping the tiller, and keeping his eyes steadily bent on the chaos of waters, into which they were driving. The launch, the largest boat of the two, was cut loose from the "gripes," and the bustle and exertion of the moment rendered the crew insensible to the horror of the scene that surrounded them. But the loud, hoarse call of the cockswain, to "look out—secure yourselves!" suspended even their efforts, and at that instant the Ariel settled on a wave that melted from under her, heavily on the rocks. The shock was so violent, as to throw all who disregarded the warning cry, from their feet, and the universal quiver that pervaded the vessel was like the last shudder of animated nature. For a time long enough to breathe, the least experienced among the men supposed the danger to be past; but a wave of great height followed the one that had deserted them, and raising the vessel again, threw her roughly still further on her bed of rocks, and at the same time its crest broke over her quarter, sweeping the length of her decks, with a fury that was almost resistless. The shuddering seamen beheld their loosened boat, driven from their grasp, and dashed against the base of the cliffs, where no fragment of her wreck could be traced, at the receding of the waters. But the passing billow had thrown the vessel into a position which, in some measure, protected her decks from the violence of those that succeeded it.

"Go, my boys, go," said Barnstable, as the moment of dreadful uncertainty passed; "you have still the whale-boat, and she, at least, will take you nigh the shore; go into her, my boys; God bless you, God bless you all; you have been faithful and honest fellows, and I believe he will not yet desert you; go, my friends, while there is a lull."

The seamen threw themselves, in a mass, into the light vessel, which nearly sunk under the unusual burthen; but when they looked around them, Barnstable, and Merry, Dillon, and the cockswain, were yet to be seen on the decks of the Ariel. The former was pacing, in deep, and perhaps bitter melancholy, the wet planks of the schooner, while the boy hung, unheeded, on his arm, uttering disregarded petitions to his commander, to desert the wreck. Dillon approached the side where the boat lay, again and again, but the threatening countenances of the seamen as often drove him back in despair. Tom had seated himself on the heel of the bowsprit; where he continued, in an attitude of quiet resignation, returning no other answers to the loud and repeated calls of his shipmates, than by waving his hand toward the shore.

"Now hear me," said the boy, urging his request to tears; "if not for my sake, or for your own sake, Mr. Barnstable, or for the hopes of God's mercy; go into the boat, for the love of my cousin Katherine."

The young lieutenant paused in his troubled walk, and for a moment, he cast a glance of hesitation at the cliffs; but, at the next instant, his eyes fell on the ruin of his vessel, and he answered—

"Never, boy, never; if my hour has come, I will not shrink from my fate."

"Listen to the men, dear sir; the boat will be swamped

along-side the wreck, and their cry is, that without you they will not let her go."

Barnstable motioned to the boat, to bid the boy enter it, and turned away in silence.

"Well," said Merry, with firmness, "if it be right that a lieutenant shall stay by the wreck, it must also be right for a midshipman; shove off; neither Mr. Barnstable nor myself will quit the vessel."

"Boy, your life has been intrusted to my keeping, and at my hands will it be required," said his commander, lifting the struggling youth, and tossing him into the arms of the seamen. "Away with ye, and God be with you; there is more weight in you, now, than can go safe to land."

Still, the seamen hesitated, for they perceived the cockswain moving, with a steady tread, along the deck, and they hoped he had relented, and would yet persuade the lieutenant to join his crew. But Tom, imitating the example of his commander, seized the latter, suddenly, in his powerful grasp, and threw him over the bulwarks, with an irresistible force. At the same moment, he cast the fast of the boat from the pin that held it, and lifting his broad hands high into the air, his voice was heard in the tempest.

"God's will be done with me," he cried; "I saw the first timber of the Ariel laid, and shall live just long enough to see it torn out of her bottom; after which I wish to live no longer."

But his shipmates were swept far beyond the sounds of his voice, before half these words were uttered. All command of the boat was rendered impossible, by the numbers it contained, as well as the raging of the surf; and, as it rose on the white crest of a wave, Tom saw his beloved little craft for the last time; it fell into a trough of the sea, and in a few moments more its fragments were ground into splinters on the adjacent rocks. The cockswain still remained where he had cast off the rope, and beheld the numerous heads and arms that appeared rising, at short intervals, on the waves; some making powerful and well-directed efforts to gain the sands, that were becoming visible as the tide fell, and others wildly tossed, in the frantic movements of helpless despair. The honest old seaman gave a cry of joy, as he saw Barnstable issue from the surf, bearing the form of Merry in safety to the sands, where, one by one, several seamen soon appeared also, dripping and exhausted. Many others of the crew were carried, in a similar manner, to places of safety; though, as Tom returned to his seat on the bowsprit, he could not conceal, from his reluctant eyes, the lifeless forms that were, in other spots, driven against the rocks, with a fury that soon left them but few of the outward vestiges of humanity.

Dillon and the cockswain were now the sole occupants of their dreadful station. The former stood, in a kind of stupid despair, a witness of the scene we have related; but as his curdled blood began again to flow more warmly through his heart, he crept close to the side of Tom, with that sort of selfish feeling that makes even hopeless misery more tolerable, when endured in participation with another.

"When the tide falls," he said, in a voice that betrayed the agony of fear, though his words expressed the renewal of hope, "we shall be able to walk to land."

"There was One, and only One, to whose feet the waters were the same as a dry deck," returned the cockswain; "and none but such as have his power will ever be able to walk from these rocks to the sands." The old seaman paused, and turning his eyes, which exhibited a mingled expression of disgust and compassion, on his companion, he added, with reverence—"Had you thought more of him in fair weather, your case would be less to be pitied in this tempest."

"Do you still think there is much danger?" asked Dillon.

"To them that have reason to fear death; listen! do you hear that hollow noise beneath ye?"

" 'Tis the wind, driving by the vessel!"

" 'Tis the poor thing herself," said the affected cockswain, "giving her last groans. The water is breaking up her decks, and in a few minutes more, the handsomest model that ever cut a wave, will be like the chips that fell from her timbers in framing!"

"Why, then, did you remain here!" cried Dillon, wildly.

"To die in my coffin, if it should be the will of God," returned Tom; "these waves, to me, are what the land is to you; I was born on them, and I have always meant that they should be my grave."

"But I—I," shrieked Dillon, "I am not ready to die!—I cannot die!—I will not die!"

"Poor wretch!" muttered his companion; "you must go, like the rest of us; when the death-watch is called, none can skulk from the muster."

"I can swim," Dillon continued, rushing, with frantic eagerness, to the side of the wreck. "Is there no billet of wood, no rope, that I can take with me?"

"None; every thing has been cut away, or carried off by the sea. If ye are about to strive for your life, take with ye a stout heart and a clean conscience, and trust the rest to God!"

"God!" echoed Dillon, in the madness of his frenzy; "I know no God! there is no God that knows me!"

"Peace!" said the deep tones of the cockswain, in a voice that seemed to speak in the elements; "blasphemer, peace!"

The heavy groaning, produced by the water, in the timbers of the Ariel, at that moment, added its impulse to the raging feelings of Dillon, and he cast himself headlong into the sea.

The water, thrown by the rolling of the surf on the beach, was necessarily returned to the ocean, in eddies, in different places, favourable to such an action of the element. Into the edge of one of these counter-currents, that was produced by the very rocks on which the schooner lay, and which the watermen call the "under-tow," Dillon had, unknowingly, thrown his person, and when the waves had driven him a short distance from the wreck, he was met by a stream that his most desperate efforts could not overcome. He was a light and powerful swimmer, and the struggle was hard and protracted. With the shore immediately before his eyes, and at no great distance, he was led, as by a false phantom, to continue his efforts, although they did not advance him a foot. The old seaman, who, at first, had watched his motions with careless indifference, understood the danger of his situation at a glance, and, forgetful of his own fate, he shouted aloud, in a voice that was driven over the struggling victim, to the ears of his shipmates on the sands—

"Sheer to-port, and clear the under-tow! sheer to the southward!"

Dillon heard the sounds, but his faculties were too much obscured by terror, to distinguish their object; he, however, blindly yielded to the call, and gradually changed his direction, until his face was once more turned towards the vessel. The current swept him diagonally by the rocks, and he was forced into an eddy, where he had nothing to contend against but the waves, whose violence was much broken by the wreck. In this state, he continued still to struggle, but with a force that was too much weakened, to overcome the resistance he met. Tom looked around him for a rope, but all had gone over with the spars, or been swept away by the waves. At this moment of disappointment, his eyes met those of the desperate Dillon. Calm, and inured to horrors, as was the veteran seaman, he involuntarily passed his hand before his brow, to exclude the look of despair he encountered; and when, a moment afterwards, he removed the rigid member, he beheld the sinking form of the victim, as it gradually settled in the ocean, still struggling, with regular but impotent strokes of the arms and feet, to gain the wreck, and to preserve an existence that had been so much abused in its hour of allotted probation.

"He will soon know his God, and learn that his God knows him!" murmured the cockswain to himself. As he yet spoke, the wreck of the Ariel yielded to an overwhelming sea, and, after an universal shudder, her timbers and planks gave way, and were swept towards the cliffs, bearing the body of the simple-hearted cockswain among the ruins.

# Chapter XXV.

"Let us think of them that sleep,
  Full many a fathom deep,
  By thy wild and stormy steep,
  Elsinore!"
        Campbell, "Battle of the Baltic," VII.6−9.

LONG AND DREARY did the hours appear to Barnstable, before the falling tide had so far receded, as to leave the
sands entirely exposed to his search for the bodies of his lost
shipmates. Several had been rescued from the wild fury of the
waves themselves, and one by one, as the melancholy conviction that life had ceased was forced on the survivors, they had
been decently interred, in graves dug on the very margin of
that element on which they had passed their lives. But still the
form longest known and most beloved was missing, and the
lieutenant paced the broad space that was now left between
the foot of the cliffs and the raging ocean, with hurried strides
and a feverish eye, watching and following those fragments of
the wreck that the sea still continued to cast on the beach.
Living and dead, he now found, that of those who had lately
been in the Ariel, only two were missing. Of the former, he
could muster but twelve, besides Merry and himself, and his
men had already interred more than half that number of the
latter, which, together, embraced all who had trusted their
lives to the frail keeping of the whale-boat.

"Tell me not, boy, of the impossibility of his being safe,"
said Barnstable, in deep agitation, which he in vain struggled
to conceal from the anxious youth, who thought it unnecessary to follow the uneasy motions of his commander, as he
strode along the sands. "How often have men been found
floating on pieces of wreck, days after the loss of their vessel?
and you can see, with your own eyes, that the falling water
has swept the planks this distance; ay, a good half league from
where she struck. Does the look-out, from the top of the
cliffs, make no signal of seeing him yet?"

"None, sir, none; we shall never see him again. The men
say, that he always thought it sinful to desert a wreck, and

that he did not even strike-out once for his life, though he has been known to swim an hour, when a whale has stove his boat. God knows, sir," added the boy, hastily dashing a tear from his eye, by a stolen movement of his hand, "I loved Tom Coffin better than any foremast-man in either vessel. You seldom came aboard the frigate but we had him in the steerage among us reefers, to hear his long-yarns, and share our cheer. We all loved him, Mr. Barnstable, but love cannot bring the dead to life again."

"I know it, I know it," said Barnstable, with a huskiness in his voice, that betrayed the depth of his emotion; "I am not so foolish as to believe in impossibilities; but while there is a hope of his living, I will never abandon poor Tom Coffin to such a dreadful fate. Think, boy, he may, at this moment, be looking at us, and praying to his Maker that he would turn our eyes upon him; ay, praying to his God, for Tom often prayed, though he did it in his watch, standing, and in silence."

"If he had clung to life so strongly," returned the midshipman, "he would have struggled harder to preserve it."

Barnstable stopped short in his hurried walk, and fastened a look of opening conviction on his companion; but, as he was about to speak in reply, the shouts of the seamen reached his ears, and, turning, they saw the whole party running along the beach, and motioning, with violent gestures, to an intermediate point in the ocean. The lieutenant and Merry hurried back, and, as they approached the men, they distinctly observed a human figure, borne along by the waves, at moments seeming to rise above them, and already floating in the last of the breakers. They had hardly ascertained so much, when a heavy swell carried the inanimate body far upon the sands, where it was left by the retiring waters.

" 'Tis my cockswain!" cried Barnstable, rushing to the spot. He stopped suddenly, however, as he came within view of the features, and it was some little time before he appeared to have collected his faculties sufficiently to add, in tones of deep horror—"what wretch is this, boy! his form is unmutilated, and yet observe the eyes! they seem as if the sockets would not contain them, and they gaze as wildly as if their owner yet had life—the hands are open and spread, as though they would still buffet the waves!"

"The Jonah! the Jonah!" shouted the seamen, with savage exultation, as they successively approached the corpse; "away with his carrion into the sea again! give him to the sharks! let him tell his lies in the claws of the lobsters!"

Barnstable had turned away from the revolting sight, in disgust, but when he discovered these indications of impotent revenge, in the remnant of his crew, he said, in that voice, which all respected, and still obeyed—

"Stand back! back with ye, fellows! would you disgrace your manhood and seamanship, by wreaking your vengeance on him whom God has already in judgment!" A silent, but significant gesture towards the earth, succeeded his words, and he walked slowly away.

"Bury him in the sands, boys," said Merry, when his commander was at some little distance; "the next tide will unearth him."

The seamen obeyed his orders, while the midshipman rejoined his commander, who continued to pace along the beach, occasionally halting, to throw his uneasy glances over the water, and then hurrying onward, at a rate that caused his youthful companion to exert his greatest power to maintain the post he had taken at his side. Every effort to discover the lost cockswain was, however, after two hours' more search, abandoned as fruitless, and with reason; for the sea was never known to give up the body of the man who might be, emphatically, called its own dead.

"There goes the sun, already dropping behind the cliffs," said the lieutenant, throwing himself on a rock; "and the hour will soon arrive to set the dog-watches; but we have nothing left to watch over, boy; the surf and rocks have not even left us a whole plank, that we may lay our heads on for the night."

"The men have gathered many articles on yon beach, sir," returned the lad; "they have found arms to defend ourselves with, and food to give us strength to use them."

"And who shall be our enemy?" asked Barnstable, bitterly; "shall we shoulder our dozen pikes, and carry England by boarding?"

"We may not lay the whole island under contribution," continued the boy, anxiously watching the expression of his commander's eye; "but we may still keep ourselves in work, until the cutter returns from the frigate. I hope, sir, you do not think our case so desperate, as to intend yielding as prisoners."

"Prisoners!" exclaimed the lieutenant; "no, no, lad, it has not got to that, yet! England has been able to wreck my craft, I must concede, but she has, as yet, obtained no other advantage over us. She was a precious model, Merry! the cleanest run, and the neatest entrance, that art ever united on the stem and stern of the same vessel! Do you remember the time, younker, when I gave the frigate my topsails, in beating out of the Chesapeake? I could always do it, in smooth water, with a whole-sail-breeze. But she was a frail thing! a frail thing, boy, and could bear but little."

"A mortar-ketch would have thumped to pieces where she lay," returned the midshipman.

"Ay, it was asking too much of her, to expect she could hold together on a bed of rocks. Merry, I loved her; dearly did I love her; she was my first command, and I knew and loved every timber and bolt in her beautiful frame!"

"I believe it is as natural, sir, for a seaman to love the wood and iron in which he has floated over the depths of the ocean, for so many days and nights," rejoined the boy, "as it is for a father to love the members of his own family."

"Quite, quite, ay, more so," said Barnstable, speaking as if he were choked by emotion. Merry felt the heavy grasp of the lieutenant on his slight arm, while his commander continued, in a voice that gradually increased in power, as his feelings predominated; "and yet, boy, a human being cannot love the creature of his own formation as he does the works of God. A man can never regard his ship as he does his shipmates. I sailed with him, boy, when every thing seemed bright and happy, as at your age; when, as he often expressed it, I knew nothing and feared nothing. I was then a truant from an old father and a kind mother, and he did that for me, which no parents could have done in my situation—he was my father and mother on the deep!—hours, days, even months, has he passed in teaching me the art of our profession; and now, in my manhood, he has followed me from ship to ship, from sea to sea, and has only quitted me to die, where I should have died—as if he felt the disgrace of abandoning the poor Ariel to her fate, by herself!"

"No—no—no—'twas his superstitious pride!" interrupted Merry; but perceiving that the head of Barnstable had sunk between his hands, as if he would conceal his emotion, the boy added no more, but he sat respectfully watching the display of feeling that his officer, in vain, endeavoured to suppress. Merry felt his own form quiver with sympathy at the shuddering which passed through Barnstable's frame; and the relief experienced by the lieutenant himself, was not greater than that which the midshipman felt, as the latter beheld large tears forcing their way through the other's fingers, and falling on the sands at his feet. They were followed by a violent burst of emotion, such as is seldom exhibited in the meridian of life, but which, when it conquers the nature of one who has buffeted the chances of the world with the loftiness of his sex and character, breaks down every barrier, and seems to sweep before it, like a rushing torrent, all the factitious defences which habit and education have created to protect the pride of manhood. Merry had often beheld the commanding severity of the lieutenant's manner, in moments of danger, with deep respect; he had been drawn towards him by kindness and affection, in times of gayety and recklessness; but he now sate, for many minutes, profoundly silent, regarding his officer with sensations that were nearly allied to awe. The struggle with himself was long and severe in the bosom of Barnstable; but, at length, the calm of relieved passions succeeded to his emotion. When he arose from the rock, and removed his hands from his features, his eye was hard and proud, his brow slightly contracted, and he spoke in a voice so harsh, that it startled his companion—

"Come, sir; why are we here and idle! are not yon poor fellows looking up to us for advice, and orders how to proceed in this exigency? Away, away, Mr. Merry; it is not a time to be drawing figures in the sand with your dirk; the flood-tide will soon be in, and we may be glad to hide our heads in some cavern among these rocks. Let us be stirring, sir, while we have the sun, and muster enough food and arms to keep life in us, and our enemies off us, until we can once more get afloat."

The wondering boy, whose experience had not yet taught him to appreciate the reaction of the passions, started at this unexpected summons to his duty, and followed Barnstable towards the group of distant seamen. The lieutenant, who was instantly conscious how far pride had rendered him unjust, soon moderated his long strides, and continued in milder tones, which were quickly converted into his usual frank communications, though they still remained tinged with a melancholy, that time only could entirely remove—

"We have been unlucky, Mr. Merry, but we need not despair—these lads have gotten together abundance of supplies, I see; and, with our arms, we can easily make ourselves masters of some of the enemy's smaller craft, and find our way back to the frigate, when this gale has blown itself out. We must keep ourselves close, though, or we shall have the redcoats coming down upon us, like so many sharks around a wreck. Ah! God bless her, Merry! there is not such a sight to be seen on the whole beach as two of her planks holding together."

The midshipman, without advertising to this sudden allusion to their vessel, prudently pursued the train of ideas, in which his commander had started.

"There is an opening into the country, but a short distance south of us, where a brook empties into the sea," he said. "We might find a cover in it, or in the wood above, into which it leads, until we can have a survey of the coast, or can seize some vessel to carry us off."

"There would be a satisfaction in waiting 'till the morning watch, and then carrying that accursed battery, which took off the better leg of the poor Ariel!" said the lieutenant—"the thing might be done, boy; and we could hold the work too, until the Alacrity and the frigate draw in to land."

"If you prefer storming works to boarding vessels, there is a fortress of stone, Mr. Barnstable, which lies directly on our beam. I could see it through the haze, when I was on the cliffs, stationing the look-out—and—"

"And what, boy? speak without a fear; this is a time for free consultation."

"Why, sir, the garrison might not all be hostile—we should liberate Mr. Griffith and the marines; besides—"

"Besides what, sir?"

"I should have an opportunity, perhaps, of seeing my cousin Cecilia, and my cousin Katherine."

The countenance of Barnstable grew animated as he listened, and he answered, with something of his usual cheerful manner—

"Ay, that, indeed, would be a work worth carrying! and the rescuing of our shipmates, and the marines, would read like a thing of military discretion—ha! boy! all the rest would be incidental, younker; like the capture of the fleet, after you have whipped the convoy."

"I do suppose, sir, that if the Abbey be taken, Colonel Howard will own himself a prisoner of war."

"And Colonel Howard's wards! now, there is good sense in this scheme of thine, Master Merry, and I will give it proper reflection. But here are our poor fellows; speak cheeringly to them, sir, that we may hold them in temper for our enterprise."

Barnstable and the midshipman joined their shipwrecked companions, with that air of authority which is seldom wanting between the superior and the inferior, in nautical intercourse, but at the same time, with a kindness of speech and looks, that might have been a little increased by their critical situation. After partaking of the food which had been selected from among the fragments that still lay scattered, for more than a mile, along the beach, the lieutenant directed the seamen to arm themselves with such weapons as offered, and, also, to make a sufficient provision, from the schooner's stores, to last them for four-and-twenty hours longer. These orders were soon executed; and the whole party, led by Barnstable and Merry, proceeded along the foot of the cliffs, in quest of the opening in the rocks, through which the little rivulet found a passage to the ocean. The weather contributed, as much as the seclusion of the spot, to prevent any discovery of the small party, which pursued its object with a disregard of caution that might, under other circumstances, have proved fatal to its safety. Barnstable paused in his march when they had all entered the deep ravine, and ascended nearly to the brow of the precipice, that formed one of its sides, to take a last and more scrutinizing survey of the sea.

His countenance exhibited the abandonment of all hope, as his eye moved slowly from the northern to the southern boundary of the horizon, and he prepared to pursue his march, by moving, reluctantly, up the stream, when the boy, who still clung to his side, exclaimed joyously—

"Sail ho! It must be the frigate in the offing!"

"A sail!" repeated his commander; "where-away do you see a sail in this tempest? Can there be another as hardy and unfortunate as ourselves!"

"Look to the starboard hand of the point of rock to windward!" cried the boy; "now you lose it—ah! now the sun falls upon it! 'tis a sail, sir, as sure as canvass can be spread in such a gale!"

"I see what you mean," returned the other, "but it seems a gull, skimming the sea! nay, now it rises, indeed, and shows itself like a bellying topsail; pass up that glass, lads; here is a fellow in the offing who may prove a friend."

Merry waited the result of the lieutenant's examination with youthful impatience, and did not fail to ask, immediately—

"Can you make it out, sir? is it the ship or the cutter?"

"Come, there seemeth yet some hope left for us, boy," returned Barnstable, closing the glass; " 'tis a ship, lying-to under her main-topsail. If one might but dare to show himself on these heights, he would raise her hull, and make sure of her character! But I think I know her spars, though even her topsail dips, at times, when there is nothing to be seen but her bare poles, and they shortened by her top-gallant-masts."

"One would swear," said Merry, laughing, as much through the excitement produced by this intelligence, as at his conceit, "that Captain Munson would never carry wood aloft, when he can't carry canvass. I remember, one night, Mr. Griffith was a little vexed, and said, around the capstern, he believed the next order would be, to rig in the bowsprit, and house lowermasts!"

"Ay, ay, Griffith is a lazy dog, and sometimes gets lost in the fogs of his own thoughts," said Barnstable; "and I suppose old Moderate was in a breeze. However, this looks as if he were in earnest; he must have kept the ship away, or she would never have been where she is; I do verily believe the old gentleman remembers that he has a few of his officers and men on this accursed island. This is well, Merry, for should we take the Abbey, we have a place at hand in which to put our prisoners."

"We must have patience till the morning," added the boy, "for no boat would attempt to land in such a sea."

"No boat could land! The best boat that ever floated, boy, has sunk in these breakers! But the wind lessens, and before morning, the sea will fall. Let us on, and find a birth for our poor lads, where they can be made more comfortable."

The two officers now descended from their elevation, and led the way still further up the deep and narrow dell, until, as the ground rose gradually before them, they found themselves in a dense wood, on a level with the adjacent country.

"Here should be a ruin at hand, if I have kept a true reckoning, and know my courses and distances," said Barnstable; "I have a chart about me, that speaks of such a land-mark."

The lieutenant turned away from the laughing expression of the boy's eye, as the latter archly inquired—

"Was it made by one who knows the coast well, sir? or was it done by some school-boy, to learn his maps, as the girls work samplers?"

"Come, younker, no sampler of your impudence. But look ahead; can you see any habitation that has been deserted?"

"Ay, sir, here is a pile of stones before us, that looks as dirty and ragged, as if it was a soldier's barrack; can this be what you seek?"

"Faith, this has been a whole town in its day! we should call it a city in America, and furnish it with a Mayor, Aldermen, and Recorder—you might stow old Faneuil-Hall in one of its lockers."

With this sort of careless dialogue, which Barnstable engaged in, that his men might discover no alteration in his manner, they approached the mouldering walls that had proved so frail a protection to the party under Griffith.

A short time was passed in examining the premises, when the wearied seamen took possession of one of the dilapidated apartments, and disposed themselves to seek that rest of which they had been deprived by the momentous occurrences of the past night.

Barnstable waited until the loud breathing of the seamen assured him that they slept, when he aroused the drowsy boy, who was fast losing his senses in the same sort of oblivion, and motioned to him to follow. Merry arose, and they stole together from the apartment, with guarded steps, and penetrated more deeply into the gloomy recesses of the place.

# Chapter XXVI.

Mercury—"I permit thee to be Sosia again."
Dryden, *Amphitryon*, V.i.306.

W E MUST LEAVE the two adventurers winding their way among the broken piles, and venturing boldly beneath the tottering arches of the ruin, to accompany the reader, at the same hour, within the more comfortable walls of the Abbey; where, it will be remembered, Borroughcliffe was left, in a condition of very equivocal ease. As the earth had, however, in the interval, nearly run its daily round, circumstances had intervened to release the soldier from his confinement—and no one, ignorant of the fact, would suppose, that the gentleman who was now seated at the hospitable board of Colonel Howard, directing, with so much discretion, the energies of his masticators to the delicacies of the feast, could read, in his careless air and smiling visage, that those foragers of nature had been so recently condemned, for four long hours, to the mortification of discussing the barren subject of his own sword-hilt. Borroughcliffe, however, maintained not only his usual post, but his well-earned reputation at the table, with his ordinary coolness of demeanour; though, at times, there were fleeting smiles, that crossed his military aspect, which sufficiently indicated, that he considered the matter of his reflection to be of a particularly ludicrous character. In the young man, who sat by his side, dressed in the deep blue jacket of a seaman, with the fine, white linen of his collar contrasting strongly with the black silk handkerchief, that was tied, with studied negligence, around his neck, and whose easy air and manner contrasted still more strongly with this attire, the reader will discover Griffith. The captive paid much less devotion to the viands than his neighbour, though he affected more attention to the business of the table than he actually bestowed, with a sort of consciousness that it would relieve the blushing maiden who presided. The laughing eyes of Katherine Plowden were glittering by the side of the mild countenance of Alice Dunscombe, and, at times, were fastened, in droll interest, on the rigid and upright exterior that

Captain Manual maintained, directly opposite to where she was seated. A chair had, also, been placed for Dillon—of course, it was vacant.

"And so, Borroughcliffe," cried Colonel Howard, with a freedom of voice, and a vivacity in his air, that announced the increasing harmony of the repast, "the sea-dog left you nothing to chew but the cud of your resentment!"

"That and my sword-hilt!" returned the immoveable recruiting officer; "gentlemen, I know not how your Congress rewards military achievements; but if that worthy fellow were in my company, he should have a halbert within a week—spurs I would not offer him, for he affects to spurn their use."

Griffith smiled, and bowed in silence to the liberal compliment of Borroughcliffe; but Manual took on himself the task of replying—

"Considering the drilling the man has received, his conduct has been well enough, sir; though a well-trained soldier would not only have made prisoners, but he would have secured them."

"I perceive, my good comrade, that your thoughts are running on the exchange," said Borroughcliffe, good humouredly; "we will fill, sir, and, by permission of the ladies, drink to a speedy restoration of rights to both parties—the statu quo ante bellum."

"With all my heart," cried the colonel; "and Cicily and Miss Katherine will pledge the sentiment in a woman's sip; will ye not, my fair wards?—Mr. Griffith, I honour this proposition of yours, which will not only liberate yourself, but restore to us my kinsman, Mr. Christopher Dillon. Kit had imagined the thing well; ha! Borroughcliffe! 'twas ingeniously contrived, but the fortune of war interposed itself to his success; and yet, it is a deep and inexplicable mystery to me, how Kit should have been conveyed from the Abbey with so little noise, and without raising the alarm."

"Christopher is a man who understands the philosophy of silence, as well as that of rhetoric," returned Borroughcliffe, "and must have learned, in his legal studies, that it is, sometimes, necessary to conduct matters sub silentio. You smile at my Latin, Miss Plowden; but, really, since I have become an inhabitant of this Monkish abode, my little learning is stimulated to unwonted efforts—nay, you are pleased to be yet more merry! I used the language, because silence is a theme in which you ladies take but little pleasure."

Katherine, however, disregarded the slight pique that was apparent in the soldier's manner; but, after following the train of her own thoughts in silent enjoyment for a moment longer, she seemed to yield to their drollery, and laughed, until her dark eyes flashed with merriment. Cecilia did not assume the severe gravity with which she sometimes endeavoured to repress, what she thought, the unseasonable mirth of her cousin, and the wondering Griffith fancied, as he glanced his eye from one to the other, that he could discern a suppressed smile playing among the composed features of Alice Dunscombe. Katherine, however, soon succeeded in repressing the paroxysm, and, with an air of infinitely comic gravity, she replied to the remark of the soldier—

"I think I have heard of such a process in nautical affairs as towing; but I must appeal to Mr. Griffith for the correctness of the term?"

"You could not speak with more accuracy," returned the young sailor, with a look that sent the conscious blood to the temples of the lady, "though you had made marine terms your study."

"The profession requires less thought, perhaps, than you imagine, sir; but is this towing often done, as Captain Borroughcliffe—I beg his pardon—as the Monks have it, sub silentio?"

"Spare me, fair lady," cried the captain, "and we will establish a compact of mutual grace; you to forgive my learning, and I to suppress my suspicions."

"Suspicions, sir, is a word that a lady must defy."

"And defiance a challenge that a soldier can never receive; so, I must submit to talk English, though the fathers of the church were my companions. I suspect that Miss Plowden has it in her power to explain the manner of Mr. Christopher Dillon's departure."

The lady did not reply, but a second burst of merriment succeeded, of a liveliness and duration quite equal to the former.

"How's this!" exclaimed the colonel; "permit me to say,

Miss Plowden, your mirth is very extraordinary! I trust no disrespect has been offered to my kinsman? Mr. Griffith, our terms are, that the exchange shall only be made on condition that equally good treatment has been extended to the parties!"

"If Mr. Dillon can complain of no greater evil than that of being laughed at by Miss Plowden, sir, he has reason to call himself a happy fellow."

"I know not, sir; God forbid that I should forget what is due to my guests, gentlemen—but ye have entered my dwelling as foes to my prince."

"But not to Colonel Howard, sir."

"I know no difference, Mr. Griffith. King George or Colonel Howard—Colonel Howard or King George. Our feelings, our fortunes, and our fate, are as one; with the mighty odds that Providence has established between the prince and his people! I wish no other fortune, than to share, at an humble distance, the weal or wo of my sovereign!"

"You are not called upon, dear sir, to do either, by the thoughtlessness of us ladies," said Cecilia, rising; "but here comes one who should turn our thoughts to a more important subject—our dress."

Politeness induced Colonel Howard, who both loved and respected his niece, to defer his remarks to another time; and Katherine, springing from her chair, with childish eagerness, flew to the side of her cousin, who was directing a servant that had announced the arrival of one of those erratic vendors of small articles, who supply, in remote districts of the country, the places of more regular traders, to show the lad into the dining-parlour. The repast was so far ended, as to render this interruption less objectionable, and as all felt the object of Cecilia to be the restoration of harmony, the boy was ushered into the room, without further delay. The contents of his small basket, consisting, chiefly, of essences, and the smaller articles of female economy, were playfully displayed on the table, by Katherine, who declared herself the patroness of the itinerant youth, and who laughingly appealed to the liberality of the gentlemen in behalf of her protégé.

"You perceive, my dear guardian, that the boy must be loyal; for he offers, here, perfume, that is patronized by no less than two royal dukes! do suffer me to place a box aside, for your especial use? you consent; I see it in your eye. And, Captain Borroughcliffe, as you appear to be forgetting the use of your own language, here is even a horn-book for you! How admirably provided he seems to be! You must have had St. Ruth in view, when you laid in your stock, child?"

"Yes, my lady," the boy replied, with a bow that was studiously awkward; "I have often heard of the grand ladies that dwell in the old Abbey, and I have journeyed a few miles beyond my rounds, to gain their custom."

"And surely they cannot disappoint you. Miss Howard, that is a palpable hint to your purse; and I know not that even Miss Alice can escape contribution, in these troublesome times. Come, aid me, child; what have you to recommend, in particular, to the favour of these ladies?"

The lad approached the basket, and rummaged its contents, for a moment, with the appearance of deep, mercenary interest; and then, without lifting his hand from the confusion he had caused, he said, while he exhibited something within the basket to the view of his smiling observer—

"This, my lady."

Katherine started, and glanced her eyes, with a piercing look, at the countenance of the boy, and then turned them, uneasily, from face to face, with conscious timidity. Cecilia had effected her object, and had resumed her seat, in silent abstraction—Alice was listening to the remarks of Captain Manual and the host, as they discussed the propriety of certain military usages—Griffith seemed to hold communion with his mistress, by imitating her silence; but Katherine, in her stolen glances, met the keen look of Borroughcliffe, fastened on her face, in a manner that did not fail instantly to suspend the scrutiny.

"Come, Cecilia," she cried, after a pause of a moment, "we trespass too long on the patience of the gentlemen; not only to keep possession of our seats, ten minutes after the cloth has been drawn! but even to introduce our essences, and tapes, and needles, among the Madeira, and—shall I add, segars, colonel?"

"Not while we are favoured with the company of Miss Plowden, certainly."

"Come, my coz; I perceive the colonel is growing particularly polite, which is a never-failing sign that he tires of our presence."

Cecilia rose, and was leading the way to the door, when Katherine turned to the lad, and added—

"You can follow us to the drawing-room, child, where we can make our purchases, without exposing the mystery of our toilets."

"Miss Plowden has forgotten my horn-book, I believe," said Borroughcliffe, advancing from the standing group who surrounded the table; "possibly I can find some work in the basket of the boy, better fitted for the improvement of a grown-up young gentleman, than this elementary treatise."

Cecilia, observing him to take the basket from the lad, resumed her seat, and her example was necessarily followed by Katherine; though not without some manifest indications of vexation.

"Come hither, boy, and explain the uses of your wares. This is soap, and this a penknife, I know; but what name do you affix to this?"

"That? that is tape," returned the lad, with an impatience that might very naturally be attributed to the interruption that was thus given to his trade.

"And this?"

"That?" repeated the stripling, pausing, with a hesitation between sulkiness and doubt; "that?—"

"Come, this is a little ungallant!" cried Katherine; "to keep three ladies dying with impatience to possess themselves of their finery, while you detain the boy, to ask the name of a tambouring-needle!"

"I should apologize for asking questions that are so easily answered; but perhaps he will find the next more difficult to solve," returned Borroughcliffe, placing the subject of his inquiries in the palm of his hand, in such a manner as to conceal it from all but the boy and himself. "This has a name, too; what is it?"

"That?—that—is sometimes called—white-line."

"Perhaps you mean a white lie?"

"How, sir!" exclaimed the lad, a little fiercely, "a lie!"

"Only a white one," returned the captain. "What do you call this, Miss Dunscombe?"

"We call it bobbin, sir, generally, in the north," said the placid Alice.

"Ay, bobbin, or white-line; they are the same thing," added the young trader.

"They are! I think, now, for a professional man, you know but little of the terms of your art," observed Borroughcliffe, with an affectation of irony; "I never have seen a youth of your years who knew less. What names, now, would you affix to this, and this, and this?"

While the captain was speaking, he drew from his pockets the several instruments that the cockswain had made use of, the preceding night, to secure his prisoner.

"That," exclaimed the lad, with the eagerness of one who would vindicate his reputation, "is ratlin-stuff; and this is marline; and that is sennit."

"Enough, enough," said Borroughcliffe; "you have exhibited sufficient knowledge, to convince me that you *do* know something of your *trade*, and nothing of these articles. Mr. Griffith, do you claim this boy?"

"I believe I must, sir," said the young sea-officer, who had been intently listening to the examination. "On whatever errand you have ventured here, Mr. Merry, it is useless to affect further concealment."

"Merry!" exclaimed Cecilia Howard; "is it you, then, my cousin? are you, too, fallen into the power of your enemies! was it not enough that—"

The young lady recovered her recollection in time to suppress the remainder of the sentence, though the grateful expression of Griffith's eye sufficiently indicated that he had, in his thoughts, filled the sentence with expressions abundantly flattering to his own feelings.

"How's this, again!" cried the colonel; "my two wards embracing and fondling a vagrant, vagabond pedler, before my eyes! is this treason, Mr. Griffith? or what means the extraordinary visit of this young gentleman?"

"Is it extraordinary, sir," said Merry himself, losing his assumed awkwardness, in the ease and confidence of one whose faculties had been early exercised, "that a boy, like myself, destitute of mother and sisters, should take a little risk on himself, to visit the only two female relatives he has in the world?"

"Why this disguise, then? surely, young gentleman, it was unnecessary to enter the dwelling of old George Howard, on such an errand, clandestinely, even though your tender years have been practised on, to lead you astray from your allegiance. Mr. Griffith and Captain Manual must pardon me, if I express sentiments, at my own table, that they may find unpleasant; but this business requires us to be explicit."

"The hospitality of Colonel Howard is unquestionable," returned the boy; "but he has a great reputation for his loyalty to the crown."

"Ay, young gentleman; and, I trust, with some justice."

"Would it, then, be safe, to intrust my person in the hands of one who might think it his duty to detain me?"

"This is plausible enough, Captain Borroughcliffe, and I doubt not the boy speaks with candour. I would, now, that my kinsman, Mr. Christopher Dillon, were here, that I might learn if it would be misprison of treason, to permit this youth to depart, unmolested, and without exchange?"

"Inquire of the young gentleman, after the Cacique," returned the recruiting officer, who, apparently satisfied in producing the exposure of Merry, had resumed his seat at the table; "perhaps he is, in verity, an ambassador, empowered to treat on behalf of his highness."

"How say you, sir," demanded the colonel; "do you know any thing of my kinsman?"

The anxious eyes of the whole party were fastened on the boy, for many moments, witnessing the sudden change from careless freedom to deep horror, expressed in his countenance. At length he uttered, in an under tone, the secret of Dillon's fate.

"He is dead."

"Dead!" repeated every voice in the room.

"Yes, dead," said the boy, gazing at the pallid faces of those who surrounded him.

A long and fearful silence succeeded the announcement of this intelligence, which was only interrupted by Griffith, who said—

"Explain the manner of his death, sir, and where his body lies."

"His body lies interred in the sands," returned Merry, with

a deliberation that proceeded from an opening perception, that if he uttered too much, he might betray the loss of the Ariel, and, consequently, endanger the liberty of Barnstable.

"In the sands!" was echoed from every part of the room.

"Ay, in the sands; but how he died, I cannot explain."

"He has been murdered!" exclaimed Colonel Howard, whose command of utterance was now amply restored to him; "he has been treacherously, and dastardly, and basely murdered!"

"He has *not* been murdered," said the boy, firmly; "nor did he meet his death among those who deserve the name either of traitors or of dastards."

"Said you not that he was dead? that my kinsman was buried in the sands of the sea-shore?"

"Both are true, sir—"

"And you refuse to explain how he met his death, and why he has been thus ignominiously interred?"

"He received his interment by my orders, sir; and if there be ignominy about his grave, his own acts have heaped it on him. As to the manner of his death, I cannot, and will not speak."

"Be calm, my cousin," said Cecilia, in an imploring voice; "respect the age of my uncle, and remember his strong attachment to Mr. Dillon."

The veteran had, however, so far mastered his feelings, as to continue the dialogue with more recollection.

"Mr. Griffith," he said, "I shall not act hastily—you and your companion will be pleased to retire to your several apartments. I will so far respect the son of my brother Harry's friend, as to believe your parole will be sacred. Go, gentlemen; you are unguarded."

The two prisoners bowed low to the ladies and their host, and retired. Griffith, however, lingered a moment on the threshold, to say—

"Colonel Howard, I leave the boy to your kindness and consideration. I know you will not forget that his blood mingles with that of one who is most dear to you."

"Enough, enough, sir," said the veteran, waving his hand to him to retire; "and you, ladies; this is not a place for you, either."

"Never will I quit this child," said Katherine, "while such a horrid imputation lies on him. Colonel Howard, act your pleasure on us both, for I suppose you have the power; but his fate shall be my fate."

"There is, I trust, some misconception in this melancholy affair," said Borroughcliffe, advancing into the centre of the agitated group; "and I should hope, by calmness and moderation, all may yet be explained—young gentleman, you have borne arms, and must know, notwithstanding your youth, what it is to be in the power of your enemies."

"Never!" returned the proud boy; "I am a captive for the first time."

"I speak, sir, in reference to our power."

"You may order me to a dungeon; or, as I have entered the Abbey in disguise, possibly, to a gibbet."

"And is that a fate to be met so calmly, by one so young!"

"You dare not do it, Captain Borroughcliffe," cried Katherine, involuntarily throwing an arm around the boy, as if to shield him from harm; "you would blush to think of such a cold-blooded act of vengeance, Colonel Howard."

"If we could examine the young man, where the warmth of feeling, which these ladies exhibit, might not be excited," said the captain, apart to his host, "we should gain important intelligence."

"Miss Howard, and you, Miss Plowden," said the veteran, in a manner that long habit had taught his wards to respect, "your young kinsman is not in the keeping of savages, and you can safely confide him to my custody. I am sorry that we have so long kept Miss Alice standing, but she will find relief on the couches of your drawing-room, Cecilia."

Cecilia and Katherine permitted themselves to be conducted to the door, by their polite, but determined guardian, where he bowed to their retiring persons, with the exceeding courtesy that he never failed to use, when in the least excited.

"You appear to know your danger, Mr. Merry," said Borroughcliffe, after the door was closed; "I trust you also know what duty would dictate to one in my situation."

"Do it, sir," returned the boy; "you have a king to render an account to, and I have a country."

"I may have a country, also," said Borroughcliffe, with a

calmness that was not in the least disturbed by the taunting air with which the youth delivered himself. "It is possible for me, however, to be lenient, even merciful, when the interests of that prince, to whom you allude, are served—you came not on this enterprise alone, sir?"

"Had I come better attended, Captain Borroughcliffe might have heard these questions, instead of putting them."

"I am happy, sir, that your retinue has been so small; and yet, even the rebel schooner called the Ariel might have furnished you with a more becoming attendance. I cannot but think, that you are not far distant from your friends."

"He is near his enemies, your honour," said Sergeant Drill, who had entered the room, unobserved; "for here is a boy who says he has been seized in the old ruin, and robbed of his goods and clothes; and, by his description, this lad should be the thief."

Borroughcliffe signed to the boy, who stood in the back ground, to advance, and he was instantly obeyed, with all that eagerness which a sense of injury on the part of the sufferer could excite. The tale of this unexpected intruder was soon told, and was briefly this:

He had been assaulted by a man and a boy, (the latter was in presence,) while arranging his effects, in the ruin, preparatory to exhibiting them to the ladies of the Abbey, and had been robbed of such part of his attire as the boy had found necessary for his disguise, together with his basket of valuables. He had been put into an apartment of an old tower, by the man, for safe keeping; but as the latter frequently ascended to its turret, to survey the country, he had availed himself of this remissness, to escape. And, to conclude, he demanded a restoration of his property, and vengeance for his wrongs.

Merry heard his loud and angry details with scornful composure, and before the offended pedler was through his narrative, had devested himself of the borrowed garments, which he threw to the other, with singular disdain.

"We are beleaguered, mine host! beset! besieged!" cried Borroughcliffe, when the other had ended. "Here is a rare plan to rob us of our laurels! ay, and of our rewards! but, harkye, Drill! they have old soldiers to deal with, and we shall look into the matter. One would wish to triumph on foot; you understand me?—there was no horse in the battle. Go, fellow, I see you grow wiser; take this young gentleman—and remember *he is* a young gentleman—put him in safe keeping, but see him supplied with all he wants."

Borroughcliffe bowed politely to the haughty bend of the body with which Merry, who now began to think himself a martyr to his country, followed the orderly from the room.

"There is metal in the lad!" exclaimed the captain; "and if he live to get a beard, 'twill be a hardy dog who ventures to pluck it. I am glad, mine host, that this 'wandering jew' has arrived, to save the poor fellow's feelings, for I detest tampering with such a noble spirit. I saw, by his eye, that he had squinted oftener over a gun, than through a needle!"

"But they have murdered my kinsman!—the loyal, the learned, the ingenious Mr. Christopher Dillon!"

"If they have done so, they shall be made to answer it," said Borroughcliffe, re-seating himself at the table, with a coolness that furnished an ample pledge of the impartiality of his judgment; "but let us learn the facts, before we do aught hastily."

Colonel Howard was fain to comply with so reasonable a proposition, and he resumed his chair, while his companion proceeded to institute a close examination of the pedler boy.

We shall defer, until the proper time may arrive, recording the result of his inquiries; but shall so far satisfy the curiosity of our readers, as to tell them, that the captain learned sufficient to convince him, a very serious attempt was meditated on the Abbey; and, as he thought, enough, also, to enable him to avert the danger.

# Chapter XXVII.

—"I have not seen
So likely an embassador of love."
*The Merchant of Venice*, III.i.91–92.

CECILIA AND KATHERINE separated from Alice Dunscombe in the lower gallery of the cloisters; and the cousins ascended to the apartment which was assigned them as a dressing-room. The intensity of feeling that was gradually accumulating in the breasts of the ladies, as circumstances brought those in whom their deepest interests were centered, into situations of extreme delicacy, if not of actual danger, perhaps, in some measure, prevented them from experiencing all that concern which the detection and arrest of Merry might be supposed to excite. The boy, like themselves, was an only child of one of those three sisters, who caused the close connexion of so many of our characters, and his tender years had led his cousins to regard him with an affection that exceeded the ordinary interest of such an affinity; but they knew, that in the hands of Colonel Howard his person was safe, though his liberty might be endangered. When the first emotions, therefore, which were created by his sudden appearance, after so long an absence, had subsided, their thoughts were rather occupied by the consideration of what consequences, to others, might proceed from his arrest, than by any reflections on the midshipman's actual condition. Secluded from the observations of any strange eyes, the two maidens indulged their feelings, without restraint, according to their several temperaments. Katherine moved to and fro, in the apartment, with feverish anxiety, while Miss Howard, by concealing her countenance under the ringlets of her luxuriant, dark hair, and shading her eyes with a fair hand, seemed to be willing to commune with her thoughts more quietly.

"Barnstable cannot be far distant," said the former, after a few minutes had passed; "for he never would have sent that child on such an errand, by himself!"

Cecilia raised her mild, blue eyes to the countenance of her cousin, as she answered—

"All thoughts of an exchange must now be abandoned; and perhaps the persons of the prisoners will be held as pledges, to answer for the life of Dillon."

"Can the wretch be dead! or is it merely a threat, or some device of that urchin? he is a forward child, and would not hesitate to speak and act boldly, on emergency."

"He is dead!" returned Cecilia, veiling her face again, in horror; "the eyes of the boy, his whole countenance, confirmed his words! I fear, Katherine, that Mr. Barnstable has suffered his resentment to overcome his discretion, when he learned the treachery of Dillon; surely, surely, though the hard usages of war may justify so dreadful a revenge on an enemy, it was unkind to forget the condition of his own friends!"

"Mr. Barnstable has done neither, Miss Howard," said Katherine, checking her uneasy footsteps, her light form swelling with pride; "Mr. Barnstable is equally incapable of murdering an enemy, or of deserting a friend!"

"But retaliation is neither deemed nor called murder, by men in arms."

"Think it what you will, call it what you will, Cecilia Howard, I will pledge my life, that Richard Barnstable has to answer for the blood of none but the open enemies of his country."

"The miserable man may have fallen a sacrifice to the anger of that terrific seaman, who led him hence as a captive!"

"That terrific seaman, Miss Howard, has a heart as tender as your own. He is—"

"Nay, Katherine," interrupted Cecilia, "you chide me unkindly; let us not add to our unavoidable misery, by such harsh contention."

"I do not contend with you, Cecilia! I merely defend the absent and the innocent from your unkind suspicions, my cousin."

"Say, rather, your sister," returned Miss Howard, their hands involuntarily closing upon each other, "for we are surely sisters! But let us strive to think of something less horrible. Poor, poor Dillon! now that he has met a fate so terrible, I can even fancy him less artful and more upright than we had thought him! You agree with me, Katherine, I see by your countenance, and we will dwell no longer on the sub-ject. — Katherine! my cousin Kate, what see you?"

Miss Plowden, as she relinquished her pressure of the hand of Cecilia, had renewed her walk with a more regulated step; but she was yet making her first turn across the room, when her eyes became keenly set on the opposite window, and her whole frame was held in an attitude of absorbed attention. The rays of the setting sun fell bright upon her dark glances, which seemed fastened on some distant object, and gave an additional glow to the mantling colour that was slowly steal-ing, across her cheeks, to her temples. Such a sudden alter-ation in the manner and appearance of her companion, had not failed to catch the attention of Cecilia, who, in conse-quence, interrupted herself by the agitated question we have related. Katherine slowly beckoned her companion to her side, and, pointing in the direction of the wood that lay in view, she said—

"See yon tower, in the ruin! Do you observe those small spots of pink and yellow that are fluttering above its walls?"

"I do. They are the lingering remnants of the foliage of some tree; but they want the vivid tints which grace the au-tumn of our own dear America!"

"One is the work of God, and the other has been produced by the art of man. Cecilia, those are no leaves, but they are my own childish signals, and without doubt Barnstable him-self is on that ruined tower. Merry, cannot, will not, betray him!"

"My life should be a pledge for the honour of our little cousin," said Cecilia. "But you have the telescope of my uncle at hand, ready for such an event! one look through it will ascertain the truth—"

Katherine sprang to the spot where the instrument stood, and with eager hands she prepared it for the necessary ob-servation.

"It is he!" she cried the instant her eye was put to the glass. "I even see his head above the stones. How unthinking to expose himself so unnecessarily!"

"But what says he, Katherine!" exclaimed Cecilia; "you alone can interpret his meaning."

The little book which contained the explanations of Miss

Plowden's signals was now hastily produced, and its leaves rapidly run over in quest of the necessary number.

" 'Tis only a question to gain my attention. I must let him know he is observed."

When Katherine, as much to indulge her secret propensities, as with any hope of its usefulness, had devised this plan for communicating with Barnstable, she had, luckily, not forgotten to arrange the necessary means to reply to his interrogatories. A very simple arrangement of some of the ornamental cords of the window-curtains, enabled her to effect this purpose; and her nimble fingers soon fastened the pieces of silk to the lines, which were now thrown into the air, when these signals in miniature were instantly displayed in the breeze.

"He sees them!" cried Cecilia, "and is preparing to change his flags."

"Keep then your eye on him, my cousin, and tell me the colours that he shows, with their order, and I will endeavour to read his meaning."

"He is as expert as yourself! There are two more of them fluttering above the stones again: the upper is white, and the lower black."

"White over black," repeated Katherine, rapidly, to herself, as she turned the leaves of her book. — " *My messenger: has he been seen?*'—To that we must answer the unhappy truth. Here it is—yellow, white, and red—'*he is a prisoner.*' How fortunate that I should have prepared such a question and answer. What says he, Cecilia, to this news?"

"He is busy making his changes, dear. Nay, Katherine, you shake so violently as to move the glass! Now he is done; 'tis yellow over black, this time."

" '*Griffith, or who?*' He does not understand us; but I had thought of the poor boy, in making out the numbers—ah! here it is; yellow, green, and red—'*my cousin Merry.*'—He cannot fail to understand us now."

"He has already taken in his flags. The news seems to alarm him, for he is less expert than before. He shows them now— they are green, red and yellow."

"The question is, '*Am I safe?*' 'Tis that which made him tardy, Miss Howard," continued Katherine. "Barnstable is ever slow to consult his safety. But how shall I answer him?

should we mislead him now, how could we ever forgive ourselves!"

"Of Andrew Merry there is no fear," returned Cecilia; "and
I think if Captain Borroughcliffe had any intimation of the
proximity of his enemies, he would not continue at the table."

"He will stay there while wine will sparkle, and man can
swallow," said Katherine; "but we know, by sad experience,
that he is a soldier on an emergency; and yet, I'll trust to his
ignorance this time—here, I have an answer: *'you are yet safe,
but be wary.'* "

"He reads your meaning with a quick eye, Katherine; and
he is ready with his answer too: he shows green over white
this time. Well! do you not hear me? 'tis green over white.
Why, you are dumb—what says he, dear?"

Still Katherine answered not, and her cousin raised her eyes
from the glass, and beheld her companion gazing earnestly at
the open page, while the glow which excitement had before
brought to her cheek, was increased to a still deeper bloom.

"I hope your blushes and his signals are not ominous,
Kate," added Cecilia; "can green imply his jealousy, as white
does your purity? what says he, coz?"

"He talks, like yourself, much nonsense," said Katherine,
turning to her flags, with a pettish air, that was singularly
contradicted by her gratified countenance; "but the situation
of things requires that I should talk to Barnstable more
freely."

"I can retire," said Cecilia, rising from her chair with a
grave manner.

"Nay, Cecilia, I do not deserve these looks—'tis you who
exhibit levity now! But you can perceive, for yourself, that
evening is closing in, and that some other medium for conversation, besides the eyes, may be adopted.—Here is a signal,
which will answer: '*When the Abbey clock strikes nine, come with
care to the wicket, which opens, at the east side of the Paddock, on
the road: until then, keep secret.*' I had prepared this very signal,
in case an interview should be necessary."

"Well, he sees it," returned Cecilia, who had resumed her
place by the telescope, "and seems disposed to obey you, for I
no longer discern his flags or his person."

Miss Howard now arose from before the glass, her obser-

vations being ended; but Katherine did not return the instrument to its corner, without fastening one long and anxious
look through it, on what now appeared to be the deserted
tower. The interest and anxiety produced by this short and
imperfect communication between Miss Plowden and her
lover, did not fail to excite reflections in both the ladies, that
furnished materials to hold them in earnest discourse, until
the entrance of Alice Dunscombe announced that their presence was expected below. Even the unsuspecting Alice, on
entering, observed a change in the countenances and demeanor of the two cousins, which betrayed that their secret
conference had not been entirely without contention. The features of Cecilia were disturbed and anxious, and their expression was not unlike melancholy; while the dark flashing eye,
flushed temples, and proud, determined step of Katherine, exhibited in an equal, if not a greater degree, a very different
emotion. As no reference to the subject of their conversation
was, however, made by either of the young ladies, after the
entrance of Alice, she led the way, in silence, to the drawing
room.

The ladies were received, by Col. Howard and Borroughcliffe, with marked attention. In the former there were moments when a deep gloom would, in spite of his very obvious
exertions to the contrary, steal over his open, generous countenance; but the recruiting officer maintained an air of immovable coolness and composure. Twenty times did he detect
the piercing looks of Katherine fastened on him, with an in-
tentness, that a less deliberative man might have had the vanity to misinterpret; but even this flattering testimonial of his
power to attract, failed to disturb his self-possession. It was in
vain that Katherine endeavoured to read his countenance,
where every thing was fixed in military rigidity, though his
deportment appeared more than usually easy and natural.
Tired at length with her fruitless scrutiny, the excited girl
turned her gaze upon the clock; to her amazement, she discovered that it was on the stroke of nine, and, disregarding a
deprecating glance from her cousin, she arose and quitted the
apartment. Borroughcliffe opened the door for her exit, and,
while the lady civilly bowed her head in acknowledgment of
his attention, their eyes once more met; but she glided

quickly by him, and found herself alone in the gallery. Katherine hesitated, more than a minute, to proceed, for she thought she had detected in that glance a lurking expression, that manifested conscious security mingled with secret design. It was not her nature, however, to hesitate, when circumstances required that she should be both prompt and alert; and, throwing over her slight person a large cloak, that was in readiness for the occasion, she stole warily from the building.

Although Katherine suspected, most painfully, that Borroughcliffe had received intelligence that might prove dangerous to her lover, she looked around her in vain, on gaining the open air, to discover any alteration in the arrangements for the defence of the Abbey, which might confirm her suspicions, or the knowledge of which might enable her to instruct Barnstable how to avoid the secret danger. Every disposition remained as it had been since the capture of Griffith and his companion. She heard the heavy, quick steps of the sentinel, who was posted beneath their windows, endeavouring to warm himself, on his confined post; and as she paused to listen, she also detected the rattling of arms from the soldier, who, as usual, guarded the approach to that part of the building where his comrades were quartered. The night had set in cloudy and dark, although the gale had greatly subsided towards the close of the day; still the wind swept heavily, and, at moments, with a rushing noise, among the irregular walls of the edifice; and it required the utmost nicety of ear, to distinguish even these well-known sounds, among such accompaniments. When Katherine, however, was satisfied that her organs had not deceived her, she turned an anxious eye in the direction of what Borroughcliffe called his "barracks." Every thing in that direction appeared so dark and still as to create a sensation of uneasiness, by its very quiet. It might be the silence of sleep that now pervaded the ordinarily gay and mirthful apartment! or it might be the stillness of a fearful preparation! There was no time, however, for further hesitation, and Katherine drew her cloak more closely about her form, and proceeded, with light and guarded steps, to the appointed spot. As she approached the wicket the clock struck the hour, and she again paused, while the mournful sounds were borne by her on the wind, as if expecting that each

stroke on the bell, would prove a signal to unmask some secret design of Borroughcliffe. As the last vibration melted
away, she opened the little gate, and issued on the highway.
The figure of a man sprung forward from behind an angle of
the wall, as she appeared; and, while her heart was still throbbing with the suddenness of the alarm, she found herself in
the arms of Barnstable. After the first few words of recognition and pleasure which the young sailor uttered, he acquainted his mistress with the loss of his schooner, and the
situation of the survivors.

"And now, Katherine," he concluded, "you have come, I
trust, never to quit me; or, at most, to return no more to that
old Abbey, unless it be to aid in liberating Griffith, and then
to join me again for ever."

"Why, truly, there is so much to tempt a young woman to
renounce her home and friends, in the description you have
just given of your condition, that I hardly know how to
refuse your request, Barnstable. You are very tolerably provided with a dwelling in the ruin; and I suppose certain pred-
atory schemes are to be adopted to make it habitable! St.
Ruth is certainly well supplied with the necessary articles, but
whether we should not be shortly removed to the Castle at
York, or the gaol at Newcastle, is a question that I put to your
discretion."

"Why yield your thoughts to such silly subjects, lovely tri-
fler!" said Barnstable, "when the time and the occasion both
urge us to be in earnest?"

"It is a woman's province to be thrifty, and to look after the
comforts of domestic life," returned his mistress; "and I
would discharge my functions with credit. But I feel you are
vexed, for, to see your dark countenance is out of the question, on such a night. When do you propose to commence
housekeeping, if I should yield to your proposals?"

"I have not concluded relating my plans, and your provoking wit annoys me! The vessel I have taken, will, unquestionably, come into the land, as the gale dies; and I intend
making my escape in her, after beating this Englishman, and
securing the liberty of Miss Howard and yourself. I could see
the Frigate in the offing, even before we left the cliffs."

"This certainly sounds better!" rejoined Katherine, in a

manner that indicated she was musing on their prospects; "and yet there may exist some difficulties in the way that you little suspect."

"Difficulties! there are none—there can be none."

"Speak not irreverently of the mazes of love, Mr. Barnstable. When was it ever known to exist unfettered or unembarrassed? even I have an explanation to ask of you, that I would much rather let alone."

"Of me! ask what you will, or how you will; I am a careless, unthinking fellow, Miss Plowden; but to you I have little to answer for—unless a foolish sort of adoration be an offence against your merits."

Barnstable felt the little hand that was supported on his arm, pressing the limb, as Katherine replied, in a tone so changed from its former forced levity, that he started as the first sounds reached his ears. "Merry has brought in a horrid report!" she said; "I would I could believe it untrue! but the looks of the boy, and the absence of Dillon, both confirm it."

"Poor Merry! he too has fallen into the trap! but they shall yet find one who is too cunning for them. Is it to the fate of that wretched Dillon that you allude?"

"He *was* a wretch," continued Katherine, in the same voice, "and he deserved much punishment at your hands, Barnstable; but life is the gift of God, and is not to be taken whenever human vengeance would appear to require a victim."

"His life was taken by him who bestowed it," said the sailor. "Is it Katherine Plowden who would suspect me of the deed of a dastard!"

"I do not suspect you—I did not suspect you," cried Katherine; "I will never suspect any evil of you again. You are not, you cannot be angry with me, Barnstable? had you heard the cruel suspicions of my cousin Cecilia, and had your imagination been busy in portraying your wrongs and the temptations to forget mercy, like mine, even while my tongue denied your agency in the suspected deed, you would—you would at least have learned, how much easier it is to defend those we love against the open attacks of others, than against our own jealous feelings."

"Those words, love and jealousy, will obtain your acquittal," cried Barnstable, in his natural voice; and, after uttering a few more consoling assurances to Katherine, whose excited feelings found vent in tears, he briefly related the manner of Dillon's death.

"I had hoped I stood higher in the estimation of Miss Howard, than to be subjected to even her suspicions," he said, when he had ended his explanation. "Griffith has been but a sorry representative of our trade, if he has left such an opinion of its pursuits."

"I do not know that Mr. Griffith would altogether have escaped my conjectures, had he been the disappointed commander, and you the prisoner," returned Katherine; "you know not how much we have both studied the usages of war, and with what dreadful pictures of hostages, retaliations, and military executions, our minds are stored! but a mountain is raised off my spirits, and I could almost say, that I am now ready to descend the valley of life in your company."

"It is a discreet determination, my good Katherine, and God bless you for it; the companion may not be so good as you deserve, but you will find him ambitious of your praise. Now let us devise means to effect our object."

"Therein lies another of my difficulties. Griffith, I much fear, will not urge Cecilia to another flight, against her—her—what shall I call it, Barnstable—her caprice, or her judgment? Cecilia will never consent to desert her uncle, and I cannot muster the courage to abandon my poor cousin, in the face of the world, in order to take shelter with even Mr. Richard Barnstable!"

"Speak you from the heart now, Katherine?"

"Very nearly—if not exactly."

"Then have I been cruelly deceived! It is easier to find a path in the trackless ocean, without chart or compass, than to know the windings of a woman's heart!"

"Nay, nay, foolish man; you forget that I am but small, and how very near my head is to my heart; too nigh, I fear, for the discretion of their mistress! but is there no method of forcing Griffith and Cecilia to their own good, without undue violence?"

"It cannot be done; he is my senior in rank, and the instant I release him he will claim the command. A question might be raised, at a leisure moment, on the merits of such a claim—

but even my own men are, as you know, nothing but a draft from the frigate, and they would not hesitate to obey the orders of the first lieutenant, who is not a man to trifle on matters of duty."

" 'Tis vexatious, truly," said Katherine, "that all my well concerted schemes in behalf of this wayward pair, should be frustrated by their own wilful conduct! But, after all, have you justly estimated your strength, Barnstable? are you certain that you would be successful, and that without hazard, too, if you should make the attempt?"

"Morally, and what is better, physically certain. My men are closely hid, where no one suspects an enemy to lie; they are anxious for the enterprise, and the suddenness of the attack will not only make the victory sure, but it will be rendered bloodless. You will aid us in our entrance, Katherine: I shall first secure this recruiting officer, and his command will then surrender without striking a blow. Perhaps, after all, Griffith will hear reason; if he do not, I will not yield my authority to a released captive, without a struggle."

"God send that there shall be no fighting!" murmured his companion, a little appalled at the images his language had raised before her imagination; "and, Barnstable, I enjoin you, most solemnly, by all your affection for me, and by every thing you deem most sacred, to protect the person of Col. Howard at every hazard. There must be no excuse, no pretence, for even an insult to my passionate, good, obstinate, but kind old guardian. I believe I have given him already more trouble than I am entitled to give any one, and Heaven forbid, that I should cause him any serious misfortune!"

"He shall be safe, and not only he, but all that are with him; as you will perceive, Katherine, when you hear my plan. Three hours shall not pass over my head before you will see me master of that old Abbey. Griffith, ay, Griffith must be content to be my inferior, until we get afloat again."

"Attempt nothing unless you feel certain of being able to maintain your advantage, not only against your enemies, but also against your friends," said the anxious Katherine. "Rely on it, both Cecilia and Griffith are refining so much on their feelings, that neither will be your ally."

"This comes of passing the four best years of his life within walls of brick, poring over Latin Grammars and Syntaxes, and such other nonsense, when he should have been rolling them away in a good box of live oak, and studying, at most, how to sum up his day's work, and tell where his ship lies after a blow. Your college learning may answer well enough for a man who has to live by his wits, but it can be of little use to one who is never afraid to read human nature, by looking his fellow creatures full in the face, and whose hand is as ready as his tongue. I have generally found the eye that was good at Latin was dull at a compass, or in a night-squall: and yet, Grif is a seaman; though I have heard him even read the testament in Greek! Thank God, I had the wisdom to run away from school the second day they undertook to teach me a strange tongue, and I believe I am the more honest man, and the better seaman, for my ignorance!"

"There is no telling what you might have been, Barnstable, under other circumstances," retorted his mistress, with a playfulness of manner that she could not always repress, though it was indulged at the expense of him she most loved; "I doubt not but, under proper training, you would have made a reasonably good priest."

"If you talk of priests, Katherine, I shall remind you that we carry one in the ship. But listen to my plan; we may talk further of priestcraft when an opportunity may offer."

Barnstable then proceeded to lay before his mistress a project he had formed for surprising the Abbey that night, which was so feasible, that Katherine, notwithstanding her recent suspicions of Borroughcliffe's designs, came gradually to believe it would succeed. The young seaman answered her objections with the readiness of an ardent mind, bent on executing its purposes, and with a fertility of resources that proved he was no contemptible enemy, in matters that required spirited action. Of Merry's remaining firm and faithful he had no doubt, and, although he acknowledged the escape of the pedler boy, he urged that the lad had seen no other of his party besides himself, whom he mistook for a common marauder.

As the disclosure of these plans was frequently interrupted by little digressions, connected with the peculiar emotions of the lovers, more than an hour flew by, before they separated.

But Katherine, at length, reminded him how swiftly the time was passing, and how much remained to be done, when he reluctantly consented to see her once more through the wicket, where they parted.

Miss Plowden adopted the same precaution in returning to the house, she had used on leaving it; and she was congratulating herself on its success, when her eye caught a glimpse of the figure of a man, who was apparently following at some little distance, in her footsteps, and dogging her motions. As the obscure form, however, paused also when she stopped to give it an alarmed, though inquiring look, and then slowly retired towards the boundary of the paddock, Katherine believing it to be Barnstable watching over her safety, entered the Abbey, with every idea of alarm entirely lost in the pleasing reflection of her lover's solicitude.

# Chapter XXVIII.

"He looks abroad and soon appears,
    O'er Horncliffe-hill, a plump of spears,
    Beneath a pennon gay."
            Scott, *Marmion*, Canto First, III.1—4.

THE SHARP SOUNDS of the supper-bell were ringing along
    the gallery, as Miss Plowden gained the gloomy passage;
and she quickened her steps to join the ladies, in order that
no further suspicions might be excited by her absence.—Alice
Dunscombe was already proceeding to the dining parlour, as
Katherine passed through the door of the drawing room, but
Miss Howard had loitered behind, and was met by her cousin
alone.

"You have then been so daring as to venture, Katherine?"
exclaimed Cecilia.

"I have," returned the other, throwing herself into a chair,
to recover her agitation—"I have, Cecilia; and I have met
Barnstable, who will soon be in the Abbey, and its master."

The blood, which had rushed to the face of Cecilia on first
seeing her cousin, now retreated to her heart, leaving every
part of her fine countenance of the whiteness of her polished
temples, as she said—

"And we are to have a night of blood!"

"We are to have a night of freedom, Miss Howard; freedom to you, and to me; to Andrew Merry, to Griffith, and to
his companion!"

"What freedom more than we now enjoy, Katherine, is
needed by two young women? Think you I can remain silent,
and see my uncle betrayed before my eyes? his life perhaps
endangered?"

"Your own life and person will not be held more sacred,
Cecilia Howard, than that of your uncle. If you will condemn
Griffith to a prison, and perhaps to a gibbet, betray Barnstable, as you have threatened—an opportunity will not be
wanting at the supper table, whither I shall lead the way,
since the mistress of the house appears to forget her duty."

Katherine arose, and, with a firm step, and proud eye, she

moved along the gallery, to the room where their presence was expected by the rest of the family. Cecilia followed, in silence, and the whole party immediately took their several places at the board.

The first few minutes were passed in the usual attentions of the gentlemen to the ladies, and the ordinary civilities of the table; during which, Katherine had so far regained the equanimity of her feelings, as to commence a watchful scrutiny of the manners and looks of her guardian and Borroughcliffe, in which she determined to persevere until the eventful hour when she was to expect Barnstable should arrive. Col. Howard had, however, so far got the command of himself, as no longer to betray his former abstraction. In its place Katherine fancied, at moments, that she could discover a settled look of conscious security, mingled a little with an expression of severe determination; such as, in her earlier days, she had learned to dread as sure indications of the indignant, but upright justice of an honourable mind. Borroughcliffe, on the other hand, was cool, polite, and as attentive to the viands as usual, with the alarming exception of discovering much less devotion to the Pride of the Vineyards, than he commonly manifested on such occasions. In this manner the meal passed by, and the cloth was removed, though the ladies appeared willing to retain their places longer than was customary. Col. Howard, filling up the glasses of Alice Dunscombe, and himself, passed the bottle to the recruiting officer, and, with a sort of effort that was intended to rouse the dormant cheerfulness of his guests, cried—

"Come, Borroughcliffe, the ruby lips of your neighbours would be still more beautiful, were they moistened with this rich cordial, and that too, accompanied by some loyal sentiment. Miss Alice is ever ready to express her fealty to her Sovereign; in her name, I can give the health of His Most Sacred Majesty, with defeat and death to all traitors!"

"If the prayers of an humble subject, and one of a sex that has but little need to mingle in the turmoil of the world, and that has less right to pretend to understand the subtilties of statesmen, can much avail a High and Mighty Prince, like him who sits on the throne, then will he never know temporal evil," returned Alice, meekly; "but I cannot wish death to any one, not even to my enemies, if any I have, and much less to a people who are the children of the same family with myself."

"Children of the same family!" the Colonel repeated, slowly, and with a bitterness of manner that did not fail to attract the painful interest of Katherine; "children of the same family! Ay! even as Absalom was the child of David, or as Judas was of the family of the holy Apostles! But let it pass unpledged—let it pass. The accursed spirit of rebellion has invaded my dwelling, and I no longer know where to find one of my household, that has not been assailed by its malign influence!"

"Assailed I may have been, among others," returned Alice; "but not corrupted, if purity, in this instance, consist in loyalty—"

"What sound is that?" interrupted the Colonel, with startling suddenness. "Was it not the crash of some violence, Captain Borroughcliffe?"

"It may have been one of my rascals who has met with a downfall in passing from the festive board, where you know I regale them to-night, in honour of our success!—to his blanket," returned the Captain, with admirable indifference; "or it may be the very spirit of whom you have spoken so freely, my host, that has taken umbrage at your remarks, and is passing from the hospitable walls of St. Ruth into the open air, without submitting to the small trouble of ascertaining the position of doors. In the latter case there may be some dozen perches or so of wall to replace in the morning."

The Colonel, who had risen, glanced his eyes, uneasily, from the speaker to the door, and was, evidently, but little disposed to enter into the pleasantry of his guest.

"There are unusual noises, Capt. Borroughcliffe, in the grounds of the Abbey, if not in the building itself," he said, advancing, with a fine military air, from the table to the centre of the room, "and, as master of the mansion, I will inquire who it is that thus unseasonably disturbs these domains. If as friends, they shall have welcome, though their visit be unexpected; and if enemies, they shall also meet with such a reception as will become an old soldier!"

"No, no," cried Cecilia, entirely thrown off her guard by the manner and language of the veteran, and rushing into his arms. "Go not out, my uncle, go not into the terrible fray, my kind, my good uncle! you are old; you have already done more than your duty; why should you be exposed to danger?"

"The girl is mad with terror, Borroughcliffe," cried the Colonel, bending his glistening eyes fondly on his niece, "and you will have to furnish my good-for-nothing, gouty old person with a corporal's guard, to watch my night-cap, or the silly child will have an uneasy pillow, till the sun rises once more. But you do not stir, sir?"

"Why should I?" cried the captain; "Miss Plowden yet deigns to keep me company, and it is not in the nature of one of the ——th, to desert his bottle and his standard at the same moment. For, to a true soldier, the smiles of a lady are as imposing in the parlour, as the presence of his colours in the field."

"I continue undisturbed, Captain Borroughcliffe," said Katherine, "because I have not been an inhabitant, for so many months, of St. Ruth, and not learned to know the tunes which the wind can play among its chimneys and pointed roofs. The noise which has taken Col. Howard from his seat, and which has so unnecessarily alarmed my cousin Cicely, is nothing but the Æolian Harp of the Abbey sounding a double bass."

The captain fastened on her composed countenance, while she was speaking, a look of open admiration, that brought, though tardily, the colour more deeply to her cheeks; and he answered, with something extremely equivocal, both in his emphasis and his air—

"I have avowed my allegiance, and I will abide by it. So long as Miss Plowden will deign to bestow her company, so long will she find me among her most faithful and persevering attendants, come who may, or what will."

"You compel me to retire," returned Katherine, rising, "whatever may have been my gracious intentions in the matter; for even female vanity must crimson, at an adoration so profound as that which can chain Capt. Borroughcliffe to a supper-table! As your alarm has now dissipated, my cousin, will you lead the way? Miss Alice and myself attend you."

"But not into the paddock, surely, Miss Plowden," said the captain; "the door, the key of which you have just turned, communicates with the vestibule. This is the passage to the drawing room."

The lady faintly laughed, as if in derision of her own forgetfulness, while she bowed her acknowledgment, and moved towards the proper passage; she observed—

"The madness of fear has assailed some, I believe, who have been able to affect a better disguise than Miss Howard."

"Is it the fear of present danger, or of that which is in reserve?" asked the captain; "but, as you have stipulated so generously in behalf of my worthy host here, and of one, also, who shall be nameless, because he has not deserved such a favour at your hands, your safety shall be one of my especial duties in these times of peril."

"There is peril then!" exclaimed Cecilia; "your looks announce it, Capt. Borroughcliffe! The changing countenance of my cousin tells me that my fears are too true!"

The soldier had now risen also, and, casting aside the air of badinage, which he so much delighted in, he came forward into the centre of the apartment, with the manner of one who felt it was time to be serious.

"A soldier is ever in peril, when the enemies of his king are at hand, Miss Howard," he answered; "and that such is now the case, Miss Plowden can testify, if she will. But you are the allies of both parties—retire, then, to your own apartments, and await the result of the struggle which is at hand."

"You speak of danger and hidden perils," said Alice Dunscombe; "know ye aught that justifies your fears?"

"I know all," Borroughcliffe coolly replied.

"All!" exclaimed Katherine.

"All!" echoed Alice, in tones of horror. "If, then, you know all, you must know his desperate courage, and powerful hand, when opposed—yield in quiet, and he will not harm ye. Believe me, believe one who knows his very nature, that no lamb can be more gentle than he would be, with unresisting women; nor any lion more fierce, with his enemies!"

"As we happen not to be of the feminine gender," returned Borroughcliffe, with an air somewhat splenetic, "we must abide the fury of the king of beasts. His paw is, even now, at the outer door; and, if my orders have been obeyed, his entrance will be yet easier than that of the wolf, to the respect-able female ancestor of the little red-riding-hood."

"Stay your hand for one single moment!" said Katherine, breathless with interest; "you are the master of my secret, Capt. Borroughcliffe, and bloodshed may be the conse-quence. I can yet go forward, and, perhaps, save many inesti-mable lives. Pledge to me your honour, that they who come hither as your enemies, this night, shall depart in peace, and I will pledge to you my life for the safety of the Abbey."

"Oh! hear her, and shed not human blood!" cried Cecilia.

A loud crash interrupted further speech, and the sounds of heavy footsteps were heard in the adjoining room, as if many men were alighting on its floor, in quick succession. Bor-roughcliffe drew back, with great coolness, to the opposite side of the large apartment, and took a sheathed sword from the table where it had been placed; at the same moment the door was burst open, and Barnstable entered alone, but heavily armed.

"You are my prisoners, gentlemen," said the sailor, as he advanced; "resistance is useless, and without it you shall re-ceive favour. Ha! Miss Plowden! my advice was, that you should not be present at this scene."

"Barnstable, we are betrayed!" cried the agitated Katherine. "But it is not yet too late. Blood has not yet been spilt, and you can retire, without that dreadful alternative, with honour. Go, then, delay not another moment; for, should the soldiers of Capt. Borroughcliffe come to the rescue of their com-mander, the Abbey would be a scene of horror!"

"Go you away; go, Katherine," said her lover, with impa-tience; "this is no place for such as you. But, Capt. Borrough-cliffe, if such be your name, you must perceive that resistance is in vain. I have ten good pikes in this outer room, in twenty better hands, and it will be madness to fight against such odds."

"Show me your strength," said the captain, "that I may take counsel with mine honour."

"Your honour shall be appeased, my brave soldier, for such is your bearing, though your livery is my aversion, and your cause most unholy! Heave-ahead, boys! but hold your hands for orders."

The party of fierce-looking sailors, whom Barnstable led, on receiving this order, rushed into the room in a medley; but, notwithstanding the surly glances, and savage characters of their dress and equipments, they struck no blow, nor committed any act of hostility. The ladies shrunk back appalled, as this terrific little band took possession of the hall; and even Borroughcliffe, was seen to fall back towards a door, which, in some measure, covered his retreat. The confusion of this sudden movement had not yet subsided, when sounds of strife were heard rapidly approaching from a distant part of the building, and presently one of the numerous doors of the apartment was violently opened, when two of the garrison of the Abbey rushed into the hall, vigorously pressed by twice their number of seamen, seconded by Griffith, Manual, and Merry, who were armed with such weapons of offence as had presented themselves to their hands, at their unexpected liberation. There was a movement on the part of the seamen, who were already in possession of the room, that threatened instant death to the fugitives; but Barnstable beat down their pikes with his sword, and sternly ordered them to fall back. Surprise produced the same pacific result among the combatants; and as the soldiers hastily sought a refuge behind their own officers, and the released captives, with their liberators, joined the body of their friends, the quiet of the hall, which had been so rudely interrupted, was soon restored.

"You see, sir," said Barnstable, after grasping the hands of Griffith and Manual, in a warm and cordial pressure, "that all my plans have succeeded. Your sleeping guard are closely watched in their barracks, by one party, our officers are released, and your sentinels cut off by another, while, with a third, I hold the centre of the Abbey, and am, substantially, in possession of your own person. In consideration, therefore, of what is due to humanity, and to the presence of these ladies, let there be no struggle! I shall impose no difficult terms, nor any long imprisonment."

The recruiting officer manifested a composure, throughout the whole scene, that would have excited some uneasiness in his invaders, had there been opportunity for minute observation; but his countenance now gradually assumed an appearance of anxiety, and his head was frequently turned, as if listening for further, and more important interruptions. He answered, however, to this appeal, with his ordinary deliberation.

"You speak of conquests, sir, before they are achieved. My venerable host and myself are not so defenceless as you may choose to imagine." While speaking, he threw aside the cloth of a side table, from beneath which, the colonel and himself were instantly armed with a brace of pistols each. "Here are the death warrants of four of your party, and these brave fellows at my back can account for two more. I believe, my transatlantic warrior, that we are now something in the condition of Cortes and the Mexicans, when the former overran part of your continent—I being Cortes, armed with artificial thunder and lightning, and you the Indians, with nothing but your pikes and slings, and such other antediluvian inventions. Shipwrecks and sea-water are fatal dampers of gunpowder!"

"That we are unprovided with fire-arms, I will not deny," said Barnstable; "but we are men who are used, from infancy, to depend on our good right arms for life and safety, and we know how to use them, though we should even grapple with death! As for the trifles in your hands, gentlemen, you are not to suppose that men who are trained to look in at one end of a thirty-two pounder, loaded with grape, while the match is put to the other, will so much as wink at their report, though you fired them by fifties. What say you, boys! is a pistol a weapon to repel boarders?"

The discordant and disdainful laughs that burst from the restrained seamen, were a sufficient pledge of their indifference to so trifling a danger. Borroughcliffe noted their hardened boldness, and taking the supper bell, which was lying near him, he rang it, for a minute, with great violence. The heavy tread of trained footsteps soon followed this extraordinary summons; and presently, the several doors of the apartment were opened, and filled with armed soldiers, wearing the livery of the English crown.

"If you hold these smaller weapons in such vast contempt," said the recruiting officer, when he perceived that his men had possessed themselves of all the avenues, "it is in my power to try the virtue of some more formidable. After this exhibition of my strength, gentlemen, I presume you cannot hesitate to submit as prisoners of war."

The seamen had been formed in something like military array, by the assiduity of Manual, during the preceding dialogue; and as the different doors had discovered fresh accessions to the strength of the enemy, the marine industriously offered new fronts, until the small party was completely arranged in a hollow square, that might have proved formidable in a charge, bristled as it was with the deadly pikes of the Ariel.

"Here has been some mistake," said Griffith, after glancing his eye at the formidable array of the soldiers; "I take precedence of Mr. Barnstable, and I shall propose to you, Capt. Borroughcliffe, terms that may remove this scene of strife from the dwelling of Col. Howard."

"The dwelling of Col. Howard," cried the veteran, "is the dwelling of his king, or of the meanest servant of the crown! so, Borroughcliffe, spare not the traitors on my behalf; accept no other terms, than such unconditional submission as is meet to exact from the rebellious subjects of the Anointed of the Lord."

While Griffith spoke, Barnstable folded his arms, in affected composure, and glanced his eyes expressively at the shivering Katherine, who, with her companions, still continued agitated spectators of all that passed, chained to the spot by their apprehensions; but to this formidable denunciation, of the master of the Abbey, he deemed proper to reply—

"Now, by every hope I have of sleeping again on salt water, old gentleman, if it were not for the presence of these three trembling females, I should feel tempted to dispute, at once, the title of his majesty—you may make such a covenant as you will with Mr. Griffith, but if it contain one syllable about submission to your king, or of any other allegiance, than that which I owe to the Continental Congress, and the state of Massachusetts, you may as well consider the terms violated at once; for not an article of such an agreement will I consider as binding on me, or on any that shall choose to follow me as leader."

"Here are but two leaders, Mr. Barnstable," interrupted the haughty Griffith; "the one of the enemy, and the other, of the arms of America. Capt. Borroughcliffe, to you, as the former, I address myself. The great objects of the contest, which now unhappily divides England from her ancient colonies, can be, in no degree, affected by the events of this night; while, on the other hand, by a rigid adherence to military notions, much private evil and deep domestic calamity, must follow any struggle in such a place. We have but to speak, sir, and these rude men, who already stand impatiently handling their instruments of death, will aim them at each other's lives; and who can say that he shall be able to stay their hands when and where he will! I know you to be a soldier, and that you are not yet to learn how much easier it is to stimulate to blood, than to glut vengeance."

Borroughcliffe, unused to the admission of violent emotions, and secure in the superiority of his own party, both in numbers and equipments, heard him with the coolest composure to the end, and then answered in his customary manner.

"I honour your logic, sir. Your premises are indisputable, and the conclusion most obvious. Commit, then, these worthy tars to the good keeping of honest Drill, who will see their famished natures revived by diverse eatables, and a due proportion of suitable fluids; while we can discuss the manner in which you are to return to the colonies, around a bottle of liquor, which my friend Manual there, assures me has come from the sunny side of the island of Madeira, to be drunk in a bleak corner of that of Britain. By my palate! but the rascals brighten at the thought! They know by instinct, sir, that a shipwrecked mariner is a fitter companion to a ration of beef and a pot of porter, than to such unsightly things as bayonets and boarding-pikes!"

"Trifle not unseasonably!" exclaimed the impatient young sailor. "You have the odds in numbers, but whether it will avail you much in a deadly struggle of hand to hand, is a question you must put to your prudence: we stand not here to ask terms, but to grant them. You must be brief, sir, for the time is wasting while we delay."

"I have offered to you the means of obtaining in perfection the enjoyment of the three most ancient of the numerous family of the arts—eating, drinking, and sleeping! What more do you require?"

"That you order these men, who fill the pass to the outer door, to fall back and give us room. I would take, in peace, these armed men from before the eyes of those who are unused to such sights. Before you oppose this demand, think how easily these hardy fellows could make a way for themselves, against your divided force."

"Your companion, the experienced Capt. Manual, will tell you that such a manœuvre would be very unmilitary, with a superior body in your rear!"

"I have not leisure, sir, for this folly," cried the indignant Griffith. "Do you refuse us an unmolested retreat from the Abbey?"

"I do."

Griffith turned, with a look of extreme emotion, to the ladies, and beckoned to them to retire, unable to give utterance to his wishes in words. After a moment of deep silence, however, he once more addressed Borroughcliffe in the tones of conciliation.

"If Manual and myself will return to our prisons, and submit to the will of your government," he said, "can the rest of the party return to the frigate unmolested?"

"They cannot," replied the soldier, who, perceiving that the crisis approached, was gradually losing his artificial deportment in the interest of the moment. "You, and all others, who willingly invade the peace of these realms, must abide the issue."

"Then God protect the innocent and defend the right!"

"Amen."

"Give way, villains!" cried Griffith, facing the party that held the outer door; "give way, or you shall be riddled with our pikes!"

"Show them your muzzles, men!" shouted Borroughcliffe; "but pull no trigger till they advance."

There was an instant of bustle and preparation, in which the rattling of fire-arms, blended with the suppressed execrations and threats of the intended combatants; and Cecilia and Katherine had both covered their faces to veil the horrid sight that was momentarily expected, when Alice Dunscombe advanced, boldly, between the points of the threatening weapons, and spoke in a voice that stayed the hands that were already uplifted.

"Hear me, men! if men ye be, and not demons, thirsting for each other's blood; though ye walk abroad in the semblance of him who died that ye might be elevated to the rank of angels! call ye this war? Is this the glory that is made to warm the hearts of even silly and confiding women? Is the peace of families to be destroyed to gratify your wicked lust for conquest; and is life to be taken in vain, in order that ye may boast of the foul deed in your wicked revels! Fall back, then, ye British soldiers! if ye be worthy of that name, and give passage to a woman; and remember that the first shot that is fired, will be buried in her bosom!"

The men, thus enjoined, shrunk before her commanding mien, and a way was made for her exit through that very door which Griffith had, in vain, solicited might be cleared for himself and party. But Alice, instead of advancing, appeared to have suddenly lost the use of those faculties which had already effected so much. Her figure seemed rooted to the spot where she had spoken, and her eyes were fixed in a settled gaze as if dwelling on some horrid object. While she yet stood in this attitude of unconscious helplessness, the doorway became again darkened, and the figure of the Pilot was seen on its threshold, clad, as usual, in the humble vestments of his profession, but heavily armed with the weapons of naval war. For an instant, he stood a silent spectator of the scene; and then advanced calmly, but with searching eyes, into the centre of the apartment.

# Chapter XXIX.

Don Pedro. "Welcome Signior: you are almost
come to part, almost a fray."
*Much Ado about Nothing*, V.i.113–114.

"DOWN WITH your arms, you Englishmen!" said the daring intruder; "and you, who fight in the cause of sacred liberty, stay your hands, that no unnecessary blood may flow. Yield yourself, proud Britons, to the power of the Thirteen Republics!"

"Ha!" exclaimed Borroughcliffe, grasping a pistol, with an air of great resolution, "the work thickens—I had not included this man in my estimate of their numbers. Is he a Sampson, that his single arm can change the face of things so suddenly! Down with your own weapon, you masquerader, or, at the report of this pistol, your body shall become a target for twenty bullets."

"And thine for a hundred!" returned the pilot—"without there! wind your call, fellow, and bring in our numbers. We will let this confident gentleman feel his weakness."

He had not done speaking, before the shrill whistle of a boatswain rose gradually on the ears of the listeners, until the sense of hearing became painfully oppressed, by the piercing sounds that rung under the arched roof of the hall, and penetrated even to the most distant recesses of the Abbey. A tremendous rush of men followed, who drove in before them the terrified fragment of Borroughcliffe's command, that had held the vestibule; and the outer room became filled with a dark mass of human bodies.

"Let them hear ye, lads!" cried their leader; "the Abbey is your own!"

The roaring of a tempest was not louder than the shout that burst from his followers, who continued their cheers, peal on peal, until the very roof of the edifice appeared to tremble with their vibrations. Numerous dark and shaggy heads were seen moving around the passage; some cased in the iron-bound caps of the frigate's boarders, and others glittering with the brazen ornaments of her marine guard. The sight of the latter did not fail to attract the eye of Manual, who rushed among the throng, and soon re-appeared, followed by a trusty band of his own men, who took possession of the posts held by the soldiers of Borroughcliffe, while the dialogue was continued between the leaders of the adverse parties.

Thus far Col. Howard had yielded to his guest, with a deep reverence for the principles of military subordination, the functions of a commander, but, now that affairs appeared to change so materially, he took on himself the right to question these intruders into his dwelling.

"By what authority, sir," the colonel demanded, "is it that you dare thus to invade the castle of a subject of this realm? Do you come backed by the commission of the lord lieutenant of the county, or has your warrant the signature of His Majesty's Secretary for the Home Department?"

"I bear no commission from any quarter," returned the pilot; "I rank only an humble follower of the friends of America; and having led these gentlemen into danger, I have thought it my duty to see them extricated. They are now safe; and the right to command all that hear me, rests with Mr. Griffith, who is commissioned by the Continental Congress for such service."

When he had spoken he fell back from the position he occupied, in the centre of the room, to one of its sides, where, leaning his body against the wainscot, he stood a silent observer of what followed—

"It appears, then, that it is to you, degenerate son of a most worthy father, that I must repeat my demand," continued the veteran. "By what right is my dwelling thus rudely assailed? and why is my quiet, and the peace of those I protect, so daringly violated?"

"I might answer you, Col. Howard, by saying that it is according to the laws of arms, or rather in retaliation for the thousand evils that your English troops have inflicted, between Maine and Georgia; but I wish not to increase the unpleasant character of this scene, and I therefore will tell you, that our advantage shall be used with moderation. The instant that our men can be collected, and our prisoners properly secured, your dwelling shall be restored to your authority. We

are no freebooters, sir, and you will find it so after our departure. Capt. Manual, draw off your guard into the grounds,
and make your dispositions for a return march to our boats—
let the boarders fall back, there! out with ye! out with ye—
tumble out, you boarders!"

The amicable order of the young lieutenant, which was delivered after the stern, quick fashion of his profession, operated on the cluster of dark figures, that were grouped around
the door, like a charm; and as the men whom Barnstable had
led, followed their shipmates into the court-yard, the room
was now left to such only, as might be termed the gentlemen
of the invading party, and the family of Col. Howard.

Barnstable had continued silent since his senior officer had
assumed the command, listening most attentively to each syllable that fell from either side; but now that so few remained,
and the time pressed, he spoke again—

"If we are to take boat so soon, Mr. Griffith, it would be
seemly that due preparations should be made to receive the
ladies, who are to honour us with their presence; shall I take
that duty on myself?"

The abrupt proposal produced a universal surprise in his
hearers; though the abashed and conscious expression of
Katherine Plowden's features, sufficiently indicated, that to
her, at least, it was not altogether unexpected. The long
silence that succeeded the question, was interrupted by Col.
Howard.

"Ye are masters, gentlemen; help yourselves to whatever
best suits your inclinations. My dwelling, my goods, and my
wards, are alike at your disposal—or, perhaps Miss Alice,
here, good and kind Miss Alice Dunscombe, may suit the
taste of some among ye! Ah! Edward Griffith! Edward Griffith! little did I ever—"

"Breathe not that name in levity again, thou scoffer, or
even your years may prove a feeble protection!" said a stern,
startling voice from behind. All eyes turned involuntarily at
the unexpected sounds, and the muscular form of the Pilot
was seen resuming its attitude of repose against the wall,
though every fibre in his frame was working with suppressed
passion.

When the astonished looks of Griffith ceased to dwell on

this extraordinary exhibition of interest in his companion, they were turned imploringly towards the fair cousins, who still occupied the distant corner, whither fear had impelled them.

"I have said, that we are not midnight marauders, Col. Howard," he replied; "but if any there be here, who will deign to commit themselves to our keeping, I trust it will not be necessary to say, at this hour, what will be their reception."

"We have not time for unnecessary compliments," cried the impatient Barnstable; "here is Merry, who, by years and blood, is a suitable assistant for them, in arranging their little baggage—what say you, urchin, can you play the ladies' maid on emergency?"

"Ay, sir, and better than I acted the pedler-boy," cried the gay youngster; "to have my merry cousin Kate, and my good cousin Cicely for shipmates, I could play our common grand-mother! Come, coz, let us be moving; you will have to allow a little lee-way in time, for my awkwardness."

"Stand back, young man," said Miss Howard, repulsing his familiar attempt to take her arm; and then advancing, with a maidenly dignity, nigher to her guardian, she continued, "I cannot know what stipulations have been agreed to by my cousin Plowden, in the secret treaty she has made this night with Mr. Barnstable; this for myself, Col. Howard, I would have you credit your brother's child when she says, that, to her, the events of the hour have not been more unexpected than to yourself."

The veteran gazed at her, for a moment, with an expression of his eye that denoted reviving tenderness; but gloomy doubts appeared to cross his mind again, and he shook his head, as he walked proudly away.

"Nay, then," added Cecilia, her head dropping meekly on her bosom, "I may be discredited by my uncle, but I cannot be disgraced without some act of my own."

She slowly raised her mild countenance again, and bending her eyes on her lover, she continued, while a rich rush of blood passed over her fine features—

"Edward Griffith, I will not, I cannot say how humiliating it is to think that you can, for an instant, believe I would again forget myself so much as to wish to desert him whom

God has given me for a protector, for one chosen by my own erring passions. And you, Andrew Merry! learn to respect the child of your mother's sister, if not for her own sake, at least for that of her who watched your cradle!"

"Here appears to be some mistake," said Barnstable, who participated, however, in no trifling degree, in the embarrassment of the abashed boy; "but, like all other mistakes on such subjects, it can be explained away, I suppose. Mr. Griffith, it remains for you to speak:—damn it, man," he whispered, "you are as dumb as a cod-fish—I am sure so fine a woman is worth a little fair weather talk:—you are muter than a four-footed beast—even an ass can bray!"

"We will hasten our departure, Mr. Barnstable," said Griffith, sighing heavily, and rousing himself, as if from a trance. "These rude sights cannot but appal the ladies. You will please, sir, to direct the order of our march to the shore. Captain Manual has charge of our prisoners, who must all be secured, to answer for an equal number of our own countrymen."

"And our countrywomen!" said Barnstable, "are they to be forgotten, in the selfish recollection of our own security!"

"With them we have no right to interfere, unless at their request."

"By Heaven! Mr. Griffith, this may smack of learning," cried the other, "and it may plead bookish authority as its precedent; but, let me tell you, sir, it savours but a little of a sailor's love."

"Is it unworthy of a seaman, and a gentleman, to permit the woman he calls his mistress to be so, other than in name?"

"Well, then, Griff, I pity you, from my soul. I would rather have had a sharp struggle for the happiness that I shall now obtain so easily, than that you should be thus cruelly disappointed. But you cannot blame me, my friend, that I avail myself of fortune's favour. Miss Plowden, your fair hand. Colonel Howard, I return you a thousand thanks for the care you have taken, hitherto, of this precious charge, and believe me, sir, that I speak frankly, when I say, that next to myself, I should choose to intrust her with you in preference to any man on earth."

The Colonel turned to the speaker, and bowed low, while he answered with grave courtesy—

"Sir, you repay my slight services with too much gratitude. If Miss Katherine Plowden has not become under my guardianship, all that her good father, Capt. John Plowden, of the Royal Navy, could have wished a daughter of his to be, the fault, unquestionably, is to be attributed to my inability to instruct, and to no inherent quality in the young lady herself. I will not say, take her, sir, since you have her in your possession already, and it would be out of my power to alter the arrangement; therefore, I can only wish that you may find her as dutiful as a wife, as she has been, hitherto, as a ward and a subject."

Katherine had yielded her hand, passively, to her lover, and suffered him to lead her more into the circle than she had before been; but now she threw off his arm, and shaking aside the dark curls which she had rather invited to fall in disorder around her brow, she raised her face and looked proudly up, with an eye that sparkled with the spirit of its mistress, and a face that grew pale with emotion at each moment, as she proceeded—

"Gentlemen, the one may be as ready to receive as the other is to reject; but has the daughter of John Plowden no voice in this cool disposal of her person! If her guardian tires of her presence, other habitations may be found, without inflicting so severe a penalty on this gentleman, as to compel him to provide for her accommodation in a vessel which must be already straitened for room!"

She turned, and rejoined her cousin with such an air of maidenly resentment, as a young woman would be apt to discover, who found herself the subject of matrimonial arrangement, without her own feelings being at all consulted. Barnstable, who knew but little of the windings of the female heart, or how necessary to his mistress, notwithstanding her previous declarations, the countenance of Cecilia was, to any decided and open act in his favour, stood in stupid wonder at her declaration. He could not conceive that a woman who had already ventured so much in secret in his behalf, and who had so often avowed her weakness, should shrink to declare it again, at such a crisis, though the eyes of a universe were on her! He looked from one of the party to the other, and met in every face an expression of delicate reserve, except in those of the guardian of his mistress, and of Borroughcliffe.

The colonel had given a glance of returning favour at her, whom, he now conceived, to be his repentant ward, while the countenance of the entrapped captain exhibited a look of droll surprise, blended with the expression of bitter ferocity it had manifested since the discovery of his own mishap.

"Perhaps, sir," said Barnstable, addressing the latter, fiercely, "you see something amusing about the person of this lady, to divert you thus unseasonably. We tolerate no such treatment of our women in America!"

"Nor do we quarrel before ours in England," returned the soldier, throwing back the fierce glance of the sailor, with interest; "but I was thinking of the revolutions that time can produce! nothing more I do assure you. It is not half an hour since I thought myself a most happy fellow; secure in my plans for overreaching the scheme you had laid to surprise me; and now I am as miserable a dog as wears a single epaulette, and has no hope of seeing its fellow!"

"And in what manner, sir, can this sudden change apply to me?" asked Katherine, with all her spirit.

"Certainly not to your perseverance in the project to assist my enemies, madam," returned the soldier with affected humility; "nor to your zeal for their success, or your consummate coolness at the supper table! But I find it is time that I should be superannuated—I can no longer serve my king with credit, and should take to serving my God, like all other worn out men of the world! My hearing is surely defective, or a paddock wall has a most magical effect in determining sounds!"

Katherine waited not to hear the close of this sentence, but walked to a distant part of the room, to conceal the burning blushes that covered her countenance. The manner in which the plans of Barnstable had become known to his foe, was no longer a mystery. Her conscience also reproached her a little, with some unnecessary coquetry as she remembered, that quite one half of the dialogue between her lover and herself, under the shadow of that very wall to which Borroughcliffe alluded, had been on a subject altogether foreign to contention and tumults. As the feelings of Barnstable were by no means so sensitive as those of his mistress, and his thoughts much occupied with the means of attaining his object, he did not so readily comprehend the indirect allusion of the soldier, but turned abruptly away to Griffith, and observed, with a serious air—

"I feel it my duty, Mr. Griffith, to suggest, that we have standing instructions to secure all the enemies of America, wherever they may be found, and to remind you, that the States have not hesitated to make prisoners of females, in many instances."

"Bravo!" cried Borroughcliffe; "if the ladies will not go as your mistresses, take them as your captives!"

" 'Tis well for you, sir, that you are a captive yourself, or you should be made to answer for this speech," retorted the irritated Barnstable. "It is a responsible command, Mr. Griffith, and must not be disregarded."

"To your duty, Mr. Barnstable," said Griffith, again arousing from deep abstraction; "you have your orders, sir; let them be executed promptly."

"I have also the orders of our common superior, Capt. Munson, Mr. Griffith; and I do assure you, sir, that in making out my instructions for the Ariel—poor thing! there are no two of her timbers hanging together!—but my instructions were decidedly particular on that head."

"And my orders now supersede them."

"But am I justifiable in obeying a verbal order from an inferior, in direct opposition to a written instruction?"

Griffith had hitherto manifested in his deportment nothing more than a cold determination to act, but the blood now flew to every vessel in his cheeks and forehead, and his dark eyes flashed fire, as he cried authoritatively—

"How, sir! do you hesitate to obey?"

"By heaven, sir, I would dispute the command of the Continental Congress itself, should they bid me so far to forget my duty to—to—"

"Add yourself, sir!—Mr. Barnstable, let this be the last of it. To your duty, sir."

"My duty calls me here, Mr. Griffith."

"I must act, then, or be bearded by my own officers. Mr.

Merry, direct Capt. Manual to send in a serjeant, and a file of marines."

"Bid him come on himself!" cried Barnstable, maddened to desperation by his disappointment; " 'tis not his whole corps that can disarm me—let them come on! Hear, there, you Ariels! rally around your captain."

"The man among them, who dares to cross that threshold without my order, dies," cried Griffith, menacing, with a naked hanger, the seamen, who had promptly advanced at the call of their old commander. "Yield your sword, Mr. Barnstable, and spare yourself the disgrace of having it forced from you by a common soldier."

"Let me see the dog who dare attempt it!" exclaimed Barnstable, flourishing his weapon in fierce anger. Griffith had extended his own arm, in the earnestness of his feelings, and their hangers crossed each other. The clashing of the steel operated on both like the sound of the clarion on a war-horse, and there were sudden and rapid blows, and as rapid parries, exchanged between the flashing weapons.

"Barnstable! Barnstable!" cried Katherine, rushing into his arms, "I will go with you to the ends of the earth!"

Cecilia Howard did not speak; but when Griffith recovered his coolness, he beheld her beautiful form kneeling at his feet, with her pale face bent imploringly on his own disturbed countenance. The cry of Miss Plowden had separated the combatants, before an opportunity for shedding blood had been afforded, but the young men exchanged looks of keen resentment, notwithstanding the interference of their mistresses. At this moment Col. Howard advanced, and raising his niece from her humble posture, said—

"This is not a situation for a child of Harry Howard, though she knelt in the presence, and before the throne of her Sovereign. Behold, my dear Cecilia, the natural consequences of this rebellion! It scatters discord in their ranks; and, by its damnable levelling principles, destroys all distinction of rank among themselves; even these rash boys know not where obedience is due!"

"It is due to me," said the Pilot, who now stepped forward among the agitated group, "and it is time that I enforce it. Mr. Griffith, sheath your sword. And you, sir, who have defied the authority of your senior officer, and have forgotten the obligation of your oath, submit, and return to your duty."

Griffith started at the sounds of his calm voice, as if with sudden recollection; and then bowing low, he returned the weapon to its scabbard. But Barnstable still encircled the waist of his mistress with one arm, while, with the other, he brandished his hanger, and laughed with scorn at this extraordinary assumption of authority.

"And who is this!" he cried, "who dares give such an order to me!"

The eyes of the Pilot flashed with a terrible fire, while a fierce glow seemed to be creeping over his whole frame, which actually quivered with passion. But, suppressing this exhibition of his feelings, by a sudden and powerful effort, he answered, in an emphatic manner—

"One who has a right to order, and who *will* be obeyed!"

The extraordinary manner of the speaker, contributed as much as his singular assertion, to induce Barnstable, in his surprise, to lower the point of his weapon, with an air that might easily have been mistaken for submission. The Pilot fastened his glowing eyes on him, for an instant, and then turning to the rest of the listeners, he continued, more mildly—

"It is true that we came not here as marauders, and that our wish is, to do no unnecessary acts of severity to the aged and the helpless. But this officer of the Crown, and this truant American, in particular, are fairly our prisoners; as such, they must be conducted on board our ship."

"But the main object of our expedition?"—said Griffith.

" 'Tis lost," returned the Pilot, hastily—" 'tis sacrificed to more private feelings; 'tis like a hundred others, ended in disappointment, and is forgotten, sir, for ever. But the interests of the Republics must not be neglected, Mr. Griffith.— Though we are not madly to endanger the lives of those gallant fellows, to gain a love-smile from one young beauty, neither are we to forget the advantages they may have obtained for us, in order to procure one of approbation from another. This Col. Howard will answer well, in a bargain with the minions of the Crown, and may purchase the freedom of some worthy patriot, who is deserving of his liberty.

Nay, nay, suppress that haughty look, and turn that proud eye on any, rather than me! he goes to the frigate, sir, and that immediately."

"Then," said Cecilia Howard, timidly approaching the spot where her uncle stood, a disdainful witness of the dissensions amongst his captors; "then, will I go with him! He shall never be a resident among his enemies alone!"

"It would be more ingenuous, and more worthy of my brother's daughter," said her uncle, coldly, "if she ascribed her willingness to depart to its proper motive." Disregarding the look of deep distress with which Cecilia received this mortifying rejection of her tender attention, the old man walked towards Borroughcliffe, who was gnawing the hilt of his sword, in very vexation at the downfall of his high-raised hopes, and placing himself by his side, with an air of infinitely dignified submission, he continued, "act your pleasure on us, gentlemen: you are the conquerors, and we must even submit. A brave man knows as well how to yield, with decorum, as to defend himself stoutly, when he is not surprised, as we have been. But if an opportunity should ever offer!—Act your pleasures, gentlemen; no two lambs were ever half so meek as Capt. Borroughcliffe and myself."

The smile of affected, but bitter resignation, that the colonel bestowed on his fellow prisoner, was returned by that officer, with an attempt at risibility that abundantly betokened the disturbed state of his feelings. The two, however, succeeded in so far maintaining appearances, as to contemplate the succeeding movements of the conquerors, with a sufficient degree of composure.

The colonel steadily, and coldly, rejected the advances of his niece, who bowed meekly to his will, and relinquished, for the present, the hope of bringing him to a sense of his injustice. She, however, employed herself in earnest, to give such directions as were necessary to enforce the resolution she had avowed, and in this unexpected employment she found both a ready and a willing assistant in her cousin. The latter, unknown to Miss Howard, had, in anticipation of some such event as the present, long since made, in secret, all those preparations which might become necessary to a sudden flight from the Abbey. In conjunction with her lover then, who, perceiving that the plan of the Pilot was furthering his own views, deemed it most wise to forget his quarrel with that mysterious individual, she flew to point out the means of securing those articles which were already in preparation. Barnstable and Merry accompanied her light steps among the narrow, dark passages of the Abbey, with the utmost delight; the former repeatedly apostrophizing her wit and beauty, and, indeed, all of her various merits, and the latter, laughing, and indulging those buoyant spirits, that a boy of his years and reflection might be supposed to feel even in such a scene. It was fortunate for her cousin, that Katherine had possessed so much forethought, for the attention of Cecilia Howard was directed much more to the comforts of her uncle, than to those which were necessary for herself. Attended by Alice Dunscombe, the young mistress of St. Ruth moved through the solitary apartments of the building, listening to the mild, religious consolation of her companion, in silence, at times yielding to those bursts of mortified feeling, that she could not repress, or again as calmly giving her orders to her maids, as if the intended movement was one of but ordinary interest. All this time, the party in the dining hall remained stationary. The Pilot, as if satisfied with what he had already done, sunk back to his reclining attitude against the wall, though his eyes keenly watched every movement of the preparations, in a manner which denoted that his was the master spirit that directed the whole. Griffith had, however, resumed, in appearance, the command, and the busy seamen addressed themselves for orders to him alone. In this manner an hour was consumed, when Cecilia and Katherine, appearing in succession, attired in a suitable manner for their departure, and the baggage of the whole party having been already entrusted to a petty officer, and a party of his men, Griffith gave forth the customary order to put the whole in motion. The shrill, piercing whistle of the boatswain once more rung among the galleries and ceilings of the Abbey, and was followed by the deep, hoarse cry of—

"Away, there! you shore-draft! away, there, you boarders! ahead, heave ahead, sea-dogs!"

This extraordinary summons was succeeded by the roll of a drum, and the strains of a fife, from without, when the whole party moved from the building in the order that had been previously prescribed by Capt. Manual, who acted as the marshal of the forces on the occasion.

The Pilot had conducted his surprise with so much skill and secrecy as to have secured every individual about the Abbey, whether male or female, soldier or civilian; and as it might be dangerous to leave any behind who could convey intelligence into the country, Griffith had ordered that every human being, found in the building, should be conducted to the cliffs; to be held in durance, at least, until the departure of the last boat to the cutter, which he was informed, lay close in to the land, awaiting their re-embarkation. The hurry of the departure had caused many lights to be kindled in the Abbey, and the contrast between the glare within, and the gloom without, attracted the wandering looks of the captives, as they issued into the paddock. One of those indefinable, and unaccountable feelings, which so often cross the human mind, induced Cecilia to pause at the great gate of the grounds, and look back at the Abbey, with a presentiment that she was to behold it for the last time. The dark and ragged outline of the edifice was clearly delineated against the northern sky, while the open windows, and neglected doors, permitted a view of the solitude within. Twenty tapers were shedding their useless light in the empty apartments, as if in mockery of the deserted walls, and Cecilia turned, shuddering, from the sight, to press nigher to the person of her indignant uncle, with a secret impression, that her presence would soon be more necessary than ever to his happiness.

The low hum of voices in front, with the occasional strains of the fife, and the stern mandates of the sea-officers, soon recalled her, however, from these visionary thoughts to the surrounding realities, while the whole party pursued their way with diligence to the margin of the ocean.

# Chapter XXX.

"A chieftain to the Highlands bound,
Cries 'Boatman, do not tarry!
And I'll give thee a silver pound,
To row us o'er the ferry.' "
Campbell, "Lord Ullin's Daughter," ll. 1–4.

THE SKY had been without a cloud during the day, the
gale having been dry and piercing, and thousands of stars
were now shining through a chill atmosphere. As the eye,
therefore, became accustomed to the change of light, it obtained a more distinct view of surrounding objects. At the
head of the line, that was stretched along the narrow path-
way, marched a platoon of the marines, who maintained the
regular, and steady front of trained warriors. They were followed, at some little distance, by a large and confused body of
seamen, heavily armed, whose disposition to disorder and
rude merriment, which became more violent from their treading on solid ground, was with difficulty restrained by the
presence and severe rebukes of their own officers. In the centre of this confused mass, the whole of the common prisoners
were placed, but were no otherwise attended to by their nautical guard, than as they furnished the subjects of fun and
numberless quaint jokes. At some distance in their rear,
marched Col. Howard and Borroughcliffe, arm in arm, both
maintaining the most rigid and dignified silence, though under the influence of very bitter feelings. Behind these again,
and pressing as nigh as possible to her uncle, was Miss
Howard, leaning on the arm of Alice Dunscombe, and surrounded by the female domestics of the establishment of St.
Ruth. Katherine Plowden moved lightly by herself, in the
shadow of this group, with elastic steps, but with a maiden
coyness, that taught her to veil her satisfaction with the semblance of captivity. Barnstable watched her movements with
delight, within six feet of her, but submitted to the air of
caprice in his mistress, which seemed to require that he
should come no nearer. Griffith, avoiding the direct line of
the party, walked on its skirts in such a situation that his eye

345

could command its whole extent, in order, if necessary, to direct the movements. Another body of the marines marched at the close of the procession, and Manual, in person, brought up the rear. The music had ceased by command, and nothing was now audible, but the regular tread of the soldiers, with the sighs of the dying gale, interrupted occasionally by the voice of an officer, or the hum of low dialogue.

"This has been a Scotch prize that we've taken," muttered a surly old seaman; "a ship without head-money or cargo! There was kitchen timber enough in the old jug of a place, to have given an outfit in crockery and knee-buckles, to every lad in the ship; but, no! let a man's mouth water ever so much for food and rainment, damme if the officers would give him leave to steal even so good a thing as a spare Bible."

"You may say all that, and then make but a short yarn of the truth," returned the messmate, who walked by his side; "if there had been such a thing as a ready-made prayer handy, they would have choused a poor fellow out of the use of it.— I say, Ben, I'll tell ye what; it's my opinion, that if a chap is to turn soldier and carry a musket, he should have soldiers' play, and leave to plunder a little—now the devil a thing have I laid my hands on to-night, except this firelock, and my cutlash—unless you can call this bit of a table-cloth something of a windfall."

"Ay! you have fallen in there with a fresh bolt of duck, I see!" said the other, in manifest admiration of the texture of his companion's prize—"why, it would spread as broad a clue as our mizen-royal, if it was loosened! well, your luck hasn't been every man's luck—for my part, I think this here hat was made for some fellow's great toe; I've rigged it on my head both fore-and-aft, and athwart ships; but curse the inch can I drive it down—I say, Sam! you'll give us a shirt off that table cloth?"

"Ay, ay, you can have one corner of it; or for that matter, ye can take the full half, Nick; but I don't see that we go off to the ship any richer than we landed, unless you may muster she-cattle among your prize money."

"No richer!" interrupted a waggish young sailor, who had been hitherto a silent listener to the conversation between his older, and more calculating shipmates; "I think we are set up for a cruise in them seas where the day watches last six months; don't you see we have caught a double allowance of midnight!"

While speaking he laid his hands on the bare and woolly heads of Col. Howard's two black slaves, who were moving near him, both occupied in mournful forebodings on the results that were to flow from this unexpected loss of their liberty. "Slue your faces this way, gentlemen," he added; "there; don't you think that a sight to put out the binnacle lamps? there's darkness visible for ye!"

"Let the niggars alone," grumbled one of the more aged speakers; "what are ye sky-larking with the like of them for? the next thing they'll sing out, and then you'll hear one of the officers in your wake. For my part, Nick, I can't see why it is that we keep dodging along shore here, with less than ten fathoms under us, when, by stretching into the broad Atlantic, we might fall in with a Jamaica-man every day or two, and have sugar hogsheads, and rum puncheons as plenty aboard us as hard fare is now."

"It is all owing to that Pilot," returned the other; "for d'ye see, if there was no bottom, there would be no Pilots. This is a dangerous cruising ground, where we stretch into five fathoms, and then drop our lead on a sand-spit, or a rock! Besides, they make night work of it too! If we had day-light for fourteen hours instead of seven, a man might trust to feeling his way for the other ten."

"Now, a'n't ye a couple of old horse-marines!" again interrupted the young sailor; "don't you see that Congress wants us to cut up Johnny Bull's coasters, and that old Blow-Hard has found the days too short for his business, and so he has landed a party to get hold of night. Here we have him! and when we get off to the ship, we shall put him under hatches, and then you'll see the face of the sun again! Come, my lilies! let these two old gentlemen look into your cabin windows — what? you won't! Then I must squeeze your woollen night-caps for ye!"

The negroes, who had been submitting to his humours with the abject humility of slavery, now gave certain low intimations that they were suffering pain, under the rough manipulation of their tormentor.

"What's that!" cried a stern voice, whose boyish tones seemed to mock the air of authority that was assumed by the speaker—"who's that, I say, raising that cry among ye?"

The wilful young man slowly removed his two hands from the woolly polls of the slaves, but as he suffered them to fall reluctantly along their sable temples, he gave the ear of one of the blacks a tweak that caused him to give vent to another cry, that was uttered with a much greater confidence of sympathy than before.

"Do ye hear, there!" repeated Merry—"who's sky-larking with those negroes?"

" 'Tis no one, sir," the sailor answered with affected gravity; "one of the pale faces has hit his shin against a cob-web, and it has made his ear ache!"

"Harkye, you mister Jack Joker! how came you in the midst of the prisoners! did not I order you to handle your pike, sir, and to keep in the outer line!"

"Ay, ay, sir, you did; and I obeyed orders as long as I could; but these niggars have made the night so dark, that I lost my way!"

A low laugh passed through the confused crowd of seamen, and even the midshipman might have been indulging himself in a similar manner at this specimen of quaint humour, from the fellow, who was one of those licensed men that are to be found in every ship. At length—

"Well, sir," he said, "you have found out your false reckoning now; so get you back to the place where I bid you stay."

"Ay, ay, sir, I'm going. By all the blunders in the purser's book, Mr. Merry, but that cob-web has made one of these niggars shed tears! Do let me stay to catch a little ink, sir, to write a letter with to my poor old mother—devil the line has she had from me since we sailed from the Chesapeake!"

"If ye don't mind me at once, Mr. Jack Joker, I'll lay my cutlass over your head," returned Merry, his voice now betraying a much greater sympathy in the sufferings of that abject race, who are still in some measure, but who formerly were much more, the butts of the unthinking and licentious among our low countrymen; "then ye can write your letter in red ink if ye will!"

"I wouldn't do it for the world," said Joker, sneaking away, towards his proper station—"the old lady wouldn't forget the hand, and swear it was a forgery—I wonder, though, if the breakers on the coast of Guinea be black! as I've heard old seamen say who have cruised in them latitudes."

His idle levity was suddenly interrupted by a voice that spoke above the low hum of the march, with an air of authority, and a severity of tone, that could always quell, by a single word, the most violent ebullition of merriment in the crew.

The low buzzing sounds of "Ay, there goes Mr. Griffith!" and of "Jack has woke up the first lieutenant, he had better now go to sleep himself;" were heard passing among the men. But these suppressed communications soon ceased, and even Jack Joker himself pursued his way with diligence, on the skirts of the party, as mutely as if the power of speech did not belong to his organization.

The reader has too often accompanied us over the ground between the Abbey and the ocean, to require any description of the route pursued by the seamen during the preceding characteristic dialogue; and we shall at once pass to the incidents which occurred on the arrival of the party at the cliffs. As the man who had so unexpectedly assumed a momentary authority within St. Ruth, had unaccountably disappeared from among them, Griffith continued to exercise the right of command, without referring to any other for consultation. He never addressed himself to Barnstable, and it was apparent that both the haughty young men felt that the tie which had hitherto united them in such close intimacy, was, for the present at least, entirely severed. Indeed, Griffith was only restrained by the presence of Cecilia and Katherine, from arresting his refractory inferior on the spot; and Barnstable, who felt all the consciousness of error, without its proper humility, with difficulty so far repressed his feelings, as to forbear exhibiting in the presence of his mistress, such a manifestation of his spirit as his wounded vanity induced him to imagine was necessary to his honour. The two, however, acted in harmony on one subject, though it was without concert or communication. The first object with both the young men, was to secure the embarkation of the fair cousins; and Barnstable proceeded instantly to the boats, in order to hasten the preparations that were necessary before they could receive these unexpected captives: the descent of the Pilot having been made in such force as to require the use of all the frigate's boats, which were left riding in the outer edge of the surf, awaiting the return of the expedition. A loud call from Barnstable gave notice to the officer in command, and in a few moments the beach was crowded with the busy and active crews of the "cutters," "launches," "barges," "jolly-boats," "pinnaces," or by whatever names the custom of the times attached to the different attendants of vessels of war. Had the fears of the ladies themselves been consulted, the frigate's launch would have been selected for their use, on account of its size; but Barnstable, who would have thought such a choice on his part humiliating to his guests, ordered the long, low barge of Capt. Munson to be drawn upon the sand, it being peculiarly the boat of honour. The hands of fifty men were applied to the task, and it was soon announced to Col. Howard and his wards, that the little vessel was ready for their reception. Manual had halted on the summit of the cliffs with the whole body of the marines, where he was busily employed in posting picquets and sentinels, and giving the necessary instructions to his men to cover the embarkation of the seamen, in a style that he conceived to be altogether military. The mass of the common prisoners, including the inferior domestics of the Abbey, and the men of Borroughcliffe, were also held in the same place, under a suitable guard; but Col. Howard and his companion, attended by the ladies and their own maids, had descended the rugged path to the beach, and were standing passively on the sands, when the intelligence that the boat waited for them, was announced.

"Where is he?" asked Alice Dunscombe, turning her head, as if anxiously searching for some other than those around her.

"Where is who?" inquired Barnstable; "we are all here, and the boat waits."

"And will he tear me—even me, from the home of my infancy! the land of my birth and my affections!"

"I know not of whom you speak, madam, but if it be of Mr. Griffith, he stands there, just without that cluster of seamen."

Griffith, hearing himself thus named, approached the ladies, and, for the first time since leaving the Abbey, addressed them:—"I hope I am already understood," he said, "and that it is unnecessary for me to say, that no female here is a prisoner; though should any choose to trust themselves on board our ship, I pledge to them the honour of an officer, that they shall find themselves protected, and safe."

"Then will I not go," said Alice.

"It is not expected of you," said Cecilia; "you have no ties to bind you to any here."—(The eyes of Alice, were still wandering over the listeners.) "Go, then, Miss Alice, and be the mistress of St. Ruth, until my return; or," she added, timidly, "until Col. Howard may declare his pleasure."

"I obey you, dear child; but the agent of Col. Howard, at B—— will undoubtedly be authorized to take charge of his effects."

While no one but his niece alluded to his will, the master of the Abbey had found, in his resentment, a sufficient apology for his rigid demeanor; but he was far too well bred to hear, in silence, such a modest appeal to his wishes, from so fair, and so loyal a subject as Alice Dunscombe.

"To relieve you, madam, and for no other reason, will I speak on this subject," he said; "otherwise, I should leave the doors and windows of St. Ruth open, as a melancholy monument of rebellion, and seek my future compensation from the Crown, when the confiscated estates of the leaders of this accursed innovation on the rights of Princes, shall come to the hammer. But you, Miss Alice, are entitled to every consideration that a lady can expect from a gentleman. Be pleased, therefore, to write to my agent, and request him to seal up my papers, and transmit them to the office of his Majesty's Secretary of State. They breathe no treason, madam, and are entitled to official protection. The house, and most of the furniture, as you know, are the property of my landlord, who, in due time, will doubtless take charge of his own interest. I kiss your hand, Miss Alice, and I hope we shall yet meet at St. James's—depend on it, madam, that the Royal Charlotte shall yet honour your merits; I know she cannot but estimate your loyalty."

"Here I was born, in humble obscurity—here I have lived, and here I hope to die in quiet," returned the meek Alice; "if

I have known any pleasure, in late years, beyond that which
every Christian can find in our daily duties, it has been, my
sweet friends, in your accidental society.—Such companions,
in this remote corner of the kingdom, has been a boon too
precious to be enjoyed without alloy, it seems, and I have
now to exchange the past pleasure for present pain. Adieu!
my young friends; let your trust be in Him, to whose eyes
both prince and peasant, the European and the American, are
alike, and we shall meet again, though it be neither in the
island of Britain, nor on your own wide continent."

"That," said Col. Howard, advancing and taking her hand
with kindness, "that is the only disloyal sentiment I have ever
heard fall from the lips of Miss Alice Dunscombe! It is to be
supposed that Heaven has established orders among men, and
that it does not respect the works of its own formation! But
adieu; no doubt if time was allowed us for suitable explanations, we should find but little or no difference of opinion on
this subject."

Alice did not appear to consider the matter as worthy of
further discussion at such a moment, for she gently returned
the colonel's leave-taking, and then gave her undivided attention to her female friends. Cecilia wept bitterly on the shoulder of her respected companion, giving vent to her regret at
parting, and her excited feelings, at the same moment; and
Katherine pressed to the side of Alice, with the kindliness
prompted by her warm, but truant heart. Their embraces
were given and received in silence, and each of the young
ladies moved towards the boat, as she withdrew herself from
the arms of Miss Dunscombe. Col. Howard would not precede his wards, neither would he assist them into the barge.
That attention they received from Barnstable, who, after
seeing the ladies and their attendants seated, turned to the
gentlemen, and observed—

"The boat waits."

"Well, Miss Alice," said Borroughcliffe, in bitter irony,
"you are entrusted, by our excellent host, with a message to
his agent; will you do a similar service to me, and write a
report to the commander of the district, and just tell him
what a dolt—ay, use the plainest terms, and say what an ass,
one Capt. Borroughcliffe has proved himself in this affair.

You may throw in, by way of episode, that he has been playing bo-peep with a rebellious young lady from the Colonies, and, like a great boy, has had his head broken for his pains! Come, my worthy host, or rather, fellow prisoner, I follow you, as in duty bound."

"Stay," cried Griffith; "Capt. Borroughcliffe does not embark in that boat."

"Ha! sir; am I to be herded with the common men? Forget you that I have the honour to bear the commission of his Britannic Majesty, and that—"

"I forget nothing that a gentleman is bound to remember, Capt. Borroughcliffe; among other things, I recollect the liberality of your treatment to myself, when a prisoner. The instant the safety of my command will justify such a step, not only you, but your men, shall be set at liberty."

Borroughcliffe started in surprise; but his feelings were too much soured by the destruction of those visions of glory, in which he had been luxuriously indulging for the last day or two, to admit of his answering as became a man. He swallowed his emotions, therefore, by a violent effort, and walked along the beach, affecting to whistle a low, but lively air.

"Well, then," cried Barnstable—"all our captives are seated. The boat waits only for its officers!"

In his turn, Griffith walked away, in haughty silence, as if disdaining to hold communion with his former friend. Barnstable paused a moment, from a deference that long habit had created for his superior officer, and which was not to be shaken off by every burst of angry passion; but perceiving that the other had no intention to return, he ordered the seamen to raise the boat from the sand and bear it bodily into the water. The command was instantly obeyed; and by the time the young lieutenant was in his seat the barge was floating in the still heavy, though no longer dangerous surf, and the crew sprang into their places.

"Bear her off, boys!" he cried; "never mind a wet jacket. I've seen many a worthy fellow tumbling on this beach in a worse time than this! Now you have her head to sea; give way, my souls, give way."

The seamen rose simultaneously at their oars, and, by an united effort, obtained the command of their boat; which, after making a few sudden ascents and as many heavy pitches in the breakers, gained the smoother seas of the swelling ocean, and stemmed the waters, in a direction for the place where the Alacrity was supposed to be in waiting.

# Chapter XXXI.

"His only plot was this—that much provoked,
He raised his vengeful arm against his country."
Thomson, *Coriolanus*, V.iv.30–31.

ALICE DUNSCOMBE remained on the sands, watching the dark spot that was soon hid amid the waves, in the obscurity of night, and listening, with melancholy interest, to the regulated sounds of the oars, which were audible long after the boat had been blended with the gloomy outline of the eastern horizon. When all traces of her departed friends were to be found only in her own recollections, she slowly turned from the sea, and hastening to quit the bustling throng, that were preparing for the embarkation of the rest of the party, she ascended the path that conducted her once more to the summit of those cliffs, along which she had so often roved, gazing at the boundless element that washed their base, with sensations that might have been peculiar to her own situation.

The soldiers of Borroughcliffe, who were stationed at the head of the pass, respectfully made way; nor did any of the sentinels of Manual heed her retiring figure, until she approached the rear guard of the marines, who were commanded by their vigilant captain in person.

"Who goes there!" cried Manual, advancing without the dusky group of soldiers, as she approached them.

"One who possesses neither the power nor the inclination to do ye harm," answered the solitary female; " 'tis Alice Dunscombe, returning, by permission of your leader, to the place of her birth."

"Ay," muttered Manual, "this is one of Griffith's unmilitary exhibitions of his politeness! does the man think that there was ever a woman who had no tongue! Have you the countersign, madam, that I may know you bear a sufficient warrant to pass?"

"I have no other warrant besides my sex and weakness, unless Mr. Griffith's knowledge that I have left him, can be so considered."

"The two former are enough," said a voice, that proceeded from a figure which had hitherto stood unseen, shaded by the trunk of an oak, that spread its wide, but naked arms above the spot where the guard was paraded.

"Who have we here!" Manual again cried; "come in; yield or you will be fired at."

"What, will the gallant Capt. Manual fire on his own rescuer!" said the Pilot, with cool disdain, as he advanced from the shadow of the tree. "He had better reserve his bullets for his enemies, than waste them on his friends."

"You have done a dangerous deed, sir, in approaching, clandestinely, a guard of marines! I wonder that a man who has already discovered, to-night, that he has some knowledge of tactics, by so ably conducting a surprise, should betray so much ignorance in the forms of approaching a picquet!"

" 'Tis now of no moment," returned the Pilot; "my knowledge and my ignorance are alike immaterial, as the command of the party is surrendered to other, and perhaps more proper hands. But I would talk to this lady alone, sir; she is an acquaintance of my youth, and I will see her on her way to the Abbey."

"The step would be unmilitary, Mr. Pilot, and you will excuse me if I do not consent to any of our expedition straggling without the sentries. If you choose to remain here to hold your discourse, I will march the picquet out of hearing; though I must acknowledge I see no ground so favourable as this we are on, to keep you within the range of our eyes. You perceive that I have a ravine to retreat into, in case of surprise, with this line of wall on my left flank, and the trunk of that tree to cover my right. A very pretty stand might be made here, on emergency; for even the oldest troops fight the best when their flanks are properly covered, and a way to make a regular retreat is open in their rear."

"Say no more, sir; I would not break up such a position on any account," returned the Pilot; "the lady will consent to retrace her path for a short distance."

Alice followed his steps, in compliance with this request, until he had led her to a place, at some little distance from the marines, where a tree had been prostrated by the late gale. She seated herself quietly on its trunk, and appeared to await with patience his own time for the explanation of his motives, in seeking the interview. The Pilot paced, for several minutes, back and forth, in front of the place where she was seated, in profound silence, as if communing with himself, when, suddenly throwing off his air of absence, he came to her side, and assumed a position similar to the one which she herself had taken.

"The hour is at hand, Alice, when we must part," he at length commenced; "it rests with yourself whether it shall be for ever."

"Let it then be for ever, John," she returned, with a slight tremor in her voice.

"That word would have been less appalling, had this accidental meeting never occurred. And yet your choice may have been determined by prudence—for what is there in my fate that can tempt a woman to wish that she might share it!"

"If ye mean your lot is that of one who can find but few, or even none, to partake of his joys, or to share in his sorrows, whose life is a continual scene of dangers and calamities, of disappointments and mishaps, then do ye know but little of the heart of woman, if ye doubt of either her ability or her willingness, to meet them with the man of her choice."

"Say you thus, Alice! then have I misunderstood your meaning, or misinterpreted your acts. My lot is not altogether that of a neglected man, unless the favour of princes, and the smiles of queens, are allowed to go for nothing. My life is, however, one of many and fearful dangers; and yet it is not filled altogether with calamities and mishaps; is it, Alice?" He paused a moment, but in vain, for her answer. "Nay, then, I have been deceived in the estimation that the world has affixed to my combats and enterprises! I am not, Alice, the man I would be, or even the man I had deemed myself."

"You have gained a name, John, among the warriors of the age," she answered, in a subdued voice; "and it is a name that may be said to be written in blood!"

"The blood of my enemies, Alice!"

"The blood of the subjects of your natural prince! The blood of those who breathe the air you first breathed, and who were taught the same holy lessons of instruction that you were first taught; but which, I fear, you have too soon forgotten!"

"The blood of the slaves of despotism!" he sternly interrupted her; "the blood of the enemies of freedom! you have dwelt so long in this dull retirement, and you have cherished so blindly the prejudices of your youth, that the promise of those noble sentiments I once thought I could see budding in Alice Dunscombe, has not been fulfilled."

"I have lived and thought only as a woman, as become my sex and station," Alice meekly replied; "and when it shall be necessary for me to live and think otherwise, I should wish to die."

"Ay, there lie the first seeds of slavery! A dependant woman is sure to make the mother of craven and abject wretches, who dishonour the name of man!"

"I shall never be the mother of children good or bad"— said Alice, with that resignation in her tones that showed she had abandoned the natural hopes of her sex.—"Singly and unsupported have I lived; alone and unlamented must I be carried to my grave."

The exquisite pathos of her voice, as she uttered this placid speech, blended as it was with the sweet and calm dignity of virgin pride, touched the heart of her listener, and he continued silent many moments, as if in reverence of her determination. Her sentiments awakened in his own breast those feelings of generosity and disinterestedness, which had nearly been smothered in restless ambition and the pride of success. He resumed the discourse, therefore, more mildly, and with a much greater exhibition of deep feeling, and less of passion, in his manner.

"I know not, Alice, that I ought, situated as I am, and contented, if not happy, as you are, even to attempt to revive in your bosom those sentiments which I was once led to think existed there. It cannot, after all, be a desirable fate, to share the lot of a rover like myself; one who may be termed a Quixote in the behalf of liberal principles, and who may be hourly called to seal the truth of those principles with his life."

"There never existed any sentiment in my breast, in which you are concerned, that does not exist there still, and unchanged," returned Alice, with her single-hearted sincerity.

"Do I hear you aright! or have I misconceived your resolution to abide in England! or have I not rather mistaken your early feelings?"

"You have fallen into no error now nor then. The weakness may still exist, John, but the strength to struggle with it, has, by the goodness of God, grown with my years. It is not, however, of myself, but of you, that I would speak. I have lived like one of our simple daisies, which in the budding may have caught your eye; and I shall also wilt like the humble flower, when the winter of my time arrives, without being missed from the fields that have known me for a season. But your fall, John, will be like that of the oak that now supports us, and men shall pronounce on the beauty and grandeur of the noble stem while standing, as well as of its usefulness when felled."

"Let them pronounce as they will!" returned the proud stranger. "The truth must be finally known, and when that hour shall come, they will say, he was a faithful and gallant warrior in his day; and a worthy lesson for all who are born in slavery, but would live in freedom, shall be found in his example!"

"Such may be the language of that distant people, whom ye have adopted in the place of those that once formed home and kin to ye," said Alice, glancing her eye timidly at his countenance, as if to discern how far she might venture, without awakening his resentment; "but what will the men of the land of your birth transmit to their children, who will be the children of those that are of your own blood?"

"They will say, Alice, whatever their crooked policy may suggest, or their disappointed vanity can urge. But the picture must be drawn by the friends of the hero as well as by his enemies! Think you that there are not pens as well as swords in America?"

"I have heard that America called a land, John, where God has lavished his favours with an unsparing hand; where he has bestowed many climes with their several fruits, and where his power is exhibited no less than his mercy. It is said her rivers are without any known end, and that lakes are found in her bosom, which would put our German ocean to shame! The plains, teeming with verdure, are spread over wide degrees, and yet those sweet valleys, which a single heart can hold, are not wanting. In short, John, I hear it is a broad land, that can furnish food for each passion, and contain objects for every affection."

"Ay, you have found those, Alice, in your solitude, who have been willing to do her justice! It is a country, that can form a world of itself; and why should they who inherit it, look to other nations for their laws?"

"I pretend not to reason on the right of the children of that soil, to do whatever they may deem most meet for their own welfare," returned Alice—"but can men be born in such a land, and not know the feeling which binds a human being to the place of his birth?"

"Can you doubt that they should be patriotic?" exclaimed the Pilot, in surprise. "Do not their efforts in this sacred cause—their patient sufferings—their long privations, speak loudly in their behalf?"

"And will they, who know so well how to love home, sing the praises of him, who has turned his ruthless hand against the land of his fathers?"

"Forever harping on that word, home!" said the Pilot, who now detected the timid approaches of Alice to her hidden meaning. "Is a man a stick or a stone, that he must be cast into the fire, or buried in a wall, wherever his fate may have doomed him to appear on the earth? The sound of home is said to feed the vanity of an Englishman, let him go where he will; but it would seem to have a still more powerful charm with English women!"

"It is the dearest of all terms to every woman, John, for it embraces the dearest of all ties! If your dames of America are ignorant of its charm, all the favours which God has lavished on their land, will avail their happiness but little."

"Alice," said the Pilot, rising in his agitation, "I see but too well the object of your allusions. But on this subject we can never agree; for not even your powerful influence can draw me from the path of glory in which I am now treading. But our time is growing brief; let us then talk of other things.— This may be the last time that I shall ever put foot on the island of Britain."

Alice paused to struggle with the feelings excited by this remark, before she pursued the discourse. But, soon shaking off the weakness, she added, with a rigid adherence to that course which she believed to be her duty—

"And now, John, that you have landed, is the breaking up of a peaceful family, and the violence ye have shown towards an aged man, a fit exploit for one whose object is the glory of which ye have spoken?"

"Think you that I have landed, and placed my life in the hands of my enemies, for so unworthy an object! No, Alice, my motive for this undertaking has been disappointed, and therefore will ever remain a secret from the world. But duty to my cause has prompted the step which you so unthinkingly condemn. This Col. Howard has some consideration with those in power, and will answer to exchange for a better man. As for his wards, you forget their home, their magical home, is in America; unless, indeed, they find them nearer at hand, under the proud flag of a frigate, that is now waiting for them in the offing."

"You talk of a frigate!" said Alice, with sudden interest in the subject—"Is she your only means of escaping from your enemies?"

"Alice Dunscombe has taken but little heed of passing events, to ask such a question of me!" returned the haughty Pilot. "The question would have sounded more discreetly, had it been, 'is she the only vessel with you that your enemies will have to escape from?'"

"Nay, I cannot measure my language at such a moment," continued Alice, with a still stronger exhibition of anxiety. "It was my fortune to overhear a part of a plan that was intended to destroy, by sudden means, those vessels of America that were in our seas."

"That might be a plan more suddenly adopted than easily executed, my good Alice. And who were these redoubtable schemers?"

"I know not but my duty to the king should cause me to suppress this information," said Alice, hesitating.

"Well, be it so," returned the Pilot, coolly; "it may prove the means of saving the persons of some of the royal officers from death or captivity. I have already said, this may be the last of my visits to this island, and consequently, Alice, the last of our interviews—"

"And yet," said Alice, still pursuing the train of her own thoughts, "there can be but little harm in sparing human blood; and least of all in serving those whom we have long known and regarded!"

"Ay, that is a simple doctrine, and one that is easily maintained," he added, with much apparent indifference; "and yet king George might well spare some of his servants—the list of his abject minions is so long!"

"There was a man named Dillon, who lately dwelt in the Abbey, but who has mysteriously disappeared," continued Alice; "or rather who was captured by your companions: know you aught of him, John?"

"I have heard there was a miscreant of that name, but we have never met. Alice, if it please heaven that this should be the last"—

"He was a captive in a schooner called the Ariel," she added, still unheeding his affected indifference to her communication, "and when permitted to return to St. Ruth, he lost sight of his solemn promise, and of his plighted honour, to wreak his malice. Instead of effecting the exchange that he had conditioned to see made, he plotted treason against his captors. Yes! it was most foul treason! for his treatment was generous and kind, and his liberation certain."

"He was a most unworthy scoundrel! But, Alice"—

"Nay, listen, John," she continued, urged to even a keener interest in his behalf, by his apparent inattention; "and yet I should speak tenderly of his failings, for he is already numbered with the dead! One part of his scheme must have been frustrated, for he intended to destroy that schooner which you call the Ariel, and to have taken the person of the young Barnstable."

"In both of which he has failed! The person of Barnstable I have rescued, and the Ariel has been stricken by a hand far mightier than any of this world! she is wrecked."

"Then is the frigate your only means of escape! Hasten, John, and seem not so proud and heedless, for the hour may come when all your daring will not profit ye against the machinations of secret enemies. This Dillon had also planned that expresses should journey to a sea-port at the south, with the intelligence that your vessels were in these seas, in order that ships might be despatched to intercept your retreat."

The Pilot lost his affected indifference as she proceeded, and before she ceased speaking, his eye was endeavouring to anticipate her words, by reading her countenance through the dusky medium of the star-light.

"How know you this, Alice?" he asked quickly—"and what vessel did he name?"

"Chance made me an unseen listener to their plan, and—I know not but I forget my duty to my prince!—but, John, 'tis asking too much of weak woman, to require that she shall see the man whom she once viewed with eyes of favour, sacrificed, when a word of caution, given in season, might enable him to avoid the danger!"

"Once viewed with an eye of favour! Is it then so!" said the Pilot, speaking in a vacant manner. "But, Alice, heard ye the force of the ships, or their names? Give me their names, and the first lord of your British admiralty shall not give so true an account of their force, as I will furnish from this list of my own."

"Their names were certainly mentioned," said Alice, with tender melancholy, "but the name of one far nearer to me was ringing in my ears, and has driven them from my mind."

"You are the same good Alice I once knew! And my name was mentioned? What said they of the Pirate? Had his arm stricken a blow that made them tremble in their Abbey? Did they call him coward, girl?"

"It was mentioned in terms that pained my heart as I listened. For, it is ever too easy a task to forget the lapse of years, nor are the feelings of youth to be easily eradicated."

"Ay, there is luxury in knowing, that with all their affected abuse, the slaves dread me in their secret holds!" exclaimed the Pilot, pacing in front of his listener, with quick steps. "This it is to be marked, among men, above all others in your calling! I hope yet to see the day when the third George shall start at the sound of that name, even within the walls of his palace."

Alice Dunscombe heard him in deep and mortified silence. It was too evident that a link in the chain of their sympathies was broken, and that the weakness in which she had been unconsciously indulging, was met by no correspondent emotions in him. After sinking her head for a moment on her bosom, she arose with a little more than her usual air of meekness, and recalled the Pilot to a sense of her presence, by saying, in a yet milder voice —

"I have now communicated all that it can profit you to know, and it is meet that we separate."

"What, thus soon!" he cried, starting and taking her hand. "This is but a short interview, Alice, to precede so long a separation."

"Be it short, or be it long, it must now end," she replied. "Your companions are on the eve of departure, and I trust you would be one of the last who would wish to be deserted. If ye do visit England again, I hope it may be with altered sentiments, so far as regards her interests. I wish ye peace, John, and the blessings of God, as ye may be found to deserve them."

"I ask no farther, unless it may be the aid of your gentle prayers! But the night is gloomy, and I will see you in safety to the Abbey."

"It is unnecessary," she returned, with womanly reserve. "The innocent can be as fearless on occasion, as the most valiant among you warriors. But here is no cause for fear. I shall take a path that will conduct me in a different way from that which is occupied by your soldiers, and where I shall find none but Him who is ever ready to protect the helpless. Once more, John, I bid ye adieu." Her voice faltered as she continued —"ye will share the lot of humanity, and have your hours of care and weakness; at such moments ye can remember those ye leave on this despised island, and perhaps among them ye may think of some whose interest in your welfare has been far removed from selfishness."

"God be with you, Alice!" he said, touched with her emotion, and losing all vain images in more worthy feelings —"but I cannot permit you to go alone."

"Here we part, John," she said firmly, "and for ever! 'Tis for the happiness of both, for I fear we have but little in common." She gently wrested her hand from his grasp, and once more bidding him adieu, in a voice that was nearly inaudible, she turned and slowly disappeared, moving, with lingering steps, in the direction of the Abbey.

The first impulse of the Pilot was, certainly, to follow, and insist on seeing her on the way; but the music of the guard on the cliffs, at that moment sent forth its martial strains, and the whistle of the boatswain was heard winding its shrill call among the rocks, in those notes that his practised ear well understood to be the last signal for embarking.

Obedient to the summons, this singular man, in whose breast the natural feelings, that were now on the eve of a violent eruption, had so long been smothered by the visionary expectations of a wild ambition, and perhaps of fierce resentments, pursued his course, in deep abstraction, towards the boats. He was soon met by the soldiers of Borroughcliffe, deprived of their arms, it is true, but unguarded, and returning peacefully to their quarters. The mind of the Pilot, happily for the liberty of these men, was too much absorbed in his peculiar reflections, to note this act of Griffith's generosity, nor did he arouse from his musing until his steps were arrested by suddenly encountering a human figure in the path-way. A light tap on his shoulder was the first mark of recognition he received, when Borroughcliffe, who stood before him, said—

"It is evident, sir, from what has passed this evening, that you are not what you seem. You may be some rebel admiral or general, for aught that I know, the right to command having been strangely contested among ye this night. But let who will own the chief authority, I take the liberty of whispering in your ear that I have been scurvily treated by you—I repeat, most scurvily treated by you all, generally, and by you in particular."

The Pilot started at this strange address, which was uttered with all the bitterness that could be imparted to it by a disappointed man, but he motioned with his hand for the captain to depart, and turned aside to pursue his own way.

"Perhaps I am not properly understood," continued the obstinate soldier; "I say, sir, you have treated me scurvily, and I would not be thought to say this to any gentleman, without wishing to give him an opportunity to vent his anger."

The eye of the Pilot, as he moved forward, glanced at the pistols which Borroughcliffe held in his hands, the one by the handle, and the other by its barrel, and the soldier even fancied that his footsteps were quickened by the sight. After gazing at him until his form was lost in the darkness, the captain muttered to himself—

"He is no more than a common pilot after all! No true gentleman would have received so palpable a hint with such a start. Ah! here comes the party of my worthy friend whose palate knows a grape of the north side of Madeira, from one of the south. The dog has the throat of a gentleman! we will see how he can swallow a delicate allusion to his faults!"

Borroughcliffe stepped aside to allow the marines, who were also in motion for the boats, to pass, and watched with keen looks for the person of the commander. Manual, who had been previously apprized of the intention of Griffith to release the prisoners, had halted to see that none but those who had been liberated by authority, were marching into the country. This accidental circumstance gave Borroughcliffe an opportunity of meeting the other at some little distance from either of their respective parties.

"I greet you, sir," said Borroughcliffe, "with all affection. This has been a pleasant forage for you, Capt. Manual."

The marine was far from being disposed to wrangle, but there was that in the voice of the other which caused him to answer—

"It would have been far pleasanter, sir, if I had met an opportunity of returning to Capt. Borroughcliffe some of the favours that I have received at his hands."

"Nay, then, dear sir, you weigh my modesty to the earth! Surely you forget the manner in which my hospitality has already been requited—by some two hours' mouthing of my sword hilt; with a very unceremonious ricochet into a corner; together with a love-tap, received over the shoulder of one of my men, by so gentle an instrument as the butt of a musket! Damme, sir, but I think an ungrateful man only a better sort of beast!"

"Had the love tap been given to the officer instead of the man," returned Manual, with all commendable coolness, "it would have been better justice; and the ramrod might have answered as well as the butt, to floor a gentleman who carried the allowance of four thirsty fiddlers under one man's jacket."

"Now, that is rank ingratitude to your own cordial of the south side, and a most biting insult! I really see but one way of terminating this wordy war, which if not discreetly ended, may lead us far into the morning."

"Elect your own manner of determining the dispute, sir; I hope, however, it will not be by your innate knowledge of mankind, which has already mistaken a captain of marines in the service of Congress, for a runaway lover, bound to some green place or other."

"You might just as well tweak my nose, sir!" said Bor-roughcliffe. "Indeed, I think it would be the milder reproach of the two! will you make your selection of these, sir? They were loaded for a very different sort of service, but I doubt not will answer on occasion."

"I am provided with a pair, that are charged for any service," returned Manual, drawing a pistol from his own belt, and stepping backward a few paces.

"You are destined for America, I know," said Borrough-cliffe, who stood his ground with consummate coolness; "but it would be more convenient for me, sir, if you could delay your march for a single moment."

"Fire and defend yourself!" exclaimed Manual furiously, retracing his steps towards his enemy.

The sounds of the two pistols were blended in one report, and the soldiers of Borroughcliffe and the marines all rushed to the place, on the sudden alarm. Had the former been provided with arms, it is probable a bloody fray would have been the consequence of the sight that both parties beheld on arriving at the spot, which they did simultaneously. Manual lay on his back, without any signs of life, and Borroughcliffe had changed his cool, haughty, upright attitude, for a recumbent posture, which was somewhat between lying and sitting.

"Is the poor fellow actually expended?" said the Englishman, in something like the tones of regret; "well, he had a soldier's metal in him, and was nearly as great a fool as myself!"

The marines had, luckily for the soldiers and their captain, by this time discovered the signs of life in their own commander, who had been only slightly stunned by the bullet which had grazed his crown, and who being assisted on his feet, stood a minute or two rubbing his head, as if awaking from a dream. As Manual came gradually to his senses he recollected the business in which he had just been engaged, and, in his turn, inquired after the fate of his antagonist.

"I am here, my worthy incognito," cried the other, with a voice of perfect good nature; "lying in the lap of mother Earth, and all the better for opening a vein or two in my right leg;—though I do think that the same effect might have been produced without treating the bone so roughly!—But I opine that I saw you also reclining on the bosom of our common ancestor."

"I was down for a few minutes, I do believe," returned Manual; "there is the path of a bullet across my scalp!"

"Humph! on the head!" said Borroughcliffe, dryly; "the hurt is not likely to be mortal, I see.—Well, I shall offer to raffle with the first poor devil I can find that has but one good leg, for who shall have both; and that will just set up a beggar and a gentleman!—Manual, give me your hand; we have drank together, and we have fought; surely there is nothing now to prevent our being sworn friends!"

"Why," returned Manual, continuing to rub his head, "I see no irremoveable objections—but you will want a surgeon? can I order any thing to be done? There go the signals again to embark—march the fellows down at quick time, sergeant: my own man may remain with me, or, I can do altogether without assistance."

"Ah! you are what I call a well made man, my dear friend!" exclaimed Borroughcliffe; "no weak points about your fortress! such a man is worthy to be the *head* of a whole corps, instead of a solitary company;—Gently, Drill, gently; handle me as if I were made of potter's clay;—I will not detain you longer, my friend Manual, for I hear signal after signal; they must be in want of some of your astonishing reasoning faculties to set them afloat."

Manual might have been offended at the palpable allusions that his new friend made to the firmness of his occiput, had not his perception of things been a little confused, by a humming sound that seemed to abide near the region of thought. As it was, he reciprocated the good wishes of the other, whom he shook most cordially by the hand, and once more renewed his offers of service, after exchanging sundry friendly speeches.

"I thank you quite as much as if I were not at all indebted to you for letting blood, thereby saving me a fit of apoplexy; but Drill has already despatched a messenger to B—— for a leech, and the lad may bring the whole dépôt down upon you.—Adieu, once more, and remember, that if you ever visit England again as a friend, you are to let me see you."

"I shall do it without fail; and I shall keep you to your promise, if you once more put foot in America."

"Trust me for that; I shall stand in need of your excellent head to guide me safely among those rude foresters! Adieu; cease not to bear me in your thoughts."

"I shall never cease to remember you, my good friend," returned Manual, again scratching the member, which was snapping in a manner that caused him to fancy he heard it. Once more these worthies shook each other by the hand, and again they renewed their promises of future intercourse; after which they separated like two reluctant lovers—parting in a manner that would have put to shame the friendship of Orestes and Pylades!

# Chapter XXXII.

"Nay, answer me: stand, and unfold yourself."
*Hamlet*, I.i.2.

D URING THE TIME occupied by the incidents that occurred after the Pilot had made his descent on the land,
the Alacrity, now under the orders of Mr. Boltrope, the master of the frigate, lay off and on, in readiness to receive the
successful mariners. The direction of the wind had been gradually changing from the north-east to the south, during the
close of the day; and long before the middle watches of the
night, the wary old seaman, who, it may be remembered, had
expressed, in the council of war, such a determined reluctance
to trust his person within the realm of Britain, ordered the
man who steered the cutter to stand in boldly for the land.
Whenever the lead told them that it was prudent to tack, the
course of the vessel was changed; and in this manner the seamen continued to employ the hours in patient attendance on
the adventurers. The sailing-master, who had spent the early
years of his life as the commander of divers vessels employed
in trading, was apt, like many men of his vocation and origin,
to mistake the absence of refinement for the surest evidence of
seamanship; and, consequently, he held the little courtesies
and punctilios of a man-of-war in high disdain. His peculiar
duties of superintending the expenditure of the ship's stores,
in their several departments; of keeping the frigate's log-
book; and of making his daily examinations into the state of
her sails and rigging, brought him so little in collision with
the gay, laughing, reckless young lieutenants, who superin-
tended the ordinary management of the vessel, that he might
be said to have formed a distinct species of the animal,
though certainly of the same genus with his more polished
messmates. Whenever circumstances, however, required that
he should depart from the dull routine of his duty, he made it
a rule, as far as possible, to associate himself with such of the
crew as possessed habits and opinions the least at variance
with his own.

By a singular fatality, the chaplain of the frigate was, as

respects associates, in a condition, nearly assimilated to that of this veteran tar.

An earnest desire to ameliorate the situation of those who were doomed to meet death on the great deep, had induced an inexperienced and simple-hearted divine to accept this station, in the fond hope, that he might be made the favoured instrument of salvation to many, who were then existing in a state of the most abandoned self-forgetfulness. Neither our limits, nor our present object, will permit the relation of the many causes that led, not only to an entire frustration of all his visionary expectations, but to an issue which rendered the struggle of the good divine with himself both arduous and ominous, in order to maintain his own claims to the merited distinctions of his sacred office. The consciousness of his backsliding had so far lessened the earthly, if not the spiritual pride of the chaplain, as to induce him to relish the society of the rude master, whose years had brought him, at times, to take certain views of futurity, that were singularly affected by the peculiar character of the individual. It might have been that both found themselves out of their places—but it was owing to some such secret sympathy, let its origin be what it would, that the two came to be fond of each other's company. On the night in question, Mr. Boltrope had invited the chaplain to accompany him in the Alacrity; adding, in his broad, rough language, that as there was to be fighting on shore, "his hand might come in play with some poor fellow or other." This singular invitation had been accepted, as well from a desire to relieve the monotony of a sea life, by any change, as perhaps with a secret yearning in the breast of the troubled divine, to get as nigh to terra firma as possible. Accordingly, after the Pilot had landed with his boisterous party, the sailing-master and the chaplain, together with a boatswain's-mate and some ten or twelve seamen, were left in quiet possession of the cutter. The first few hours of this peaceable intercourse, had been spent by the worthy messmates, in the little cabin of the vessel, over a can of grog, the savoury relish of which was much increased by a characteristic disquisition on polemical subjects, which our readers have great reason to regret it is not our present humour to record. When, however, the winds invited the nearer approach to the hostile shores already mentioned, the prudent sailing-master adjourned the discussion to another and more suitable time, removing himself and the can, by the same operation, to the quarter-deck.

"There," cried the honest tar, placing the wooden vessel, with great self-contentment, by his side on the deck, "this is ship's comfort! There is a good deal of what I call a lubber's fuss, parson, kept up on board a ship that shall be nameless, but which bears, about three leagues distant, broad off in the ocean, and which is lying-to under a close-reefed maintopsail, a foretopmast-staysail and foresail—I call my hand a true one in mixing a can—take another pull at the halyards! 'twill make your eye twinkle like a light-house, this dark morning! You won't? well we must give no offence to the English-man's rum."—After a potent draught had succeeded this con-siderate declaration, he added—"You are a little like our first lieutenant, parson, who drinks, as I call it, nothing but the elements—which is, water stiffened with air!"

"Mr. Griffith may indeed be said to set a wholesome exam-ple to the crew," returned the chaplain, perhaps with a slight consciousness that it had not altogether possessed its due weight with himself.

"Wholesome!" cried Boltrope; "let me tell you, my worthy leaf-turner, that if you call such a light diet wholesome, you know but little of salt water and sea-fogs! However, Mr. Grif-fith is a seaman; and if he gave his mind less to trifles and gimcracks, he would be, by the time he got to about our years, a very rational sort of a companion.—But you see, par-son, just now, he thinks too much of small follies; such as man-of-war disciplyne.—Now there is rationality in giving a fresh nip to a rope, or in looking well at your mats, or even in crowning a cable; but damme, priest, if I see the use—luff, luff, ye lubber; don't ye see, sir, you are steering for Gar-many!—if I see the use, as I was saying, of making a rumpus about the time when a man changes his shirt; whether it be this week, or next week, or for that matter, the week after, provided it be bad weather. I sometimes am mawkish about attending muster, (and I believe I have as little to fear on the score of behaviour as any man,) lest it should be found I car-ried my tobacco in the wrong cheek!"

"I have indeed thought it somewhat troublesome to myself, at times; and it is in a striking degree vexatious to the spirit, especially when the body has been suffering under sea-sickness."

"Why, yes, you were a little apt to bend your duds wrong for the first month, or so," said the master; "I remember you got the marine's scraper on your head, once, in your hurry to bury a dead man! Then you never looked as if you belonged to the ship, so long as those cursed black knee-breeches lasted! For my part, I never saw you come up the quarter-deck ladder, but I expected to see your shins give way across the combing of the hatch—a man does look like the devil, priest, scudding about a ship's decks in that fashion, under bare poles! But now the tailor has found out the articles ar'n't sea-worthy, and we have got your lower stanchions cased in a pair of purser's slops, I am puzzled often to tell your heels from those of a main-top-man!"

"I have good reason to be thankful for the change," said the humbled priest, "if the resemblance you mention existed, while I was clad in the usual garb of one of my calling."

"What signifies a calling?" returned Boltrope, catching his breath after a most persevering draught; "a man's shins are his shins, let his upper works belong to what sarvice they may. I took an early prejudyce against knee-breeches, perhaps from a trick I've always had of figuring the Devil as wearing them. You know, parson, we seldom hear much said of a man, without forming some sort of an idea concerning his rigging and fashion-pieces—and so as I had no particular reason to believe that Satan went naked—keep full ye lubber; now you are running into the wind's eye, and be d——d to ye!—but as I was saying, I always took a conceit that the devil wore knee-breeches and a cock'd hat. There's some of our young lieutenants, who come to muster on Sundays in cock'd hats, just like soldier-officers; but, d'ye see, I would sooner show my nose under a night cap, than under a scraper!"

"I hear the sound of oars!" exclaimed the chaplain, who finding this image more distinct than even his own vivid conceptions of the great Father of evil, was quite willing to conceal his inferiority by changing the discourse—"Is not one of our boats returning?"

"Ay, ay, 'tis likely; if it had been me, I should have been land-sick before this—ware round, boys, and stand by to heave-to on the other tack."

The cutter, obedient to her helm, fell off before the wind, and rolling an instant in the trough of the sea, came up again easily to her oblique position, with her head towards the cliffs, and gradually losing her way, as her sails were brought to counteract each other, finally became stationary. During the performance of this evolution, a boat had hove up out of the gloom, in the direction of the land, and by the time the Alacrity was in a state of rest, it had approached so nigh as to admit of hailing.

"Boat ahoy!" murmured Boltrope, through a trumpet, which, aided by his lungs, produced sounds not unlike the roaring of a bull.

"Ay, ay," was thrown back from a clear voice, that swept across the water with a fulness that needed no factitious aid to render it audible.

"Ay, there comes one of the lieutenants, with his ay, ay," said Boltrope—"pipe the side, there, you boatswain's-mate! But here's another fellow more on our quarter! boat a-hoy!"

"Alacrity"—returned another voice, in a direction different from the other.

"Alacrity! There goes my commission of Captain of this craft, in a whiff," returned the sailing-master.—"That is as much as to say, here comes one, who will command when he gets on board. Well, well, it is Mr. Griffith, and I can't say, notwithstanding his love of knee-buckles, and small wares, but I'm glad he's out of the hands of the English! Ay, here they all come upon us at once! here is another fellow, that pulls like the jolly-boat, coming up on our lee-beam, within hail—let us see if he is asleep—boat a-hoy!"

"Flag," answered a third voice from a small, light-rowing boat which had approached very near the cutter, in a direct line from the cliffs, without being observed.

"Flag!" echoed Boltrope, dropping his trumpet in amazement—"that's a big word to come out of a jolly-boat! Jack Manly himself could not have spoke it with a fuller mouth—but I'll know who it is that carries such a weather helm, with a Yankee man-of-war's prize! Boat a-hoy! I say."

This last call was uttered in those short menacing tones, that are intended to be understood as intimating that the party hailing is in earnest; and it caused the men who were rowing, and who were now quite close to the cutter, to suspend their strokes, simultaneously, as if they dreaded that the cry would be instantly succeeded by some more efficient means of ascertaining their character. The figure that was seated by itself in the stern of the boat, started at this second summons, and then, as if with sudden recollection, a quiet voice replied—

"No—no."

" 'No—no,' and 'flag,' are very different answers," grumbled Boltrope; "what know-nothing have we here!"

He was yet muttering his dissatisfaction at the ignorance of the individual that was approaching, whoever it might be, when the jolly-boat came slowly to their side, and the Pilot stepped from her stern-sheets on the decks of the prize.

"Is it you, Mr. Pilot?" exclaimed the sailing-master, raising a battle lantern within a foot of the other's face, and looking with a sort of stupid wonder at the proud and angry eye he encountered—"is it you! well, I should have rated you for a man of more experience than to come booming down upon a man-of-war in the dark, with such a big word in your mouth, when every boy in the two vessels knows that we carry no swallow-tailed bunting abroad! Flag! why you might have got a shot, had there been soldiers."

The Pilot threw him a still fiercer glance, and turning away with a look of disgust, he walked along the quarter-deck towards the stern of the vessel, with an air of haughty silence, as if disdaining to answer. Boltrope kept his eyes fastened on him for a moment longer, with some appearance of scorn, but the arrival of the boat first hailed, which proved to be the barge, immediately drew his attention to other matters. Barnstable had been rowing about in the ocean for a long time, unable to find the cutter, and as he had been compelled to suit his own demeanour to those with whom he was associated, he reached the Alacrity in no very good-humoured mood. Col. Howard and his niece had maintained, during the whole period, the most rigid silence, the former from pride, and the latter touched with her uncle's evident displeasure;

and Katherine, though secretly elated with the success of all her projects, was content to emulate their demeanour for a short time, in order to save appearances. Barnstable had several times addressed himself to the latter, without receiving any other answer than such as was absolutely necessary to prevent the lover from taking direct offence, at the same time that she intimated by her manner her willingness to remain silent. Accordingly, the lieutenant, after aiding the ladies to enter the cutter, and offering to perform the same service to Col. Howard, which was coldly declined, turned, with that sort of irritation that is by no means less rare in vessels of war than with poor human nature generally, and gave vent to his spleen where he dared.

"How's this! Mr. Boltrope!" he cried, "here are boats coming alongside with ladies in them, and you keep your gaff swayed up till the leach of the sail is stretched like a fiddle-string—settle away your peak-halyards, sir, settle away!"

"Ay, ay, sir," grumbled the master; "settle away that peak there; though the craft wouldn't forge ahead a knot in a month, with all her gibs hauled over!" He walked sulkily forward among the men, followed by the meek divine; and added, "I should as soon have expected to see Mr. Barnstable come off with a live ox in his boat as a petticoat! The Lord only knows what the ship is coming to next, parson! what between cocked hats and epaulettes, and other knee-buckle matters, she was a sort of no-mans-land before, and now, what with the women, and their band-boxes, they'll make another Noah's Ark of her. I wonder they didn't all come aboard in a coach and six, or a one horse shay!"

It was a surprising relief to Barnstable to be able to give utterance to his humour, for a few moments, by ordering the men to make sundry alterations in every department of the vessel, in a quick, hurried voice, that abundantly denoted, not only the importance of his improvements, but the temper in which they were dictated. In his turn, however, he was soon compelled to give way by the arrival of Griffith, in the heavily rowing launch of the frigate, which was crowded with a larger body of the seamen who had been employed in the expedition. In this manner, boat after boat speedily arrived, and the whole party were once more happily embarked in safety, under their national flag.

The small cabin of the Alacrity was relinquished to Col. Howard and his wards, with their attendants. The boats were dropped astern, each protected by its own keeper; and Griffith gave forth the mandate, to fill the sails and steer broad off into the ocean. For more than an hour the cutter held her course in this direction, gliding gracefully through the glittering waters, rising and settling heavily on the long, smooth billows, as if conscious of the unusual burden that she was doomed to carry; but at the end of that period, her head was once more brought near the wind, and she was again held at rest; awaiting the appearance of the dawn, in order to discover the position of the prouder vessel, on which she was performing the humble duty of a tender. More than a hundred and fifty living men were crowded within her narrow limits; and her decks presented, in the gloom, as she moved along, the picture of a mass of human heads.

As the freedom of a successful expedition was unavoidably permitted, loud jokes, and louder merriment, broke on the silent waters, from the reckless seamen, while the exhilarating can passed from hand to hand, strange oaths, and dreadful denunciations breaking forth, at times, from some of the excited crew against their enemy. At length the bustle of re-embarking gradually subsided, and many of the crew descended to the hold of the cutter, in quest of room to stretch their limbs, when a clear, manly voice, was heard rising above the deep in those strains that a seaman most loves to hear. Air succeeded air, from different voices, until even the spirit of harmony grew dull with fatigue, and verses began to be heard where songs were expected, and fleeting lines succeeded stanzas. The decks were soon covered with prostrate men, seeking their natural rest, under the open heavens, and perhaps dreaming, as they yielded heavily to the rolling of the vessel, of scenes of other times in their own hemisphere. The dark glances of Katherine were concealed beneath her falling lids; and even Cecilia, with her head bowed on the shoulder of her cousin, slept sweetly in innocence and peace. Boltrope groped his way into the hold among the seamen, where, kicking one of the most fortunate of the men from his birth, he established himself in his place, with all that cool indifference to the other's comfort, that had grown with his experience, from the time when he was treated thus cavalierly in his own person, to the present moment. In this manner, head was dropped after head, on the planks, the guns, or on whatever first offered for a pillow, until Griffith and Barnstable, alone, were left pacing the different sides of the quarter-deck, in haughty silence.

Never did a morning watch appear so long to the two young sailors, who were thus deprived, by resentment and pride, of that frank and friendly communion, that had for so many years sweetened the tedious hours of their long, and at times, dreary service. To increase the embarrassment of their situation, Cecilia and Katherine, suffering from the confinement of the small and crowded cabin, sought the purer air of the deck, about the time when the deepest sleep had settled on the senses of the wearied mariners. They stood, leaning against the taffrail, discoursing with each other, in low and broken sentences; but a sort of instinctive knowledge of the embarrassment which existed between their lovers, caused a guarded control over every look or gesture which might be construed into an encouragement for one of the young men to advance at the expense of the other. Twenty times, however, did the impatient Barnstable feel tempted to throw off the awkward restraint, and approach his mistress; but in each instance was he checked by the secret consciousness of error, as well as by that habitual respect for superior rank that forms a part of the nature of a sea-officer. On the other hand, Griffith manifested no intention to profit by this silent concession in his favour, but continued to pace the short quarter-deck with strides more hurried than ever; and was seen to throw many an impatient glance towards that quarter of the heavens, where the first signs of the lingering day might be expected to appear. At length Katherine, with a ready ingenuity, and perhaps with some secret coquetry, removed the embarrassment, by speaking first, taking care to address the lover of her cousin—

"How long are we condemned to these limited lodgings, Mr. Griffith?" she asked; "truly, there is a freedom in your nautical customs, which, to say the least, is novel to us females, who have been accustomed to the division of space!"

"The instant that there is light to discover the frigate, Miss Plowden," he answered, "you shall be transferred from a vessel of an hundred, to one of twelve hundred tons. If your situation there be less comfortable, than when within the walls of St. Ruth, you will not forget that they who live on the ocean, claim it as a merit to despise the luxuries of the land."

"At least, sir," returned Katherine, with a sweet grace, which she well knew how to assume on occasion, "what we shall enjoy will be sweetened by liberty, and embellished by a sailor's hospitality. To me, Cicely, the air of this open sea is as fresh and invigorating, as if it were wafted from our own distant America!"

"If you have not the arm of a patriot, you at least possess a most loyal imagination, Miss Plowden," said Griffith, laughing; "this soft breeze blows in the direction of the fens of Holland, instead of the broad plains of America.—Thank God, there come the signs of day, at last! unless the currents have swept the ship far to the north, we shall surely see her with the light."

This cheering intelligence drew the eyes of the fair cousins towards the east, where their delighted looks were long fastened, while they watched the glories of the sun rising over the water. As the morning had advanced, a deeper gloom was spread across the ocean, and the stars were gleaming in the heavens, like balls of twinkling fire. But now, a streak of pale light showed itself along the horizon, growing brighter, and widening at each moment, until long, fleecy clouds became visible, where nothing had been seen before but the dim base of the arch that overhung the dark waters. This expanding light, which, in appearance, might be compared to a silvery opening in the heavens, was soon tinged with a pale flush, which quickened with sudden transitions into glows yet deeper, until a belt of broad flame bounded the water, diffusing itself more faintly towards the zenith, where it melted into the pearl-coloured sky, or played on the fantastic volumes of a few light clouds with inconstant glimmering. While these beautiful transitions were still before the eyes of the youthful

admirers of their beauties, a voice was heard above them, crying as if from the heavens—

"Sail—ho! The frigate lies broad off to sea-ward, sir!"

"Ay, ay; you have been watching with one eye asleep, fellow," returned Griffith, "or we should have heard you before!
Look a little north of the place where the glare of the sun is
coming, Miss Plowden, and you will be able to see our gallant
vessel."

An involuntary cry of pleasure burst from the lips of
Katherine, as she followed his directions, and first beheld the
frigate through the medium of the fluctuating colours of the
morning. The undulating outline of the lazy ocean, which
rose and fell heavily against the bright boundary of the heavens, was without any relief to distract the eye, as it fed eagerly
on the beauties of the solitary ship. She was riding sluggishly
on the long seas, with only two of her lower and smaller sails
spread, to hold her in command; but her tall masts and heavy
yards were painted against the fiery sky, in strong lines of
deep black, while even the smallest cord in the mazes of her
rigging, might be distinctly traced, stretching from spar to
spar, with the beautiful accuracy of a picture. At moments,
when her huge hull rose on a billow, and was lifted against
the back ground of sky, its shape and dimensions were
brought into view, but these transient glimpses were soon
lost, as it settled into the trough, leaving the waving spars
bowing gracefully towards the waters, as if about to follow
the vessel into the bosom of the deep. As a clearer light gradually stole on the senses, the delusion of colours and distance
vanished together, and when a flood of day preceded the immediate appearance of the sun, the ship became plainly visible, within a mile of the cutter, her black hull checkered with
ports, and her high tapering masts exhibiting their proper
proportions and hues.

At the first cry of "a sail," the crew of the Alacrity had been
aroused from their slumbers, by the shrill whistle of the boatswain, and long before the admiring looks of the two cousins
had ceased to dwell on the fascinating sight of morning
chasing night from the hemisphere, the cutter was again
in motion to join her consort. It seemed but a moment before their little vessel was in what the timid females thought,

a dangerous proximity to the frigate, under whose lee she slowly passed, in order to admit of the following dialogue between Griffith and his aged commander:

"I rejoice to see you, Mr. Griffith!" cried the captain, who stood in the channel of his ship, waving his hat, in the way of cordial greeting. "You are welcome back, Capt. Manual; welcome, welcome, all of you, my boys! as welcome as a breeze in the calm latitudes." As his eye, however, passed along the deck of the Alacrity, it encountered the shrinking figures of Cecilia and Katherine, and a dark shade of displeasure crossed his decent features, while he added—"How's this, gentlemen! The frigate of Congress is neither a ball-room, nor a church, that it is to be thronged with women!"

"Ay, ay," muttered Boltrope to his friend the chaplain, "now the old man has hauled out his mizzen, you'll see him carry a weather helm! He wakes up about as often as the trades shift their points, and that's once in six months. But when there has been a neap-tide in his temper for any time, you're sure to find it followed by a flood with a vengeance. Let us hear what the first lieutenant can say in favour of his petticoat quality!"

The blushing sky had not exhibited a more fiery glow, than gleamed in the fine face of Griffith for a moment; but struggling with his disgust, he answered with bitter emphasis—

"'Twas the pleasure of Mr. Gray, sir, to bring off the prisoners."

"Of Mr. Gray!" repeated the captain, instantly losing every trace of displeasure, in an air of acquiescence. "Come-to, sir, on the same tack with the ship, and I will hasten to order the accommodation ladder rigged, to receive our guests!"

Boltrope listened to this sudden alteration in the language of his commander, with sufficient wonder; nor was it until he had shaken his head repeatedly, with the manner of one who saw deeper than his neighbours into a mystery, that he found leisure to observe—

"Now, parson, I suppose if you held an almanack in your fist, you'd think you could tell which way we shall have the wind to-morrow! but damn me, priest, if better calculators than you havn't failed! Because a lubberly—no, he's a thorough seaman, I'll say that for the fellow!—because a pilot chooses to say, 'bring me off these here women,' the ship is to be so cluttered with she-cattle, that a man will be obligated to spend half his time in making his manners! Now mind what I tell you, priest, this very frolic will cost Congress the price of a year's wages for an able-bodied seaman, in bunting and can-vass for screens; besides the wear and tear of running-gear in shortening sail, in order that the women need not be 'stericky in squalls!"

The presence of Mr. Boltrope being required, to take charge of the cutter, the divine was denied an opportunity of dissenting from the opinions of his rough companion; for the loveliness of their novel shipmates, had not failed to plead loudly in their favour, with every man in the cutter whose habits and ideas had not become rigidly set in obstinacy.

By the time the Alacrity was hove-to, with her head to-wards the frigate, the long line of boats that she had been towing during the latter part of the night, were brought to her side, and filled with men. A wild scene of unbridled merriment and gayety succeeded, while the seamen were ex-changing the confinement of the prize for their accustomed lodgings in the ship, during which the reins of discipline were slightly relaxed. Loud laughter was echoed from boat to boat, as they glided by each other; and rude jests, interlarded with quaint humours and strange oaths, were freely bandied from mouth to mouth. The noise, however, soon ceased, and the passage of Col. Howard and his wards was then effected, with less precipitancy, and due decorum. Capt. Munson, who had been holding a secret dialogue with Griffith and the Pilot, received his unexpected guests with plain hospitality, but with an evident desire to be civil. He politely yielded to their service his two convenient state-rooms, and invited them to partake, in common with himself, of the comforts of the great cabin.

# Chapter XXXIII.

"Furious press the hostile squadron,
 Furious he repels their rage,
 Loss of blood at length enfeebles;
 Who can war with thousands wage?"
     Percy (tr.), "Gentle River, Gentle River," ll. 53−56.

W E CANNOT DETAIN the narrative, to detail the scenes which busy wonder, aided by the relation of divers marvellous feats, produced among the curious seamen who remained in the ship, and their more fortunate fellows, who had returned in glory from an expedition to the land. For nearly an hour the turbulence of a general movement was heard, issuing from the deep recesses of the frigate, and the boisterous sounds of hoarse merriment were listened to by the officers in indulgent silence; but all these symptoms of unbridled humour ceased by the time the morning repast was ended, when the regular sea-watch was set, and the greater portion of those whose duty did not require their presence on the vessel's deck, availed themselves of the opportunity to re-pair the loss of sleep sustained in the preceding night. Still no preparations were made to put the ship in motion, though long and earnest consultations, which were supposed to relate to their future destiny, were observed by the younger officers, to be held between their captain, the first lieutenant, and the mysterious Pilot. The latter threw many an anxious glance along the eastern horizon, searching it minutely with his glass, and then would turn his impatient looks at the low, dense bank of fog, which, stretching across the ocean like a barrier of cloud, entirely intercepted the view towards the south. To the north and along the land, the air was clear, and the sea without spot of any kind; but in the east a small white sail had been discovered since the opening of day, which was gradually rising above the water, and assuming the appear-ance of a vessel of some size. Every officer on the quarter-deck in his turn, had examined this distant sail, and had ventured an opinion on its destination and character; and even Kather-ine, who with her cousin was enjoying, in the open air, the novel beauties of the ocean, had been tempted to place her sparkling eye to a glass, to gaze at the stranger.

"It is a collier," Griffith said, "who has hauled from the land in the late gale, and who is luffing up to his course again. If the wind holds here in the south, and he does not get into that fog bank, we can stand off for him and get a supply of fuel before eight bells are struck."

"I think his head is to the northward, and that he is steering off the wind," returned the Pilot, in a musing manner. "If that Dillon succeeded in getting his express far enough along the coast, the alarm has been spread, and we must be wary. The convoy of the Baltic trade is in the North Sea, and news of our presence could easily have been taken off to it by some of the cutters that line the coast—I could wish to get the ship as far south as the Helder!"

"Then we lose this weather tide!" exclaimed the impatient Griffith; "surely we have the cutter as a look-out! besides, by beating into the fog, we shall lose the enemy, if enemy it be, and it is thought meet for an American frigate to skulk from her foes!"

The scornful expression that kindled the eye of the Pilot, like a gleam of sunshine lighting for an instant some dark dell and laying bare its secrets, was soon lost in the usually quiet look of his glance, though he hesitated like one who was struggling with his passions, before he answered—

"If prudence and the service of the States require it, even this proud frigate must retreat and hide from the meanest of her enemies. My advice, Capt. Munson, is, that you make sail, and beat the ship to windward, as Mr. Griffith has suggested, and that you order the cutter to precede us, keeping more in with the land."

The aged seaman, who evidently suspended his orders, only to receive an intimation of the other's pleasure, immediately commanded his youthful assistant to issue the necessary mandates to put these measures in force. Accordingly, the Alacrity, which vessel had been left under the command of the junior lieutenant of the frigate, was quickly under way; and making short stretches to windward, she soon entered the bank of fog, and was lost to the eye. In the mean time the canvass of the ship was loosened, and spread leisurely in order not to disturb the portion of the crew who were sleeping, and following her little consort, she moved heavily through the water, bearing up against the dull breeze.

The quiet of regular duty had succeeded to the bustle of making sail, and as the rays of the sun fell less obliquely on the distant land, Katherine and Cecilia were amusing Griffith by vain attempts to point out the rounded eminences which they fancied lay in the vicinity of the deserted mansion of St. Ruth. Barnstable, who had resumed his former station in the frigate, as her second lieutenant, was pacing the opposite side of the quarter-deck, holding under his arm the speaking trumpet, which denoted that he held the temporary control of the motions of the ship, and inwardly cursing the restraint that kept him from the side of his mistress. At this moment of universal quiet, when nothing above low dialogues interrupted the dashing of the waves as they were thrown lazily aside by the bows of the vessel, the report of a light cannon burst out of the barrier of fog, and rolled by them on the breeze, apparently vibrating with the rising and sinking of the waters.

"There goes the cutter!" exclaimed Griffith, the instant the sound was heard.

"Surely," said the captain. "Somers is not so indiscreet as to scale his guns, after the caution he has received!"

"No idle scaling of guns is intended there," said the Pilot, straining his eyes to pierce the fog, but soon turning away in disappointment at his inability to succeed—"that gun is shotted, and has been fired in the hurry of a sudden signal!— can your look-outs see nothing, Mr. Barnstable?"

The lieutenant of the watch hailed the man aloft, and demanded if any thing were visible in the direction of the wind, and received for answer, that the fog intercepted the view in that quarter of the heavens, but that the sail in the east was a ship, running large or before the wind. The Pilot shook his head doubtingly at this information, but still he manifested a strong reluctance to relinquish the attempt of getting more to the southward. Again he communed with the commander of the frigate, apart from all other ears, and while they yet deliberated, a second report was heard, leaving no doubt that the Alacrity was firing signal guns for their particular attention.

"Perhaps," said Griffith, "he wishes to point out his position, or to ascertain ours; believing that we are lost like himself in the mist."

"We have our compasses!" returned the doubting captain; "Somers has a meaning in what he says!"

"See!" cried Katherine, with girlish delight, "see, my cousin! see, Barnstable! how beautifully that vapour is wreathing itself in clouds above the smoky line of fog! It stretches already into the very heavens like a lofty pyramid!"

Barnstable sprang lightly on a gun, as he repeated her words—

"Pyramids of fog! and wreathing clouds! By heaven!" he shouted, " 'tis a tall ship! Royals, skysails, and studding-sails all abroad! She is within a mile of us, and comes down like a race horse, with a spanking breeze, dead before it! Now know we why Somers is speaking in the mist!"

"Ay," cried Griffith, "and there goes the Alacrity, just breaking out of the fog, hovering in for the land!"

"There is a mighty hull under all that cloud of canvass, Capt. Munson," said the observant but calm Pilot—"it is time, gentlemen, to edge away to leeward."

"What, before we know from whom we run!" cried Griffith; "my life on it, there is no single ship king George owns, but would tire of the sport before she had played a full game of bowls with"—

The haughty air of the young man was daunted by the severe look he encountered in the eye of the Pilot, and he suddenly ceased, though inwardly chafing with impatient pride.

"The same eye that detected the canvass above the fog, might have seen the flag of a vice-admiral fluttering still nearer the heavens," returned the collected stranger; "and England, faulty as she may be, is yet too generous to place a flag-officer in time of war, in command of a frigate, or a captain in command of a fleet. She knows the value of those who shed their blood in her behalf, and it is thus that she is so well served! believe me, Capt. Munson, there is nothing short of a ship of the line under that symbol of rank, and that broad show of canvass!"

"We shall see, sir, we shall see," returned the old officer, whose manner grew decided, as the danger appeared to thicken; "beat to quarters, Mr. Griffith, for we have none but enemies to expect on this coast."

The order was instantly issued, when Griffith remarked, with a more temperate zeal—

"If Mr. Gray be right, we shall have reason to thank God that we are so light of heel!"

The cry of "a strange vessel close aboard the frigate," having already flown down the hatches, the ship was in an uproar at the first tap of the drum. The seamen threw themselves from their hammocks and lashing them rapidly into long, hard bundles, they rushed to the decks, where they were dexterously stowed in the netting, to aid the defences of the upper part of the vessel. While this tumultuous scene was exhibiting, Griffith gave a secret order to Merry, who disappeared, leading his trembling cousins to a place of safety in the inmost depths of the ship.

The guns were cleared of their lumber, and loosened. The bulk-heads were knocked down, and the cabin relieved of its furniture, and the gun deck exhibited one unbroken line of formidable cannon, arranged in all the order of a naval battery ready to engage. Arm chests were thrown open, and the decks strewed with pikes, cutlasses, pistols, and all the various weapons for boarding. In short, the yards were slung, and every other arrangement was made with a readiness and dexterity that were actually wonderful, though all was performed amid an appearance of disorder and confusion that rendered the ship another Babel during the continuance of the preparations. In a very few minutes every thing was completed, and even the voices of the men ceased to be heard answering to their names, as they were mustered at their stations, by their respective officers. Gradually the ship became as quiet as the grave, and when even Griffith or his commander found it necessary to speak, their voices were calmer, and their tones more mild than usual. The course of the vessel was changed to an oblique line from that in which their enemy was approaching, though the appearance of flight was to be studiously avoided to the last moment. When nothing further remained to be done, every eye became fixed on the enormous pile of swelling canvass that was rising, in cloud over cloud, far above the fog, and which was manifestly moving, like driving vapour, swiftly to the north. Presently the dull, smoky boundary of the mist which rested on the water, was pushed aside in vast volumes, and the long taper spars that projected from the bowsprit of the strange ship, issued from the obscurity, and were quickly followed by the whole of the enormous fabric, to which they were merely light appendages. For a moment, streaks of reluctant vapour clung to the huge, floating pile, but they were soon taken off by the rapid vessel, and the whole of her black hull became distinct to the eye.

"One, two, three rows of teeth!" said Boltrope, deliberately counting the tiers of guns that bristled along the sides of the enemy; "a three decker! Jack Manly would show his stern to such a fellow! and even the bloody Scotchman would run!"

"Hard up with your helm, quarter-master!" cried Capt. Munson; "there is indeed no time to hesitate, with such an enemy within a quarter of a mile! Turn the hands up Mr. Griffith, and pack on the ship from her trucks to her lower studding-sail booms. Be stirring, sir, be stirring! Hard up with your helm! Hard up, and be damn'd to you!"

The unusual earnestness of their aged commander acted on the startled crew like a voice from the deep, and they waited not for the usual signals of the boatswain and drummer to be given, before they broke away from their guns, and rushed tumultuously to aid in spreading the desired canvass. There was one minute of ominous confusion, that, to an inexperienced eye would have foreboded the destruction of all order in the vessel, during which every hand, and each tongue, seemed in motion; but it ended in opening the immense folds of light duck which were displayed along the whole line of the masts, far beyond the ordinary sails, overshadowing the waters for a great distance, on either side of the vessel. During the moment of inaction that succeeded this sudden exertion, the breeze which had brought up the three decker, fell fresher on the sails of the frigate, and she started away from her dangerous enemy with a very perceptible advantage in point of sailing.

"The fog rises!" cried Griffith; "give us but the wind for an hour, and we shall run her out of gun-shot!"

"These ninety's are very fast off the wind;" returned the captain, in a low tone, that was intended only for the ears of his first lieutenant and the Pilot, "and we shall have a struggle for it."

The quick eye of the stranger was glancing over the movements of his enemy, while he answered—

"He finds we have the heels of him already! he is making ready, and we shall be fortunate to escape a broadside! Let her yaw a little, Mr. Griffith; touch her lightly with the helm; if we are raked, sir, we are lost!"

The captain sprang on the taffrail of his ship, with the activity of a younger man, and in an instant he perceived the truth of the other's conjecture.

Both vessels now ran for a few minutes, keenly watching each other's motions like two skilful combatants; the English ship making slight deviations from the line of her course, and then, as her movements were anticipated by the other, turning as cautiously in the opposite direction, until a sudden and wide sweep of her huge bows, told the Americans plainly on which tack to expect her. Capt. Munson made a silent, but impressive gesture with his arm, as if the crisis were too important for speech, which indicated to the watchful Griffith, the way he wished the frigate sheered, to avoid the weight of the impending danger. Both vessels whirled swiftly up to the wind, with their heads towards the land, and as the huge black side of the three-decker, checkered with its triple batteries, frowned full upon her foe, it belched forth a flood of fire and smoke, accompanied by a bellowing roar that mocked the surly moanings of the sleeping ocean. The nerves of the bravest man in the frigate contracted their fibres, as the hurricane of iron hurtled by them, and each eye appeared to gaze in stupid wonder, as if tracing the flight of the swift engines of destruction. But the voice of Capt. Munson was heard in the din, shouting, while he waved his hat earnestly in the required direction—

"Meet her! meet her with the helm, boy! meet her, Mr. Griffith, meet her!"

Griffith had so far anticipated this movement, as to have already ordered the head of the frigate to be turned in its former course when, struck by the unearthly cry of the last tones uttered by his commander, he bent his head, and beheld the venerable seaman driven through the air, his hat still waving, his gray hair floating in the wind, and his eye set in the wild look of death.

"Great God!" exclaimed the young man, rushing to the side of the ship, where he was just in time to see the lifeless body disappear in the waters that were dyed in his blood; "he has been struck by a shot! Lower-away the boat, lower-away the jolly-boat, the barge, the tiger, the—"

"'Tis useless," interrupted the calm, deep voice of the Pilot; "he has met a warrior's end, and he sleeps in a sailor's grave! The ship is getting before the wind again, and the enemy is keeping his vessel away."

The youthful lieutenant was recalled by these words to his duty, and reluctantly turned his eyes away from the bloody spot on the waters, which the busy frigate had already passed, to resume the command of the vessel with a forced composure.

"He has cut some of our running gear," said the master, whose eye had never ceased to dwell on the spars and rigging of the ship, "and there's a splinter out of the main-top-mast, that is big enough for a fid! He has let day-light through some of our canvass too, but taking it by-and-large, the squall has gone over and little harm done.—Didn't I hear something said of Capt. Munson getting jamm'd by a shot?"

"He is killed!"—said Griffith, speaking in a voice that was yet husky with horror—"he is dead, sir, and carried overboard; there is more need that we forget not ourselves, in this crisis."

"Dead!" said Boltrope, suspending the operation of his active jaws for a moment, in surprise; "and buried in a wet jacket! well, it is lucky 'tis no worse, for, damme if I did not think every stick in the ship would have been cut out of her!"

With this consolatory remark on his lips, the master walked slowly forward, continuing his orders to repair the damages with a singleness of purpose that rendered him, however uncouth as a friend, an invaluable man in his station.

Griffith had not yet brought his mind to the calmness that was so essential to discharge the duties which had thus suddenly and awfully devolved on him, when his elbow was lightly touched by the Pilot, who had drawn closer to his side—

"The enemy appear satisfied with the experiment," said the stranger, "and as we work the quicker of the two, he loses too much ground to repeat it, if he be a true seaman."

"And yet, as he finds we leave him so fast," returned Griffith, "he must see that all his hopes rest, in cutting us up aloft. I dread that he will come by the wind again, and lay us under his broadside; we should need a quarter of an hour to run without his range, if he were anchored!"

"He plays a surer game—see you not that the vessel we made in the eastern board, shows the hull of a frigate? 'Tis past a doubt that they are of one squadron, and that the expresses have sent them in our wake. The English admiral has spread a broad clue, Mr. Griffith, and as he gathers in his ships, he sees that his game has been successful."

The faculties of Griffith had been too much occupied with the hurry of the chase to look at the ocean; but startled at the information of the Pilot, who spoke coolly, though like a man sensible of the existence of approaching danger, he took the glass from the other, and with his own eye examined the different vessels in sight. It is certain that the experienced officer, whose flag was flying above the light sails of the three-decker, saw the critical situation of his chase, and reasoned much in the same manner as the Pilot, or the fearful expedient apprehended by Griffith, would have been adopted. Prudence, however, dictated that he should prevent his enemy from escaping by pressing so closely on his rear, as to render it impossible for the American to haul across his bows and run into the open sea between his own vessel and the nearest frigate of his squadron. The unpractised reader will be able to comprehend the case better by accompanying the understanding eye of Griffith as it glanced from point to point, following the whole horizon. To the west lay the land, along which the Alacrity was urging her way industriously, with the double purpose of keeping her consort abeam, and of avoiding a dangerous proximity to their powerful enemy. To the east, bearing off the starboard bow of the American frigate, was the vessel first seen, and which now began to exhibit the hostile appearance of a ship of war, steering in a line converging towards themselves, and rapidly drawing nigher, while far in the north-east, was a vessel, as yet faintly discerned, whose evolutions could not be mistaken by one who understood the movements of nautical warfare.

"We are hemmed in, effectually," said Griffith, dropping the glass from his eye; "and I know not but our wisest course would be to haul in to the land, and cutting every thing light adrift, endeavour to pass the broadside of the flag-ship?"

"Provided she left a rag of canvass to do it with!" returned the Pilot. "Sir, 'tis an idle hope! She would strip your ship, in ten minutes, to her plank shears. Had it not been for a lucky wave on which so many of her shot struck and glanced upward, we should have nothing to boast of left from the fire she has already given; we must stand on, and drop the three decker as far as possible."

"But the frigates!" said Griffith, "what are we to do with the frigates?"

"Fight them!" returned the Pilot, in a low, determined voice, "fight them! Young man, I have borne the stars and stripes aloft in greater straits than this, and even with honour! Think not that my fortune will desert me now!"

"We shall have an hour of desperate battle!"

"On that we may calculate; but I have lived through whole days of bloodshed! you seem not one to quail at the sight of an enemy."

"Let me proclaim your name to the men!" said Griffith; " 'twill quicken their blood, and at such a moment, be a host in itself."

"They want it not," returned the Pilot, checking the hasty zeal of the other with his hand. "I would be unnoticed, unless I am known as becomes me. I will share your danger, but would not rob you of a tittle of your glory. Should we come to a grapple," he continued, while a smile of conscious pride gleamed across his face, "I will give forth the word as a war-cry, and, believe me, these English will quail before it!"

Griffith submitted to the stranger's will, and after they had deliberated further on the nature of their evolutions, he gave his attention again to the management of the vessel. The first object which met his eye, on turning from the Pilot, was Col. Howard, pacing the quarter-deck, with a determined brow, and a haughty mien, as if already in the enjoyment of that triumph which now seemed certain.

"I fear, sir," said the young man, approaching him with respect, "that you will soon find the deck unpleasant and dangerous: your wards are—"

"Mention not the unworthy term!" interrupted the colonel. "What greater pleasure can there be than to inhale the odour of loyalty that is wafted from yonder floating tower of the king!—And danger! you know but little of old George Howard, young man, if you think he would for thousands miss seeing that symbol of rebellion levelled before the flag of his Majesty."

"If that be your wish, Col. Howard," returned Griffith, biting his lip as he looked around at the wondering seamen who were listeners, "you will wait in vain—but I pledge you my word, that when that time arrives, you shall be advised, and that your own hands shall do the ignoble deed."

"Edward Griffith, why not this moment? This is your moment of probation—submit to the clemency of the crown, and yield your crew to the royal mercy! In such a case I would remember the child of my brother Harry's friend; and believe me, my name is known to the ministry. And you, misguided and ignorant abettors of rebellion! cast aside your useless weapons, or prepare to meet the vengeance of yonder powerful and victorious servant of your prince."

"Fall back! back with ye, fellows!" cried Griffith, fiercely, to the men who were gathering around the colonel, with looks of sullen vengeance. "If a man of you dare approach him, he shall be cast into the sea."

The sailors retreated at the order of their commander; but the elated veteran had continued to pace the deck for many minutes before stronger interests diverted the angry glances of the seamen to other objects.

Notwithstanding the ship of the line was slowly sinking beneath the distant waves, and in less than an hour from the time she had fired the broadside, no more than one of her three tiers of guns was visible from the deck of the frigate, she yet presented an irresistible obstacle against retreat to the south. On the other hand the ship first seen, drew so nigh as to render the glass no longer necessary in watching her movements. She proved to be a frigate, though one so materially lighter than the American, as to have rendered her conquest easy, had not her two consorts continued to press on for the scene of battle with such rapidity. During the chase the scene had shifted from the point opposite to St. Ruth, to the verge of those shoals where our tale commenced. As they approached the latter, the smallest of the English ships drew so nigh as to render the combat unavoidable. Griffith and his crew had not been idle in the intermediate time, but all the usual preparations against the casualties of a sea-fight had been duly made, when the drum once more called the men to their quarters, and the ship was deliberately stripped of her unnecessary sails, like a prizefighter about to enter the arena, casting aside the incumbrances of dress; at the instant she gave this intimation of her intention to abandon flight, and trust the issue to the combat, the nearest English frigate also took in her light canvass in token of her acceptance of the challenge.

"He is but a little fellow," said Griffith to the Pilot, who hovered at his elbow with a sort of fatherly interest in the other's conduct of the battle, "though he carries a stout heart."

"We must crush him at a blow," returned the stranger; "not a shot must be delivered until our yards are locking."

"I see him training his twelves upon us already; we may soon expect his fire."

"After standing the brunt of a Ninety-gun-ship," observed the collected Pilot, "we shall not shrink from the broadside of a Two-and-thirty!"

"Stand to your guns, men!" cried Griffith, through his trumpet—"not a shot is to be fired without the order."

This caution, so necessary to check the ardour of the seamen, was hardly uttered, before their enemy became wrapped in sheets of fire and volumes of smoke, as gun after gun hurled its iron missiles at their vessel in quick succession. Ten minutes might have passed, the two vessels sheering closer to each other every foot they advanced, during which time the crew of the American were compelled, by their commander, to suffer the fire of their adversary, without returning a shot. This short period, which seemed an age to the seamen, was distinguished in their vessel by deep silence. Even the wounded and dying, who fell in every part of the ship, stifled their groans, under the influence of the severe discipline, which gave a character to every man and each movement of the vessel; and those officers who were required to speak, were heard only in the lowest tones of resolute preparation. At length the ship slowly entered the skirts of the smoke that enveloped their enemy, and Griffith heard the man who stood at his side whisper the word "now."

"Let them have it!" cried Griffith, in a voice that was heard in the remotest parts of the ship.

The shout that burst from the seamen, appeared to lift the decks of the vessel, and the affrighted frigate trembled like an aspen, with the recoil of her own massive artillery, that shot forth a single sheet of flame, the sailors having disregarded, in their impatience, the usual order of firing. The effect of the broadside on the enemy was still more dreadful, for a death-like silence succeeded to the roar of the guns, which was only broken by the shrieks and execrations that burst from her, like the moanings of the damned. During the few moments in which the Americans were again loading their cannon, and the English were recovering from their confusion, the vessel of the former moved slowly past her antagonist, and was already doubling across her bows, when the latter was suddenly, and, considering the inequality of their forces, it may be added desperately, headed into her enemy. The two frigates grappled. The sudden and furious charge made by the Englishman, as he threw his masses of daring seamen along his bowsprit, and out of his channels, had nearly taken Griffith by surprise; but Manual, who had delivered his first fire with the broadside, now did good service, by ordering his men to beat back the intruders, by a steady and continued discharge. Even the wary Pilot lost sight of their other foes, in the high daring of that moment, and smiles of stern pleasure were exchanged between him and Griffith, as both comprehended at a glance their advantages.

"Lash his bowsprit to our mizzen-mast," shouted the lieutenant, "and we will sweep his decks as he lies!"

Twenty men sprang eagerly forward to execute the order, among the foremost of whom were Boltrope and the stranger.

"Ay, now he's our own!" cried the busy master, "and we

will take an owner's liberties with him, and break him up—
for by the eternal—"

"Peace, rude man," said the Pilot, in a voice of solemn remonstrance; "at the next instant you may face your God;
mock not his awful name!"

The master found time, before he threw himself from the
spar on the deck of the frigate again, to cast a look of amazement at his companion, who, with a steady mien, but with an
eye that lighted with a warrior's ardour, viewed the battle
that raged around him, like one who marked its progress, to
control the result.

The sight of the Englishmen, rushing onward with shouts,
and bitter menaces, warmed the blood of Col. Howard, who
pressed to the side of the frigate, and encouraged his friends,
by his gestures and voice, to come on.

"Away with ye, old croaker!" cried the master, seizing him
by the collar; "away with ye to the hold, or I'll order you fired
from a gun."

"Down with your arms, rebellious dog!" shouted the colonel, carried beyond himself by the ardour of the fray; "down
to the dust, and implore the mercy of your injured prince!"

Invigorated by a momentary glow, the veteran grappled
with his brawny antagonist, but the issue of the short struggle
was yet suspended, when the English, driven back by the fire
of the marines, and the menacing front that Griffith, with his
boarders presented, retreated to the forecastle of their own
ship, and attempted to return the deadly blows they were receiving in their hull from the cannon that Barnstable directed.
A solitary gun was all they could bring to bear on the Americans, but this, loaded with cannister, was fired so near as to
send its glaring flame into the very faces of the enemies. The
struggling colonel, who was already sinking beneath the arm
of his foe, felt the rough grasp loosen from his throat, at the
flash, and the two combatants sunk powerless on their knees,
facing each other.

"How now, brother!" exclaimed Boltrope, with a smile of
grim fierceness; "some of that grist has gone to your mill,
ha!"

No answer could, however be given, before the yielding
forms of both fell to the deck, where they lay helpless, amid

the din of the battle and the wild confusion of the eager combatants.

Notwithstanding the furious struggle they witnessed, the elements did not cease their functions; and urged by the breeze, and lifted irresistibly on a wave, the American ship was forced through the water still further across the bows of her enemy. The idle fastenings of hemp and iron, were snapped asunder, like strings of tow, and Griffith saw his own ship borne away from the Englishman at the instant that the bowsprit of the latter was torn from its lashings, and tumbled into the sea, followed by spar after spar, until nothing of all her proud tackling was remaining, but the few parted and useless ropes that were left dangling along the stumps of her lower masts. As his own stately vessel moved from the confusion she had caused, and left the dense cloud of smoke in which her helpless antagonist lay, the eye of the young man glanced anxiously towards the horizon, where he now remembered he had more foes to contend against.

"We have shaken off the thirty-two most happily!" he said to the Pilot, who followed his motions with singular interest; "but here is another fellow sheering in for us, who shows as many ports as ourselves, and who appears inclined for a closer interview; besides the hull of the Ninety is rising again, and I fear she will be down but too soon!"

"We must keep the use of our braces and sails," returned the Pilot, "and on no account close with the other frigate — we must play a double game, sir, and fight this new adversary with our heels as well as with our guns."

" 'Tis time then that we were busy, for he is shortening sail, and as he nears so fast we may expect to hear from him every minute; what do you propose, sir?"

"Let him gather in his canvass," returned the Pilot, "and when he thinks himself snug, we can throw out a hundred men at once upon our yards and spread every thing alow and aloft; we may then draw ahead of him by surprise; if we can once get him in our wake I have no fears of dropping them all."

"A stern chase is a long chase," cried Griffith, "and the thing may do! Clear up the decks, here, and carry down the wounded; and as we have our hands full, the poor fellows who have done with us, must go overboard at once."

This melancholy duty was instantly attended to, while the young seaman who commanded the frigate returned to his duty, with the absorbed air of one who felt its high responsibility. These occupations, however, did not prevent his hearing the sounds of Barnstable's voice, calling eagerly to young Merry. Bending his head towards the sound, Griffith beheld his friend, looking anxiously up the main hatch, with a face grimed with smoke, his coat off, and his shirt bespattered with human blood—"Tell me, boy," he said, "is Mr. Griffith untouched? They say that a shot came in upon the quarter deck that tripped up the heels of half a dozen."

Before Merry could answer, the eyes of Barnstable, which even while he spoke were scanning the state of the vessel's rigging, encountered the kind looks of Griffith, and from that moment perfect harmony was restored between the friends.

"Ah! you are there Griff. and with a whole skin, I see," cried Barnstable, smiling with pleasure; "they have passed poor Boltrope down into one of his own store-rooms! If that fellow's bowsprit had held on ten minutes longer, what a mark I should have made on his face and eyes!"

"'Tis perhaps best as it is," returned Griffith; "but what have you done with those whom we are most bound to protect?"

Barnstable made a significant gesture towards the depths of the vessel as he answered—

"On the cables; safe as wood, iron, and water can keep them—though Katherine has had her head up three times to—"

A summons from the Pilot drew Griffith away, and the young officers were compelled to forget their individual feelings, in the pressing duties of their stations.

The ship which the American frigate had now to oppose, was a vessel of near her own size and equipage, and when Griffith looked at her again, he perceived that she had made her preparations to assert her equality in manful fight.

Her sails had been gradually reduced to the usual quantity, and, by certain movements on her decks, the lieutenant and his constant attendant the Pilot, well understood that she only wanted to lessen her distance a few hundred yards to begin the action.

"Now spread every thing," whispered the stranger.

Griffith applied the trumpet to his mouth, and shouted in a voice that was carried even to his enemy—"Let fall—out with your booms—sheet home—hoist away of every thing!"

The inspiriting cry was answered by a universal bustle; fifty men flew out on the dizzy heights of the different spars, while broad sheets of canvass rose as suddenly along the masts, as if some mighty bird were spreading its wings. The Englishman instantly perceived his mistake, and he answered the artifice by a roar of artillery. Griffith watched the effects of the broadside with an absorbing interest, as the shot whistled above his head, but when he perceived his masts untouched and the few unimportant ropes only that were cut, he replied to the uproar with a burst of pleasure. A few men were however seen clinging with wild frenzy to the cordage, dropping from rope to rope like wounded birds fluttering through a tree, until they fell heavily into the ocean, the sullen ship sweeping by them, in cold indifference. At the next instant the spars and masts of their enemy exhibited a display of men similar to their own, when Griffith again placed the trumpet to his mouth, and shouted aloud:

"Give it to them; drive them from their yards, boys; scatter them with your grape—unreeve their rigging!"

The crew of the American wanted but little encouragement to enter on this experiment with hearty good will, and the close of his cheering words were uttered amid the deafening roar of his own cannon. The Pilot had, however, mistaken the skill and readiness of their foe, for notwithstanding the disadvantageous circumstances under which the Englishman increased his sail, the duty was steadily and dexterously performed.

The two ships were now running rapidly on parallel lines, hurling at each other their instruments of destruction, with furious industry, and with severe and certain loss to both, though with no manifest advantage in favour of either. Both Griffith and the Pilot witnessed with deep concern this unexpected defeat of their hopes, for they could not conceal from themselves, that each moment lessened their velocity through the water, as the shot of their enemy, stripped the canvass from the yards, or dashed aside the lighter spars in their terrible progress.

"We find our equal here!" said Griffith to the stranger.
"The Ninety is heaving up again, like a mountain, and if we
continue to shorten sail at this rate, she will soon be down
upon us!"

"You say true, sir," returned the Pilot, musing; "the man
shows judgment as well as spirit; but—"

He was interrupted by Merry, who rushed from the forward part of the vessel, his whole face betokening the eagerness of his spirit, and the importance of his intelligence—

"The breakers!" he cried, when nigh enough to be heard
amid the din; "we are running dead on a ripple, and the sea is
white not two hundred yards ahead!"

The Pilot jumped on a gun, and bending to catch a glimpse
through the smoke, he shouted, in those clear, piercing tones,
that could be even heard among the roaring of the cannon.
"Port, port your helm! we are on the Devil's Grip! pass up the
trumpet, sir; port your helm, fellow; give it them, boys—give
it to the proud English dogs!" Griffith unhesitatingly relinquished the symbol of his rank, fastening his own firm look
on the calm but quick eye of the Pilot, and gathering assurance from the high confidence he read in the countenance of
the stranger. The seamen were too busy with their cannon
and their rigging to regard the new danger, and the frigate
entered one of the dangerous passes of the shoals, in the heat
of a severely contested battle. The wondering looks of a few
of the older sailors glanced at the sheets of foam that flew by
them, in doubt whether the wild gambols of the waves were
occasioned by the shot of the enemy, when suddenly the
noise of cannon was succeeded by the sullen wash of the disturbed element, and presently the vessel glided out of her
smoky shroud, and was boldly steering in the centre of the
narrow passages. For ten breathless minutes longer the Pilot
continued to hold an uninterrupted sway, during which the
vessel ran swiftly by ripples and breakers, by streaks of foam
and darker passages of deep water, when he threw down his
trumpet and exclaimed—

"What threatened to be our destruction has proved our salvation!—keep yonder hill crowned with wood, one point
open from the church tower at its base, and steer east and by
north; you will run through these shoals on that course in an

hour, and by so doing, you will gain five leagues of your enemy, who will have to double their tail."

The moment he stepped from the gun, the Pilot lost the air of authority that had so singularly distinguished his animated form, and even the close interest he had manifested in the incidents of the day, became lost in the cold, settled reserve he had affected during his intercourse with his present associates. Every officer in the ship, after the breathless suspense of uncertainty had passed, rushed to those places where a view might be taken of their enemies. The Ninety was still steering boldly onward, and had already approached the Two-and-thirty, which lay, a helpless wreck, rolling on the unruly seas, that were rudely tossing her on their wanton billows. The frigate last engaged was running along the edge of the ripple, with her torn sails flying loosely in the air, her ragged spars tottering in the breeze, and every thing above her hull exhibiting the confusion of a sudden and unlooked-for check to her progress. The exulting taunts and mirthful congratulations of the seamen, as they gazed at the English ships, were, however, soon forgotten in the attention that was required to their own vessel. The drums beat the retreat, the guns were lashed, the wounded again removed, and every individual, able to keep the deck, was required to lend his assistance in repairing the damages of the frigate and securing her masts.

The promised hour carried the ship safely through all the dangers, which were much lessened by daylight, and by the time the sun had begun to fall over the land, Griffith, who had not quitted the deck during the day, beheld his vessel once more cleared of the confusion of the chase and battle, and ready to meet another foe. At this period he was summoned to the cabin, at the request of the ship's chaplain. Delivering the charge of the frigate to Barnstable, who had been his active assistant, no less in their subsequent labours than in the combat, he hastily divested himself of the vestiges of the fight, and proceeded to obey the repeated and earnest call.

# Chapter XXXIV.

"Whither, 'midst falling dew,
While glow the heavens with the last steps of day,
Far, through their rosy depths, dost thou pursue
Thy solitary way?"
                    Bryant, "To a Waterfowl," ll. 1–4.

W HEN THE YOUNG SEAMAN, who now commanded the
frigate, descended from the quarter-deck in compliance
with the often repeated summons, he found the vessel restored to the same neatness as if nothing had occurred to disturb its order. The gun-deck had been cleansed of its horrid
stains, and the smoke of the fight had long since ascended
through the hatches, and mingled with the clouds that flitted
above the ship. As he walked along the silent batteries, even
the urgency of his visit could not prevent him from glancing
his eyes towards the splintered sides, those terrible vestiges,
by which the paths of the shot of their enemy might be
traced; and by the time he tapped lightly at the door of the
cabin, his quick look had embraced every material injury the
vessel had sustained in her principal points of defence. The
door was opened by the surgeon of the frigate, who, as he
stepped aside to permit Griffith to enter, shook his head with
that air of meaning, which, in one of his profession, is understood to imply the abandonment of all hopes, and then immediately quitted the apartment, in order to attend to those who
might profit by his services.

The reader is not to imagine that Griffith had lost sight of
Cecilia and her cousin during the occurrences of that eventful
day; on the contrary, his troubled fancy had presented her
terror and distress, even in the hottest moments of the fight,
and the instant that the crew were called from their guns, he
had issued an order to replace the bulk-heads of the cabin,
and to arrange its furniture for their accommodation, though
the higher and imperious duties of his station had precluded
his attending to their comfort in person. He expected, therefore, to find the order of the rooms restored, but he was by

no means prepared to encounter the scene he was now to witness.

Between two of the sullen cannon, which gave such an air of singular wildness to the real comfort of the cabin, was placed a large couch, on which the Colonel was lying, evidently near his end. Cecilia was weeping by his side, her dark ringlets falling in unheeded confusion around her pale features, and sweeping in their rich exuberance the deck on which she kneeled. Katherine leaned tenderly over the form of the dying veteran, while her dark, tearful eyes seemed to express self-accusation blended with deep commiseration. A few attendants of both sexes surrounded the solemn scene, all of whom appeared to be under the influence of the hopeless intelligence which the medical officer had but that moment communicated. The servants of the ship had replaced the furniture with a care that mocked the dreadful struggle that so recently disfigured the warlike apartment, and the stout, square frame of Boltrope occupied the opposite settee, his head resting on the lap of the Captain's Steward, and his hand gently held in the grasp of his friend the Chaplain. Griffith had heard of the wound of the master, but his own eyes now conveyed the first intelligence of the situation of Colonel Howard. When the shock of this sudden discovery had a little subsided, the young man approached the couch of the latter, and attempted to express his regret and pity, in a voice that afforded an assurance of his sincerity.

"Say no more, Edward Griffith," interrupted the Colonel, waving his hand feebly for silence; "it seemeth to be the will of God that this rebellion should triumph, and it is not for vain man to impeach the acts of Omnipotence! To my erring faculties, it wears an appearance of mystery, but doubtless it is to answer the purpose of his own inscrutable providence! I have sent for you, Edward, on a business that I would fain see accomplished before I die, that it may not be said old George Howard neglected his duty, even in his last moments. You see this weeping child at my side; tell me, young man, do you love the maiden?"

"Am I to be asked such a question?" exclaimed Griffith.

"And will you cherish her—will you supply to her the

places of father and mother, will you become the fond guardian of her innocence and weakness?"

Griffith could give no other answer than a fervent pressure
of the hand he had clasped.

"I believe you," continued the dying man; "for however he
may have forgotten to inculcate his own loyalty, worthy
Hugh Griffith could never neglect to make his son a man of
honour. I had weak, and perhaps evil wishes in behalf of my
late unfortunate kinsman, Mr. Christopher Dillon; but they
have told me that he was false to his faith. If this be true, I
would refuse him the hand of the girl, though he claimed the
fealty of the British realms! But he has passed away, and I am
about to follow him into a world where we shall find but one
Lord to serve, and it may have been better for us both had we
more remembered our duty to Him, while serving the Princes
of the earth. One thing further—know you this officer of
your congress well; this Mr. Barnstable?"

"I have sailed with him for years," returned Griffith, "and
can answer for him as myself."

The veteran made an effort to rise, which in part succeeded,
and he fastened on the youth a look of keen scrutiny that gave
to his pallid features an expression of solemn meaning, as he
continued—

"Speak not now, sir, as the companion of his idle pleasures,
and as the unthinking associate commends his fellow, but remember that your opinion is given to a dying man who leans
on your judgment for advice. The daughter of John Plowden
is a trust not to be neglected, nor will my death prove easy, if
a doubt of her being worthily bestowed shall remain!"

"He is a gentleman," returned Griffith, "and one whose
heart is not less kind than gallant—he loves your ward, and
great as may be her merit, he is deserving of it all—like myself, he has also loved the land that gave him birth, before the
land of his ancestors, but—"

"That is now forgotten," interrupted the Colonel; "after
what I have this day witnessed I am forced to believe that it is
the pleasure of Heaven that you are to prevail! But, sir, a
disobedient inferior will be apt to make an unreasonable commander. The recent contention between you—"

"Remember it not, dear sir," exclaimed Griffith with generous zeal—" 'twas unkindly provoked, and it is already forgotten and pardoned. He has sustained me nobly throughout the day, and my life on it, that he knows how to treat a woman as a brave man should!"

"Then am I content!" said the veteran, sinking back on his couch; "let him be summoned."

The whispered message, which Griffith gave requesting Mr. Barnstable to enter the cabin, was quickly conveyed, and he had appeared before his friend deemed it discreet to disturb the reflections of the veteran by again addressing him. When the entrance of the young sailor was announced, the Colonel again roused himself, and addressed his wondering listener, though in a manner much less confiding and familiar, than that which he had adopted towards Griffith.

"The declarations you made last night, relative to my ward, the daughter of the late Captain John Plowden, sir, have left me nothing to learn on the subject of your wishes. Here, then, gentlemen, you both obtain the reward of your attentions! Let that reverend divine hear you pronounce the marriage vows, while I have strength to listen, that I may be a witness against ye, in heaven, should ye forget their tenor!"

"Not now, not now," murmured Cecilia; "Oh ask it not now, my uncle!"

Katherine spoke not, but deeply touched by the tender interest her guardian manifested in her welfare, she bowed her face to her bosom, in subdued feeling, and suffered the tears that had been suffusing her eyes to roll down her cheeks in large drops, till they bathed the deck.

"Yes, now, my love," continued the Colonel, "or I fail in my duty. I go shortly to stand face to face with your parents, my children; for the man, who dying, expects not to meet worthy Hugh Griffith and honest Jack Plowden in heaven, can have no clear view of the rewards that belong to lives of faithful service to the country, or of gallant loyalty to the King! I trust no one can justly say, that I ever forgot the delicacy due to your gentle sex; but it is no moment for idle ceremony when time is shortening into minutes, and heavy duties remain to be discharged. I could not die in peace, children, were I to leave you here in the wide ocean, I had almost said in the wide world, without that protection which be-

comes your tender years and still more tender characters. If it
has pleased God to remove your guardian, let his place be
supplied by those he wills to succeed him!"

Cecilia no longer hesitated, but she arose slowly from her
knees, and offered her hand to Griffith with an air of forced
resignation. Katherine submitted to be led by Barnstable to
her side, and the chaplain who had been an affected listener to
the dialogue, in obedience to an expressive signal from the
eye of Griffith, opened the prayer book from which he had
been gleaning consolation for the dying master, and commenced reading, in trembling tones, the marriage service. The
vows were pronounced by the weeping brides in voices more
distinct and audible than if they had been uttered amid the
gay crowds that usually throng a bridal; for though they were
the irreclaimable words that bound them forever to the men,
whose power over their feelings they thus proclaimed to the
world, the reserve of maiden diffidence was lost in one engrossing emotion of solemnity, created by the awful presence
in which they stood. When the benediction was pronounced,
the head of Cecilia dropped on the shoulder of her husband,
where she wept violently, for a moment, and then resuming
her place at the couch, she once more knelt at the side of her
uncle. Katherine received the warm kiss of Barnstable, passively, and returned slowly to the spot whence she had been
led.

Colonel Howard succeeded in raising his person, to witness
the ceremony, and had answered to each prayer with a fervent
"amen." He fell back with the last words, and a look of satisfaction shone in his aged and pallid features, that declared the
interest he had taken in the scene.

"I thank you, my children," he at length uttered, "I thank
you, for I know how much you have sacrificed to my wishes.
You will find all my papers relative to the estates of my wards,
gentlemen, in the hands of my banker in London, and you
will also find there my will, Edward, by which you will learn
that Cicely has not come to your arms an unportioned bride.
What my wards are in persons and manners your eyes can
witness, and I trust the vouchers in London will show that
I have not been an unfaithful steward to their pecuniary
affairs!"

"Name it not—say no more, or you will break my heart," cried Katherine, sobbing aloud, in the violence of her remorse at having ever pained so true a friend. "Oh! talk of yourself, think of yourself; we are unworthy—at least I am unworthy of another thought!"

The dying man extended a hand to her in kindness, and continued, though his voice grew feebler as he spoke—

"Then to return to myself—I would wish to lie, like my ancestors, in the bosom of the earth—and in consecrated ground."

"It shall be done," whispered Griffith; "I will see it done myself."

"I thank thee, my son," said the veteran; "for such thou art to me in being the husband of Cicely—you will find in my will, that I have liberated and provided for all my slaves—except those ungrateful scoundrels who deserted their master—they have seized their own freedom, and they need not be indebted to me for the same. There is, Edward, also an unworthy legacy to the King; his Majesty will deign to receive it—from an old and faithful servant, and you will not miss the trifling gift." A long pause followed, as if he had been summing up the account of his earthly duties, and found them duly balanced, when he added, "kiss me Cicely—and you, Katherine—I find you have the genuine feelings of honest Jack, your father.—My eyes grow dim—which is the hand of Griffith? Young gentleman, I have given you all that a fond old man had to bestow—deal tenderly with the precious child—we have not properly understood each other—I had mistaken both you and Mr. Christopher Dillon, I believe; perhaps I may have also mistaken my duty to America—but I was too old to change my politics or my religion—I—I—I lov'd the King—God bless him—"

His words became fainter and fainter as he proceeded, and the breath deserted his body with this benediction on his livid lips, which the proudest monarch might covet from so honest a man.

The body was instantly borne into a state-room by the attendants, and Griffith and Barnstable supported their brides into the after-cabin, where they left them seated on the sofa that lined the stern of the ship, weeping bitterly, in each other's arms.

No part of the preceding scene had been unobserved by Boltrope, whose small, hard eyes, were observed by the young men to twinkle, when they returned into the state apartment, and they approached their wounded comrade to apologize for the seeming neglect that their conduct had displayed.

"I heard you were hurt, Boltrope," said Griffith, taking him kindly by the hand; "but as I know you are not unused to being marked by shot, I trust we shall soon see you again on deck."

"Ay, ay," returned the master, "you'll want no spy-glasses to see the old hulk as you launch it into the sea. I have had shot, as you say, before now to tear my running gear, and even to knock a splinter out of some of my timbers, but this fellow has found his way into my bread-room; and the cruise of life is up!"

"Surely the case is not so bad, honest David," said Barnstable; "you have kept afloat, to my knowledge, with a bigger hole in your skin than this unlucky hit has made!"

"Ay, ay," returned the master, "that was in my upper works, where the doctor could get at it with a plug; but this chap has knocked away the shifting-boards, and I feel as if the whole cargo was broken up. — You may say, that Tourniquet rates me all the same as a dead man, for after looking at the shot-hole, he has turned me over to the parson here, like a piece of old junk which is only fit to be worked up into something new. Captain Munson had a lucky time of it! I think you said, Mr. Griffith, that the old gentleman was launched overboard with every thing standing, and that Death made but one rap at his door, before he took his leave!"

"His end was indeed sudden!" returned Griffith; "but it is what we seamen must expect."

"And for which there is so much the more occasion to be prepared," the chaplain ventured to add, in a low, humble, and, perhaps, timid voice.

The sailing-master looked keenly from one to the other as they spoke, and, after a short pause, he continued with an air of great submission —

" 'Twas his luck; and I suppose it is sinful to begrudge a man his lawful luck. As for being prepared, parson, that is your business and not mine; therefore, as there is but little time to spare, why, the sooner you set about it the better; and to save unnecessary trouble, I may as well tell you not to strive to make too much of me, for, I must own it to my shame, I never took learning kindly. If you can fit me for some middling birth in the other world, like the one I hold in this ship, it will suit me as well, and, perhaps, be easier to all hands of us."

If there was a shade of displeasure, blended with the surprise, that crossed the features of the divine at this extraordinary limitation of his duties, it entirely disappeared when he considered, more closely, the perfect expression of simplicity with which the dying master uttered his wishes. After a long and melancholy pause, which neither Griffith nor his friend felt any inclination to interrupt, the chaplain replied—

"It is not the province of man to determine on the degrees of the merciful dispensations of the Deity, and nothing that I can do, Mr. Boltrope, will have any weight in making up the mighty and irrevocable decree. What I said to you last night, in our conversation on this very subject, must still be fresh in your memory, and there is no good reason why I should hold a different language to you now."

"I can't say that I log'd all that pass'd," returned the master, "and that which I do recollect chiefly fell from myself, for the plain reason that a man remembers his own, better than his neighbor's ideas. And this puts me in mind, Mr. Griffith, to tell you, that one of the forty-two's from the three-decker, travelled across the forecastle, and cut the best bower within a fathom of the clinch, as handily as an old woman would clip her rotten yarn with a pair of tailor's shears!—If you will be so good as to order one of my mates to shift the cable end-for-end, and make a new bend of it, I'll do as much for you another time."

"Mention it not," said Griffith; "rest assured that every thing shall be done for the security of the ship in your department—I will superintend the whole duty in person; and I would have you release your mind from all anxiety on the subject, to attend to your more important interests elsewhere."

"Why," returned Boltrope, with a little show of pertinacity,

"I have an opinion, that the cleaner a man takes his hands into the other world, of the matters of duty in this, the better he will be fitted to handle any thing new.—Now the parson, here, undertook to lay down the doctrine last night, that it was no matter how well or how ill a man behaved himself, so that he squared his conscience by the lifts and braces of faith, which I take to be a doctrine that is not to be preach'd on shipboard, for it would play the devil with the best ship's company that was ever mustered."

"Oh! no—no—dear Mr. Boltrope, you mistook me and my doctrine altogether!" exclaimed the chaplain; "at least you mistook—"

"Perhaps, sir," interrupted Griffith, gently, "our honest friend will not be more fortunate now. Is there nothing earthly that hangs upon your mind, Boltrope? no wish to be remembered to any one, nor any bequest to make of your property?"

"He has a mother, I know," said Barnstable in a low voice; "he often spoke of her to me in the night watches; I think she must still be living."

The master, who distinctly heard his young shipmates, continued for more than a minute rolling the tobacco, which he still retained, from one side of his mouth to the other, with an industry that denoted singular agitation for the man, and raising one of his broad hands, with the other he picked the worn skin from fingers, which were already losing their brownish yellow hue in the fading colour of death, before he answered—

"Why, yes, the old woman still keeps her grip upon life, which is more than can be said of her son David. The old man was lost the time the Susan and Dorothy was wrecked on the back of Cape Cod; you remember it, Mr. Barnstable? you were then a lad, sailing on whaling voyages from the island! well, ever since that gale, I've endeavoured to make smooth water for the old woman myself, though she has had but a rough passage of it, at the best; the voyage of life, with her, having been pretty much crossed by rugged weather and short stores."

"And you would have us carry some message to her?" said Griffith, kindly.

"Why, as to messages," continued the master, whose voice was rapidly growing more husky and broken, "there never has been many compliments—passed between us, for the reason—that she is not more used to receive them—than I am to make them. But if any one of you will overhaul—the purser's books, and see what there is standing there—to my side of the leaf—and take a little pains to get it to the old woman—you will find her moor'd in the lee side of a house—ay, here it is, No. 10 Cornhill, Boston. I took care— to get her a good warm birth, seeing that a woman of eighty, wants a snug anchorage—at her time of life, if ever."

"I will do it myself, David," cried Barnstable, struggling to conceal his emotion; "I will call on her the instant we let go our anchor in Boston harbor, and as your credit can't be large, I will divide my own purse with her!"

The sailing-master was powerfully affected by this kind offer, the muscles of his hard weather-beaten face working convulsively, and it was a moment before he could trust his voice in reply.

"I know you would, Dickey, I know you would," he at length uttered, grasping the hand of Barnstable with a portion of his former strength; "I know you would give the old woman one of your own limbs, if it would do a service—to the mother of a messmate—which it would not—seeing that I am not the son of a—cannibal; but you are out of your own father's books, and it's too often shoal water in your pockets to help any one—more especially since you have just been spliced to a pretty young body—that will want all your spare coppers."

"But I am master of my own fortune," said Griffith, "and am rich."

"Ay, ay, I have heard it said you could build a frigate and set her afloat all a-taunt-o without thrusting your hand—into any man's purse—but your own!"

"And I pledge you the honor of a naval officer," continued the young sailor, "that she shall want for nothing; not even the care and tenderness of a dutiful son."

Boltrope appeared to be choking; he made an attempt to raise his exhausted frame on the couch, but fell back exhausted and dying, perhaps a little prematurely, through the powerful and unusual emotions that were struggling for utterance. "God forgive me my misdeeds!" he, at length, said, "and chiefly for ever speaking a word against your disciplyne; remember the best bower—and look to the slings of the lower yards—and—and—he'll do it Dickey, he'll do it! I'm casting off—the fasts—of life—and so God bless ye all—and give ye good weather—going large—or on a bowline!"

The tongue of the master failed him, but a look of heart-felt satisfaction gleamed across his rough visage, as its muscles suddenly contracted, when the faded lineaments slowly settled into the appalling stiffness of death.

Griffith directed the body to be removed to the apartment of the Master, and proceeded with a heavy heart to the upper deck. The Alacrity had been unnoticed during the arduous chase of the frigate, and favored by day-light, and her light draught of water, she had easily effected her escape also among the mazes of the shoals. She was called down to her consort by signal, and received the necessary instructions how to steer during the approaching night. The British ships were now only to be faintly discovered, like small white specks on the dark sea, and as it was known that a broad barrier of shallow water lay between them, the Americans no longer regarded their presence as at all dangerous.

When the necessary orders had been given, and the vessels were fully prepared, they were once more brought up to the wind, and their heads pointed in the direction of the coast of Holland. The wind, which freshened towards the decline of day, hauled round with the sun, and when that luminary retreated from the eye, so rapid had been the progress of the mariners, it seemed to sink in the bosom of the ocean, the land having long before settled into its watery bed. All night the frigate continued to dash through the seas with a sort of sullen silence, that was soothing to the melancholy of Cecilia and Katherine, neither of whom closed an eye during that gloomy period. In addition to the scene they had witnessed, their feelings were harrowed by the knowledge that, in conformity to the necessary plans of Griffith, and in compliance with the new duties he had assumed, they were to separate in the morning for an indefinite period, and possibly forever.

With the appearance of light, the boatswain sent his rough

summons through the vessel, and the crew were collected in solemn silence in her gang-ways, to "bury the dead." The bodies of Boltrope, of one or two of her inferior officers, and of several common men, who had died of their wounds in the night, were, with the usual formalities, committed to the deep; when the yards of the ship were again braced by the wind, and she glided along the trackless waste, leaving no memorial in the midst of the ever-rolling waters, to mark the place of their sepulture.

When the sun had gained the meridian the vessels were once more hove-to, and the preparations were made for a final separation. The body of Colonel Howard was transferred to the Alacrity, whither it was followed by Griffith and his cheerless bride, while Katherine hung fondly from a window of the ship, suffering her own scalding tears to mingle with the brine of the ocean. After every thing was arranged, Griffith waved his hand to Barnstable, who had now succeeded to the command of the frigate, and the yards of the latter were braced sharp to the wind, when she proceeded to the dangerous experiment of forcing her way to the shores of America, by attempting the pass of the streights of Dover, and running the gauntlet through the English ships that crowded their own channel; an undertaking, however, for which she had the successful example of the Alliance frigate, which had borne the stars of America along the same hazardous path but a few months previously.

In the meanwhile the Alacrity, steering more to the west, drew in swiftly towards the shores of Holland, and about an hour before the setting of the sun, had approached so nigh as to be once more hove into the wind, in obedience to the mandate of Griffith. A small light boat was lowered into the sea, when the young sailor, and the pilot, who had found his way into the cutter unheeded, and almost unseen, ascended from the small cabin together. The stranger glanced his eyes along the range of coast, as if he would ascertain the exact position of the vessel, and then turned them on the sea and the western horizon to scan the weather. Finding nothing in the appearance of the latter to induce him to change his determination, he offered his hand frankly to Griffith, and said—

"Here we part. As our acquaintance has not led to all we wished, let it be your task, sir, to forget we ever met."

Griffith bowed respectfully, but in silence, when the other continued, shaking his hand contemptuously towards the land—

"Had I but a moiety of the navy of that degenerate republic, the proudest among those haughty islanders should tremble in his castle, and be made to feel there is no security against a foe that trusts his own strength and knows the weakness of his enemy! But," he muttered in a lower and more hurried voice, "this has been like Liverpool, and—Whitehaven—and Edinburgh, and fifty more! it is past, sir; let it be forgotten."

Without heeding the wondering crew, who were collected as curious spectators of his departure, the stranger bowed hastily to Griffith, and springing into the boat, he spread her light sail with the readiness of one who had nothing to learn even in the smallest matters of his daring profession. Once more, as the boat moved briskly away from the cutter, he waved his hand in adieu, and Griffith fancied, that even through the distance, he could trace a smile of bitter resignation, lighting his calm features with a momentary gleam. For a long time the young man stood an abstracted gazer at his solitary progress, watching the small boat as it glided towards the open ocean, nor did he remember to order the head sheets of the Alacrity drawn, in order to put the vessel again in motion, until the dark speck was lost in the strong glare that fell, obliquely across the water, from the setting sun.

Many wild and extraordinary conjectures were uttered among the crew of the cutter, as she slowly drew in towards her friendly haven, on the appearance of the mysterious pilot, during their late hazardous visit to the coast of Britain, and on his still more extraordinary disappearance, as it were, amid the stormy wastes of the North sea. Griffith himself was not observed to smile, nor to manifest any other evidence of his being a listener to their rude discourse, until it was loudly announced that a small boat was seen pressing for their own harbor, across the fore foot of the cutter, under a single lugsail. Then, indeed, the sudden and cheerful lighting of his troubled eye, might have betrayed to more accurate observers, the vast relief that was imparted to his feelings by the interesting discovery.

# Chapter XXXV.

"Come all you kindred Chieftains of the deep!
In mighty phalanx, round your brother bend;
Hush every murmur that invades his sleep—
And guard the laurels that o'ershade your friend!"
*Lines on Tripp.*

---

HERE, perhaps it would be wise to suffer the curtain of our imperfect drama to fall before the reader, trusting that the imagination of every individual can readily supply the due proportions of health, wealth, and happiness, that the rigid rules of poetic justice would award to the different characters of the legend. But as we are not disposed to part so coldly from those with whom we have long held amicable intercourse, and as there is no portion of that in reservation which is not quite as true as all that has been already related, we see no unanswerable reason for dismissing the dramatis personae so abruptly. We shall therefore proceed to state briefly, the outlines of that which befel them in after-life, regretting, at the same time, that the legitimate limits of a modern tale will not admit of such a dilatation of many a merry or striking scene, as might create the pleasing hope of beholding hereafter, some more of our rude sketches quickened into life, by the spirited pencil of Dunlap.

Following the course of the frigate, then, towards those shores, from which, perhaps, we should never have suffered our truant pen to have wandered, we shall commence the brief task with Barnstable, and his laughing, weeping, gay, but affectionate, bride—the black-eyed Katherine. The ship fought her way, gallantly, through swarms of the enemy's cruisers, to the port of Boston, where Barnstable was rewarded for his services by promotion, and a more regular authority to command his vessel.

During the remainder of the war, he continued to fill that station with ability and zeal, nor did he return to the dwelling of his fathers, which he soon inherited, by regular descent, until after peace had established not only the independence of his country, but his own reputation, as a brave and successful sea-officer. When the Federal Government laid the foundation of its present navy, Captain Barnstable was once more tempted by the offer of a new commission to desert his home; and for many years he was employed among that band of gallant seamen who served their country so faithfully in times of trial and high daring. Happily, however, he was enabled to accomplish a great deal of the more peaceful part of his service accompanied by Katherine, who, having no children, eagerly profited by his consent, to share his privations and hardships on the ocean. In this manner they passed merrily, and we trust happily, down the vale of life together, Katherine entirely discrediting the ironical prediction of her former guardian, by making, every thing considered, a very obedient, and certainly, so far as attachment was concerned, a most devoted wife.

The boy, Merry, who in due time became a man, clung to Barnstable and Katherine, so long as it was necessary to hold him in leading strings; and when he received his regular promotion, his first command was under the shadow of his kinsman's broad pendant. He proved to be in his meridian, what his youth had so strongly indicated, a fearless, active, and reckless sailor, and his years might have extended to this hour, had he not fallen untimely, in a duel with a foreign officer.

The first act of Captain Manual, after landing once more on his native soil, was to make interest to be again restored to the line of the army. He encountered but little difficulty in this attempt, and was soon in possession of the complete enjoyment of that which his soul had so long pined after, "a steady drill." He was in time to share in all the splendid successes which terminated the war, and also to participate in his due proportion of the misery of the army. His merits were not forgotten, however, in the reorganization of the forces, and he followed both St. Clair and his more fortunate successor, Wayne, in the western campaigns. About the close of the century, when the British made their tardy relinquishment of the line of posts along the frontiers, Captain Manual was ordered to take charge, with his company, of a small stockade on our side of one of those mighty rivers, that sets bounds to the territories of the Republic in the north. The British flag was waving over the ramparts of a more regular fortress, that

had been recently built, directly opposite, within the new
lines of the Canadas. Manual was not a man to neglect the
observances of military etiquette, and understanding that the
neighbouring fort was commanded by a field officer, he did
not fail to wait on that gentleman, in proper time, with a
view to cultivate the sort of acquaintance that their mutual
situations would render not only agreeable, but highly convenient. The American martinet, in ascertaining the rank of the
other, had not deemed it at all necessary to ask his name, but
when the red-faced, comical-looking officer with one leg, who
met him, was introduced as Major Borroughcliffe, he had not
the least difficulty in recalling to recollection his quondam
acquaintance of St. Ruth. The intercourse between these
worthies was renewed with remarkable gusto, and at length
arrived to so regular a pass, that a log cabin was erected on
one of the islands in the river, as a sort of neutral territory,
where their feastings and revels might be held without any
scandal to the discipline of their respective garrisons. Here the
qualities of many a saddle of savory venison were discussed,
together with those of sundry pleasant fowls, as well as of
divers strange beasts that inhabit those western wilds, while,
at the same time, the secret places of the broad river were
vexed, that nothing might be wanting that could contribute
to the pleasures of their banquets. A most equitable levy was
regularly made on their respective pockets, to sustain the foreign expenses of this amicable warfare, and a suitable division
of labour was also imposed on the two Commandants, in
order to procure such articles of comfort as were only to be
obtained from those portions of the globe, where the art of
man had made a nearer approach to the bounties of nature,
than in the vicinity of their fortifications. All liquids in which
malt formed an ingredient, as well as the deep-coloured wines
of Oporto, were suffered to enter the Gulf of St. Lawrence,
and were made to find their way, under the superintendence
of Borroughcliffe, to their destined goal; but Manual was,
solely, entrusted with the more important duty of providing
the generous liquor of Madeira, without any other restriction
on his judgment, than an occasional injunction from his coadjutor, that it should not fail to be the product of the "South-
side!"

It was not unusual for the younger officers of the two garrisons to allude to the battle in which Major Borroughcliffe had lost his limb—the English ensign invariably whispering to the American on such occasions, that it occurred during the late contest, in a desperate affair on the North Eastern coast of their island, in which the Major commanded, in behalf of his country, with great credit and signal success; and for which service he obtained his present rank "without purchase!" A sort of national courtesy prevented the two veterans, for by this time both had earned that honourable title, from participating at all in these delicate allusions; though whenever, by any accident, they occurred near the termination of the revels, Borroughcliffe would so far betray his consciousness of what was passing, as to favor his American friend with a leer of singular significance, which generally produced in the other that sort of dull recollection, which all actors and painters endeavour to represent by scratching the head. In this manner year after year rolled by, the most perfect harmony existing between the two posts, notwithstanding the angry passions that disturbed their respective countries, when an end was suddenly put to the intercourse by the unfortunate death of Manual. This rigid observer of discipline, never trusted his person on the neutral island without being accompanied by a party of his warriors, who were posted as a regular picquet, sustaining a suitable line of sentries; a practice which he also recommended to his friend, as being highly conducive to discipline, as well as a salutary caution against a surprise on the part of either garrison. The Major, however, dispensed with the formality in his own behalf, but was sufficiently good-natured to wink at the want of confidence it betrayed in his boon companion. On one unhappy occasion, when the discussions of a new importation had made a heavy inroad on the morning, Manual left the hut to make his way towards his picquet, in such a state of utter mental aberration, as to forget the countersign when challenged by a sentinel, when, unhappily, he met his death by a shot from a soldier, whom he had drilled to such an exquisite state of insensibility, that the man cared but little whether he killed friend or enemy, so long as he kept within military usage, and the hallowed limits established by the articles of war.

He lived long enough, however, to commend the fellow for the deed, and died while delivering an eulogium to Borroughcliffe, on the high state of perfection to which he had brought his command!

About a year before this melancholy event, a quarter cask of wine had been duly ordered from the South side of the island of Madeira, which was, at the death of Manual, toiling its weary way up the rapids of the Mississippi and the Ohio; having been made to enter by the port of New-Orleans, with the intention of keeping it as long as possible under a genial sun! The untimely fate of his friend imposed on Borroughcliffe the necessity of attending to this precious relick of their mutual tastes; and he procured a leave of absence from his superior, with the laudable desire to proceed down the streams and superintend its farther advance in person. The result of his zeal was a high fever, that set in the day after he reached his treasure, and as the Doctor and the Major espoused different theories, in treating a disorder so dangerous in that climate, the one advising abstemiousness, and the other administering repeated draughts of the cordial that had drawn him so far from home, the disease was left to act its pleasure. Borroughcliffe died in three days; and was carried back and interred by the side of his friend, in the very hut which had so often resounded with their humours and festivities! We have been thus particular in relating the sequel of the lives of these rival chieftains, because, from their want of connexion with any kind heart of the other sex, no widows and orphans were left to lament their several ends, and furthermore, as they were both mortal, and might be expected to die at a suitable period, and yet did not terminate their career until each had attained the mature age of three-score, the reader can find no just grounds of dissatisfaction at being allowed this deep glance into the womb of fate.

The chaplain abandoned the seas in time to retrieve his character, a circumstance which gave no little satisfaction to Katherine, who occasionally annoyed her worthy husband on the subject of the informality of their marriage.

Griffith and his mourning bride conveyed the body of Colonel Howard in safety to one of the principal towns in Holland, where it was respectfully and sorrowfully interred;

after which the young man removed to Paris, with a view of erasing the sad images, which the hurried and melancholy events of the few preceding days had left on the mind of his lovely companion.—From this place Cecilia held communion, by letter, with her friend Alice Dunscombe, and such suitable provision was made in the affairs of her late uncle as the times would permit. Afterwards, when Griffith obtained the command which had been offered him, before sailing on the cruise in the North Sea, they returned together to America. The young man continued a sailor until the close of the war, when he entirely withdrew from the ocean, and devoted the remainder of his life to the conjoint duties of a husband and a good citizen.

As it was easy to reclaim the estates of Colonel Howard, which, in fact, had been abandoned more from pride than necessity, and which had never been confiscated, their joint inheritances made the young couple extremely affluent, and we shall here take occasion to say, that Griffith remembered his promise to the dying master, and saw such a provision made for the childless mother, as her situation and his character required.

It might have been some twelve years after the short cruise, which it has been our task to record in these volumes, that Griffith, who was running his eyes carelessly over a file of newspapers, was observed by his wife to drop the bundle from before his face, and pass his hand slowly across his brow, like a man who had been suddenly struck with renewed impressions of some former event, or who was endeavouring to recall to his mind images that had long since faded.

"See you any thing in that paper, to disturb you Griffith?" said the still lovely Cecilia. "I hope that now we have our confederate government, the States will soon recover from their losses—but it is one of those plans to create a new navy, that has met your eye! Ah! truant! you sigh to become a wanderer again, and pine after your beloved ocean!"

"I have ceased sighing and pining since you have begun to smile," he returned, with a vacant manner, and without removing his hand from his brow.

"Is not the new order of things, then, likely to succeed? Does the Congress enter into contention with the President?"

"The wisdom and name of Washington will smooth the way for the experiment, until time shall mature the system. Cecilia, do you remember the man who accompanied Manual and myself to St. Ruth, the night we became your uncle's prisoners, and who afterwards led the party which liberated us, and rescued Barnstable?"

"Surely I do; he was the pilot of your ship, it was then said; and I remember the shrewd soldier we entertained, even suspected that he was one greater than he seemed."

"The soldier surmised the truth; but you saw him not on that fearful night, when he carried us through the shoals! and you could not witness the calm courage with which he guided the ship into those very channels again, while the confusion of battle was among us!"

"I heard the dreadful din! And I can easily imagine the horrid scene," returned his wife, her recollections chasing the colour from her cheeks even at that distance of time; "but what of him? is his name mentioned in those papers? Ah! they are English prints! you called his name Gray, if I remember?"

"That was the name he bore with us! he was a man who had formed romantic notions of glory, and wished every thing concealed in which he acted a part that he thought would not contribute to his renown. It has been, therefore, in compliance with a solemn promise made at the time, that I have ever avoided mentioning his name—he is now dead!"

"Can there have been any connexion between him and Alice Dunscombe?" said Cecilia, dropping her work in her lap, in a thoughtful manner.—"She met him alone, at her own urgent request, the night Katherine and myself saw you in your confinement, and even then my cousin whispered that they were acquainted! The letter I received yesterday, from Alice, was sealed with black, and I was pained with the melancholy, though gentle manner, in which she wrote of passing from this world into another!"

Griffith glanced his eye at his wife, with a look of sudden intelligence, and then answered like one who began to see with the advantages of a clearer atmosphere.

"Cecilia, your conjecture is surely true! Fifty things rush to my mind at that one surmise—his acquaintance with that

particular spot—his early life—his expedition—his knowledge of the abbey, all confirm it! He, altogether, was indeed a
man of marked character!"

"Why has he not been among us," asked Cecilia; "he appeared devoted to our cause?"

"His devotion to America proceeded from desire of distinction, his ruling passion, and perhaps a little also from resentment at some injustice which he claimed to have suffered
from his own countrymen. He was a man, and not therefore
without foibles—among which may have been reckoned the
estimation of his own acts; but they were most daring, and
deserving of praise! neither did he at all merit the obloquy
that he received from his enemies. His love of liberty may be
more questionable; for if he commenced his deeds in the
cause of these free States, they terminated in the service of a
despot! He is now dead—but had he lived in times and under circumstances, when his consummate knowledge of his
profession, his cool, deliberate, and even desperate courage,
could have been exercised in a regular, and well-supported
Navy, and had the habits of his youth better qualified him to
have borne, meekly, the honors he acquired in his age, he
would have left behind him no name in its lists that would
have descended to the latest posterity of his adopted countrymen with greater renown!"

"Why, Griffith," exclaimed Cecilia, in a little surprise, "you
are zealous in his cause! Who was he?"

"A man who held a promise of secrecy while living, which
is not at all released by his death. It is enough to know, that
he was greatly instrumental in procuring our sudden union,
and that our happiness might have been wrecked in the voyage of life had we not met the unknown pilot of the German
Ocean."

Perceiving her husband to rise, and carefully collect the
papers in a bundle, before he left the room, Cecilia made no
further remark at the time, nor was the subject ever revived
between them!

# THE RED ROVER

## A TALE

*"Ye speak like honest men: pray God ye prove so!"*
*Henry VIII*, III.i.69

TO
W. B. SHUBRICK,
ESQUIRE,
U. S. NAVY

In submitting this hastily-composed and imperfect picture of a few scenes, peculiar to the profession, to your notice, dear SHUBRICK, I trust much more to your kind feelings than to any merit in the execution. Such as it may be, however, the book is offered as another tribute to the constant esteem and friendship of

THE AUTHOR

# Preface
[1827]

THE WRITER felt it necessary, on a former occasion, to state, that, in sketching his marine life, he did not deem himself obliged to adhere, very closely, to the chronological order of nautical improvements. It is believed that no very great violation of dates will be found in the following pages. If any keen-eyed critic of the ocean, however, should happen to detect a rope rove through the wrong leading-block, or a term spelt in such a manner as to destroy its true sound, he is admonished of the duty of ascribing the circumstances, in charity, to any thing but ignorance on the part of a brother. It must be remembered that there is an undue proportion of landsmen employed in the mechanical as well as the more spiritual part of book-making; a fact which, in itself, accounts for the numberless imperfections that still embarrass the respective departments of the occupation. In due time, no doubt, a remedy will be found for this crying evil; and then the world may hope to see the several branches of the trade a little better ordered. The true Augustan age of literature can never exist until works shall be as accurate, in their typography, as a "log-book," and as sententious, in their matter, as a "watch-bill."

On the less important point of the materials, which are very possibly used to so little advantage in his present effort, the Writer does not intend to be very communicative. If their truth be not apparent, by the manner in which he has set forth the events in the tale itself, he must be content to lie under the imputation of having disfigured it, by his own clumsiness. All testimony must, in the nature of things, resolve itself into three great classes—the positive, the negative, and the circumstantial. The first and the last are universally admitted to be entitled to the most consideration; since the third can only be resorted to in the absence of the two others. Of the positive evidence of the verity of its contents, the book itself is a striking proof. It is hoped, also, that there is no want of circumstance to support this desirable character. If these two opening points be admitted, those who may be still disposed to cavil are left to the full enjoyment of their negation, with which the Writer wishes them just as much success as the question may merit.

# *Preface*
## [1834]

FROM THE TIME when this Tale originally appeared, till now, it has never even been read by its author, except to make the corrections for the present edition in "The Standard Novels." On examination the book has been found to be full of errors in style, orthography, and taste. It is hoped that a good deal has been done to correct all three of these faults, and that the work will now be thought much more worthy of the favor with which it has been received, than it was before.

As respects the subject of the tale, the author has little to say. America is a country nearly without traditions, the few there are being commonly too familiar to be worked up in fiction. The object of the book is to paint sea scenes and to describe nautical usages and nautical character, and not at all to embody any real events. There never was any such free-booter as the hero of this tale, nor did the writer ever hear of the appellation which he has given him. As respects himself, the name of Red Rover is as much invention as any other part of the book. All that has been aimed at, in the way of moral, is to show the manner in which men of the fairest promise can be led astray by their wayward passions, and to prove how narrow the boundaries become between virtue and vice, when education or neglect gives a false tendency to such minds as may contain the seeds of better things. It was also believed it might be useful to show that crime can be commit-ted under a fair exterior, and that men are not always to be thought monsters because they fail in some one important quality, by which they have justly forfeited the esteem of their fellow creatures; for, in general, as much harm is done by the ruthless denunciations of those, who, favored by fortune are removed from the dangers of temptation themselves, as by the example of the criminal.

*London, Oct. 1833*

# Preface

SMOLLETT had obtained so much success as a writer of nautical tales, that it probably required a new course should be steered in order to enable the succeeding adventurer in this branch of literature to meet with any favour. This difficulty was fully felt when this book was originally written, and probably has as much force to-day as it had then, though nearly a quarter of a century has intervened.

The history of this country has very little to aid the writer of fiction, whether the scene be laid on the land or on the water. With the exception of the well-known, though meagre incidents connected with the career of Kidd, indeed, it would be very difficult to turn to a single nautical occurrence on this part of the continent, in the hope of conferring on a work of the imagination any portion of that peculiar charm which is derived from facts clouded a little by time. The annals of America are surprisingly poor in such events; a circumstance that is doubtless owing to the staid character of the people, and especially to that portion of them which is most addicted to navigation.

These difficulties were duly appreciated by the writer of this book, who found it necessary to invent his legend without looking for the smallest aid from traditions or facts. There is no authority whatever for any incident, character or scene, of the book now offered to the reader, unless nature may be thought to furnish originals, in a greater or less degree, to some of the pictures.

A good deal of speculation has been resorted to by different writers, in order to discover the history and uses of the little stone ruin in which one of our incidents is laid. Those who are not content to accept of a simple solution of this antiquarian problem, have assailed the irreverent manner in which we have termed it a mill, and have claimed for the little structure an original as remote as the times of the Northmen who are supposed to have preceded Columbus in his voyage to this western hemisphere. We pretend to no exclusive knowledge on the subject, never having seen this much-talked of ruin but once, and then only in a hurried visit of a single half-hour. It must be confessed that it struck the writer as the very obvious remains of a wind-mill, and as nothing else; though there may be better reasons than any he can give to the contrary, for supposing it to have been erected as a fortress, several centuries ago! We can imagine the use in placing a mill on arches, as it is a very simple process, and one often had recourse to, in order to prevent the ravages of the mice; but it is not so easy to see why the extra labour of forming arches, the loss of room, and the additional risk from fire, should all be voluntarily incurred to raise up a fortress against savages. Under no circumstances, it would seem, could such a tower be less expensive, less difficult to construct, and less secure, by building it up as a solid structure from the ground, than by raising it in the air, on senseless because useless pillars, as must have been the case, if we are to suppose the building to have been erected for the purposes of defence. The lower apartment, which, on this antiquarian theory, would be thrown away, might have been of great daily utility, as it certainly would have added to the strength of the tower; thus reducing these poor Northmen to the dilemma of having it inferred that their intelligence was of so low a stamp as to lead them to expend their time and labour in raising an elaborate structure that would be less likely to effect all their objects than one much more simple.

We trust this denial of the accuracy of what may be a favourite local theory, will not draw down upon us any new evidence of the high displeasure of the Rhode Island Historical Society, an institution which displayed such a magnanimous sense of the right, so much impartiality, and so profound an understanding of the laws of nature and of the facts of the day, on a former occasion when we incurred its displeasure, that we really dread a second encounter with its philosophy, its historical knowledge, its wit, and its signal love of justice. Little institutions, like little men, very naturally have a desire to get on stilts, a circumstance that may possibly explain the theory of this extraordinary, and very useless fortification.

We prefer the truth and common sense, to any other mode

of reasoning, not having the honour to be an Historical Society, at all. That which we have elsewhere written, and in a graver capacity, we think has been triumphantly vindicated, and we have given our reasons here, for disbelieving the theory of the citadel of the Northmen. If others prefer to tilt with a windmill, we commend them to their own gallantry and the sympathy of Sancho Panza. Thank Heaven! we have never published any thing which involves the necessity of believing that four vessels, with their topsails aback, drifted round the whole earth in two hours and a half, in straight lines regardless of islands and continents, which creates the necessity of supposing that a crippled craft will drift to windward, or have asserted that any particular battle, the property of the whole nation, belongs to "the naval annals of New York." They who have maintained these historical and philosophical *tours de force*, are quite right to top off their mental labours by maintaining that the "Newport Ruin" was a dwelling of the Cæsars!

Cooperstown, January 1, 1850

# Chapter I

Par. "Mars dote on you for his novices!"
*All's Well That Ends Well*, II.i.47.

N O ONE, who is familiar with the bustle and activity of an American commercial town, would recognise, in the repose which now reigns in the ancient mart of Rhode Island, a place that, in its day, has been ranked amongst the most important ports along the whole line of our extended coast. It would seem, at the first glance, that nature had expressly fashioned the spot, to anticipate the wants, and to realize the wishes of the mariner. Enjoying the four great requisites of a safe and commodious haven, a placid basin, an outer harbor, and a convenient roadstead with a clear offing, Newport appeared, to the eyes of our European ancestors, designed to shelter fleets and to nurse a race of hardy and expert seamen. Though the latter anticipation has not been entirely disappointed, how little has reality answered to expectation in respect to the former! A successful rival has arisen even in the immediate vicinity of this seeming favorite of nature, to defeat all the calculations of mercantile sagacity and to add another to the thousand existing evidences that "the wisdom of man is foolishness."

There are few towns of any magnitude, within our broad territories, in which so little change has been effected in half a century, as in Newport. Until the vast resources of the interior were developed the beautiful island on which it stands was a chosen retreat of the affluent planters of the South from the heats and diseases of their burning climate. Here they resorted in crowds to breathe the invigorating breezes of the sea. Subjects of the same government the inhabitants of the Carolinas and of Jamaica, met here, in amity, to compare their respective habits and policies, and to strengthen each other in a common delusion which the descendants of both, in the third generation, are beginning to perceive and to regret.

The communion left on the simple and unpractised offspring of the Puritans its impression both of good and evil. The inhabitants of the country, while they derived from the intercourse a portion of that bland and graceful courtesy for which the gentry of the Southern British Colonies were so distinguished, did not fail to imbibe some of those peculiar notions, concerning the distinctions in the races of men, for which they are no less remarkable. Rhode-Island was the foremost among the New-England Provinces to recede from the manners and opinions of their simple ancestors. The first shock was given through her, to that rigid and ungracious deportment which was once believed a necessary concomitant of true religion, a sort of outward pledge of the healthful condition of the inward man, and it was also through her, that the first palpable departure was made from those purifying principles, which might serve as an apology for even more repulsive exteriors. By a singular combination of circumstances and qualities, which is, however no less true than perplexing, the Merchants of Newport were becoming, at the same time, both slave-dealers and gentlemen.

Whatever might have been the moral condition of its proprietors, at the precise period of 1759, the island itself was never more enticing and lovely. Its swelling crests were then crowned with the wood of centuries, its little vales were covered with the living verdure of the north, and its unpretending but neat and comfortable villas lay sheltered in groves and embedded in flowers. The beauty and fertility of the place gained for it a name which probably expressed far more than was properly understood at that early day. The inhabitants of the country styled their possessions the "Garden of America." Neither were their guests from the scorching plains of the South reluctant to concede this imposing title. The appellation descended even to our own time, nor was it entirely abandoned until the traveller had the means of contemplating the thousand broad and lovely vallies, which fifty years ago lay buried in the dense shadows of the forest.*

The date which we have just named, was a period fraught with the deepest interest to the British possessions on this

*There are both a state and island which bear the same name. Rhode Island (the state) is the smallest of the twenty-four sisters which compose the American Union. It is not so large as many English counties, has to-day a population of only about one hundred thousand souls, and is well known for its manufacturing industry.

Continent. A bloody and vindictive war, which had been commenced in defeat and disgrace, was about to end in triumph. France was deprived of the last of her possessions on the main, while the immense region which lies between the Bay of Hudson and the territories of Spain submitted to the power of England. The Colonists had shared largely in contributing to the success of the Mother Country. Losses and contumely that had been incurred by the besotting prejudices of European commanders were beginning to be forgotten in the pride of success. The blunders of Braddock, the indolence of Loudon and the impotency of Abercrombie were repaired by the vigor of Amherst and the Genius of Wolfe. In every quarter of the Globe the arms of Britain were triumphant. The loyal Provincials were among the loudest in their exultations and rejoicings; willfully shutting their eyes to the scanty meed of applause, that a powerful people ever reluctantly bestows on its dependents, as if love of glory like avarice increases by its means of indulgence.

The system of oppression and misrule which hastened a separation, that sooner or later must have occurred in the natural order of events, had not yet commenced. The Mother Country if not just was still complaisant. Like all old and great nations she was indulging in the pleasing but dangerous enjoyment of self-contemplation. The qualities and services of a race who were believed to be inferior were however soon forgotten, or if remembered it was in order to be misrepresented and vituperated. As this feeling increased with the discontent of the civil dissentions it led to still more striking injustice, and greater folly. Men, who from their observations should have known better, were not ashamed to proclaim even in the highest council of the nation their ignorance of the character of a people with whom they had mingled their blood. Self-esteem gave value to the opinions of fools. It was under this soothing infatuation, that veterans were heard to disgrace their noble profession by boastings that should have been hushed in the mouth of a soldier of the carpet; it was under this infatuation that Burgoyne gave in the Commons of England that memorable promise of marching from Quebec to Boston with a force he saw fit to name, a pledge that he afterwards redeemed by going over the same ground with twice the number of followers as captives and it was under this infatuation that England subsequently threw away her hundred thousand lives and lavished her hundred millions of treasure. We forbear to dwell longer on the ungrateful recollections of those days of mistaken pride and ignorance. Contumely as usual brought upon itself a just retribution.

The History of that memorable struggle is familiar to every American. Content with the knowledge that his country triumphed, he is willing to let the glorious result take its proper place in the pages of History. He sees that her empire rests on a broad and natural foundation, which needs no support from venal pens, and, happily for his peace of mind no less than for his character, he feels that the prosperity of the Republic is not to be sought in the degradation of surrounding nations.

Our present purpose leads us back to the period of calm which preceded the storm of the Revolution. In the early days of the month of October 1759, Newport, like every other town in America, was filled with the mingled sentiments of grief and joy. The inhabitants mourned the fall of Wolfe while they triumphed in his victory. Quebec, the strong hold of the Canadas, and the last place of any importance held by a people whom they had been educated to believe were their natural enemies, had just changed its masters. That loyalty to the crown of England, which endured so much before the strange principle became extinct, was then at its height, and probably the colonist was not to be found, who did not in some measure identify his own honor with the fancied glory of the house of Brunswick. The day on which the action of our tale commences had been expressly set apart to manifest the sympathy of the good people of the town and its vicinity, in the success of the Royal Arms. It had opened, as thousands of days have opened since, with the ringing of bells and the firing of cannon, and the population, at an early hour, had poured into the streets of the place with that determined zeal in the cause of merriment, which ordinarily makes preconcerted joy so dull an amusement. The chosen orator of the day had exhibited his eloquence in a sort of prosaic monody in praise of the dead hero, and had sufficiently manifested his loyalty by laying the glory not only of that sacrifice, but all that had been reaped by so many thousands of his brave companions also, most humbly, at the foot of the throne.

Content with these demonstrations of their allegiance the inhabitants began to retire to their dwellings as the sun settled towards those immense regions, which then lay an endless and unexplored wilderness, but which, now, are teeming with the fruits and enjoyments of civilized life. The countrymen from the environs, and even from the adjoining main, were beginning to turn their faces towards their distant homes, with that frugal care which still distinguishes the inhabitants of this portion of our country even in the midst of their greatest abandonment to pleasures, in order that the approaching evening might not lead them into expenditures, which were not deemed germain to the proper feelings of the occasion. In short, the excess of the hour was passed, and each individual was returning into the sober channels of his ordinary avocations, with an earnestness and discretion which proved he was not altogether unmindful of the time that had been squandered in the display of a spirit, that he already appeared half disposed to consider as supererogatory.

The sounds of the hammer, the axe and the saw were again heard in the place; the windows of more than one shop were half-opened, as if its owner had made a sort of compromise between his interests and his conscience, and the masters of the only three inns in the town were to be seen standing before their doors, regarding the retiring countrymen, with eyes which plainly betrayed that they were seeking customers among a people who were always much more ready to sell than to buy. A few noisy and thoughtless seamen belonging to the vessels in the haven, together with some half dozen notorious tavern-hunters, were, however the sole fruits of all their nods of recognition, inquiries into the welfare of wives and children, and in some instances of open invitations to alight and drink.

Worldly care, with a constant, though sometimes an oblique look at the future state, formed the great characteristic of all that people who then dwelt in what were called the Provinces of New-England. Still the business of the day was not forgotten, though it was deemed unnecessary to digest its

proceedings in idleness, or over the bottle. The travellers
along the different roads that led into the interior of the island, formed themselves into little knots, in which the policy
of the great national events they had just been commemorat-
ing and the manner they had been treated by the different
individuals selected to take the lead in the offices of the day,
were freely handled, though still with great deference to the
established reputations of the distinguished parties most concerned. It was every where conceded that the prayers, which
had been in truth a little conversational and historical, were
faultless and searching exercises, and, on the whole, though to
this opinion there were some clients of an advocate adverse to
the orator who were moderate dissentients, it was established
that a more eloquent oration had never issued from the
mouth of man, than had that day been delivered in their presence. Precisely in the same temper, was the subject discussed
by the workmen on a ship, which was then building in the
harbor, and which, in the same spirit of Provincial admiration, that has since immortalized so many edifices, bridges
and even individuals within their several precincts, was confi-
dently affirmed to be the rarest specimen then extant of the
nice proportions of Naval Architecture.

Of the orator himself it may be necessary to say a word, in
order that so remarkable an intellectual prodigy should fill his
proper place, in our frail and short-lived catalogue of the worthies of that day. He was the usual oracle of his neighborhood
when a condensation of its ideas, on any great event, like the
one just mentioned, became necessary. His learning was justly
reputed, by comparison, to be of the most profound and
erudite character, and it was very truly affirmed to have astonished more than one European scholar, who had been
tempted, by a fame, which, like heat was only the more intense, from its being so confined, to grapple with him on the
arena of ancient Literature. He was a man who knew how to
improve these high gifts to his exclusive advantage. In but
one instance had he ever been thrown enough off his guard to
commit an act that had a tendency to depress the reputation
he had thus gained; and that was in permitting one of his
labored flights of eloquence to be printed: or, as his more
witty though less successful rival, the only other lawyer in the

place expressed it "in suffering one of his *fugitive* essays to be *caught*." But even this experiment, whatever might have been its effects abroad, served to confirm his renown at home. He now stood before his admirers in the dignity of types, and it was in vain for that miserable tribe of "animalculæ who live by feeding on the body of genius," to attempt to undermine a reputation that was embalmed in the faith of so many parishes. The brochure was diligently scattered through the Provinces, lauded around the tea-pot, openly extolled in the prints by some kindred spirit, as was manifest in the similarity of style, and by one believer, more zealous or perhaps more interested than the rest, it was actually put on board the next ship which sailed for "home," as England was then affectionately termed, enclosed in an envelope which bore an address no less imposing than that of the Majesty of Britain. Its effects on the straight-going mind of the dogmatic German who then filled the throne of the Conqueror were never accurately known, though they who were in the secret of the transmission long looked in vain for the signal reward that was to follow so favourable an exhibition of human intellect.

Notwithstanding these high and beneficent gifts, their possessor was now as unconsciously engaged in that portion of his professional labors which bore the strongest resemblance to the occupation of a scrivener, as if nature, in bestowing such rare endowments, had denied him the phrenological quality of self-esteem. A critical observer might, however, have seen, or fancied that he saw, in the forced humility of his countenance, certain gleamings of a triumph that might not be traced to the fall of Quebec. The habit of appearing meek had, however, united with a frugal regard for the precious and irreclaimable minutes, in producing this extraordinary diligence in a pursuit of a character that was so humble when compared with his recent mental efforts.

Leaving this gifted favorite of fortune and nature we shall now pass to an entirely different individual and to another quarter of the place. The spot to which we wish to transport the reader was neither more nor less than the shop of a tailor who did not disdain to perform the most minute offices of his vocation in his own heedful person. The humble edifice stood, at no great distance from the water, in the skirts of the town, and in such a situation as to enable its occupants to look out upon the loveliness of the inner basin, and through a vista cut by the element between islands, even upon the lake-like scenery of the outer harbor. A small though little frequented wharf lay before its door, while a certain air of negligence and the absence of bustle sufficiently manifested that the place itself was not the immediate site of the much boasted commercial prosperity of the port.

The afternoon was like a morning in spring. The breeze which occasionally rippled the basin possessed that peculiarly bland influence which is so often felt in the American autumn, and the worthy mechanic labored at his calling, seated on his shop-board at an open window far better satisfied with himself, than many of those whose fortune it is to be placed in state beneath canopies of velvet and gold. On the outer side of the little building a tall, awkward, but vigorous and well formed countryman was lounging, with one shoulder placed against the side of the shop, as if his legs found the task of supporting his heavy frame too grievous to be endured without assistance, seemingly in waiting for the completion of the garment at which the other toiled, and with which he intended to adorn his person in an adjoining parish, on the succeeding Sabbath.

In order to render the minutes shorter, and possibly in the indulgence of a very ungovernable propensity to talk, of which he who wielded the needle was somewhat the subject, but few of the passing moments were suffered to escape without a word from one or the other of the parties. As the subject of their discourse had a direct reference to the principal matter of our tale, we shall take leave to give such portions of it to the reader as we deem most relevant to a clear exposition of that which is to follow. The latter will always bear in mind that he who worked was a man drawing into the wane of life, that he bore about him the appearance of one, who either from incompetency, or from some fatality of fortune had been doomed to struggle through the world, keeping poverty from his residence only by the aid of great industry and rigid frugality, and that the idler was a youth of that age and condition that the acquisition of an entire set of habiliments, formed a sort of era in his adventures.

"Yes," exclaimed the indefatigable shaper of cloth, a species of sigh which might have been equally construed into an evidence of the fullness of his mental enjoyment or of the excess of his bodily labours struggling from his lips; "yes, smarter sayings may have fallen from the lips of man, than such as the squire pour'd out to day, but we in the provinces have never heard them. When he spoke of the plains of Father Abraham, and of the smoke and thunder of the battle, Pardon, it stirred up such stomachy feelings in my bosom that I verily believe I could have had the heart to throw aside the thimble and go forth myself, to seek glory in battling in the cause of the King!"

The youth, whose christian or "given" name, as it is even now generally termed in New-England, had been intended by his pious sponsors, humbly to express his future hopes, turned his head towards the heroic tailor, with an expression of drollery about the eye that proved nature had not been niggardly in the gift of humour, however the quality was suppressed by the restraints of a very peculiar manner and no less peculiar education.

"There's an opening, now, neighbor Homespun, for an ambitious man," he said, "sin' his Majesty has lost his stoutest general."

"Yes, yes," returned the individual who, either in his youth or in his age had made so capital a blunder in the choice of a profession, "a fine and promising chance it is for one who counts only five-and-twenty; but most of my day has gone by, and I must spend the rest of it here, where you see me, between buckram and ossenbricks! who put the dye into this cloth, Pardy? it is the best laid-in bark I've fingered this fall."

"Let the old woman alone for giving the lasting colour to her web; I'll engage, neighbor Homespun, provided you furnish the proper fit there'll not be a better dressed lad on the island than my own mother's son. But sin' you cannot be a general, good-man, you'll have the comfort of knowing there'll be no more fighting without you. Every body agrees the French won't hold out much longer, and then we must have a peace for want of enemies."

"So best, so best, boy; for one, who has seen as much of

the horrors of war as I, knows how to put a rational value on the blessings of tranquility!"

"Then you ar'n't altogether unacquainted, good-man, with the new trade, you thought of setting up?"

"I! I have been through five long and bloody wars, and I've reason to thank God that I've gone through them all without a scratch as big as one this needle would make! Five long and bloody, ay, and I may say glorious wars have I lived through, in safety!"

"A perilous time it must have been for you, neighbor. But I don't remember to have heard of more than two quarrels with the Frenchmen in my day."

"You are but a boy, compared to one who has seen the end of his third score of years. Here is this war, that is now so likely to be soon ended—Heaven, which rules all things in wisdom, be praised for the same! Then there was the business of '45 when the bold Warren sailed up and down our coasts, a scourge to his Majesty's enemies and a safeguard to all loyal subjects. Then, there was a business in Garmany, concerning which we had awful accounts of battles fou't, in which men were mowed down like grass falling before the scythe of a strong arm. That makes three;" cocking his spectacles and counting with his thimble on the fingers of the other hand. "The fourth was the rebellion of '15, of which I pretend not to have seen much, being but a youth at the time, and the fifth was a dreadful rumour that was spread through the Provinces, of a general rising among the blacks and Indians, which was to sweep all us Christians into eternity at a minute's warning."

"Well, I had always reckoned you for a home-staying and a peaceable man, neighbor," returned the admiring country-man, "nor did I ever dream that you had seen these serious movings."

"I have not boasted, Pardon, or I might have added other heavy matters to the list. There was a great struggle in the East, no longer than the year '32, for the Persian throne. You have read of the laws of the Medes and the Persians: Well, for the very throne that gave forth those unalterable laws was there a frightful struggle in which blood ran like water; but as it was not in Christendom I do not account it, among my own experiences, though I might have spoken of the Porteous

Mob, with great reason, as it took place in another portion of the very Kingdom in which I lived."

"You must have journeyed much, and been stirring late and early, good-man, to have seen all these things, and to have got no harm."

"I have been something of a traveller, too, Pardy. Twice have I been over land to Boston, and once have I sailed through the Great Sound of Long Island, down to the Town of York. It is an awful undertaking the latter, as it respects the distance, and more especially because it is needful to pass a place that is likened, by its name to the entrance of Tophet."

"I have often heard the spot called 'Hell Gate' spoken of, and I may say, too, that I know a man *well*, who has been through it twice; once in going to York, and once in coming homeward."

"He had enough of it, as I'll engage! Did he tell you of the pot, which tosses and roars as if the biggest of Beelzebub's fires was burning beneath, and of the hogs-back, over which the water pitches as it may tumble over the Great Falls of the West! Owing to reasonable skill in our seamen and uncommon resolution in the passengers, we happily had a good time of it through ourselves, though I care not who knows it, I will own it is a severe trial to the courage to enter that dreadful straight. We cast out our anchors at certain islands which lie a few furlongs this side the place, and sent the pinnace with the captain and two stout seamen to reconnoitre the spot, in order to see if it were in a peaceful state or not. The report being favorable, the passengers were landed, and the vessel was got through, by the blessing of Heaven, in safety! We had all reason to rejoice that the Prayers of the Congregation were asked before we departed from the peace and security of our own homes!"

"You journeyed round the 'Gate' on foot?" demanded the attentive boor.

"Certain! It would have been a sinful and a blasphemous tempting of Providence to have done otherwise, seeing that our duty called us to no such sacrifice. But all that danger is gone by, and so do I trust will that of this bloody war in which we have both been actors. And then I humbly hope his sacred Majesty will have leisure to turn his royal mind to the pirates who infest the coast, and to order some of his stout naval captains to mete out to the rogues the treatment they are so fond of giving to others. It would be a joyful sight to my old eyes to see the famous and long-hunted Red Rover brought into this very port, towing at the poop of a King's cruiser."

"And is it a desperate villain, he of whom you now make mention?"

"He! There are many he's in that one lawless ship, and bloody minded and nefarious thieves are they to the smallest boy! It is heart-searching and grievous, Pardy, to hear of their evil-doings on the high-seas of the King!"

"I have often heard mention made of the Rover," returned the countryman, "but never to enter into any of the intricate particulars of his knavery."

"How should you, boy, who live up in the country, know so much of what is passing on the Great Deep, as we who dwell in a port that is resorted to by mariners! I am fearful, you'll be making it late home, Pardon," he added, glancing his eye at certain lines drawn on his shop-board by the aid of which, he was enabled to note the progress of the setting sun. "It is drawing towards the hour of five, and you have twice that number of miles to go, before you can by any manner of means, reach the nearest boundary of your father's farm!"

"The road is plain and the people honest," returned the countryman, who cared not if it were midnight provided he could be the bearer of the particulars of some dreadful sea-robbery to the ears of those, whom he well knew, would throng around him, at his return, to hear the tidings from the port. "And is he in truth, so much feared and sought-for, as people say?—"

"Is he sought for! Is Tophet sought by a praying Christian? Few there are on the Mighty Deep, let them even be as stout for battle as was Joshua the great Jewish-Captain, that would not rather behold the land, than see the top-gallants of that wicked pirate! Men fight for glory, Pardon, as I may say I have seen after living through so many wars, but none love to meet an enemy who hoists a bloody flag, at the first blow, and who is ready to cast both parties into the air, when he finds the hand of Satan has no longer the mind to help him."

"If the rogue is so desperate," returned the youth, straightening his powerful limbs with a look of rising pride, "why do not the Island and the Plantations fit out a coaster, in order to bring him in that he might get a sight of a wholesome gibbet? Let the drum beat on such a message, through our neighborhood, and I'll engage that it don't leave it without one volunteer, at least!"

"So much for not having seen war! Of what use would flails and pitch-forks prove against men who have sold themselves to the devil? Often has the Rover been seen, at night, or just as the sun has been going down, by the King's cruisers, who, having fairly surrounded the thieves, had good reason to believe that they had them already in the bilboes, but when the morning has come, the prize was vanished, by fair means or by foul."

"And are the villains so bloody-minded that they are called red?"

"Such is the title of their leader," returned the worthy tailor, who by this time was swelling with the importance of possessing so interesting a legend to communicate, "and such is also the name they give to his vessel, because no man who has put foot on board her, has ever come back to say, that she has a better or a worse. That is, no honest mariner or lucky voyager. The ship is of the size of a King's sloop they say, and of like equipments and form, but she has miraculously escaped from the hands of many a gallant frigate, and once, it is whispered, for no loyal subject would like to say so scandalous a thing openly, Pardon, that she lay under the guns of a fifty for an hour, and seemingly to all eyes she sunk like hammered lead to the bottom. But just as every body was shaking hands and wishing his neighbor joy at so happy a punishment coming over the knaves, a West-Indiaman came into port, that had been robbed by the Rover on the morning after the night in which it was thought they had all gone into eternity together. And what makes the matter worse, boy, while the King's ship was heeling her keel out, to stop the holes of cannon balls, the pirate was sailing up and down the coast, as sound as the day that the wrights first turned her from their hands!"

"Well this is unheard of!" returned the countryman, on

whom the tale was beginning to make a sensible impression. "Is she a well turned and comely ship to the eye, or is it by any means certain that she is an actual, living, vessel at all?"

"Opinions differ. Some say yes, some say no. But I am well acquainted with a man, who travelled a week in company with a mariner, who passed within a hundred fathoms of her, in a gale of wind. Lucky it was for them, that the hand of the Lord was felt so powerfully on the deep, and that the Rover had enough to do to keep his own ship from foundering. The acquaintance of my friend, had a good view of both vessel and captain, therefore, in perfect safety. He said that the pirate was a man, maybe half as big again as the tall preacher over on the main, with hair of the color of the sun in a fog, and eyes that no man would like to look upon a second time. He saw him as plainly as I see you, for the knave stood in the rigging of his ship, beckoning with a hand as big as a coat-flap for the honest trader to keep off, in order that the two vessels might not do one another damage by coming foul."

"He was a bold mariner, that trader, to go so nigh such a merciless rogue!"

"I warrant you, Pardon, it was desperately against his will. But it was on a night so dark—"

"Dark!" interrupted the other, who had the inquisitive shrewdness of a New Englander, notwithstanding his disposition to credulity; "by what contrivance then, did he manage to see, so well?"

"No man can say!" answered the tailor, "but see he did, just in the manner, and the very things that I have named to you. More than that, he took good note of the vessel that he might know her, if chance or Providence, should ever happen to throw her again into his way. She was a long black ship, lying low in the water, like a snake in the grass, with a desperate wicked look, and altogether of dishonest dimensions. Then every body says that she appears to sail faster than the clouds above her, seeming to care little which way the wind blows, and that no one is a jot safer from her speed than her honesty. According to all that I have heard she is something such a craft as yonder slaver that has been lying, the week past, the Lord knows why, in our outer harbor."

As the gossiping tailor had necessarily lost many precious

moments, in relating the preceding history, he now set about redeeming them, with the utmost diligence, keeping time to the rapid movement of his needle-hand, by corresponding jerks of his head and shoulders. In the mean while the bumpkin, whose wondering mind was, by this time charged nearly to bursting, with what he had heard, turned his look towards the vessel the other had pointed out, in order to get the only image that was now required, to enable him to do credit to so moving a tale, suitably engraved on his imagination. There was necessarily a pause while the respective parties were thus severally occupied. It was suddenly broken, by the tailor, who clipped the thread with which he had just finished the garment, cast every thing from his hands, threw his spectacles upon his forehead and leaning his arms on his knees in such a manner as to form a perfect labyrinth with the limbs, he stretched his body forward so far, as to lean out of the window, rivetting his eyes, also, on the ship which still attracted the gaze of his companion.

"Do you know, Pardy," he said, "that strange thoughts and cruel misgivings have come over me, concerning that very vessel! They say she is a slaver come in for wood and water, and yet there she has been a week, and not a stick bigger than an oar has gone up her side, and I'll engage that ten drops from Jamaica have gone on board her, to one from the spring. Then you may see she is anchored in such a way that but one of the guns from the battery can touch her, whereas had she been a real timid trader, she would naturally have got into a place where, if a straggling picaroon should come into the port, he would have found her in the very hottest of the fire!"

"You have an ingenious turn with you, good-man," returned the wondering Countryman; "now, a ship might have lain on the battery island, itself, and I would have, hardly, noticed the thing!"

" 'Tis use and experience, Pardon, that makes men of us all. I should know something of batteries, having seen so many wars, and I served a campaign of a week, in that very fort, when the rumour came that the French were sending cruisers from Louisbourg down the coast. For that matter, my duty was to stand sentinel over that very cannon, and if I have done the thing once, I have twenty times squinted along the piece to see in what quarter it would send its shot, provided such a calamity should arrive as that it might become necessary to fire it, loaded with real, warlike balls."

"And who are these?" demanded Pardon, with that species of sluggish curiosity which had been awakened by the wonders related by the other. "Are these mariners of the slaver, or are they idle Newporters?"

"They!" exclaimed the tailor; "sure enough they are newcomers; it may be well to have a closer look at them, in these troublesome times! Here, Nab, take the garment and press down the seams, you idle hussy, for neighbor Hopkins is straightened for time, while your tongue is going like a young lawyer's in a justice's court. Don't be sparing of your elbow, girl, for it is no India muslin that you'll have under the iron, but cloth that would do to side a house with. Ah! your mother's loom, Pardy, robs the seamster of many an honest job."

Having thus transferred the remainder of the job, from his own hands to those of an awkward, pouting girl of seventeen who was compelled to abandon her gossip with a neighbor, in order to obey his injunctions, he quickly removed his own person, notwithstanding a miserable limp with which he had come into the world, from the shop board to the open air. As more important characters are, however, about to be introduced to the reader we shall defer the ceremony to the opening of another chapter.

# Chapter II

Sir Toby. "Excellent! I smell a device."
*Twelfth Night*, II.iii.162.

THE STRANGERS were three in number; for strangers the good-man Homespun, who knew not only the names but most of the private histories of every man and woman within ten miles of his own residence, immediately proclaimed them to be, in a whisper to his companion, and strangers, too, of a mysterious and threatening aspect. In order that others may have an opportunity of judging of the probability of the latter conjecture, it becomes necessary that a more minute account should be given of the respective appearances of these individuals, who, unhappily for their reputations, temporarily at least, had the misfortune to be unknown to the gossiping tailor of Newport.

The one, by far the most imposing in his general mien, was a youth who had apparently seen some six or seven and twenty seasons. That those seasons had not been entirely made of sunny days and nights of repose was betrayed, by the tinges of brown, which had been laid on his features, layer after layer, in such constant succession, as to have changed to a deep olive, a complexion which had once been fair, through which the rich blood was still mantling with the finest glow of vigorous health. His features were rather noble and manly than distinguished for their exactness and symmetry; his nose being far more bold and prominent than regular in its form, with his brows projecting and sufficiently marked to give to the whole of the superior parts of his face, that decided intellectual expression which is already becoming so common to the character of American physiognomy. The mouth was firm and manly, and while he muttered to himself and smiled, as the curious tailor drew slowly nigher, it discovered a set of glittering teeth, that shone the brighter from being cased in so dark a setting. The hair was a jet black, in thick and confused ringlets. The eyes were very little larger than common; gray, and though evidently of a changing expression, rather leaning to mildness than severity. The form of this young man was of that happy size, which unites activity with strength. It seemed to be well-knit, while it was justly proportioned and graceful. Though these several personal qualifications, were exhibited under the disadvantages of the perfectly simple, though neat and rather tastefully disposed attire of a common mariner, they were sufficiently imposing to cause the suspicious dealer in buckram to hesitate before he would venture to address the stranger, whose eye appeared fastened, by a species of fascination, on the reputed slaver in the outer harbor. A curl of the upper lip, and another inexplicable smile, in which some strong feeling was mingled with the muttering, decided the vacillating mind of the good-man. Without venturing to disturb a reverie that seemed so profound, he left the youth leaning against the head of the pile, where he had long been standing perfectly unconscious of the presence of any intruder, and turned a little hastily, to examine the rest of the party.

One of the remaining two, was a white-man and the other a negro. Both had passed the middle age, and both, in their appearances, furnished the strongest proofs of long exposure to the severity of many climates, and to numberless tempests. They were dressed in the plain, weather soiled, and tarred habiliments of common seamen, bearing about their persons the other never-failing evidences of their peculiar profession. The former was of a short, thick-set, powerful frame, in which, by a happy ordering of nature, a little confirmed perhaps by long habit, the strength was principally seated, about the broad and brawny shoulders and sinewy arms, as if in the construction of the man, the inferior members had been considered of little other use than to transfer the superior, to the different situations in which the former were to display their energies. His head was in proportion to the more immediate members; the forehead low, and nearly covered with hair; the eyes small, obstinate, sometimes fierce and often droll; the nose snub, coarse and vulgar; the mouth large and voracious; the teeth short, clean and perfectly sound, and the chin broad, manly, and even expressive. This singularly constructed personage had taken his seat on an empty barrel, and, with folded arms he sat examining the often-mentioned slaver, occasionally favoring his companion the black, with such remarks as were suggested by his observation and experience.

The negro occupied a more humble post; one better suited to his subdued habits and inclinations. In stature and the peculiar division of animal force, there was a great resemblance between the two, with the exception that the latter enjoyed the advantage in height and even in proportions. While nature had stamped on his lineaments those distinguishing marks which characterize the race from which he sprung, she had not done it to that revolting degree to which her displeasure against that stricken people is sometimes carried. His features were more elevated than common; his eye was mild, easily excited to joy, and, like that of his companion sometimes humorous. His head was beginning to be sprinkled with gray, his skin had lost the shining jet colour which had distinguished it, in his youth, and all his limbs and movements bespoke a man whose frame had been equally indurated and stiffened by toil. He sat on a low stone, and seemed intently employed in tossing pebbles into the air, showing his dexterity by catching them in the hand from which they had just been cast, an amusement which betrayed alike, the natural tendency of his mind to seek pleasure in trifles, and the absence of the more elevating feelings which are the fruits of education. The process however furnished a striking exhibition of the physical force of the negro. In order to conduct this trivial pursuit without incumbrance, he had rolled the sleeve of his light canvass jacket to the elbow, laying bare, by the process, an arm that might have served as a model for the limb of Hercules.

There was certainly nothing sufficiently imposing about the persons of either of these individuals to repel the investigations of one as much influenced by curiosity as our tailor. Instead, however, of yielding directly to the strong impulse, the honest shaper of cloth chose to conduct his advance in a manner that should give the bumpkin a striking proof of his sagacity. After making a sign of caution and intelligence to the latter, he approached slowly from behind, with a light step that might give him an opportunity of overhearing any secret that should unwittingly fall from either of the seamen. His forethought was followed by no very important results, though it served to supply him with all the additional testimony of the treachery of their characters that could be furnished by evidence so simple as the mere sound of their voices. As to the words themselves, though the good-man believed they might possibly contain treason, he was compelled to acknowledge to himself that it was so artfully concealed as to escape even his astute capacity. We leave the reader himself to judge of the correctness of both opinions.

"This is a pretty bight of a basin, Guinea," observed the white, rolling his tobacco in his mouth, and turning his eyes for the first time in many minutes from the vessel; "and a spot is it, that a man who lay on a lee-shore without sticks, might be glad to see his craft in! Now, do I call myself something of a seaman, and yet I cannot weather upon the philosophy of that fellow, in keeping his ship in the outer harbor, when he might warp her into this mill-pond, in half an hour. It gives his boats hard duty, dusky S'ip—, and that I call making foul weather of fair!"

The negro had been christened Scipio Africanus, by a species of witticism which was much more common to the Provinces than it is to the States of America, and which filled so many of the meaner employments of the country, in name at least, with the counterparts of the philosophers, heroes, poets and Princes of Rome. To him it was a matter of small moment whether the vessel lay in the offing or in the port, and without discontinuing his childish amusement, he manifested the same, by replying with great indifference,—

"I s'pose he t'ink all the water inside, lie on a top."

"I tell you, Guinea," returned the other, in a harsh positive tone, "the fellow is a know-nothing! Would any man who understands the behaviour of a ship, keep his craft in a road-stead, when he might tie her, head and heels, in a basin like this!"

"What he call road-stead!" interrupted the negro, seizing at once, with the avidity of ignorance on the little oversight of his adversary in confounding the outer-harbor of Newport with the wilder anchorage below, and with the usual indifference of all similar people to the more material matter of whether his objection was at all germain to the point at issue;

"I never hear 'em call anchoring ground with land around it, roadstead, afore."

"Harkee, Mister Gold-coast," muttered the white, bending his head aside in a threatening manner, though he still disdained to turn his eyes on his humble adversary, "if you've no wish to wear your shins parcelled, for the next month, gather in the slack of your wit and have an eye to the manner in which you let it run again. Just tell me this; isn't a port a port; and isn't an offing, an offing?"

As these were two propositions to which even the ingenuity of Scipio could raise no plausible objection, he wisely declined touching on either, contenting himself with shaking his head, in great self-gratulation, and laughing as heartily at his imaginary triumph over his companion, as if he had never known care, nor been the subject of wrong and humiliation so long and so patiently endured.

"Ay, ay," grumbled the white, re-adjusting his person in its former composed attitude, and again crossing the arms which had been a little separated to give force to the menace against the tender member of the black, "now you are piping the wind out of your throat like a flock of 'long-shore crows, you think you've got the best of the matter. The Lord made a nigger an unrational animal, and an experienced seaman, who has doubled both capes and made all the head-lands atween Fundy and Horn, has no right to waste his breath in teaching common sense to any of the breed! I tell you, Scipio, since Scipio is your name on the ship's books, though I'll wager a month's pay against a wooden fid that your Father was known at home as Quashee and your Mother as Quasheeba, therefore, do I tell you, Scipio Africa, which is a name for all your colour, I believe, that yonder chap, in the outer harbor of this here sea-port, is no judge of an anchorage, or he would drop a kedge, mayhap, hereaway in a line with the southern end of that there small matter of an island, and hauling his ship up to it, fasten her to the spot, with good hempen cables and iron mud-hooks. Now look you here, S'ip, at the reason of the matter," he continued, in a manner that showed the little skirmish that had just passed, was like one of those sudden squalls of which they had both seen so many, and which were usually so soon succeeded by corresponding seasons of calm, "look you at the rationality of what I say. He has come into this anchorage either for something, or for nothing. I suppose you are ready to admit that. If for nothing he might have found that much outside, and I'll say no more about it; but, if for something, he could get it off easier provided the ship lay, hereaway, just where I told you, boy, not a fathom ahead or astern, than where she is now riding, though the article was no heavier than a fresh handful of feathers for the captain's pillow. Now, if you have any thing to gainsay the reason of this, why I'm ready to hear it as a reasonable man, and one who has not forgotten his manners in picking up his learning."

"S'pose a wind come out fresh, here, at nor-west," answered the other, stretching his brawny arm towards the point of the compass he named, "and a vessel want to get to sea, in a hurry, how you t'ink he get her far enough up, to lay through the weather reach! Ha! you answer me dat; you great scholar, Mister Dick, but you never see ship go in wind's teeth, or hear a monkey talk."

"The black is right!" exclaimed the youth, who it would seem had overheard the dispute, while he appeared otherwise engaged—"the slaver has left his vessel in the outer harbour, knowing that the wind holds so much to the west-ward at this season of the year. And then you see, he keeps his light spars aloft, although it is plain enough by the manner in which his sails are furled, that he is strong-handed. Can you make out, boys, whether he has an anchor under-foot or is he merely riding by a single cable?"

"The man must be a driveller to lie in such a tides-way without dropping his stream, or at least a kedge, to steady the ship by," returned the white, without appearing to think any thing more than the received practice of seamen necessary to decide the point. "That he is no great judge of an anchorage I am ready to allow, but no man who can keep things so snug aloft would think of fastening his ship, for any length of time by a single cable to sheer starboard and port, like that kicking colt tied to the tree, by a long halter, that we fell in with, in our passage over land, from Boston."

" 'Em got a stream down, and all a rest of he anchor stowed," said the black, whose dark eye was glancing understandingly at the vessel, while he still continued to cast his pebbles into the air. "S'pose he jam he helm hard a-port, Misser Harry, and take a tide on he larboard bow, what you t'ink make him kick and gallop about! Golly! I like to see Dick, without a foot-rope, ride a colt tied to he tree!"

Again the negro enjoyed his own humour by shaking his head, as if his whole soul was amused by the whimsical image his rude fancy had conjured, indulging in a hearty laugh till the tears came, and again his white companion muttered heavy and sententious denunciations. The young man, who seemed to enter very little into the quarrels and witticisms of his singular associates, still kept his gaze intently fastened on the vessel, which to him, appeared, for the moment, to be the subject of some extraordinary interest. Shaking his own head, though in a far graver manner, as if his doubts were drawing to a close, he added, when the boisterous merriment of the negro had ceased,—

"Scipio, you are right. He rides altogether by his stream, and he keeps every thing in readiness for a sudden move. In ten minutes he could carry his ship beyond the fire of the battery, provided he had but a cap-full of wind."

"You appear to be a capital judge in these matters!" said a voice behind him.

The youth turned, suddenly on his heel, and then for the first time, was he apprised of the presence of intruders. The surprise, however, was not confined to himself, for as there was another new-comer to be added to the company, the gossiping tailor was quite as much, or even more, the subject of astonishment, than any of that party, which he had been so intently watching, as to have prevented him from observing the approach of another, utter stranger.

This new comer was a man between thirty and forty, and of a mien and attire, not a little adapted to quicken the active curiosity of the good-man Homespun. His person was slight, but it afforded the promise of exceeding agility, and even of vigor, especially when contrasted with his stature, which was scarcely equal to the medium height of man. His skin had been dazzling as that of woman, though a deep red which had taken possession of the lower lineaments of his face, and was particularly conspicuous on the outline of a fine aquiline nose, served to destroy all appearance of effeminacy. His hair was like his complexion, fair, and fell about his temples in rich, glossy and exuberant curls. His mouth and chin were beautiful in their formation, but the former was a little scornful, and the two together bore a decided character of voluptuousness. The eye was blue, full, without being prominent, and though in common placid and even soft, there were moments when it seemed a little unsettled and wild. He wore a high conical hat, placed a little on one side, so as to give a slightly rakish expression to his physiognomy, a riding-frock of light green, breeches of buck-skin, high-boots, and spurs. In one of his hands he carried a small whip, with which, when first seen he was cutting the air with an appearance of the utmost indifference to the surprise occasioned by his sudden interruption.

"I say, sir, you seem to me to be an excellent judge in these matters," he repeated, when he had endured the frowning examination of the young seaman quite as long as comported with his own patience. "You speak like a man who at least feels that he has a right to give an opinion!"

"Do you find it remarkable that one should not be ignorant of a profession that he has diligently pursued for a whole life?"

"Hum! I find it a little remarkable that one whose business is that of a handicraft, should dignify his trade with such a sounding name as *profession*. We of the science of the law, and who enjoy the particular smiles of the learned Universities cannot say much more!"

"Then call it trade, for nothing in common with gentlemen of your craft is acceptable to a seaman," retorted the young mariner, turning away from the intruder with a disgust that he did not affect to conceal.

"A lad of some metal!" muttered the other, with a rapid utterance and a meaning smile. "Let not such a trifle as a word part us, friend. I confess my ignorance of all maritime matters, and would gladly learn a little from one as skilful as yourself in the noble—*profession*. I think you said something concerning the manner in which yonder ship 'has anchored,' and of the condition in which they keep things alow and aloft?"

"*Alow* and aloft!" exclaimed the young sailor, facing his

interrogator with a stare that was quite as expressive as his recent disgust.

"A-low and aloft," calmly repeated the other.

"I spoke of her neatness aloft, but do not affect to judge of things below at this distance."

"Then it was my error; but you will have pity on the ignorance of one who is so new to the *profession*. As I have intimated, I am no more than an unworthy barrister, in the service of his Majesty, expressly sent from home on a particular errand. If it were not a pitiful pun, I might add, I am not yet a—judge."

"No doubt you will soon arrive at that distinction," returned the other, "if his Majesty's ministers have any just conceptions of modest merit; unless indeed you should happen to be prematurely"—

The youth bit his lip, made a quick inclination of the head, and walked leisurely up the wharf, followed with the same appearance of deliberation by the two seamen who had accompanied him in his visit to the place. The stranger in green, watched the whole movement with a calm, and apparently an amused, eye, tapping his boot with his whip and seeming to reflect like one who would willingly find means to continue the discourse.

"Hanged!" he at length uttered, as if to complete the sentence the other had left unfinished. "It is droll enough that such a fellow should dare to foretell so elevated a fate for *me*"—

He was evidently preparing to follow the retiring party, when he felt a hand laid a little unceremoniously on his arm, and his step was arrested.

"One word in your ear, Sir," said the attentive tailor, making a significant sign that he had matters of importance to communicate. "A single word, Sir, since you are in the particular service of his majesty. Neighbor Pardon," he continued with a patronising air, "the sun is getting low, and you will make it late home, I fear. The girl will give you the garment, and God speed you. Say nothing of what you have heard and seen until you have word from me to that effect, for it is seemly that two men, who have had so much experience in a war like this, should not lack in discretion. Fare-ye-well, lad!—pass the good word to the worthy farmer your father, not forgetting a refreshing hint of friendship to the thrifty housewife, your mother. Fare-ye-well, honest youth, fare-ye-well."

Homespun, having thus disposed of his admiring companion, waited with much elevation of mien, until the gaping bumpkin had left the wharf, before he again turned his look on the stranger in green. The latter had continued in his tracks, with an air of undisturbed composure, until he was once more addressed by the tailor, whose character and dimensions he seemed to have taken in, at a single glance of his rapid eye.

"You say, Sir, that you are a servant of his Majesty?" demanded the latter, determined to solve all doubts as to the other's claims on his confidence, before he committed himself, by any precipitate disclosure.

"I may say more; his familiar confident."

"It is an honour to converse with such a man, that I feel in every bone in my body," returned the cripple, smoothing his scanty hairs and bowing nearly to the earth. "A high and loyal honour do I feel this gracious privilege to be!"

"Such as it is, my friend, I take on myself, in his Majesty's name, to bid you welcome."

"Such munificent condescension would open my whole heart, though treason and all other unrighteousness were locked up in it. I am happy, honoured and I doubt not honorable Sir, to have this opportunity of proving my zeal to the King, before one who will not fail to report my humble efforts to his royal ears"—

"Speak freely," interrupted the stranger in green, with an air of princely condescension, though one, less simple and less occupied with his own budding honors than the tailor, might have easily discovered that he began to grow weary of the other's prolix loyalty. "Speak without reserve, friend; it is what we always do at court." Then switching his boot with his riding whip, he muttered to himself as he swung his light frame on his heel, with an indolent indifferent air, "if the fellow swallows that, he is as heavy as his own goose!"

"I shall, Sir, I shall; and a great proof of charity is it in one like your noble self to listen! You see yonder tall ship, Sir, in the outer harbor of this loyal sea-port?"

"I do. She seems to be an object of general attention among the worthy lieges of the place!"

"Therein I conceive, Sir, you have overrated the sagacity of my townsmen. She has been lying where you now see her, for many days, and not a syllable have I heard whispered against her character from mortal man except myself!"

"Indeed!" muttered the stranger, biting the handle of his whip, and fastening his glittering eyes intently on the features of the good-man, which were literally swelling with the importance of his discovery; "and what may be the nature of *your* suspicions?"

"Why, Sir, I may be wrong—and God forgive me if I am—but this is no more nor less than what has arisen in my mind on the subject: Yonder ship and her crew bear the reputation of being innocent and harmless slavers, among the good people of Newport, and as such, are they received and welcomed in the place, the one to a safe and easy anchorage and the others among the taverners and shop dealers. I would not have you imagine that a single garment has ever gone from my fingers for one of all her crew; no, let it be forever remembered that the whole of their dealings have been with the young tradesman named Tape, who entices customers to barter, by backbiting and otherwise defiling the fair names of his betters in the business; not a garment has been made by my hands for even the smallest boy."

"You are lucky," returned the stranger in green, "in being so well quit of the knaves! And yet have you forgotten to name the particular offense with which I am to charge them before the face of the King."

"I am coming as fast as possible to the weighty matter. You must know, worthy and commendable Sir, that I am a man that has seen much and suffered much in his Majesty's service. Five bloody and cruel wars have I gone through, besides other adventures and experiences, such as becomes a humble subject to suffer meekly and in silence."

"All of which shall be communicated to the royal ear. And now, worthy friend, relieve your mind by a direct communication of your suspicions."

"Thanks, honorable Sir, your goodness in my behalf cannot be forgotten, though it shall never be said that impatience to seek the relief you mention hurried me into a light and improper manner of unburthening my mind. You must know, honored gentleman, that yesterday, as I sat alone, at this very hour on my board, reflecting in my thoughts, for the plain reason that my envious neighbor had enticed all the newly arrived customers to his own shop, well, Sir, the head will be busy when the hands are idle; there I sat, as I have briefly told you, reflecting in my thoughts, like any other accountable being, on the calamities of life and on the great experiences that I have had in the wars. For you must know, valiant gentleman, besides the affair in the land of the Medes and Persians, and the Porteous mob in Edinbro', five cruel and bloody"—

"There is that in your air which sufficiently proclaims the soldier," interrupted his listener, who struggled to keep down his rising impatience. "But as my time is so precious, I would now more especially hear what you have to say concerning yonder ship?"

"Yes, Sir, one gets a military look, after seeing numberless wars; and so happily for the need of both, I have now come to the part of my secret which touches more particularly on the character of that vessel. There sat I, reflecting on the manner in which the strange seamen had been deluded by my tonguey neighbor, for as you should know, Sir, a desperate talker is that Tape and a younker who has seen but one war at the utmost, therefore was I thinking of the manner in which he had enticed my lawful customers from my shop, when, as one thought is the father of another, the following concluding reasoning, as our pious priest has it weekly in his reviving and searching discourses, came uppermost in my mind. If these mariners were honest and conscientious slavers, would they overlook a laboring man with a large family, to pour their well earned gold into the lap of a common babbler? I proclaimed to myself at once, Sir, that they would not. I was bold to say the same, in my own mind; and, thereupon, I openly put the question to all in hearing—if they are not slavers, what are they? A question which the King himself, would, in his Royal wisdom, allow to be a question easier asked than answered; upon which I replied, if the vessel be no fair-trading slaver nor a common cruiser of his Majesty, it is as tangible as the best man's reasoning, that she may be neither more nor less than the ship of that nefarious pirate the Red Rover."

"The Red Rover!" exclaimed the stranger in green, with a start so natural as to evidence that his dying interest in the tailor's narrative was suddenly and powerfully revived. "That indeed would be a secret worth having!—but why do you suppose this?"

"For sundry reasons, which I am now about to name, in their respective order. In the first place, she is an armed ship, Sir. In the second, she is no lawful cruiser, or the same would be publicly known, and by no one sooner than myself, inasmuch as it is seldom that I do not finger a penny from the King's ships. In the third place, the burglarious and unfeeling conduct of the few seamen who have landed from her, go to prove it, and lastly, what is well proved may be considered as substantially established. These are what, Sir, I should call the opening premises of my inferences, all of which I hope you will properly lay before the royal mind of his Majesty."

The barrister in green listened to the somewhat wire-drawn deductions of Homespun with great attention notwithstanding the confused and obscure manner in which they were delivered by the aspiring tradesman. His keen eye rolled quickly and often from the vessel to the countenance of his companion, but several moments elapsed before he saw fit to make any reply. The reckless gaiety with which he had introduced himself, and which he had hitherto maintained in the discourse was entirely superseded by a musing and abstracted air, which sufficiently betrayed that whatever levity he might display in common, he was far from being a stranger on proper occasions to deep and becoming thought. Suddenly throwing off his air of gravity, however, he assumed one, in which irony and sincerity were singularly blended, and laying his hand familiarly on the shoulder of the expecting tailor, he replied—

"You have communicated such matter as becometh a faithful and loyal servant of the King. It is well known that a heavy price is set on the head of the meanest follower of the Rover, and that a rich, ay, a splendid reward will be the fortune of him who is the instrument of delivering the whole knot of miscreants into the hands of the executioner. Indeed I know not but some marked evidence of the royal pleasure might follow such a service. There was Phipps, a man of humble origin, who received knighthood—"

"Knighthood!" echoed the tailor in awful admiration.

"Knighthood;" coolly repeated the stranger, "honorable and chivalric knighthood. What may have been the appellation you received from your sponsors in baptism?"

"My given name, gracious and grateful Sir, is Hector."

"And the house itself—the distinctive appellation of the family?"

"We have *always* been called Homespun."

"Sir Hector Homespun will sound as well as another! But to secure these rewards, my friend, it is necessary to be discreet. I admire your ingenuity, and am a perfect convert to your logic. You have so entirely demonstrated the truth of your own suspicions that I have no more doubt of yonder vessel being the pirate, than I have of your wearing spurs, and being called Sir Hector. The two things are equally established in my mind, but it is needful that we proceed in the matter with caution. I understand you to say, that no one else has been enlightened by your erudition, in this affair?"

"Not a soul. Tape would swear that the crew are conscientious slavers."

"So best. We must first render conclusions certain; then to our reward. Meet me at the hour of eleven this night, at yonder low point, where the land juts into the outer harbour. From that stand will we make our observations, and having removed every doubt, let the morning produce a discovery that shall ring from the Colony of the Bay to the settlements of Oglethorpe. Until then we part, for it is not wise that we be longer seen in conference. Remember silence, punctuality, and the favor of the King. These are our watch-words."

"Adieu, honorable Gentleman," said his companion, making a reverence nearly to the earth, as the other slightly touched his hat in passing.

"Adieu, Sir Hector," returned the stranger in green, with an affable smile and a gracious wave of the hand. He then walked slowly up the wharf, and disappeared behind the mansion of the Homespuns, leaving the head of that ancient family, like many a predecessor and many a successor, so rapt in the admiration of his own good-fortune, and so blinded by his folly, that while, physically, he saw to the right and to the left as well as ever, his mental vision was completely obscured in the clouds of ambition.

# Chapter III

Alonzo. "Good boatswain, have care."
*The Tempest*, I.i.9.

THE INSTANT the stranger had separated from the credulous tailor he lost his assumed air in one more natural
and sedate. Still it would seem that thought was either an
unwonted or an unwelcome tenant of his mind, for, switching his boot with his little riding-whip, he entered the principal street of the place, with a light step and a wandering
eye. Though his look was unsettled, few of the individuals
whom he passed escaped his quick glances; and it was quite
apparent from the hurried manner in which he began to regard objects, that his mind was not less active than his body.
A stranger thus accoutred, and one bearing about his person
so many evidences of his recent acquaintance with the road
did not fail to attract the attention of the provident publicans
we have had occasion to mention in our opening chapter.
Declining the civilities of the most favored of the inn-keepers,
he suffered his steps to be oddly enough arrested by the one
whose house was the usual haunt of the hangers-on of the
port.

On entering the bar-room of this tavern as it was called,
but which in another country would probably have aspired to
be termed no more than a pot-house, he found the hospitable
apartment thronged with its customary revelers. A slight interruption was produced by the appearance of a guest who
was altogether superior in mien and attire to the ordinary customers of the house, but it ceased the moment the stranger
had thrown himself on a bench, and intimated to the host the
nature of his wants. As the latter furnished the required
draught, he made a sort of apology which was intended for
the ears of all his customers nigh the stranger for the manner
in which an individual in the farther end of the long, narrow
room not only monopolized the discourse, but appeared to
extort the attention of all within hearing to some portentous
legend he was recounting.

"It is the boatswain of the slaver in the outer harbor,

Squire," the worthy minister of Bacchus concluded; "a man who has followed the water many a day, and who has seen sights and prodigies enough to fill a smart volume: old Boreus the people call him, though his lawful name is Jack Nightingale. Is the toddy to the Squire's relish?"

The stranger assented to the latter query by smacking his lips and bowing, as he put down the nearly untouched draught. He then turned his head to examine the individual, who might by the manner in which he declaimed have been termed in the language of the Country another "orator of the day."

A stature which greatly exceeded six feet, enormous whiskers that quite concealed a moiety of his grim countenance, a scar which was the memorial of a badly healed gash that had once threatened to divide that moiety in quarters, limbs in proportion, the whole rendered striking by the dress of a seaman, a long tarnished silver chain and a little whistle of the same metal, served to render the individual in question sufficiently remarkable. Without appearing to be in the smallest degree diverted from his self-importance by the entrance of one altogether so superior to the class of his usual auditors, this son of the ocean continued his narrative as follows, and in a voice that seemed given to him by nature in very mockery of his musical name—indeed so very near did his tones approach to the low murmurings of a bull, that some little practice was necessary to accustom the ear to the strangely uttered words.

"Well," he continued, thrusting his brawny arm forth with the fist clenched, indicating the necessary point of the compass by the thumb; "the coast of Guinea might have lain, hereaway, and the wind, you see, was dead off shore, blowing in squalls, as a cat spits, all the same as if the old fellow, who keeps it bagged for the use of us seamen, sometimes let the stopper slip through his fingers, and was sometimes fetching it up again with a double turn round the end of his sack— you know what a sack is, brother?"

This abrupt question was put to the gaping bumpkin already known to the reader, who with the nether garment just received from the tailor under his arm, had lingered to add the incidents of the present legend to the stock of lore that he had already obtained for the ears of his kins-folk in the country. A general laugh at the expense of the admiring Pardon succeeded; Nightingale bestowed a knowing wink on one or two of his familiars, and profiting by the occasion to "freshen his nip," as he quaintly styled swallowing a pint of rum and water, he continued his narrative, by saying in a sort of admonitory tone,

"And the time may come when you will know what a round-turn is, too, if you let go your hold of honesty. A man's neck was made, brother, to keep his head above water, and not to be stretched out of shape, like a pair of badly fitted dead-eyes. Therefore have your reckoning worked up, in season, and the lead of conscience going when you find yourself drifting on the shoals of temptation." Then rolling his tobacco over in his mouth, he looked boldly about him, like one who had acquitted himself of a moral obligation, and continued—"Well, here lay the land, and as I was saying, the wind was here at East and by South, or mayhap, at East and by South half South, sometimes blowing like a fin-back in a hurry, and sometimes leaving all the canvass chafing ag'in the rigging and spars, as if a bolt of duck cost no more than a rich man's blessing. I didn't like the looks of the weather, seeing that there was altogether too much unsartainty for a quiet watch, so I walked aft, in order to put myself in the way of giving an opinion, if-so-be such a thing should be asked. You must know, brothers, that according to my notions of religion and behaviour, a man is not good for much, unless he has a full share of manners; therefore I am never known to put my spoon into the captain's mess unless I am invited, for the plain reason that my berth is for'rard and his'n aft. I do not say in which end of a ship the better man is to be found. That is a matter concerning which, there are different opinions; though most good judges in the business are agreed. But aft I walked to put myself in the way of giving an opinion if one should be asked, nor was it long before the thing came to pass, just as I had foreseen. 'Mister Nightingale,' says he, for our captain is a gentleman and never forgets his behaviour on deck, or when any of the ship's company are at hand— *Mister* Nightingale,' says he, 'what do you think of that rag of a cloud, hereaway, at the north-west?' says he. 'Why, Sir,' says I boldly, for I'm never backward in speaking when properly spoken to, so, 'why, Sir,' says I, 'saving your honor's better judgment,' which was all a flam, for he was but a chicken to me in years and experience, but then I never throw hot-ashes to windward, or any thing else that is warm; so, 'Sir,' says I, 'it is my advice to hand the three topsails and to stow the jib. We are in no hurry, for the plain reason that Guinea will be to-morrow just where Guinea is to-night. As for keeping the ship steady, in these matters of squalls, we have the mainsail on her—' "

"You should have furl'd your mainsail too," exclaimed a voice from behind, that was quite as dogmatical, though a little less grum than that of the loquacious boatswain.

"What know-nothing says that?" demanded Nightingale fiercely, all his latent ire excited by so rude and daring an interruption.

"A man who has run Africa down from Bon to Good-hope more than once, and who knows a white squall from a rainbow," returned Dick Fid, edging his short person, stoutly towards his furious adversary, and making his way through the crowd by which the important boatswain was environed, by dint of his massive shoulders; "ay, brother, and a man, know much or know-nothing, who would never advise his officer to keep so much after sail on a ship, when there was the likelihood of the wind taking her aback."

To this bold vindication of an opinion which all present deemed to be so audacious there succeeded a general and loud murmur. Encouraged by this evidence of his popularity, Nightingale was not slow nor very meek with his retort, and then followed a clamorous concert, in which the voices of the company in general served for the higher and shriller notes, and through which the pithy and vigorous assertions, contradictions and opinions of the two principal disputants were heard running in a sort of thorough bass.

For some time no part of the discussion was very distinct, so great was the confusion of tongues, and there were certain symptoms of an intention on the part of Fid and the boatswain to settle their controversy by the last appeal. During this moment of suspense, the former squared his firm-built frame in front of his gigantic opponent, and there were vehement passings and counter passings in the way of gestures, from four athletic arms, each of which was knobbed, like a fashionable rattan, with a lump of bones, knuckles and sinews that threatened annihilation to any thing that should oppose it. As the general clamour, however, gradually abated the chief reasoners began to be heard, and as if content to rely on their respective powers of eloquence, each gradually relinquished his hostile attitude, and appeared disposed to maintain his ground by a member scarcely less terrible than his brawny arm.

"You are a bold seaman, brother," said Nightingale, resuming his seat; "and if saying was doing, no doubt you would make a ship talk. But I, who have seen fleets of two and three-deckers, and that of all nations except your Mohawks, may-hap, whose cruisers I will confess never to have fallen in with—lying as snug as so many white gulls, under reefed mainsails, know how to take the strain off a ship, and to keep my bulkheads in their places."

"I deny the judgment of heaving-to a boat, under her after square sails," retorted Dick. "Give her the staysails if you will, and no harm done; but a true seaman will never get a bagful of wind between his main-mast and his lee-swifter, if-so-be he knows his business. But words are like thunder, which only rumbles aloft without ever striking, as I have yet seen; let us therefore put the question to some one who has been on the water, and who knows a little of life and of ships as well as ourselves."

"If the oldest Admiral in his Majesty's fleet was here, he wouldn't be backward in saying who is right and who is wrong. I say, brothers, if there is a man among you all who has had the advantage of a sea-education, let him speak, in order that the truth of this matter may not be hid, like a marlingspike jammed between a brace block and a yard."

"Here then is the man," returned Fid; and stretching out his arm, he seized Scipio by the collar, and drew him without ceremony into the centre of the circle, that had opened around the two disputants. "There is a man for you, who has made one more passage between this and Africa than myself, for the reason that he was born there. Now, answer as if you were hallowing from a lee-earing, S'ip, under what sail would you heave-to a ship, on the coast of your native country, with the danger of a white-squall at hand?"

"I no heave-'em-to," said the black. "I make 'em scud."

"Ay, boy; but to be in readiness for the puff—would you jam her up under a mainsail, or would you let her lie a little off under a fore course?"

"Any fool know dat," returned Scipio grumly, and evidently tired already of being thus catechised. "If you want 'em to fall off, how you'm expect in reason he do it, under a main course—you answer me dat, Misser Dick!"

"Gentlemen," said Nightingale, looking about him with an air of offended dignity, "I put it to your honors. Is it genteel behaviour to bring a nigger, in this out of the way fashion, to give an opinion in the teeth of a white man!"

This appeal to the prejudices of the company was answered, by a common murmur. Scipio, who was prepared to maintain, and would have maintained his professional opinion, after his positive and peculiar manner, against any disputant, had not the heart to resist so general an evidence of the impropriety of his presence. Without uttering a word, in vindication or apology, he folded his arms, and walked out of the house with the submission and meekness of one, who had been too long trained in humility to rebel. This desertion on the part of his companion was not, however, so quietly acquiesced in by Fid, who found himself thus unexpectedly deprived of the testimony of the black. He loudly remonstrated against his retreat, but, finding it in vain, he crammed the end of several inches of tobacco into his mouth, swearing as he followed the African and keeping his eye, at the same time, firmly fastened on his adversary that in his opinion, "the lad if he was fairly skinned would be found to be the whiter man of the two."

The triumph of the boatswain was now complete, nor was he at all sparing of his exultation.

"Gentlemen," he said, addressing himself with increased confidence to the motley audience who surrounded him, "you see that reason is like a ship bearing down with studdingsails on both sides, leaving a straight wake and no favors. Now, I scorn boasting, nor do I know who the fellow is that has just sheered off, in time to save his character, but this I will say, that the man is not to be found between Boston and the West-Indies, who knows better than myself, how to make a ship walk, or how to make her stand still, provided I"—

The deep voice of Nightingale became suddenly hushed, and his eye was riveted by a sort of enchantment on the keen glance of the stranger in green, whose countenance was now seen blended among the more vulgar faces of the crowd.

"Mayhap," continued the boatswain, swallowing his words, in the surprise of seeing himself unexpectedly confronted by so imposing an eye, "mayhap this gentleman has some knowledge of the sea, and can decide the matter in dispute."

"We do not study naval tactics at the Universities," returned the other, briskly, "though I will confess I am, from the little I have heard, altogether in favor of *scudding*."

He pronounced the latter word with an emphasis, which rendered it questionable if he did not mean to pun; the more especially as he threw down his reckoning, and instantly left the field to the quiet possession of Nightingale. The latter, after a short pause resumed his narrative, though either from weariness or some other cause, it was observed that his voice was far less positive than before, and that his tale was cut prematurely short. After completing his narrative and his grog, he staggered to the beach, whither a boat was shortly after despatched to convey him on board the ship, which, during all this time had not ceased to be the constant subject of the suspicious examination of the good-man Homespun.

In the mean while the stranger in green, had pursued his walk along the main street of the Town. As Fid had given chase to the disconcerted Scipio, grumbling as he went and uttering no very delicate remarks on the knowledge and seamanship of the boatswain, they soon joined company again, the former changing his attack to the negro, whom he liberally abused for abandoning a point which he maintained was as simple and as true as, "that yonder bit of a schooner would make more way, going wing-and-wing, than jammed up on a wind."

Probably diverted with the touches of peculiar character he had detected in this singular pair of confederates, or possibly led by his own wayward humour, the stranger followed their footsteps. After turning from the water they mounted a hill, the latter a little in the rear of his pilots, until he lost sight of them in a bend of the street, or rather road, for by this time, they were past even the little suburbs of the town. Quickening his steps, the barrister, as he had announced himself to be, was glad to catch a glimpse of the two worthies seated under a fence, several minutes after he had believed them lost. They were making a frugal meal, from the contents of a little bag, which the white had borne under his arm, portions from which he now dispensed liberally to his companion, who had taken his post sufficiently nigh to proclaim that perfect amity was restored, though he still observed the distance which was becoming his colour and debased condition.

Approaching the spot, the stranger observed—

"If you make so free with the bag, my lads, your third man may have to go supperless to bed."

"Who hails?" said Dick, looking up from his bone, with an expression much like that of a mastiff, when interrupted at a similar employment.

"I merely wished to remind you that you had another messmate," cavalierly returned the other.

"Will you take a cut, brother?" said the seaman, offering the bag with the liberality of a sailor, the moment he fancied that there was an indirect demand made on its contents.

"You still mistake my meaning. On the wharf you had another companion."

"Ay, ay. He is in the offing there, overhauling that bit of a light-house, which is badly enough moored, unless they mean it to show the channel to your ox teams, and inland traders. Hereaway, gentleman, where you see that pile of stones, which seems likely to be coming down shortly by the run."

The stranger looked in the direction indicated by the other, and saw the young mariner to whom he had alluded, standing at the foot of a ruined tower, which was crumbling under the slow operations of time, at no great distance from the place where he stood. Throwing a handful of small change to the seamen, he wished them a better meal and crossed the fence, with an apparent intention, of examining the ruin, also.

"The lad is free with his coppers," said Dick, suspending the movements of his teeth, to give the stranger another and a better look; "but, as they will not grow where he has planted them, S'ip, you may turn them over to my pocket. An off-handed and a free-handed chap, that, Africa, but then these law-dealers get all their pence of the devil, and they are sure of more when the shot begins to run low in their lockers."

Leaving the negro to collect the money, and to transfer it, as in duty bound, to the hands of him, who, if not his master, was at all times ready and willing to exercise the authority of one, we shall follow the stranger in his walk toward the tottering edifice. There was little about the ruin itself to attract the attention of one, who, from his assertions, had probably often enjoyed the opportunities of examining far more imposing remains of former ages on the other side of the Atlantic. It was a small circular tower, which stood on rude pillars connected by arches, and might have been constructed, in the infancy of the country, as a place of defence, though it is far more probable that it was a work of a less warlike nature. More than half a century after the period of which we are writing, this little edifice, peculiar in its form, its ruinous condition, and its materials, has suddenly become the study and the theme of that very learned sort of individual, the American antiquarian. It is not surprising that a ruin thus honored should have become the subject of divers hot and erudite discussions. While the chivalrous in the arts and in the antiquities of the Country have been gallantly breaking their lances around the mouldering walls, the less instructed and the less zealous have regarded the combatants with the same species of wonder, as they would have manifested had they been present when the renowned knight of La Mancha tilted against those other windmills so ingeniously described by the immortal Cervantes.

On reaching the place, the stranger in green, gave his boot a smart blow with the riding whip, as if to attract the attention of the abstracted young sailor, freely commencing a conversation at the same time, like one who was a regular companion, rather than an intruder on the other's time.

"A very pretty object this would be, if covered with ivy, to be seen peeping through an opening in a wood," he said. "But I beg pardon; gentlemen of your *profession* have little to do with woods and crumbling stones. Yonder is the tower," pointing to the masts of the ship in the outer-harbor, "you love to look on; and your only ruin is a wreck."

"You seem familiar with our tastes, Sir," coldly returned the seaman.

"It is by instinct then. For it is certain I have had but little opportunity of acquiring my knowledge by actual communion with any of the—cloth, nor do I perceive that I am likely to be more fortunate at present. Let us be frank, my friend, and talk in amity. What do you see about this pile of stones that can keep you so long from your study of yonder noble and gallant ship?"

"Did it then surprise you, that a seaman out of employment should examine a vessel that he finds to his mind, perhaps with an intention to ask for service?"

"Her commander must be a dull fellow if he refuse it to so proper a lad! But you seem to be too well instructed for any of the meaner berths."

"Berths!" repeated the other, again fastening his eyes with a singular expression on the stranger in green.

"Berths. It is your nautical word for situation or station, is it not? We know but little of the marine vocabulary, we barristers, but I think I may venture on that as the true Doric. Am I justified by your authority?"

"The word is certainly not yet obsolete, and by a figure, it is proper in the sense you used it."

"Obsolete!" repeated the stranger in green, returning the meaning look he had just received. "Is that the name of any part of a ship? Perhaps by figure you mean figure-head, and by obsolete the long-boat!"

The young seaman laughed, and, as if this sally had broke through the barrier of his reserve, his manner lost some of its restraint during the remainder of their conference.

"It is just as plain," he said, "that you have been at sea, as it is, that I have been at school. Since we have both been so fortunate we may afford to be generous, and cease speaking in parables. For instance what do you think has been the object and use of this ruin when it was in better condition than it is at present?"

"In order to judge of that," returned the stranger in green, "it may be necessary to examine it more closely. Let us ascend."

As he spoke, the barrister mounted by a crazy ladder to the floor, which lay just above the crown of the arches, through which he passed by an open trap-door. His companion hesitated to follow; but observing that the other expected him at the summit of the ladder, and that he very kindly pointed out a defective round, he sprang forward and went up the ascent with the agility and steadiness peculiar to his calling.

"Here we are!" exclaimed the stranger in green, looking about at the naked walls, which were formed of such small and irregular stones as to give the building the appearance of dangerous frailty, "with good oaken plank for our deck, as you would say, and the sky for our roof, as we call the upper part of a house, at the universities. Now let us speak of things on the lower world—a—a—I forget what you said was your usual appellation?"

"That might depend on circumstances. I have been known by different names in different situations. However, if you call me Wilder, I shall not fail to answer."

"Wilder! a good name; though I dare say it would have been as true, were it Wild-one. You young ship-boys have the character of being a little erratic in your humours. How many tender hearts have you left to sigh, for your errors amid shady bowers, while you have been ploughing—that is the word I believe—ploughing the 'salt-sea ocean?'"

"Few sigh for me," returned Wilder, thoughtfully, who began to chafe under this free sort of catechism. "Let us return to our study of the tower. What think you has been its object?"

"Its present use is plain, and its former uses can be no great mystery. It holds, at this moment, two light hearts, and if I am not mistaken as many light heads, not overstocked with the stores of wisdom. Formerly it had its granaries of corn, at least, and I doubt not certain little quadrupeds, who were quite as light of fingers as we are of head and heart. In plain English it has been a mill."

"There are those who think it has been a fortress."

"Hum. The place might do at need," returned he in green, casting a rapid and peculiar glance around him. "But mill it has been, notwithstanding one might wish it a nobler origin. The windy situation, the pillars to keep off the invading vermin; the shape, the air, the very complexion prove it. Whir-r-r —whir-r-r—there has been clatter enough here, in time past, I warrant you. Hist! It is not done yet."

Stepping lightly to one of the little perforations which had once served as windows to the tower, he cautiously thrust his head through the opening, and after gazing there half a minute, he withdrew it again, making a gesture to the attentive Wilder to be silent. The latter complied, nor was it long, before the nature of the interruption was sufficiently explained.

The silvery voice of woman was first heard at a little distance, and then as the speakers drew nigher, the sounds arose directly from beneath, within the very shadow of the tower. By a sort of tacit consent, Wilder and the barrister chose spots, favorable to the execution of such a purpose, and each continued, during the time the visiters remained near the ruin, examining their persons, unseen themselves and, we are sorry we must do so much violence to the breeding of two such important characters in our legend, amused and attentive listeners to their conversation.

# Chapter IV

"They fool me to the top of my bent."
*Hamlet*, III.ii.384.

---

THE PARTY, below, consisted of four individuals, all of whom were females. One was a lady in the decline of her years, another was past the middle age, the third was on the very threshold of what is called life, as it is applied to intercourse with the world, and the fourth was a negress who might have seen some five and twenty revolutions of the seasons. The latter, at that time and in that country, of course appeared only in the character of a humble though perhaps favored domestic.

"And now, my child, that I have given you all the advice, which circumstances and your own excellent heart need," said the older lady, among the first words that were distinctly intelligible to the listeners, "I will change the ungracious office to one more agreeable. You will tell your Father of my continued affection, and of the promise he has given, that you are to return, once again, before we separate for the last time."

This speech was addressed to the younger female, and was apparently received with as much tenderness and sincerity as it was uttered. The one who was addressed raised her eyes, which were glittering with tears she evidently struggled to conceal, and answered, in a voice that sounded in the ears of the two youthful listeners, like the notes of the Syren, so very sweet and musical were its tones.

"It is useless to remind me of a promise, my beloved aunt, which I have so much interest in remembering," she said. "I hope for even more than you have perhaps dared to wish; if my father himself does not return with me in the spring it shall not be for want of urging on my part."

"Our good Wyllys will lend her aid," returned the aunt, smiling and bowing to the third female, with that mixture of suavity and form which was peculiar to the stately manners of the time, and which was rarely neglected when a superior addressed an inferior: "She is intitled to command some interest with Gen. Grayson, from her fidelity and services."

"She is entitled to every thing that love and heart can give!" exclaimed the niece, with a haste and earnestness that proclaimed how willingly she would temper the formal politeness of the other, by the warmth of her own affectionate manner. "My father will scarcely refuse *her* any thing!"

"And have we the assurance of Mrs Wyllys that she will be in our interests?" demanded the aunt, without permitting her own sense of propriety to be overcome by the stronger feelings of her niece. "With so powerful an ally, our league will be invincible."

"I am so entirely of opinion that the salubrious air of this healthful island is of great importance to my young charge, Madam, that were all other considerations wanting, the little I can do to aid your wishes, shall be sure to be done."

Wyllys spoke with dignity, and perhaps with some portion of that reserve which distinguished all the communications between the wealthy and high born aunt and the salaried and dependant governess of her brother's heiress; still her manner was gentle, and the voice, like that of her pupil, soft and feminine.

"We may then consider the victory as atchieved, as my late husband, the rear-admiral was accustomed to say. Admiral de Lacey, my dear Mrs Wyllys, adopted it in early life as a maxim, by which all his future conduct was governed, and by adhering to which he acquired no small share of his professional reputation, that in order to be successful it was only necessary to be *determined* one would be so. A noble and inspiriting rule, and one that could not fail to lead to those signal results which as we all know them, I need not mention."

Wyllys bowed her head in acknowledgement of the truth of the opinion and in testimony of the renown of the deceased Admiral, but did not appear to think it necessary to make any reply. Instead of allowing the subject to occupy her mind any longer she turned to her young pupil, and observed, speaking in a voice and with a manner from which every appearance of restraint was banished—

"Gertrude, my love, you will have pleasure in returning to this charming island and to these cheering sea breezes?"

"And to my aunt!" exclaimed Gertrude. "I wish my father

could be persuaded to dispose of his estates in Carolina, and come northward to reside the whole year."

"It is not quite as easy for an affluent proprietor to remove, as you may imagine, my child," returned Mrs de Lacey. "Much as I wish that some such plan could be adopted, I never press my brother on the subject; besides I am not certain, that if we were ever to make another change in the family, it would not be to return *home*, altogether. It is now more than a century, Mrs Wyllys, since the Graysons came into the colonies, in a moment of dissatisfaction with the Government in England. My great-grandfather, Sir Everard, was displeased with his second son, and the dissension led my grandfather to the Province of Carolina. But as the breach has long since been healed I often think my brother and myself may yet return to the Halls of our ancestors. Much will however depend on the manner in which we dispose of our treasure on this side of the Atlantic."

As the really well-meaning, though perhaps a little too much self-satisfied old lady concluded her remark, she glanced her eye at the perfectly unconscious subject of the close of her speech. Gertrude had, as usual when her aunt chose to favor her governess with any of the family reminiscences, turned her head aside, and was now offering her cheek, burning with health, and perhaps a little with shame to the cooling influence of the evening breeze. The instant the voice of Mrs de Lacey ceased, she turned hastily to her companions and pointing to a noble looking ship whose masts, as it lay in the inner harbor, were seen rising above the roofs of the town, she exclaimed, glad to change the subject in any manner—

"And yonder gloomy prison is to be our home, dear Mrs Wyllys, for the next month!"

"I hope your dislike to the sea has magnified the time," mildly returned her governess: "The passage between this place and the Carolinas has been often made in a much shorter period."

"That it has been so done, I can testify," resumed the Admiral's widow, adhering a little pertinaciously to a train of thoughts, which once thoroughly awakened in her bosom, was not easily diverted into another channel—"since my late estimable, and, I feel certain all who hear me will acquiesce when I add, gallant husband once conducted a squadron of his Royal Master, from one extremity of his Majesty's American Dominions to the other, in a time less than that named by my niece. It may have made some difference in his speed, certainly, that he was in pursuit of the enemies of his King and Country, but still the fact proves that the voyage can be made within the month."

"There is that dreadful Henlopen, with its sandy shoals and shipwrecks on one hand and that stream they call the Gulph on the other!" exclaimed Gertrude, with a shudder and a burst of natural terror, which makes timidity sometimes attractive when exhibited in the person of youth and beauty. "If it were not for Henlopen and its gales, and its shoals, and its Gulphs, I could think only of the pleasures of meeting my father!"

Mrs Wyllys, who never encouraged her pupil in these natural weaknesses, however pretty and becoming they might appear to other eyes, turned, with a steady mien to the young lady, and remarked with a brevity and decision that were intended to put the question of fear at rest for ever—

"If all the dangers you appear to apprehend existed in reality, the passage would not be made daily or even hourly in safety. You have often, Madam, come from the Carolinas by sea, in company with Admiral de Lacey?"

"Never," the widow promptly and a little dryly replied. "The water never agreed with my constitution, and I have always made the journey by land. But then you know, Wyllys, as the consort and relict of a flag-officer, it was not seemly that I should be ignorant of naval science. I believe there are few ladies in the British empire, who are more familiar with ships, either singly or in squadron, particularly the latter, than myself. This information I have naturally acquired as the companion of an officer whose fortune it was to lead fleets. I presume these are matters of which you are profoundly ignorant."

The calm, dignified countenance of Wyllys, on which it would seem long cherished and painful recollections had left a settled but mild expression of sorrow, that rather tempered than destroyed the traces of character which still were remarkable in her eye, became clouded for a moment with a shade of melancholy. After hesitating, as if willing to change the subject, she replied—

"I have not been altogether a stranger to the sea. It has been my lot to have made many long and some perilous voyages."

"As a mere passenger. But we wives of sailors only, among our sex, can lay claim to any real knowledge of the noble profession. What natural object is there or can there be," exclaimed the nautical dowager in a burst of professional enthusiasm, "finer than a stately ship, bore down by its canvass, breasting the billows, with, as I have heard the admiral say a thousand times, its taffrail ploughing the main, and its cut-water gliding after like a sinuous serpent, pursuing its shining wake as a living creature choosing its path on the land, and leaving the 'bone under its fore-foot,' a beacon for those that follow! I know not, my dear Wyllys, if I make myself intelligible to you, but to my instructed eye this charming description conveys a picture of all that is grand and beautiful!"

The latent smile of the governess might have betrayed that she was imagining the deceased Admiral had not been altogether devoid of the waggery of his vocation, had not a slight noise, which sounded like the rustling of the wind, but which in truth was suppressed laughter, proceeded from the upper room of the tower. The words "It is lovely!" were still on the lips of the youthful Gertrude, who saw all the beauty of the picture her aunt had essayed to describe, without descending to the humble employment of verbal criticism. But her voice became hushed and her attitude that of startled attention.

"Did you hear nothing?" she said.

"The rats have not yet altogether deserted the mill," was the calm reply of Wyllys.

"Mill! my dear Mrs Wyllys, will you persist in calling this picturesque ruin a mill!"

"However fatal it may be to its charms in the eyes of eighteen, I must call it a mill. Would not a rose by any other name, be found as sweet?"

"Ruins are not so plenty in this country, my dear governess," returned her pupil, laughing, while the ardor of her eye denoted how serious she was in defending her favourite opinion, "as to justify us, in robbing them of any little claims to interest they may happen to possess."

"Then happier is the Country! Ruins in a land are, like most of the signs of decay in the human form, sad evidences of abuses and passions, which have hastened the inroads of time. These provinces are like yourself, my Gertrude, in their freshness and their youth, and comparatively in their innocence also. Let us hope for both a long, an useful and a happy existence."

"Thank you for myself and for my country, but still I can never admit that this picturesque ruin has been a mill!"

"Whatever it may have been, it has long occupied its present place, and has the appearance of continuing where it is much longer; which is more than can be said of our prison, as you call yonder stately ship, in which we are so soon to embark. Unless my eyes deceive me, Madam, those masts are moving slowly past the chimneys of the town."

"You are very right, Wyllys. The seamen are towing the vessel into the outer harbor, where they will warp her fast to the anchors, and thus secure her until they shall be ready to unmake their sails, in order to put to sea in the morning. This is a manoeuvre often performed and one which the Admiral has so clearly explained, that I should find little difficulty in superintending it in my own person, were it suitable to my sex."

"This is then a hint that all our own preparations are not completed. However lovely this spot may seem, Gertrude, we must now leave it for some months at least."

"Yes," continued Mrs de Lacey, slowly following the footsteps of the governess, who had already moved from beneath the ruin—"whole fleets have often been towed to their anchors, and there warped, waiting for wind and tide to serve! None of our sex know the dangers of the ocean but we who have been bound in the closest of all ties to officers of rank and great service, and none others can ever truly enjoy the real grandeur of the ennobling profession. A charming object is a vessel cutting the waves with her taffrail, and chasing her wake on the trackless waters, like a courser that ever keeps in his path, though dashing madly on at the very top of his speed—"

The reply of Mrs Wyllys was not audible to the covert

listeners. Gertrude had followed her companions, but when at some little distance from the tower, she paused, and turning, shook back the raven tresses that fell about her rich glowing cheeks; she lifted her lovely face, full toward the ruin, as if to take a parting look at its mouldering walls. A profound stillness succeeded for more than a minute.

"There is something in that pile of stones, Cassandra," she said to the jet-black maiden at her elbow, "that could make me wish it had been something more than a mill."

"There rat in 'em," returned the literal and simple minded black. "You hear what Missee Wyllys say!"

Gertrude turned, laughed, patted the dark cheek of her attendant, with fingers that looked like snow by the contrast, as if to chide her for wishing to destroy the pleasing illusion she would so gladly harbor, and then bounded down the hill, after her aunt and governess, like a joyous and youthful Atalanta.

The two singularly consorted listeners in the tower, stood gazing at their respective look-outs, so long as the smallest glimpse of the flowing robe of her light form was to be seen, and then they turned to each other, and stood confronted, the eyes of each endeavoring to read the expression of his neighbour's countenance.

"I am ready to make an affidavit before my Lord High Chancellor," suddenly exclaimed the barrister, "that this has never been a mill!"

"Your opinion has undergone a sudden change!"

"I am open to conviction, as I hope ever to be a judge. The case has been argued by a powerful advocate and I have lived to see my error."

"And yet there are rats in the place."

" 'Land rats, or water rats?' " quickly demanded the other, giving his companion one of those startling and searching glances, which his keen eye had so freely at command.

"Both, I believe," was the caustic reply—"Certainly the former or the gentlemen of the long-robe are much injured by report."

The barrister laughed, nor did his temper appear in the slightest degree ruffled at so free a hit at his learned and honorable profession.

"You gentlemen of the Ocean have such an honest and amusing frankness about you," he said, "that I vow to God, you are overwhelming. I am a down right admirer of your noble calling, and something skilled in its terms. What spectacle, for instance, can be finer than a noble ship, stemming the waves with her taffrail and chasing her wake, like a racer on the course!"

"Leaving the 'bone in her mouth' under her stern, as a light-house for all that come after."

Then, as if they found singular satisfaction in dwelling on these images of the worthy relict of the Admiral, they broke out simultaneously into a fit of clamorous merriment, which caused the old ruin to ring as in its best days of windy power. The barrister was the first to regain his self-command, for the mirth of the young mariner was joyous and without the least restraint.

"But this is dangerous ground for any but a seaman's widow to touch," the former observed, as suddenly causing his laughter to cease as he had admitted of its indulgence. "The younger, she who is no lover of a mill, is a rare and lovely creature! It would seem that she is the niece of the nautical critic."

The young mariner ceased laughing, in his turn, as if he were suddenly convinced of the glaring impropriety of making so near a relative of the fair vision he had seen the subject of his merriment. Whatever might have been his secret thoughts, he was content with replying—

"She so declared herself."

"Tell me," said the Barrister, walking close to the other, like one who communicated an important secret in the question, "was there not something remarkable, searching, extraordinary, heart-touching, in the voice of her they called Wyllys?"

"Did you note it!"

"It sounded to me like the tones of an oracle—the whisperings of fancy—the very words of truth! It was a strange and persuasive voice!"

"I confess I felt its influence. And in a way for which I cannot account!"

"It amounts to infatuation!" returned the barrister, pacing up and down the little apartment, every trace of humour and irony having disappeared in a look of settled and abstracted care. His companion appeared little disposed to interrupt his meditations, but stood leaning against the naked walls, himself the subject of reflection. At length the former shook off his air of thought, with that startling quickness, which seemed common to his manner; he approached a window, and directing the attention of Wilder to the ship in the outer harbor, abruptly demanded—

"Has all your interest in yonder vessel ceased?"

"Far from it. It is just such a boat as a seaman's eye loves to study!"

"Will you venture to board her?"

"At this hour! alone!—I know not her commander or her people."

"There are other hours beside this, and a sailor is certain of a frank reception from his messmates."

"These slavers are not always willing to be boarded. They carry arms, and know how to keep strangers at a distance."

"Are there no watch-words, in the masonry of your trade, by which a brother is known? Such terms, as stemming the waves with the taffrail for instance, or some of those knowing phrases we have lately heard?"

Wilder kept his own keen look on the countenance of the other as he thus questioned him, and seemed to ponder on what he heard before he ventured a reply—

"Why do you demand this of me?" he coldly asked.

"Because as I believe, that 'faint heart never won fair lady,' so do I believe that indecision never won a ship. You wish a situation, you say, and if I were an Admiral I would make you my flag-captain. At the assizes when we wish a brief, we throw out the proper feelers. But perhaps I am talking too much at random for an utter stranger. You will, however, remember, that though it is the advice of a lawyer it is given gratuitously."

"Is it the more to be relied on for such extraordinary liberality?"

"Of that you must judge for yourself," said the stranger in green, very deliberately putting his foot on the ladder and descending, until no part of his person but his head was seen. "Here I go, literally cutting the waves with my taffrail," he

added, descending backwards, and seeming to take great pleasure in laying particular emphasis on the words. "Adieu, my
friend. If we do not meet again, I enjoin you never to forget
the rats in the Newport ruin."

He disappeared as he concluded, and in another instant his
light form was on the ground. Turning with the most admirable coolness, he gave the bottom of the ladder a trip with
one of his feet, and laid the only means of descent prostrate
on the earth. Then looking up, at the wondering Wilder, he
nodded his head familiarly, repeated his adieus, and passed
with a swift step from beneath the arches.

"This is extraordinary, not to say insolent, conduct," muttered Wilder, who by the process was left a prisoner in the
ruin. After ascertaining that a fall from the trap might endanger his legs, the young sailor ran to one of the windows of the
place, in order to reproach his treacherous comrade, or indeed
to assure himself that he was serious in thus deserting him.
The Barrister was already out of hailing-distance, and before
Wilder had time to decide on what course to take, his active
footsteps had led him into the skirts of the town, among the
buildings of which his person became immediately lost to the
eye.

During all the time occupied by the foregoing scenes and
dialogues, Fid and the negro were diligently discussing the
contents of the bag, under the fence where they were last
seen. As the appetite of the former became appeased, his
didactic disposition returned, and at the precise moment
when Wilder was left alone in the tower he was intently engaged in admonishing the black on the delicate subject of behaviour in mixed society.

"And so you see, Guinea," he concluded, "in order to keep
a weather helm in company you are never to throw all aback,
and go stern foremost out of a dispute as you have this day,
seen fit to do. According to my l'arning, that Master Nightingale is better in a bar-room than in a squall, and if you had
just luffed up on his quarter, when you saw me laying myself
athwart his hawse in the argument, we should have given him
a regular jam in the discourse, and then the fellow would have
been shamed in the eyes of the byestanders. Who hails? what
cook is sticking his neighbour's pig now!"

"Lor'! Misser Fid," cried the black, "here Masser Harry wid a head out of port-hole, up dere-away in a light house, singing out like a marine in a boat wid a plug out!"

"Ay, ay, let him alone for hailing a top-gallant-yard or a flying-jib-boom! The lad has a voice like a French horn when he has a mind to tune it! And what the devil is he manning the guns of that weather beaten wreck for! At all events if he has to fight his craft alone, there is no one to blame but himself, since he has gone to quarters without beat of drum, or without, in any other manner, seeing fit to muster his people."

As Dick and the negro had both been making the best of their way towards the ruin, from the moment they discovered the situation of their friend, by this time, they were within speaking distance of the spot itself. Wilder in those brief, pithy tones, that distinguish the manner in which a sea officer issues his orders, directed them to raise the ladder. When he was liberated he demanded with a sufficiently significant air if they had observed the direction in which the stranger in green had made his retreat.

"Do you mean the chap in boots, who was for shoving his oar into another man's rullock, a bit ago, on the wharf?"

"The very same."

"He made a slant on the wind until he had weathered yonder bit of a barn, and then he tacked and stretched away off here to the East-and-by-South, going large, with studding sails alow and aloft, as I think, for he made a devil of a head-way."

"Follow!" cried Wilder, starting forward in the direction indicated by Fid, without waiting to hear any more of the other's explanations.

The search was vain. Although they continued their inquiries until long after the sun had set, no one could give them the smallest tidings of what had become of the Stranger in Green. Some had seen him, and marvelled at his singular costume and bold and wandering look, but, by all accounts, he had disappeared from the town as strangely and as mysteriously as he had entered it.

# Chapter V

"Are you so brave? I'll have you talked with anon."
*Coriolanus*, IV.v.17–18.

THE GOOD PEOPLE of the Town of Newport sought their rest at an early hour. They were remarkable for that temperance and discretion which, even to this day, distinguish the manners of the inhabitants of New England. By ten the door of every house in the place was closed for the night, and it is quite probable that before another hour had passed scarcely an eye was open, among all those which had been sufficiently alert, throughout the day, not only in superintending the interests of their proper owners, but in bestowing wholesome glances, at the concerns of the rest of the neighborhood.

The landlord of the "Foul Anchor," as the inn where Fid and Nightingale had so nearly come to blows, was called, scrupulously closed his doors at eight; a sort of expiation, by which he endeavored to atone while he slept for any moral peccadilloes that he might have committed during the day. Indeed, it was to be observed as a rule, that those who had the most difficulty in maintaining their good name, on the score of temperance and moderation, were the most rigid in withdrawing in season from the daily cares of the world. The Admiral's widow had given no little scandal, in her time, because lights were so often seen burning in her house long after the hour prescribed by custom for their extinction. There were several other little particulars in which this good lady had also rendered herself obnoxious to the whispered remarks of some of her female visitants. An Episcopalian herself, she was always observed to be employed with her needle on the evenings of Saturdays, though by no means distinguished for her ordinary industry. It was, however, a sort of manner the good lady had of exhibiting her adherence to the belief that the night of Sunday was the orthodox evening of the Sabbath. On this subject there was, in truth, a species of silent warfare between her and the wife of the principal clergyman of the town. It resulted happily, in no very striking

487

marks of hostility. The latter was content to retaliate, by bringing her work, on the evenings of Sundays to the house of the dowager, and occasionally interrupting their discourse, by a diligent application of the needle for some five or six minutes at a time. Against this contamination Mrs de Lacey took no other precaution, than to play with the leaves of a prayer book, precisely on the principle that one uses holy water to keep the devil at that distance which the Church has considered safest for its proselytes.*

Let these matters be as they would, by ten o'clock on the night of the day our tale commences the Town of Newport was as still as if it did not contain a living soul. Watchmen there were none; for roguery had not yet begun to thrive openly in the provinces. When, therefore, Wilder and his two companions issued, at that hour, from their place of retirement into the empty streets, they found them as still as though man had never trod there. Not a candle was to be seen, nor the smallest evidence of human life to be heard. It would seem our adventurers knew their errand well, for instead of knocking up any of the drowsy publicans to demand admission, they held their way steadily to the water's side, Wilder leading, Fid coming next, and Scipio, in conformity to all usage, bringing up the rear, in his ordinary, quiet, submissive manner.

At the margin of the water they found several small boats, moored under the shelter of a neighboring wharf. Wilder gave his companions their directions, and walked to a place, convenient for embarking. After waiting the necessary time, the bows of two boats came to the land, at the same moment,

---

*The puritans believed that the Sabbath commenced with the setting of the sun on Saturday, and ended at the same hour on Sunday. Thus the latter evening throughout all New England was, and in some measure is still, more observed as a fête than as a time of worship, while the preceding evening is respected with the most rigid observances. The writer once had a discussion on this point with a New England divine. The latter had no very high biblical authority for the usage; but he very justly remarked, that there was something consolatory and grand in the idea that the whole of Christendom was keeping holy the Sabbath at precisely the same moment! It is scarcely necessary to add, that this opinion, besides the fact that the usage was confined to a sect or sects, was met by the objection, that as we proceed east or west, there is a known difference in time to defeat the calculation.

one of which was governed by the hands of the negro and the other by those of Fid.

"How's this!" demanded Wilder, "is not one enough! There is some mistake between you."

"No mistake at all," responded Dick, suffering his oar to float on its blade, and running his fingers into his hair, content with his atchievement. "No more mistake than there is in taking the sun on a clear day and in smooth water. Guinea is in the boat you hired; but a bad bargain you made of it, as I thought at the time, and so, as 'better late than never,' is my rule, I have just been casting an eye over all the craft; if this is not the tightest and fastest rowing clipper of them all, then am I no judge, and yet the parish priest would tell you if he were here, that my father was a boat-builder; ay, and swear it too; that is to say, if you paid him well for the same!"

"Fellow," returned Wilder, angrily, "you will one day, induce me to turn you adrift. Take the boat to the place where you found it, and see it secured as before."

"Turn me adrift!" deliberately repeated Fid. "That would be cutting all your weather-lanyards at one blow, Master Harry. Little good would come of Scipio Africa and you, after I should part company. Have you ever fairly logg'd the time, we have sailed together?"

"Ay, have I; but it is possible to break even a friendship of twenty years."

"Saving your presence, Master Harry, I'll be d—d if I believe any such thing. Here is Guinea, who is no better than a nigger, and therein far from being a fitting messmate to a white-man, but being used to look at his black face for four and twenty years, d'ye see, the colour has got into my eye, and now it suits as well as another. Then at sea, in a dark night, it is not so easy a matter to tell the difference. I am not tired of you, yet, Master Harry, and it is no trifle that shall part us."

"Then abandon your habit of making free with the property of others."

"I abandon nothing. No man can say, he ever knowed me to quit a deck while a plank stuck to the beams, and shall I abandon, as you call it, my rights? What is the mighty matter, that all hands must be call'd to see an old sailor punished! You gave a lubberly fisherman, a fellow who has never been in deeper water than his own line will sound, you gave him I say, a glittering spaniard, just for the use of a bit of a skiff, for the night, or mayhap for a small reach into the morning. Well, what does Dick do? He says to himself, for d—e if he's any blab to run round a ship grumbling at his officer—so, he just says to himself, 'That's too much,' says he; and he looks about to find the worth of it, in some of the fisherman's neighbors.' Money can be eaten, and what is better it may be drunk, therefore it is not to be pitched overboard with the cook's ashes. I'll warrant me, if the truth could be fairly come by, it would be found that, as to the owners of this here yawl and that there skiff, their mothers are cousins, and that the dollar will go in snuff and strong drink among the whole family, so no great harm done, after all."

Wilder made an impatient gesture to the other to obey, and walked up the bank, to give him time to comply. Fid never disputed a positive and distinct order, though he often took so much discretionary latitude in executing those which were less precise. He did not hesitate, therefore, to return the boat, but he did not carry his subordination so far as to do it without complaint. When this act of justice was performed Wilder entered the skiff, and seeing that his companions were seated at their oars, he bad them pull down the harbor, admonishing them at the same time to make as little noise as possible.

"The night I rowed you into Louisbourg, a-reconnoitring," said Fid, thrusting his left hand into his bosom, while with his right he applied sufficient force to the light oar to make the skiff glide swiftly over the water, "that night we muffled every thing, even to our tongues. When there is occasion to put stoppers on the mouths of a boat's crew, why I'm not the man to gainsay it, but as I'm one of them that thinks tongues were just as much made to talk with, as the sea was made to live on, I uphold rational conversation in sober society—S'ip, thou Guinea, where the devil are you shoving the skiff to! Hereaway lies the island, and you are for going into yonder bit of a church."

"Lay on your oars," interrupted Wilder. "Let the boat drift by this vessel."

They were now in the act of passing the ship, which had been warping from the wharves to an anchorage, and in which the young sailor had so clandestinely learned, that Mrs Wyllys and the fascinating Gertrude were to embark, on the following morning, for the distant Province of Carolina. As the skiff floated past, Wilder examined the vessel by the dim light of the stars with a seaman's eye. No part of her hull, her spars, or her rigging escaped his notice, and when the whole became confounded, by the distance, in one dark mass of shapeless matter, he leaned his head over the side of his little bark, and mused. To this abstraction, Fid presumed to offer no interruption. It had the appearance of professional duty, a subject that, in his eyes, was endowed with a species of character that might be called sacred. Scipio was habitually silent. After losing many minutes in this manner, Wilder suddenly regained his recollection, and abruptly observed—

"It is a tall ship, and one that should make a long chase!"

"That's as may be," returned the ready Fid. "Should that fellow get a free wind, and his canvass all abroad it might worry a King's cruiser to get nigh enough to throw the iron on his decks, but jammed up close haul'd, why, I'd engage to lay on his weather quarter, with the saucy He—"

"Boys," interrupted Wilder, "it is now proper that you should know something of my future movements. We have been shipmates, I might almost say messmates, for more than twenty years. I was no better than an infant, Fid, when you brought me to the commander of your ship, and not only was instrumental in saving my life, but in putting me into a situation to make an officer."

"Ay, ay, you were no great matter, Master Harry, as to bulk, and a short hammock served your turn as well as the captain's berth."

"I owe you a heavy debt, Fid, for that one generous act, and something I may add for your steady adherence to me since."

"Why yes, I have been pretty steady in my conduct, Master Harry, in this here business, more particularly, seeing that I have never let go my grapplings, though you have so often sworn to turn me adrift. As for Guinea, here, the chap makes fair weather with you, blow high or blow low, whereas it is no hard matter to get up a squall between us, as might be seen in that small affair about the boat."

"Say no more of it," interrupted Wilder, whose feelings appeared sensibly touched as his recollection ran over long past and bitterly remembered scenes. "You know that little else than death can part us—unless indeed you choose to quit me now. It is right you should know, that I am engaged in a desperate pursuit, and one that may easily end in ruin to myself and all who accompany me. I feel reluctant to separate from you, my friends, for it may be a final parting, but at the same time you should know all the danger."

"Is there much more travelling by land?" bluntly demanded Fid.

"No. The duty such as it is, will be done entirely on the water."

"Then bring forth your ship's books, and find room for such a mark as a pair of crossed anchors, which stand for all the same as so many letters reading Richard Fid."

"But perhaps when you know"—

"I want to know nothing about it, Master Harry. Haven't I sailed with you often enough under sealed orders, to trust my old body once more in your company without forgetting my manners, and asking saucy questions? What say you, Guinea, will you ship, or shall we land you, at once, on yonder bit of a low point and leave you to scrape acquaintance with the clams?"

"Em berry well off, here," muttered the perfectly contented negro.

"Ay, ay, Guinea is like the launch of one of the coasters, always towing in your wake, Master Harry, whereas I am often luffing athwart your hawse or getting foul in some fashion or other on one of your quarters. Howsomever, we are both shipped, as you see, in this here cruise, with the particulars of which we are both well satisfied. So pass the word among us, what is to be done next, and no more parley."

"Remember the cautions you have already received," returned Wilder, who saw that the devotion of his followers was too infinite to need quickening, and who knew from long and perilous experience how implicitly he might rely on their fidelity notwithstanding certain failings, that were perhaps peculiar to their condition. "Remember what I have already given in charge. And, now, pull directly for the ship in the outer harbor."

Fid and the black promptly complied, and the boat was soon skimming the water between the little island, and what might, by comparison, be called the main. As they approached the vessel, the strokes of the oars were moderated and finally abandoned, altogether, Wilder preferring to let the skiff drop down with the tide upon the object, he wished well to examine, before venturing to board.

"Has not that ship her nettings triced to the rigging!" he demanded, in a voice that was lowered to the tones necessary to escape observation, and which betrayed, at the same time the interest he took in the reply.

"According to my sight she has," returned Fid. "Your slavers are a little pricked by conscience, and are never over bold unless when they are chasing a young nigger on the coast of Congo. Now there is about as much danger of a Frenchman's looking in here to night, with this land breeze and clear sky, as there is of my being made Lord High Admiral of England; a thing not likely to come to pass soon, seeing that the King don't know a great deal of my merit."

"They are to a certainty ready to give a warm reception to any boarders!" continued Wilder, who rarely paid much attention to the amplifications with which Fid so often saw fit to embellish the discourse. "It would be no easy matter to carry a ship thus prepared, if her people were true to themselves!"

"I warrant ye there is a full quarter-watch at least sleeping among her guns at this very moment, with a bright look out from her cat-heads and taffrail. I was once, on the weather fore-yard-arm of the Hebe, when I made, here-a-way to the South-west, a sail coming large upon us"—

"Hist—They are stirring on her decks!"

"To be sure they are. The cook is splitting a log. The captain has most likely sung out for his night-cap."

The voice of Fid was lost in a summons from the ship, that sounded like the roaring of some sea-monster which had unexpectedly raised its head above the water. The practised ears of our adventurers instantly comprehended it to be what it truly was, the manner in which it was not unusual to hail a boat. Without taking time to ascertain that the plashing of oars was to be heard in the distance, Wilder raised his form in the skiff and answered.

"How now!" exclaimed the same strange voice, "this is no one victualled aboard here! Whereaway is he that answers?"

"A little on your larboard bow, here in the shadow of the ship."

"And what are ye about within the sweep of my hawse?"

"Cutting the waves with my taffrail—" returned Wilder, after a moment's hesitation.

"What fool has broke adrift here!" muttered his interrogator. "Pass a blunderbuss forward, and let us see, if a civil answer can be drawn from the fellow."

"Hold!" said a calm authoritative voice from the most distant part of the ship. "It is, as it should be. Let them approach."

The man in the bows of the vessel bad them "come alongside," and the conversation ceased. Wilder had now an opportunity to discover that as the hail had been intended for another boat, which was still at a distance, he had answered prematurely. But perceiving that it was too late to retreat with safety, or perhaps only acting in conformity to his original determination, he directed his companions to obey.

"Cutting the waves with the taffrail, is, of a surety, not the civillest answer a man can give to a hail," muttered Fid, dropping the blade of his oar into the water, "nor is it matter to be logged, that they have taken some offense at the same. However, Master Harry, if they are so minded as to make a quarrel about the thing, give them as good as they send, and count on manly backers."

No reply was made to this encouraging assurance for, by this time, the skiff was within a few feet of the ship. Wilder ascended the side of the vessel amid a deep, and, as he felt it to be at the moment, an ominous silence. The night was dark, though enough light fell from the stars, that were, here and there, visible, to render objects sufficiently distinct to the eyes of a seaman. When our young adventurer touched the deck, he cast a hurried and scrutinizing look about him, as if doubts and impressions which had long been harbored, were all to be resolved by that first view.

An ignorant landsman would have been struck with the order and symmetry, with which the tall spars, rose towards the heavens, from the black mass of the hull, and with the rigging that hung in the air, one dark line crossing another, until all design seemed confounded in the confusion and intricacy of the studied maze. But to Wilder these familiar objects furnished no immediate attraction. His first, rapid glance had, like that of all seamen it is true, been thrown upward, but it was instantly succeeded by the brief though keen examination to which we have just alluded. With the exception of one who, though his form was muffled in a large sea-cloak, seemed to be an officer, not a living creature was visible on the decks. On each side was a dark, frowning battery, arranged in the beautiful and imposing order of marine architecture; but no where could he find a trace of the crowd of human beings which usually throng the deck of an armed ship, or that was necessary to render the engines effective. It was quite in rule that most of her people should be in their hammocks at that hour, but still it was customary to leave a sufficient number in the watch to look to the safety of the vessel. Finding himself so unexpectedly confronted with a single individual, our adventurer began to be sensible of the awkwardness of his situation, and of the necessity of some explanation.

"You are no doubt surprised, Sir," he said, "at the lateness of the hour that I have chosen for my visit?"

"You were certainly expected earlier," was the laconic answer.

"Expected!"

"Ay, expected. Have I not seen you, and your two companions who are in the boat, reconnoitring us half the day, from the wharves of the town, and even from the old tower on the hill! What did all this curiosity foretell but an intention to come on board?"

"This is odd, I will acknowledge!" exclaimed Wilder, in some alarm. "And then you had notice of my intentions?"

"Harkee, friend," interrupted the other, indulging in a low laugh. "From your outfit and appearance, I think I am right in calling you a seaman. Do you imagine that glasses were forgotten in the inventory of this ship, or do you fancy that we don't know how to use them?"

"You must have strong reasons for looking so closely into the movements of strangers on the land."

"Hum—Perhaps we expect our cargo from the country. But I suppose you have not come so far in the dark to look at our manifest. You would see the captain?"

"Do I not see him?"

"Where!" demanded the other with a start, that proved he stood in salutary awe of his superior.

"In yourself."

"I! I have not got so high in the books; though my time may yet come some fair day. Harkee, friend; you passed under the stern of yonder ship, which has been hauling into the stream, in coming out to us."

"Certainly—She lies, as you see, directly in my course."

"A wholesome looking craft that! And one well found, I warrant you. She is quite ready to be off they tell me?"

"It would so seem. Her sails are bent, and she floats like a ship that is full."

"Of what?" abruptly demanded the other.

"Of Articles mentioned in her manifest, no doubt. But you seem light yourself. If you are to load at this port, it will be some days before you put to sea."

"Hum—I don't think we shall be long after our neighbour," the other remarked a little drily. Then as if he might have said too much, he added hastily, "We slavers carry little else, you know, than our shackles and a few extra terces of rice. The rest of our ballast is made up of these guns and the stuff to put into them."

"And is it usual for ships in the trade to carry so heavy an armament?"

"Perhaps it is, perhaps not. To own the truth there is not much law on the coast, and the strong arm often does as much as the right. Our owners, therefore, I believe, think it quite as well there should be no lack of guns and ammunition on board."

"They should also give you people to work them."

"They have forgotten that part of their wisdom certainly—"

His words were nearly drowned by the same gruff voice that had brought-to the skiff of Wilder, which sent another hoarse summons across the water, rolling out sounds that were intended to say—

"Boat ahoy."

The answer was quick, short and nautical, but it was rendered in a low and cautious tone. The individual with whom Wilder had been holding such equivocating parlance, seemed embarrassed by the sudden interruption, and a little at a loss to know how to conduct himself. He had already made a motion towards leading his visiter to the cabin, when the sounds of oars were heard clattering in a boat, along side of the ship, announcing that he was too late. Bidding the other remain where he was, he sprang to the gangway, in order to receive those who had just arrived.

By this sudden desertion Wilder found himself in entire possession of the part of the vessel where he stood. It gave him a better opportunity to renew his examination, and to cast a scrutinizing eye over the new comers.

Some five or six athletic looking seamen ascended from the boat in profound silence. A short and whispered conference took place between them and their officer who appeared both to receive a report and to communicate an order. When these preliminary matters were ended, a line was lowered, from a whip on the main yard, the end evidently dropping into the boat. In a moment the burthen it was intended to transfer to the ship was seen swinging in the air, midway between the water and the spar. It then slowly descended, inclining inboard, until it was safely and somewhat carefully landed on the decks of the vessel.

During the whole of this process, which in itself had nothing extraordinary or out of the daily practice of large vessels in port, Wilder had strained his eyes, until they appeared nearly ready to start from their sockets. The black mass which had been lifted from the boat, seemed while it lay against the back-ground of sky, to possess the proportions of the human form. The seamen gathered about this object. After much bustle and a good deal of low conversation, the burthen or body, whichever it might be called, was raised by the men, and the whole disappeared together, behind the masts, boats, and guns which crowded the forward part of the vessel.

The whole event was of a character to attract the attention of Wilder. His eye was not however so intently rivetted on the groupe in the gangway as to prevent his detecting a dozen black objects that were suddenly thrust forward from behind the spars and other dark masses of the vessel. They might be blocks swinging in the air, but they bore also a strong resemblance to human heads. The simultaneous manner in which they appeared and disappeared served to confirm this impression, nor, to confess the truth, had our adventurer any doubt, that curiosity had drawn so many eager countenances from their respective places of concealment. He had not much leisure however to reflect on all these little accompaniments of his situation before he was rejoined by his former companion, who, to all appearance, was again left to himself in entire possession of the deck.

"You know the trouble of getting off the people from the shore," the officer observed, "when a ship is ready to sail."

"You seem to have a summary method of hoisting them in!" returned Wilder.

"Ah! you speak of the fellow on the whip! Your eyes are good, friend, to tell a jack-knife from a marlingspike at this distance! But the lad was mutinous—that is, not absolutely mutinous—but drunk. As mutinous as a man can be who can neither speak, sit nor stand."

Then as if as well content with his humour as with this simple explanation the other laughed and chuckled in a manner that showed he was in perfect good humour with himself.

"But all this time you are left on deck," he quickly added, "and the captain is waiting your appearance in the cabin. Follow; I will be your pilot."

"Hold!" said Wilder, "will it not be as well to announce my visit?"

"He knows it already. Little takes place aboard here, that does not reach his ears before it gets into the log-book."

Wilder made no further objection, but indicated his readiness to proceed. The other led the way to the bulkhead which separated the principal cabin from the quarter-deck of the ship; pointing to a door, he then whispered,—

"Tap twice; if he answers, go in."

Wilder did as directed. His first summons was either un-heard or disregarded. On repeating it, he was commanded to enter. The young seaman opened the door, with a crowd of sensations which will find their solution in the succeeding parts of our narrative, and instantly stood, under the light of a powerful lamp, in the presence of the stranger in green.

# Chapter VI

——"The good old plan,
That they should get, who have the power,
And they should keep, who can."
Wordsworth, "Rob Roy's Grave," ll. 37, 39–40.

THE APARTMENT, in which our adventurer now found
himself, afforded no bad illustration of the character of
its occupant. In its form, and proportions it was a cabin of
the usual size and arrangements, but in its furniture and
equipments, it exhibited a singular admixture of luxury and
martial preparation. The lamp which swung from the upper
deck was of solid silver, and though adapted to its present
situation, by mechanical ingenuity, there was that in its shape
and ornaments which betrayed it had once been used before
some shrine of a more sacred character. Massive candlesticks
of the same precious metal, and which partook of the same
ecclesiastical formation, were on a venerable table, whose
mahogany was glittering with the polish of half a century, and
whose gilded claws and carved supporters also bespoke an
original destination very different from the ordinary service of
a ship. A couch, covered with cut velvet, stood along the tran-
som, while a divan, of blue silk, lay against the bulkhead opposite, manifesting by its fashion, its materials and its piles of
pillows that even Asia had been made to contribute to the
ease of its luxurious owner. In addition to these prominent
articles, there were cut glass, mirrors, plate, and even hangings, each of which by something peculiar in its fashion or
materials, bespoke an origin different from that of its neighbor. In short splendor and elegance seemed to have been
much more consulted than propriety or taste, in the selection
of most of those articles which had been, oddly enough, made
to contribute to the caprice or to the comfort of their singular
possessor.

In the midst of this medley of wealth and luxury appeared
the frowning appendages of war. The cabin included four of
those dark cannon, whose weight and number had been first
to catch the attention of Wilder. Notwithstanding they were

placed in such close proximity to the articles of ease just enumerated, it only needed a seaman's eye to perceive that they
stood ready for immediate service, and that five minutes of
preparation would strip the place of all its tinsel, and leave it a
warm and well protected battery. Pistols, sabres, half-pikes,
boarding axes and all the minor implements of marine warfare
were arranged about the cabin, in such a manner as to aid in
giving it an appearance of wild embellishment, while, at the
same time, each was convenient to the hand.

Around the mast was placed a stand of muskets. Strong
wooden bars, that were evidently made to fit in brackets on
each side of the door, sufficiently showed that the bulkhead
might easily be converted into a barrier. The entire arrangement proclaimed that the cabin was considered as the citadel
of the ship. In support of this latter opinion there was also a
hatch, communicating with the apartments of the inferior
officers, and which opened a direct passage into the magazine. These dispositions, a little different from what he had
been accustomed to see, instantly struck the eye of Wilder,
though leisure was not then given to reflect on their usages
and objects.

There was a latent expression of satisfaction, something
modified perhaps by irony, on the countenance of the
stranger in green (for he was still clad as when first introduced to the reader) as he arose on the entrance of his visiter.
The two stood several moments without speaking, when the
pretended barrister saw fit to break the awkward silence.

"To what happy circumstance is this ship indebted for the
honor of such a visit?" he demanded.

"I believe I may answer, to the invitation of her captain,"
Wilder answered, with a steadiness and calmness equal to that
displayed by the other.

"Did he show you his commission in assuming that office?
They say at sea, I believe, that no cruiser should be found
without a commission."

"And what say they at the Universities, on this material
point?"—

"I see I may as well lay aside my gown and own the
marlingspike!" returned the other, smiling. "There is something about the trade—profession, though, I believe, is your

favorite word—there is something about the profession, which betrays us to each other. Yes, Mr Wilder," he added, with dignity, motioning to his guest to imitate his example and take a seat, "I am, like yourself, a seaman bred, and I am happy to add, the commander of this gallant vessel."

"Then must you admit that I have not intruded without a sufficient warrant."

"I confess the same. My ship has filled your eye agreeably, nor shall I be slow to acknowledge that I have seen enough about your air and person to make me wish to be an older acquaintance. You want service?"

"One should be ashamed of idleness in these stirring times."

"It is well. This is an oddly constructed world in which we live, Mr Wilder. Some think themselves in danger with a foundation beneath them, no less solid than terra firma, while others are content to trust their fortunes on the sea. So, again, some there are who believe praying is the business of man, and then come others who are sparing of their breath, and take those favors for themselves which they have not always the leisure, or perhaps the inclination to ask for—No doubt you thought it prudent, to inquire into the nature of our trade before you came hither in quest of employment."

"You are said to be a slaver, among the Townsmen of Newport."

"They are never wrong, your village gossips! If witchcraft ever truly existed on earth, the first of the cunning tribe has been a village innkeeper, the second its doctor, and the third its priest. The right to the fourth honor may be disputed between the barber and the tailor—Roderick!"

The captain accompanied the word with which he so unceremoniously interrupted himself, by striking a light blow on a Chinese gong, which, among other curiosities, was suspended from one of the beams of the upper deck within reach of his hand.

"I say, Roderick, dost sleep!"

A light and active boy darted out of one of the two little state-rooms, which were constructed on the quarters of the ship, and answered to the summons by announcing his presence.

"Has the boat returned?"

The reply was in the affirmative.

"Has she been successful?"

"The General is in his room, Sir, and can give you an answer better than I."

"Then let the General appear and report the result of his campaign."

Wilder was by far too deeply interested to break the sudden reverie into which his companion had now fallen, even by breathing as loud as usual. The boy descended through the hatch like a serpent gliding into his hole, or rather a fox darting into his burrow, and then a profound stillness reigned in the cabin. The commander of the ship leaned his head on his hand, appearing unconscious of the presence of a stranger. The silence might have been of much longer duration, had it not been interrupted by the appearance of a third person. A straight, rigid form slowly elevated itself through the little hatchway, very much in the manner that theatrical spectres are seen to make their appearance on the stage, until about half of the person was visible, when it ceased to rise and turned its disciplined countenance on the captain.

"I wait for orders," said a mumbling voice, which issued from lips that were hardly perceived to move.

Wilder started at this unexpected vision, nor was the stranger wanting in an aspect sufficiently remarkable to produce surprise in any spectator. The face was that of a man of fifty, with the lineaments thoroughly indurated by service. Its colour was an uniform red, with the exception of one of those expressive little fibrous tell-tales on each cheek, which bear so striking a resemblance to the mazes of the vine, and which would seem to be the true origin of the proverb which says that "good wine needs no bush." The crown of the head was bald; but around each ear was a mass of grizzled hair, pomatumed and combed into military bristles. The neck was long and supported by a black stock; the shoulders, arms and body were those of a tall man; and the whole were enveloped in an over-coat, which, while it had something methodical in its fashion, was evidently intended as a sort of domino. The Captain raised his head, as the other spoke, exclaiming, as if taken by surprise, —

"Ah! General, are you at your post! Did you find the land?"

"Yes."

"And the point—and the man?"

"Both."

"What did you?"

"Obey orders."

"That was right. You are a jewel, for an executive officer, general; as such I wear you near my heart. Did the fellow complain?"

"He was gagged."

"A summary method of closing remonstrance. It is as it should be, General. As usual you have merited my approbation."

"Then reward me for it."

"In what manner! You are already as high in rank, as I can elevate you. The next step must be knighthood."

"Pshaw! my men are no better than militia. They want coats."

"They shall have them. His Majesty's guards shall not be half so well equipt. General, I wish you a good night."

The figure descended in the same rigid spectral manner as it had risen on the sight, leaving Wilder, again, alone with the Captain of the ship. The latter seemed suddenly struck with the fact that this odd interview had occurred in the presence of one who was nearly a stranger, and that, in his eyes, at least, it might appear to require some explanation.

"My friend," he said with an air, something explanatory while it was, at the same time, not a little haughty, "commands what, in a more regular cruiser, would be called the marine guard. He has gradually risen, by service, from the rank of a subaltern to the high station which he now fills. You perceive he smells of the camp?"

"More than of the ship. Is it usual for slavers to be so well provided with military equipments? I find you armed at all points."

"You would know more of us, before we proceed to drive our bargain," the captain answered, with a smile. He then opened a little casket that stood on the table, and drew from it a parchment which he coolly handed to Wilder, saying as he did so, with one of the quick, searching glances of his restless eye—"you will see by that, we have 'letters of marque,' and are duly authorised to fight the battles of the King, while we are conducting our own more peaceable affairs."

"This is the commission of a brig!"

"True—true. I have given you the wrong paper. I believe you will find this more accurate."

"This is truly a commission for the 'good ship Seven-Sisters' but you surely carry more than ten guns, and then these in your cabin throw nine instead of four pound shot!"

"You are as precise as if you had been the barrister, and I the blundering seaman! I dare say you have heard of such a thing as stretching a commission," continued the captain, carelessly throwing the parchment back among a pile of similar documents. Then rising from his seat, he began to pace the cabin with quick steps as he continued. "I need not tell you, Mr Wilder, that ours is a hazardous pursuit. Some call it lawless. But as I am little addicted to theological disputes we will wave the question. You have not come here, without knowing your errand."

"I am in search of a berth."

"Doubtless you have reflected well on the matter, and know your own mind as to the trade in which you would sail. In order that no time may be wasted, and that our dealings may be frank as becomes two honest seamen, I will confess to you at once that I have need of you. A brave and skilful man, one older though I dare say not better than yourself, occupied that larboard state-room within the month; poor fellow, he is food for fishes ere this!"

"He was drowned."

"Not he! He died as a brave man should in open battle with a King's ship."

"A King's ship! Have you then stretched your commission so far as to find a warranty for giving battle to his Majesty's cruisers?"

"Is there no King but George IId.! Perhaps she bore the white flag, perhaps a Dane. But he was truly a gallant fellow, and there lies his berth as empty as the day he was carried from it, to be cast into the sea. He was a man fit to succeed to the command should an evil star shine on my fate. I think I could die easier, were I to know this noble vessel was to be transmitted to one who would make such use of her as should be."

"Doubtless your owners would provide a successor in the event of such a calamity!"

"My owners are very reasonable—" returned the other, casting another searching glance at his guest, which compelled Wilder to lower his own eyes to the cabin floor. "They seldom trouble me, with importunities or orders!"

"They are indulgent! I see that flags at least were not forgotten in your inventory; do they also give you permission to wear any of those ensigns, as you may please?"

As this question was put the expressive and understanding looks of the two seamen met. The Captain drew a flag from the half open locker where it had caught the attention of his visiter, and letting the roll unfold itself on the deck, he answered—

"This is the Lily of France you see. No bad emblem of your stainless Frenchman: an escutcheon of pretence without spot, but nevertheless a little soiled by use. Here you have the calculating Dutchman; plain, substantial and cheap. It is a flag I little like. If the ship be of value, her owners are not often willing to dispose of her without a price. This is your swaggering Hamburgher: He is rich in the possession of one town, and makes his boast of it, in these towers. Of the rest of his mighty possessions he wisely says nothing, in his allegory. These, are the crescents of Turkey: a moon-struck nation, that believe themselves the inheritors of Heaven. Let them enjoy their birth-right in peace; it is seldom they are found looking for its blessings on the high seas. And these the little satellites that play about the mighty moon—your barbarians of Africa. I hold but little communion with these wide-trowsered gentry, for they seldom deal in aught gainful. And yet—" he added, glancing his eye at the silken divan before which Wilder was seated, "I have met the rascals, nor have we parted entirely without communication! Ah! Here comes the man I like; your gorgeous Spaniard! This field of yellow reminds one of the riches of his mines. And this crown! one might fancy it of beaten gold, and stretch forth a hand to grasp the treasure. What a blazonry is this for a Galleon! Here is the humbler Portuguese; and yet is he not without a wealthy look. I have often fancied there were true Brazilian diamonds in this kingly bauble. Yonder crucifix, which you see hanging in pious proximity to my state-room door, is a specimen of the sort I mean." Wilder turned his head to throw a look on the valuable emblem that was really suspended from the bulk-head, within a few inches of the spot the other named. After satisfying his curiosity, he was in the act of giving his attention again to the flags, when he detected another of those penetrating but stolen glances, with which his companion so often read the countenances of his associates. It is probable that the captain was endeavoring to discover the effect his profuse display of wealth had produced on the mind of his visiter. Let that be as it would, Wilder smiled, for at that moment the idea first occurred, that the ornaments of the cabin had been thus studiedly arranged with an expectation of his arrival and with the wish that their richness might strike him favorably. The other caught the expression of his eye, and perhaps he mistook its meaning when he suffered his construction of what it said, to animate him to pursue his whimsical analysis of the flags, with an air, still more cheerful and vivacious than before.

"These double-headed monsters are land-birds and seldom risk a flight over deep waters," he continued; "they are not for me. Your hardy, valiant Dane; your sturdy Swede; a nest of smaller fry," he continued, passing his hand rapidly over a dozen little rolls as they lay, each in its own repository, "who spread their bunting like larger states, and your luxurious Ne-apolitan. Ah! here come the Keys of Heaven! This is a flag to die under! I lay yard arm and yard arm once, under that very bit of bunting, with a heavy corsair from Algiers"—

"What! Did you choose to fight under the banners of the Church!"

"In mere devotion. I pictured to myself the surprise that would overcome the barbarian when he should find that we did not go to prayers. We gave him but a round or two, be-fore he swore that Allah had decreed he might surrender. There was a moment while I luffed up on his weather quarter, I believe, that the Mussulman thought the whole of the holy conclave was afloat, and that the downfal of Mahomet and his offspring was nigh. I provoked the conflict, I will confess, in showing him these peaceful keys, which he is dull enough to think open half the strong-boxes of Christendom."

"When he had confessed his error, you let him go?"

"Hum. With my blessing. There was some interchange of commodities between us, and we parted. I left him, smoking his pipe, in a heavy sea, with his foretopmast over the side, his mizzen mast under his counter, and some six or seven holes in his bottom that let in the water just as fast as the pumps discharged it. You see he was in a fair way to acquire his portion of the inheritance. But heaven had ordained it all, and he was satisfied."

"And what flags are these, which you have passed? They seem rich and many."

"These are England; like herself, aristocratic, party-coloured and a good deal touched by humour. Here is bunting to note all ranks and conditions, as if men were not made of the same flesh, and the people of one Kingdom might not all sail honestly under the same emblems. Here is my Lord High Admiral; your St George; your field of red and of blue, as chance may give you a leader, or the humour of the moment prevail. The stripes of Mother India, and the Royal Standard itself!"

"The Royal Standard!"

"Why not! a commander is termed a monarch in his ship. Ay; this is the standard of the King. And what is more it has been worn in presence of an Admiral."

"This needs explanation!" exclaimed his listener, who seemed to feel much that sort of horror that a churchman would discover at the detection of sacrilege. "To wear the Royal Standard in presence of a flag! We all know how difficult and even dangerous it becomes to sport a simple pennant, with the eyes of a King's cruiser on us."

"I love to flaunt the rascals!" interrupted the other, with a smothered but bitter laugh. "There is pleasure in the thing. In order to punish they must possess the power; an experiment that has failed as often as it has been tryed. You understand balancing accounts with the law, by showing a broad sheet of canvass! I need say no more."

"And which of all these flags do you most use?" demanded Wilder, after a moment of intense thought.

"As to mere sailing, I am as whimsical as a girl in her teens, in the choice of her ribbons. I will often show you a dozen in a day. Many is the worthy trader, who has gone into port with his veritable account of this Dutchman, or that Dane with whom he has spoken in the offing. As to fighting, though I have been known to indulge a humour too, in that particular, still there is one which I most affect."

"And that is —?"

The captain kept his hand for a moment on the roll he had touched and seemed to read the very soul of his visiter, so intent and keen was his look the while. Then suffering the bunting to fall, a deep, blood-red field, without relief or ornament of any sort unfolded itself, as he answered with emphasis—

"This."

"That is the colour of a rover!"

"Ay, it is red. I like it better than your gloomy fields of black, with death's heads and other childish scare-crows. It threatens nothing; but merely says, 'Such is the price at which I am to be bought.' Mr Wilder," he added, losing the mixture of irony and pleasantry with which he had supported the previous dialogue, in an air of authority, "we understand each other. It is time, that each should sail under his proper colours. I need not tell you who I am."

"I believe it is unnecessary," said Wilder. "If I can comprehend these palpable signs, I stand in presence of—of—"

"The Red Rover," continued the other, observing that he hesitated to pronounce the appalling name. "It is true, and I hope this interview is the commencement of a durable and firm friendship. I know not the secret cause, but from the moment of our meeting a strong and indefinable interest has drawn me towards you. Perhaps I felt the void, which my situation has drawn about me—be that as it may, I receive you with a longing heart and open arms."

Though it must be very evident from what preceded this open avowal, that Wilder was not ignorant of the character of the ship on board of which he had thus ventured, yet did he not receive the acknowledgment without embarrassment. The reputation of this renowned freebooter, his daring, his acts of liberality and licentiousness so frequently blended, and his desperate disregard of life on all occasions were probably crowding together in the recollection of our more youthful adventurer, and caused him to feel that species of responsible hesitation, to which we are all, more or less subject, on the occurrence of important events, be they ever so much expected.

"You have not mistaken my purpose or my suspicions," he at length answered, "for I own that I have come in search of this very ship. I accept the service; from this moment you will rate me in whatever station you may think me best able to discharge my duty, with credit."

"You are next to myself. In the morning the same shall be proclaimed on the quarter deck; and in the event of my death, unless I am deceived in my man, you will prove my successor. This may strike you as sudden confidence. It is so in part, I must acknowledge; but our shipping lists cannot be opened like those of the King, by beat of drum in the streets of the Metropolis; and then am I no judge of the human heart, if my frank reliance on your faith does not in itself, strengthen your good feelings in my favor."

"It does!" exclaimed Wilder, with sudden and strong emphasis.

The Rover smiled calmly, as he continued—

"Young gentlemen of your years are apt to carry no small portion of their hearts in their hands. But notwithstanding this seeming sympathy, in order that you may have sufficient respect for the discretion of your leader, it is necessary that I should say we have met before. I was apprised of your intention to seek me out, and to offer to join me."

"It is impossible!" cried Wilder. "No human being—"

"Can ever be certain his secrets are safe," interrupted the other, "when he carries a face as ingenuous as your own. It is but four-and-twenty hours since you were in the good town of Boston?"

"I admit that much; but—"

"You will soon admit the rest. You were too curious in your inquiries of the dolt who declares he was robbed by us, of his provisions and sails. The false-tongued villain! It may be well for him to keep from my path, or he may get a lesson that shall prick his honesty. Does he think such pitiful game as he, would induce me to spread a single inch of canvass or even to lower a boat into the sea!"

"Is not his statement then true?" demanded Wilder in a surprise he took no pains to conceal.

"True! Am I what report has made me? Look keenly at the monster, that nothing may escape you," returned the Rover with a hollow laugh, in which scorn struggled to keep down the feelings of wounded pride. "Where are the horns, and the cloven foot! Snuff the air: is it not tainted with sulphur? But enough of this. I knew of your inquiries, and liked your mien. In short, you were my study, and though my approaches were made with some caution, they were sufficiently nigh to effect the object. You pleased me, Wilder, and I hope the satisfaction may be mutual."

The newly engaged buccanier bowed to the compliment of his superior, and appeared at some little loss for a reply. As if to get rid of the subject at once, he hurriedly observed—

"As we now understand each other, I will intrude no longer, but leave you for the night, and return to my duty in the morning."

"Leave me!" returned the Rover, stopping short in his walk, and fastening his eye keenly on the other. "It is not usual for my officers to leave me at this hour. A sailor should love his ship, and never sleep out of her, unless on compulsion."

"We may as well understand each other," said Wilder quickly. "If it is to be a slave, and like one of the bolts, a fixture in the vessel, that you need me, our bargain is at an end."

"Hum. I admire your spirit, Sir, much more than your discretion. You will find me an attached friend, and one who little likes a separation however short. Is there not enough to content you here! I will not speak of such low considerations as those which administer to the ordinary appetites—but you have been taught the value of reason—here are books; you have taste—here is elegance. You are poor—here is wealth."

"They amount to nothing without liberty," coldly returned the other.

"And what is this liberty you ask? I hope, young man, you would not so soon betray the confidence you have just received! Our acquaintance is but short, and I may have been too hasty in my faith."

"I must return to the land," Wilder added firmly, "if it be only to know that I am intrusted, and not a prisoner."

"There is generous sentiment, or deep villainy in all this," resumed the Rover, after a minute of thought. "I will believe the former. Declare to me that while in the Town of Newport, you will inform no soul of the true character of this ship."

"I will swear it," eagerly interrupted Wilder.

"On this cross," rejoined the Rover with a sarcastic laugh— "on this diamond mounted cross! No, Sir," he added with a proud curl of the lip, as he cast the jewel contemptuously aside, "oaths are made for men who need laws to keep them to their promises. I need no more than the clear and unequivocal affirmation of a gentleman."

"Then plainly and unequivocally do I declare, that while in Newport, I will discover the character of this ship to no one, without your wish or order so to do. Nay more"—

"No more. It is wise to be sparing of our pledges, and to say no more than the occasion requires. The time may come when you can do good to yourself without harming me by being unfettered by a promise. In an hour, you shall land; that time will be needed, to make you acquainted with the terms of your enlistment, and to grace my rolls with your name. Roderick," he added, again touching the gong—"you are wanted, boy."

The same active lad, that had made his appearance at the first summons, ran up the steps from the cabin beneath, and announced his presence again by his voice.

"Roderick," continued the Rover, "this is my future Lieutenant, and of course, your officer and my friend—Will you take refreshment, Sir? there is little that man needs, which Roderick cannot supply."

"I thank you. I have need of none."

"Then have the goodness to follow the boy. He will show you into the dining apartment beneath, and give you the written regulations. In an hour you will have digested the code, and by that time I shall be with you. Throw the light more upon the ladder, boy—you can descend *without* a ladder though, it would seem, or I should not now have the pleasure of your company."

The intelligent smile of the Rover was unanswered by any corresponding evidence from the subject of his joke, that he found satisfaction in the remembrance of the awkward situation in which he had been left in the tower. The former caught the displeased expression of the other's countenance, as he gravely prepared to follow the boy, who already stood in the hatchway with a light. Advancing a step, with the grace and tones of a man of breeding he said quickly—

"Mr Wilder, I owe you an apology, for my seeming rudeness, at parting on the hill. Though I believed you mine, I was not sure of my acquisition. You will readily see, how necessary it might be to one in my situation to throw off a companion at such a moment."

Wilder turned with a countenance from which every shade of displeasure had vanished, and motioned to him to say no more.

"It was awkward enough, certainly, to find one's self in such a prison, but I feel the justice of what you say. I might have done the very thing myself, if the same presence of mind were at hand to help me."

"The Good-man who grinds in the Newport ruin, must be in a sad way, since all the rats are leaving his mill," cried the Rover, beckoning his temporary adieus, as his companion followed the boy. Wilder freely returned the open, cordial laugh, and then, as he descended, the cabin was left to him, who, a few minutes before, had been found in its quiet possession.

# Chapter VII

"The world affords no law to make thee rich;
Then be not poor, but break it, and take this."
*Apoth.* "My poverty, but not my will, consents."
*Romeo and Juliet*, V.i.73–75.

THE ROVER arrested his step, as the other disappeared, and stood for more than a minute in an attitude of high and self-gratulating triumph. He was exulting in his success. But though his intelligent face betrayed the satisfaction of the inward man, it was illumined by no expression of vulgar joy. It was the countenance of one who was suddenly relieved from intense care, rather than that of a man who was greedy of profiting by the services of others. Indeed, it would not have been difficult for a close observer to detect a shade of regret, in the lightings of his seductive smile, or in the momentary flashes of his changeful eye. The feeling however quickly passed away, and his whole figure and countenance resumed the ordinary careless mien, in which he most indulged in his hours of ease.

After allowing sufficient time for the boy to conduct Wilder to the cabin below, and to put him in possession of the regulations for the police of the ship, the captain again touched the gong and once more summoned the former to his presence. The lad had, however, to approach the elbow of his master and to speak thrice before the other was conscious that he had answered his call.

"Roderick," said the Rover, after a long pause, "are you there?"

"I am here," returned a low, and a mournful voice.

"Ah! you gave him the Regulations?"

"I did."

"And he reads?"

"He reads."

"It is well. I would speak to the General. Roderick, you must have need of rest. Good night. Let the General be summoned to a Council, and—Good night, my Roderick."

The boy made an assenting reply, but instead of springing

with his former alacrity to execute the order, he lingered for a moment nigh his master's chair. Failing however, in his wish to catch his eye, he reluctantly descended the stairs which led into the lower cabins, and was seen no more that night.

It is needless to describe the manner in which the General made his second appearance. It differed in no particular from his former entrée, except that, on this occasion, the whole of his person was developed. He appeared a tall, upright form, that was far from being destitute of natural proportions, but which had been so exquisitely drilled into simultaneous movement, that the several members appeared to have so far lost the power of volition, as to render it impossible for any one of them to stir, without producing something like a correspondent demonstration in all of its fellows. This rigid and well regulated personage, after making a military bow to his superior, helped himself to a chair, in which, after some little time lost in preparation, he seated himself in silence. The Rover seemed conscious of his presence, for he acknowledged his salute, by a gentle inclination of his own head, though he did not appear to think it necessary to suspend his ruminations, the more, on that account. At length, however, he turned short upon his companion, and said abruptly—

"General, the campaign is not finished."

"What remains? The field is won, and the enemy is a prisoner."

"Ay, your part of the adventure is well achieved, but much of mine remains to be done. You saw the youth in the lower cabin?"

"I did."

"And how do you like his appearance?"

"Maritime."

"That is as much as to say you like him not."

"I like discipline."

"I am much mistaken if you do not find him to your taste on the quarter-deck. Let that be as it may, I have still a favor to ask of you."

"A favor! It is getting late."

"Did I say a favor? There is duty to be done."

"I wait your orders."

"It is necessary that we use great precaution, for as you know"—

"I wait your orders," laconically repeated the other.

The Rover compressed his mouth, and a smile struggled about the nether lip, but it changed into a look half bland and half authoritative as he continued—

"You will find two seamen in a skiff alongside the ship. The one is white and the other is a black. These men you will have conducted into the vessel—into one of the forward state-rooms, and you will have them both thoroughly intoxicated."

"It shall be done," returned he who was called the general, rising and marching with long strides towards the door of the cabin.

"Pause a moment!" added the Rover. "What agent will you use?"

"Nightingale has the strongest head, but one, in the ship."

"He is too far gone already. I sent him ashore to look about for any straggling seamen who might like our service, and I found him, in a tavern, with all the fastenings off his tongue, declaiming like a lawyer who had taken a fee from both par-ties. Besides he had a quarrel with one of these very men, and it is probable they would get to blows in their cups. You must employ another agent."

"I will do it myself. My night-cap is waiting for me, and it is only to lace it a little tighter than common."

The Rover seemed content, with this assurance, for he expressed his satisfaction with a familiar nod of the head. The soldier was now about to depart when he was again interrupted—

"One thing more. General—there is your captive"—

"Shall I make him drunk too?"

"By no means. Let him be conducted hither."

The General made an ejaculation of assent and left the cabin. "It were weak," thought the Rover, as he resumed his walk up and down the apartment, "to trust too much to an ingenuous face and youthful enthusiasm. I am deceived if the boy has not had reason to think himself disgusted with the world and ready to embark in any romantic enterprise, but still to be deceived might be fatal. Therefore will I be prudent even to excess of caution. He is tied, in an extraordinary manner to these two seamen. I could wish to know his history! But that will come in proper time. The men must remain as hostages for his own return and for his faith. If he prove false—why they are seamen and many men are expended in this wild service of ours. It is well arranged, and no suspicion of any plot on our part will wound the sensitive pride of the boy, if he be, as I would gladly think, a true man."

Such was, in a great measure, the train of thought, in which the Rover indulged for many minutes after his military companion had left him. His lips moved; smiles and dark shades of thought, in turn, chased each other from his speaking countenance, which betrayed all the sudden and violent changes that denoted the workings of a busy spirit within. While thus engrossed in mind, his step became more rapid, and at times, he even gesticulated a little extravagantly, when he found himself, in a sudden turn unexpectedly confronted by a form, that seemed to rise on his sight like a vision.

While most engaged in his own humours, two powerful seamen had unheeded entered the cabin, and after silently depositing a human figure in a seat, they withdrew without speaking. It was before this personage that the Rover now found himself. The gaze was mutual, long and uninterrupted by a syllable from either party. Surprise and indecision held the Rover mute, while wonder and alarm appeared to have literally frozen the faculties of the other. At length the former, suffering a quaint and peculiar smile to gleam for a moment across his countenance, said abruptly—

"I welcome Sir Hector Homespun!"

The eyes of the confounded tailor—for it was no other than that garrulous acquaintance of the reader who had fallen into the toils of the Rover, the eyes of the good-man rolled from right to left, embracing in their wanderings the medley of elegance and warlike preparation that they everywhere met, never failing to return from each greedy look, to devour the figure that stood before him.

"I say welcome, Sir Hector Homespun," repeated the Rover.

"The Lord will be lenient to the sins of the miserable father of seven small children," ejaculated the tailor. "It is but little, valiant Pirate, that can be gotten from a hard-working, upright tradesman, who sits from the rising to the setting sun, bent over his labor"—

"These are debasing terms for chivalry, Sir Hector," interrupted the Rover, laying his hand on the little riding-whip, which had been thrown carelessly on the cabin table, and tapping the shoulder of the tailor with the same, as if he were a sorcerer, and would disenchant the other with a touch. "Cheer up, honest and loyal subject; fortune has at length ceased to frown. It is but a few hours since you complained that no custom came to your shop from this vessel, and now are you in a fair way to do the business of the whole ship."

"Ah! honorable and magnanimous Rover," rejoined Homespun, whose fluency returned with his senses, "I am an impoverished and undone man. My life has been one of weary and probationary hardships. Five bloody and cruel wars"—

"Enough. I have said that fortune was just beginning to smile. Clothes are as necessary to gentlemen of our profession, as to the Parish priest. You shall not baste a seam without your reward. Behold," he added, touching the spring of a secret drawer, which flew open and discovered a confused pile of gold, in which the coins of nearly every christian people were blended, "we are not without the means of paying those who serve us faithfully."

The sudden exhibition of a horde of wealth, which not only greatly exceeded any thing of the kind he had ever before witnessed, but which actually surpassed his limited imaginative powers, was not without its effect on the sensitive feelings of the good-man. After feasting on the sight for the few moments that his companion left the treasure exposed to view, he turned to the envied possessor of so much gold, and demanded, the tones of increasing confidence gradually stealing into his voice, as the inward man felt additional motives of encouragement—

"And what am I expected to perform, Mighty Seaman, for my portion of this wealth?"

"That which you daily perform on the land—To cut, to fashion and to sew. Perhaps, too, your talent at a masquerade dress may occasionally be taxed."

"Ah! they are lawless and irreligious devices of the enemy, to lead man into sin and worldly abominations! But, worthy

Mariner, there is my disconsolate consort, Desire; though stricken in years and given to wordy strife, yet is she the lawful partner of my bosom and the mother of a numerous offspring!"

"She shall not want. This is an asylum for distressed husbands. Your men who have not force enough to command at home, come to my ship as to a city of refuge. You will make the seventh who has found peace, by fleeing to this sanctuary. Their families are supported by ways, best known to ourselves, and all parties are content. This is not the least of my benevolent acts."

"It is praiseworthy and just, honorable captain, and I hope that Desire and her offspring may not be forgotten. The 'laborer is surely worthy of his hire,' and if peradventure I should toil in your behalf, through stress of compulsion, I hope the good-woman and her young may fatten on your liberality."

"You have my word. They shall not be neglected."

"Perhaps, just gentleman, if an allotment should be made in advance from that stock of gold, the mind of my consort would be relieved, her enquiries after my fate not so searching and her spirit less troubled. I have reason to understand the temper of Desire, and am well identified that while the prospect of want is before her eyes, there will be a clamor in Newport. Now that the Lord has graciously given me the hopes of a respite, there can be no sin in wishing to enjoy it in peace!"

Although the Rover was far from believing, with his captive, that the tongue of Desire could disturb the harmony of his ship, he was in the humor to be indulgent. Touching the spring, again, he took a handful of the gold, and extending it towards Homespun, demanded—

"Will you take the bounty and the oath? The money will then be your own."

"The Lord defend us from the evil one, and deliver us all, from temptation!" ejaculated the tailor. "Heroic Rover, I have a dread of the law. Should any evil overcome you, in the shape of a King's cruiser, or a tempest cast you on the land, there might be danger in being contaminated too closely with your crew. Any little services which I may render, on compulsion, will be overlooked I humbly hope, and I trust to your magnanimity, honest and honorable commodore, that the same will not be forgotten in the division of your upright earnings."

"This is but the spirit of cabbaging a little distorted," muttered the Rover, as he turned lightly on his heel, and tapped the gong, with an impatience that sent the startling sound through every cranny of the ship. Four or five heads were thrust in at the different doors of the cabin, and the voice of one was heard desiring to know the wishes of their leader.

"Take him to his hammock," was the sudden order.

The good-man Homespun, who, from fright or policy appeared to be utterly unable to move, was quickly lifted from his seat and conveyed to the door which communicated with the quarter-deck.

"Pause," he exclaimed to his unceremonious bearers, as they were about to transport him to the place designated by their captain; "I have one word yet to say. Honest and Loyal Rebel, though I do not accept your service, neither do I refuse it, in an unseemly and irreverent manner. It is a sore temptation and I feel it at my fingers' ends. But a covenant may be made between us by which neither party shall be a loser, and in which the law shall find no grounds of displeasure. I would wish, mighty Commodore, to carry an honest name to my grave, and I would also wish to live out the number of my days; for, after having past with so much credit and unharmed through five bloody and cruel wars"—

"Away with him!"

Homespun vanished as if magic had been employed in transporting him, and the Rover was again left to himself. His meditations were not interrupted for a long time, by human footstep or voice. That breathing stillness, which unbending and stern discipline can alone impart pervaded the ship. A landsman seated in the cabin, might have fancied himself, although surrounded by a crew of lawless and violent men, in the solitude of a deserted church, so suppressed and deadened were even those sounds that were absolutely necessary. There were heard at times, it is true, the high and harsh notes of some reveller, who appeared to break forth in the strains of a sea song, which, as they issued from the depths of the vessel and were not very musical in themselves, broke on the silence like the first discordant strains of a new practitioner on a bugle. But even these interruptions, gradually grew less frequent, and finally became inaudible. At length the Rover heard a hand fumbling about the handle of the cabin-door, and then his military friend once more made his appearance.

There was that in the step, the countenance, and the whole air of the General, which proclaimed, that his recent service, if successful, had not been atchieved without great personal hazard. The Rover, who had started from his seat, the moment he saw, who entered, instantly demanded his report.

"The white is so drunk, that he cannot lie down without holding on to the mast, but the negro is either a cheat, or his head is made of flint."

"I hope you have not too easily abandoned the design."

"I would as soon batter a mountain! My retreat was not made a minute too soon."

The Rover fastened his eye on the General in order to assure himself of the precise condition of his subaltern, and changed his purpose.

"It is well. We will now retire for the night."

The other, carefully dressed his tall person, and brought his face in the direction of the little hatchway so often named. Then by a sort of desperate effort, he essayed to march to the spot, with his customary military step. As one or two erratic movements and crossings of the legs were not commented on by his captain, the worthy martinet descended the stairs, slowly and as he believed with sufficient dignity, the moral man not being in the precise state which is the best adapted to discover any little blunders that might be made by his physical coadjutor. The Rover looked at his watch, and after allowing sufficient time for the deliberate retreat of the General, he stepped lightly on the stairs and descended also.

The lower apartments of the vessel, though less striking in their equipments than the upper cabin, were arranged with great attention to neatness and comfort. A few offices for the servants occupied the extreme after-part of the ship, communicating by doors with the dining apartment of the secondary officers, or as it was called in technical language, the wardroom. On each side of this, again, were the state rooms, an imposing name, by which the dormitories of those who are entitled to the honors of the quarter-deck are called. Forward of the ward-room came the apartments of the minor officers, and immediately in front of them, the corps of the individual, who was called the General, were lodged, forming by their discipline a barrier between the more lawless seamen and their superiors.

There was little departure, in this disposition of the accommodations, from the ordinary arrangements of vessels of war of the same description and force as the rover, but Wilder had not failed to remark, that the bulk-heads which separated the cabins from the berth-deck, or the part occupied by the crew, were far stouter than common, and that a small-howitzer was at hand, to be used as a physician might say, internally, should occasion require. The doors were of extraordinary strength, and the means of barricadoing them, resembled more a preparation for battle, than the usual securities against petty encroachments on private property. Muskets, blunderbusses, pistols, sabres, half-pikes, &c., were fixed to the beams and carlines, or were made to serve as ornaments against the different bulkheads, in a profusion that plainly told they were there as much for use as for show. In short to the eye of a seaman the whole betrayed a state of things, in which the superiors felt that their whole security, against the violence and insubordination of their inferiors depended on their influence and their ability to resist united, and that the former had not deemed it prudent to neglect any of the precautions which might aid their comparatively less powerful physical force.

In the principal of the lower apartments, or the ward-room, the Rover found his newly enlisted Lieutenant apparently busy in studying the regulations of the service in which he had just embarked. Approaching the corner in which the latter had seated himself, the former said in a frank, encouraging and even confidential manner—

"I hope you find our laws, sufficiently firm, Mr Wilder."

"Want of firmness is not their fault; if the same quality can always be observed in administering them, it is well," returned the other, rising to salute his superior. "I have never found such rigid rules even in"—

"Even in what, Sir?" demanded the Rover, perceiving that his companion hesitated.

"I was about to say, even in his Majesty's service," returned Wilder, slightly coloring. "I know not whether it may be a fault or a recommendation to have served in a King's ship."

"It is the latter. At least I, for one, should think it so, since I learned my trade in the same service."

"In what ship?" eagerly interrupted Wilder.

"In many," was the cold reply. "But, speaking of rigid rules, you will soon perceive, that in a service where there are no Courts on shore to protect us, nor any sister cruisers to look after our welfare, no small portion of power is necessarily vested in the commander. You find my authority a good deal extended?"

"A little unlimited," said Wilder with a smile that might have passed for ironical.

"I hope you will have no occasion to say that it is arbitrarily executed," returned the Rover, without observing, or perhaps without letting it appear that he observed the expression of his companion's countenance. "But your hour is come; you are at liberty to land."

The young man thanked him with a courteous inclination of the head, and expressed his readiness to go. As they ascended the ladder into the upper cabin, the Captain expressed his regret, that the hour and the necessity of preserving the incognito of his ship would not permit him to send an officer of his rank, ashore in the manner he could wish.

"But then there is the skiff, in which you came off, still along-side, and your own two stout fellows will soon twitch you to yon point. Apropos of those two men; are they included in our arrangements?"

"They have never quitted me since my childhood, and would not wish to do it now."

"It is a singular tie, that unites two men so oddly constituted to one so different by habits and education from themselves," returned the Rover, glancing his eye keenly at the other, and withdrawing it, the instant he perceived his interest in the answer was observed.

"It is," Wilder calmly replied. "But as we are all seamen, the difference is not so great, as one would, at first imagine. I will now join them, and take an opportunity to let them know, that they are to serve in future, under your orders."

The Rover suffered him to leave the cabin, following to the quarter-deck, with a careless step, as if he had come abroad to breathe the open air of the night.

The weather had not changed, but it still continued dark though mild. The same stillness as before, reigned on the decks of the ship, and no where with a solitary exception, was a human form to be seen, amid the collection of dark objects that rose on the sight, all of which Wilder well understood to be necessary fixtures in the vessel. The exception was the same individual that had first received our adventurer, and who still paced the quarter-deck, wrapped, as before in a watch-coat. To this personage the youth now addressed himself, announcing his intention, temporarily, to quit the vessel. His communication was received with a respect, that satisfied him, his new rank was already known, although, as it would seem, it was to be made to succumb to the superior authority of the Rover.

"You know, Sir, that no one, of whatever station can leave the ship at this hour, without an order from the captain," was the steady reply.

"So I presume; but I have the order, and transmit it to you. I shall land in my own boat."

The other, seeing a figure within hearing, which he well knew to be that of his commander, waited an instant to ascertain if what he heard was true. Finding that no objection was made, he merely indicated the place where the other would find his boat.

"The men have left it!" exclaimed Wilder, stepping back in surprise as he was about to descend the vessel's side.

"Have the rascals run?"

"Sir, they have not run, neither are they rascals. They are in this ship and must be found."

The other waited to witness the effect of these authoritative words, too, on the individual, who still lingered in the shadow of a mast. As no answer was however, given from that quarter, he saw the necessity of obedience. Intimating his intention to seek the men, he passed into the forward parts of the vessel, leaving Wilder, as he thought, in the sole possession of the quarter-deck. The latter was however, soon undeceived. The Rover, advancing carelessly to his side, made an allusion to the condition of his vessel, in order to divert the thoughts of his new Lieutenant, who, by his hurried manner of pacing the deck, he heard was beginning to indulge in uneasy meditations.

"A charming sea-boat, Mr Wilder," he continued, "and one that never throws a drop of spray abaft her mainmast. She is just the craft a seaman loves: easy on her rigging and lively in a sea. I call her the Dolphin, from the manner in which she cuts the water, and perhaps because she has as many colours as that fish, you will say. Jack must have a name for his ship, you know, and I dislike your cut-throat appellations; your Spit-fires, and Bloody-Murders."

"You were fortunate in finding such a vessel. Was she built to your orders?"

"Few ships under six hundred tons, sail from these Colonies, that are not built to serve my purposes," returned the Rover, with a smile, as if he would cheer his companion, by displaying the mine of wealth that was opening to him, through the new connexion he had made. "This vessel was originally built for his most Faithful Majesty, and I believe was either intended as a present or a scourge to the Algerines, but—but she has changed owners as you see, and her fortune is a little altered, though how or why, is a trifle with which we will not just now, divert ourselves. I think she is all the better handled for the transfer. I have had her in port; she has undergone some improvements, and is now altogether suited to a running trade."

"You then venture sometimes inside the forts?"

"When you have leisure, my private journal may afford some interest," the other evasively replied. "I hope, Mr. Wilder, you find the vessel in such a state that a seaman need not blush for her?"

"Her beauty and neatness first caught my eye, and induced me to make closer enquiries into her character."

"You were quick in seeing that she was kept at a single anchor!" returned the other laughing. "But I never risk any thing without a reason, not even the loss of my ground tackle. It would be no great atchievement for so warm a battery, as this I carry, to silence yonder apology for a fort, but in doing it, we might receive an unfortunate hit, and therefore I keep ready for an instant departure."

"It must be a little awkward to fight in a war, where one cannot lower his flag in any emergency!" said Wilder more like one who mused, than one who intended to express the opinion aloud.

"The bottom is always beneath us," was the laconick answer. "But to you I may say, that I am on principle tender on my spars. They are examined daily, like the heels of a racer, for it often happens that our valour must be well tempered by discretion."

"And how and where do you refit, when damaged in a gale, or in a fight?"

"Hum. We contrive to refit, Sir, and to take the sea again in tolerable condition."

He stopped, and Wilder, perceiving that he was not yet deemed entitled to entire confidence, continued silent. In this pause, the officer returned, followed by the black alone. A few words served to explain the condition of Fid. It was very apparent that the young man was not only disappointed, but that he was deeply mortified. The frank and ingenuous air, however, with which he turned to the Rover to apologise for the dereliction of his follower, satisfied the latter, that he was far from suspecting any improper agency in bringing about his awkward condition.

"You know the character of seamen too well, Sir," he said, "to impute this oversight to my poor fellow as a heinous fault. A better sailor never lay on a yard, or stretched a ratlin, than Dick Fid; but I must allow that he carries the quality of good-fellowship to excess."

"You are fortunate in having one man left you, to pull the boat ashore," carelessly returned the other.

"I am more than equal to that little exertion myself—nor do I like to separate the men. With your permission the black shall be berthed, too, in the ship to-night."

"As you please. Empty hammocks are not scarce among us, since the last brush."

Wilder then directed the negro to return to his messmate, and to watch over him so long as he should be unable to look after himself. The black, who was far from being as clear headed as common, willingly complied. The young man then took leave of his companions and descended into the skiff. As he pulled, with vigorous arms, away from the dark ship, his eyes were cast upward, with a seaman's pleasure in the order and neatness, of her gear, and thence they fell on the frowning mass of the hull. A light-built, compact form was seen standing on the heel of the bowsprit, apparently watching his movements, and notwithstanding the gloom of the clouded star-light, he was enabled to detect, in the individual who took so much apparent interest in his proceedings, the person of the Rover.

# Chapter VIII

―――"What is yon gentleman?"
Nurse. "The son and heir of old Tiberio."
Juliet. "What's he that follows there, that would not dance?"
Nurse. "Marry, I know not."
*Romeo and Juliet*, I.v.128−29, 132−33.

THE SUN was just heaving up out of the field of waters in which the blue islands of Massachusetts lie, when the inhabitants of Newport were seen opening their doors and windows, and preparing for the different employments of the day, with the freshness and alacrity of people who had wisely adhered to the natural allotments of time, in seeking their rests, or in pursuing their pleasures. The morning salutations passed cheerfully from one to another, as each undid the slight fastenings of his shop, and many a kind enquiry passed from one to the other concerning a daughter's fever, or the rheumatism of some aged grandam. As the landlord of the Foul Anchor was so wary in protecting the character of his house from any unjust imputations of unseemly revelling, so was he among the foremost in opening his doors to catch any transient customer who might feel the necessity of washing away the damps of the past night with an invigorating stomachic. This cordial was then very generally taken in the British Provinces, under the various names of "bitters," "juleps," "morning drams," "fogmatics," &c., as the situation of different districts appeared to require particular preventives. The custom is getting a little into disuse, it is true; but still it retains much of that sacred character which is the consequence of antiquity. It is not a little extraordinary that this venerable and laudable practice of washing away the unwholesome impurities engendered in the human system at a time when, as it is entirely without any moral protector, it is left exposed to the attacks of 'all the evils to which flesh is heir,' should subject the American to the witticisms of his European brother. We are not among the least grateful to those foreign philanthropists, who take so deep an interest in our welfare as seldom to let any republican foible pass without applying to it, as it merits, the caustic application of their purifying monarchical pens. We are, perhaps, the more sensible of this generosity, because we have had occasion to witness, that so great is their zeal in behalf of our infant states, (robust and a little unmanageable perhaps, but still infant) they are wont in the warmth of their ardor to reform cisatlantic sins, to overlook some of their own backslidings. Numberless are the moral missionaries that the Mother Country, for instance, has sent among us on these pious and benevolent errands. We can only regret that their efforts have been crowned with so little success. It was our fortune to be familiarly acquainted with one of these worthies, who never lost an opportunity of declaiming, above all, against the infamy of the particular practice to which we have alluded. The ground he took was so broad, that he held it to be not only immoral, but, what was hideous, it was ungenteel, to swallow any thing stronger than small beer before the hour allotted to dinner. After that important period it was not only permitted to assuage the previous mortifications of the flesh, but so liberal did he show himself in the indulgence, after the clock had settled the point of orthodoxy, that he was regularly carried to bed at midnight, from which he as regularly issued in the course of the following day, to discourse again, on the deformities of premature drunkenness. And here we would take occasion to say, that, as to our own insignificant person, we eschew the abomination altogether, and only regret that those of the two nations, who find pleasure in the practice, could not come to some amicable understanding as to the precise period of the twenty four hours, when it is permitted to such Christian gentlemen as speak English to steep their senses in liquor, without bringing scandal on good breeding. That the negotiators who framed the last treaty of amity should have overlooked this important moral topic, is another evidence that both parties were so tired of an unprofitable war as to patch up a peace in a hurry. It is not too late to name a commission for this purpose, and in order that the question may be fairly treated on its merits, we presume to suggest to the Executive the propriety of nominating as our Commissioner, some confirmed advocate of the system of Juleps: it is believed our worthy and indulgent Mother can have no difficulty in selecting a suitable coadjutor from the ranks of her numerous and well-trained diplomatic corps.

With this manifestation of our personal liberality, united to so much interest in the proper, and we hope final disposition of this important question we may be permitted to resume the narrative without being set down as advocates for morning stimulants or evening intoxication, which is a very just division of the whole subject, as we believe, from an observation that is far from being limited.

The landlord of the "Foul Anchor," as has just been said, was early afoot to gain an honest penny from any of the supporters of the former system who might chance to select his bar, for their morning sacrifices to Bacchus, in preference to that of his neighbor, he who endeavored to entice the lieges, by exhibiting a red faced man in a scarlet coat, that was called The Head of George IId. The activity of the alert publican did not go without its reward. The tide of custom set strongly for the first half-hour towards the haven of his hospitable bar, nor did he appear entirely to abandon the hopes of a further influx, even after the usual period for such arrivals began to pass away. Finding, however, that his customers were beginning to depart on their several pursuits, he left his station, and appeared at the outer door, with a hand in each pocket, as if he found a secret pleasure in the manipulation of their new tenants. A stranger who had not entered with the others, and who of course had not partaken of the customary libations, was standing at a little distance, with a hand thrust into the bosom of his vest, apparently more occupied with his own reflections than with the success of the publican. This figure caught the understanding eye of the latter, who conceived that no man who had recourse to the proper morning stimulants could wear so meditative a face at that early period in the cares of the day, and that consequently something was yet to be gained, by opening a communication between them.

"A clean air this, friend, to brush away the damps of the night," he said, snuffing the really delicious, and invigorating breathings of a fine October morning. "It is such purifiers as this, that give our island its character, and make it, perhaps, the very healthiest, as it is universally admitted to be the beautifullest spot in creation. A stranger here, 'tis likely?"

"But quite lately arrived, Sir," was the reply.

"A sea-faring man by your dress and one in search of a ship as I am ready to qualify to," continued the publican, chuckling at his own penetration. "We have many such that pass hereaway, but people mustn't think because Newport is so flourishing, that berths can always be had for asking. Have you tried your luck in the capital of the Bay Province?"

"I left Boston no later, than the day before yesterday."

"What, couldn't the proud towns-folks* find you a ship! Ay, they are a mighty people at talking, and it isn't often that they put their candle under the bushel, and yet there are what I call good judges, who think Narragansett Bay is in a fair way, shortly, to count as many sail as Massachusetts. Yonder is a wholesome brig, that is going within the week to turn her horses into rum and sugar; and here is a ship that hauled into the stream no longer ago than yesterday sun-down. That is a noble vessel, and her cabins are fit for a Prince! She'll be off with the change of the wind, and I dare say a good hand wouldn't go a begging aboard her just now. Then there is a slaver off the fort, if you like a cargo of wool-heads for your money."

"Is it thought the ship in the inner harbor will sail with the first wind?" demanded the stranger.

"It is downright. My wife is a full cousin to the wife of the collector's clerk, and I have it quite straight that the papers are ready, and that nothing but the wind detains them. I keep some short scores you know, friend, with the blue jackets, and it behoves an honest man to look to his interests in these hard times. Yes, there she lies; a well known ship, the Royal Caroline; she makes a regular v'yage once a year between the Provinces and Bristol, touching here, out and home, to give us certain supplies, and to wood and water, and then she goes home, or to the Carolinas, as the case may be."

"Pray, Sir, has she much of an armament?" continued the stranger, who began to lose his thoughtful air, in the more evident interest he was beginning to take in the discourse.

"Yes, yes; she is not without a few bull-dogs, to bark in

*Boston was called the *town* of Boston, not being incorporated as a city, until quite lately. The government was that of a "town" until it had more than fifty thousand inhabitants.

defence of her own rights, and to say a word in support of his Majesty's honor too, God bless him! Judy! you Jude," he shouted at the top of his voice, to a negro girl who was gathering kindling-wood among the chips of a ship yard, "scamper over to neighbor Homespun's, and rattle away at his bed-room windows. The man has over-slept himself; it is oncommon to hear seven o'clock strike and the thirsty tailor, not appear for his bitters."

A short cessation took place in the dialogue, while the wench was executing her master's orders. The summons produced no other effect than to draw a shrill reply from Desire, whose voice penetrated through the thin board coverings of the little dwelling, as readily as sound would be conveyed through a sieve. In another moment a window was opened, and the worthy housewife thrust her disturbed visage into the fresh air of the morning.

"What next—what next!" demanded the offended, and as she was fain to believe, neglected wife under the impression that it was her truant husband making a tardy return to his domestic allegiance, who had thus presumed to disturb her slumbers. "Is it not enough that you have eloped from my bed and board for a whole night, but you must break in on the natural rest of a whole family, seven blessed children without counting their mother—Oh! Hector—Hector—An example are you getting to be to the young and giddy, and a warning will you yet prove to the unthoughtful!"

"Bring hither the black book," said the publican to his wife, who had been drawn to a window by the lamentations of Desire. "I think the woman said something about starting on a journey between two days; if such has been the philosophy of the good-man, it behoves honest people to look into their accounts. Ay, as I live, Keziah, you have let the limping beggar get seventeen and sixpence into arrears, and that for such trifles as morning drams and night-caps!"

"You are wrathy, friend, without reason; the man made a garment for the boy at school, and found the"—

"Hush, good woman—" interrupted her husband, returning the book and making a sign for her to retire. "I dare say it will all come round in proper time, and the less noise we make about the backslidings of a neighbor, the less will be said of our own transgressions. A worthy and a hard working mechanic, Sir," he continued, addressing the stranger; "but a man who could never get the sun to shine in at his windows, though Heaven knows, the glass is none too thick for such a blessing."

"And do you imagine, on evidence as slight as this we have seen, that such a man has actually absconded?"

"Why it is a calamity that has befallen his betters!" returned the publican, interlocking his fingers across the rotundity of his person with an air of grave consideration. "We innkeepers, who live, as it were, in plain sight of every man's secrets, for it is after a visit to us, that one is most apt to open his heart, should know something of the affairs of a neighborhood. If the good-man Homespun could smooth down the temper of his companion, as easily as he lays a seam into its place, the thing might not occur, but—do you drink this morning, Sir?"

"A drop of your best."

"As I was saying," continued the other, furnishing his customer, according to his desire, "if a tailor's goose would take the wrinkles out of the ruffled temper of a woman, as it does out of the cloth, and then, if after it had done this task, a man might eat it, as he would yonder bird, hanging behind my bar—Perhaps you will have occasion to make your dinner with us too, Sir—"

"I cannot say I shall not," returned the stranger, paying for the dram he had barely tasted; "it greatly depends on the result of my enquiries concerning the different vessels in the port."

"Then would I, though perfectly disinterested as you know, Sir, recommend you to make this house your home, while you sojourn in the town. It is the resort of most of the sea-faring men, and I may say this much of myself without conceit, no man can tell you more of what you want to know, than the landlord of the 'Foul Anchor.' "

"You advise an application to the commander of this vessel in the stream for a berth—will she sail so soon as you have named?"

"With the first wind. I know the whole history of the ship, from the day they laid the blocks for her keel, to the minute when she let her anchor go where you now see her. The great Southern heiress, General Grayson's fine daughter, is to be a passenger; she, and her overlooker, Government lady, I believe they call her, a Mrs Wyllys, are waiting for the signal up here, at the residence of Madam de Lacey, she that is the relick of the rear-admiral of that name, who is full sister to the general, and therefore, an aunt to the young lady according to my reckoning. Many people think the two fortunes will go together, in which case he will be not only a lucky man, but a rich one, who gets Miss Getty Grayson for a wife."

The stranger, who had maintained rather an indifferent manner during the close of the foregoing dialogue, appeared now disposed to enter into it with a degree of interest suited to the sex and condition of the present subject of their discourse. After waiting to catch the last syllable that the publican chose to expend his breath on, he demanded a little abruptly—

"And you say the house near us, on the rising ground is the residence of Mrs. de Lacey?"

"If I did, I know nothing of the matter. By up here, I mean half a mile off. It is a place fit for a lady of her quality, and none of your elbowing dwellings like these crowded about us. One may easily tell the house, by its pretty blinds and its shades. I'll engage there are no such shades, in all Europe, as the very trees that stand before the door of Madam de Lacey."

"It is very probable," muttered the stranger, who, not appearing quite as sensitive in his provincial admiration as the publican, had already relapsed into his former musing air. Instead of pushing the discourse, he suddenly turned the subject, by making some common-place remark, and then repeating the probability of his being obliged to return, he walked deliberately away, taking the direction of the residence of Mrs de Lacey. The observing publican would probably have found sufficient matter for observation in this abrupt termination of the interview, had not Desire, at that precise moment, broken out of her habitation, and diverted his attention, by the peculiarly lively manner in which she delineated the character of her delinquent husband.

The reader has probably, ere this, suspected that the individual, who had conferred with the publican as a stranger, was not unknown to himself. It was in truth, no other than Wilder. But in the completion of his own secret purposes, the young mariner, left the wordy war in his rear, and turning up the gentle ascent against the side of which the town is built, he proceeded towards the suburbs.

It was not difficult to distinguish the house he sought among a dozen other similar retreats, by its shades, as the innkeeper, in conformity with a provincial use of the word, had termed a few really noble elms that grew in the little court before its door. In order, however, to assure himself that he was right, he confirmed his surmises by actual en-quiry, and continued thoughtfully on his path.

The morning had by this time fairly opened with every appearance of another of those fine, bland, autumnal days for which the climate is, or ought to be so distinguished. The little air there was, came from the south, fanning the face of our adventurer, as he occasionally paused in his ascent to gaze at the different vessels in the harbor, like a mild breeze in June. In short it was just such a time as one who is fond of strolling in the fields is apt to seize on with rapture, and which a seaman sets down as a day lost in his reckoning.

Wilder was first drawn from his musings, by the sound of a dialogue, that came from persons who were evidently ap-proaching. There was one voice, in particular, that caused his blood to thrill, he knew not why, and which appeared unac-countably even to himself, to set in motion every latent fac-ulty of his system. Profiting by the formation of the ground, he sprang, unseen, up a little bank, and approaching an angle in a low wall, he found himself in the immediate proximity of the speakers.

The wall enclosed the garden and pleasure grounds of a mansion, that he now perceived was the residence of Mrs de Lacey. A rustic summer house, which in the proper season, had been nearly buried in leaves and flowers, stood at no great distance from the road. By its elevation and position it commanded a view of the Town, the harbor, the isles of Mas-sachusetts to the East, those of the Providence Plantations to the West, and to the South an illimitable expanse of Ocean. As it had now lost its leafy covering there was no difficulty in looking directly into its interior, through the rude pillars which supported its little dome. Here Wilder discovered the very party, of whose conversation he had been a listener, the previous day, while caged with the Rover in the loft of the ruin. Though the Admiral's Widow and Mrs Wyllys were most in advance, evidently addressing some one, who, like himself, was in the public road, the young sailor soon detected the more enticing person of the blooming Gertrude, in the back ground. His observations were, however, interrupted by a reply from the individual who as yet, was unseen. Directed by the voice, Wilder was soon enabled to perceive the person of a man in a green old age, who, seated on a stone by the way side, appeared to be resting his weary limbs, while he answered to certain interrogations that were made from the summer-house. His head was white, and the hand which grasped a long walking staff, sometimes trembled but there was that in the costume, the manner, and the voice of the speaker, which furnished sufficient evidence of his having once been a veteran of the sea.

"Lord, your Ladyship, Ma'am," he said in tones that were getting tremulous, even while they retained the deep intonations of his profession, "we old sea-dogs, never stop to look into an almanack to see which way the wind will come after the next thaw before we put to sea. It is enough for us, that the sailing orders are aboard, and that the captain has taken leave of his lady."

"Ah! The very words of the poor, lamented Admiral!" exclaimed Mrs de Lacey, who had great satisfaction in pursuing the discourse with a superannuated mariner. "And then you are of opinion, honest friend, that when a ship is ready she should sail, whether the wind is"——

"Here is another follower of the sea, opportunely come to lend us his advice," interrupted Gertrude, with a hurried air as if to divert the attention of her aunt from something very like a dogmatical termination of an argument that had just occurred between her and Mrs Wyllys; "or perhaps to serve as an umpire."

"What think you, Sir," demanded Mrs Wyllys, who caught a glimpse of Wilder's form as he stood leaning on the garden wall, after hesitating a single moment to be sure of his character; "are we to have a calm month or is there much prospect of Northern gales?"

The young mariner, reluctantly withdrew his eyes from the blushing Gertrude, who in her eagerness to point him out, had advanced to the front, and was now shrinking back, timidly, to the centre of the building again like one who already repented of her temerity. He then fastened his look on her who put the question, and so long and rivetted was his gaze, that she saw fit to repeat it, believing that what she had first said, was not properly understood.

"There is little faith to be put in the weather, Madam," was the dilatory reply. "A man has followed the sea to but little purpose who is tardy in making that discovery."

There was something so sweet and gentle, at the same time that it was manly in the voice of Wilder, that the ladies by a common impulse were won to listen. The neatness of his attire, which, while it was strictly professional, was worn with an air of smartness and even of gentility, that rendered it difficult to suppose he was not entitled to lay claim to a higher station in society, than that in which he actually appeared aided him also, in producing a favourable impression. Bending her head, with a manner that was intended to be polite, a little more perhaps in self-respect than out of consideration to the other, Mrs de Lacey resumed the discourse.

"These ladies," she said, "are about to embark in yonder ship for the Province of Carolina, and we were consulting concerning the quarter in which the wind will probably blow next. But in such a vessel it cannot matter much, I should think, Sir, whether the wind were fair or foul."

"I think not," was the reply. "She looks to me like a ship that will not do much, let the wind be as it may."

"She has the reputation of being a very fast sailer — reputation! we know she is such, having come from home to the Colonies in the incredibly short passage of seven weeks! But seamen have their favorites and prejudices, I believe, like us poor mortals ashore. You will therefore excuse me if I ask this honest veteran for an opinion on this particular point, also. What do you imagine, friend, to be the sailing qualities of yonder ship — she with the peculiarly high top-gallant-booms, and such conspicuous round-tops?"

A smile struggled on the lip of Wilder, but he continued silent. On the other hand the old mariner arose, appearing to examine the ship like one who perfectly comprehended the somewhat untechnical language of the Admiral's Widow.

"The ship in the inner harbor, your ladyship," he answered, when his examination was finished, "which is, I suppose the vessel that Madam means, is just such a ship as does a sailor's eyes good to look at. A gallant and a safe boat she is, as I will swear, and as to sailing, though she may not be altogether a witch, yet is she a fast craft, or I am no judge of blue-water, or of those that live on it."

"Here is at once an extraordinary difference of opinion!" exclaimed Mrs de Lacey. "I am glad, however, you pronounce her safe, for although seamen love a fast-sailing vessel, these ladies will not like her the less for the security. I presume, Sir, you will not dispute her being *safe*?"

"The very quality I should most deny," was the laconic answer of Wilder.

"It is very remarkable! This is a veteran seaman, Sir, and he appears to think differently?"

"He may have seen more in his time than myself, Madam; but I doubt whether he can just now see as well. This is a great distance to discover the merits or demerits of a ship. I have been nigher."

"Then you really think there is danger to be apprehended, Sir?" demanded the soft voice of Gertrude, whose fears had gotten the better of her diffidence.

"I do. Had I a mother, or a sister," touching his hat, and bowing to his fair interrogator, as he uttered the latter word with marked emphasis, "I would hesitate to let her embark in that ship. On my honor, ladies, I do assure you, that I think this very vessel in more danger, than any ship which has left, or probably will leave a port in the provinces this autumn."

"This is extraordinary!" observed Mrs Wyllys. "It is not the character we have received of the vessel, which has been greatly exaggerated, or she is entitled to be considered as uncommonly convenient and safe! May I ask, Sir, on what circumstances you have founded this opinion?"

"They are sufficiently plain. She is too lean in the harpen and too full in the counter to steer. Then she is as wall-sided as a church and stows too much above the water line. Besides this she carries no head sail, but all the press upon her will be aft, which will jam her into the wind, and more than likely throw her aback. The day will come when that ship will go down stern foremost."

His auditors listened to this opinion, which Wilder delivered in an oracular and very decided manner, with that sort of secret faith and humble dependance which the uninstructed are very apt to lend to those who are initiated in the mysteries of any imposing profession. Neither of them certainly had a very clear perception of his meaning, but there were danger and death in his very words. Mrs de Lacey, felt it incumbent on her own particular advantages, however, to manifest how well she comprehended the subject.

"These are certainly very serious evils!" she gravely rejoined. "It is quite unaccountable that my agent should have neglected to mention them. Is there any other quality, Sir, that strikes your eye at this distance, and which you deem alarming?"

"Too many. You observe that her top-gallant-masts are fidded abaft, none of her lofty sails set flying, and then, Madam, she has depended on bobstays and gammonings for the security of that very important part of a vessel the bowsprit!"

"Too true! too true!" said Mrs de Lacey with a start of professional horror. "These things had altogether escaped me, but I see them all plain enough now they are mentioned. Such neglect is highly culpable; more especially to rely on bobstays and gammonings for the security of a bowsprit. Really, Mrs Wyllys, I can never consent that my niece should embark in such a vessel!"

The calm eye of Wyllys had been fastened on the countenance of Wilder while he was speaking, and she now turned it, with undisturbed serenity on the Admiral's widow.

"Perhaps the danger has been a little magnified to our uninformed senses," she observed. "Let us enquire of this other seaman what he thinks on these points. And do you see all these serious dangers to be apprehended, friend, in trusting our selves, at this season of the year in a passage to the Carolinas, aboard of yonder ship?"

"Lord, Madam," said the gray headed mariner, with a

chuckling laugh, "these are new-fashioned fears and difficulties, if they be difficulties at all. In my time such matters were
never heard of, and I confess I am so stupid as not to understand half the young gentleman has been saying."

"It is some time I fancy, old man, since you were last at
sea," Wilder coolly observed.

"Some five or six years since the last time, and fifty since the
first."

"Then you do not see the same causes for apprehension?"
Mrs Wyllys once more demanded.

"Old and worn out as I am, lady, if her captain will give me
a berth aboard her, I will thank him for the same as a favor."

"Misery seeks any relief," whispered Mrs de Lacey, bestowing on her companions a significant glance, that paid no great
compliment to the old man's motives. "I incline to the opinion of the younger seaman; he supports it with substantial
professional reasons."

Mrs Wyllys suspended her questions just as long as com-
plaisance to the last speaker seemed to require, and then she
resumed them as follows, addressing her next inquiry to
Wilder.

"And how do you explain this difference in judgement,
Sir," she continued, "between two men, who ought both to
be so well qualified to decide right?"

"I believe there is a well-known proverb, which will answer
that question," returned the young man, smiling: "But some
allowance must be made for the improvements in ships, and
perhaps some little deference to the stations we have respec-
tively filled on board them."

"Both very true. Still one would think the changes of half a
dozen years cannot be so very considerable, in a profession
that is so exceedingly ancient."

"Your pardon, Madam. They require constant practice to
be known. Now I dare say that yonder worthy old tar, is
ignorant of the manner in which a ship, when pressed by her
canvass is made to cut the waves with her taffrail."

"Impossible!" cried the Admiral's widow; "the youngest
and the meanest mariner must have been struck with the
beauty of such a spectacle!"

"Yes—yes," returned the old tar, who wore the air of an

offended man, and who probably had he been ignorant of any part of his art was not just then in the temper to confess it. "Many is the proud ship that I have seen, doing the very same. And as the lady says a grand and comely sight it is!"

Wilder was confounded. He bit his lip like one who was over reached either by excessive ignorance or exceeding cunning; but the self-complacency of Mrs de Lacey spared him the necessity of an immediate reply.

"It would have been an extraordinary circumstance truly," she said, "that a man should have grown white-headed on the seas, and never have been struck with so noble a spectacle. But then, my honest tar, you appear to be wrong in overlooking the striking faults in yonder ship, which this—a—a—this gentleman has just, and so properly, named."

"I do not call them faults, your ladyship. Such is the way, my late brave and excellent commander always had his own ship rigged, and I am bold to say, that a better seaman or a more honest man never served in his Majesty's fleet."

"And you have served the King? How was your beloved commander named?"

"How should he be; by us who knew him well, he was called Fair-Weather, for it was always smooth-water and prosperous times under his orders—though on shore he was known as the gallant and victorious Rear-Admiral de Lacey."

"And did my late revered and skilful husband cause his ships to be rigged in this manner!" said the Widow, with a tremor in her voice that bespoke how much, and how truly, she was overcome by surprise and gratified pride.

The aged tar lifted his bending frame from the stone, gazed wistfully at the relict of him he had just named, and bowing low, he answered—

"If I have the honor of seeing my Admiral's lady, it will prove a joyful sight to my old eyes. Sixteen years did I serve in his own ship, and five more in the same squadron. I dare say, your ladyship may have heard him speak of the captain of the main-top, Bob Bunt."

"I dare say—I dare say—He loved to talk of those who served him faithfully."

"Ay, God bless him, and make his memory glorious! He was a kind officer, and one that never forgot a friend, whether his duty kept him on a yard, or in the cabin. He was the sailor's friend, that very same Admiral!"

"This is a grateful man," said Mrs de Lacey, wiping a tear from her eye, "and I dare say, a most competent judge of a vessel. And are you quite sure, worthy friend, that my late, revered husband had all his ships arranged like the one, of which we have been talking?"

"Very sure, Madam; for with my own hands did I assist to rig them."

"Even to the bobstays?"

"And the gammonings, my Lady. Were the Admiral, alive and here, he would call yon, a safe and well fitted ship, as I am ready to swear."

Mrs de Lacey turned with an air of great dignity and entire decision to Wilder, as she continued—

"I have then made a small mistake in memory, which is not surprising, when one recollects that he who taught me so much of the profession is no longer here to continue his lessons. We are much obliged to you, Sir, for your opinion, but we must think that you have overrated the danger."

"On my honor, Madam," interrupted Wilder, laying his hand on his heart, and speaking with singular emphasis, "I am sincere in what I say. I do affirm, that I believe there will be great danger in embarking in yonder ship, and I call Heaven to witness, that in so saying, I am actuated by no malice to her commander, her owners, or any connected with her."

"We dare say, Sir, you are very sincere. We only think you a little in error," returned the Admiral's Widow with a commiserating and what she intended for a condescending smile. "We are your debtors for your good intentions at least. Come, worthy veteran. We must not part here. You will gain admission, by knocking at my door, and we shall talk further of these matters."

Then bowing coolly to Wilder, she led the way up the garden followed by all her companions. The step of Mrs de Lacey was proud like the tread of one conscious of all her advantages, while that of Wyllys was slow as if she were buried in thought. Gertrude kept close at the side of the latter, her face hid beneath the shade of a gipsy hat. But Wilder, fancied that he could discover the stolen and anxious glance that she threw back towards one, who had excited a decided emotion in her sensitive bosom, though it was a feeling no more attractive than alarm. He lingered until they were lost amid the shrubbery; then turning to pour out his disappointment on his brother tar, he found that the old man, had made such good use of his time, as to be already within the gate, most probably felicitating himself on the prospect of reaping the reward of his recent adulation.

# Chapter IX

"He ran this way, and leap'd this orchard wall."
*Romeo and Juliet*, II.i.5.

WILDER RETIRED from the field like a defeated man. Accident, or as he was willing to term it, the sycophancy of the old mariner, had counteracted his own little artifice, and he was now left without the remotest chance of being again favored with such another opportunity of effecting his purpose. We shall not, at this period of the narrative enter into a detail of the feelings and policy which induced our adventurer to plot against the apparent interests of those with whom he had so recently associated himself; it is enough for our present object that the facts themselves should be distinctly set before the reader.

The return of the disappointed young sailor, towards the town, was moody, and slow. More than once he stopped short in the descent and fastened his eyes for minutes together on the different vessels in the harbor. But in these frequent halts no evidence of the particular interest he took in any one of the ships escaped him. Perhaps his gaze at the Southern trader was longer and more earnest than at any other, though his eye, at times, wandered curiously, and even anxiously, over every craft that lay within the shelter of the haven.

The customary hour for exertion had now arrived, and the sounds of labor were beginning to be heard, issuing from every quarter of the place. The songs of the mariners were rising on the calm of the morning with their peculiar intonations and long-drawn cadences. The ship in the inner harbor was among the first to furnish this proof of the industry of her people and of her approaching departure. It was only as these movements caught his eye that Wilder seemed to be thoroughly awakened from his abstraction and to pursue his observations with an undivided mind. He saw the seamen ascending the rigging, in that lazy manner which is so strongly contrasted by their activity in moments of need, and here and there, a human form was showing itself on the black and ponderous yards. In a few moments the foretopsail fell from its compact compass on the yard, into graceful and care-less festoons. This the attentive Wilder well knew, was among all trading vessels the signal of sailing. In a few more minutes the lower angles of this important sail were drawn to the ex-tremities of the corresponding spar beneath, and then the heavy yard was seen slowly ascending the mast, dragging after it the opening folds of the sail, until the latter was tightened at all its edges, displaying itself in one broad, snow-white sheet of canvass. Against this wide surface the light currents of air fell and as often receded, the sail bellying and collapsing in a manner to show that as yet they were powerless. At this point the preparations appeared suspended, as if the mariners, having thus invited the breeze, were awaiting to see if their invocation was likely to be attended with success.

It was a natural transition for him who so closely observed these indications of departure in the ship so often named to turn his eyes on the vessel which lay without the fort, in order to witness the effect so manifest a signal had produced in her also. But the closest and the keenest scrutiny could detect no sign of any bond of interest between the two. While the former was making the movements just described, the latter lay at her anchors, without the smallest proof that man existed within the mass of her black and inanimate hull. So quiet and motionless did she seem, that one, who had never been instructed in the matter, might readily have believed her a fixture in the sea; some symmetrical and enormous excres-cence thrown up by the waves, with its mazes of lines and pointed fingers, or one of those fantastic monsters that are believed to exist in the bottom of the ocean, darkened by the fogs and tempests of ages. To the understanding eye of Wilder, however, she exhibited a very different spectacle. He easily saw, through all this, apparently, drowsy quietude, those signs of readiness which none but a seaman could dis-cover. The cable, instead of stretching in a long declining line towards the water, was "short" or, nearly "up and down" as it is equally termed in technical language, just "scope" enough being allowed outboard to resist the power of the lively tide that acted on the deep keel of the vessel. All her boats were in the water, so disposed and prepared as to convince him they were in a state to be employed in towing in the shortest possible time. Not a sail, or a yard was out of its place, under-going those repairs and examinations, which the mariner is wont to make, when lying within the security of a suitable haven, nor was there a single rope wanting, amid the hundreds which interlaced the blue sky that formed the background of the picture, that might be necessary in bringing every art of facilitating motion into use. In short, the vessel while seeming least prepared, was most in a condition to move, or if neces-sary to resort to her means of offence and defence. The boarding-nettings it is true were triced to the rigging, as on the previous day, but a sufficient apology was to be found for this act of extreme caution, in the war which exposed her to attacks from the light French cruisers, that so often ranged from the islands of the West-Indies along the whole coast of the continent, and in the position the ship had taken without the ordinary defences of the harbor. In this state, the vessel, to one who knew her real character, appeared like some beast of prey, or venomous reptile, that lay in an assumed lethargy to delude the unconscious victim within the limits of its leap or nigh enough to receive the deadly blow of its fangs.

Wilder shook his head, in a manner which said plainly enough, how well he understood this treacherous tranquility, and continued his walk towards the town, with the same de-liberate step as before. He had whiled away many minutes unconsciously, and would probably have lost the reckoning of as many more, had not his attention been suddenly diverted by a slight touch on the shoulder. Starting at this unexpected diversion, he turned and saw that, in his dilatory progress, he had been overtaken by the seaman whom he had last seen in that very society in which he would have given so much to have been included himself.

"Your young limbs should carry you ahead, Master," said the latter, when he had succeeded in attracting the attention of Wilder, "like a 'Mudian going with a clean full, and yet I have forereached upon you with my old legs, in such a man-ner as to bring us again within hail."

"Perhaps you enjoy the extraordinary advantage of 'cutting the waves with your taffrail,'" returned Wilder with a sneer. "There can be no accounting for the head-way one makes when sailing in that remarkable manner."

"I see, brother, you are offended that I followed your motions, though in so doing I did no more than obey a signal of your own setting. Did you expect an old sea-dog like me, one who has stood his watch so long in a flag-ship, to confess ignorance in any matter that of right belongs to blue water? How the devil was I to know, that there is not some sort of craft, among the thousands that are getting into fashion, which sails best stern foremost! They say a ship is modelled from a fish, and if such be the case, it is only to make one after the fashion of a crab or an oyster, to have the very thing you named."

"It is well, old man; you have had your reward I suppose, in a handsome present from the Admiral's Widow, and you may now lie by for a season, without caring much as to the manner in which they build their ships in future. Pray, do you intend to shape your course much further down this hill?"

"Until I get to the bottom."

"I am glad of it, for it is my especial intention to go up it again. As we say at sea when our conversation is ended, 'a good time to you.'"

The old seaman laughed, when he saw the young man turn abruptly on his heel, and begin to retrace the very ground along which he had just before descended.

"Ah! you have never sailed with a rear-admiral," he said, continuing his own course in the former direction, and picking his way with a care suited to his age and infirmities. "No, there is no getting the finish, even at sea, without a cruise or two under a flag and that at the mizzen, too!"

"Intolerable old hypocrite!" muttered Wilder between his teeth. "The rascal has seen better days, and is now perverting his knowledge to juggle a foolish woman. I am well quit of the knave, who I dare say has adopted begging for his trade, when lying is unproductive. I will go back. The coast is now clear, and who can say what may happen next."

Most of the foregoing paragraph was actually uttered, in the suppressed manner already described, while the rest was merely meditated, which, considering the fact that our adventurer had no auditor, was quite as well as if he had spoken it through a trumpet. The expectation thus vaguely expressed, however, was not likely to be soon realized. Wilder sauntered up the hill, endeavoring to assume the unconcerned air of an idler if by chance his return should excite attention, but, though he lingered long in open view of the windows of Mrs de Lacey's villa, he was not able to catch another glimpse of its tenants. There were very evident symptoms of the approaching journey, in the trunks and packages that left the building for the town, and in the hurried and busy manner of the few servants that he occasionally saw, but it would seem that the principal personages of the establishment had withdrawn into the secret recesses of the building, probably for the very natural purpose of confidential communion and affectionate leave-taking. He was turning, vexed and disappointed from his anxious and fruitless watch, when he once more heard female voices on the inner side of the low wall against which he had been leaning. The sounds approached, nor was it long before his quick ears again recognised the musical voice of Gertrude.

"It is tormenting ourselves without sufficient reason, my dear Madam," she said, as the speakers drew sufficiently nigh to be distinctly overheard, "to allow any thing that may have fallen from such a—such an individual to make the slightest impression."

"I feel the justice of what you say, my love," returned the mournful voice of her governess, "and yet am I so weak as to be unable entirely to shake off a sort of superstitious feeling on this subject. Gertrude, would you not wish to see that youth again?"

"Me, Ma'am!" exclaimed her élève in a sort of alarm. "Why should you or I, wish to see an utter stranger, again—and one so low—not low perhaps—but one is surely not altogether a very suitable companion for"—

"Well-born ladies, you would say. Why do you imagine the young man to be so much our inferior?"

Wilder thought there was a melody in the intonations of the youthful voice of the maiden as she answered which in some measure excused the personality.

"I am certainly not so fastidious in my notions of birth and station as aunt de Lacey," she said, laughing, "but I should forget some of your own instructions, dear Mrs Wyllys, did I not feel that education and manners make a sensible difference in the opinions and characters of all us poor mortals."

"Very true, my child. But I confess I saw or heard nothing that induces me to believe the young man of whom we are speaking either uneducated or vulgar. On the contrary his language and pronunciation were those of a gentleman, and his air was quite suited to his utterance. He had the frank and simple manner of his profession, but you are not now to learn that youths of the first families in the Provinces or even in the Kingdom are often placed in the service of the Marine."

"But they are officers, dear Madam, this—this individual wore the dress of a common mariner."

"Not altogether. It was finer in its quality and more tasteful in its fashion than is customary. I have known Admirals do the same in their moments of relaxation. Sailors of condition, often love to carry about them, the testimonials of their profession, without any of the trappings of their rank."

"You then think he was an officer—perhaps in the King's service?"

"He might well have been so. Though the fact that there is no cruiser in the port would seem to contradict it. But it was not so trifling a circumstance that awakened the unaccountable interest that I feel. Gertrude, my love, it was my fortune to have been much with seamen in early life. I seldom see one of that age, and of that spirited and manly mien without feeling emotion. But I tire you—let us talk of other things."

"Not in the least, dear Madam," Gertrude hurriedly interrupted. "Since you think the stranger a gentleman there can be no harm—that is, it is not quite so improper, I believe, to speak of him. Can there then be the danger he would make us think, in trusting ourselves in a ship of which we have had so good a report?"

"There was a strange, I had almost said—wild admixture of irony and concern in his manner, that is inexplicable! He certainly uttered nonsense part of the time, but then he did not appear to do it, without a serious object. Gertrude, you are not as familiar with nautical expressions as myself, and perhaps you are ignorant that your good aunt, in her admiration of a profession that she has certainly a right to love, sometimes makes"—

"I know it—I know it. At least I often think so," the other interrupted, in a manner which plainly manifested that she found no pleasure in dwelling on the disagreeable subject. "It was exceedingly presuming, Madam, in a stranger, however, to amuse himself, if he did it, with so amiable and so trivial a weakness, if indeed weakness it be."

"It was," Mrs Wyllys steadily continued; "and yet he did not appear to me like one of those empty minds, that find pleasure in exposing the follies of others. You may remember, Gertrude, that yesterday while at the ruin, Mrs de Lacey made some remarks expressive of her admiration of a ship under sail."

"Yes, yes. I remember them," said the niece a little impatiently.

"One of her terms was particularly incorrect, as I happen to know from my own familiarity with the language of sailors."

"I thought as much, by the expression of your eye," returned Gertrude; "but"—

"Listen, my love. It certainly was not remarkable that a lady should make a trifling error in the use of so peculiar a language, but it is singular, that a seaman himself should commit the same fault in precisely the same words. This the youth of whom we are speaking did; and what is no less surprising the old man assented to the same just as if they had been correctly uttered."

"Perhaps," said Gertrude in a low tone, "they may have heard that attachment to this description of conversation is a foible of Mrs de Lacey. I am sure after this, dear Madam, you cannot any longer consider the stranger a gentleman."

"I should think no more about it, love, were it not for a feeling that I can neither account for nor define. I would I could, again, see him"—

A slight exclamation from her companion interrupted her words, and the next instant the subject of her thoughts leaped the wall apparently in quest of the rattan that had fallen at the feet of Gertrude, occasioning her alarm. After apologizing for his intrusion, and recovering his lost property, Wilder was slowly preparing to retire, as if nothing had happened. There was a softness and delicacy in his manner, which was probably intended to convince the younger of the ladies that he was not entirely without some claims to the title she had so recently denied him, and which was certainly not without its effect. The countenance of Mrs Wyllys was pale; her lip quivered, though the steadiness of her voice proved it was not with alarm, and she hastily said—

"Remain, a moment, Sir, if your presence is not required elsewhere. There is something so remarkable in this meeting that I could wish to improve it."

Wilder bowed, and again faced the ladies whom he had just been about to quit, like one who felt he had no right to intrude a moment longer than had been necessary to recover that, which had been lost by his pretended awkwardness. When Mrs Wyllys found that her wish was so unexpectedly realized, she hesitated as to the manner in which she should next proceed.

"I have been thus bold, Sir," she said, in some embarrassment, "on account of the opinion you so lately expressed concerning the vessel which now lies ready to put to sea, the instant she is favored with a wind."

"The Royal Caroline!" Wilder carelessly added.

"That is her name, I believe."

"I hope, Madam, that nothing which I have said," he hastily continued, "will have an effect to prejudice you against the ship. I will pledge myself that she is made of excellent materials, and then I have not the least doubt but she is very ably commanded."

"And, yet, have you not hesitated to say, that you consider a passage in this very vessel more dangerous than one in any other ship that will probably leave a port of the Provinces in many months to come!"

"I did," answered Wilder, with a manner not to be mistaken.

"Will you explain your reasons for this opinion?"

"If I remember rightly, I gave them to the lady whom I had the honor to see an hour ago."

"That individual, sir, is no longer here, neither is she to trust her person in the vessel. This young lady and myself, with our attendants will be the only passengers."

"I understood it so," returned Wilder, keeping his gaze riveted on the speaking countenance of Gertrude.

"And now that there is no apprehension of any mistake may I ask you to repeat the reasons why you think there will be danger in embarking in the 'Royal Caroline?'"

Wilder started, and even had the grace to colour when he met the attentive look with which Mrs Wyllys awaited his answer.

"You would not have me repeat, Madam," he stammered, "what I have already said on the subject?"

"I would not, Sir. Once will suffice for such an explanation. Still I am persuaded that you have other reasons for your words."

"It is exceedingly difficult for a seaman to speak of ships in any other than technical language, which must be the next thing to being unintelligible to one of your sex. You have never been at sea, Madam?"

"Very often."

"Then I may hope possibly to make myself understood. You must be conscious, Madam, that no small part of the safety of a ship depends on the very material point of keeping her right side uppermost. Sailors call it, 'making her stand up.' Now I need not say, I am quite sure to a lady of your intelligence, that if the 'Caroline' fall on her beam ends, there will be imminent hazard to all on board."

"Nothing can be clearer; the same risk would be incurred in any other vessel."

"Without doubt if any other vessel should trip. But I have pursued my profession for many years without meeting with such a misfortune but once. Then the fastenings of her bow-sprit"—

"Are good as ever came from the hand of rigger," said a voice behind them.

The whole party turned, and beheld at a little distance the old seaman already introduced, mounted on some object on the other side of the wall, against which he was very coolly leaning, and whence he overlooked the whole of the interior of the grounds.

"I have been to the water side to look at the boat, at the wish of Madam de Lacey, the widow of my late noble commander and Admiral, and let other men think as they may, I am ready to swear, that the 'Royal Caroline' has as well secured a bowsprit, as any ship that carries the British flag! Ay, nor is that all I will say in her favor. She is throughout neatly and lightly sparred, and has no more of a wall side, than the walls of yonder church tumble home. I am an old man and my reckoning is got to the last leaf of the Log-book, therefore it is little interest that I have or can have in this brig or that schooner, but thus much will I say, which is, that it is just as wicked and as little likely to be forgiven to speak scandal of a wholesome and stout ship, as it is to talk amiss of a Christian!"

The old man spoke with energy and with a show of honest indignation, which did not fail to make an impression on the ladies, at the same time that it brought certain ungrateful admonitions to the conscience of the understanding Wilder.

"You perceive, Sir," said Mrs Wyllys, after waiting in vain for the reply of the young seaman, "that it is very possible for two men of equal advantages to disagree on a professional point. Which am I to believe?"

"Whichever your own excellent sense should tell you is most likely to be correct. I repeat, and in a sincerity to whose truth I call Heaven to witness, that no mother or sister of mine should with my consent embark in the Caroline!"

"This is incomprehensible!" said Mrs Wyllys, turning to Gertrude and speaking only for her ear. "My reason tells me we have been trifled with by this young man and yet his protestations are so earnest and apparently so sincere that I cannot shake off the impression they have made. To which of the two, my love, do you feel most inclined to yield credence?"

"You know how very ignorant I am, dear Madam, of all these things," said Gertrude, dropping her eyes to the faded sprig she was plucking, "but to me that old wretch has a very presuming and vicious look."

"You then think the younger most entitled to belief?"

"Why not; since you think he is a gentleman?"

"I know not that his superior situation in life entitles him to greater credit. Men often obtain such advantages only to abuse them. I am afraid, Sir," continued Mrs Wyllys, turning to the expecting Wilder, "that unless you see fit to be more frank, we shall be compelled to refuse you our faith and must persevere in the intention to profit by the opportunity of the 'Royal Caroline' to get to the Carolinas."

"From the bottom of my heart, Madam, I regret the determination."

"It may still be in your power to change it, by being explicit."

Wilder appeared to muse; once or twice his lips moved as if he were about to speak. Mrs Wyllys and Gertrude awaited his intentions with intense interest but after a long and seemingly hesitating pause, he disappointed both, by saying—

"I am sorry that I have not the ability to make myself better understood. It can only be the fault of my dulness, for I again affirm that the danger is as apparent to my eyes as the sun at noon-day."

"Then must we continue blind, Sir," returned Mrs Wyllys, with a cold salute. "I thank you for your good intentions, but you cannot blame us for not consenting to follow advice which is buried in so much obscurity. Although in our own grounds, we shall be pardoned the rudeness of leaving you. The hour appointed for our departure has arrived."

Wilder returned the grave bow of Mrs Wyllys with one quite as formal as her own, though he bent with greater grace and with more cordiality to the deep hurried courtesy of Gertrude Grayson. He remained in the precise spot in which they left him, until he saw them enter the villa, and he even fancied he could catch the anxious expression of another timid glance which the latter threw in his direction as her light form appeared to float from before his sight. Placing one hand on the wall, the young sailor then leaped into the highway. As his feet struck the ground the slight shock seemed to awake him from his abstraction, and he became conscious that he stood within six feet of the old mariner who had now twice stepped rudely between him and the object he had so much at heart. The latter did not allow him time to give utterance to his disappointment, for he was the first, himself to speak.

"Come, brother," he said in friendly, confidential tones, and shaking his head like one, who wished to show to his companion that he was aware of the deception he had attempted to practice, "come, brother, you have stood far enough on this tack, and it is time to try another. I've been young myself in my time, and I know what a hard matter it is to give the devil a wide berth, when there is fun to be found in sailing in his company. But old age brings us to our reckonings, and when life is getting on short allowance with a poor fellow, he begins to think of being sparing of his tricks, just as water is saved in a ship when the calms set in, after it has been split about decks like rain, for weeks and months on end. Thought comes with gray hairs, Master, and no one is the worse for providing a little of it, among his other small stores!"

"I had hoped, when I gave you the bottom of this hill and took the top myself," returned Wilder, without even deigning to look at his disagreeable companion, "that we had parted company forever. As you seem, however, to prefer the high ground, I leave you to enjoy it, at your leisure; I shall now descend into the town."

The old man shuffled after him with a gait that rendered it difficult for Wilder, who was by this time in a fast walk, to outstrip him, without resorting to the undignified expedient of actual flight. Vexed alike with himself and his tormentor he was tempted to offer some violence to the latter, and then recalled to his recollection by the dangerous impulse, he moderated his pace and continued his route, with a determination to be superior to any emotions that such a pitiful object could excite.

"You were going under such a press of sail, young master," said the stubborn old mariner, who still kept a pace or two in his rear, "that I had to set every thing to hold way with you; but you now seem to be getting reasonable, and we may as well lighten the passage by a little profitable talk. You had nearly made the oldish lady believe the good ship 'Royal Caroline' was the flying Dutchman"—

"And why did you see fit to undeceive her?" bluntly demanded Wilder.

"Would you have a man who has followed blue water fifty years, scandalize wood and iron after so wild a manner! The character of a ship is as dear to an old sea-dog, as the character of his wife or his sweetheart."

"Harkee, friend, you live I suppose like other people, by eating and drinking?"

"A little of the first, and a good deal of the last," returned the other with a chuckle.

"And you get both, like most seamen, by hard work, great risk, and the severest exposure."

"Hum; 'making our money like horses, and spending it like asses.' That is said to be the way with us all."

"Now, then, you have an opportunity of making some with less labour; you may spend it to suit your own fancy. Will you engage in my service for a few hours, with this for your bounty, and as much more for wages, provided you deal honestly?"

The old man stretched out a hand and took the guinea which Wilder had showed over his shoulder, without appearing to deem it at all necessary to face his recruit.

"It's no sham?" said the latter, stopping to ring the metal on a stone.

" 'Tis gold as pure as ever came from the mint."

The other very coolly pocketed the coin and then with a certain hardened and decided way, as if he were ready for any thing, he demanded—

"What hen-roost am I to rob for this?"

"You are to do no such feat. You have only to perform a little of that, which I fancy you are no stranger to. Can you keep a false log?"

"Ay, and swear to it, on occasion. I understand you. You are tired of twisting the truth like a new laid rope, and you wish to turn the job over to me."

"Something so. You must unsay all you have said concerning yonder ship, and as you have had cunning enough to get on the weather of Mrs de Lacey, you must improve your advantage, by making matters a little worse than I have represented them to be. Tell me, that I may judge of your qualifications—did you, in truth, ever sail with the worthy rear-admiral?"

"As I am an honest and religious christian, I never heard of the honest old man, before yesterday. Oh, you may trust me in these matters! I am not likely to spoil a history for want of facts."

"I think you will do. Now listen to my plan—"

"Stop, worthy messmate," interrupted the other. "Stones

can hear, they say on shore. We sailors know that the pumps have ears on board a ship. Have you ever seen such a place as the Foul-Anchor tavern in this town?"

"I have been there."

"I hope you like it well enough to go again. Here we will part. You shall haul on the wind, being the lightest sailer, and make a stretch or two, among these houses until you are well to windward of yonder church. You will then have plain sailing down upon hearty Joe Joram's, where is to be found as snug an anchorage, for an honest trader, as in any inn in the colonies. I will keep away down this hill, and considering the difference in our rate of sailing, we shall not be long after one another in port."

"And what is to be gained by so much manœuvring? Can you listen to nothing which is not steeped in rum!"

"You offend me by the word. You shall see what it is to send a sober messenger on your errands when the time comes. But suppose we are seen speaking each other in the highway—why, as you are in such low repute, just now, I shall lose my character with the ladies, altogether."

"There may be reason in that. Hasten, then, to meet me, for as they spoke of embarking soon, there is not a minute to lose."

"No fear of their breaking ground so suddenly," returned the old man, holding the palm of his hand above his head to catch the wind. "There is not yet air enough, to cool the burning cheeks of that young beauty, and depend on it, the signal will not be given to them, until the sea breeze is fairly come in."

Wilder waved his hand, and stepped lightly along the road, the other had indicated to him, ruminating on the figure which the fresh and youthful charms of Gertrude had extorted from one even as old and as coarse as his new ally. His companion followed his person, for a moment, with an amused look, and an ironical cast of the eye, and then he also quickened his pace, in order to reach the place of rendezvous in sufficient season.

# Chapter X

"Forewarn him, that he use no scurrilous words."
*The Winter's Tale*, IV.iv.213.

A s WILDER approached the "Foul Anchor," he beheld
every symptom of a strong excitement existing within
the bosom of the hitherto peaceful town. More than half
the women, and perhaps one fourth of all the men, within a
reasonable proximity of that well known inn, were assembled
before its door, listening to one of the former sex, who declaimed in tones so shrill and penetrating as not to leave the
proprietors of the curious and attentive countenances, in the
outer circle of the crowd, the smallest rational ground of
complaint, on the score of impartiality. Our adventurer hesitated, with the sudden consciousness of one but newly embarked in such enterprises as that in which he had so recently
enlisted, when he first saw these signs of commotion; nor did
he determine to proceed, until he caught a glimpse of his
aged confederate elbowing his way through the mass of
bodies, with a perseverance and energy that promised to
bring him right speedily into the very presence of her who
uttered such piercing plaints. Encouraged by this example,
the young man advanced, but was content to take his position, for the moment, in a situation that left him entire command of his limbs, and consequently in a condition to make a
timely retreat should the latter measure prove expedient.

"I call on you, Earthly Potter, and you, Preserved Green,
and you, Faithful Wanton," cried Desire, as he came within
hearing, pausing to catch a morsel of breath, before she proceeded in this affecting appeal to the neighbourhood, "and
you too, Upright Crook, and you too, Relent Flint, and you,
Wealthy Poor,* to be witnesses and testimonials in my behalf!
You, and all and each of you can qualify, if you will, that I
have ever been a slaving and loving consort of the man who
has deserted me in my age, leaving so many of his own children on my hands to feed and to rear, besides"—

*This whimsical collection of names may strike the reader as overcharged,
and yet they are all taken from the local history of Rhode Island.

"What certainty is there," interrupted the Landlord of the "Foul Anchor" most inopportunely, "that the good-man has absconded? It was a merry day, the one that is just gone, and it is quite in reason to believe that your husband was, like some others I can name, a thing I shall not be so unwise as to do, a little of what I call 'how-come-ye-so,' and that his nap holds on longer than common. I'll engage we shall all see the honest tailor creeping out of some of the barns shortly, as fresh and as ready for his bitters as if he had not wet his throat with cold water since the last time of general rej'icing."

A low but pretty general laugh followed this effort of tavern wit, though it failed in exciting even a smile on the disturbed visage of Desire, which, by its doleful outline, appeared to have taken leave of all its risible properties forever.

"Not he—not he—" exclaimed the disconsolate consort of the good-man; "he has not the heart to get himself courageous in loyal drinking on such an occasion as a merrymaking on account of his Majesty's glory; he was a man altogether for work, and it is chiefly for his hard labor that I have reason to complain. After being so long used to rely on his toil, it is a sore cross to a dependant woman to be thrown suddenly and altogether on herself for support. But I'll be revenged on him, if there's law to be found in Rhode-Island or in the Providence Plantations! Let him dare to keep his pitiful image out of my sight the lawful time, and then when he returns, he shall find himself as many a vagabond has been before him, without wife as he will be without a house to lay his graceless head in."* Then catching a glimpse of the inquiring face of the old seaman, who by this time had worked his way to her very side, she abruptly added—"Here is a stranger in the place, and one who has lately arrived! Did you meet, a straggling runaway, friend, in your journey hither?"

---

*It would seem from this declaration that certain legal authorities, who have contended that the community is indebted to Desire for the unceremonious manner of clipping the nuptial knot, which is so well known to exist, even to this hour, in the community of which she was a member are entirely in the wrong. It evidently did not take its rise in her example, since she clearly alludes to it, as a means before resorted to, by the injured innocents of her own sex.

"I had too much trouble in navigating my old hulk on dry land, to log the name and rate of every craft I fell in with," returned the other, with infinite composure; "and yet now you speak of such a thing, I do remember to have come within hail, of a poor fellow, just about the beginning of the morning watch somewhere, here-away, up in the bushes, between this town and the bit of a ferry that carries one on to the main."

"What sort of a man was he?" demanded five or six anxious voices, in a breath; among which the tones of Desire, however, maintained their supremacy, rising above those of all the others, like the strains of a first-rate artist flourishing a quaver above the more modest thrills of the rest of the troupe.

"What sort of a man! Why, a fellow with his arms rigged athwart-ship, and his legs stepped like those of all other christians to be sure—but now you speak of it, I remember that he had a bit of a sheep-shank in one of his legs, and that he rolled a good deal as he went ahead."

"It was he!" added the same chorus of voices. Five or six of the speakers, instantly stole, out of the throng, with the intention of hurrying after the delinquent in order to secure the payment of certain small balances of account, in which the unhappy and much traduced good-man stood indebted to the several parties. Had we leisure to record the manner, in which these praiseworthy efforts to save an honest penny were conducted, the reader might find much subject of amusement in the secret diligence with which each worthy tradesman endeavored to outwit his neighbor on the occasion, as well as in the cunning subterfuges which were adopted to conceal their real designs when all met at the ferry, deceived and disappointed in their object. As Desire, however, had neither legal demand on, nor hope of favor from her truant husband, she was content to pursue on the spot such further enquiries in behalf of the fugitive, as she saw fit to make. It is possible the pleasures of freedom, in the shape of the contemplated divorce, were already floating before her active mind, with the soothing perspective of second nuptials backed by the influence of such another picture, as might be drawn from the recollections of her first love, the whole having a manifest tendency to pacify her awakened spirit, and to give a certain

portion of directness and energy to the subsequent interrogatories.

"Had he a thieving look?" she demanded, without attending to the manner in which she was so suddenly deserted by
all those who had just expressed the strongest sympathy in
her loss, "was he a man, that had the air of a sneaking run-a-
way?"

"As for his head-piece, I will not engage to give a very true
account," returned the old mariner, "though, he had the look
of one who had been kept a good deal of his time in the
lee-scuppers. If I should give an opinion, the poor devil has
had too much"—

"Idle time, you would say; yes, yes, it has been his misfortune to be out of work a good deal latterly, and wickedness
has got into his head, for want of something better to think
of. Too much"—

"Wife," interrupted the old man, emphatically. Another
general and a far less equivocal laugh at the expense of Desire,
succeeded this blunt declaration. Nothing intimidated by such
a manifest assent to the opinion of the hardy seaman, the undaunted virago, resumed—

"Ah! you little know the suffering and forbearance I have
endured with the man in so many long years. Had the fellow
you met the look of one, who had left an injured woman
behind him?"

"I can't say that there was any thing about him, which said
in so many words that the woman he had left at her moorings
was more or less injured;" returned the tar, with commendable discrimination, "but there was enough about him to
show, that, however and wherever he may have stowed his
wife, if wife she was, he had not seen fit to leave all her outfit
at home. The man had plenty of female toggery around his
neck; I suppose he found it more agreeable than her arms!"

"What!" exclaimed Desire, looking aghast, "has he dared to
rob me! What had he of mine? Not the gold beads!"

"I'll not swear they were gold."

"The villain!" continued the enraged termagant, catching
her breath, like a person that had just been submerged in water, longer than is agreeable to human nature, and forcing her
way through the crowd, with such vigor, as soon to be in a

situation to fly to her secret hordes in order to ascertain the extent of her misfortune; "the sacrilegious villain! to rob the wife of his bosom, the mother of his own children, and"—

"Well—well—" again interrupted the landlord of the "Foul Anchor," with his unseasonable voice, "I never before heard the good-man suspected of roguery, though the neighborhood was never backward in calling him chicken-hearted."

The old seaman looked the publican full in the face, with much meaning in his eye, as he answered—

"If the honest tailor never robbed any but that virago, there would be no great thieving sin to be laid to his account, for every bead he had about him, wouldn't serve to pay his ferry-age. I could carry all the gold on his neck in my eye, and see none the worse for it. But it is a shame to stop the entrance into a licensed tavern with such a mob, as if it were an embargoed port, and so I have sent the woman after her valuables, and all the idlers, as you see, in her wake."

Joe Joram gazed on the speaker like a man enthralled by some mysterious charm, neither answering nor altering the direction of his eye, for near a minute. Then suddenly breaking out in a deep and powerful laugh, as if he were not backward in enjoying the artifice, which certainly had produced the effect of removing the crowd from his own door to that of the absent tailor's, he flourished his arm, in the way of greeting and exclaimed—

"Welcome, Tarry Bob, welcome, old boy, welcome! From what cloud have you fallen, and before what wind have you been running that Newport is again your harbor?"

"Too many questions to be answered, in an open road-stead, friend Joram, and altogether too dry a subject for a husky conversation. When I am berthed in one of your inner cabins, with a mug of flip, and a kid of good Rhode-Island beef, within grappling distance, why as many questions as you choose, and as many answers, you know, as suits my appetite."

"And who's to pay the piper, honest Bob; whose ship's purser will pay your check now?" continued the publican, showing the old sailor in, however, with a readiness that seemed to contradict the doubt expressed by his words of any reward for his extraordinary civility.

"Who!" interrupted the other, displaying the money so lately received from Wilder, in such a manner that it might he seen by the few bystanders who remained, as if he would himself furnish a sufficient apology for the distinguished manner in which he was received; "who, but this gentleman? I can boast of being backed by the countenance of his Sacred Majesty himself, God bless him!"

"God bless him!" echoed several of the loyal lieges; and that too in a place which has since heard such different cries, and where the same words would now excite nearly as much surprise, though less alarm, than an earthquake.

"God bless him," repeated Joram, opening the door of an inner room, and pointing the way to his customer, "and all that are favored with his countenance. Walk in, old Bob; you shall soon grapple with half an ox."

Wilder, who had approached the outer door of the tavern as the mob receded, witnessed the retreat of the two worthies into the recesses of the house, and immediately entered the bar-room himself. While deliberating on the manner in which he should arrive at a communication with his new confederate without attracting too much attention to so odd an association, the land-lord returned in person to relieve him. After casting a hasty glance around the apartment, his look settled on our adventurer, whom he approached in a manner half-doubting, half-decided.

"What success, Sir, in looking for a ship?" he demanded, now recognizing for the first time the stranger with whom he had before held converse that morning. "More hands than places to employ them!"

"I am not sure it will so prove. In my walk on the hill I met an old seaman, who"—

"Hum—" interrupted the publican, with an intelligible, though stolen sign to follow. "You will find it more convenient, Sir, to take your breakfast in another room." Wilder followed his conductor, who left the public apartment by a different door from that by which he had led his other guest into the interior of the house, wondering at the air of mystery that the inn-keeper saw fit to assume on the occasion. After leading him by a circuitous passage, the latter showed Wilder, in profound silence, up a private stair-way into the very attic of the building. Here he rapped lightly at a door and was bid to enter, by a voice that caused our adventurer to start by its deepness and severity. On finding himself, however, in a low and confined room, he saw no other occupant than the seaman who had just been greeted by the publican as an old acquaintance, and by a name to which he might, by his attire, well lay claim to be entitled—that of *Tarry* Bob. While Wilder was staring about him, a good deal surprised at the situation in which he was placed, the landlord retired, and he found himself alone with his confederate. The latter was already engaged in discussing the fragment of the ox, just mentioned, and in quaffing of some liquid that seemed equally adapted to his taste, although sufficient time, had not, certainly, been allowed to prepare the beverage he had seen fit to order. Without allowing his visiter leisure for much further reflection the old mariner, made a motion to him to take the only vacant chair in the room, while he continued his employment on the surloin with as much assiduity as if no interruption had taken place.

"Honest Joe Joram, always makes a friend of his butcher," he said, after ending a draught that threatened to drain the mug to the bottom. "There is such a flavor about his beef, that one might mistake it for the fin of a halibut. You have been in foreign parts, shipmate, or I may now call you 'messmate,' since we are both anchored nigh the same kid—but you have doubtless been in foreign countries?"

"Often. I should else be but a miserable seaman."

"Then tell me frankly, have you ever been in the Kingdom which can furnish such rations, fish, flesh, fowl and fruits, as this very noble land of America, in which we are now both moored, and in which, as I suppose, we both of us were born!"

"It would be carrying the love of home a little too far to believe in such universal superiority," returned Wilder, willing to divert the conversation from his real object until he had time to arrange his ideas, and assure himself he had no other auditor but his visible companion. "It is generally admitted that England excels us, in all these articles."

"By whom! By your know-nothings and bold-talkers. But I, a man that has seen the four quarters of the earth and no small part of the water besides, give the lie to such empty-boasters. We are colonies, friend, we are colonies, and it is as bold in a colony to tell the mother that it has the advantage in this or that particular, as it would be in a foremast Jack to tell his officer he was wrong, though he knew it to be true. I am but a poor man, Mr—by what name may I call your honor?"

"Me! my name—Harris."

"I am but a poor man, Mr Harris, but I have had charge of a watch in my time, old and rusty as I seem, nor have I spent so many long nights on deck without keeping thoughts at work, though I may not have overhauled as much philosophy in so doing, as a paid parish priest or a fee'd lawyer. Let me tell you, it is a disheartening thing to be nothing but a dweller in a colony. It keeps down the pride and spirit of a man, and lends a hand in making him what his masters would be glad to have him. I shall say nothing of fruits and meats and other eatables that come from the land, of which both you and I have heard and know too much, unless it be to point to yonder sun and then to ask the question, whether you think King George has the power to make it shine on the bit of an island where he lives, as it shines here in his broad Provinces of America?"

"Certainly not—and yet you know that every one allows that the productions of England are so much superior"—

"Ay, ay; a colony always sails under the lee of its mother! Talk does it all, friend Harris. Talk—talk—talk. A man can talk himself into a fever, or set a ship's company by the ears. He can talk a cherry into a peach or a flounder into a whale. Now here is the whole of this long coast of America, and all her rivers and lakes and brooks swarming with such treasures as any man might fatten on, and yet his Majesty's servants, who come among us, talk of their turbots and their sole and their carp, as if the Lord had only made such fish, and the devil had let the others slip through his fingers without asking leave."

Wilder turned and fastened a look of surprise on the old man, who continued to eat, however, as if he had uttered nothing but what might be considered as a matter of course opinion.

"You are more attached to your birth-place than loyal, friend," said the young mariner, a little austerely.

"I am not fish-loyal at least. What the Lord made, one may speak of, I hope, without offence. As to the government, that is a rope twisted by the hands of man, and"—

"And what?" demanded Wilder, perceiving that the other hesitated.

"Hum. Why, I fancy man will undo his own work when he can find nothing better to busy himself in. No harm in saying that either, I hope."

"So much, that I must call your attention to the business that has brought us together. You have not so soon forgotten the earnest money you received?"

The old sailor, shoved the dish from before him, and folding his arms, he looked his companion full in the eye, as he calmly answered.

"When I am fairly enlisted in a service, I am a man to be counted on. I hope you sail under the same colours, friend Harris?"

"It would be dishonest to be otherwise. There is one thing you will excuse, before I proceed to detail my plans and wishes? I must take occasion to examine this closet, in order to be sure that we are actually alone."

"You will find little there, except the toggery of some of honest Joe's female gender. As the door is not fastened with any extraordinary care, you have only to look for yourself, since seeing is believing."

Wilder did not seem disposed to wait for this permission. He opened the door while the other was speaking, and finding that the closet actually contained little else than the articles named by his companion, he turned away like a man who was disappointed.

"Were you alone, when I entered?" he demanded, after a thoughtful pause.

"Honest Joram and yourself."

"No one else?"

"None that I saw," returned the other, his manner betraying slight uneasiness. "If you think otherwise, let us overhaul the room. Should my hand fall on a listener, the salute will not be light."

"Hold. Answer a single question. Who bade me 'enter'?"

Tarry Bob, who had arisen with a good deal of alacrity, now reflected, in his turn, for an instant, and closed his musing by indulging in a low laugh.

"Ah, I see that you have got your ideas a little jammed. A man cannot talk the same with a small portion of ox in his mouth, as if his tongue had as much sea-room, as a ship four and twenty hours out."

"Then it was you."

"I'll swear to that much," returned Bob, resuming his seat, like one who had settled the whole affair to his own entire satisfaction. "And now, friend Harris, if you are ready to lay bare your mind, I'm just as ready to look at it."

Wilder did not appear to be quite as well content with the explanation, as his companion, but he drew a chair, and prepared to open his subject.

"I am not to tell you, friend, after what you have heard and seen that I have no very strong desire that the lady with whom we have both spoken this morning and her companion, should sail in the Royal Caroline. I suppose it is enough for our purposes that you should know the fact: the reason why I prefer they should remain where they are, can be of no moment as to the duty you are to undertake."

"You need not tell an old seaman how to gather in the slack of a running idea!" cried Bob, chuckling and winking at his companion in a way that displeased the latter, by its familiarity. "I have not lived fifty years on blue water to mistake it for the skies!"

"You then fancy, Sir, that my motive is no secret to you?"

"It needs no spy-glass to see that while the old people say go, the young people would like to stay where they are."

"You do both of the young people much injustice then. Until yesterday, I never laid eyes on the person you mean."

"Ah! I see how it is, the owners of the Caroline, have not been so civil as they ought and you are paying them a small debt of thanks."

"That is possibly a means of retaliation, that might suit your taste," said Wilder, gravely; "but which is not much in accordance with mine. The whole of the parties are utter strangers to me."

"Hum. I suppose you belong to the vessel in the outer-harbor, and though you don't hate your enemies, you love your friends. We must contrive the means to coax the ladies to take passage in the slaver."

"God forbid!"

"God forbid! Now I think, friend Harris, you set up the back-stays of your conscience a little too taut. Though I cannot and do not agree with you in all you have said concerning the Royal Caroline, I see no reason to doubt that we shall have but one mind about the other vessel. I call her a wholesome-looking and well proportioned craft, and one that a king might sail in, with comfort!"

"I deny it not. Still I like her not."

"Well, I am glad of that, and since the matter is fairly before us, Master Harris, I have a word or two to say concerning that very ship. I am an old sea dog, and one not easily blinded in matters of the trade. Do you not find something that is not in character for an honest trader, in the manner in which they have laid that vessel at her anchors, without the fort, and the sleepy look she bears, at the same time that any one may see she is not built to catch oysters or to carry cattle to the islands?"

"As you have said, I think her a wholesome and a tight-built ship. Of what evil practice, however, do you suspect her? Perhaps she robs the revenue?"

"Hum. I am not sure it would be pleasant to smuggle in such a vessel, though your contraband is a merry trade after all. She has a pretty battery, as well as one can see from this distance."

"I dare say her owners are not tired of her yet, and would gladly keep her from falling into the hands of the French."

"Well, well,—I may be wrong, but unless sight is going with my years, all is not as it would be on board that slaver, provided her papers were true, and she had the lawful name to her letters of marque. What think *you*, honest Joe, in this matter?"

Wilder turned impatiently, and found that the landlord had entered the room with a step so light as to have escaped his attention, which had been drawn, to his companion, with a force that the reader will readily comprehend. The air of surprise with which Joram regarded the speaker was certainly not affected, for the question was repeated, and in still more definite terms before he saw fit to reply.

"I ask *you*, honest Joe, if you think the slaver in the outer-harbor of this port a true man?"

"You come across one, Bob, in your bold way, with such startling questions," returned the publican, casting his eyes obliquely around him as if to make sure of the character of his audience, "such stirring opinions, that really I am often non-plushed to know how to get the ideas together to make a saving answer."

"It is droll enough, truly, to see the landlord of the 'Foul Anchor' dumb-foundered," returned the old man with perfect composure in mien and eye. "I ask you, in plain English, if you do not suspect something wrong about that slaver?"

"Wrong! Good heavens, Mister Robert, recollect what you are saying. I would not for the custom of His Majesty's Lord High Admiral have any discouraging words uttered in my house against the reputation of any virtuous and fair-dealing slavers! The Lord protect me from blacking the character of any honest subject of the King!"

"Do you see nothing wrong, worthy and tender Joram, about the ship in the outer harbor?" repeated Mister Robert, without moving eye, limb or muscle.

"Well, since you press me so hard for an opinion, and see-ing that you are a customer who pays freely for what he orders, I will say, that if there is any thing unreasonable or even illegal in the deportment of the gentlemen"—

"You sail so nigh the wind, friend Joram," coolly inter-rupted the old man, "as to keep every thing shaking, your teeth included. Just bethink you of a plain answer; have you seen any thing wrong about the slaver?"

"Nothing, on my conscience then," said the Publican, puffing not unlike a cetaceous fish, that had come to the sur-face to breathe: "as I am an unworthy sinner, sitting under the preaching of good and faithful Dr Dogma, nothing—nothing."

"No! Then are you a duller man than I had rated you at! Do you *suspect* nothing?"

"Heaven protect me from suspicions. The devil besets all

our minds with doubts, but weak and evil inclined is he who submits to them! The officers and crew of that ship are free drinkers, and as generous as Princes: Moreover as they never forget to clear the score before they leave the house, I call them honest."

"And I call them pirates!"

"Pirates!" echoed Joram, fastening his eye with marked distrust on the countenance of the attentive Wilder. "Pirate, is a harsh word, Mister Robert, and should not be thrown in any gentleman's face without testimony enough to clear one in an action of defamation, should such a thing get fairly before twelve sworn and conscientious men. But I suppose you know what you say, and before whom you say it."

"I do; and now as it seems that your opinion in this matter, amounts to just nothing at all, you will please"—

"To do any thing you order," cried Joram, delighted to change the subject.

"To go and ask the customers below, if they are dry," continued the other, beckoning for the publican to retire by the way he entered, with the air of one who felt certain of being obeyed. As soon as the door was closed on the retiring landlord, he turned to his remaining companion and continued, "You seem as much struck aback, as unbelieving Joe, himself, at what you have just heard!"

"It is a harsh suspicion, and should be well supported, old man, before you venture to repeat it. What Pirate has lately been heard of on this coast?"

"There is the well-known Red Rover," returned the other, dropping his voice, and casting a furtive look around him, as if even he thought extraordinary caution was necessary in uttering the formidable name, "who may be here as well as in another place."

"But he is said to keep chiefly in the Caribbean sea."

"He is a man to be any where and every where. The King would pay him well, who put the rogue into the hands of the law!"

"A thing easier planned than executed," Wilder thoughtfully answered.

"That is as it may be. I am an old fellow, and fitter to point out the way than to go ahead. But you are like a newly fitted ship, with all your rigging tight and your spars without a warp in them. What say you to make your fortune, by selling the knaves to the King? It is only giving the devil his own, a few months sooner or later!"

Wilder started and turned away from his companion like one who was little pleased by the manner in which he expressed himself. Perceiving the necessity of a reply however, he demanded,—

"And what reason have you for believing your suspicions true, or what means have you for effecting your object, if true, in the absence of the Royal cruisers?"

"I cannot swear that I am right; but if sailing on the wrong tack, we can only go about when we find out the mistake. As to means, I confess they are easier named than mustered."

"Go, go. This is idle talk—a mere whim of your old brain," said Wilder, coldly, "and the less said the soonest mended. All this time we are forgetting our proper business. I am half inclined to think, Mister Robert, you are holding out false lights, in order to get rid of the duty for which you are already half paid."

There was a look of satisfaction in the countenance of the old tar, while Wilder was speaking, that might have struck his companion, had not the young man risen, to pace the narrow room, with a thoughtful and hurried step.

"Well, well," the former rejoined, endeavouring to disguise his contentment, in his customary selfish, but shrewd expression. "I am an old dreamer, and often have I thought myself swimming in the sea when I have been safe moored on dry land! I believe there must soon be a reckoning with the devil, in order that each may take his share of my poor carcass, and I be left the captain of my own ship. Now for your honor's orders."

Wilder returned to his seat, and disposed himself to give the necessary instructions to his confederate, in order that he might counteract all he had already said in favor of the outward-bound vessel.

# Chapter XI

—"The man is, notwithstanding, sufficient;—three
thousand ducats;—I think I may take his bond."
*The Merchant of Venice*, I.iii.25—27.

A S THE DAY advanced, the appearances of a fresh sea breeze
setting in gradually grew stronger; and, with the increase of the wind, were to be seen all the symptoms of an
intention to leave the harbour on the part of the Bristol
trader. The sailing of a large ship was an event of much more
importance in an American port, sixty years ago, than at the
present hour, when a score is frequently seen to arrive and
depart from one haven in a single day. Although claiming to
be inhabitants of one of the principal towns of the colony, the
good people of Newport did not witness the movements on
board the Caroline with that species of indolent regard which
is the fruit of satiety in sights as well as in graver things, and
with which, in the course of time, the evolutions of even a
fleet come to be contemplated. On the contrary, the wharves
were crowded with boys, and indeed with idlers of every
growth. Even many of the more considerate and industrious
of the citizens were seen loosening the close grasp they usually kept on the precious minutes, and allowing them to
escape uncounted, though not entirely unheeded, as they
yielded to the ascendancy of curiosity over interest, and
strayed from their shops, and their work-yards, to gaze upon
the noble spectacle of a moving ship.

The tardy manner in which the crew of the Caroline made
their preparations, however, exhausted the patience of more
than one time-saving citizen. Quite as many of the better sort
of the spectators had left the wharves as still remained, and
yet the vessel had spread to the breeze but the solitary sheet of
canvass which has been already named. Instead of answering
the wishes of hundreds of weary eyes, the noble ship was seen
sheering about her anchor, inclining from the passing wind,
as her bows were alternately turned to the right and to the
left, like a restless courser restrained by the grasp of the
groom, chafing his bit, and with difficulty keeping those

limbs upon the earth with which he is shortly to bound around the ring. After more than an hour of unaccountable delay, a rumour was spread among the crowd that an accident had occurred, by which some important individual, belonging to the complement of the vessel, was severely injured. But this rumour passed away also, and was nearly forgotten, when a sheet of flame issued from a bow-port of the Caroline, driving before it a cloud of curling and mounting smoke, and was succeeded by the roar of artillery. A bustle, like that which usually precedes the immediate announcement of a long ex-pected event, took place among the weary expectants on the land, and every one now felt certain, that, whatever might have occurred, it was settled that the ship should proceed.

Of all this delay, the several movements on board, the sub-sequent signal for sailing, and of the impatience in the crowd, Wilder had been a close observer. Posted with his back against the upright fluke of a condemned anchor, on a wharf a little apart from that occupied by most of the spectators, he had remained an hour in the same position, scarcely bending his look to his right hand or to his left. When the gun was fired he started, not with the nervous impulse which had made a hundred others do precisely the same thing, but to turn a glance along the streets that came within the range of his eye. From this hasty and uneasy examination, he soon returned into his former reclining posture, though the wandering of his glances, and the whole expression of his countenance, would have told an observer that some event, to which the young mariner looked forward with excessive interest, was on the eve of its consummation. As minute after minute, how-ever, rolled by, his composure was gradually restored, and a smile of satisfaction lighted his features, while his lips moved like those of a man who expressed his pleasure in a soliloquy. In the midst of these agreeable meditations, the sound of many voices met his ears; and, turning, he saw a large party within a few yards of the spot where he stood. He was not slow to detect among them the forms of Mrs Wyllys and Ger-trude, attired in such a manner as to leave no doubt that they were on the eve of embarking.

A cloud, driving before the sun, does not produce a greater change in the aspect of the earth, than was wrought in the expression of Wilder's countenance, by this unexpected sight. He was just implicitly relying on the success of an artifice, which, though sufficiently shallow, he flattered himself was deep enough to act on the timidity and credulity of woman; and, now, he was suddenly awoke from his self-gratulation, to prove the utter disappointment of his hopes. Muttering a suppressed but deep execration against the perfidy of his confederate, he shrunk as much as possible behind the fluke of the anchor, fastening his eyes sullenly on the ship.

The party which accompanied the travellers to the water side was, like all other parties made to take leave of valued friends, taciturn and restless. Those who spoke, did so with a rapid and impatient utterance, as if they wished to hurry the very separation they regretted; and the features of those who said nothing looked full of meaning. Wilder heard several affectionate and warm-hearted wishes given, and promises extorted, from youthful voices, all of which were answered in the mournful tones of Gertrude; and yet he obstinately refused to bend even a stolen look in the direction of the speakers.

At length, a footstep within a few feet of him induced a hasty glance aside. His eye met that of Mrs Wyllys. The lady started, as well as our young mariner, at the sudden recognition; but, recovering her self-possession, she observed, with admirable coolness,—

"You perceive, Sir, that we are not to be deterred from an enterprize once undertaken, by any ordinary dangers."

"I hope you may not have reason, Madam, to repent your courage."

A short, but painfully thoughtful pause succeeded, on the part of Mrs Wyllys. Casting a look behind her, in order to ascertain that she was not overheard, she drew a step nigher to the youth, and said, in a voice even lower than before—

"It is not yet too late. Give me but the shadow of a reason for what you have said, and I will wait for another ship. My feelings are foolishly inclined to believe you, young man, though my judgment tells me there is but too much probability that you trifle with our womanish fears."

"Trifle! On such a matter I would trifle with none of your sex—and least of all with you!"

"This is extraordinary! For a stranger it is inexplicable! Have you a fact, or a reason, which I can plead to the friends of my young charge?"

"You know them, already."

"Then, Sir, I am compelled, against my will, to believe your motive is one that you have some powerful considerations for wishing to conceal," coldly returned the disappointed and even mortified governess. "For your own sake, I hope it is not unworthy. I thank you for all that is well intended; if you have spoken aught which is otherwise, I forgive it."

They parted, with the restraint of people who feel that distrust exists between them. Wilder again shrunk behind his cover, maintaining a proud position, and a countenance that was grave to austerity. His situation, however, compelled him to become an auditor of most of what was now said.

The principal speaker, as was meet on such an occasion, was Mrs de Lacey, whose voice was often raised in sage admonitions and professional opinions, blended in a manner that all would admire, though none of her sex, but they who had enjoyed the singular good fortune of sharing in the intimate confidence of a flag-officer, might ever hope to imitate.

"And now, my dearest niece," concluded the relict of the rear-admiral, after exhausting her breath, and her stores of wisdom, in numberless exhortations to be careful of her health, to write often, to repeat the actual words of her private message to her brother the general, to keep below in gales of wind, to be particular in the account of any extraordinary sights she might have the good fortune to behold in the passage, and, in short, in all other matters likely to grow out of such a leave-taking, "and now, my dearest niece, I commit you to the mighty deep, and one far mightier—to him who made it. Banish from your thoughts all recollections of any thing you may have heard concerning the imperfections of the Royal Caroline, for the opinion of the aged seaman, who sailed with the lamented Admiral, assures me they are all founded in mistake." ("The treacherous villain!" muttered Wilder.) "Who spoke?" said Mrs de Lacey; but, receiving no reply, she continued. "His opinion is also exactly in accordance with my own, on more mature reflection. To be sure it is a culpable neglect to depend on bobstays and gammonings for the security of the bow-sprit, but even this is an oversight which, as my old friend has just told me, may be remedied by 'preventers and lashings.' I have written a note to the Master—Gertrude, my dear, be careful ever to call the Master of the ship *Mister* Nichols; for none, but those who bear his Majesty's commission, are entitled to be termed *Captains*; it is an honorable station, and should always be treated with reverence, it being, in fact, next in rank to a flag-officer,—I have written a note to the Master on the subject, and he will see the neglect repaired; and so, my love, God bless you; take the best possible care of yourself; write me by every opportunity; remember my kindest love to your father, and be very minute in your description of the whales."

The eyes of the worthy and kind-hearted widow were filled with tears, and there was a touch of nature, in the tremor of her voice, that produced a sympathetic feeling in all who heard her. The final parting took place under the impression of these kind emotions, and, before another minute, the oars of the boat, which bore the travellers to the ship, were stirring the water.

Wilder listened to the well known sounds with a feverish interest, that he might have found it difficult to explain to himself. A light touch on the elbow first drew his attention from the disagreeable subject. Surprised at the circumstance, he faced the intruder, who appeared to be a lad of apparently some fifteen years. A second look was necessary, to tell the abstracted young mariner that he again saw the attendant of the Rover; he who has already been introduced in our pages under the name of Roderick.

"Your pleasure?" he demanded, when his amazement, at being thus interrupted had a little subsided.

"I am directed to put these orders into your own hands," was the answer.

"Orders!" repeated the young man with a curling lip. "The authority should be respected which issues its mandates through such a messenger."

"The authority is one that it has ever proved dangerous to disobey," gravely returned the boy.

"Indeed! Then will I look into the contents without delay, lest I fall into some fatal negligence. Are you bid to wait an answer?"

On raising his eyes from the note, after breaking its seal, the young man found that the messenger had already vanished. Perceiving how useless it would be to pursue so light a form, amid the mazes of lumber that loaded the wharf, and most of the adjacent shore, he opened the letter and read as follows: —

"An accident has disabled the Master of the outward bound ship called the Royal Caroline. Her consignee is reluctant to intrust her to the officer next in rank; but sail she must. I find she has credit for speed. If you have any credentials of *character* and *competency*, profit by the occasion, and earn the station you are finally destined to fill. You have been named to some who are interested, and you have been sought diligently. If this reach you in season, be on the alert, and be decided. Show no surprise at any co-operation you may unexpectedly meet. My agents are more numerous than you probably believe. The reason is obvious; gold is yellow, though I am

Red"

The signature, the matter, and the style of this letter, left Wilder in no doubt as to its author. Casting a glance around him, he sprang into a skiff; and, before the boat of the travellers had reached the ship, that of Wilder had skimmed the water over half the distance between her and the land. As he plied his sculls with vigorous and skilful arms, he soon stood upon her decks. Forcing his way among the crowd of attendants from the shore, that are apt to cumber a departing ship, he reached the part of the vessel where a circle of busy faces told him he should find those most concerned in her fate. Until now, he had hardly breathed clearly, much less reflected on the character of his sudden enterprise. It was too late, however, to retreat, had he been so disposed, or to abandon his purpose, without incurring the hazard of exciting dangerous suspicions. A single instant served to recal his thoughts, ere he demanded, —

"Do I see the owner of the Caroline?"

"The ship is consigned to our house," returned a sedate,

deliberate, and shrewd-looking individual, in the attire of a
wealthy, thrifty trader.

"I have heard that you have need of an experienced officer."

"Experienced officers are comfortable things to an owner in
a vessel of value," returned the merchant. "I hope the Caroline is not without her portion."

"But I had heard, one to supply her commander's place for
a time, was greatly needed?"

"If her commander were incapable of doing his duty, such a
thing might certainly come to pass. Are you seeking a berth?"

"I have come to apply for the vacancy."

"It would have been wiser, had you first ascertained there
existed a vacancy to fill. But you have not come to ask authority, in such a ship as this, without sufficient testimony of your
ability and fitness?"

"I hope these documents may prove satisfactory," said
Wilder, placing in his hands a couple of unsealed letters.

During the time the other was reading the certificates, for
such they proved to be, his shrewd eye was looking over his
spectacles at the subject of their contents, and returning to the
paper, in alternate glances, in such a way as to render it very
evident that he was endeavouring to assure himself of the
fidelity of the words he read, by actual observation:

"Hum—This is certainly very excellent testimony in your
favor, young gentleman; and coming, as it does, from two so
respectable and affluent houses as Spriggs, Boggs & Tweed,
and Hammer & Hacket, entitled to great credit. A richer and
broader bottomed firm than the former, is not to be found in
his Majesty's colonies; and I have great respect for the latter,
though envious people do say that they overtrade a little."

"Since, then, you esteem them so highly, I shall not be considered hasty in presuming on their friendship."

"Not at all, not at all, Mr—a—a—" glancing his eye again
into one of the letters, "ay—Mr Wilder; there is never any
presumption in a fair offer, in a matter of business. Without
offers to sell and offers to buy, our property would never
change hands, Sir, ha, ha, ha; never change to a profit, you
know, young gentleman."

"I am aware of the truth of what you say, and therefore I
beg leave to repeat my offer."

"All perfectly fair and perfectly reasonable. But you cannot expect us, Mr Wilder, to make a vacancy expressly for you to fill, though it must be admitted that your papers are excellent. As good as the note of Spriggs, Boggs & Tweed themselves—not to make a vacancy, expressly"—

"I had supposed the Master of the ship so seriously injured"—

"Injured, but not seriously," interrupted the wary consignee, glancing his eye around at sundry shippers and one or two spectators, who were within ear-shot—"injured certainly, but not so much as to quit the vessel. No, no, gentlemen; the good ship Royal Caroline proceeds on her voyage as usual, under the care of that old and well tried mariner, Nicholas Nichols."

"Then, Sir, I am sorry to have intruded on your time at so busy a moment," said Wilder, bowing with a disappointed air, and falling back a step, as if about to withdraw.

"Not so hasty—not so hasty; bargains are not to be concluded, young man, as you let a sail fall from the yard. It is possible that your services may be of use, though not perhaps in the responsible situation of Master. At what rate do you value the title of Captain?"

"I care little for the name, provided the trust and the authority are mine."

"A very sensible youth!" muttered the discreet merchant; "and one who knows how to distinguish between the shadow and the substance! A gentleman of your good sense and character must know however that the reward is always proportioned to the nominal dignity. If I were acting for myself, in this business, the case would be materially changed, but as an agent it is a duty to consult the interest of my principal."

"The reward is of no account," said Wilder with an eagerness that might have overreached itself had not the individual with whom he was bargaining fastened his thoughts on the means of cheapening the other's services, with a steadiness from which they rarely swerved, when bent on so commendable an object as saving. "I seek for service."

"Then service you shall have; nor will you find us niggardly in the operation. You cannot expect an advance, for a run of

no more than a month, nor any perquisites in the way of
stowage, since the ship is now full to her hatches; nor, indeed, any great price in the shape of wages, since we take you
chiefly to accommodate so worthy a youth, and to honor the
recommendations of so respectable a house as Spriggs, Boggs
& Tweed—but you will find us liberal, excessive liberal—
Stay—how know we that you are the person named in the
invoi—I should say, recommendation?"

"Does not the fact of possessing the letters establish my
character?"

"It might in peaceable times, when the realm was not
scourged by war. A description of the person should have
accompanied the documents like a letter of advice with the
bill. As we take you at some risk in this matter, you are not to
be surprised that the price will be affected by the circumstance. We are liberal; I believe no house in the Colonies pays
more liberally, but then we have a character for prudence
too."

"I have already said, Sir, that the price shall not interrupt
our bargain."

"Good. There is pleasure in transacting business on such
liberal and honorable views! And yet I wish a notarial seal or
a description of the person had accompanied the letters! This
is the signature of Robert Tweed; I know it well, and would
be glad to see it at the bottom of a promissory note for ten
thousand pounds, that is, with a responsible endorser; but—
the uncertainty is much against your pecuniary interest,
young man, since we become, as it were, underwriters that
you are the individual named."

"In order that your mind may be at ease on this subject, Mr
Bale," said a voice from among the little circle that was listening with characteristic interest to the progress of the bargain,
"I can testify, or should it be necessary, qualify, to the person
of the gentleman."

Wilder turned in some haste, and in no little astonishment
to discover the acquaintance whom chance had thrown in so
extraordinary and possibly in so disagreeable a manner across
his path; and that, too, in a portion of the country where he
wished to believe himself an entire stranger. To his utter
amazement he found that the new speaker was no other than

the landlord of the "Foul Anchor."—Honest Joe stood with a perfectly composed look, and with a face that might readily have been trusted to confront a far more imposing tribunal, awaiting the result of his testimony on the wavering mind of the consignee.

"Ah! you have lodged the gentleman, for a night, and you can testify that he is a punctual paymaster and a civil inmate. But I want documents fit to be filed with the correspondence of the owners *at home*."

"I know not what sort of testimony you think fit for such good company," returned the unmoved publican, holding up his hand with an air of admirable innocence; "but if the sworn declaration of a housekeeper is of the sort you need, you are a magistrate, and may begin to say over the words at once."

"Not I, not I, man. Though a magistrate, the oath is informal, and would not be binding in law. But what do you know of the person in question?"

"That he is as good a seaman for his years as any in the colonies. There may be some of more practice and greater experience; I dare say such are to be found; but as to activity, watchfulness and prudence it would be hard to find his equal—especially for prudence."

"You then are quite certain that this person is the individual named in these papers?"

Joram received the certificates with the same admirable coolness he had maintained from the commencement, and prepared to read them with the most scrupulous care. In order to effect this necessary operation he had to put on his spectacles, for the landlord of the "Foul Anchor" was in the wane of life, and Wilder fancied that he stood during the process a notable example of how respectable depravity may become, in appearance, when supported by a reverend air.

"This is all very true, Mr Bale," continued the publican, removing his glasses and returning the papers. "They have forgotten to say any thing of the manner in which he saved the Lively Nancy off Hatteras, and how he run the Peggy and Dolly over the Savannah bar without a pilot, blowing great guns from the Northward and Eastward at the time; but I, who followed the water as you know in my younger days, have often heard both circumstances mentioned among sea-faring men, and I am a judge of the difficulty. I have an interest in this ship, neighbour Bale (for though a rich man and I a poor one we are nevertheless neighbours)—I say I have an interest in this ship since she is a vessel that seldom quits Newport without leaving something to jingle in my pocket, or I should not be here to day, to see her lift her anchor."

As the publican concluded he gave audible evidence that his visit had not gone unrewarded by raising a music that was no less agreeable to the ears of the thrifty merchant than to his own. The two worthies laughed in an understanding way and like two men who had found a particular profit in their intercourse with the Royal Caroline. The latter then beckoned Wilder apart, and after a little further preliminary discourse the terms of the young mariner's engagement were finally settled. The true master of the ship was to remain on board, both as a security for the insurance and in order to preserve her reputation, but it was frankly admitted that his hurt, which was no less than a broken leg, and which the surgeons were then setting, would probably keep him below for a month to come. During the time he was kept from his duty his functions were to be discharged by our adventurer. These arrangements occupied another hour, and then the consignee left the vessel perfectly satisfied with the prudent and frugal manner in which he had discharged his duty towards his principal. Before stepping into the boat, however, with a view to be equally careful of his own interests, he took an opportunity to request the publican to make a proper and legal affidavit of all that he knew "of his own knowledge," concerning the officer just engaged. Honest Joram was liberal of his promises, but as he saw no motive, now that all was so happily effected, for incurring useless risks, he contrived to evade their fulfilment, finding no doubt his apology for this breach of faith in the absolute poverty of his information when the subject came to be duly considered in his own mind.

It is unnecessary to relate the bustle, the reparation of half-forgotten and consequently neglected business, the duns, good-wishes, injunctions to execute commissions in some distant port and all the confused and seemingly interminable duties that crowd themselves into the last ten minutes that precede the sailing of a merchant vessel, more especially if she is fortunate or rather unfortunate enough to have passengers. A certain class of men quit a vessel in such a situation with the reluctance that they would part with any other well established means of profit, creeping down her sides as lazily as the leech, filled to repletion, rolls from his bloody repast. The common seaman with an attention divided by the orders of the pilot and the adieus of acquaintances runs in every direction but the right one and perhaps at the only time in his life seems ignorant of the uses of the ropes he has so long been accustomed to handle. Notwithstanding all these vexatious delays and customary incumbrances, the Royal Caroline, finally got rid of all her visiters but one, and Wilder was enabled to indulge in a pleasure that a seaman alone can appreciate, that of clear decks and an orderly ship's company.

# Chapter XII

—"Good: Speak to the mariners: Fall to't yarely, or we
run ourselves aground."

*The Tempest*, I.i.3–4.

A GOOD DEAL of the day had wasted during the time occupied by the scenes just related. The breeze had come
in steady, but far from fresh. So soon, however, as Wilder
found himself left without the molestation of idlers from the
shore and the busy interposition of the consignee, he cast his
eyes about him, with the intention of immediately submitting
the ship to its power. Sending for the pilot, he announced his
determination, and withdrew himself to a part of the deck
whence he might take a proper survey of the materials of his
new command, and where he might reflect on the unexpected
and extraordinary situation in which he found himself.

The Royal Caroline was not entirely without pretensions to
her lofty name. She was a vessel of that happy size in which
comfort and convenience have been equally consulted. The
letter of the Rover affirmed she had a reputation for speed,
and her young and intelligent commander saw, with great inward satisfaction, that she was not destitute of the means of
enabling him to exhibit her properties. A healthy, active, and
skilful crew, justly proportioned spars, little top-hamper, and
an excellent trim with a superabundance of light sails offered
all the advantages his experience could suggest. His eye
lighted as it glanced rapidly over these several particulars of
his command, and his lips moved, like those of a man who
uttered inward gratulations, or who indulged in some vaunt
that propriety suggested should go no farther than his own
thoughts.

By this time the crew, under the orders of the pilot, were
assembled at the windlass, and had commenced heaving in
upon the cable. The labor was of a nature to exhibit their
individual powers, as well as their collective force to the greatest advantage. Their motion was simultaneous, quick and full
of muscle. The cry was clear and cheerful. As if to feel his
influence, our adventurer lifted his own voice amid the song

of the mariners, in one of those sudden and inspiriting calls with which a sea officer is wont to encourage his people. His utterance was deep, animated and full of authority. The seamen started, like mettled coursers when they first hear the signal, each man casting a glance behind him, as if he would scan the qualities of his new superior. Wilder smiled like one satisfied with his success and turning to pace the quarter deck, he found himself once more confronted by the calm, considerate, but certainly astonished eye of Mrs Wyllys.

"After the opinions you were pleased to express of this vessel," said the lady in a manner of the coldest irony, "I did not expect to find you filling a place of so much responsibility here."

"You probably know, Madam," returned the young mariner, "that a sad accident has happened to her master?"

"I do; and I had heard that another officer had been found temporarily to supply his place. Still, I should presume, that on reflection, you will not think it remarkable, I am amazed in finding who this person is."

"Perhaps you may have conceived, from our conversations, an unfavorable opinion of my professional skill. I hope that, on this head you will place your mind at ease, for "—

"You are doubtless a master of the art! It would seem, at least, that no trifling danger can deter you from seeking proper opportunities to display this knowledge. Are we to have the pleasure of your company during the whole passage, or do you leave us at the mouth of the port?"

"I am engaged to conduct the ship to the end of her voyage."

"We may then hope that the danger you either saw or imagined is lessened in your judgment; otherwise you would not surely be so ready to encounter it in our company!"

"You do me injustice, Madam," returned Wilder with warmth, glancing his eye unconsciously towards the grave but attentive Gertrude: "There is no danger that I would not cheerfully encounter to save you—or this young lady from harm!"

"Even this young lady must be sensible of so much chivalry!" Then losing the constrained manner which she had hitherto maintained, in one more natural and one far more consonant to her usually mild and thoughtful mien, Mrs Wyllys continued. "You have a powerful advocate, young man, in the unaccountable interest which I feel in your truth; an interest that my reason would condemn. As the ship must need your services, I will no longer detain you. Opportunities cannot be wanting to enable us to judge both of your inclination and ability to serve us. Gertrude, my love, females are usually considered as incumbrances in a vessel, more particularly when there is any delicate duty to perform, like this before us."

Gertrude started, blushed, and followed her governess to the opposite side of the quarter-deck, though a look from our adventurer seemed to say that he considered her presence any thing but an incumbrance. As the ladies, took a position apart from every body, and one where they were least in the way of working the ship, at the same time, that they could command an entire view of her manœuvres, the disappointed sailor, was obliged to cut short a communication which he would gladly have continued, until compelled to take the charge of the vessel from the hands of the pilot. By this time, however, the anchor was a-weigh, and the seamen were actively engaged in the process of making sail. Wilder lent himself with feverish excitement to the duty, and taking the words from the Officer who was issuing the orders, he assumed the immediate superintendance in person.

As sheet after sheet of canvass fell from the yards and became distended by the complicated mechanism, the interest that a seaman seldom fails to take in his vessel began to gain the ascendancy over all other feelings. By the time every thing was set from the royals down, and the ship was cast with her head towards the harbor's mouth our adventurer had momentarily forgotten that he was a stranger among those he was in so extraordinary a manner selected to command, and how precious a stake was intrusted to his firmness and decision. Every thing being set to advantage, alow and aloft, and the ship brought close upon the wind, his eye scanned each yard and sail from the truck to the hull, concluding by casting a glance along the outer side of the vessel in order to see that not even the smallest rope was in the water to impede her progress. A small skiff, occupied by a boy, was towing under the lee, and, as the mass of the vessel began to move, it was skipping along the surface of the water, light and buoyant as a feather. Perceiving it was a boat belonging to the shore, Wilder walked forward and demanded who was its owner. A mate pointed to Joram, who at that moment, ascended from the interior of the vessel where he had been settling the balance due from a delinquent or what was in his eyes the same thing, a departing debtor.

The sight of this man recalled Wilder to a recollection of all that had occurred that morning, and of the whole delicacy of the task he had undertaken to perform. But the publican, whose ideas appeared always concentrated when occupied on the subject of gain, seemed troubled by no particular emotions at the interview. He approached the young mariner, and saluting him by the title of Captain, wished him a good voyage, with the customary compliments which seamen express, when about to separate on such an occasion.

"A lucky trip you have made of it, Captain Wilder," he concluded; "and I hope your passage will be short. You'll not be without a breeze this afternoon, and by stretching well over towards Montauk, you'll be able to make such an offing on the other tack, as to run the coast down in the morning. If I am any judge of the weather the wind will have more Easting in it, than you may happen to find to your fancy."

"And how long do you think my voyage is likely to last?" demanded Wilder, dropping his voice so low as to reach no ear but that of the Publican.

Joram cast a furtive glance aside; perceiving that they were alone, he suffered an expression of hardened cunning to take possession of a countenance that ordinarily seemed set in dull physical contentment, and laying a finger on his nose, he muttered,—

"Didn't I tender the consignee a beautiful oath, Master Wilder!"

"You certainly exceeded my expectations with your promptitude and"—

"Information!" added the landlord of the Foul Anchor, perceiving the other a little at a loss for a word—"yes, I have always been remarkable for the activity of my mind in these matters! But when a man once knows a thing thoroughly it is a great folly to spend his breath in words."

"It is certainly a great advantage to be thoroughly instructed. I suppose you improve your knowledge to a good account."

"Ah! bless me, Master Wilder, what would become of us all in these difficult times, if we did not turn an honest penny in every way that offers? I have brought up several fine children, in credit, and it sha'n't be my fault if I don't leave them something too, besides my good name! Well, well, they say a nimble sixpence is as good as a lazy shilling, but give me the man who don't stand shilly shally when a friend has need of his good word, or a lift from his hand. You always know where to find such a man as our politicians say, after they have gone through thick and thin in the cause, be it right or be it wrong."

"Very commendable principles, and such as will surely be the means of exalting you in the world, sooner or later. But you forget to answer my question. Will the passage be long or short?"

"Heaven bless you, Master Wilder; is it for a poor publican like me, to tell the master of this noble ship which way the wind will blow next! There is the worthy and notable commander, Nichols, lying in his state-room below, he could do any thing with the vessel, and why am I to expect that a gentleman so well recommended as yourself will do less? I expect to hear that you have made a famous run, and have done credit to the good word I have had occasion to say in your favor."

Wilder execrated, in his heart, the wary cunning of the rogue with whom he was compelled for the moment, to be in league; for he saw plainly that a determination not to commit himself, a tittle further than he might conceive to be absolutely necessary, was likely to render Joram too circumspect to answer his own immediate wishes. After hesitating a moment, to reflect, he continued, hastily—

"You see that the ship is gathering way, too fast to admit of trifling. You know of the letter, I received this morning?"

"Bless me, Captain Wilder, do you take me for a Post-

Master! How should I know what letters arrive at Newport, and what stop on the main!"

"As timid a villain as he is thorough!" muttered the young mariner. "But this much you may surely say. Am I to be followed immediately or is it expected that I shall detain the ship in the offing, under any pretence that I can devise?"

"Heaven keep you, young gentleman! these are strange questions coming from one, who is fresh off the sea, to a man that has done no more than look at it from the land these five and twenty years. According to my memory, Sir, you will keep the ship about South, until you are clear of the islands, and then you must make your calculations according to the wind, in order not to get into the 'gulph,' where you know the stream will be setting you one way, while your orders say, go another."

"Luff! Mind your luff, Sir," cried the pilot in a reproving voice, to the man at the helm, "luff you can; on no account go to leeward of the slaver!"

Wilder and the Publican started, as if they both found something alarming in the proximity of the vessel just named; and the former pointed to the skiff as he said—

"Unless you wish to go to sea with us, Mr Joram, it is time your boat held its master."

"Ay, ay, I see you are fairly under way, and I must leave you, however much I like your company," returned the landlord of the Foul Anchor, bustling over the side, and getting into his skiff in the best manner he could. "Well, boys, a good time to ye, a plenty of wind and of the right sort, a safe passage out, and a quick return—cast off—"

His order was obeyed; the light skiff, no longer impelled by the ship, immediately deviated from its course, and after making a little circuit it became stationary while the mass of the vessel passed on, with the steadiness of an elephant from whose back a butterfly had just taken its flight. Wilder followed the boat with his eyes for a moment, but his thoughts were recalled by the voice of the pilot, who again called from the forward part of the ship—

"Let the light sails lift a little, boy; let them lift I say; keep every inch you can, or you'll not weather the slaver. Luff, I say, Sir, luff!"

"The slaver!" muttered our adventurer, hastening to a part of the ship, whence he could command a view of that important, and to him doubly interesting ship; "ay, the slaver, it may be difficult, indeed, to weather upon the slaver!"

He had unconsciously placed himself near Mrs Wyllys and Gertrude, the latter of whom, was leaning on the rail of the quarter deck, regarding the strange vessel at anchor with a pleasure far from unnatural to her years.

"You may laugh at me, and call me fickle and perhaps credulous, dear Mrs Wyllys," the unsuspecting girl said, just as Wilder took the position mentioned, "but I wish we were well out of this Royal Caroline, and that our passage was to be made in yonder beautiful ship!"

"It is indeed a beautiful ship!" returned Wyllys—"but I know not that it would be safer or more comfortable than the one we are in."

"With what symmetry and order the ropes are arranged, and how like a bird it floats upon the water!"

"Had you particularised the duck, the comparison, would have been nautical," said the governess, smiling mournfully; "you show capabilities, my love, to become one day a seaman's wife."

Gertrude blushed a little and turning back her head to answer in the playful vein of her governess, her eye met the look of Wilder, fastened on herself. The colour on her cheek deepened to carnation, and she was mute; the large gipsy hat she wore, serving to conceal both her face and the confusion which suffused it.

"You make no answer, child, as if you reflected seriously on the chances," continued Mrs Wyllys, whose thoughtful and abstracted mien, however, proved that she scarcely knew what she uttered.

"The sea is too unstable an element for my taste," Gertrude coldly answered. "Pray tell me, Mrs Wyllys, if the vessel we are approaching is a King's ship? She has a warlike not to say a threatening exterior!"

"The pilot has twice called her a slaver."

"A slaver! How deceitful is all her beauty and symmetry! I will never trust to appearances again, since so lovely an object can be devoted to so vile a purpose!"

"Deceitful, indeed!" said Wilder aloud, under an impulse that he found as irresistible as it was involuntary. "I will take upon myself to say that a more treacherous vessel does not float the ocean, than yonder finely proportioned and admirably equipped"—

"Slaver—" added Mrs Wyllys, who had time to turn, and to look her astonishment, before the young man, appeared disposed to finish his sentence.

"Slaver—" he said, with emphasis, bowing at the same time, as if to thank her for the word.

After this interruption, there was a profound silence. Mrs Wyllys studied the disturbed features of the young man, for a moment, with a countenance that denoted a singular, though a complicated, interest, and then she gravely bent her eyes on the water, deeply occupied with intense and painful reflection. The light symmetrical form of Gertrude continued leaning on the rail, it is true, but Wilder was unable to catch another glimpse of her averted face. In the mean while, events, that were of a character to withdraw his attention from even so pleasing a study, were hastening to their accomplishment.

The ship, by this time, had passed between the little island and the point where Homespun embarked, and she might now be said to have fairly left the inner harbour. The slaver lay directly in her track, and every man in the vessel was watching with interest, to see whether they would be able to pass her weather-beam. The measure was desirable; because a seaman has a pride in keeping on the honorable side of every thing he encounters, but chiefly because, from the position of the stranger, it would be the means of preventing the necessity of tacking before the Caroline reached a point more advantageous for such a manœuvre. The reader will, however, readily understand that the interest of her new commander took its rise in feelings very different from professional pride or momentary convenience.

Wilder felt, in every nerve, the probability that a crisis was at hand. It will be remembered that he was profoundly ignorant of the immediate intentions of the Rover. As the fort was not in a state for service, it would not be difficult for the latter to seize upon his prey in open view of the townsmen, and bear it off, in contempt of their feeble means of defence. The position of the two ships was favorable to such an enterprize. Unprepared, and unsuspecting, the Caroline, at no times a match for her powerful adversary, must fall an easy victim, nor would there be much reason to apprehend that a single shot from the battery could reach them, before the captor, and his prize, would be at such a distance as to render the blow next to impotent, if not utterly innocuous. The wild and audacious character of such an enterprise was in accordance with the reputation of the desperate freebooter, on whose caprice, alone, the act now seemed solely to depend.

Under these impressions, and with the prospect of such a speedy termination to his new-born authority, it is not to be considered wonderful that our adventurer awaited the result with an interest greatly exceeding that of any of those by whom he was surrounded. He walked into the waist of the ship, and endeavoured to read the plan of his secret confederates, by some of those indications that are familiar to a seaman. Not the smallest sign of any intention to depart, or in any manner to change her position, was discoverable in the pretended slaver. She lay in the same deep, beautiful, but treacherous quiet, as that in which she had reposed throughout the whole of the eventful morning. But a solitary individual could be seen amid the mazes of her rigging, or along the wide reaches of her spars. It was a seaman seated on the extremity of a lower yard, where he appeared to busy himself with one of those repairs that are so constantly required in the gear of a ship. As the man was placed on the weather side of his own vessel, Wilder instantly conceived the idea that he was thus stationed to cast a grapnel into the rigging of the Caroline should such a measure become necessary in order to bring the two ships foul of each other. With the view to prevent so rude an encounter, he instantly determined to defeat the plan. Calling to the pilot, he told him the attempt to pass to windward was of very doubtful success, and reminded him that the safer way would be to go to leeward.

"No fear—no fear, Captain," returned the stubborn conductor of the ship, who, as his authority was so brief, was only the more jealous of its unrestrained exercise, and who, like the usurper of a throne, felt a jealousy of the more legitimate power which he had temporarily dispossessed. "No fear of me, Captain. I have trolled over this ground oftener than you have crossed the ocean, and I know the name of every rock on the bottom as well as the town crier knows the streets of Newport. Let her luff, boy; luff her into the very eye of the wind; luff, you can"—

"You have the ship shivering as it is, sir; should you get us foul of the slaver, who is to pay the cost?"

"I am a general underwriter," returned the opinionated pilot. "My wife shall mend every hole I make in your sails, with a needle no bigger than a hair, and with such a palm as a fairy's thimble!"

"This is fine talking, Sir; but you are already losing the ship's way, and before you have ended your boasts, she will be as fast in irons as a condemned thief. Keep the sails full, boy; keep them a rap full, sir."

"Ay, ay, keep her a good full," echoed the Pilot, who, as the difficulty of passing to windward became more obvious, began to waver in his resolution. "Keep her full, and by—I have always told you full, and by—I don't know, Captain, seeing that the wind has hauled a little, but we shall have to pass to leeward yet; you will acknowledge, that, in such case, we shall be obliged to go about."

Now, in point of fact, the wind, though a little lighter than it had been, was, if any thing, a trifle more favorable; nor had Wilder ever, in any manner, denied that the ship would not have to tack, some twenty minutes sooner, by going to leeward of the other vessel, than if she had succeeded in her delicate experiment of passing on the more honorable side. But as the vulgarest minds are always the most reluctant to confess their blunders, the discomfited pilot was disposed to qualify the concession he found himself compelled to make, by some salvo of the sort, that he might not lessen his reputation for foresight, among his auditors.

"Keep her away at once," cried Wilder, who was beginning to change the tones of remonstrance for those of command; "keep the ship away, Sir, while you have room to do it, or by the"—

His lips became motionless; for his eye happened to fall on the pale features of the frightened Gertrude.

"I believe it must be done, seeing that the wind is hauling.

Hard up, boy, and run her under the stern of the ship at anchor. Hold! Keep your luff again; eat into the wind to the bone, boy; lift again; let the light sails lift. The slaver has run a warp directly across our track. If there's law in the Plantations, I'll have her Captain before the courts for this!"

"What does the fellow mean?" demanded Wilder, jumping hastily on a gun, to get a better view.

His mate pointed to the lee quarter of the other vessel, where, sure enough, a large rope was seen whipping the water in the very process of being extended. The truth instantly flashed on the mind of our young mariner. The Rover lay secretly moored with a spring with a view to bring his guns more readily to bear upon the battery should his defence become necessary, and he now profited by the circumstance in order to prevent the trader from passing to leeward. The whole arrangement excited a good deal of surprise, and not a few execrations among the officers of the Caroline, though none but her commander had the smallest twinkling of the real reason why the kedge had thus been laid, and why a warp was so awkwardly stretched across their path. Of the whole number, the Pilot alone saw cause to rejoice in the circumstance. He had, in fact, got the ship in such a situation, as to render it nearly as difficult to proceed in one way as in the other; and he was now furnished with a sufficient justification, should any accident occur, in the course of the exceedingly critical manœuvre, from whose execution there was now no retreat.

"This is an extraordinary liberty to take in the mouth of a harbour," muttered Wilder, when his eyes put him in possession of the fact just related. "You must shove her by to windward, Pilot; there is no remedy."

"I wash my hands of the consequences, as I call all on board to witness," returned the other, with the air of an offended man, though secretly glad of the appearance of being driven to the very measure he was a minute before so obstinately bent on executing. "Law must be called in here, if sticks are snapped, or rigging parted. Luff to a hair, boy; luff her short into the wind, and try a half-board."

The man at the helm obeyed the order. Releasing his hold of its spokes, the wheel made a quick evolution; and the ship, feeling a fresh impulse of the wind, turned her head heavily towards the quarter whence it came, the canvass fluttering with a noise like that produced by a flock of water-fowl taking wing. But, met by the helm again, she soon fell off as before, powerless from having lost her way, and settling bodily down toward the fancied slaver, impelled by the air, which seemed to have lost much of its force, at the critical instant it was most needed.

The situation of the Caroline was one which a seaman will readily understand. She had forged so far ahead as to lie directly on the weather-beam of the stranger, but too near to enable her to fall-off in the least, without imminent danger that the vessels would fall foul of each other. The wind was inconstant, sometimes blowing in puffs, while at moments there was a lull. As the ship felt the former, her tall masts bent gracefully towards the slaver, as if to make the parting salute; but, relieved from the momentary pressure of the inconstant air, she as often rolled heavily to windward, without advancing a foot. The effect of each change, however, was to bring her still nigher to her dangerous neighbour, until it became evident, to the judgment of the youngest seaman in the vessel, that nothing but a sudden shift of wind could enable her to pass ahead, the more especially as the tide was on the change.

The inferior officers of the Caroline were not delicate in making their comments on the dullness which had brought them into so awkward and so mortifying a position, and the Pilot endeavoured to conceal his vexation, by the number and vociferousness of his orders. From blustering, he soon passed into confusion, until the men themselves stood idle, not knowing which of the uncertain and contradictory mandates ought to be obeyed. In the mean time, Wilder had folded his arms with an appearance of entire composure, and taken his station near his female passengers. Mrs Wyllys studied his eye, with the wish of ascertaining, by its expression, the nature and extent of their danger, if danger there might be, in the approaching collision of two ships in water that was perfectly smooth, and where one was stationary, and the motion of the other scarcely perceptible. The stern, determined look she saw settling about the brow of the young man excited an uneasiness that she would not otherwise have felt under circumstances that, in themselves, bore no very vivid appearance of hazard.

"Have we aught to apprehend, Sir?" demanded the Governess, endeavouring to conceal from her charge the nature of her own disquietude.

"I told you, Madam, the Caroline would prove an unlucky ship."

Both females regarded the peculiarly bitter smile with which Wilder made his reply as an evil omen, and Gertrude clung to her companion as to one on whom she had long been accustomed to lean.

"Why do not the mariners of the slaver appear, to assist us—to keep us from coming too nigh?" anxiously demanded the latter.

"Why do they not, indeed; we shall see them, I think, ere long."

"You speak and look, young man, as if you thought there would be danger in the interview!"

"Keep near to me," returned Wilder, in a voice that was nearly smothered by the manner in which he compressed his lips. "In every event, keep as nigh my person as possible."

"Haul the spanker-boom to windward," shouted the Pilot; "lower away the boats, and tow the ship's head round—clear away the stream anchor—aft gib sheet—Board main tack, again."

The astonished men stood like statues, not knowing whither to turn, some calling to the rest to do this or that, and some as loudly countermanding the order, when an authoritative voice was heard calmly to say—

"Silence in the ship."

The tones were of that sort which, while they denote the self-possession of the speaker, never fail to inspire the inferior with a portion of the confidence of him who commands. Every face was turned towards the quarter of the vessel whence the sound proceeded, each ear ready to catch the smallest additional mandate. Wilder was standing on the head of the capstern, where he could command a full view on every side of him. With a quick and understanding glance, he had made himself a perfect master of the situation of his ship. His eye was at the instant fixed anxiously on the slaver to pierce the treacherous calm which still reigned on all about her, in order to know how far his exertions might be permitted to be useful. But it appeared as if the stranger lay like some enchanted vessel on the water, not a human form appearing about her complicated machinery, except the seaman already named, who still continued his employment, with as much indifference as if the Caroline was a hundred miles from the place where he sat. The lips of Wilder moved, whether in bitterness or in satisfaction it would be difficult to say; and he motioned to the attentive crew to be quick.

"Throw all aback—Lay every thing flat to the masts, forward and aft," he said.

"Ay!" echoed the Pilot, "lay every thing flat to the masts."

"Is there a shore-boat alongside the ship?" demanded our adventurer.

The answer, from a dozen voices, was in the affirmative.

"Show that pilot into her."

"This is an unlawful order," exclaimed the other; "I forbid any voice but mine to be obeyed."

"*Throw* him in," repeated Wilder.

Amid the bustle and exertion of bracing round the yards, the resistance of the Pilot produced little sensation. He was raised on the extended arms of the two mates; and, after exhibiting his limbs in sundry contortions in the air, he was dropped into the boat, with as little ceremony as a billet of wood. The end of the painter was cast after him; and the discomfited guide was left, with singular indifference, to his own meditations.

In the mean time, the order of Wilder was executed. Those vast sheets of canvass which, a moment before, had been either fluttering in the air, or were bellying inward or outward, as they touched or filled, as it is technically called, were now pressing against their respective masts, impelling the vessel to retrace her mistaken path. The manœuvre required the utmost attention, and the nicest delicacy in its direction. But her young commander proved himself, in every particular, competent to the task. Here, a sail was lifted; there, another was brought, with a flatter surface, to the air; now, the lighter canvass was spread; and, now it disappeared, like thin vapour dispelled by the sun. The voice of Wilder, throughout, though calm, was breathing with authority. The ship itself seemed, like an animated being, conscious that her destinies were reposed in different, and more intelligent, hands than before. Obedient to the new impulse they had received, the immense clouds of canvass, with the tall forest of spars and rigging, rolled to and fro; and then, having overcome its state of rest, the vessel heavily yielded to the pressure, and began to recede.

Throughout the whole of the time necessary to extricate the Caroline, the attention of Wilder was divided between his own ship and his inexplicable neighbour. Not a sound was heard to issue from the imposing stillness of the latter. Not a single anxious countenance, not even one lurking eye, was to be detected, at any of the numerous outlets by which the inmates of an armed vessel can look abroad upon the deep. The seaman on the yard continued his labour, like a man unconscious of any thing but his own employment. There was, however, a slow, though nearly imperceptible, motion in the ship itself, which was apparently made, like the lazy movement of a slumbering whale, more by listless volition, than through any agency of human hands.

Not the smallest of these changes escaped the keen examination of Wilder. He saw, that, as his own ship retired, the side of the slaver was gradually exposed to the Caroline. The muzzles of the threatening guns gaped constantly on his vessel, as the eye of the couching tiger follows the movement of its prey; and at no time, while nearest, did there exist a single instant that the decks of the latter ship could not have been swept, by a general discharge from the battery of the former. As each successive order issued from his own lips, our adventurer turned his eye, with increasing interest, to ascertain whether he would be permitted to execute it; and never did he feel certain that he was left to the sole management of the Caroline, until he found that she had backed from her dangerous proximity to the other; and that, obedient to a new disposition of her sails, she was falling off, before the light air, in a place where he could hold her entirely at command.

Finding that the tide was getting unfavourable, and the wind too light to stem it, the sails were drawn to the yards, and an anchor was dropped.

# Chapter XIII

"What have we here? A man, or a fish?"
*The Tempest*, II.ii.24–25.

THE CAROLINE now lay within a cable's length of the supposed slaver. In dismissing the Pilot, Wilder had assumed a responsibility from which a seaman usually shrinks; since, in the case of any untoward accident in leaving the port, it would involve a loss of insurance, and his own probable punishment. How far he had been influenced, in taking so decided a step, by a knowledge of his being beyond, or above, the reach of the law, will be made manifest in the course of the narrative; the only immediate effect of the measure, was, to draw the whole of his attention, which had before been so much divided between his passengers and the ship, to the care of the latter. But, so soon as his vessel was secured, for a time at least, and his mind was no longer excited by the expectation of a scene of immediate violence, our adventurer found leisure to return to his former occupation. The success of his delicate manœuvre had imparted to his countenance a glow of something like triumph; and his step, as he advanced towards Mrs Wyllys and Gertrude, was that of a man who enjoyed the consciousness of having acquitted himself dexterously, in circumstances that required no small exhibition of professional skill. At least, such was the construction the former lady put upon his kindling eye and exulting air; though the latter might, possibly, be disposed to judge of his motives with greater indulgence. Both, however, were ignorant of the true reasons of his self-felicitation, for a sentiment more generous than either of them could imagine, had a full share in his present feelings.

Let the cause of his exultation be what it would, Wilder no sooner saw the Caroline swinging to her anchor, and that his services were of no further immediate use, than he sought an opportunity to renew a conversation which had hitherto been so vague, and so often interrupted. Mrs Wyllys had been viewing the neighbouring vessel with a steady look; nor did she now turn her gaze from the motionless and silent object, until the young mariner was near her person. She was then the first to speak.

"Yonder vessel must possess an extraordinary, not to say an insensible, crew!" exclaimed the Governess, in a tone bordering on astonishment. "If such things were, it would not be difficult to fancy her a spectre-ship."

"She is truly an admirably proportioned and a beautifully equipped trader!"

"Did my apprehensions deceive me? or were we in actual danger of getting the two vessels entangled?"

"There was certainly some reason for apprehension; but we are now safe."

"For which we have to thank your skill. The manner in which you have just extricated us from the late danger, has a direct tendency to contradict all that you have foretold of that which is to come."

"I well know that my conduct may bear an unfavourable construction, but"—

"You thought it no harm to laugh at the weakness of three credulous females," resumed Mrs Wyllys, smiling. "You have had your amusement; and now, I hope, you will be more disposed to pity what is said to be a natural infirmity of woman's mind."

The governess glanced her eye at Gertrude, with an expression that seemed to say, it would be cruel to trifle further with the apprehensions of one so innocent and so young. The look of Wilder followed her own; and he answered with a sincerity that was well calculated to carry conviction,—

"On the faith which a gentleman owes to all of your sex, Madam, what I have already told you I continue to believe."

"The gammonings and the top-gallant-masts!"

"No, no," interrupted the young mariner, slightly laughing, and at the same time colouring a good deal; "perhaps not all of that. But neither mother, wife, nor sister of mine, should make this passage in the Royal Caroline."

"Your look, your voice, and your air of good faith, form a strange contradiction to your words, young man; for, while the former almost tempt me to believe you honest, the latter have not a shade of reason to support them. Perhaps I ought to be ashamed of such a weakness, and yet I will acknowledge, that the mysterious quiet, which seems to have settled forever, on yonder ship, has excited an inexplicable uneasiness, that may in some way be connected with her character. —She is certainly a slaver?"

"She is certainly beautiful," exclaimed Gertrude.

"Very beautiful!" Wilder rejoined.

"There is a man still seated on one of her yards, who appears to be entranced in his occupation," continued Mrs Wyllys, leaning her chin thoughtfully on a hand, as she gazed at the object of which she was speaking. "Not once, during the time we were in so much danger of getting the ships entangled, did that seaman bestow so much as a stolen glance towards us. He resembles the solitary individual in the city of the transformed; for not another mortal is there to keep him company, so far as we may discover."

"Perhaps his comrades sleep," said Gertrude.

"Sleep! Mariners do not sleep in an hour and a day like this! Tell me, Mr Wilder, you that are a seaman should know, is it usual for the crew to sleep when a strange vessel is so nigh—near even to touching, I might almost say?"

"It is not."

"I thought as much; for I am not an entire novice in matters of your daring—your hardy—your *noble* profession!" returned the governess, with emphasis. "Had we gone foul of the slaver, do you think her crew would have maintained their apathy?"

"I think not."

"There is something in all this assumed tranquillity, which might induce one to suspect the worst. Is it known that any of her crew have had communication with the town, since her arrival?"

"It is."

"I have heard that false colours have been seen on the coast, and that ships have been plundered, and their people and passengers maltreated, during the past summer. It is even thought that the famous Rover has tired of his excesses on the Spanish Main, and that a vessel was not long since seen in the Caribbean Sea, which was thought to be the cruiser of that desperate Pirate!"

Wilder made no reply. His eyes, which had been fastened

steadily, though respectfully, on those of the speaker, fell to the deck, and he appeared to await her further pleasure. The Governess mused a moment, and then, with a change in the expression of her countenance which proved that her suspicion of the truth was too light to continue without further and better confirmation, she added,—

"After all, the occupation of a slaver is bad enough, and unhappily by far too probable, to render it necessary to attribute any worse character to the stranger. I would I knew the motive of your singular assertions, Mr Wilder?"

"I cannot better explain them, Madam: unless my manner produces its effect, I fail altogether in my intentions, which at least are sincere."

"Is not the risk lessened by your presence?"

"Lessened, but not removed."

Until now, Gertrude had rather listened, as if unavoidably, than seemed to make one of the party. But here she turned quickly, and perhaps a little impatiently, to Wilder, and, while her cheeks glowed, she demanded, with a smile that might have brought even a more obdurate man to his confession,—

"Is it forbidden to be more explicit?"

The young commander hesitated, perhaps as much to dwell upon the ingenuous features of the speaker, as to decide upon his answer. The colour mounted into his own embrowned cheek, and his eye lighted with a gleam of pleasure. Then, suddenly reminded that he was delaying to reply, he said,—

"I am certain, that, in relying on your discretion, I shall be safe."

"Doubt it not," returned Mrs Wyllys. "In no event shall you ever be betrayed."

"Betrayed! For myself, Madam, I have little fear. If you suspect me of personal apprehension, you do me great injustice."

"We suspect you of nothing unworthy," said Gertrude hastily, "but—we are very anxious for ourselves."

"Then will I relieve your uneasiness, though at the expense of"—

A call, from one of the mates to the other, arrested his words for the moment, and drew his attention to the other ship.

"The slaver's people have just found out that their ship is

not made to put in a glass case, to be looked at by women and children," cried the speaker, in tones loud enough to send his words into the fore-top, where the messmate he addressed was attending to some especial duty.

"Ay, ay," was the answer; "seeing us in motion, has put him in mind of his next voyage. They keep watch aboard the fellow, like the sun in Greenland; six months on deck and six months below!"

The witticism produced, as usual, a laugh among the seamen, who continued their remarks in a similar vein, but in tones more suited to the deference due their superiors.

The eyes of Wilder, however, had fastened on the other ship. The man so long seated on the end of the main-yard had disappeared, and another sailor was deliberately walking along the opposite quarter of the same spar, steadying himself by the boom, and holding in one hand the end of a rope, which he was apparently about to reeve in the place where it properly belonged. The first glance told Wilder that the latter was Fid, who was so far recovered from his debauch as to tread the giddy height with as much, if not greater steadiness than he would have rolled along the ground, had his duty called him to terra firma. The countenance of the young man, which an instant before had been flushed with excitement and which was beaming with the pleasure of an opening confidence, changed directly to a look of gloom and reserve. Mrs Wyllys, who had lost no shade of the varying expression of his face, resumed the discourse with some earnestness where he had seen fit so abruptly to break it off.

"You would relieve us," she said, "at the expense of"—

"Life, Madam; but not of honor."

"Gertrude, we can now retire to our cabin," observed Mrs Wyllys with an air of cold displeasure, in which disappointment was a good deal mingled with resentment at the trifling of which she believed herself the subject. The eye of Gertrude was no less averted and distant than that of her governess, while the tint that gave lustre to its beam was brighter if not quite so resentful. As they moved past the silent Wilder, each dropped a distant salute, and then our adventurer found himself the sole occupant of the quarter deck. While his crew were busied in coiling ropes and clearing the decks, their

young commander leaned his head on the taffrail, that part of
the vessel which the good relict of the rear-admiral had so
strangely confounded with a very different object in the other
end of the ship, remaining for many minutes in an attitude of
abstraction. From this reverie, he was at length aroused by a
sound like that produced by the lifting and falling of a light
oar into the water. Believing himself about to be annoyed by
visiters from the land, he raised his head, casting a dissatisfied
glance over the vessel's side to see who was approaching.

A light skiff, such as is commonly used by fishermen in the
bays and shallow waters of America, was lying within ten feet
of the ship, and in a position where it was necessary to take
some little pains in order to observe it. It was occupied by a
single man, whose back was towards the vessel, and who was
apparently abroad on the ordinary business of the owner of
such a boat.

"Are you in search of rudder-fish, my friend, that you hang
so closely under my counter?" demanded Wilder. "The bay is
said to be full of delicious bass and other scaly gentlemen,
that would far better repay your trouble."

"He is well paid who gets the bite he baits for," returned
the other, turning his head and exhibiting the cunning eye and
chuckling countenance of old Bob Bunt, as Wilder's recent
and treacherous confederate had announced his name to be.

"How now! Dare you trust yourself with me in five fathom
water after the villanous trick you have seen fit"—

"Hist! noble Captain; hist!" interrupted Bob, holding up a
finger to repress the other's animation, and intimating by a
sign that their conference must be held in lower tones. "There
is no need to call all hands to help us through a little chat. In
what way have I fallen to leeward in your favour, Captain?"

"In what way, Sirrah! Did you not receive money to give
such a character of this ship to the ladies, as you said, yourself, would make them sooner pass the night in a churchyard
than trust foot on board her?"

"Something of the sort passed between us, Captain; but
you forgot one half of the conditions and I overlooked the
other; and I need not tell so expert a navigator that two
halves make a whole. No wonder, therefore, that the affair
dropp'd through between us!"

"How! Do you add falsehood to perfidy! What part of my engagement did I neglect?"

"What part!" returned the pretended fisherman, leisurely drawing in a line which the quick eye of Wilder saw, though abundantly provided with lead at the end was destitute of the equally material implement, the hook. "What part, Captain! No less a particular than the second guinea."

"It was to have been the reward of a service done, and not an earnest, like its fellow to induce you to undertake the duty."

"Ah, you have helped me to the very word I wanted. I fancied it was not in earnest, like the one I got, and so I left the job half-finished."

"Half-finished, scoundrel! you never commenced what you swore so stoutly to perform."

"Now are you on as wrong a course, my master, as if you steered due East to get to the pole. I religiously performed one half my undertaking, and you will acknowledge, I was only half paid."

"You would find it difficult to prove that you even did that little!"

"Let us look into the Log. I enlisted to walk up the hill, as far as the dwelling of the good admiral's widow, and there to make certain alterations in my sentiments, which it is not necessary to speak of between us."

"Which you did not make; but on the contrary, which you thwarted by telling an exactly contradictory tale."

"True."

"True, knave! Were justice done you, an acquaintance with a rope's end, would be your reward!"

"A squall of words!—If your ship steer as wild as your ideas, captain, you will make a crooked passage to the South. Do you not think it an easier matter for an old man like me, to tell a few lies, than to climb yonder long and heavy hill? In strict justice, more than half my duty was done when I got into the presence of the believing widow, and then I concluded to refuse the half of the reward that was unpaid, and to take bounty from t'other side—"

"Villain!" exclaimed Wilder, a little blinded by resentment, "even your years shall no longer protect you. Forward, there! Send a crew into the jolly-boat, Sir, and bring me this old fellow in the skiff on board the ship. Pay no attention to his outcries; I have an account to settle with him, that cannot be balanced without a little noise."

The mate to whom this order was addressed, and who had answered the hail, jumped on the rail, where he got sight of the craft he was commanded to chase. In less than a minute he was in the boat, with four men, and pulling round the bows of the ship in order to get on the side necessary to effect his object. The self-styled Bob Bunt, gave one or two strokes with his sculls and sent the skiff some twenty or thirty fathoms off, where he lay chuckling, like a man who saw only the success of his cunning without any apparent apprehensions of the consequences. But the moment the boat appeared in view, he laid himself to the work with vigorous arms, and soon convinced the spectators that his capture was not to be easily achieved.

For some little time it was doubtful what course the fugitive meant to take, for he kept whirling and turning in swift and sudden circles, completely confusing and baffling his pursuers, by his skilful and light evolutions. But tiring of this amusement, or perhaps apprehensive of exhausting his own strength, which was powerfully and most dexterously exerted, it was not long before he darted on in a perfectly straight line, taking the direction of the rover.

The chase now grew hot and earnest, exciting the clamour and applause of most of the nautical spectators. The result, for a time, seemed doubtful; but, if any thing, the jolly-boat, though some distance astern began to gain, as it gradually overcame the resistance of the water. In a very few minutes, however, the skiff shot under the stern of the other ship and disappeared, bringing the hull of the vessel in a line with the Caroline and its course. The pursuers were not long in taking the same direction, and then the seamen of the latter ship, began laughingly to climb the rigging, in order to command a view over the intervening object.

Nothing, however, was to be seen beyond but water, and the still more distant island, with its little fort. In a few minutes the crew of the jolly boat were observed pulling back in their path; returning slowly, like men who were disappointed. All crowded to the side of the ship, in order to hear the termination of the adventure; the noisy assemblage even draw-ing the two passengers from the cabin to the deck. Instead, however, of meeting the questions of their ship-mates with the usual wordy narrative of men of their condition, the crew of the boat were silent and perplexed. Their officer sprang to the deck without speaking, and he immediately sought his commander.

"The skiff was too light for you, Mr Knighthead," Wilder calmly observed, as the other approached, having never moved, himself, from the place where he had been standing during the whole proceeding.

"Too light, Sir! are you acquainted with the man who pulled it?"

"Not particularly well. I only know him for a knave."

"He should be one, since he is of the family of the devil."

"I will not take on myself to say, he is as bad as you appear to think, though I have little reason to believe he has any honesty to cast into the sea. What has become of him?"

"A question easily asked, but hard to answer. In the first place, though an old and a gray-headed fellow, he twitched his skiff along as if it floated in air. We were not a minute, or two at the most, behind him, but when we got by the other side of the slaver, boat and man had vanished!"

"He doubled her bows, while you were crossing the stern."

"Did you see him, then?"

"I confess we did not."

"It could not be, Sir, since we pulled far enough ahead to examine on both sides at once; besides, the people of the slaver knew nothing of him."

"You saw the slaver's people?"

"I should have said her man, for there is seemingly but one hand on board her."

"And how was he employed?"

"He was seated in the chains, and seem'd to have been asleep. It is a lazy ship, Sir, and one that takes more money from her owners, I fancy, than it ever returns!"

"It may be so. Well, let the rogue escape. There is the pros-pect of a breeze coming in from the sea, Mr Earing; we will get our topsails to the mast-heads, again, and be in readiness for it. I could like yet to see the sun set in the waters."

The mates and the crew went cheerfully to their task, though many a curious question was asked by the wondering seamen of their ship-mates who had been in the boat, and many a solemn answer was given, while they were again spreading the canvass to invite the breeze. Wilder turned, in the mean time, to Mrs Wyllys, who had been an auditor of his short conversation with the mate.

"You perceive, Madam," he said, "that our voyage does not commence without its omens!"

"When you tell me, inexplicable young man, with the air of singular sincerity you sometimes possess, that we are unwise in trusting to the ocean, I am half inclined to put faith in what you say; but when you attempt to enforce your advice with the machinery of witchcraft you only induce me to proceed."

"Man the windlass!" cried Wilder, with a look that seemed to tell his companions, If you are so stout of heart, the opportunity to show your resolution shall not be wanting. "Man the windlass, there: we will try the breeze, again, and work the ship into the offing while there is light."

The clattering of handspikes preceded the mariners' song. Then the heavy labor by which the ponderous iron was lifted from the bottom was again resumed, and in a few more minutes the ship was once more released from her hold upon the land.

The wind soon came fresh off the ocean, charged with the saline dampness of the element. As the air fell upon the distended and balanced sails, the ship bowed to the welcome guest, and then rising gracefully from its low inclination, the breeze was heard singing, through the maze of rigging, the music that is so grateful to a seaman's ear. The inspiriting sounds and the freshness of the peculiar air, gave additional energy to the movements of the men. The anchor was stowed, the ship cast, the lighter sails set, the courses had fallen, and the bows of the Caroline were throwing the spray before her, ere ten minutes more had gone by.

Wilder had now undertaken the task of running his vessel through the passage between the islands of Conanicut and Rhode. Fortunately for the heavy responsibility he had assumed the channel was not difficult, and the wind had veered so far to the east, as to give him a favorable opportunity, after making a short stretch to windward, of laying through in a single reach. But this stretch would bring him under the necessity of passing very near the rover, or of losing no small portion of his vantage ground. He did not hesitate. When the vessel was as nigh the weather shore as his busy lead told him was prudent, the ship was tacked and her head laid directly towards the still motionless and seemingly unobservant slaver.

The approach of the Caroline was more propitious than before. The wind was steady, and her crew held her in hand, as a skilful rider governs the action of a fiery and mettled steed. Still the passage was not made without exciting a breathless interest in every soul in the Bristol trader. Each individual had his own secret cause of curiosity. To the seamen, the strange ship began to be the subject of wonder, the governess and her ward scarce knew the reasons of their own interest, while Wilder was but too well instructed in the nature of the hazard that all but himself were running. As before, the man at the wheel was about to indulge his nautical pride by going to windward. But, although the experiment would now have been attended with no hazard, he was commanded to proceed differently.

"Pass the slaver's lee-beam, Sir," said Wilder with a gesture of authority, and then the young captain went himself to lean on the weather rail, like every other idler on board, to examine the object they were so fast approaching. As the Caroline came boldly up, seeming to bear the breeze before her, the sighing of the wind, as it murmured through the rigging of the stranger vessel was the only sound that issued from her. Not a single human face, not even a secret and curious eye, was any where to be seen. The passage was rapid, and as the two vessels lay with heads and sterns nearly in a line, Wilder thought it was to be made without the slightest notice from the imaginary slaver. He was mistaken. A light active form, in the undress attire of a naval officer, sprang upon the taffrail, and waved a sea cap in salute. The instant the fair hair was blowing about the countenance of this individual, Wilder recognised the features of the Rover.

"Think you the wind will hold, here, Sir?" shouted the latter, at the top of his voice.

"It has come in fresh enough to be steady," was the answer.

"A wise mariner would get all his easting in time; to me there is a smack of West-Indies about it."

"You believe we shall have it more at South?"

"I do. But a taught bowline for the night, will carry you clear."

By this time the Caroline had swept by, and she was now luffing across the slaver's bows into her course again. The figure on the taffrail waved the sea-cap in adieu, and disappeared.

"Is it possible that such a man, can traffic in human beings!" exclaimed Gertrude, when the sounds of both voices had ceased.

Receiving no reply, she turned to regard her companion. The Governess was standing, like a being entranced, her eyes looking on vacancy. They had not changed their direction since the motion of the vessel had carried her beyond the view of the countenance of the stranger. Gertrude took her hand, and repeated the question, when the recollection of Mrs Wyllys returned. Passing her own hand over her brow with a bewildered air, she forced a smile and said—

"The meeting of vessels or the renewal of any maritime experience, never fails to revive my earliest recollections, love. But, surely that was an extraordinary being who has at length shown himself in the slaver!"

"For a slaver, most extraordinary!"

Wyllys leaned her head on a hand for an instant, and then turned to look for Wilder. The young mariner was standing near, watching the expression of her countenance with an interest scarcely less remarkable than her own air of thought.

"Tell me, young man, is yonder individual the commander of the slaver?"

"He is."

"You know him?"

"We have met."

"And, he is called—?"

"The master of yon ship. I know no other name."

"Gertrude, we will seek our cabin. When we are quitting so the land, Mr Wilder will have the goodness to let us know."

The latter bowed his assent, and the ladies left the deck. The Caroline had now the prospect of getting speedily to sea. In order to effect this object, Wilder had every thing that would draw set to the utmost advantage. One hundred times, at least, however, did he turn his head to steal a look at the vessel he left behind. She lay as when they passed, a regular, beautiful but motionless object in the bay. From each of these furtive examinations our adventurer invariably cast an excited and impatient glance at the sails of his own ship, ordering this to be drawn tighter to the spar beneath, or that to be more distended along its mast.

The effect of so much solicitude united with so much skill was to urge the Bristol trader through her element at a rate she had rarely if ever surpassed. It was not long before the land ceased to be seen on her two beams, and then it was only to be traced in the blue islands in their rear, or in a long dim horizon to the North and West, where the vast continent stretched for countless leagues. The passengers were now summoned to take their parting look at the land, and the officers were seen noting their departures. Just before the day shut in, and ere the islands were entirely sunk into the waves, Wilder ascended to an upper yard, bearing a glass. His gaze towards the haven he had left was long, anxious and occupied. But his descent was distinguished by a more quiet eye, and a calmer mien. A smile, like that of success played about his lips, and he gave his orders clearly, in a more cheerful voice. They were obeyed as briskly. The elder mariners pointed to the seas as they cut through them, and affirmed that the Caroline had never made such progress. The Mates cast the log, and nodded their approbation as one announced to the other the unusual speed of the ship. In short, content and hilarity reigned on board, for it was thought that the passage was commenced under favourable auspices, and there was the hope of a speedy and a prosperous termination of the run. In the midst of these encouraging omens the sun dipped into the sea, illuming, as it fell, a wide reach of the chill and gloomy element. Then the shades of night gathered over the illimitable waste.

# Chapter XIV

"So foul and fair a day I have not seen."
*Macbeth*, I.iii.38.

THE FIRST WATCH of the night brought no change. Wilder had joined his passengers, cheerful, and with that air of enjoyment which every officer of the sea is apt to exhibit when he has disengaged his vessel from the land, and has fairly launched her on the trackless and fathomless abyss of the ocean. He no longer alluded to the hazards of the passage, but strove by the thousand nameless assiduities which his station enabled him to manifest, to expel all recollection of what had passed from their minds. Mrs Wyllys lent herself to his evident efforts to remove their apprehensions, and one, ignorant of what had occurred between them would have thought the little party around the evening's repast was a contented and unsuspecting groupe of travellers, who had commenced their enterprise under the happiest auguries.

Still there was that in the thoughtful eye and clouded brow of the Governess, as at times she turned her bewildered look on our adventurer, which denoted a mind far from being at ease. She listened to the gay, and peculiar because professional sallies of the young mariner, with smiles that were indulgent while they were melancholy, as if his youthful spirits, enlivened by touches of a humour that was thoroughly and quaintly nautical, recalled familiar but sad images to her fancy. Gertrude had less alloy in her pleasure. Home and a beloved and indulgent father were before her, and she felt while the ship yielded to each fresh impulse of the wind, as if another of those weary miles which had so long separated them, was passed.

During these short, but pleasant hours, the mariner who had been so oddly called to the command of the Bristol trader appeared in a new character. Though his conversation was characterized by the frank manliness of a seaman it was nevertheless tempered by the delicacy of one whose breeding had not been neglected. The beautiful mouth of Gertrude often struggled to conceal the smiles which dimpled her cheeks at his sallies, like a soft air ruffling the surface of some limpid spring, and once or twice when the humour of Wilder came unexpectedly, and in stronger colours than common, across her youthful fancy, she yielded to an irresistible merriment.

One hour of the free intercourse of a ship can do more towards softening the cold exterior in which the world encrusts the best of human feelings, than weeks of the unmeaning ceremonies of the land. He who has not felt this truth, would do well to distrust his own companionable qualities. It would seem that man, when he finds himself in the solitude of the ocean, most feels his dependancy on others for happiness. He yields to sentiments with which he trifled, in the wantonness of security, and is glad to seek relief in the sympathies of his kind. A community of hazard makes a community of interest, whether person or property composes the stake. Perhaps a literal reasoner might add, that, as each is conscious the condition and fortunes of his neighbour are the indexes of his own, they acquire value from their affinity to self. If this conclusion be true, Providence has happily so constituted some of the species, that the sordid feeling is too latent to be discovered; and least of all was any one of the three who passed the first hours of the night around the cabin table of the Royal Caroline to be included in this selfish class. The nature of the intercourse, which had rendered the first hours of their acquaintance so singularly equivocal, appeared to be forgotten in the freedom of the moment, or if it were remembered at all, it merely served to give the young seaman additional interest in the eyes of the females, as much by the mystery of the circumstances as by the concern he had manifested in their behalf.

The bell had struck eight; and the hoarse call was heard which summoned another set of watchers to the deck, before the party was aware of the lateness of the hour.

"It is the middle watch," said Wilder, smiling when he observed that Gertrude started at the strange sounds, listening like a timid doe that catches the note of the hunter's horn. "We seamen are not always musical, as you may judge by the strains of the present spokesman. There are, however, ears in the ship to whom his notes are even more discordant than to your own."

"You mean the sleepers?" said Mrs Wyllys.

"I mean the watch below. There is nothing so sweet to the foremast mariner as his sleep, for it is the most precarious of all his enjoyments; on the other hand, perhaps, it is the most treacherous companion the commander knows."

"And why is the rest of the superior so much less grateful than that of the common man?"

"Because he pillows his head on responsibility."

"You are young, Mr Wilder, for a trust like this you bear."

"It is a service which makes all prematurely old."

"Then, why not quit it?" said Gertrude, a little hastily.

"Quit it!" he replied, gazing at her intently, while he suspended his reply. "It would be like quitting the air I breathe."

"Have you so long been devoted to your profession?" resumed Mrs Wyllys, bending her thoughtful eye from the ingenuous countenance of her pupil, once more towards the features of the young man.

"I have reason to think I was born on the sea."

"Think! you surely know your birth-place!"

"We are all of us dependant on the testimony of others," said Wilder, smiling, "for the account of that important event. My earliest recollections are blended with the sight of the ocean, and I can hardly say that I am a creature of the land at all."

"You have at least been fortunate in those who have had the charge of your education and of your younger days?"

"I have!" he answered with emphasis. Then shading his face an instant with his hands, he arose and added with a melancholy smile—"And now to my last duty for the twenty four hours. Have you a disposition to look at the night? So skilful and so stout a sailor should not seek her berth, without passing an opinion on the weather."

The governess took his arm, and they ascended the stairs of the cabin in silence, each finding sufficient employment in meditation. She was followed by the more active Gertrude, who joined them on the weather side of the quarter deck.

The night was misty rather than dark. A full and bright moon had arisen, but it pursued its path through the heavens behind a body of dusky clouds, that was much too dense for the borrowed rays to penetrate. Here and there, a straggling gleam appeared to find its way through a covering of vapour less dense than the rest, falling upon the water like the dim illumination of a distant taper. As the wind was fresh and easterly,* the sea seemed to throw upward from its agitated surface more light than it received, long lines of glittering foam following each other, and lending a distinctness to the waters that the heavens themselves wanted. The ship was bowed low on its side, and as it entered each rolling swell, a wide crescent of foam was driven ahead, the element appearing to gambol along its path. But though the time was propitious, the wind not absolutely adverse, and the heavens rather gloomy than threatening, an uncertain and to a landsman it might seem an unnatural light gave a character of the wildest loneliness to the view.

Gertrude shuddered on reaching the deck, while she murmured an expression of strange delight. Even Mrs Wyllys gazed upon the dark waves, that were heaving and setting in the horizon, around which was shed most of that radiance that seemed so supernatural with a deep conviction that she was now entirely in the hands of the being who had created the waters and the land. But Wilder looked upon the scene as one fastens his gaze on a placid sky. To him the view possessed neither novelty, nor dread, nor charm. Not so with his more youthful and enthusiastic companion. After the first sensations of awe had a little subsided, she exclaimed, in the ardour of admiration, —

"One such sight would repay a month of imprisonment in a ship! You must find great enjoyment in these scenes, Mr Wilder, you who have them always at command."

"There is pleasure to be found in them without doubt. I would that the wind had veer'd a point or two! I do not like the sky nor yonder misty horizon nor this breeze hanging so dead at east."

"The vessel makes great progress," calmly returned Mrs Wyllys, observing that the young man spoke without consciousness, and fearing the effect of his words on the mind of

---

*The writer will not pretend to give the philosophical reason for the phenomenon; but he thinks that every seaman must have observed that the sea has more of the peculiar light alluded to in an eastern than in a western breeze, especially within the limits of the Atlantic.

her pupil. "If we are going on our course, there is the appearance of a quick and prosperous passage."

"True!" exclaimed Wilder, who had become conscious of his indiscretion. "Quite probable, and very true. Mr Earing, the air is getting too heavy for that duck. Hand all your topgallant sails, and haul the ship up closer. Should the wind hang here at East-with-southing, we may want all the offing we can get."

The mate replied in the obedient manner which seamen use to their superiors, and after scanning the signs of the weather for a moment himself, he proceeded to see the order executed. While the men were on the yards furling the light canvass, the females walked apart, leaving the young commander to the uninterrupted discharge of his duty. But Wilder, so far from deeming it necessary to lend his attention to so ordinary a service, the moment after he had spoken, seemed perfectly unconscious that the mandate had issued from his mouth. He stood on the precise spot where the view of the ocean and the heavens first caught his eye, and his gaze still continued fastened on the aspect of the two elements. His look was always in the direction of the wind, which, though far from a gale, frequently fell upon the sails in heavy and sullen puffs. After a long examination, the young mariner muttered his thoughts to himself, and commenced pacing the deck rapidly. Still he would make sudden and short pauses, rivetting his gaze on the point of the compass whence the blasts came, as if he distrusted the weather, and would fain penetrate the gloom of night, in order to relieve some painful doubt. At length his step became arrested, in one of those quick turns that he made at each end of his narrow walk. Mrs Wyllys and Gertrude stood nigh, and were enabled to read the anxious character of his countenance, as his eye became suddenly fastened on a distant point of the ocean, though in a quarter exactly opposite to that in which his former looks had been directed.

"Do you see reason to distrust the weather?" asked the governess, when she thought his examination had endured long enough to become ominous of evil.

"One does not look to leeward for the signs of the weather, in a breeze like this."

"What is there, that you fasten your eye so intently?"

Wilder raised his arm, and was about to speak, when the limb suddenly fell.

"It was delusion!" he muttered, turning and pacing the deck more rapidly than ever.

His companions watched the extraordinary and apparently unconscious movements of the young commander with amazement and not without a little secret dismay. Their own looks wandered over the expanse of troubled water to leeward, but no where could they see more than the tossing element capped with those ridges of garish foam which served only to make the chilling waste more dreary and imposing.

"We see nothing," said Gertrude, when Wilder again stopped to gaze, as before, on the seeming void.

"Look!" he answered, directing their eyes with his finger. "Is there nothing there?"

"Nothing."

"You look into the sea. Here, just where the heavens and the waters meet, along that streak of misty light, into which the waves are tossing themselves like little hillocks. There, now 'tis smooth again, and my eyes did not deceive me. By heavens, it is a ship!"

"Sail, ho!" shouted a voice from a-top. The cry sounded in the ears of our adventurer like the croaking of a sinister spirit.

"Where-a-way?" he sternly demanded.

"Here on our lee quarter, Sir," returned the seaman at the top of his voice. "I make her out a ship close-hauled, but for an hour past she has looked more like mist than a vessel."

"He is right," muttered Wilder, "and yet 'tis a strange thing that a ship should be just there."

"And why stranger than that we are here?"

"Why!" said the young man, regarding Mrs Wyllys, who had put this question, with a perfectly unconscious eye. "I say, 'tis strange she should be there. I would she were any where else, or steering northward."

"You give no reason. Are we always to have warnings from you," she continued, "without reasons? Do you deem us so utterly unworthy of a reason? or do you think us incapable of thought on a subject connected with the sea? You have failed to make the essay, and are too quick to decide. Try us this once. We may possibly deceive your expectations."

Wilder laughed faintly, and bowed, as if he recollected himself. Still he entered into no explanation but he turned his gaze on the quarter of the ocean where the strange sail was said to be. The females followed his example, and always with the same want of success. Gertrude expressed her disappointment aloud, and her complaints found their way to the ears of the young man.

"You see the streak of dim light," he said, again pointing across the waste. "The clouds have lifted a little there, but the spray of the sea is floating between us and the opening. Her spars look like the delicate work of a spider, against the sky, and yet you see there are all the proportions, with the three masts, of a noble ship."

Aided by these minute directions, Gertrude at length caught a glimpse of the faint object, and soon succeeded in giving the true direction to the look of her governess also. Nothing was visible but the dim outline, not unaptly described by Wilder himself as resembling a spider's web.

"It must be a ship!" said Mrs Wyllys. "But at a vast distance."

"Hum. Would it were farther. I could wish that vessel any where but there."

"And why not there? Have you reason to dread an enemy has been waiting for us in this particular spot?"

"No. Still I like not her position. Would to God she were going North."

"It is some vessel from the port of New York, steering to his Majesty's islands in the Caribbean Seas?"

"Not so," said Wilder, shaking his head. "No vessel, from under the heights of Navesink, could gain that offing with a wind like this!"

"It is then some ship going into the same place, or perhaps a vessel bound for one of the bays of the Middle Colonies!"

"Her road would be too plain to be mistaken. See; the stranger is close upon a wind."

"It may be a trader, or a cruiser coming *from* one of the places I have named."

"Neither. The wind has had too much northing the last two days for that."

"It is a vessel that we have overtaken, and which, like ourselves, has come out of the waters of Long-Island Sound."

"That, indeed, is our last hope," muttered Wilder.

The Governess, who had put the foregoing questions in order to extract from the commander of the Caroline, the information he so pertinaciously withheld, had now exhausted all her own knowledge on the subject, and was compelled to await his further pleasure in the matter, or resort to the less equivocal means of direct interrogatories. But the busy state of Wilder's thoughts left her no immediate opportunity to pursue the subject. He soon summoned the Officer of the watch to his councils, and they consulted together apart for many minutes. The hardy, but far from quick-witted, seaman, who filled the second station in the ship, saw nothing so remarkable in the appearance of a strange sail in the precise spot where the dim and nearly aerial image of the unknown vessel was still visible; nor did he hesitate to pronounce her some honest trader, bent, like themselves, on her purpose of lawful commerce. His commander thought otherwise, as will appear by the short dialogue that passed between them.

"Is it not extraordinary that she should be just there?" demanded Wilder, after each, in turn, had made a closer examination of the faint object by the aid of an excellent night-glass.

"She would certainly be better off here," returned the literal seaman, who had an eye only for the nautical situation of the stranger; "we should be none the worse for being a dozen leagues more to the eastward, ourselves. If the wind holds here, at East by South, half-South, we shall have need of all that offing. I got jammed once between Hatteras and the Gulph"—

"Do you not perceive that she is where no vessel could or ought to be, unless she has run exactly the same course with ourselves?" interrupted Wilder. "Nothing from any harbor South of New-York, could have such northing as the wind has held; while nothing from the Colony of York would stand on this tack if bound East, or would be there, if going Southward."

The plain-going ideas of the honest mate were open to a

reasoning which the reader may find a little obscure, for his mind contained a sort of chart of the ocean, to which he could at any time refer, with a proper discrimination between the various winds and all the different points of the compass. When properly directed, he was not slow to see the probable justice of his young commander's inferences, and then wonder, in its turn, began to take possession of his more obtuse faculties.

"It is downright unnatural, truly, that the fellow should be just there!" he replied, shaking his head, but meaning no more than that it was entirely out of the order of nautical propriety. "I see the reason of what you say, Captain Wilder, and I don't know how to explain it. It is a ship to a moral certainty!"

"Of that there is no doubt. But a ship most strangely placed!"

"I doubled the Good-Hope in the year '46," continued the other, "and we saw a vessel, lying as it might be here on our weather bow, which is just opposite to this fellow, since *he* is on our lee quarter—but there I saw a ship standing for an hour across our forefoot, and yet, though we set the azimuth, not a degree did he budge, starboard or larboard during all that time, which as it was heavy weather was to say the least, something out of the common order!"

"It was remarkable!" returned Wilder with an air so vacant as to prove that he rather communed with himself than attended to his companion.

"There are mariners who say that the Flying Dutchman cruises off that Cape, and that he often gets on the weather side of a stranger and bears down upon him, like a ship about to lay him aboard. Many is the King's cruiser, as they say, that has turned her hands up from a sweet sleep, when the look-outs have seen a double-decker coming down in the night, with ports up and batteries lighted—but then this can't be any such craft as the Dutchman, since she is at the most no more than a large sloop-of-war, if a cruiser at all."

"No," said Wilder, "this can never be the Dutchman."

"Yon vessel shows no lights, and, for that matter, she has such a misty look that one might well question its being a ship at all—then again the Dutchman is always seen to windward, and the strange sail we have here, lies broad upon our lee-quarter!"

"It is no Dutchman," said Wilder, drawing a long breath, like a man awaking from a trance. "Main-top-mast-cross trees, there!"

The man stationed aloft answered the hail in the customary manner, the short conversation that succeeded being necessarily maintained in shouts rather than in speeches.

"How long have you seen the stranger?" was the first demand of Wilder.

"I have just come aloft, Sir; but the man I relieved tells me more than an hour."

"And has the man you relieved come down; or who is that I see sitting on the lee-side of the mast-head?"

" 'Tis Bob Roband, Sir, who says he cannot sleep, and so he stays upon the yard to keep me company—"

"Send the man down. I would speak to him."

While the wakeful seaman was descending the rigging, the two officers continued silent, finding sufficient occupation in musing on what had already passed.

"Why are you not in your hammock?" said Wilder, a little sternly to the man, who in obedience to his order had descended to the quarter deck.

"I am not sleep-bound, your honour, and I had a mind to pass another hour aloft."

"And why are you who have two night-watches to keep already, so willing to enlist in a third?"

"To own the truth, Sir, my mind has been a little misgiving about this passage since the moment we lifted our anchor."

Mrs Wyllys and Gertrude, who were auditors, insensibly drew nigher to listen with a species of interest which betrayed itself by the thrilling of nerves, and an accelerated movement of the pulse.

"And you have your doubts, Sir!" exclaimed the Captain in a tone of slight contempt. "Pray, may I ask, what you have seen on board here to make you distrust the ship."

"No harm in asking, your honour," returned the seaman, crushing the hat he held between two hands, that had a gripe like a couple of vices, "and, so, I hope, there is none in answering. I pulled an oar in the boat after the old man this morning, and I cannot say I like the manner in which he got from the chase. Then there is something in the ship to lee-ward that comes athwart my fancy like a drag, and I confess, your honor, that I should make but little head-way in a nap, though I should try the swing of a hammock."

"How long is it since you made out the ship to leeward?"

"I will not swear that a real, living ship has been made out at all, Sir. Something I did see, just before the bell struck seven, and there it is just as clear and just as dim to be seen, now, by them that have good eyes."

"And how did she bear when you first saw her?"

"Two or three points more upon the beam than now."

"Then we are passing her!" exclaimed Wilder, with a plea-sure too evident to be concealed.

"No, your honour, no. You forget, Sir, the ship has come closer to the wind since the middle watch was set."

"True—" returned his young commander in disappoint-ment—"true; too true. And her bearing has not changed since you first made her out?"

"Not by compass, Sir. It is a quick boat, that, or it would never hold such way with the Royal Caroline, and that too upon a stiffened bow-line, which every body knows is the real play of this ship."

"Go, get you to your hammock. In the morning we may have a better look at the fellow."

"And—you hear me, Sir," added the attentive mate, "do not keep the men's eyes open below with a tale as long as the short cable, but take your own natural rest, and leave all others, that have clear consciences to do the same."

"Mr Earing," said Wilder, as the seaman reluctantly proceeded to his place of rest, "we will bring the ship upon the other tack, and get more easting, while the land is so far from us. This course will be setting us upon Hatteras. Besides"—

"Yes, Sir," the mate replied, observing his superior to hesi-tate, "as you were saying, besides, no one can foretell the length of a gale nor the real quarter from which it may come."

"Precisely. No one can answer for the weather. The men can scarcely be in their hammocks. Turn them up at once, Sir, before their eyes are heavy, and we will get the ship's head the other way."

The mate instantly sounded the well known cry which summoned the watch below to the assistance of their ship-mates on deck. Little delay occurred and not a word was uttered, but the short authoritative mandates which Wilder saw fit to deliver from his own lips. No longer pressed up against the wind, the ship, obedient to her helm, gracefully began to incline her head from the waves, and to bring the wind abeam. Then, instead of breasting and mounting the endless hillocks, like a being that toiled heavily along its path, she fell into the trough of the sea, from which she issued like a courser that, having conquered an ascent, shoots along the track with redoubled velocity. For an instant the wind appeared to lull, though the wide ridge of foam that rolled along on each side the vessel's bows, sufficiently proclaimed that she was skimming before it. In another moment the tall spars began to incline again to the west, and the vessel came swooping up to the wind, until her plunges and shocks against the seas were renewed as violently as before. When every yard and sheet were properly trimmed to meet the new position of the vessel, Wilder turned to get a glimpse of the stranger. A minute was lost in ascertaining the precise point where he ought to appear: for in such a chaos of water, and with no guide but the judgement the eye was apt to deceive itself by referring to the nearer and more familiar objects by which the spectator was surrounded.

"The stranger has vanished!" said Earing, with a voice in which mental relief and distrust were oddly manifesting themselves.

"He should indeed be on this quarter; but I see him not!"

"Ay, ay, Sir; this is the way that the midnight cruiser off the Hope is said to come and go. There are men who have seen that vessel shut in by a fog, in as fine a star-light night as was ever met in a Southern latitude—but then this cannot be the Dutchman, since it is so many long leagues from the pitch of the Cape to the coast of North America!"

"Here he lies; and by Heavens he has already gone about!"

The truth of what Wilder affirmed was sufficiently evident to the eye of a seaman. The same diminutive and misty tracery as before was to be seen on the lighter background of the horizon, looking not unlike the faintest shadows cast upon some brighter surface, by the deception of the Phantasmagoria. But to the mariners, who so well knew how to distinguish between the different lines of her masts, it was very evident that her course had been suddenly and dexterously changed, and that she was now no longer steering to the South and West, but like themselves, holding her way towards the northeast, or broadly off towards the middle of the Atlantic. The fact appeared to make a sensible impression on them all, though probably, had their reasons been sifted they would have been found to be entirely different.

"That fellow has truly tacked!" said Earing, after a long meditative pause, and with a voice, in which awe was beginning to get the ascendency of doubt. "Long as I have followed the sea, have I never before seen a vessel tack against such a head-beating sea! He must have been all shaking in the wind, when we gave him the last look, or we should not have lost sight of him!"

"A lively and quick-working vessel might do it—" said Wilder—"especially if strong-handed."

"Ay, the hand of Belzebub is always strong; and a light job would he make of it, in forcing a craft to sail upon her trucks"—

"Mr Earing," said Wilder, "we will pack upon the Caroline, and try our sailing with this stranger. Get the main tack aboard, and set the top-gallant sail."

The slow-minded mate would have remonstrated against the order had he dared, but there was that, in the calm manner of his young commander, which admonished him of the hazard. He was not wrong, however, in considering the duty he was now to perform, as one that was not entirely free from risk. The ship was already moving under quite as much canvass as he deemed it prudent to show, at such an hour and with so many threatening symptoms of still heavier weather hanging about the horizon. The necessary orders were, however, repeated as promptly as they had been given. The seamen had already begun to consider the stranger, and to converse among themselves concerning his appearance and situation, and they obeyed with an alacrity that might perhaps have been traced to a secret but common wish to escape from his vicinity. The sails were successively and speedily set, and then each man folded his arms, and stood gazing steadily and intently at the shadowy object to leeward, in order to witness the effect of the change.

The Royal Caroline seemed, like her crew, sensible of the necessity of increasing her speed. As she felt the pressure of the broad sheets of canvass that had just been distended, the ship bowed lower, appearing to recline on the bed of water, which rose under her lee nearly to the scuppers. On the other side, the dark planks and polished copper lay bare, for many feet, though often washed by the waves that came sweeping along her length, green and angrily, still capped as usual with crests of lucid foam. The shocks, as the vessel tilted against the billows, were becoming every moment more severe, and from each encounter, a bright cloud of spray arose, which either fell glittering on the deck, or drove in brilliant mist across the rolling water far to leeward.

Wilder long watched the ship with a clouded brow, but with the steady intelligence of a seaman. Once or twice, when she trembled, and appeared to stop in her violent encounter with a wave, as suddenly as if she had struck a rock, his lips severed, and he was about to give the order to reduce the sail. But a glance at the misty looking image in the western horizon caused him to change his purpose. Like a desperate adventurer who had cast his fortunes on some hazardous experiment, he appeared to await the issue with a resolution as haughty as it was unconquerable.

"That top-mast is bending like a whip," muttered the careful Earing at his elbow—

"Let it go; we have spare spars enough to put in its place."

"I have always found the Caroline leaky, after she has been strained by driving her against the sea."

"We have our pumps."

"True, Sir; but, in my poor judgement it is idle to think of outsailing a craft that the devil commands, if he does not altogether handle."

"One will never know that, Mr Earing, 'till he tries."

"We gave the Dutchman a chance of that sort, and I must say we not only had the most canvass spread, but much the best of the wind. And what good did it do! There he lay under his three topsails, driver and jib, and we with studding sails alow and aloft couldn't alter his bearing a foot."

"The Dutchman is never seen in a Northern latitude."

"Well, I cannot say he is," returned Earing, in a sort of compelled resignation; "but he who has put that flyer off the Cape may have found the cruise so profitable as to wish to send another ship into these seas."

Wilder made no reply. He had either humoured the superstitious apprehensions of his mate, enough, or his mind was too intent on its principal object, to dwell longer on a foreign subject.

Notwithstanding the seas that met her advance, in such quick succession as greatly to retard her progress, the Bristol trader had soon toiled her way through a league of the troubled element. At every plunge she took, the bows divided a mass of water, that appeared to be fast getting more vast and more violent, and more than once the struggling hull was nearly buried forward, in some wave which it had equal difficulty in mounting or penetrating.

The mariners narrowly watched the smallest movements of their vessel. Not a man left her deck for hours. The superstitious awe which had taken such deep hold of the untutored faculties of the chief mate had not been slow in extending its influence to the meanest of her crew. Even the accident which had befallen their former commander, and the sudden and mysterious manner in which the young officer who now trod the quarter deck, so singularly firm and calm under circumstances deemed so imposing, had their influence in heightening the wild impression. The impunity with which the Caroline bore such a press of canvass under the circumstances in which she was placed added to their kindling admiration, and ere Wilder had determined in his own mind on the powers of his ship in comparison with those of the vessel that so strangely hung in the horizon, he was himself becoming the subject of unnatural and revolting suspicions to his own crew.

# Chapter XV

—"I' the name of truth,
Are ye fantastical, or that indeed
Which outwardly ye show?"
*Macbeth*, I.iii.52—54.

Superstition is a quality that seems indigenous to the ocean. Few common mariners are exempt from its influence in a greater or less degree, though it is found to exist among the seamen of different people in forms that are tempered by their respective national habits and peculiar opinions. The sailor of the Baltic has his secret rites and his manner of propitiating the gods of the wind; the Mediterranean mariner tears his hair and kneels before the shrine of some impotent saint, when his own hand might better do the service he implores; while the more skilful Englishman sees the spirits of the dead in the storm and hears the cries of a lost messmate in the gusts that sweep the waste he navigates. Even the better-instructed and still more reasoning American has not been able to shake off entirely the secret influence of a sentiment that seems to be the concomitant of his condition.

There is a majesty in the might of the great deep, that has a tendency to keep open the avenues of that dependant credulity which more or less besets the mind of every man, however he may have fortified his intellect by thought. With the firmament above him and wandering on an interminable waste of water, the less gifted seaman is tempted at every step of his pilgrimage to seek the relief of some propitious omen. The few which are supported by scientific causes, give support to the many that have their origin only in his own excited and doubting fancy. The gambols of the dolphin, the earnest and busy passage of the porpoise, the ponderous sporting of the unwieldy whale and the screams of the marine birds have all, like the signs of the ancient soothsayers, their attendant consequences of good or evil. The confusion between things which are explicable and things which are not, gradually brings the mind of the mariner to a state in which any exciting and unnatural sentiment is welcome, if it be for no other reason than that, like the vast element on which he passes his life, it bears the impression of what is thought a supernatural, because it is an incomprehensible, cause.

The crew of the Royal Caroline were all from that distant island that has been and still continues to be the hive of nations, which are probably fated to carry her name to a time when the site of her own fallen power shall be sought as a curiosity, like the remains of a city in a desert.

The whole events of the day had a tendency to arouse the latent superstition of these men. It has already been said that the calamity which had befallen their former commander and the manner in which a stranger had succeeded to his authority had their influence in increasing their disposition to doubt. The sail to leeward appeared most inopportunely for the character of our adventurer, who had not yet enjoyed a fitting opportunity to secure the confidence of his inferiors, before such untoward circumstances occurred as threatened to deprive him of it forever.

There has existed but one occasion for introducing to the reader the mate who filled the station in the ship next to that of Earing. He was called Knighthead; a name that was, in sound at least, indicative of a certain misty obscurity that beset his superior member. The qualities of his mind may be appreciated by the few reflections he saw fit to make on the escape of the old mariner whom Wilder had intended to punish. As this individual was but one degree removed from the common men in situation, he was much more nearly associated with them in habits and opinions than Earing. His influence among them was accordingly much greater than that of his brother mate, while his authority was less, and his sentiments were very generally received as the rule by which all things, that did not actually depend on the mere right to command, were to be judged.

After the ship had been wore, and during the time that Wilder, with a view to lose sight of his unwelcome neighbour, was endeavouring to urge her through the seas in the manner already described, this stubborn and mistified tar remained in the waist of the vessel, surrounded by a few of the older and more experienced seamen, holding converse on the remarkable appearance of the phantom to leeward and on the extraordinary manner in which their unknown officer saw fit to attest the enduring qualities of their own vessel. We shall commence our relation of the dialogue at a point where Knighthead saw fit to discontinue his distant innuendos in order to deal more directly with the subject he had under discussion.

"I have heard it said by older sea-faring men than any in this ship," he continued, "that the devil has been known to send one of his mates aboard a lawful trader, to lead her astray among shoals and quicksands, in order that he might make a wreck and get his share of the salvage, among the souls of the people. What man can say, who gets into the cabin, when an unknown name stands first in the shipping list of a vessel?"

"The stranger is shut in by a cloud!" exclaimed one of the mariners, who while he listened to the philosophy of his officer, still kept an eye riveted on the mysterious object to leeward.

"Ay, ay; it would occasion no surprise to me to see that craft steering into the moon! Luck is like a fly-block and its yard. When one goes up, the other comes down. They say the red-coats ashore have had their turn of fortune, and it is time we honest seamen look out for our squalls. I have doubled the Horn, brothers, in a King's ship, and I have seen the bright cloud that never sets, and I have held a living corposant in my own hand. But these are things which any man may look on, who will go upon a yard in a gale, or ship aboard a Southseaman; still I pronounce it uncommon for a vessel to see her shadow in the haze, as we have ours at this moment; there it comes again—hereaway between the after-shroud and the backstay—or for a trader to carry sail in a fashion that would make every knee in a bomb-ketch work, like a tooth-brush fiddling across a passenger's mouth after he has had a smart bout with the sea sickness."

"And yet the lad holds the ship in hand," said the oldest of all the seamen, who kept his gaze fastened on the proceedings of Wilder; "he is driving her through it, in a mad manner I will allow, but yet so far he has not parted a yarn!"

"Yarns!" repeated the mate in a tone of contempt, "what signify yarns when the whole cable is to snap, and in such a fashion as to leave no hope for the anchor, except in a buoy rope! Harkee, old Bill; the devil never finishes his jobs by halves; what is to happen will happen bodily, and no easing off as if you were lowering the captain's lady into a boat, and he on deck to see fair play."

"Mr Knighthead knows how to keep a ship's reckoning in all weathers!" said another, whose manner sufficiently announced the dependance he himself placed on the capacity of the second mate.

"And no credit to me for the same. I have seen all services and handled every rig, from a lugger to a double decker! Few men can say more in their own favour than myself; for the little I know, has been got by much hardship and small schooling. But what matters information or even seamanship against witchcraft or the workings of one whom I don't choose to name, seeing there is no use in offending any gentleman unnecessarily? I say, brothers, that this ship is packed upon in a fashion that no prudent seaman ought to or would allow."

A common murmur announced that most if not all of his hearers were of the same mind.

"Let us examine calmly and reasonably and in a manner becoming enlightened Englishmen into the whole state of the case," the mate continued, casting an eye obliquely over his shoulder to make sure that the individual of whose displeasure he stood in so salutary awe was not actually at his elbow. "We are all of us, to a man, native born islanders without a drop of foreign blood among us; not so much as a Scotchman or an Irishman in the ship; let us therefore look into the philosophy of this affair with the judgment which becomes our breeding. In the first place, here is honest Nicholas Nichols slips from this here water-cask and breaks me a leg! Now, brothers, I've known men to fall from tops and yards and lighter damage done. But what matters it to a certain person how far he throws his man since he has only to lift a finger to get us all hanged! Then comes me aboard here, a stranger with a look of the colonies about him, and none of your plain dealing out-and-out smooth

English faces such as a man can cover with the flat of his hand."—

"The lad is well enough to the eye," interrupted the old mariner.

"Ay, therein lies the whole deviltry of this matter! He is good looking I grant ye, but it is not such good looking as an Englishman loves. There is a meaning about him, that I don't like; I never likes too much meaning in a man's countenance, seeing that it is not always easy to understand what he would be doing. Then this stranger gets to be Master of the Ship, or what is the same thing, next to master, while he who should be on deck giving his orders, in a time like this, is lying in his berth unable to tack himself, much less to put the vessel about; and yet no man can say how the thing came to pass!"

"He drove a bargain with the consignee for the station, and right glad did the cunning merchant seem to get so tight a youth to take charge of the Caroline."

"A merchant, after all, like the rest of us, is made of nothing better than clay—and what is worse, it is seldom that in putting him together, he is dampened with salt water. Many is the trader that has doused his spectacles and shut his account books to step aside to overreach his neighbour, and then come back to find that he has overreached himself. Mr Bale, no doubt, thought he was doing the clever thing for the owners when he shipped this Mr Wilder, but then perhaps he did not know that the vessel was sold to—it becomes a plain-going seaman to have a respect for all he sails under, so I will not unnecessarily name the person, who, I believe, has got, whether he came by it in a fair purchase or not, no small right in this vessel."

"I have never seen a ship got out of irons more handsomely than he handled the Caroline this very morning."

Knighthead indulged in a low, but what to his listeners appeared to be an exceedingly meaning laugh.

"When a ship has a certain sort of captain one is not to be surprised at any thing!" he answered, the instant his merriment ceased. "For my own part, I shipped to go from Bristol to the Carolinas and Jamaica, touching at Newport out and home, and I will say, boldly, I have no wish to go any where else. As to backing the Caroline from her awkward berth alongside the slaver, why it was well done; too well for so young a mariner. Had I done the thing myself it could not have been better. But what think you, brothers, of the old man in the skiff? There was a chase and an escape such as few old sea-dogs have the fortune to behold! I have heard of a smuggler that was chased a hundred times by his Majesty's cutters in the chops of the Channel, and which always had a fog handy to run into, but from which no man could truly say he ever saw her come out again! This skiff may have plied between the land and that Gurnseyman for any thing I know to the contrary but it is not a boat I wish to pull a scull in."

"That *was* a remarkable flight!" exclaimed the elder seaman, whose faith in the character of our adventurer began to give way gradually before such an accumulation of testimony.

"I call it so; though other men may possibly know better than I, who have only followed the water five and thirty years. Then, here is the sea getting up in an unaccountable manner; and look at these rags of clouds which darken the heavens, and yet there is light enough coming from the ocean for a good scholar to read by!"

"I've often seen the weather as it is now."

"Ay, who has not? It is seldom that any man, let him come from what part he will, makes his first voyage as captain. Let who will be out to night upon the water, I'll engage he has been there before. I have seen worse looking skies and even worse looking water than this but I never knew any good come of either. The night I was wreck'd in the Bay of"—

"In the waist there!" cried Wilder.

Had a warning voice arisen from the turbulent and rushing ocean itself it would not have sounded more alarming in the startled ears of the conscious seamen than this sudden hail. Their young commander found it necessary to repeat it before even Knighthead, the proper and official spokesman, could muster resolution to answer.

"Get the fore-top-gallant sail on the ship, Sir," continued Wilder when the customary reply let him know that he had been heard.

The mate and his companions regarded each other for a moment in dull admiration, and many a melancholy shake of the head was exchanged, before one of the party threw himself into the weather rigging, proceeding aloft, with a doubting mind, in order to loosen the sail in question.

There was certainly enough in the desperate manner with which Wilder pressed the canvass on the vessel to excite distrust, either of his intentions or judgment, in the opinions of men less influenced by superstition than those it was now his lot to command. It had long been apparent to Earing, and his more ignorant and consequently more obstinate brother officer, that their young superior had the same desire to escape from the spectral looking ship which so strangely followed their movements as they had themselves. They only differed in the mode. But this difference was so very material that the two mates consulted together apart, and then Earing, something stimulated by the hardy opinions of his coadjutor, approached his commander with the determination of delivering the results of their united judgments, with the directness which he thought the occasion now demanded. But there was that in the steady eye and calm mien of Wilder that caused him to touch on the dangerous subject with a discretion and circumlocution that were a little remarkable for the individual. He stood watching the effect of the sail recently spread for several minutes, before he even presumed to open his mouth. But a terrible encounter between the vessel and a wave that lifted its angry crest apparently some dozen feet above the approaching bows, gave him courage to proceed, by admonishing him afresh of the danger of continuing silent.

"I do not see that we drop the stranger, though the ship is wallowing through the water so heavily," he commenced, determined to be as circumspect as possible in his advances.

Wilder bent another of his frequent glances on the misty object in the horizon, and then turned his frowning eye towards the point whence the wind proceeded, as if he would invite its heaviest blasts; he, however, made no answer.

"We have ever found the crew discontented at the pumps, Sir," resumed the other, after a sufficient pause for the reply he in vain expected, "I need not tell an officer who knows his duty so well that seamen rarely love their pumps."

"Whatever I may find necessary to order, Mr Earing, this ship's company will find it necessary to execute."

There was a settled air of command in the manner with which this tardy answer was given, that did not fail of its effect. Earing recoiled a step submissively, affecting to be lost in consulting the driving masses of clouds. Then, summoning his resolution, he attempted to renew the attack in a different quarter.

"Is it your deliberate opinion, Capt. Wilder," he said, using the title to which the claim of our adventurer might well be questioned with a view to propitiate him, "is it, then, your deliberate opinion that the Royal Caroline can, by any human means, be made to outsail yonder vessel?"

"I fear not," returned the young man, drawing a breath so long, that all his secret concern seemed struggling in his breast for utterance.

"And, Sir, with proper submission to your better education and authority in this ship I *know* not. I have often seen these matches tried, in my time, and well do I know that nothing is gained by straining a vessel with the hope of getting to windward of one of these flyers!"

"Take the glass, Earing, and tell me under what canvass the stranger is going, and what you think his distance may be," said Wilder, without appearing to advert at all to what the other had just observed.

The honest and really well-meaning mate deposed his hat on the quarter deck, and did as desired. When his look had been long, grave and deeply absorbed, he closed the glass with the palm of his broad hand, and replied in the manner of one whose opinion was sufficiently matured—

"If yonder sail had been built and fitted like other craft," he said, "I should not be backward in pronouncing her a full-rigged ship, under three single reefed topsails, courses, spanker and jib."

"Has she no more!"

"To that I would qualify, provided an opportunity were given me to make sure that she is in all respects, like other vessels."

"And, yet, Earing, with all this press of canvass by the compass we have not left her a foot!"

"Lord, Sir," returned the mate, shaking his head like one who was well convinced of the folly of such efforts, "if you were to split every cloth in the mainsail, you will never alter the bearings of that craft an inch 'till the sun shall rise! Then, indeed, such as have eyes that are good enough, might perhaps see her sailing about among the clouds, though it has never been my fortune, be it bad or be it good, to fall in with one of these cruisers, after the day has fairly dawned."

"And the distance?—" said Wilder; "you have not yet spoken of her distance."

"That is much as people choose to measure. She may be here, nigh enough to toss a biscuit into our tops; or she may be there, where she seems to be, hull-down, in the horizon."

"But if where she seems to be—?"

"Why, she *seems* to be a vessel of about six hundred tons, and judging from appearances only, a man might be tempted to say she was a couple of leagues, more or less, under our lee."

"I put her at the same! Six miles to windward is not a little advantage in a hard chase. By Heavens! Earing, I'll drive the Caroline out of water but I'll leave him!"

"That might be done, if the ship had wings like a curlew or a sea-gull; but, as it is I think we are more likely to drive her under."

"She bears her canvass well so far. You know not what the boat can do when urged!"

"I have seen her sailed in all weathers, Capt. Wilder, but"—

His mouth was suddenly closed. A vast black wave reared itself between the ship and the Eastern horizon and came rolling onward, seeming to threaten to engulf all before it. Even Wilder watched the shock with breathless anxiety, conscious for the moment that he had exceeded the bounds of sound discretion in urging his ship so powerfully against such a mass of water. Luckily the sea broke a few fathoms from the bows of the Caroline, sending its surge in a flood of foam upon her decks. For half a minute, the forward part of the vessel disappeared, as if, unable to mount the swell, it were striving to go through it and then she heavily emerged, gemmed with a million of the scintillating insects of the ocean. The ship stopped, trembling in every joint of her massive and powerful frame like some affrighted courser, and when she resumed her course it was with a moderation that appeared to warn those who governed her movements of their indiscretion.

Earing faced his commander in silence, perfectly conscious that nothing he could utter contained an argument like this. The seamen no longer hesitated to mutter their disapprobation aloud, and many a prophetic opinion was ventured concerning the consequences of such reckless risks. To all this Wilder turned an insensible ear. Firm in his secret purpose, he would have braved a greater hazard to accomplish his object. But a distinct though smothered shriek, from the stern of the vessel reminded him of the fears of others. Turning quickly on his heel, he approached the still trembling Gertrude and her governess, who had both been, throughout the whole of those long and tedious hours, inobtrusive but deeply interested observers of his smallest movements.

"The vessel bore that shock so well, I have great reliance on her powers," he said in a soothing voice, but with words that were intended to lull her into a blind security. "With a firm ship, a thorough seaman is never at a loss!"

"Mr Wilder," returned the Governess, "I have seen much of this terrible element on which you live. It is vain to think of deceiving me. I know that you are urging the vessel beyond what is usual. Have you sufficient motive for this hardihood?"

"Madam—I have."

"And is it, like so many of your motives, to continue locked for ever in your own breast, or may we who are equal participators in its consequences claim to share equally in the reason?"

"Since you know so much of the profession," returned the young man, slightly laughing, but in a way that rendered what he said more alarming by the sounds produced in the unnatural effort, "you need not be told that in order to get a ship to windward, it is necessary to show her canvass."

"You can at least answer one of my questions more directly. Is this wind sufficiently favorable to pass the dangerous shoals of Hatteras?"

"I doubt it."

"Then why not return to the place, whence we came!"

"Will you consent to that?" demanded the youth with the swiftness of thought.

"I would go to my father," said Gertrude, with a rapidity so nearly resembling his own, that the ardent girl appeared to want breath to utter the little she said.

"And I am willing, Mr Wilder, to abandon this ship entirely," calmly resumed the Governess. "I require no explanation of all your mysterious warnings; restore us to our friends in Newport, and no further questions shall ever be asked."

"It might be done!" muttered our adventurer. "It might be done! A few busy hours would do it with this wind. Mr Earing—"

The Mate was instantly at his elbow. Wilder pointed to the dim object to leeward, and handing him the glass, desired that he would take another view. Each again looked in turn long and closely.

"He shows no more sail!" said the commander impatiently, when his own prolonged gaze was ended.

"Not a cloth, Sir. But what matters it to such a craft how much canvass is spread, or how the wind blows!"

"Earing, I think there is too much Southing in this breeze; and there is more brewing in yonder streak of dusky clouds on our beam. Let the ship fall off a couple of points or more, and take the strain off the spars, by a pull upon the weather braces."

The simple minded mate heard this order with an astonishment he did not care to conceal. There needed no explanation to teach one of his experience that the effect would be to go over the same track they had just passed, and that it was in substance, abandoning the objects of the voyage. He presumed to defer his compliance in order to remonstrate.

"I hope there is no offence for an elderly seaman, like myself, Capt. Wilder, in venturing an opinion on the weather," he said. "My judgement approved of going about, for I have no taste for land that the wind blows on, instead of off, but, by easing the ship with a reef or two, she would be always jogging sea-ward and all we gain would be clear gain, because it is so much off the Hatteras—besides who can say that to-morrow, or the next day, we shan't have a puff out of America, here at North-West!"

"A couple of points fall off, and a pull upon your weather braces," said Wilder in a way to show that he was in earnest.

It would have exceeded the peaceful and submissive disposition of the honest Earing to delay any longer. The orders were given to the inferiors, and as a matter of course they were obeyed, though ill-suppressed and portentous sounds of discontent, at the undetermined and seemingly unreasonable changes in their officer's mind might have been heard issuing from the mouths of Knighthead and the other veterans of the crew.

To all these symptoms of disaffection, Wilder, remained utterly indifferent. If he heard them at all, he either disdained to yield them any notice, or guided by a temporizing policy, he chose to appear unconscious of their import. In the mean time, the vessel, like a bird whose wing had wearied with struggling against the tempest, and which inclines from the gale to choose an easier course, glided swiftly away, quartering the crests of the waves, or sinking gracefully into their troughs, as she yielded to the force of a wind that was now made to be favorable. The seas rolled on in a direction no longer adverse to her course, and by receding from the breeze, the quantity of sail spread was no longer trying to her powers of endurance. Still, in the opinions of all her crew she had quite enough canvass exposed to a night of so portentous aspect. But not so, in the judgment of the stranger who was charged with the guidance of her destinies. In a voice, that still admonished his inferiors of the danger of disobedience, he commanded several broad sheets of studding-sails to be set, in quick succession. Urged by these new impulses the ship went careering over the waves, piling a mass of foam in her track, that rivalled, in its volume and brightness the tumbling summit of the largest swell.

When sail after sail had been set, until even Wilder was obliged to confess to himself, that the Royal Caroline, staunch as she was, would bear no more, our adventurer began to pace the deck again, and to cast his eyes about him, to watch the fruits of his new experiment. The change in the course of the Bristol trader, had made a corresponding change in the apparent direction of the stranger, who yet floated in the horizon like a diminutive and misty shadow. Still the unerring compass told the watchful mariner, that she continued to maintain the same relative position as when first seen.* No effort on the part of Wilder, could alter her bearing an inch. An hour soon passed away, during which, as the log told him, his own ship had rolled through three leagues of water, and still there lay the stranger in the west, as if he were merely a lessened shadow of herself, cast by the Caroline upon the distant and dusky clouds. An alteration in his course exposed a broader surface of his canvass to the eyes of those who watched him, but in nothing else was there a visible change. If his sail had been materially increased the distance and the obscurity prevented even the understanding Earing from detecting it. Perhaps the excited mind of the worthy mate was too much predisposed to believe in the miraculous powers possessed by his unaccountable neighbor, to admit of the full exercise of his experienced faculties on the occasion, but even Wilder, who vexed his sight, in often repeated examinations, was obliged to confess to himself, that the stranger seemed to glide across the waste of waters, more like a body floating in air, than a ship resorting to the known expedients of mariners.

Mrs Wyllys and her charge, by this time, had retired to their cabin, the former secretly felicitating herself on the prospect of soon quitting a vessel that had commenced its voyage under such sinister circumstances, as to have deranged the equilibrium of even her governed and well disciplined mind. Gertrude was left in ignorance of the change. To her uninstructed eye, all appeared the same on the wilderness of the ocean, Wilder having it in his power to alter the direction of his vessel as often as he pleased without his fairer and more youthful passenger being any the wiser.

Not so with the intelligent commander of the Caroline, himself. To him there was neither obscurity nor doubt in the midst of his midnight path. His eye had long been familiar with every star that rose from out the dark and ragged outline of the sea, nor was there a blast that swept across the ocean, that his burning cheek could not tell from what quarter of the heavens it poured out its power. He understood each inclination made by the bows of his ship, his mind kept even pace

*The reader will understand that the *apparent* direction of a ship at sea, seen from the deck of another, changes with the change of course, but that the *true* direction can only be varied by a change of relative position.

with her windings and turnings in all her trackless wanderings, and he had little need to consult any of the accessories of his art to tell him what course to steer, or in what manner to guide the movements of the nice machine he governed. Still, he was unable to explain the extraordinary evolutions of the stranger. The smallest change he ordered seemed rather anticipated than followed, and his hopes of eluding a vigilance that proved so watchful were baffled by a facility of manœuvring and a superiority of sailing that really began to assume, even to his intelligent eyes, the appearance of some unaccountable agency.

While our adventurer was engaged in the gloomy musings that such impressions were not ill adapted to excite, the heavens and the sea began to exhibit new aspects. The bright streak which had so long hung along the eastern horizon, as if the curtain of the firmament had been slightly opened to admit a passage for the winds, was now suddenly closed, and heavy masses of black clouds began to gather in that quarter, until vast volumes of the vapour were piled upon the water, blending the two elements in one. On the other hand, the gloomy canopy lifted in the west, and a long belt of lurid light, was shed athwart the view. In this flood of bright and portentous mist, the stranger still floated, though there were moments, when his faint and fanciful outlines seemed to be melting into air.

# Chapter XVI

—"Yet again? What do you here? Shall we give o'er,
and drown? Have you a mind to sink?"

*The Tempest*, I.i.38–39.

O UR WATCHFUL ADVENTURER was not blind to these sinister omens. No sooner did the peculiar atmosphere by
which the mysterious image that he so often examined was
suddenly surrounded, catch his eye, than his voice was raised
in the clear, powerful and exciting notes of warning.

"Stand by," he called aloud, "to in all studding-sails! Down
with them!" he added, scarcely giving his former words time
to reach the ears of his subordinates. "Down with every rag of
them, fore and aft the ship! Man the top-gallant-clew lines,
Mr Earing. Clew up and clew down. In with every thing,
cheerily, men. In!"

This was a language to which the crew of the Caroline were
no strangers, and it was doubly welcome, since the meanest seaman amongst them had long thought that his unknown commander had been heedlessly trifling with the safety of the
vessel, by the hardy manner in which he disregarded the wild
symptoms of the weather. But they undervalued the keen-
eyed vigilance of Wilder. He had certainly driven the Bristol
trader through the water at a rate she had never been known
to go before, but thus far the facts themselves gave evidence
in his favor, since no injury was the consequence of what they
deemed temerity. At the quick, sudden order just given, however, the whole ship was in an uproar. A dozen seamen called
to each other from different parts of the vessel, each striving
to lift his voice, above the roaring ocean, and there was every
appearance of a general and inextricable confusion. But the
same authority which had so unexpectedly aroused them into
activity, produced order from their ill directed though vigorous efforts.

Wilder had spoken to awaken the drowsy and to excite the
torpid. The instant he found each man on the alert, he resumed his orders, with a calmness that gave a direction to the
powers of all, and yet with an energy that he well knew was

called for by the occasion. The enormous sheets of duck, which had look'd like so many light clouds in the murky and threatening heavens, were soon seen fluttering wildly as they descended from their high places, and in a few minutes the ship was reduced to the action of her more secure and heavier canvass. To effect this object every man in the ship exerted his powers to the upmost, under the guidance of the steady but rapid mandates of their commander. Then followed a short and apprehensive pause. All eyes were turned toward the quarter where the ominous signs had been discovered, and each individual endeavoured to read their import, with an intelligence correspondant to the degree of skill he might have acquired during his particular period of service on that treacherous element, which was now his home.

The dim tracery of the stranger's form had been swallowed by the flood of misty light, which, by this time, rolled along the sea like drifting vapour, semipellucid, preternatural and seemingly tangible. The ocean itself appeared admonished that a quick and violent change was nigh. The waves ceased to break in their former foaming and brilliant crests, and black masses of the water, lifted their surly summits against the eastern horizon, no longer shedding their own peculiar and lucid atmosphere around them. The breeze which had been so fresh, and which had even blown with a force that nearly amounted to a gale, was lulling and becoming uncertain, as it might be awed by the more violent power that was gathering along the borders of the sea, in the direction of the neighboring Continent. Each moment the eastern puffs of air lost their strength, becoming more and more feeble, until in an incredibly short period, the heavy sails were heard flapping against the masts, a frightfully ominous calm succeeding. At this instant, a gleam flashed from the fearful obscurity of the ocean, and a roar, like that of a sudden burst of thunder, bellowed along the waters. The seamen turned their startled looks on each other, standing aghast, as if a warning of what was to follow had come out of the heavens themselves. But their calm and more sagacious commander put a different construction on the signal. His lip curled in high professional pride, and he muttered with scorn.

"Does he think we sleep! Ay, he has got it, himself, and

would open our eyes to what is coming! What does he imagine we have been about since the middle watch was set?"

Wilder made a swift turn or two on the quarter-deck, turning his quick glances, from one quarter of the heavens to another, from the black and lulling water on which his vessel was rolling, to the sails, and from his silent and profoundly expectant crew to the dim lines of spars, that were waving above his head, like so many pencils tracing their curvilinear and wanton images over the murky volumes of the superincumbent clouds.

"Lay the after yards square," he said, in a voice, which was heard by every man on deck, though his words were apparently spoken but little above his breath. The creaking of the blocks, as the spars came slowly and heavily round to the indicated position contributed to the imposing character of the moment, sounding like notes of fearful preparation.

"Haul up the courses," resumed Wilder with the same eloquent calmness of manner. Then taking another glance at the threatening horizon, he added slowly but with emphasis—"Furl them. Furl them both—Away aloft and hand your courses," he continued in a shout, "roll them up, cheerily; in with them, boys, cheerily; in!"

The conscious seamen took their impulses from the tones of their commander. In a moment twenty dark forms were leaping up the rigging with the activity of so many quadrupeds. In another minute the vast and powerful sheets of canvass were effectually rendered harmless, by securing them in tight rolls to their respective spars. The men descended as swiftly as they had mounted to the yards, and then succeeded another breathing pause. At this appalling moment a candle would have sent its flame perpendicularly towards the heavens. The ship, missing the steadying power of the wind, rolled heavily in the troughs of the seas, which began to lessen at each instant, as if the startled element was recalling into the security of its own vast bosom that portion of its particles which had so lately been permitted to gambol madly over its surface. The water washed sullenly along the side of the ship, or, as she laboring rose from one of her frequent falls into the hollows of the waves, it shot back into the ocean from her decks, in glittering cascades. Every hue of the heavens, every sound of the element, and each dusky and anxious countenance helped to proclaim the intense interest of the moment. In this brief interval of expectation and inactivity the mates again approached their commander.

"It is an awful night, Capt. Wilder!" said Earing, presuming on his rank to be the first to speak.

"I have known far less notice given of a shift of wind," was the answer.

"We have had time to gather in our kites 'tis true, Sir; but there are signs and warnings that come with this change, which the oldest seaman must dread!"

"Yes," continued Knighthead, with a voice that sounded hoarse and powerful even amid the fearful accessories of that scene—"yes, it is no trifling commission that can call people that I shall not name out upon the water, in such a night as this! It was in just such weather, that I saw the Vesuvius ketch go to a place so deep, that her own mortar would not have been able to have sent a bomb into the open air, had hands and fire been there fit to have let it off!"

"Ay, and it was in such a time the Greenlandman was cast upon the Orkneys, in as flat a calm as ever lay on the sea"—

"Gentlemen," said Wilder, with a peculiar, and perhaps an ironical, emphasis on the word, "what would ye have! There is not a breath of air stirring, and the ship is naked to her topsails!"

It would have been difficult for either of the two malcontents to give a very satisfactory answer to this question. Both were secretly goaded by mysterious and superstitious apprehensions, that were powerfully aided by the more real and intelligible aspect of the night, but neither had so far forgotten his manhood and his professional pride as to lay bare the full extent of his own weakness, at a moment when he was liable to be called upon for the exhibition of qualities of a more positive and determined character. The feeling that was uppermost betrayed itself in the reply of Earing though in an indirect and covert manner.

"Yes, the vessel is snug enough now," he said, "though eyesight has shown us it is no easy matter to drive a freighted ship through the water as fast as one of those flying craft aboard which no man can say who stands at the helm, by what compass she steers, or what is her draught!"

"Ay," resumed Knighthead, "I call the Caroline fast for an honest trader. There are few square rigged boats who do not wear the pennants of the King, that can eat her out of the wind on a bowline, or bring her into their wake with studding sails set. But this is a time and an hour to make a seaman think. Look at that hazy light here in with the land, that is coming so fast down upon us and then tell me whether it comes from the coast of America, or whether it comes from out of the stranger who has been so long running under our lee, but who has got, or is fast getting the wind of us, at last, while none here can say how or why. I have just this much, and no more to say: Give me for a consort a craft whose captain I know, or give me none!"

"Such is your taste, Mr Knighthead," said Wilder coldly. "Mine may, by some accident, be different."

"Yes, yes," observed the more cautious and prudent Earing, "in time of war, and with letters of Marque aboard, a man may honestly hope the sail he sees, should have a stranger for her master, or otherwise he would never fall in with an enemy. But though an Englishman born myself, I should rather give the ship in that mist, a clear sea, seeing that I neither know her nation nor her cruise. Ah, Captain Wilder, this is an awful sight for the morning watch! Often and often have I seen the sun rise in the east, and no harm done, but little good can come of a day, when the light first breaks in the west! Cheerfully would I give the owners the last month's pay, hard as it has been earned, did I but know under what flag the stranger sails."

"Frenchman, Don, or Devil, yonder he comes!" cried Wilder. Then turning towards the attentive crew, he shouted in a voice that was appalling by its vehemence and warning, "Let run the after halyards—round with the fore-yard! round with it, men, with a will!"

These were cries that the startled crew but too well understood. Every nerve and muscle were exerted to execute the orders, to be in readiness for the tempest. No man spoke, but each expended the utmost of his power and skill in direct and manly efforts. Nor was there, in verity, a moment to lose, or a particle of human strength expended here, without a sufficient object.

The lurid and fearful looking mist which, for the last quarter of an hour, had been gathering in the North-West, was driving down upon them with the speed of a race-horse. The air had already lost the damp and peculiar feeling of an Easterly breeze, and little eddies were beginning to flutter among the masts, precursors of the coming squall. Then a rushing, roaring sound was heard booming along the ocean, whose surface was first dimpled, next ruffled and finally covered with a sheet of clear, white, and spotless foam. At the next moment the power of the wind fell upon the inert and labouring Bristol trader.

While the gust was approaching, Wilder had seized the slight opportunity afforded by the changeful puffs of air to get the ship, as much as possible before the wind. But the sluggish movement of the vessel met neither the wishes of his own impatience nor the strong exigencies of the moment. Her bows slowly and heavily fell off from the North, leaving her precisely in a situation to receive the first shock on her broadside. Happy it was for all who had life at risk in that defenceless vessel that she was not fated to receive the whole weight of the tempest at a blow. The sails fluttered, and trembled on their massive yards, bellying and collapsing alternately for a minute, and then the rushing wind swept over them in a hurricane.

The Caroline received the blast like a stout and buoyant trader, as she was, yielding readily to its impulse until her side lay nearly incumbent on the element; and then, as if the fearful fabric were conscious of its jeopardy, it seemed to lift its reclining masts again, struggling to work its way through the water.

"Keep the helm a-weather! Jam it a-weather, for your life!" shouted Wilder, amid the roar of the gust.

The veteran seaman at the wheel obeyed the order with steadiness, but in vain did he keep his eyes on the margin of his head sail, to watch the manner the ship would obey its power. Twice more, in as many moments, the giddy masts fell towards the horizon, waving as often gracefully upward, and then they yielded to the mighty pressure of the wind, until the whole machine lay prostrate on the water.

"Be cool!" said Wilder, seizing the bewildered Earing by the arm as the latter rushed madly up the steep of the deck; "it is our duty to be calm. Bring hither an axe!"

Quick as the thought which gave the order, the admonished mate complied, jumping into the mizzen-channels of the ship to execute with his own hands the mandate that he knew must follow.

"Shall I cut?" he demanded with uplifted arms, and in a voice that atoned for his momentary confusion, by its steadiness and force.

"Hold. Does the ship mind her helm at all?"

"Not an inch, Sir."

"Then cut," Wilder clearly and calmly added.

A single blow sufficed for the discharge of this important duty. Extended to the utmost powers of endurance by the vast weight it upheld, the lanyard struck by Earing no sooner parted, than each of its fellows snapped in succession, leaving the mast dependant on its wood for the support of all the ponderous and complicated hamper it upheld. The cracking of the spar came next, and then the mizzen fell, like a tree that had been sapped at its foundation.

"Does she fall off?" called Wilder to the observant seaman at the wheel.

"She yielded a little, Sir, but this new squall is bringing her up again."

"Shall I cut?" shouted Earing from the main rigging, whither he had leaped, like a tiger who had bounded on his prey.

"Cut."

A louder and more imposing crash succeeded this order, though not before several heavy blows had been struck into the massive mast itself. As before, the sea received the tumbling maze of spars, rigging, and sails, the vessel surging, at the same instant, from its recumbent position, and rolling far and heavily to windward.

"She rights, she rights!" exclaimed twenty voices, which had been mute in a suspense that involved life and death.

"Keep her dead away—" added the calm, but authoritative

voice of the young commander. "Stand by, to furl the fore-topsail—let it hang a moment, to drag the ship clear of the wreck—cut—cut—cheerily, men—hatchets and knives—cut *with* all, and cut *of* all!"

As the men now worked with the vigor of hope, the ropes that still confined the fallen spars to the vessel were quickly severed, and the Caroline by this time dead before the gale, appeared barely to touch the foam that covered the sea. The wind came over the waste in gusts that rumbled like distant thunder, and with a power that seemed to threaten to lift the ship from its proper element. As a prudent and sagacious sea-man had let fly the halyards of the solitary sail that remained, at the moment the squall approached, the loosened but low-ered topsail was now distended in a manner that threatened to drag after it, the only spars which still stood. Wilder saw the necessity of getting rid of this sail, and he also saw the utter impossibility of securing it. Calling Earing to his side, he pointed out the danger, and gave the necessary order—

"The spar cannot stand such shocks much longer," he con-cluded; "should it go over the bows, some fatal blow might be given to the ship, at the rate she is moving. A man or two must be sent aloft to cut the sail from the yards."

"The stick is bending like a willow whip," returned the mate, "and the lower mast itself is sprung. There would be great danger in trusting a hand in that top while these wild squalls are breathing around us."

"You may be right," returned Wilder, with a sudden con-viction of the truth of what the other had said; "stay you then here; if any thing befal me, try to get the vessel into port as far north as the capes of Virginia, at least—on no account attempt Hatteras in the present condition of"—

"What would you do, Capt. Wilder?" interrupted the mate, laying his hand on the shoulder of his commander, who had already thrown his sea-cap on the deck and was preparing to divest himself of some of his outer garments.

"I go aloft, to ease the mast of that sail, without which we lose the spar and possibly the ship."

"I see that plain enough, sir; but shall it be said that an-other did the duty of Edward Earing? It is your business to carry the vessel into the capes of Virginia, and mine to cut that topsail adrift. If harm comes to me—why put it in the log, with a word or two about the manner in which I played my part: that is the most proper epitaph for a sailor."

Wilder made no resistance. He resumed his watchful and reflecting attitude with the simplicity of one, who had been too long trained to the discharge of certain obligations himself, to manifest surprise that another should acknowledge their imperative character. In the mean time Earing proceeded steadily to perform what he had just promised. Passing into the waist of the ship, he provided himself with a suitable hatchet and then without speaking a syllable to any of the mute but attentive seamen, he sprang into the fore-rigging, every strand and even rope-yarn of which was tightened by the strain nearly to snapping. The understanding eyes of his observers, comprehended his intention and with precisely the same pride of station as had urged him to the dangerous undertaking four or five of the oldest mariners jumped upon the railings to mount into an air that apparently teemed with a hundred hurricanes.

"Lie down out of that fore-rigging," shouted Wilder through a deck trumpet; "lie down—all but the mate lie down." His words were borne past the inattentive ears of the excited and mortified followers of Earing, but for once they failed of their effect. Each man was too earnestly bent on his purpose to listen to the sounds of recall. In less than a minute the whole were scattered along the yards, prepared to obey the signal of their officer. The mate cast a look about him; perceiving that the time was comparatively favorable, he struck a blow upon the large rope that confined one of the lower angles of the distended and bursting sail to the yard. The effect was much the same as would be produced by knocking away the key-stone of an ill cemented arch. The canvass broke from its fastenings with a loud explosion, and, for an instant, it was seen sailing in the air ahead of the ship, as if it were sustained on wings. The vessel rose on a sluggish wave, the lingering remains of the former breeze, and settled heavily over the rolling surge, borne down alike by its own weight and the renewed violence of the gusts. At this critical instant, while the seamen aloft were still gazing in the direction in which the little cloud of canvass had disappeared, a lanyard of the lower rigging parted, with a crack that reached the ears of Wilder.

"Lie down—" he shouted wildly through his trumpet—"down by the backstays—down for your lives, every man of you, down!"

A solitary individual profited by the warning, gliding to the deck with the velocity of the wind. But rope parted after rope, and the fatal snapping of the wood followed. For a moment the towering maze tottered, seeming to wave towards every quarter of the heavens, and then yielding to the movements of the hull, the whole fell with a heavy crash into the sea. Cord, lanyard, and stay snapped like thread, as each received in succession the strain of the ship, leaving the naked and despoiled hull of the Caroline to drive before the tempest, as if nothing had occurred to impede its progress.

A mute and eloquent pause succeeded the disaster. It seemed as if the elements themselves were appeased by their work, and something like a momentary lull in the awful rushing of the winds might have been fancied. Wilder sprang to the side of the vessel and distinctly beheld the victims, who still clung to their frail support. He even saw Earing waving his hand in adieu with a seaman's heart, like a man who not only felt how desperate was his situation, but who knew how to meet it with resignation. Then the wreck of spars, with all who clung to it, was swallowed up, in the body of frightful preternatural looking mist which extended on every side of them from the ocean to the clouds.

"Stand by to clear away a boat!" shouted Wilder, without pausing to think of the impossibility of one's swimming or of effecting the least good in so violent a tornado.

But the amazed and confounded seamen who remained needed no instruction in this matter. Not a man moved, nor was the smallest symptom of obedience given. The mariners looked wildly around them, each endeavoring to trace in the dusky countenance of some shipmate his opinion of the extent of the evil, but not a mouth opened among them all.

"It is too late—it is too late!" murmured Wilder; "human skill and human efforts could not save them!"

"Sail, ho!" Knighthead shouted in a voice that was teeming with superstitious awe.

"Let him come on," returned his young commander bitterly. "The mischief is ready done to his hands!"

"Should this be a true ship, it is our duty to the owners and the passengers to speak her, if man can make his voice heard in this tempest," the second mate, continued, pointing through the haze at the dim object that was certainly at hand.

"Speak her! passengers!" muttered Wilder, involuntarily repeating his words. "No, any thing is better than speaking her. Do you see the vessel that is driving down upon us so fast?" he sternly demanded of the watchful seaman who still clung to the wheel of the Caroline.

"Ay, ay, Sir."

"Give her a berth—sheer away hard to port—perhaps he may pass us, in the gloom, since we are now no higher than our decks. Give the ship a broad sheer, I say, Sir."

The usual laconic answer was given, and for a few moments the Bristol trader was seen diverging a little from the line in which the other approached. But a second glance assured Wilder that the attempt was useless. The strange ship (every man on board felt certain it was the same that had so long been seen hanging in the North-Western horizon) came on through the mist, with a swiftness that nearly equalled the velocity of the tempestuous winds themselves. Not a thread of canvass was seen on board her. Each line of spars, even to the tapering and delicate top-gallant-masts, was in its place, preserving the beauty and symmetry of the whole fabric, but no where was there the smallest fragment of a sail opened to the gale. Under her bows rolled a volume of foam, that was even discernible amid the universal agitation of the ocean, and as she came within sound the sullen roar of the water, might have been likened to the noise of a cascade. At first the spectators on the decks of the Caroline believed they were not seen, and some of the men called madly for lights, in order that the disasters of the night might not terminate in an encounter.

"Too many see us there, already!" said Wilder.

"No, no," muttered Knighthead; "no fear but we are seen, and by such eyes too, as never yet looked out of mortal head!"

The seaman paused. In another instant the long-seen and mysterious ship was within a hundred feet of them. The very power of that wind which was wont usually to raise the billows, now pressed the element with the weight of mountains into its bed. The sea was every where a sheet of froth but the water did not rise above the level of the surface. The instant a wave lifted itself from the security of the vast depths, the fluid was borne away before the tornado in glittering spray. Along this frothy but comparatively motionless surface, then, the stranger came booming, with the steadiness and grandeur with which a cloud is seen sailing in the hurricane. No sign of life was discovered about her. If men looked out from their secret places, upon the straightened and discomfited wreck of the Bristol trader, it was covertly, and as darkly as the tempest before which they drove. Wilder held his breath for the moment the stranger was nighest, in the very excess of suspense. But as he saw no signal of recognition, no human form, nor any intention to arrest, if possible the furious career of the other, a smile gleamed across his countenance, and his lips moved rapidly as if he found pleasure in being abandoned to his distress. The stranger drove by like a dark vision, and, ere another minute, her form was beginning to grow less distinct, in the body of spray to leeward.

"She is going out of sight in the mist!" exclaimed Wilder, when he drew his breath after the fearful suspense of the few last moments.

"Ay, in mist, or clouds," responded Knighthead, who now kept obstinately at his elbow, watching, with the most jealous distrust, the smallest movement of his unknown commander.

"In the heavens or in the sea, I care not, provided she be gone."

"Most seamen would rejoice to see a strange sail, from the hull of a vessel shaved to the deck like this."

"Men often court their destruction, from ignorance of their own interests. Let him drive on, say I, and pray I! He goes four feet to our one, and I ask no better favor than that this hurricane may blow until the sun shall rise."

Knighthead started, and cast an oblique glance, which resembled denunciation, at his companion. To his superstitious mind there was profanity in thus invoking the tempests, at a moment, when the winds seemed already to be pouring out their utmost wrath.

"This is a heavy squall, I will allow," he said; "and such a one, as many mariners pass whole lives without seeing; but he knows little of the sea, who thinks there is not more hurricane left where this comes from!"

"Let it blow!" cried the other, striking his hands together, a little wildly. "I pray for wind!"

All the doubts of Knighthead as to the character of the young stranger, who had so unaccountably got possession of the office of Nicholas Nichols, if any remained, were now removed. He walked forward among the silent and thoughtful crew, with the air of a man whose opinion was settled. Wilder, however, paid no attention to the movements of his subordinate, but continued pacing the deck, for hours, now casting his eyes at the Heavens and now sending frequent and anxious glances around the limited horizon while the Royal Caroline, still continued drifting before the wind, a shorn and naked wreck.

# Chapter XVII

"Sit still, and hear the last of our sea sorrow."
*The Tempest*, I.ii.170

THE WEIGHT of the tempest had been felt at that fatal moment when Earing and his hapless companions were precipitated from their giddy elevation into the sea. Though the wind continued to blow long after this event, it was with a constantly diminishing power. As the gale decreased the sea began to rise, and the vessel to labor in proportion. Then followed two hours of anxious watchfulness on the part of Wilder during which the whole of his professional knowledge was needed in order to keep the despoiled hull from becoming a prey to the greedy waters. His consummate skill however proved equal to the task that was required at his hands, and just as the symptoms of day were becoming visible along the East, both wind and waves were rapidly subsiding together. During the whole of this doubtful period, our adventurer did not receive the smallest assistance from any of the crew, with the exception of two experienced seamen whom he had previously stationed at the wheel. But to this neglect he was indifferent since little more was required than his own judgment seconded as it faithfully was, by the exertions of the mariners more immediately under his eye.

The day dawned on a scene entirely different from that which had marked the tempestuous deformity of the night. The whole fury of the winds appeared to have been expended in their precocious effort. From the moderate gale to which they had fallen by the end of the middle watch they further altered to a vacillating breeze, and ere the sun rose, the changeful element subsided into a flat calm. The sea went down as suddenly as the power which had raised it, vanished, and by the time the broad golden light of the sun was shed fairly and fully upon the unstable ocean, it lay unruffled, and polished though still gently heaving in swells so long and heavy as to resemble the placid respiration of a sleeping infant.

The hour was still early, and the serene appearance of the

sky gave every promise of a day which might be passed in devising the expedients necessary to bring the ship under the command of her people.

"Sound the pumps," said Wilder, observing that the crew were appearing from the different places in which they had bestowed their cares and their persons together, during the later hours of the night.

"Do you hear me, Sir?" he added sternly, observing that no one moved to obey his order. "Let the pumps be sounded, and the ship cleared of every inch of water."

Knighthead, to whom Wilder addressed himself, regarded his commander with an oblique and sullen eye, exchanging intelligent glances with his comrades, before he saw fit to make the smallest motion towards compliance. But there was still that in the authoritative mien of his superior, which induced him to comply. The dilatory manner in which the seamen performed the duty was quickened, however, as the rod ascended, and the well known signs of a formidable leak met their eyes. The experiment was repeated with greater activity and with more precision.

"If witchcraft can clear the hold of a ship that is already half full of water," said Knighthead, casting another menacing glance towards the attentive Wilder, "the sooner it is done the better; for, the whole cunning of something more than a bungler will be needed, to make the pumps of the Royal Caroline suck!"

"Does the ship leak!" demanded his superior with a quickness which proclaimed how important the intelligence was deemed.

"Yesterday, I would have boldly put my name to the articles of any craft that floats the ocean, and had the Captain asked me, if I understood her nature and character, as certain as that my name is Francis Knighthead, I should have told him, yes. But I find that the oldest seaman may still learn something of the water, though it should be got in crossing a ferry in a flat."

"What mean you, Sir?" demanded Wilder, who for the first time, began to note the mutinous looks assumed by his mate, no less than the threatening manner in which he was seconded by the crew. "Have the pumps rigged without delay, and clear the ship of water."

Knighthead slowly complied with the former part of this order, and in a few moments, every thing was arranged to commence the necessary and as it would seem the urgent duty of pumping. But no man lifted his hand to the laborious employment. Wilder, who had taken the alarm, was not slow in detecting this reluctance, and he repeated the order more sternly, calling to two of the seamen by name to set the example of obedience. The men hesitated, giving an opportunity to the mate to confirm them by his voice, in their mutinous intentions.

"What need of hands to work a pump in a vessel like this!" he said, coarsely laughing, secret terror struggling strangely at the same time with open malice. "After what we have seen, this night, none here will be amazed should the vessel begin to spout out the brine like a whale."

"What am I to understand by this hesitation, and by this language?" said Wilder, approaching Knighthead with a firm step and an eye that threw back the defiance of his inferior, in more than equal measure. "Is it you, who should be foremost in exertion at a moment like this, who dare to set an example of disobedience?"

The mate recoiled a pace, and his lips moved; still he uttered no audible reply. Wilder ordered him, in a calm authoritative tone, to lay his own hands to the labor. Knighthead then found his voice, making a flat refusal. At the next moment he was felled to the feet of his indignant commander, by a blow he had neither the address nor the power to resist. Awed by this act of decision, one single moment of breathless silence reigned among the crew, and then the common cry, and the general rush upon our defenceless and solitary adventurer were signals for open hostility. A shriek from the quarter deck arrested the struggle, just as a dozen hands were laid violently upon the person of Wilder, and, for the moment, there was a truce. The cry came from Gertrude, and happily it possessed sufficient influence to check the savage intentions of a set of beings rude and unnurtured enough to be guilty of any act of violence when their passions were thoroughly aroused. Wilder was reluctantly released; and the surly mariners turned towards her whose interference had stopped, if it had not changed, their intentions.

During the more momentous hours of the night that was past, the very existence of the passengers had been forgotten by those whose duty kept them on deck. If they had been recalled at all to the recollection of any, it was at those fleeting moments, when the mind of the young seaman, who directed the movements of the ship, found leisure to catch stolen glimpses of softer scenes than the wild warring of the elements that was raging before his eyes. Knighthead had named them, as he would have made allusion to a part of the cargo, but their fate had little influence on his hardened nature. Mrs Wyllys and her charge had, therefore remained below during the whole period, perfectly unapprized of the disasters of the intervening time. Buried in the recesses of their berths, they had heard the roaring of the winds and the incessant washing of the waters. But these usual accompaniments of a storm served to conceal the crashing of masts, and the hoarse cries of the mariners. During the moments of terrible suspense, while the Bristol trader lay on her side the better informed Governess had, indeed, some fearful glimmerings of the truth; but conscious of her uselessness and unwilling to alarm her less instructed companion, she had sufficient self-command to be mute. The subsequent silence and comparative calm induced her to believe that she had been mistaken in her apprehensions, and long ere morning dawned, both she and Gertrude had sunk into refreshing slumbers. They had risen, and mounted to the deck together, and were still in the first burst of their wonder at the desolation which met their eyes, when the long meditated attack on Wilder was made.

"What means this awful change!" demanded Mrs Wyllys with a lip that quivered and a cheek which, notwithstanding the extraordinary power she possessed over her feelings, was blanched to the colour of death.

The eye of Wilder was glowing and his brow was dark as those heavens from which they had just so happily escaped as he answered, still menacing his assailants with an arm,—

"It means mutiny, Madam—rascally, cowardly mutiny!"

"Could mutiny strip a vessel of her masts, and leave her a helpless log upon the sea!"

"Harkee! Madam," roughly interrupted the mate, "to you I will speak freely, for it is well known who you are, and that you came on board the Caroline a paying passenger. This night have I seen the heavens and the ocean behave as I have never seen them behave before. Ships have been running afore the wind light and buoyant as corks, with all their spars stepped and steady, when other ships have been shaved of every mast, as the razor sweeps the chin. Cruisers have been fallen in with, sailing without living hands to work them, and all together, no man, here, has ever before passed a middle watch like the one gone by."

"And what has this to do with the violence I have just witnessed? Is the vessel fated to endure every evil! Can *you* explain this, Mr Wilder?"

"You cannot say, at least, you had no warning of danger," returned Wilder bitterly.

"Ay, the devil is obliged to be honest, on compulsion," resumed the mate. "Each of his imps sails with his orders and, thank Heaven, however willing he may be to overlook them, he has neither courage nor power to do so. Otherwise a peaceful voyage would be such a rarity in these unsettled times, that few men would be found hardy enough to venture on the water for a livelihood—A warning! we will own you gave us open and frequent warning. It was a notice that the consignee should not have overlooked, when Nicholas Nichols met with the hurt as the anchor was leaving the bottom. I never knew an accident happen at such a time, and no evil come of it. Then we had a warning with the old man in the boat, besides the never-failing ill luck of sending the Pilot violently out of the ship. As if all this wasn't enough, instead of taking a hint and lying peaceably at our anchors, we got the ship under way and left a safe and friendly harbor of a Friday, of all the days in a week!* So far from being surprised at what has happened, I only wonder at still finding myself a living man, the reason of which is simply this, that I have

*The superstition, that Friday is an evil day, was not peculiar to Knighthead; it prevails, more or less, among seamen, to this hour. An intelligent merchant of Connecticut had a desire to do his part in eradicating an impression that is sometimes inconvenient. He caused the keel of a vessel to be laid on a Friday; she was launched on a Friday; named "The Friday"; and sailed on her first voyage on a Friday. Unfortunately for the success of this well-intentioned experiment, neither vessel nor crew were ever again heard of!

given my faith where faith is due, and not to unknown mariners and strange commanders. Had Edward Earing done the same, he might still have had a plank between him and the bottom; but though half inclined to believe in the truth, he had, after all, too much leaning to superstition and credulity."

This labored profession of faith in the mate, though sufficiently intelligible to Wilder, was still an enigma to his female listeners. But Knighthead had not formed his resolution by halves, neither had he gone thus far with any intention to stop short of the whole design. In summary words he explained to Mrs Wyllys the desolate condition of the ship, and the utter improbability that she could continue to float many hours, since actual observation had told him that her lower hold was already half full of water.

"And what is to be done!" demanded the Governess, casting a glance of bitter distress towards the pallid and attentive Gertrude. "Is there no sail in sight to take us from the wreck, or must we perish in our helplessness?"

"God protect us from any more strange sails!" exclaimed the surly Knighthead. "We have the pinnace hanging at the stern, and here must be the land yet some forty leagues to the North-West. Water and food are plenty, and twelve stout hands, can soon pull a boat to the continent of America, that is, provided America is left where it was seen no later than at sunset yesterday."

"You propose to abandon the vessel?"

"I do. The interest of the owners is dear to all good seamen, but life is sweeter than gold."

"The will of Heaven be done! But surely you meditate no violence against this gentleman, who, I am quite certain, has governed the vessel in very critical circumstances with a discretion beyond his years!"

Knighthead muttered his intentions, whatever they might be to himself, and he walked apart, apparently to confer with the men, who seemed but too well disposed to second any of his views however mistaken or lawless. During the few moments of suspense that succeeded, Wilder was silent and composed, a smile resembling that of contempt struggling about his lip, and maintaining the air rather of one who had power to decide on the fortunes of others, than of a man who knew that his own fate was at that very moment in discussion. When the dull minds of the seamen had arrived at their conclusion the Mate advanced to proclaim the result. Indeed, words were unnecessary in order to make known a very material part of their decision, for a party of the men proceeded instantly to lower the stern boat into the water, while others set about supplying it with the necessary means of subsistence.

"There is room for all the Christians in the ship, to stow themselves in this pinnace," resumed Knighthead; "as for those that place their dependance on any particular persons, why, let them call for aid, where they have been used to receive it."

"From all which I am to infer, that it is your intention," said Wilder, calmly, "to abandon the wreck, and your duty?"

The half-awed, but still resentful mate, returned a look in which fear and triumph struggled for the mastery, as he answered—

"You can never want a boat, you who know how to sail a ship without a crew! Besides, you shall never say to your friends whoever they may be, that we leave you, without the means of reaching the land, if you are indeed a land-bird at all. There is the launch."

"There is the launch, but well do you know, that without masts, our united strengths could not lift it from the deck; else would it not be left."

"They that took the masts out of the Caroline can put them in, again," rejoined a grinning seaman. "It will not be an hour after we leave you, before a sheer-hulk will come alongside, to step the spars again, and then you may go cruise in company."

Wilder was superior to a reply. He began to pace the deck, thoughtful, it is true, but composed and entirely self-possessed. In the mean time, as a common desire to quit the wreck as soon as possible actuated the men, their preparations advanced with great activity. The wondering and alarmed females had hardly time to think clearly on the extraordinary situation in which they found themselves, before they saw the form of the helpless Master borne past them to the boat; in another minute they were summoned to take their places at his side.

Thus called upon to act, they began to feel the imperious necessity of decision. Remonstrance they feared would be useless, for the fierce and malignant looks which were cast, from time to time, at Wilder, as the labor proceeded, proclaimed the danger of awakening such obstinate and ignorant minds into renewed acts of violence. The Governess bethought her of an appeal to the wounded man, but the look of wild care which he had cast about him on being lifted to the deck, and the expression of bodily and mental pain that gleamed across his rugged features, as he buried them in the blankets by which he was enveloped, too plainly announced that little assistance was to be expected from him.

"What remains for us to do?" she at length demanded of the seemingly insensible object of her concern.

"I would I knew!" he answered quickly, casting a keen, but hurried glance around the whole horizon. "It is not at all improbable that they will reach the shore. Four and twenty hours of calm will assure it."

"If otherwise—?"

"A blow at North-West, or from any quarter off the land, will prove their ruin."

"And the ship—?"

"If deserted, she must sink."

"Then will I speak in your favor to these hearts of flint! I know not why I feel such interest in your welfare, inexplicable young man, but I would suffer much, rather than leave you to incur this peril."

"Stop, dearest Madam," said Wilder, respectfully arresting her movement with his hand. "I cannot leave the vessel."

"We know not yet. The most stubborn natures may be subdued—even ignorance can be made to open its ears at the voice of intreaty. I may prevail."

"There is one temper to be quelled—one reason to convince—one prejudice to conquer over which you have no power."

"Whose is that?"

"My own."

"What mean you, Sir! Surely, you are not weak enough to

suffer resentment against such beings to goad you to an act of madness."

"Do I seem mad!" demanded Wilder. "The feeling by which I am governed may be false, but such as it is, it is grafted on my habits—my opinions—I will say my princi- ples. Honor forbids me to quit a ship that I command while a plank of her is afloat!"

"Of what use can a single arm prove in such a crisis?"

"None," he answered, with a melancholy smile. "I must die, in order that others who may be serviceable hereafter, should do their duty."

Both Mrs Wyllys and Gertrude regarded his kindling eye, but otherwise placid countenance, with looks whose concern amounted to horror. The former read in the very composure of his mien the unalterable character of his resolution, and the latter, shuddering as the prospect of the cruel fate which awaited him crowded on her mind, felt a glow about her own youthful heart, that almost tempted her to believe his self- devotion commendable. But the Governess saw new reasons for apprehension in the determination of Wilder. If she had hitherto felt reluctance to trust herself and her ward with a band like that which now possessed the sole authority, it was more than doubly increased by the rude and noisy summons she received to hasten and take her place among them.

"Would to Heaven I knew in what manner to decide!" she exclaimed. "Speak to us, young man; counsel us, as you would counsel a mother and a sister."

"Were I so fortunate as to possess relatives so near and dear, nothing should separate us, at a time like this."

"Is there hope for those who remain on the wreck?"

"But little."

"And in the boat—?"

It was near a minute before Wilder made an answer. He again turned his eye to the bright and broad horizon, study- ing the heavens in the direction of the distant continent with infinite care. No omen that could indicate the probable character of the weather escaped his vigilance, while his countenance reflected the various emotions by which he was governed.

"As I am a man," he said with fervor, "and one who is

bound not only to counsel but to protect your sex, I distrust the time. I think the chance of being seen by some passing sail, equal to the probability that those who adventure in the pinnace will ever reach the land."

"Then let us remain," said Gertrude, the blood for the first time, since her re-appearance on deck, rushing in a torrent into her colourless cheeks. "I like not the wretches who would be our companions in that boat."

"Away—away—" impatiently shouted Knighthead. "Each minute of light is a week of life to us all, and every moment of calm a year. Away. Away, or we leave you."

Mrs Wyllys answered not, but she stood the image of doubt and indecision. The plash of oars was heard in the water, and at the next moment the pinnace was seen gliding over the element, impelled by the strong arms of six powerful rowers.

"Stay!" shrieked the Governess, no longer undetermined. "Receive my child, though you abandon me!"

A wave of the hand and an indistinct rumbling in the coarse tones of the mate were the answers to her appeal. A long, deep and breathing silence followed, among the deserted. The grim countenances of the seamen in the pinnace soon became confused and indistinct, and then the boat itself, began to lessen on the eye, until it seemed no more than a dark and distant speck rising and falling, with the flow and reflux of the blue waters. During all this time, not even a whispered word was spoken. Each of the party gazed until eyes grew dim at the receding object, and it was only when his sight refused to convey the tiny image to his brain, that Wilder, himself, shook off the impression of the trance into which he had fallen. His look then turned on his companions, and he pressed his hand upon his forehead, as if the brain were bewildered by the responsibility he had assumed in advising them to remain. But the sickening apprehension passed away, leaving in its place a firmer mind, and a resolution too often tried in scenes of doubtful issue to be long or easily shaken from its calmness and self-possession.

"They are gone!" he said, breathing heavily, like one whose respiration had been long and unnaturally suspended.

"They are gone!" echoed the governess, turning an eye that

was contracting with the intensity of her care, on the marble like and motionless form of her pupil. "There is no longer hope."

The look that Wilder threw on the same silent but lovely statue, was scarcely less expressive than the gaze of her who had nurtured her infancy. His brow grew thoughtful, and his lips became compressed, while he gathered all the resources of his fertile imagination and long experience.

"Is there hope?" demanded the governess, who was watching the changes of his working countenance, with an attention that never swerved.

The gloom passed away from his features, and the smile that lighted them, was like the radiance of the sun as it breaks through the blackest vapours of the gust.

"There is!" he said, with firmness. "Our case is not yet desperate."

"Then may He who rules the ocean and the land receive the praise!" cried the grateful governess, giving vent to her long suppressed agony in a flood of tears.

Gertrude cast herself upon the neck of Mrs Wyllys, and for a minute their unrestrained emotions were mingled.

"And now, dearest Madam," said Gertrude, leaving the arms of her Governess, "let us trust to the skill of Mr Wilder; he has foreseen and foretold this danger; equally well may he predict our safety."

"Foreseen and foretold!" returned the other, shaking her head in a manner to show, that her faith in the professional prescience of the stranger was not altogether so unbounded as that of her more youthful and ardent pupil. "No mortal could have foreseen this awful calamity, and least of all foreseeing it, would he have sought to incur its danger! Mr Wilder, I will not annoy you with further requests for explanations that might now be useless, but you will not refuse to communicate your grounds of hope."

Wilder hastened to relieve a curiosity that he knew must be as painful as it was natural. The mutineers had left the largest and much the safest of the two boats belonging to the wreck, from a desire to improve the calm, well knowing that hours of severe labour would be necessary to launch it into the ocean from the place it occupied between the stumps of the two principal masts. This operation, which might have been executed in a few minutes, with the ordinary purchases of the ship, would have required all their strength united, and that too to be exercised with a discretion and care that would have consumed too many of those moments which they rightly deemed to be so precious, at that wild and unstable season of the year. Into this little ark Wilder proposed to convey such articles of comfort and necessity, as he might hastily collect from the abandoned vessel, and then, entering it with his companions, to await the critical instant when the wreck should sink from beneath them.

"Call you this hope!" exclaimed Mrs Wyllys when his short explanation was ended, her cheek blanching with disappointment. "I have heard that the gulph which foundering vessels leave, swallows all lesser objects that are floating nigh!"

"It sometimes happens. For worlds I would not deceive you; and I now say, that I think our chance for escape equal to that of being engulphed with the vessel."

"This is terrible!" murmured the Governess, "but the will of Heaven be done. Cannot ingenuity supply the place of strength and the boat be cast from the decks before the fatal moment shall arrive?"

Wilder shook his head in the negative.

"We are not so weak as you may think us," said Gertrude. "Give a direction to our efforts, and let us see what may yet be done. Here is Cassandra," she added, turning to the black girl already introduced to the reader, who stood behind her young and ardent mistress with the mantle and shawls of the latter thrown over her arm, as if about to attend her, on an excursion for the morning— "Here is Cassandra, who alone has nearly the strength of a man."

"Had she the strength of twenty, I should despair of launching the boat without the aid of machinery. But we lose time in words: I will go below in order to judge of the probable duration of our doubt, and then to our preparations. Even you, fair and fragile as you seem, lovely being, may aid, in the latter."

He then pointed out such lighter objects as would be necessary to their comfort, should they be so fortunate as to get clear of the wreck, and advised their being put into the boat without delay. While the three females were thus usefully employed he descended into the hold of the ship in order to note the increase of the water, and to make his calculations on the time that would elapse before the sinking fabric must entirely disappear. The fact proved their case to be more alarming than even Wilder had been led to expect. Stripped of her masts, the vessel had laboured so heavily as to open many of her seams, and as the upper-works began to settle beneath the level of the ocean the influx of the element was increasing with frightful rapidity. As the young mariner looked understandingly about him, he cursed in the bitterness of his heart, the ignorance and superstition that had caused the desertion of the crew. There existed, in reality, no evil that exertion and skill could not have remedied, but deprived of aid, he saw the folly of even attempting to procrastinate a catastrophe that was now unavoidable. Returning with a heavy heart to the deck, he immediately set about those dispositions which were necessary to afford them the only chance of escape.

While his companions deadened the sense of apprehension by their lighter employment, Wilder stepped the two masts of the boat, and disposed of the sails and the other implements that might be useful in the event of success. Thus occupied, a couple of hours flew by as swiftly as if minutes were compressed into moments. At the expiration of that period, his labour ceased. He then cut the gripes that had kept the launch in its place when the ship was in motion, leaving it standing, upright on its wooden beds, but in no other manner connected with the hull, which, by this time had settled so low, as to create the apprehension, that at any moment it might sink from beneath them. After this measure of precaution was taken, the females were summoned to the boat, lest the crisis might be nearer than he supposed, for he well know that a foundering ship, was like a tottering wall, liable at any moment to yield to the impulse of the downward pressure. He then commenced the scarcely less necessary operation of selection among the chaos of articles with which the ill-directed zeal of his companions had so cumbered the boat, that there was hardly room to dispose of their more precious persons. Notwithstanding the often repeated and vociferous remonstrances of the negress, boxes, trunks, and packages flew from the launch, Wilder having no consideration for more than their ultimate safety. The boat was soon cleared of what, under their circumstances was literally lumber, leaving, however, far more than enough to meet all their wants, and not a few of their comforts, in the event that they should escape the greedy element.

Then, and not till then, did the exertions of Wilder relax. He had arranged his sails, ready to be hoisted in an instant; he had carefully examined that no straggling rope, connected the boat to the wreck, to draw them under with the foundering mass, and he had assured himself that food, water, compass and the imperfect instruments that were then in use to ascertain the position of a ship, were carefully disposed of in their several places, and ready to his hand. When all was in a state of preparation, he disposed of himself in the stern of the boat, and endeavored by the composure of his manner to inspire his less resolute companions with a portion of his own firmness.

The bright sunshine was sleeping in a thousand places on every side of the silent and deserted wreck. The sea had subsided to such a state of rest, that it was only at long intervals that the huge and helpless mass on which the ark of the expectants lay, was lifted from its dull quietude, to roll heavily for a moment in the washing waters, and then to settle lower and lower into the absorbing element. Still the disappearance of the hull was slow,—it was even tedious to those who looked forward with restless impatience to its total immersion as the crisis of their own fortunes.

During these hours of weary and awful suspense the discourse between the watchers, though conducted in tones of confidence and often of tenderness, was broken by long intervals of musing silence. Each forbore to dwell upon the danger of their situation in consideration of the feelings of the rest, but neither could conceal the imminent risk they run from that jealous love of life which was common to them all. In this manner, minutes, hours, and the day itself rolled by, and the darkness was seen stealing along the deep, gradually narrowing the boundary of their view towards the east, until the whole of the empty scene was limited to a little dusky circle around the spot on which they lay. To this change succeeded another fearful hour, during which it appeared that death was about to visit them environed by its most revolting horrors. The heavy plunges of the wallowing whale, as he cast his huge form upon the surface of the sea, were heard, accompanied by the mimic blowings of a hundred imitators that followed in the train of the monarch of the ocean. It appeared to the alarmed and feverish imagination of Gertrude that the brine was giving up all its monsters, and, notwithstanding the calm assurances of Wilder that these accustomed sounds were rather the harbingers of peace than signs of any new danger, they filled her mind with images of the secret recesses over which they seemed suspended by a thread, and painted them replete with the disgusting inhabitants of the caverns of the deep. The intelligent seaman himself was startled when he saw, on the surface of the water, the dark fins of the voracious shark stealing around the wreck, apprised by his instinct that the contents of the devoted vessel were shortly to become the prey of his tribe. Then came the moon with its mild and deceptive light to throw the delusion of its glow, on the varying but frightful scene.

"See," said Wilder, as the luminary lifted its pale and melancholy orb out of the bed of the ocean; "we shall at least have light for our hazardous launch!"

"Is it at hand?" demanded Mrs Wyllys, summoning all the resolution she could in so trying a situation.

"It is—the ship has already brought her scuppers to the water. Sometimes a vessel will float until saturated with the brine—if ours sink at all, it will be soon."

"If at all! is there the smallest hope that she can float?"

"None—" said Wilder, pausing to listen to the hollow sounds which issued from the depths of the vessel, as the water broke through her divisions in passing from side to side, and which sounded like the groaning of some heavy monster in the last agony of nature. "None. She is already losing her level!"

His companions saw the change, but, not for the empire of the world could either of them have uttered a syllable. Another low, threatening, rumbling sound was heard, and the pent air beneath blew up the forward part of the deck with an explosion like that of a gun.

"Now, grasp the ropes I have given you," cried Wilder, breathless with his eagerness to speak.

His words were smothered by the rushing and gurgling of water. The vessel made a plunge like a dying whale, and raising its stern high into the air, it glided into the depths of the sea, like the leviathan seeking his secret places. The motionless boat was lifted with the ship, until it stood in an attitude fearfully approaching to the perpendicular. As the wreck descended, the bows of the launch met the element, burying themselves nearly to filling; but buoyant and light, they rose again, and, struck powerfully on the stern by the settling mass, the little ark shot ahead as if driven by the hand of man. Still as the water rushed into the vortex, every thing within its influence yielded to the suction, and at the next instant the launch was seen darting down the declivity, as if eager to follow the vast machine of which it had so long formed a dependent through the same gaping whirlpool to the bottom: but it rose, rocking, to the surface, and for a moment was tossed and whirled like a bubble in the eddies of a pool. After which, the ocean moaned, and slept again.

# Chapter XVIII

—"Every day, some sailor's wife,
The masters of some merchant, and the merchant,
Have just our theme of woe."
*The Tempest*, II.i.4—6.

W E ARE SAFE!" said Wilder, who had stood, with his person firmly braced against a mast, steadily watching the manner of their escape. "Thus far at least, are we safe; for which may Heaven alone be praised, since no art of mine could avail us a feather."

The females had buried their faces in the folds of the vestments and cloths on which they were sitting; nor did even the Governess raise her countenance until twice assured by her companion that the imminency of the risk was passed. Another minute went by, during which Mrs Wyllys and Gertrude were rendering their thanksgivings in a manner and in words less equivocal than the expression which had just broken from the lips of the young seaman. When this grateful duty was performed, they stood erect as if emboldened by the offering, to look their situation more steadily in the face.

On every side lay the seemingly illimitable waste of waters. To them, their small and frail tenement was the world. So long as the ship, sinking and dangerous as she was, remained beneath them, there had appeared to be a barrier between their existence and the ocean. A single minute had deprived them of even this failing support, and they now found themselves cast upon the sea in a vessel that might be likened to one of the bubbles of the element. Gertrude felt, at that instant, that she would have given half her hopes in life for the sight of one foot of the vast and nearly untenanted continent, which stretched for so many thousands of miles along the west, and kept the world of waters to their limits.

But the rush of emotions, that belonged to their forlorn condition, soon subsided, and their thoughts returned to the study of the means necessary to further safety. Wilder had anticipated these feelings, and even before Mrs Wyllys and Gertrude recovered their recollections, he was occupied, aided by the terrified but loquacious Cassandra, in arranging the contents of the boat in such a manner, as would enable her to move through the element with the least possible resistance.

"With a well trimmed ship, and a fair breeze," cried our adventurer cheerfully, so soon as his little task was ended, "we may yet hope to reach the land, in one day and another night. I have seen the hour, when in this good launch, I would not have hesitated to run the length of the American coast, provided—"

"You have forgotten your provided—" said Gertrude, observing that he hesitated, probably from a reluctance to express any exception to the opinion, which might increase the fears of his companions.

"Provided it were two months earlier in the year," he added with less confidence.

"The season is then against us; it only requires the greater resolution in ourselves."

Wilder turned his head to regard the fair speaker, whose placid countenance as the moon silvered her features expressed any thing but the force necessary to endure the hardships, he knew she was liable to encounter before they might hope to gain the continent. After musing, he lifted his open hand towards the South West, and held its palm, some little time, to the air of the night.

"Any thing is better than idleness, for people in our condition," he said. "There are some symptoms of the breeze coming in this quarter; I will be ready to meet it."

He then spread his two lug sails, and trimming aft the sheets, placed himself at the helm, like one who expected his services might be shortly needed. The result did not disappoint him. Ere long, the light canvass of the boat began to flutter, and then as he brought the stem in the proper direction, the little vessel commenced moving slowly along its blind and watery path.

The wind, charged with the dampness of night, soon came fresher upon the sails. Wilder urged the latter reason, as a motive for the females to seek their rest, beneath a little canopy of tarpaulins, which his foresight had provided, and on mattresses he had brought from the ship. Perceiving that their protector wished to be alone, Mrs Wyllys and her pupil, did as he desired, and in a few minutes if not asleep, no one could have told that any other than our adventurer had possession of the solitary launch.

The middle hour of the night went by, without any material change in the prospects of these lonely travellers. The wind had freshened to a smart breeze, and by the calculations of Wilder he had already moved across several leagues of ocean, directly in a line for the eastern end of that long and narrow isle that separates the waters which wash the shores of Connecticut from those of the open sea. The minutes flew swiftly by, for the time was propitious, and the thoughts of the young seaman, were busy with the recollections of a short, but adventurous life. He leaned forward to catch the gentle respiration of those who slept. Then his form fell back into its seat, and his lip moved as he gave inward utterance to the wayward fancies of his imagination. But at no time, not even in the midst of his greatest abandonment to reverie and thought, did he forget the constant and nearly instinctive duties of his station. A rapid glance at the heavens, an oblique look at the compass, and an occasional but more protracted examination of the pale face of the melancholy moon, were the usual directions taken by his practised eyes. The latter was still in the zenith, and Wilder saw with uneasiness that she was shining through an atmosphere without a haze. He would have better liked those portentous and watery circles, by which she is so often environed, and which are thought to foretel the tempest, than the hard and dry medium through which her beams fell so clear upon the face of the waters. The humidity with which the breeze had commenced was also gone, and in its place, the sensitive organs of the seaman detected the often grateful though at that moment, unwelcome taint of the land. All these were signs that the airs from the continent were about to prevail, and as he dreaded, from certain wild looking, long, narrow clouds that were gathering over the Western horizon, to prevail with the force that was usual at that turbulent season.

If any doubts had existed in the mind of Wilder as to the accuracy of his prognostics, they would have been effectually solved about the commencement of the morning-watch. At that hour, the inconstant breeze began again to die, and even before its last breathing was felt upon the flapping canvass, it was met by counter currents from the west. Our mariner saw, at once, that the struggle was now truly to commence and he made his dispositions accordingly. The square sheets of duck which had so long been exposed to the mild airs of the South, were reduced to one third their original size by double reefs, and several of the more cumbrous of the remaining articles, such as were of doubtful use to persons in their situation were cast without pausing to hesitate into the sea. Nor was this care without a sufficient object. The air soon came hoarsely sighing over the deep, from the North-West, bringing with it, the chilling asperity of the inhospitable regions of the Canadas.

"Ah! well do I know you," muttered Wilder, as the first puff of this unwelcome wind struck his sails, and forced the little boat to bend to its power in passing. "Well do I know you, with your fresh-water flavor, and your smell of the land! Would to God you had blown your fill upon the Lakes, without coming down to drive many a weary seaman back upon his wake, and to eke out a voyage already too long, by your bitter colds and steady obstinacy."

"Do you speak?" said Gertrude, half-appearing from beneath her canopy, and then shrinking back shivering into its cover again, as she felt the influence in the change of air.

"Sleep, lady, sleep," he answered, for he liked not, at such a moment, to be disturbed by even her gentle voice.

"Is there new danger?" she asked, stepping lightly from the mattress, unwilling to disturb the repose of her governess. "You need not fear to tell me the worst. I am a soldier's child."

He pointed to the signs so well comprehended by himself, but continued silent.

"I feel that the wind is colder than it was, but I see no other change."

"And do you know whither the boat is going?"

"To the land, I think. You assured us of that, and I do not believe you would willingly deceive."

"You do me justice; as a proof of it, I will now tell you that you are mistaken. I know that to your eyes, all points of the compass, on this void, must seem the same, but I cannot so easily deceive myself."

"And we are not sailing for our homes?"

"So far from it, that should this course continue, we must cross the whole Atlantic before we can again see land."

Gertrude made no reply, but retired in sorrow to the side of her Governess. In the mean time, Wilder, left to himself, began to consult his compass and the direction of the wind. Perceiving that he might approach nearer to the continent of America by changing the position of the boat, he wore round, and brought its head as nigh up to the South-West, as the wind would permit.

But there was little hope in this trifling change. At each minute the power of the breeze was increasing, until it freshened to a degree that compelled him to furl his after sail. The slumbering ocean was not long in awakening, and by the time the launch was snug under a close-reefed foresail the boat was rising on the growing waves, or sinking into the momentary calm of their furrows. The dashing of the waters and the rushing of the wind, which now began to sweep heavily across the waste, drew the females to the side of their protector. To their hurried and anxious questions he made considerate, but brief replies, answering like a man who felt that the time was better suited to action than to words. Indeed, his utmost skill and attention soon became requisite, if not to the safety of the boat, at least for the comfort of those it contained.

In this manner the lingering minutes of the night went by, loaded with a care that each moment rendered heavier, and which each successive freshening of the breeze had a tendency to render more and more anxious. The day came only to give more distinctness to the cheerless prospect. The waves were looking green and angrily, while, here and there, large crests of foam were beginning to break on their summits, the certain evidence that a conflict between the elements was at hand. Then came the sun over the ragged margin of the Eastern horizon, climbing slowly into the blue arch above, which lay clear, chilling, distinct and without a cloud.

Wilder noted all the changes of the hour with a closeness that proved how critical he deemed their case. He seemed rather to consult the signs of the heavens, than to regard the tossings and rushings of the water, which dashed against the side of his little vessel, in a manner that often appeared to threaten their total destruction. To the latter, however, he was too much accustomed to anticipate the true moment of alarm, though to the less instructed senses of his companions it already seemed so dangerous. It was to him, as is the thunder when compared to the lightning to the mind of the philosopher; or, rather he knew that if harm might come from the one on which he floated, its ability to injure must first be called into action by the power of the sister element.

"What do you think of our case now?" asked Mrs Wyllys, keeping her look fastened on his countenance as if she would rather trust to its expression than even to his words for the answer.

"So long as the wind continue thus, we may yet hope to keep within the route of ships passing to and from the great Northern Ports. But if it freshen to a gale and the sea begin to break with violence, I doubt the ability of this boat to lie-to."

"Then our resource must be in endeavoring to run before the gale."

"Then, we must scud."

"What would be our direction, in such an event?" demanded Gertrude, to whose mind, in the agitation of the ocean and the naked view on every hand, all idea of places and distances was lost in the most inextricable confusion.

"In such an event," returned our adventurer, regarding her with a look, in which commiseration and indefinite concern were so singularly mingled, that her own mild gaze, was changed into a timid and furtive glance, "in such an event, we should be leaving that land, it is so important to reach."

"What 'em 'ere!" cried Cassandra, whose large dark eyes were rolling on every side of her with a curiosity that no care or sense of danger could extinguish; " 'em berry big fish on a water."

"It is a boat!" cried Wilder, springing upon a thwart to catch a glimpse of a dark object that was driving on the glittering crest of a wave within a hundred feet of the spot where the launch itself was struggling through the brine. "What ho! boat, ahoy! Hilloa, there—boat, ahoy!"

The breathing of the wind swept past them, but no human sound answered his shout. They had already fallen between two seas into a deep vale of water, where the narrow view extended no farther than the rolling barriers on each side.

"Merciful Providence!" exclaimed the Governess, "can there then be others as unhappy as ourselves!"

"It was a boat, or my sight is not true as usual!" returned Wilder, still keeping his stand to watch the moment when he might catch another view.

His wish was quickly realized. He had trusted the helm to the hands of Cassandra, who suffered the launch to vary a little from its course. The words were still on his lips when the same black object came sweeping down the wave to windward, and a pinnace bottom upwards washed past them in the trough. Then followed a shriek from the negress, who abandoned the tiller, and sinking on her knees, hid her face in her hands. Wilder instinctively caught the helm, bending his look at the same time in the direction of the object from which the eye of Cassandra had revolted. A human form was seen, erect and half exposed, advancing in the midst of the broken crest, which was still covering the dark declivity to windward with foam. For a moment it stood, with the brine dripping from the drenched locks, like some being that had issued from the deep to turn its frightful features on the spectators; and then the lifeless body of a drowned man drove past the launch.

Not only Wilder, but Gertrude and Mrs Wyllys, had seen this startling spectacle so nigh them, as to recognise the grim countenance of Knighthead, rendered stern and forbidding by death. Neither spoke, or gave any other evidence of their intelligence. Wilder hoped, that his companions had at least escaped the shock of recognising the victim, and the females themselves, saw in the hapless fortune of the mutineer too much of their own probable though more protracted fate to be able to give vent to the horror they felt in words. For some time the elements were heard sighing a sort of hoarse requiem over their victims.

"The pinnace has filled," Wilder at length ventured to say, when he saw by the pallid features of his companions that it was useless to affect reserve any longer. "Their boat was frail, and loaded to the water's edge."

"Think you all are lost!" observed Mrs Wyllys, in a voice

that scarcely amounted to a whisper. "All! not even a soul escaped?"

"There is no hope for any! Gladly would I part with an arm for the assistance of the poorest of those misguided seamen, who have hurried on their evil fortune, by their own disobedience and ignorance."

"And of all the happy and thoughtless human beings who so lately left the harbor of Newport, we alone remain!"

"There is not another. This boat and its contents are the sole memorials of the Royal Caroline."

"It was not within the ken of human knowledge to foresee this evil?" continued the Governess, fastening her eye on the countenance of Wilder, as if she would ask a question which conscience told her, at the same time, betrayed a portion of that very superstition which had hastened the fate of the rude being they had so lately passed.

"It was not."

"And the danger to which you so often and so inexplicably alluded, had no reference to this we have incurred?—"

"It had not."

"It has gone with the change in our situation?"

"I hope it has."

"See," interrupted Gertrude, laying a hand in her haste on the arm of Wilder. "Heaven be praised! yonder is something at last to relieve the view."

"It is a ship!" exclaimed her governess; but an envious wave lifting its green side between them and the object, they sunk into a trough, as if the vision had been placed, momentarily, before their eyes, merely to taunt them with its image. Wilder had caught, however, a glimpse of the well known outlines of a ship against the heavens as they descended. When the boat rose again, his look was properly directed and he was enabled to be certain of the reality of the vessel. Wave succeeded wave, and moments followed moments, during which the stranger as often appeared and disappeared, as the launch unavoidably rose and fell with the seas. These short and hasty glimpses sufficed, however, to convey all that was necessary to one who had been nurtured on that element where circumstances now exacted of him such constant and unequivocal evidences of his skill.

At the distance of a mile there was a ship rolling and pitching gracefully, and without any apparent shock, on those waves through which the launch was struggling with so much difficulty. A solitary sail was set to steady the vessel, and that so reduced by reefs as to look like a little snowy cloud waving in the air. At times her tapering masts, appeared pointing to the zenith, or rolling as if inclining against the wind, and then again with slow and graceful sweeps they seemed to fall towards the ruffled surface of the ocean, as if to seek refuge from their endless motion in the bosom of the agitated element itself. There were moments when the long, low and black hull was seen distinctly resting on the summit of a sea, and glittering in the sun-beams with the water washing from her sides, and then as boat and vessel sunk together, all was lost to the eye, even to the attenuated lines of her tallest and most delicate spars.

Both Mrs Wyllys and Gertrude bowed their faces to their knees, when assured of the truth of their hopes, and poured out their gratitude, in silent and secret thanksgivings. The joy of Cassandra was more clamourous and less restrained. The simple negress laughed, shed tears and exulted on the prospect that was now afforded for the escape of her young mistress and herself from a death that the recent sight, had set before her imagination in the most frightful form. But no answering look of congratulation was to be traced in the anxious eye of their companion.

"Now," said Mrs Wyllys, seizing his hand in both her own, "we may surely hope to be delivered, and then will follow, brave and excellent young man, an opportunity of proving how highly we rate your services!"

Wilder permitted this burst of feeling, but he neither spoke, nor exhibited himself the smallest sympathy in her joy.

"Surely you are not grieved, Mr Wilder," added the wondering Gertrude, "that the prospect of escape from these awful waves, is, at length, so mercifully held forth to us!"

"I would gladly die to shelter you from harm," returned the young sailor—"but—"

"This is not a time for any thing but gratitude," interrupted the Governess. "I cannot hearken to any cold exceptions now. What means that 'but?'"

"It may not be easy as you think to reach the ship—the gale may prevent—in short, many is the vessel that is seen at sea, which cannot be spoken."

"Happily, such is not our cruel fortune. I understand your wish to dampen hopes, that may possibly be thwarted; but I have too long and too often trusted this dangerous element not to know that he who has the advantage of being to windward can speak or not as he shall please."

"You are right in saying that we are to windward; and were I in a ship nothing would be easier than to run within hail of the stranger—That ship is certainly lying-to; and yet the gale is not fresh enough to bring so stout a vessel to so short canvass."

"They see us then, and await our arrival!"

"No—no. Thank God we are not yet seen. This little rag of ours is blended with the spray. They take it for a gull or a comb of the sea, for the moment it is in view."

"And do you thank Heaven for this!" exclaimed Gertrude, regarding the anxious Wilder with a wonder, that her more cautious Governess had the power to restrain.

"Did I thank Heaven for not being seen? I may have mistaken the object of my thanks—it is an armed ship!"

"Perhaps a cruiser of the King's! We are the more likely to meet with a welcome reception! Delay not to hoist some signal, lest they increase their sail and leave us."

"You forget that the enemy is often found upon our coast. This might prove a Frenchman!"

"I have no fears of a generous enemy. Even a pirate would give shelter and welcome to females in our distress."

A profound silence succeeded. Wilder still stood upon the thwart, straining his eyes to read each sign that a seaman understands, nor did he appear to find much pleasure in the task.

"We will draw ahead," he said, "and as the ship is lying on a different tack, we may yet gain a position that will leave us masters of our movements."

To this his companions knew not well how to make any objection. Mrs Wyllys was so much struck with the remarkable air of coldness with which he met this prospect of refuge against the forlorn condition in which he had just before confessed they were placed, that she was much more disposed to ponder on the cause, than to trouble him with questions she had the discernment to see would be useless. Gertrude wondered, while she was disposed to think he might be right, though she knew not why. Cassandra alone was rebellious. She made stout objections, against even a moment's delay, assuring the inattentive young seaman, that should any evil come to her young Mistress by his obstinacy, General Grayson would be angered, and she left him to reflect on the results of a displeasure that to her simple mind teemed, with more danger than would attend the frown of a monarch. Provoked by his contumacious disregard of her remonstrances, the negress, forgetting her respect, in boldness in behalf of her, whom she not only loved but had been taught to reverence, seized the boat-hook, and unperceived by Wilder, fastened to it one of the linen cloths that had been brought from the wreck, exposing the fluttering drapery above the diminished sail, ere her device, caught the attention of her companions. Then indeed, she lowered the signal, before the dark look of Wilder. Short as was the triumph of the negress it was crowned with success.

The restrained silence, which is so apt to succeed a sudden burst of displeasure was still reigning in the boat, when a cloud of smoke broke out of the side of the ship, the deadened roar of artillery struggling heavily up against the wind, immediately after.

"It is now too late to hesitate," said Mrs Wyllys; "we are seen, let the stranger be friend or enemy."

Wilder did not answer, but continued to watch the movements of the stranger. In another moment, the spars were seen receding before the breeze, and in a couple of minutes more, the head of the ship was changed to the direction in which they lay. Four or five broader sheets of canvass appeared in different parts of the complicated machinery, while the vessel inclined to the breeze. As she mounted on the seas, her bows seemed issuing from the element altogether, and high jets of glittering spray were cast into the air, falling in gems upon the sails and rigging.

"It is now too late, indeed," murmured our adventurer, bearing up the helm of his own little craft, and letting its sheet slip through his hands until the sail was bagging with the breeze nearly to bursting. The boat, which had so long been laboring through the water, with a wish to cling as nigh as possible to the continent, flew over the seas, leaving a long trail of foam behind; and before either of the females had regained their entire self-possession, she was floating in the comparative calm, that the hull of a large vessel never fails to create. A light form stood in the rigging of the ship, issuing the necessary orders for her manœuvres; and, in the midst of the confusion and trepidation that such a scene was likely to cause in the bosom of woman, Gertrude and Mrs Wyllys with their two companions were transferred in safety to the decks of the stranger. The moment they and their effects were secured, the launch was cut adrift like useless lumber. Twenty mariners were then seen climbing among the ropes, and sail after sail was opened still wider, until, bearing the vast folds of all her canvass spread, the vessel was urged along her trackless course, like a swift cloud drifting through the thin medium of the upper air.

# Chapter XIX

"Now let it work: Mischief, thou art afoot,
Take then what course thou wilt!"
*Julius Cæsar*, III.ii.260–61.

W HEN THE VELOCITY with which the vessel flew before
the wind is properly considered, the reader will not be
surprised to learn that at the end of a week from the time
when the foregoing incidents close, we are enabled to open
the scene of the present chapter in a very different quarter of
the same sea. It is unnecessary to follow the rover in the
windings of her devious and uncertain course, during which
her keel furrowed more than a thousand miles of ocean, eluding more than one cruiser of the King and avoiding sundry
less dangerous rencontres as much from inclination as any
other visible cause. It is sufficient for our purpose to lift the
curtain which must conceal her movements during this week,
when the gallant vessel is in a milder climate and, the season
of the year considered, in a more propitious sea.

Exactly seven days after Gertrude and her Governess became the inmates of a ship, whose character it is no longer
necessary to conceal from the reader, though it remained a
secret from the females, the sun rose upon her flapping sails,
symmetrical spars and dark hull within sight of a few low,
small, and rocky islands. The colour of the element would
have told a seaman had no mound of blue land been seen in
the west, that the bottom of the sea was heaving up nearer to
its surface, and that it was necessary to guard against the
known and dreaded dangers of a coast. Wind there was none;
for the vacillating and uncertain air, which, from time to time,
distended the lighter canvass of the vessel was the breathing
of a morning that was breaking upon the main, so soft, mild
and bland as to impart to the sleeping ocean the appearance
of a placid lake.

Every thing having life in the ship, was up and stirring.
Fifty stout and healthful looking seamen were hanging in
different parts of her rigging, some laughing and holding
low converse with messmates who lay indolently on the neigh-

boring spars, and others leisurely performing the light duty that was the ostensible employment of the moment. More than as many others loitered carelessly about the decks below, somewhat similarly engaged, the whole having the appearance of men, who were set to perform their trivial tasks, more to escape the imputation of idleness, than from any actual necessity of their being executed. The quarter-deck, the hallowed spot of every vessel that pretends to discipline, was occupied by a set of seamen who could not lay much greater claim to activity. In short, the vessel partook of the character of the ocean and of the weather, both of which seemed to be reserving their powers to some occasion more suitable for their display.

Three or four young, and considering the nature of their service, far from unpleasant looking men appeared in a sort of undress, nautical uniform, in which the fashion of no people in particular was very studiously consulted. Notwithstanding the calm that reigned on all around them each of them wore a short, straight dirk at his girdle, and as one of them bent over the side of the vessel, the handle of a little pistol was discovered through an opening in the folds of his professional frock. There were however no other immediate signs of distrust by which an observer might infer that this armed precaution was more than the usual custom of the ship. A couple of grim and callous looking sentinels, attired and accoutred like soldiers of the land, contrary to marine usages were posted on the line which separated the place sacred to uses of the officers from the forward part of the deck, bespeaking additional caution. Still, these arrangements were regarded by the seamen with incurious eyes, a proof that use had rendered them familiar.

The individual who has been introduced to the reader under the high sounding title of General, stood upright and rigid as one of the masts of the ship, studying with a critical eye the equipments of his two mercenaries, and apparently as regardless of what else was passing around him, as if he literally considered himself a fixture. One form, however, was to be distinguished from all around it, by the air of authority that breathed even in its repose. It was the Rover. He stood alone, none presuming to approach the spot where he had chosen to plant his person. There was a constant expression of investigation in his wandering eye, as it roved from object to object in the equipment of the vessel, and at moments, as his eye examined the blue vacuum above him, the cloud that denotes a seaman's responsibility gathered about his brow. This lowering look became so marked, at times, that the fair hair which broke out in ringlets from beneath a black velvet sea-cap from whose top depended a tassel of gold, could no longer impart to his countenance the gentleness, which formed its natural expression in moments of quiet. Disdaining concealment, and as if he wished to announce the nature of the powers he wielded, he wore his pistols openly in a leathern belt through which he had thrust with the same disregard of concealment, a light and curved yattagan which, by the chasings of its handle, had probably come from the manufactory of an eastern artisan.

On the deck of the poop overlooking the rest, and retired from the crowd beneath, stood Mrs Wyllys and her charge, neither of whom announced in the slightest degree by eye or air that anxiety, which might be supposed natural to females who found themselves in a condition so critical as that in which they were. On the contrary, while the former pointed out to the latter, the hillock of pale blue, which rose from the water, like a dark and strongly defined cloud, in the distance, hope was strongly blended with the ordinary expression of her features. She also called to Wilder in a cheerful voice, and the youth, who had long been standing, with a sort of jealous watchfulness, at the foot of the ladder which led from the quarter-deck, was at her side in an instant.

"I am telling Gertrude," said the governess, "that yonder is her home; that when the breeze shall be felt, we may speedily hope to reach it. But the wilfully timid girl insists that she cannot believe her senses, after the frightful risks we have run, until at least she shall see the dwelling of her childhood and the face of her father. You have often been on this coast before, Mr Wilder?"

"Often, Madam."

"Then you can tell us the name of the distant land we see."

"Land!" repeated our adventurer, affecting a look of surprise—"is there land in view!"

"Is there land in view!—have not hours gone by since it was proclaimed from the masts?"

"It may be so. We seamen are dull after a night of watching, and we often hear but little of what passes."

A suspicious glance was shot from the eye of the Governess as if she apprehended she knew not what.

"Has the sight of the cheerful, blessed, safe soil of America so soon lost its charm in your eye, that you approach it with so heedless an ear? The infatuation, of men of your profession, in favour of so dangerous and so treacherous an element is an enigma I could never explain."

"Do seamen, then, really love their calling with so devoted an affection?" innocently demanded Gertrude.

"It is a folly of which we are at least accused," rejoined Wilder, turning his eye on the speaker, and smiling in a manner that had lost every shade of reserve.

"And justly?—"

"I fear justly."

"Too justly!" said Mrs Wyllys, with emphasis; "better than their quiet and peaceful homes!"

Gertrude pursued the idea, no further; but her eye fell to the deck, as if she reflected on a perversity of taste which could render man so insensible to domestic pleasures, and incline him to court the dangers of which she had been a witness.

"I, at least, am free from the latter charge," exclaimed Wilder. "A ship has always been my home."

"Much of my life, too, has been wasted in one—" continued the Governess, who was pursuing, in her own mind, some images of a time long past. "Happy and miserable alike, have been the hours that I have passed upon the sea. Nor is this the first King's ship, in which it has been my fortune to be thrown. And yet, the customs seem changed, since the days I mean; or else my memory is beginning to lose some of the impressions of an age, when memory is apt to be most tenacious. Is it usual, for instance, Mr Wilder, to admit an utter stranger, like yourself to exercise authority in a vessel of war?"

"Certainly, not."

"And yet you have been acting, so far as my recollections are true, as second here, since the moment we entered this vessel, wrecked and helpless fugitives from the waves!"

Our adventurer again averted his eye, and evidently searched for words ere he replied—

"A commission is always respected. Mine procured for me, the consideration you have witnessed."

"You are then an Officer of the Crown?"

"Would any other authority be respected in a vessel of the Crown? Death had left a vacancy, in the second station of this—cruiser. Fortunately for the wants of the service—perhaps for myself—I was at hand to fill it."

"But tell me further," continued the Governess who appeared disposed to profit by the occasion to solve more doubts than one—"is it usual for the officers of a vessel of war, to appear armed among their crew, in the manner I see here?"

"It is the pleasure of our Commander."

"That Commander is evidently a skilful seaman, but his caprices and tastes are as extraordinary as his mien. I have surely seen him before; and, it would seem, but lately."

Mrs Wyllys was silent for several minutes. During the whole time her eye was never averted from the form of the calm and motionless being who still maintained his attitude of repose, aloof from all that throng whom he had the address to render so entirely dependent on his authority. The Governess studied the smallest peculiarity of his person, as if she would never tire of her gaze. Drawing a heavy and relieving breath, she remembered, however, that she was not alone, and that others were silently awaiting the process of her thoughts. Without manifesting embarrassment at an absence of mind that was far too common to surprise her pupil, she resumed the discourse where she had herself dropped it, turning again towards Wilder.

"Is Capt. Heidegger an old acquaintance?" she demanded.

"We have met before."

"It should be a name of German origin, by the sound. I am certain it is new to me. And yet there was a time when few officers of his rank were unknown to me, at least by name. Is his family of long standing in England?"

"That is a question, he may better answer himself," said Wilder, glad to perceive that the subject of their discourse, was approaching. "For the moment, Madam, my duty calls me elsewhere."

Wilder withdrew with reluctance, and had suspicion been active in the breasts of either of his companions they would not have failed to note the glance of distrust, with which he watched the manner of his Commander in making his salutations. There was nothing, however, in the air of the Rover that should have given ground to so much jealous vigilance. On the contrary he was cold and abstracted, appearing to mingle in their discourse more from a sense of the obligations of hospitality, than from any satisfaction that he might derive from the intercourse. Still his deportment was kind, and his voice bland as the airs that were wafted from the healthful islands in view.

"There is a sight," he said, pointing towards the low blue ridges of the land, "that forms the landsman's delight, and the seaman's terror."

"Are seamen so averse to the view of regions where so many millions of their fellow creatures find pleasure in dwelling?" demanded Gertrude, to whom he more particularly addressed his words, with a frankness, that would in itself, have sufficiently proved no glimmerings of his real character had ever dawned on her spotless and unsuspicious mind.

"Miss Grayson included—" he returned, with a slight bow, and a smile in which, perhaps, irony was concealed by playfulness. "After the risk you have run, even I, confirmed and obstinate sea-monster as I am, have no reason to complain of your distaste for our element. And yet, you see, it is not entirely without its charms. No lake that lies within the limits of yonder continent can be more calm and sweet than this bit of ocean. Were we a few degrees more Southward, I would show you landscapes, of rock, and mountain; of bays, and of hillsides sprinkled with verdure; of tumbling whales, and lazy fishermen, and distant cottages and lagging sails, that would make a figure even in pages that the bright eye of a lady might love to read."

"And yet for most of your picture would you be indebted to the land: In return for this sketch, I would take you north and show you black and threatening clouds, a green and angry sea; shipwrecks and shoals; cottages and hill-sides, and mountains in the imagination only of the drowning man, and sails bleached by waters, that contain the voracious shark or the disgusting polypus."

Gertrude had answered in his own vein, but it was too evident from a tremor that stole into her voice, that memory was also busy with its frightful images. The Rover was not slow to detect the change. Desirous of banishing every recollection that might give her pain, he artfully but delicately, gave a new direction to the discourse.

"There are people who think the sea has no amusements," he said. "To a pining, home-sick-sea-sick miserable lubber, this may well be true enough; but the man who has sufficient spirit to keep down the qualms of the animal, may tell a different tale. We have our balls regularly, for instance, and there are artists on board this ship, who, though they cannot, perhaps, make as accurate a right-angle with their legs as the first dancer of a ballet, can go through their figures in a gale of wind, which is more than can be said of the highest jumper of them all, on shore."

"A ball without females would, at least, be thought an unsocial amusement, with us uninstructed people of terra firma."

"Hum. It might be all the better for a lady or two. Then have we our theatre. Farce, comedy and the buskin take their turns to help along the time. Yon fellow that you see lying on the foretopsail-yard, like an indolent serpent basking on the branch of a tree, will 'roar you as gently as any sucking dove,' and here is a votary of Momus who would raise a smile on the lips of a sea-sick friar. I believe I can say no more in his commendation."

"All this is well in the description," returned Mrs Wyllys, "but something is due to the merit of the—Poet or Painter shall I term you?"

"Neither—but a grave and veritable chronologer. However, since you doubt, and since you are so new to the ocean"—

"Pardon me," the lady, gravely interrupted. "On the contrary, I have seen much of it."

The Rover, who had rather suffered his unsettled glances to wander over the youthful countenance of Gertrude than towards her companion, now bent his eyes on the last speaker, where he kept them fastened so long, as to create some little embarrassment in the subject of his gaze.

"You seem surprised, that the time of a female should have been thus employed," she observed, with a view to arouse his attention to the impropriety of his observation.

"We are speaking of the sea, if I remember," he continued, like a man, that was suddenly awakened from a reverie. "Ay, I know it was of the sea, for I had grown boastful, in my panegyrics. I had told you that this ship was faster, than"—

"Nothing!" exclaimed Gertrude, laughing at his blunder. "You were playing master of ceremonies at a nautical ball."

"Will you figure in a minuet? Will you honor my boards with the graces of your person?"

"I, Sir! and with whom? With the gentleman, who knows so well the manner of keeping his feet in a gale!"

"You were about to relieve any doubts we might have, concerning the amusements of seamen," said the Governess, reproving the too playful spirit of her pupil by a glance of her grave eye.

"Ay. It was the humour of the moment, nor will I balk it."

He turned to Wilder, who had posted himself within earshot of what was passing and continued—

"These ladies doubt our gaiety, Mr Wilder. Let the boatswain give the magical wind of his call, and pass the word 'to mischief' among the people."

Our adventurer, bowed his acquiescence, and issued the order. In a few moments, the individual who made acquaintance with the reader in the bar-room of the Foul Anchor appeared in the centre of the vessel, near the main-hatchway, decorated as before with his silver chain and whistle, and accompanied by two mates, who were humbler scholars of the same gruff school. A long, shrill whistle followed from the instrument of Nightingale, who, when the sound had died away on the ear, roared, in his least sonorous tones—

"All hands to mischief, ahoy!"

We have before had occasion to liken these sounds to the muttering of a bull, nor shall we see fit to disturb the comparison, since no other similitude so apt, presents itself. The example of the boatswain was followed by each of his mates, in turn, when the summons was deemed sufficient. However

unintelligible and grum the call might sound in the ears of
Gertrude, it produced no unpleasant effects on the organs of
a majority of those who heard it. When the first note of the
call mounted on the air, each idle and extended young seaman, as he lay stretched upon a spar, or hung dangling from
a ratlin, lifted his head to catch the words that were to follow,
as an obedient spaniel pricks his ears to catch his master's
voice. But no sooner was the emphatic word pronounced,
which preceded the long drawn and customary exclamation
with which Nightingale closed his summons, than the low
murmur of voices, which had so long been maintained among
the men, broke out in a common shout. Every symptom of
lethargy disappeared, in an instant. The young and nimble
topmen bounded into the rigging of their respective masts,
ascending the shaking ladders of ropes, like so many squirrels
hastening to their holes, at the signal of alarm. The graver
and heavier seamen of the forecastle, the quarter-gunners and
quarter-masters, the less instructed and half-startled waisters,
and the raw and actually alarmed after-guard, all hurried
by a sort of instinct to their several points, the more practised
to plot mischief against their shipmates, and the less intelligent, conscious of their ignorance, to concert the means of
defence.

In an instant the tops and yards were ringing with laughter
and jokes, as each exulting mariner aloft proclaimed his device
to his fellows, or urged his own inventions at the expense of
some less ingenious mode of annoyance. On the other hand,
the distrustful and often repeated glances, that were thrown
upward, from the men who had clustered on the quarter deck
and around the foot of the mainmast, sufficiently proclaimed
the diffidence with which the novices on deck were about to
enter into the expected contest of practical wit. The steady
and more earnest seamen forward, however, maintained their
places, with a stern resolution, which proved their reliance on
their physical force and on their long familiarity with the
humours, as well as with the dangers of the ocean.

Another little cluster of men assembled in the midst of the
general clamour and confusion, with a haste and steadiness,
that announced both a consciousness of the entire necessity
of unity, on the present occasion, and the habit of acting in

concert. These were the drilled and military dependants of the General, between whom and the less artificial seamen, there existed not only an antipathy that might almost be called instinctive, but which, for obvious reasons, had been so strongly encouraged in the vessel of which we write, as often to manifest itself in turbulent and nearly mutinous broils. About twenty in number, they collected quickly, and although obliged to dispense with their fire-arms in such an amusement, there was a sternness in the visage of each of the whiskered worthies that showed how readily he could appeal to the bayonet that was suspended from his shoulder, should there be need. Their commander withdrew with the rest of the officers to the poop, in order that their presence should prove no incumbrance to the freedom of the sports.

A couple of minutes might have been lost in producing the different changes we have just related. But so soon as the top-men were sure that no unfortunate laggard of their party was within reach of the resentment of the different groupes beneath, they complied literally with the summons of the boat-swain, by commencing their mischief.

Sundry buckets, most of which had been provided for the extinction of fire, were quickly pendant from as many whips* on the outer extremity of the different yards and descending towards the sea. In spite of the awkward opposition of the men below these leathern vessels were speedily filled and run up to the yards again. Many a gaping waister and rigid marine now made a more familiar acquaintance with the element on which he had enlisted than suited either his convenience or his humour. So long as the jokes were confined to these semi-initiated tyros, the top-men enjoyed their fun with impunity. But the instant the dignity of a quarter gunner's person was invaded the whole gang of petty officers and forecastle men rose, in a body, to resent the insult. With a readiness and dexterity that manifested how much at home the elder mariners were with all that belonged to their art, a small fire-engine was transferred to the head, and brought to bear on the nearest top, like a well planted battery clearing the way for

*A rope rove through a single block is termed "a whip" in nautical language.

the expected charge. The laughing and chattering top-men were soon dispersed, some ascending beyond the power of the engine and others fleeing into the neighboring top, along ropes and across giddy heights that would have seemed impracticable to any animal less agile than a squirrel or a monkey.

The Marines were now summoned forward by the successful and malicious mariners, to improve their advantage. Thoroughly drenched already and eager to resent their wrongs, a half-dozen of the soldiers, led on by a corporal, the coating of whose powdered poll had been converted into a sort of paste, by too great an intimacy with a bucket of water, essayed to mount the rigging, an exploit that to them was much more arduous than it would have been to enter a breach. The waggish quarter-gunners and quarter-masters, satisfied with their own success, stimulated them to the enterprise, and Nightingale and his mates, while they rolled their tongues into their cheeks, gave forth with their whistles the cheering sound of "heave away." The sight of these adventurers slowly and cautiously mounting the rigging, acted on the scattered top-men, very much in the manner that the appearance of so many flies in the immediate vicinity of a web is known to act on their concealed and rapacious enemy the spider. The sailors aloft understood, by expressive glances from those below, that a soldier was considered legal game. No sooner, therefore, had the latter fairly entered into the toils, than twenty top-men rushed out upon them, in order to make sure of their prizes. In an incredibly short time the assailants were captured to a man. Two or three of the aspiring adventurers were lashed where they had been found, unable to make any resistance in a spot, where instinct itself urged them to devote both hands to the necessary duty of holding fast; while the rest were transferred, by the means of whips, to different spars, very much as a light sail or a yard would have been swayed into its place.

In the midst of the clamorous rejoicings that attended this success, one individual made himself conspicuous for the gravity and business-like air with which he performed his particular part of the comedy. Seated on the outer end of a lower yard, with as much steadiness as if he had been placed on an ottoman, he was gravely occupied in examining into the condition of a captive, who had been run up at his feet, with an order from the waggish captain of the top, "to turn him in, for a jewel-block," an appellation that is given to the blocks that are pendant from the ends of certain yards, and which appears to have been taken from the precious stones that are so often seen dangling from the ears of the fair.

"Ay, ay," returned this deliberate and grave looking tar, who was no other than Richard Fid. "The stropping you've sent up with the fellow is none of the best, and if he squeaks so now, what will he do when you come to reeve a rope through him? By the Lord, masters, you should have furnished the lad a better outfit if you meant to send him into good company aloft. Here are more holes in his jacket, than there are cabin windows to a Chinese junk. Hilloa! on deck there! you Guinea, pick me up a tailor and send him aloft to keep the wind out of this waister's tarpaulin."

The athletic African, who, on account of his great strength, had been posted on the forecastle, cast an eye upward, and with both arms thrust into his bosom, he rolled along the deck, with just as serious a mien as if he had been sent on a duty of the gravest kind. The uproar over head had drawn a most hapless looking mortal from a retired corner of the berth-deck to the ladder of the forward hatch, where with a body half above the combings, a skein of strong, coarse thread around his neck, a piece of bees-wax in one hand and a needle in the other, he stood staring about him, with just that sort of bewildered air that a Chinese mandarin would manifest were he to be suddenly initiated into the mysteries of the ballet. On this object the eye of Scipio fell. Stretching out an arm, he cast him upon his shoulder, and before the startled subject of his attack knew into whose hands he had fallen, a hook was passed beneath the waistband of his trowsers, and he was half way between the water and the spar, on his way to Fid.

"Have a care, lest you let the man fall into the sea!" cried Wilder, sternly, from his stand on the distant poop.

"He'm a tailor, Masser Harry," returned the deliberate black; "if he breeches give way, he nobody to blame but he-self."

During this brief parlance the goodman Homespun had

safely arrived at the termination of his flight. Here he was suitably received by Fid, who raised him to his side, and having placed him comfortably between the yard and the boom, he proceeded to secure him by a lashing that should give the tailor the proper disposition of his hands.

"Bouse a bit, on this waister!" called out Richard, when he had properly secured the goodman. "So; belay all that."

He then put one foot on the neck of his prisoner, and seizing his lower member as it swung uppermost, he coolly placed it in the lap of the awe-struck tailor.

"There, friend," he said, "handle your needle and palm, now, as if you were at job work. Your knowing handicraft always begins with the foundation; whereby he makes sure that his upper gear, will stand—"

"The Lord protect me, and all other sinful mortals from an untimely end!" exclaimed Homespun, gazing at the vacant view, from his giddy elevation with a sensation a little resembling that with which the aeronaut, in his first experiment, regards the prospect beneath.

"Settle away this waister," again called Fid. "He interrupts rational conversation by his noise, and, as his gear is condemned by this here tailor, why, you may turn him over to the purser for a new outfit."

The real motive however for getting rid of his pendant companion was a twinkling of humanity that still glimmered through the rough humour of the tar, who well knew that his prisoner must hang where he did, at a good deal of expense of bodily ease. As soon as his request was complied with, he turned to the good-man to renew the discourse, with just as much composure as if they were both seated on the deck, or as if a dozen practical jokes of the same character were not in the process of enactment in as many different parts of the vessel.

"Why do you open your eyes, brother, in this port-hole fashion?" commenced the top-man. "This is all water, that you see about you, except that hommoc of blue, off here in the eastern board, which is a morsel of upland in the Bahamas, d'ye see."

"A sinful and presuming world is this we live in!" returned the Goodman; "nor can any one tell at what moment his life is to be taken from him. Five bloody and cruel wars have I lived to see in safety, and yet am I reserved to meet this disgraceful and profane end at last!"

"Well, since you have had your luck in the wars, you've the less reason to grumble at the bit of a surge you may have felt in your garments, as they run you up to this here yard arm. I say, brother; I have known stouter fellows take the same ride, who never knew when or how they got down again."

Homespun, who did not more than half comprehend the allusion of Fid, now regarded him in a way that announced some little desire for an explanation mingled with great admiration of the unconcern with which his companion maintained his position without the smallest aid from any thing but his self-balancing powers.

"I say, brother," resumed Fid, "that many a stout seaman has been whipt up to the end of a yard who has started by the signal of a gun, and who has staid, there, just as long as the President of a court-martial was pleased to believe might be necessary to improve his honesty."

"It would be a fearful and frightful trifling with Providence in the least offending and conscientious mariner to take such awful punishments in vain, by acting them in his sports but doubly so do I pronounce it, in the crew of a ship, on which no man can say at what hour retribution and compunction are to alight! It seemeth to me unwise to tempt providence by these provocating exhibitions."

Fid cast a glance of more than usual significance at the goodman, and even postponed his reply until he had freshened his ideas by an ample addition to the morsel of weed which he had kept all along thrust into one of his cheeks. Then casting his eyes about him in order to see that none of his noisy and riotous companions of the top were within earshot, he fastened a still more meaning look on the countenance of the tailor, and responded as follows: —

"Harkee, brother, whatever may be the other good points of Richard Fid, his friends cannot say he is much of a scholar. This being the case he has not seen fit to ask for a look at the sailing orders, on coming aboard this wholesome vessel. I suppose, howsomever, that they can be forthcoming at need, and that no honest man need be ashamed to be found cruising under the same."

"Ah! Heaven protect such unoffending innocents, as serve here against their will, when the allotted time of the cruiser shall be filled!" returned Homespun. "I take it however, that you, as a sea-faring and an understanding man, have not entered into this enterprise without receiving the bounty and knowing the whole nature of the service."

"The devil a bit have I entered at all; either in the Enterprise or in the Dolphin as they call the craft. There is Master Harry, the lad on the poop there; he who hails a yard like a bull-whale roaring—I follow his signals, d'ye see, and it is seldom that I bother him with questions as to what tack he means to lay his boat on next."

"What! would you sell your soul in this manner to Beelzebub; and that, too, without a price!"

"I say, friend, it may be as well to overhaul your ideas before you let them slip in this no-man's fashion from your tongue. I would wish to treat a gentleman who has come aloft to pay me a visit with such civility as may do credit to my top, though the crew be at 'mischief' d'ye see, but an officer like him I follow, has a name of his own, without stooping to borrow one of the person you've just seen fit to name. I scorn such a pitiful thing as a threat, but a man of your years needn't be told that it is just as easy to go down from this here spar as it was to come up to it."

The tailor cast a glance beneath him into the brine, and hastened to do away the unfavorable impression which his last unfortunate interrogation had so evidently left on the mind of his brawny associate.

"Heaven forbid that I should call any one but by their given and family names as the law commands," he said. "I meant merely to enquire if you would follow the gentleman you serve, to so unseemly and pernicious a place as a gibbet?"

Fid ruminated some little time, before he could muster his ideas to reply to so comprehensive a question. During this unusual process, he agitated the weed with which his mouth was nearly gorged, with great industry, and then terminating both processes by casting a jet of the juice nearly to the sprit-sail yard, he said in a very decided tone—

"If I wouldn't, may I be d——d— After sailing in company for four and twenty years, I should be no better than a sneak to part company because such a trifle as a gallows hove in sight."

"The pay of such a service should be both generous and punctual, and the cheer of the most inspiriting character?" the goodman observed in a way which manifested that he would not be displeased were he to receive a circumstantial reply. Fid was in no disposition to balk his curiosity, but rather deemed himself bound, since he had entered on the subject to leave no part of it unexplained.

"As for the pay, d'ye see," he said, "it is seaman's wages. I should despise myself to take less than falls to the share of the best foremast hand in a ship, since it would be all the same as owning that I got my deserts. But Master Harry has a way of his own, in rating men's services, and if his ideas get jamm'd in an affair of this sort, it is no marlingspike that I handle which can loosen them. I once just named the propriety of getting me a quarter-master's berth, but devil the bit, would he be doing the thing, seeing, as he says himself, that I have a fashion of getting a little hazy at times, which would only be putting me in danger of disgrace, since every body knows that the higher a monkey climbs in the rigging of a ship, the easier every body on deck can see that he has a spar abaft which isn't human. Then as to cheer, it is seaman's fare—sometimes a cut to spare for a friend and sometimes a hungry stomach."

"But then there are often divisions of the a—a—the prize money, in this successful cruiser," observed the goodman averting his face as he spoke, perhaps from a consciousness that it might betray an unseemly interest in the answer. "I dare say, you receive amends for all your sufferings when the purser gives forth the spoils?"

"Harkee, brother," said Fid, again assuming a look of significance; "can you tell me where the Admiralty Court sits, which condemns her prizes?"

The tailor returned the glance with interest, but an extraordinary uproar in another part of the vessel cut short the dialogue, just as there was a rational probability it might lead to some consolatory explanations between the parties.

As the action of the tale is shortly to be set in motion again, we shall defer the cause of the commotion to the opening of the succeeding chapter.

# Chapter XX

——"Come, and get thee a sword, though made
of a lath: They have been up these two days."
*II Henry VI*, IV.ii.1–2.

---

W HILE THE little bye-play that we have just related was
enacting on the fore-yard-arm of the rover, scenes, that
partook equally of the nature of Tragedy and Farce were in
the process of exhibition elsewhere. The contest between the
possessors of the deck and the active tenants of the tops was
far from having reached its termination. Blows had in more
than one instance succeeded to angry words, and as the
former was a part of the sports in which the marines and
waisters were on an equality with their more ingenious
tormentors, the war was beginning to be waged with some
appearances of a doubtful success. Nightingale, however, was
always ready to recall the combatants to their sense of propriety, with his well known wind of the call and his murmuring
voice. A long, shrill whistle with the words, "good-humour,
ahoy," had hitherto served to keep down the rising tempers of
the different parties, when the joke bore too hard on the
high-spirited soldier or the resentful, though perhaps, less
mettlesome member of the after-guard. But an oversight on
the part of him, who, in common, kept so vigilant an eye on
the movements of all beneath his orders, had nearly led to
results of a most serious nature.

No sooner had the crew commenced the rough sports we
have just related, than the vein which had induced the Rover
momentarily to loosen the reins of discipline seemed suddenly
to subside. The gay and cheerful air that he had maintained in
his dialogue with his female guests (or prisoners, whichever
he might be disposed to consider them,) had disappeared in a
thoughtful and clouded brow. His eye no longer lighted with
those glimmerings of wayward and sarcastic humour in which
he loved occasionally to indulge, but its expression became
settled and austere. His mind had relapsed into one of those
brooding reveries, that so often obscured his mien, as a
shadow darkens the golden tints of the ripe and waving corn.

While most of those who were not actors in the humorous achievements of the crew, steadily regarded the same, some with wonder, others, with distrust, and all with more or less of the humour of the hour, the Rover, to all appearance, was quietly unconscious of all that was going on. It is true, that at times he raised his eyes to the active beings who clung like squirrels to the ropes or suffered them to fall on the duller movements of the men below, but it was always, with a vacancy which proved that the image they carried to the brain was dim and illusory. The looks he cast, from time to time, on Mrs Wyllys, and her fair and interested pupil, betrayed the workings of the temper of the inward man. It was only in these brief but comprehensive glances, that the feelings by which he was governed might have been in any manner traced to their origins. Still the nicest observer would have been puzzled, in endeavoring to pronounce on the entire character of the emotions uppermost in his mind. At instants it might have been fancied that some unholy and licentious passion was getting the ascendancy, and then, as his eye ran rapidly over the chaste and matronly, though still attractive countenance of the governess, the look of doubt, as well as of respect, with which he gazed, was too obvious to be misinterpreted.

While the Rover was thus occupied, the sports proceeded, sometimes humourous and forcing smiles from the lips of the half-terrified Gertrude, but always tending to that violence and outbreaking of anger which might at any moment, set at naught the discipline of a vessel in which there were no other means of enforcing authority than such as its officers could on the instant command. Water had been so lavishly expended, that the decks were running with the fluid, more than one flight of spray having invaded the privileged precincts of the poop; every ordinary device of similar scenes had been resorted to by the men aloft to annoy their less advantageously posted shipmates, beneath, and such means of retaliation had been adopted as use or facility rendered obvious. Here a hog and a waister were seen swinging against each other, pendant beneath a top, there a marine lashed in the rigging was obliged to suffer the manipulation of a pet monkey, which, drilled to the duty and armed with a comb, was posted on his shoulder, with an air as grave and an eye as observant as if he had been regularly educated in the art of the perruquier, and every where some coarse and practical joke proclaimed the licentious liberty which had been momentarily accorded to a set of beings, who were in common kept in that restraint which comfort no less than safety, requires for the well ordering of an armed ship.

In the midst of the noise and turbulence a voice was heard apparently issuing from the ocean, hailing the vessel by name, with the aid of a speaking trumpet that had been applied to the outer circumference of a hawse-hole.

"Who speaks the Dolphin?" demanded Wilder, when he perceived that the summons had fallen on the ear of his commander without recalling him to the recollection of what was in action.

"Father Neptune, is under your fore-foot."

"What wills the God?"

"He has heard that certain strangers have come into his dominions, and he wishes leave to come aboard the saucy Dolphin, to inquire into their errands, and to overhaul the log-book for their characters."

"He is welcome. Show the old man aboard through the head; he is much too experienced a sailor to wish to come in by the cabin windows."

Here the parlance ceased, for Wilder turned upon his heel, disgusted with his part of the mummery.

An athletic seaman soon appeared, seemingly issuing from that element whose deity he personated. Mops, dripping with brine, supplied the place of hoary locks; gulf-weed, of which acres were floating within a league of the ship, composed a sort of negligent mantle, and, in his hand he bore a trident made of three marlingspikes, properly arranged and borne on the staff of a half-pike. Thus accoutred, the God of the Ocean, who was no less a personage than the captain of the forecastle, advanced with a suitable air of dignity along the deck, attended by a train of bearded water-nymphs and Naids, in costumes as grotesque as his own. Arrived on the quarter-deck, in front of the post occupied by the officers, the principal personage saluted the groupe with a wave of his sceptre, and resumed the discourse as follows; Wilder, from the continued abstraction of his commander, finding himself under the necessity of maintaining one portion of the dialogue.

"A wholesome and prettily rigged boat have you come out in this time, my son, and one well filled with a noble set of my children. How long is it since you left the land?"

"Some eight days."

"Hardly time enough to give the green-ones the use of their sea-legs. I shall be able to find them, by the manner in which they hold on in a calm." (Here the General, who was standing with a scornful and averted eye, let go his hold of a mizzen shroud, which he had grasped for no other visible reason than to render his person utterly immoveable; Neptune smiled and continued.) "I sha'n't ask concerning the port you are last from, seeing that the Newport soundings are still hanging about the flukes of your anchors. I hope you haven't brought out many fresh hands with you, for I smell the stock fish aboard a Baltic man, who is coming down with the trades, and who can't be more than a hundred leagues from this; I shall therefore, have but little time to overhaul your people, in order to give them their papers."

"You see them all before you. So skilful a mariner as Neptune needs no advice when or how to tell a seaman."

"I shall, then, begin with this gentleman," continued the waggish head of the forecastle, turning towards the still motionless chief of the marines. "There is a strong look of the land about him, and I should like to know how many hours it is since he first floated over blue water."

"I believe he has made many voyages, and I dare say has long since paid the proper tribute to your Majesty."

"Well, well, the thing is like enough, thof I will say I have known scholars make better use of their time, if he has been as long on the water as you pretend. How is it with these ladies; the—"

"Both have been at sea before, and have a right to pass without a question," returned Wilder a little hastily.

"The youngest is comely enough to have been born in my dominions," said the gallant Sovereign of the sea; "but no one can refuse to answer a hail that comes straight from the mouth of old Neptune, so, if it makes no great difference in your honour's reckoning, I will just beg the young woman to do her own talking." Then, without paying the least attention to the angry glance of Wilder, the sturdy representative of the God, addressed himself directly to Gertrude. "If, as report goes, my pretty damsel, you have seen blue water before this passage, you may be able to recollect the name of the vessel, and some other small particulars of the run?"

The face of Gertrude changed its colour from red to pale, as rapidly and as glowingly as the evening sky flushes and returns to its pearl-like loveliness, but she kept down her feelings sufficiently to answer with an air of entire self-possession—

"Were I to enter into all these little particulars it would detain you from more worthy subjects. Perhaps this certificate will convince you, that I am no novice on the sea." As she spoke a guinea fell from her white hand, into the broad and extended palm of her interrogator.

"I can only account for my not remembering your ladyship, by the great extent and heavy nature of my business," returned the audacious freebooter, bowing with an air of rude politeness as he pocketed the offering. "Had I looked into my books before I came aboard this here ship I should have seen through the mistake at once, for I now remember that I ordered one of my limners to take your pretty face, in order that I might show it to my wife at home. The fellow did it well enough in the shell of an East-India oyster; I will have a copy set in coral and sent to your husband whenever you may see fit to choose one."

Then repeating his bow with a scrape of the foot, he turned to the Governess in order to continue his examination.

"And you, Madam," he said; "is this the first time you have ever come into my dominions or not?"

"Neither the first nor the twentieth; I have often seen your Majesty before."

"An old acquaintance! In what latitude might it be that we first fell in with each other?"

"I believe I first enjoyed that honour, quite thirty years since, under the Equator."

"Ay, ay, I'm often there looking out for India-men, and your homeward-bound Brazil traders. I boarded a particularly great number that very season, but can't say I remember your countenance."

"I fear that thirty years have made some changes in it," returned the Governess with a smile, which though mournful, was far too dignified in its melancholy to induce the suspicion that she regretted a loss so vain as that of her personal charms. "I was in a vessel of the King, and one that was a little remarkable for its size, since it was of three decks."

The God, received the guinea which she now secretly offered, but it would seem that success had quickened his covetousness for instead of returning thanks he rather appeared to manifest a disposition to increase the amount of the bribe.

"All this may be just as your ladyship says," he rejoined, "but the interest of my kingdom, and a large family at home, make it necessary that I should look sharp to my rights. Was there a flag in the vessel?"

"There was."

"Then it's likely they hoisted it as usual, at the end of the jib-boom?"

"It was hoisted as is usual with a Vice Admiral at the fore."

"Well answered for petticoats!" muttered the deity, a little baffled in his artifice. "It is d—d queer, (saving your ladyship's presence) that I should have forgotten such a ship. Was there any thing of the extraordinary sort, that one would be likely to remember?"

The features of the Governess had already lost their forced pleasantry, in a shade of reflection, and her eye was fastened on vacancy as she answered like one who thought aloud—

"I can at this moment see the arch and roguish manner with which that wayward boy, who then had but eight years, overreached the cunning of the mimic Neptune and retaliated for his devices, by turning the laugh of all on board on his own head!"

"Was he but eight!" demanded a deep voice at her elbow.

"Eight in years; but mature in artifice," returned Mrs Wyllys, seeming to awake from a trance as she turned her eyes full upon the face of the Rover.

"Well, well," interrupted the captain of the forecastle, who cared not to continue an enquiry in which his dreaded commander saw fit to take a part. "I dare say it is all right. I will look into my journal and if I find it so, well—if not, why it is only giving the ship a head-wind, until I've overhauled the Dane and then it will be all in good time to receive the balance of the fee."

So saying, the God hurried past the Officers, and turned his attention to the marine guard, who had grouped themselves in a body, secretly aware of the necessity each man might be under of receiving support from his fellows in so searching a scrutiny. Perfectly familiar with the career each individual among them had run in his present lawless profession, and secretly apprehensive that his authority might be suddenly forced from him, the chief of the forecastle selected a raw landsman from among them, ordering his attendants to drag the victim forward, where he believed they might act the cruel revels he contemplated with less danger of interruption. Already irritated by the laughs which had been created at their expense and resolute to defend their comrade, the marines resisted. A long, clamorous and angry dispute succeeded, during which each party maintained its right to pursue the course it had adopted. From words the disputants were not long in passing to the verge of hostilities. While the peace of the ship thus hung as it were suspended by a hair, the general saw fit to express the disgust of such an outrage upon discipline which had throughout the whole scene possessed his mind.

"I protest against this riotous and unmilitary procedure," he said, addressing himself to his still abstracted and thoughtful superior. "I have taught my men, I trust, the proper spirit of soldiers, and there is no greater disgrace can happen to one of them, than to lay hands on him, except it be in the regular and wholesome way of a cat—I give open warning to all, that if a finger is put upon one of my bullies, unless as I have said, in the way of discipline, it will be answered with a blow."

As the general had not essayed to smother his voice it was heard by his followers, and produced the effect which might have been expected. A vigorous thrust from the fist of the sergeant drew mortal blood from the visage of the God of the sea, at once establishing his terrestrial origin. Thus compelled to vindicate his manhood, in more senses than one, the stout seaman returned the salutation with such additional embellishments, as the exigencies of the moment seemed to require.

Such an interchange of civilities between two so prominent personages was the signal of general hostilities among their respective followers. It was the uproar which attended this onset that caught the attention of Fid, who, the instant he saw the nature of the sports below, abandoned his companion on the yard, and slid down to the deck, by the aid of a backstay, with as much facility as a monkey could have shown in the same manœuvre. His example was followed by all the topmen, and there was every appearance that the audacious marines would be borne down by the sheer force of numbers. But stout in their resolution and bitter in their hostility, these drilled warriors, instead of seeking refuge in flight, fell back upon each other for support. Bayonets were seen gleaming in the sun, while some of the seamen in the exterior of the crowd, were already laying their hands on the half-pikes that formed a warlike ornament to the foot of the mast.

"Hold—stand back, every man of you," cried Wilder, dashing into the centre of the throng, and forcing them aside, with a haste that was possibly quickened by the recollection of the increased danger that would surround the unprotected females, were the bands of subordination once broken, among so lawless and desperate a crew. "On your lives, fall back, and obey. And you, Sir, who claim to be so good a soldier, I call on you to bid your men refrain."

The General, however disgusted he might have been by the previous scene, had too many important interests involved in the interior peace of the vessel, not to exert himself at this appeal. He was seconded by all the inferior officers, who well knew that their lives, as well as their comfort, depended on staying the torrent that had so unexpectedly broken loose. But they only proved how hard it is to uphold an authority that is not erected on the foundation of legitimate power. Neptune had cast aside his masquerade, and backed by his stout forecastle-men, was preparing for a conflict that might speedily give him greater pretensions to an immortal nature than those he had just rejected. Until now, the officers, partly by threats and partly by remonstrances, had so far controlled the outbreaking, that the time had been passed rather in preparations than in violence. But the marines had seized their arms, while two crowded masses of the mariners were forming on each side of the mainmast, abundantly provided with pikes and such other weapons as could be made of the bars and handspikes of the vessel. One or two of the cooler heads among the latter, had even proceeded so far as to clear away a gun, which they were pointing inboard, and in a direction that might have swept a moiety of the quarter-deck. In short the broil had reached that pass, when another blow struck from either side would have given up the vessel to plunder and blood-shed. The danger of such a crisis was heightened, by the taunts that broke forth from profane lips, which were only opened to lavish the coarsest revilings on the persons and characters of their enemies.

During the five minutes that might have flown by in these sinister and threatening symptoms of insubordination, the individual who was chiefly interested in the maintenance of discipline had manifested the most extraordinary indifference to, or rather unconsciousness of, all that was passing near him. With his arms folded on his breast and his eyes fastened on the placid sea, he stood motionless as the mast near which he had placed his person. Long accustomed to the noise of scenes similar to the one he had himself provoked, he heard, in the confused sounds which rose unheeded on his ear, no more than the commotion which ordinarily attended the licence of such sports.

His subordinates in command however were far more active. Wilder had already beaten back the boldest of the seamen, and a space was cleared between the hostile parties, into which his assistants threw themselves, with the haste of men who knew how much was required at their hands. This momentary success might have been pushed too far, for believing that the spirit of mutiny was subdued, our adventurer was proceeding to improve his advantage, by seizing the most audacious of the offenders, when his prisoner was immediately torn from his grasp, by twenty of his confederates.

"Who's this, that sets himself up for a commodore, aboard the Dolphin!" exclaimed a voice in the crowd, at a most unhappy moment for the authority of the new lieutenant. "In what fashion did he come aboard us, or in what service did he learn his trade?"

"Ay, ay," continued another sinister voice, "where is the

Bristol trader, he was to lead into our net, and for which we lost so many of the best days in the season at a lazy anchor!"

A general and simultaneous murmur followed, which, had such testimony been wanting, would in itself have manifested that the unknown officer was scarcely more fortunate in his present than in his recent service. Both parties united in condemning his interference, and from both sides were heard scornful opinions of his origin, mingled with unequivocal denunciations against his person. Nothing daunted by these evidences of the danger he was in, our adventurer answered their taunts with the most scornful smiles, challenging a single individual of them all to dare to step forth, and maintain his words by suitable actions.

"Hear him!" exclaimed his auditors. "He speaks like a King's Officer in chase of a smuggler!" cried one. "Ay, he's a bold'un in a calm!" said a second. "He's a Jonah, that has slipped into the cabin windows," cried a third, "and while he stays in the Dolphin, luck will keep upon our weather beam." "Into the sea with him, overboard with the upstart, into the sea with him, where he'll find that a bolder and a better man has gone before him," shouted a dozen at once; some of whom immediately made very plain demonstrations of an intention to put their threat in execution. But two forms instantly sprang from the crowd, and threw themselves, like angry lions, between Wilder and his foes. The one who was foremost in the rescue faced short upon the advancing seamen, and with a blow from an arm that was irresistible, levelled the representative of Neptune to his feet, as if he had been a waxen image of a man. The other was not slow to imitate his example, and as the throng receded before this secession from its own numbers, the latter, who was Fid, flourished a fist, that was as big and almost as solid as a twelve-pound shot, while he vociferated, fairly frothing at the mouth with rage,—

"Away with you, ye lubbers; away with you! Would you run foul of a single man, and he an officer, and such an officer as ye never set eyes on before, except, mayhap, in the fashion, that a 'cat looks upon a King?' I should like to see the man among ye all who can handle a heavy ship in a narrow channel, as I have seen Master Harry, here, handle the saucy—"

"Stand back—" cried Wilder, forcing himself between his defenders and his foes. "Stand back, I say, and leave me alone to meet the audacious villains."

"Overboard with him—overboard with them all!" cried the seamen, "he and his knaves together!"

"Will you remain silent and see murder done, before your eyes?" exclaimed Mrs Wyllys, rushing from her place of retreat, and laying a hand eagerly on the arm of the Rover.

He started, like one who was awakened suddenly from a light sleep, looking her full and intently in the eye.

"See!" she added, pointing to the violent throng below, where every sign of a bloody struggle was exhibiting itself. "See. They kill your officer, and there is none to help him!"

The look of faded marble, which had so long been seated on his features, vanished. Taking in the whole nature of the scene at the glance, the blood came rushing into every vein and fibre of his face. Seizing a rope which hung from the yard above his head, he swung his person off the poop and fell lightly into the very centre of the crowd. Both parties fell back, while a sudden silence succeeded to a clamour that a moment before would have drowned the roar of a cataract. Making a haughty and repelling motion with his arm, he spoke, and in a voice, that, if any change could be noted, was even pitched on a key less high and threatening than common. But the lowest and the deepest of its intonations reached the most distant ear, so that no one who heard was left in doubt of its meaning.

"Mutiny!" he said, in a tone that strangely balanced between irony and scorn—"open, violent and blood-seeking mutiny! Are ye tired of your lives, men! Is there one among ye all, who is willing to make himself an example for the good of the rest? If there be, let him lift a hand, a finger, a hair. Let him speak—look me in the eye, or dare to show that life is in him, by sign, breath or motion!"

He paused, and so general and absorbing was the spell produced by his presence and his mien, that in all that crowd of fierce and excited spirits, there was not one so bold, as to presume to brave his anger. Sailors and marines stood alike, passive, humbled and obedient, as faulty children when arraigned before an authority from which they feel that escape is impossible. Perceiving that no voice answered, no limb moved, nor even an eye among them all was bold enough to meet his own steady but glowing look, he continued in the same deep and commanding tone—

"It is well. Reason has come of the latest, but happily for ye all, it has returned. Fall back—fall back, I say, ye taint the quarter deck." (The men receded a pace or two on every side of him.) "Let those arms be stacked, it will be time to use them, when I say there is need. And you, fellows, who have been so bold as to lift a pike, without an order, have a care they do not burn your hands." (A dozen staves fell upon the deck together.) "Is there a drummer in this ship? let him appear."

A terrified and cringing looking being presented himself, having found his instrument by a sort of desperate instinct—

"Now speak aloud, and let me know, at once, whether I command a crew of orderly and obedient men, or a set of miscreants that require some purifying before I can trust them."

The first few taps of the drum sufficed to tell the men that it was the "beat to quarters." Without hesitating, the crowd dissolved, and each of the delinquents stole silently to his station, the crew of the gun that had been turned inboard managing to thrust it, through its port, again, with a dexterity that might have availed them greatly in time of combat. Throughout the whole affair the Rover manifested neither anger nor impatience. Deep and settled scorn with a high reliance on himself had, indeed, been exhibited in his bearing, but not for an instant did it seem that he suffered passion to get the mastery of reason. And now that he had recalled his crew to their duty, he appeared no more elated with his success than he had been daunted by the storm which, a minute before, had threatened the dissolution of his authority. Instead of pursuing his further purpose in haste, he awaited the observance of the minutest form which etiquette as well as use had rendered customary on such occasions.

The Officers approached to report their several divisions in readiness to engage with exactly the same regularity as if an enemy had been in sight. The top-men and sail-trimmers were enumerated and found prepared, shot-plugs and stoppers were handled, the magazine was even opened, the arm-chests were emptied of their contents and in short more than the ordinary preparations of an every-day exercise was observed.

"Let the yards be slung, the sheets and halyards stoppered," he said to the first Lieutenant, who now displayed as intimate an acquaintance with the military as he had hitherto discovered with the nautical part of his profession— "give the boarders their pikes and boarding-axes, Sir. We will show these fellows that we dare trust them with arms!"

The orders were obeyed to the letter; and then succeeded that deep and grave silence, which renders a crew at quarters a sight so imposing even to those who have witnessed it from boyhood. In this manner the skilful leader of this band of desperate marauders knew how to curb their violence with the fetters of discipline. When he believed their minds brought within the proper limits, by the situation of restraint in which he had placed them, where they well knew that a word or even an offensive look would be met by instant punishment, he walked apart with Wilder of whom he demanded an explanation of what had passed.

Whatever might have been the natural tendency of our adventurer to mercy, he had not been educated on the sea to look with lenity on the crime of mutiny. Had his recent escape from the wreck of the Bristol trader been already banished from his mind, the impressions of a whole life still remained to teach the necessity of keeping tight those cords which experience has so often proved are absolutely necessary to quell such turbulent bands, when removed from the pale of society, the influence of woman and when excited by the constant collision of tempers rudely provoked and equally disposed to violence. Though he "set down naught in malice," it is certain that he did "nothing extenuate," in the account he rendered. The whole of the facts were laid before the Rover in the direct, unvarnished language of truth.

"One cannot keep these fellows to their duty by preaching," returned the irregular chief, when the other had done. "We have no 'Execution Dock' for our delinquents, no 'yellow flag' for fleets to gaze at, no grave and wise-looking courts to thumb a book or two, and end by saying, 'hang him.' The rascals knew my eye was off them. Once before

they turned my vessel into a living evidence of that passage in
the testament, which teaches humility to all, by telling us 'that
the last shall be first, and the first last.' I found a dozen round-
abouts drinking and making free with the liquors of the
cabin, and all the Officers prisoners forward—a state of
things, as you will allow, a little subversive of decency as well
as decorum!"

"I am amazed you should have succeeded in restoring discipline!"

"I got among them, single-handed, and with no other aid
than a boat from the shore; but I ask no more than a place for
my foot, and room for an arm to keep a thousand such spirits
in order. Now they know me, it is rare that we misunderstand
each other."

"You must have punished, severely!"

"There was justice done. Mr Wilder, I fear you find our
service a little irregular; but a month of experience will put
you on a level with us, and remove all danger of such another
scene." As the Rover spoke he faced his recruit with a countenance that endeavored to be cheerful, but whose gaiety
could force itself no further than a frightful smile. "Come," he
quickly added, "this time, I set the mischief afoot myself, and
as we are completely masters, we may afford to be lenient.
Besides," glancing his eyes towards the spot where Mrs
Wyllys and Gertrude still remained in deep suspense, awaiting
his decision, "it may be well to consult the sex of our guests,
at such a moment."

Then leaving his subordinate, the Rover advanced to the
centre of the quarter-deck, whither he immediately summoned the principal offenders. The men listened to his
rebukes, which were not altogether free from admonitory
warnings of what might be the consequences of a similar
transgression, like creatures who stood in presence of a being
of a nature superior to their own. Though he spoke in his
usual quiet tone, the lowest of his syllables went into the ears
of the most distant of the crew, and when his brief lesson was
ended, the men stood before him not only like delinquents
who had been reproved, though pardoned, but with the air of
criminals who were as much condemned by their own consciousness as by the general voice. Among them all was only

one seaman, who perhaps from past service, was emboldened to venture a syllable in his own justification.

"As for the matter with the marines," he said, "your honour knows there is little love between us; though I allow that a quarter deck is no place to settle our begrudgings—but as to the gentleman who has seen fit to step into the shoes of—"

"It is my pleasure that he should remain there," interrupted his commander. "Of his merit, I alone am judge."

"Well—well. Since it is your pleasure, Sir, why no man may dispute it. But no account has been rendered of the Bristol man, and great expectations were had aboard here, from that very ship. Your honor is a reasonable gentleman, and will not be surprised that people who were on the look-out for an outward-bound West-India-man, should be unwilling to take up with a battered and empty launch in her stead."

"Ay, Sir, if I will it, you shall take an oar—a tiller, a thole, for your portion. No more of this! You saw the condition of his ship with your own eyes, and where is the seaman, who has not, on some evil day, been compelled to admit that his art is nothing when the elements are against him! Who saved this ship, in the very gust that has robbed us of our prize? Was it your skill, or was it that of a man who has often done it before, and who may one day leave you to your ignorance to manage your own interests? It is enough that I believe him faithful; there is no time to convince your dullness of the propriety of all that is done. Away, and send me the two men who so nobly stepped between their officer and mutiny."

Then came Fid, followed by the Negro, rolling along the deck, and thumbing his hat with one hand, while the other sought an awkward retreat in a certain part of his vestments.

"You have done well, my lad, you and your messmate—"

"No messmate, your honor, seeing that he is a nigger," interrupted Fid. "The chap messes with the other blacks, but we take a pull at the cann, now and then, in company."

"Your friend, then, if you prefer that term."

"Ay, ay, Sir. We are friendly enough at odd times, though a breeze often springs up between us. Guinea has a d——d awkward fashion of luffing up in his talk, and your honor knows it isn't always comfortable to a white man to be driven to leeward by a black. I tell him, that it is inconvenient; he is a good enough fellow in the main, howsomever, Sir, and as he is just an African bred and born, I hope you'll be good enough to overlook his little failings."

"Were I otherwise disposed," returned the Rover, "his steadiness and activity to day would plead in his favour."

"Yes, yes, Sir, he is somewhat steady, which is more than I can always say in my own behalf. Then as for seamanship, there are few men who are his betters; I wish your honour would take the trouble to walk forward and look at the heart he turned into the mainstay, no later than the last calm—it takes the strain as easy as a small sin sits upon a rich man's conscience."

"I am satisfied with your description—you call him Guinea?"

"Call him by any thing along that coast, for he is no way particular, seeing he was never christened, and knows nothing at all of the bearings and distances of religion. His lawful name is S'ip or Shipio Africa, taken as I suppose from the circumstance that he was first shipp'd from that quarter of the world. But as respects names the fellow is as meek as a lamb. You may call him any thing provided you don't call him too late to his grog."

All this time, the African stood rolling his large dark eyes in every direction except towards the speakers, perfectly content that his long-tried ship-mate should serve as his interpreter. The spirit which had so recently been awakened in the Rover, seemed already, to be subsiding; for the frown which had gathered on his brow, was dissipating in a look which bore rather the character of curiosity, than any fiercer emotion.

"You have sailed long in company, my lads," he carelessly continued, addressing his words to neither of the men, in particular.

"Full and by, in many a gale and many a calm, your honour. 'Tis four and twenty years the last equinox, Guinea, since Master Harry fell athwart our hawse, and then we had been together three years in the Thunderer, besides the run we made round the Horn in the Bay Privateer."

"Ah! you have been four and twenty years with Mr Wilder! It is not so remarkable that you should set a value on his life"—

"I should as soon think of setting a price on the King's crown!" interrupted the straight-going seaman. "I overheard the lads, d'ye see, sir, just plotting to throw the three of us overboard, and so we thought it time to say something in our own favor, and words not always being at hand, the black saw fit to fill up the time with something that might answer the turn quite as well. No—no—he is no great talker that Guinea, nor, for that matter, can I say much in my own favor in this particular. But seeing that we clapp'd a stopper on their movements, your honour will allow that we did as well as if we had spoken as smartly as a young Midshipman fresh from college, who is always for hailing a top in Latin, you know, Sir, for want of understanding the proper language."

The Rover smiled, and he glanced his eye aside, apparently in quest of our adventurer. Not seeing him at hand, he was tempted to push his enquiries a little further, though too much governed by self respect to let the intense curiosity by which he was influenced, escape him in any direct and manifest interrogation. But an instant's recollection recalled him to himself, and he discarded the idea as unworthy of his character.

"It is well, your services shall not be forgotten. Here is gold," he said, offering a handful of the metal to the Negro, as the one nearest his own person. "You will divide it like honest shipmates; and you may ever rely on my protection."

Scipio drew back, and with a motion of his elbow replied—

"His Honor will give 'em Masser Harry."

"Your Master Harry has enough of his own, lad; he has no need of money."

"S'ip no need 'em eider."

"You will please to overlook the fellow's manners, Sir," said Fid, very coolly interposing his own hand, and deliberately pocketing the offering—"but I needn't tell as old a seaman as your honor that Guinea is no country to scrape down the seams of a man's behaviour in. Howsomever I can say this much for him, which is, that he thanks your honor, just as heartily as if you had given him twice the sum. Make a bow to his honour, boy, and do some credit to the company you have kept. And now since this little difficulty about the money is gotten over by my presence of mind, with your honour's leave, I'll just step aloft and cast loose the lashings of that bit of a tailor on the larboard-fore-yard-arm. The chap was never made for a top-man, as you may see, Sir, by the fashion in which he crosses his lower staunchions. That fellow will make a carrick bend with his legs, as handily as I could do the same with a yarn of white line!"

The Rover signed for him to retire, and turning, where he stood, he found himself confronted by Wilder. The eyes of the confederates met, and a slight colour bespoke the consciousness of the former. Regaining his self-possession on the instant, however, he smilingly alluded to the character of Fid, and then he directed his Lieutenant to have the "retreat from quarters" beat.

The guns were secured, the stoppers loosened, the magazine closed, the ports lashed, and the crew withdrew to their several duties like men whose violence had been completely subdued by the triumphant influence of a master spirit. The Rover then disappeared from the deck, which, for a time was left to the care of an officer of the proper rank.

# Chapter XXI

Thief. " 'Tis in the malice of mankind, that he thus advises us; not to have us thrive in our mystery."
*Timon of Athens*, IV.iii.452–53.

THROUGHOUT the whole of that day no change occurred in the weather. The sleeping ocean lay like a waving and a glittering mirror, smooth and polished on its surface, though, as usual the long rising and falling of a heavy ground swell announced the commotion that was in action, at a distant place. From the time that he left the deck until the sun laved its burnished orb in the sea, the Rover was seen no more. Satisfied with his victory he no longer seemed to apprehend that it was possible any should be bold enough to plot the overthrow of his power. This apparent confidence in himself did not fail to impress his people favourably. As no neglect of duty was overlooked, nor any offence left to go unpunished, an eye that was not seen was believed to be ever on them, and an invisible hand was thought to be at all times uplifted, ready to strike or to reward. It was by a similar system of energy in moments of need and of forbearance when authority was irksome, that this extraordinary man had so long succeeded not only in keeping down domestic treason, but in eluding the address and industry of more open enemies.

When the watch was set for the night, however, and the ship lay in profound silence, the Rover was again seen walking swiftly to and fro, across the poop, of which he was now the solitary occupant. The vessel had drifted in the Gulf stream so far to the northward that the little mound of blue had long sunk below the edge of the ocean; and, she was again surrounded, far as human eye might see, by an interminable world of water. As not a breath of air was stirring, the sails had been handed, the naked spars rearing themselves, in the gloom of the evening, like those of a ship at anchor. In short, it was one of those hours of entire repose, that the elements occasionally grant to such adventurers as trust their fortunes to the capricious and treacherous winds.

Even the men whose duty it was to be on the alert, were

emboldened by the general tranquility to become careless on their watch, and to cast their persons between the guns or on different portions of the vessel, seeking that rest which the forms of discipline and good order prohibited them from enjoying in their hammocks. Here and there, indeed, the head of a drowsy officer was seen nodding with the lazy heaving of the ship, as he leaned against the bulwarks, or rested his person on the carriage of some gun, that was placed beyond the sacred limits of the quarter-deck. One form alone was erect and vigilant, maintaining a watchful eye over the whole. This was Wilder, whose turn it was again to keep the deck.

For two hours not the slightest communication occurred between the Rover and his Lieutenant. Both rather avoided than sought the intercourse, for each had his own secret sources of meditation. After the long and unusual silence the former stopped short in his walk, and looked steadily at the still motionless figure on the deck beneath him.

"Mr Wilder," he at length said, "the air is fresher on this poop, and more free from the impurities of the vessel: Will you ascend?"

The other complied, and they walked mechanically and silently together, as seamen are wont to pace the deck in the hours of night.

"We had a troublesome morning, Wilder," the Rover resumed, unconsciously betraying the subject of his thoughts, and speaking always in a voice so guarded that no ears but those of his new lieutenant could hear him: "Were you ever so near that pretty precipice, a mutiny, before?"

"The man who is hit is nigher to danger, than he who feels the wind of the ball."

"Ah, you have then been bearded in your ship. Give yourself no uneasiness, however, on account of the personal animosity which a few of the fellows saw fit to manifest against yourself. I am acquainted with their most secret thoughts, as you shall shortly know."

"I confess that, in your place, I should sleep on a thorny pillow, with such evidences of the temper of my men before my mind. A few hours of disorder might deliver the vessel, on any day, into the hands of government, and your own life to"—

"The Executioner. And, why not yours?" demanded the

Rover so quickly, as to give, in a slight degree, an air of distrust to his manner. "But the eye that has often seen battles seldom winks. Mine has too often and too steadily look'd danger in the face to be alarmed at the sight of a King's pennant. Besides it is not usual for us to be on this ticklish coast. The islands and the Spanish Main are less dangerous cruising grounds."

"And yet have you ventured here at a time when success against the enemy, has given the Admiral leisure to employ a powerful force in your pursuit!"

"I had a reason for it! It is not always easy to separate the commander from the man. If I have temporarily forgotten the obligations of the former in the wishes of the latter, so far at least, no harm has come of it. I may have tired of chasing your indolent Don, and of driving guarda-costas, into port. This life of ours is full of excitement which I love. To me, there is interest even in a mutiny."

"I like not treason. In this particular I confess myself like the boor who loses his resolution in the dark. While the enemy is in view, I hope you will find me true as other men, but sleeping over a mine is not an amusement to my taste."

"So much for want of practice! Hazard is hazard, come in what shape it may, and the human mind can as readily be taught to be indifferent to secret machinations, as to open risk. Hark! struck the bell six or seven?"

"Seven—you see the men slumber as before. Instinct would wake them were their hour at hand."

" 'Tis well. I fear'd the time had passed. Yes, Wilder, I love suspense; it keeps the faculties from dying, and throws a man upon the better principles of his nature. Perhaps I owe it to a wayward spirit, but to me there is sometimes enjoyment in an adverse wind."

"And in a calm?"

"Calms may have their charms for your quiet spirits; but in them there is nothing to be overcome. One cannot stir the elements, though one may counteract their workings."

"You have not entered on this trade of yours"—

"Yours!"

"I might, now, have said of ours, since I too have become a rover."

"You are still in your noviciate," resumed the other, whose quick mind, had already passed the point at which the conversation had arrived; "and high enjoyment had I in being the one who shrived you in your wishes. You manifested a skill in playing round your subject without touching it, which gives me hopes of an apt scholar."

"But no penitent, I trust."

"That, as it may be. We are all liable to have our moments of weakness, when we look on life as book-men paint it and think of being probationers where we are put to enjoy. I angled for you, as the fisherman plays with the trout. Nor did I overlook the danger of deception. You were faithful on the whole, though I protest against your ever again acting so much against my interests as to intrigue to keep the game from coming to my net."

"When and how, have I done this! You have yourself admitted—"

"That the Royal Caroline was prettily handled, and wrecked by the will of Heaven. I speak of nobler quarries, now, than such as any hawk may fly at. Are you a woman-hater, that you would fain frighten the noble minded woman and the sweet girl, who are beneath our feet at this minute, from enjoying the high privilege of your company?"

"Was it treacherous to wish to save a woman from a fate like that, for instance, which hung over them both this very day? For while your authority exists in this ship I do not think there can be danger even to her who is so lovely."

"By Heavens, Wilder, you do for me no more than justice. Before harm should come to that fair innocent, with this hand would I put the match into the magazine, and send her, all spotless as she is, to the place from which she seems to have fallen!"

Our adventurer listened greedily to these words, though he little liked the strong language of admiration with which the Rover was pleased to clothe his generous sentiments.

"How did you know of my wish to save them?" he demanded, after a pause which neither seemed in any hurry to break.

"Could I mistake your language! I thought it plain enough, when I heard it."

"Heard! My confession was then made when I least believed it."

The Rover did not answer; but his companion now understood, from his smile, that he had been the dupe of an audacious and completely successful masquerade, and that in the old seaman Bob Bunt, he had in truth been communing with his commander in person. The deportment of Joram and the unaccountable disappearance of the skiff were now completely explained. Startled at discovering how intricate were the toils into which he had rushed, and possibly vexed at being so thoroughly overreached, he made several turns across the deck without speaking.

"I confess myself deceived," he at length said, "and, henceforth, I shall submit to you as a master from whom one may learn, but who can never be surpassed. The landlord of the Foul Anchor, at least, acted in his proper person, whoever might have been the aged seaman?"

"Honest Joe Joram! An useful man to a distressed mariner, you must allow. How did you like the Newport Pilot?"

"Was he an agent too?"

"For the job, merely. I trust such knaves no further than their own eyes can see. But—hist—heard you nothing?"

"I thought a rope had fallen in the water."

"Ay. It is so. Now shall you find how thoroughly I overlook these turbulent gentlemen!"

The Rover then cut short the dialogue, which was growing deeply interesting to his companion, and moved with a light step to the stern, over which he hung for a few moments by himself, like a man who found a pleasure in gazing at the surface of the sea. But a slight noise, like that produced by agitated ropes caught the ear of his companion, who placed himself at the side of his commander, where he did not wait long without gaining another proof of the manner in which he as well as all the rest of the crew were circumvented by the devices of their leader.

A man was guardedly, and from his situation, with some difficulty, moving round the quarter of the ship, by the aid of the ropes and mouldings, which afforded him sufficient means to effect his object. He soon reached a stern ladder, where he stood suspended, endeavoring to discern which of the two forms that were overlooking his proceedings was that of the individual he sought.

"Are you there, Davis!" said the Rover, in a voice but little above a whisper, first laying his hand lightly on Wilder, as if he would tell him to attend. "I fear you have been seen or heard."

"No fear of either, your honor. I got out at the port by the cabin bulkhead; the after-guard are all as sound asleep, as if they had the watch below."

"It is well. What news do you bring from the people?"

"Lord, your honour may tell them to go to church, and the stoutest sea-dog of them all, wouldn't dare to say he had forgotten his prayers!"

"You think them in a better temper, than they were?"

"I know it, Sir. Not but what the will to work mischief is to be found in two or three of the men; but they dare not trust each other; your honour, has such winning ways with you, that one never knows when he is on safe grounds in setting up to be master."

"This is ever the way with your disorganizers," muttered the Rover, just loud enough to be heard by Wilder. "A little more honesty might make them dangerous; as it is, their knavery defeats itself. And how did the fellows receive the lenity? Did I well, or must there yet be punishment?"

"It is better as it stands, Sir. The people know you have a good memory, and they talk already of the danger of adding another reckoning to this they feel certain you have not forgotten. There is the captain of the forecastle, who is a little bitter, as usual, and the more so, just now, on account of the knock-down blow he got from the black."

"He is a troublesome rascal; a settling day must come at last between us."

"It will be easy to expend him in boat service, Sir, and the ship's company will be all the better for his absence—"

"Well—well—no more of him," interrupted the Rover a little impatiently, as if he liked not that his companion should look too deeply into the policy of his government, so early in his initiation. "I will see to him. If I mistake not, fellow, you overacted your own part to-day and were a little too forward in leading on the trouble."

"I hope your honor, will remember that the crew had been piped to mischief—besides there could be no great harm in washing the powder out of a few marines—"

"Ay, but you pressed the point, after your officer had seen fit to interfere. Be wary in future, lest you make the acting too true to nature, and get applauded in a manner quite as natural."

The fellow promised caution and amendment, and then he was dismissed with his reward in gold, and with an injunction to be secret in his return. So soon as this interview was ended, the Rover and Wilder resumed their walk, the former having made sure that no eaves-dropper was at hand to pry into the secret of his connexion with the spy. The silence was, again, long and thoughtful.

"Good ears," re-commenced the Rover, "are nearly as important in a ship like this, as a stout heart. The rogues forward must not be permitted to eat of the fruit of knowledge, lest we who are in the cabins, die."

"This is a perilous service in which we are embarked," observed his companion, involuntarily exposing his real thoughts.

The Rover made many turns across the deck before he answered. When he spoke, it was in a voice so bland and gentle, that his words sounded more like the admonitory tones of a considerate friend, than like the language of a man who had long been associated with a set of beings so rude and unprincipled as those whom he commanded.

"You are still on the threshold of life, Mr Wilder," he said, "and it is all before you, to choose the path on which you will go. As yet you have been present at no violation of what the world calls its laws, nor is it too late to say you never will be. I may have been selfish in my wish to gain you, but try me, and you will find that self, though often active, cannot nor does not long hold its dominion over my mind. Say but the word, and you are free; it is easy to destroy the little evidence which exists of your having made one of my crew. The land is not far beyond that streak of fading light; before to-morrow's sun shall set, your foot may be on it."

"Then why not both! If this irregular life be not fit for me, it is unfit for you. Could I hope—"

"What would you say?" calmly demanded the Rover, after waiting sufficiently long to be sure his companion hesitated to continue. "Speak freely; your words are for the ears of a friend."

"Then as a friend, will I unbosom myself! You say the land is here in the West. It would be easy for you and me, men nurtured on the sea, to lower this boat into the water, and profiting by the darkness, long ere our absence could be known, we should be lost to the eye of any who might seek us."

"Whither would you steer?"

"To the shores of America, where shelter and peace might be found in a thousand secret places."

"Would you have a man who has so long lived a prince among his followers, become a beggar in a land of strangers?"

"But you have gold. Are we not masters here? Who is there, that might dare even to watch our movements until we were pleased ourselves to throw off the authority with which we are clothed? Ere the middle watch was set, all might be done."

"Alone! Would you go alone?"

"No—not entirely—that is—it would scarcely become us as men to desert the females to the brutal power of those we should leave behind."

"And would it become us as men to desert those who put faith in our fidelity? Mr Wilder, your proposal would make me a villain! Lawless, in the opinion of the world, have I long been, but a traitor to my faith and plighted word never. The hour may come when the beings whose world is in the ship shall part, but the separation must be open, voluntary and manly. You never knew what drew me into the haunts of men, when we first met in the town of Boston?"

"Never," returned Wilder, in a tone of deep disappointment; for hope had caused his very heart to beat quicker.

"You shall hear. A sturdy follower had fallen into the hands of the minions of the law. It was necessary to save him. He was a man I little loved, but he was one who had been honest, after his own opinions. I could not desert the victim; nor could any but I effect his escape. Gold and artifice succeeded; the fellow is now here to sing the praises of his commander to the crew. Could I forfeit a good name obtained at so much hazard?"

"You would forfeit the good opinions of knaves, to gain a reputation among those whose commendations are an honor."

"I know not. You little understand the nature of man if you are now to learn, that he has pride in maintaining even a reputation for vice when he has once purchased notoriety by its exhibition. Besides I am not fitted for the world, as it is found among your dependant Colonists."

"You claim your birth perhaps from the Mother Country?"

"I am no better than a poor Provincial, Sir; a humble satellite of the Mighty Sun. You have seen my flags, Mr Wilder, but there was one wanting among them all. Ay, and one, which had it existed, it would have been by pride, my glory to have upheld with my heart's best blood!"

"I know not what you mean."

"I need not tell a seaman like you, how many noble rivers pour their waters into the sea along this coast of which we have been speaking; how many wide and commodious havens abound there; or, how many sails whiten the ocean that are manned by men, who first drew breath on that spacious and peaceful soil."

"Surely I know the advantages of my native country."

"I fear not," quickly returned the Rover. "Were they known as they should be, by you and others like you, the flag I mentioned would soon be found in every sea, nor would the natives of our country have to succumb to the hirelings of a foreign Prince."

"I will not affect to misunderstand your meaning, for I have known others as visionary as yourself in fancying that such an event may arrive—"

"May! As certain as that star will set in the ocean, or that day is to succeed to night, it *must*. Had that flag been abroad, Mr Wilder, no man would have ever heard the name of the Red Rover."

"The King has a service of his own, and it is open to all his subjects alike—"

"I could be a subject of a King, but to be the subject of his subjects, Wilder, exceeds the bounds of my poor patience. I was educated, I might have almost said born in one of his vessels, and how often have I been made to feel, in bitterness, that an ocean separated my birth-place from the footstool of his throne! Would you think it, Sir, one of his commanders dar'd to couple the name of my country with an epithet I will not wound your ear by repeating!"

"I hope you taught the scoundrel manners."

The Rover faced his companion, and there was a ghastly smile on his face, as he answered—

"He never repeated the offence. 'Twas his blood or mine; dearly did he pay the forfeit of his brutality."

"You fought like men, and fortune favored the injured party."

"We fought, Sir. But I had dared to raise my hand against a native of the holy Isle! It is enough, Mr Wilder; the King rendered a faithful subject desperate, and he has had reason to repent it. Enough for the present; another time I may say more. Good night."

Wilder saw the figure of his companion descend the ladder to the quarter-deck, and then he was left to pursue the current of his thoughts alone during the remainder of a watch which to his impatience, seemed without an end.

# Chapter XXII

"She made good view of me; indeed so much,
That sure, methought, her eyes had lost her tongue,
For she did speak in starts, distractedly."
Twelfth Night, II.ii.19–21.

THOUGH MOST of the crew of the Dolphin slept, there were bright and anxious eyes still open in a different part of the vessel. The Rover had relinquished his cabin to Mrs Wyllys and Gertrude, from the moment they entered the ship, and we shall shift the scene to that apartment, already sufficiently described to render the reader familiar with the objects it contained, resuming the action of the tale, at an early part of the discourse just related in the preceding chapter.

It will not be necessary to dwell upon the feelings with which the females had witnessed the disturbances of that day; the conjectures and suspicions to which they gave rise may be apparent in what is about to follow. A mild soft light fell, from the lamp of wrought and massive silver that was suspended from the upper deck, obliquely upon the pensive countenance of the Governess, while a few of its strongest rays lighted the more youthful features of her companion. The back ground was occupied, like a dark shadow in a picture, by the dusky form of the slumbering and wearied Cassandra. At the moment when the curtain must be drawn from before this quiet scene, the pupil was seeking in the averted eyes of her instructress, an answer to a question, which the tongue of the latter appeared reluctant to accord.

"I repeat, my dearest Madam," said Gertrude, "that the fashion of these ornaments, no less than their materials, is extraordinary in a ship!"

"And what would you infer from the fact?"

"I know not. I would that we were safe in the house of my father!"

"God grant it! It may be imprudent to be longer silent. Gertrude, frightful, horrible suspicions have been engendered in my mind, by what we have this day witnessed!"

The cheek of the young girl blanched, while she demanded an explanation with her eyes.

"I have long been familiar with the usages of a vessel of war," continued the Governess, who had only paused, in order to review the causes of her suspicions, in her own mind, "but never have I seen such customs as each hour unfolds in this vessel."

"Of what do you suspect her?"

The look of engrossing, maternal anxiety that the lovely interrogator received in reply to this question, might have startled one whose mind had been more accustomed to muse on the depravity of human nature, than the spotless being who received it, but to Gertrude it conveyed no more than a general and vague sensation of alarm.

"Why do you thus regard me, my governess, my mother?" she exclaimed, bending forward, and laying a hand imploringly on the arm of the other as if to arouse her from a trance. "Speak, dearest Mrs Wyllys; it is Gertrude who asks it."

"Yes, I will speak. It is safer that you should know the worst, than that your innocence should be liable to be abused. I distrust the character of this ship, and of all that belong to her."

"All!"

"Yes, of all."

"There may be wicked and evil-intentioned men in his Majesty's fleet, but we are surely safe from them, since fear of punishment, if not fear of disgrace, will be our protector."

"I dread lest we find that the lawless spirits who harbor here, submit to no laws except those of their own enacting, nor acknowledge any authority, but that which exists among themselves."

"This would make them Pirates!"

"And Pirates I fear we shall find them."

"Pirates—What! all?"

"Even all. Where one is guilty of such a crime, it is clear that the associates cannot be free from suspicion."

"But, dear Madam, we know that one among them, at least, is innocent, since he came with ourselves, and under circumstances that will not admit of deception."

"I know not. There are different degrees of turpitude as

there are different tempers to commit it. I fear that all who may lay claim to be honest in this vessel, are here."

The eyes of Gertrude sunk to the floor, and her lips quivered, partly in a tremor she could not control, and in part through an emotion, that she found inexplicable to herself.

"Since we know whence our late companion came," she said in an under tone, "I think you do him wrong, however right your suspicions may prove as to the rest."

"I may possibly be wrong as to him, I admit, but it is important that we know the worst. Command yourself, my love—our young attendant ascends; some knowledge of the truth may be gained from him."

Mrs Wyllys gave her pupil an expressive sign to compose her features, while she herself resumed a calmness of mien that might have deceived one far more practised than the boy who now came slowly into the cabin. Gertrude buried her face in a part of her attire, while the former addressed the youth, in a tone equally divided between kindness and unconcern.

"Roderick, child," she commenced, "your eye-lids are getting heavy. The service of a ship must be new to you?"

"It is so old as to keep me from sleeping on my watch," coldly returned the boy.

"A careful mother would be better for one of your years than the school of the boatswain. What is your age, Roderick?"

"I have seen years enough to be both wiser and better," he answered, not without a shade of thought on his brow. "Another month will make me twenty."

"Twenty! you trifle with my curiosity, urchin."

"Did I say twenty, Madam! Fifteen would be much nearer to the truth."

"I believe you. And how many of those years have you passed upon the water?"

"But two in truth—though I often think them ten; and yet there are times when they seem but a day!"

"You are romantic early, boy. And how do you like the trade of war?"

"War!"

"Of war—I speak plainly, do I not? Those who serve in a

vessel that is constructed expressly for battle, follow the trade of war."

"Oh, yes. War is certainly our trade."

"And have you, yet, seen any of its horrors? Has this ship been in combat, since your service began?"

"This ship!"

"Surely this ship. Have you ever sailed in another?"

"Never."

"Then it is of this ship that one must question you. Is prize-money plenty among your crew?"

"Abundant. They never want."

"Then the vessel and captain are both favorites. The sailor loves the ship and commander that give him an active life."

"Ay, Madam; our lives are active here. And some there are among us, too, who love both ship and commander."

"And have you Mother or friend to profit by your earnings?"

"Have I—"

Struck with the tone of stupor with which the boy responded to her queries, the Governess turned her head to cast a rapid glance at the language of his countenance. He stood, in a sort of senseless amazement, looking her full in the face, but with an eye so vacant as to prove that he was not sensible of the image that filled it.

"Tell me, Roderick," she continued, careful not to awaken his jealousy, by any sudden allusion to his manner. "Tell me of this life of yours. You find it merry."

"I find it sad."

"'Tis strange. The young ship-boys are usually among the merriest of mortals. Perhaps your officer treats you with severity."

No answer was given.

"I am right. Your captain is a tyrant?"

"You are wrong. Never has he said a harsh or unkind word to me."

"Ah, then he is gentle and kind. You are very happy, Roderick."

"I; happy, Madam!"

"I speak plainly, and in English—happy—"

"Oh, yes. We are all very happy, here."

"It is well. A discontented ship, is no paradise. And you are often in port, Roderick, to taste the sweets of the land?"

"I care but little for the land, Madam, could I only have friends in the ship that love me."

"And have you not? Is not Mr Wilder your friend?"

"I know but little of him. I never saw him, before—"

"When, Roderick?"

"Before we met in Newport."

"In Newport!"

"Surely you know we both came from Newport, last."

"Ah! I comprehend you. Then your acquaintance with Mr Wilder commenced in Newport. It was while the ship was lying off the fort?"

"It was. I carried him the order to take command of the Bristol trader. He had only joined us the night before."

"So lately! It was a young acquaintance, indeed! But I suppose your commander knew his merit."

"It is so hoped among the people. But—"

"You were speaking, Roderick."

"None, here, dare question the captain for his reasons. Even *I* am obliged to be mute."

"Even *you!*" exclaimed Mrs Wyllys in a surprise that, for the moment, overcame her self-restraint. But the abstracted thought in which the boy was lost, appeared to prevent his observing the sudden change in her manner. Indeed so little did he know what was passing, that the Governess touched the hand of Gertrude, and silently pointed out the insensible figure of the lad, without the slightest apprehension that the movement would be observed.

"What think you, Roderick?" continued his interrogator. "Would he refuse to answer *us* also?"

The boy, started, and as consciousness shot into his glance it fell upon the countenance of Gertrude.

"Though her beauty be so rare," he answered with vehemence, "let her not prize it too highly. Woman cannot tame his temper!"

"Is he then so hard of heart? Think you that a question from this fair one would be denied?"

"Hear me, lady," he said, with an earnestness that was no less remarkable than the plaintive softness of the tones in which he spoke. "I have seen more in the last two crowded years of my life than many youths would witness between childhood and the age of man. This is no place for innocence and beauty. Oh! quit the ship if you leave it as you came, without a deck to lay your head under!"

"It may be too late to follow such advice," Mrs Wyllys gravely replied, glancing her eye at the silent Gertrude as she spoke. "But tell me more of this extraordinary vessel, Roderick; you were not born to fill this station in which I find you?"

The boy shook his head, but remained with downcast eyes, apparently indisposed to answer.

"How is it that I find the Dolphin bearing different hues to-day, from what she did yesterday; and why is it that neither then nor now does she resemble in her paint, the slaver of Newport harbor?"

"And why is it," returned the boy with a smile in which melancholy struggled powerfully with bitterness, "that none can look into the secret heart of him who makes these changes at will! If all remained the same, but the paint of the ship, one might still be happy in her!"

"Then, Roderick, you are not happy? Shall I intercede with Capt. Heidegger for your discharge?"

"I could never wish to serve another."

"How! do you complain, and yet embrace your fetters!"

"I complain not."

The Governess eyed him closely, and after a moment's pause she continued:

"Is it usual to see such riotous conduct among the crew, as we have this day witnessed?"

"It is not. You have little to fear from the people; he who brought them under knows how to keep them down."

"They are enlisted by order of the King."

"The King! Yes, surely; a King who has no equal."

"But, they dared to threaten the life of Mr Wilder. Is a seaman in a King's ship usually so bold?"

The boy glanced a look at Mrs Wyllys, as if he would say, he understood her affected ignorance of the character of the vessel, but he chose to continue silent.

"Think you, Roderick," continued the Governess, who no

longer deemed it necessary to pursue her covert inquiries on that particular subject—"think you, Roderick, that the Rov—that is, that Capt. Heidegger will suffer us to land, at the first port which offers?"

"Many have been passed since you reached the ship."

"Ay, many that are inconvenient—but when one shall be gained where his pursuits will allow his ship to enter?"

"Such places are not common."

"But should it occur do you not think he will permit us to land? We have gold to pay him for his trouble."

"He cares not for gold. I never ask him for it, that he does not fill my hand."

"You must be happy, then. Plenty of gold, will compensate for a cold look at times."

"Never!" returned the boy with quickness and energy. "Had I the ship filled with the dross, I would give it, then, to bring a look of kindness into his eye!"

Mrs Wyllys started, no less at the fervid manner of the lad than at the language. Rising from her seat, she approached nigher to him, and in a situation where the light of the lamp fell fuller upon his person. She saw the large drop that broke out from beneath a long and silken lash, to roll down a cheek, which though embrowned by the sun was gradually blushing with the colour that stole into it, as her own gaze became more settled, and then her eyes fell, slowly and keenly along the whole form of the lad, until they reached even the feet that were so delicate, that they seemed barely able to uphold him. The usually mild countenance of the Governess changed to a look of cold regard, and her whole form elevated itself in chaste matronly dignity, as she sternly asked—

"Boy, have you a mother?"

"I know not," was the answer that came from lips, that scarcely severed to permit the smothered sounds to escape.

"It is enough. Another time, I will speak further with you. Cassandra will, in future, do the service of this cabin. When I have need of you, the gong shall be touched."

The head of Roderick fell to his bosom. He shrunk from before the cold and searching eye, which followed his form until it had disappeared through the hatch. The moment he had disappeared Mrs. Wyllys caught Gertrude to her bosom, straining the astonished but affectionate girl to her heart in a way to show how precious she was at that fearful moment.

A gentle tap at the door, broke in upon the flood of reflections which were crowding on the mind of the Governess; she gave the customary answer, and before time was allowed for any interchange of ideas between her and her pupil, the Rover entered.

# Chapter XXIII

"I melt, and am not of stronger earth than others."
*Coriolanus*, V.iii.28−29.

THE FEMALES received their visiter with a restraint, which will be easily understood, when the subject of their recent conversation is recollected. The sinking of Gertrude's form was hurried, but her governess maintained the coldness of her air with greater self-composure. Still there was anxious concern in the watchful glance that she threw towards her guest as if she would anticipate the motive of his visit before he spoke.

The countenance of the Rover, himself, was thoughtful to gravity. He bowed, as he came within the influence of the lamp, and his voice was heard muttering some low and hasty syllables that conveyed no meaning to the ears of the listeners. Indeed so great was the abstraction in which he was lost, that he had evidently prepared to throw his person on the vacant divan, without explanation or apology, like one who took possession of his own, though recollection returned just in time to prevent this breach of decorum. Smiling, and repeating his bow with a still deeper inclination, he advanced with perfect self-possession to the table, where he expressed his fears, that Mrs Wyllys might deem his visit unseasonable, or perhaps not announced with sufficient ceremony. During this short introduction his voice was bland as woman's, and his mien as courteous as if he actually felt himself an intruder in the cabin of a vessel in which he was literally a monarch.

"—But, unseasonable as the hour is," he continued, "I should have gone to my cott with a consciousness of not having discharged all the duties of an attentive and considerate host, had I forgotten to reassure you of the tranquility of the ship, after the scene you have witnessed. I have pleasure in saying that the humour of my people is already expended, and that lambs in their nightly folds, are not more placid than they are at this minute in their hammocks."

"The authority that so promptly quelled the disturbance is happily ever present to protect us," returned the cautious

735

Governess; "we repose entirely on your discretion and generosity."

"You have not misplaced your confidence. From the danger
of mutiny, at least, you are exempt."

"And from all others I trust?"

"This is a wild and fickle element we dwell on," he answered, while he bowed his acknowledgment, taking the seat
to which the other invited him by a motion of the hand.
"But, you know its character, and need not be told we seamen
are seldom certain of any of our movements. I loosened the
cords of discipline myself, to day, and in some measure, invited the broil that followed. But it is passed, like the hurricane and the squall; the ocean is not now smoother than the
tempers of my knaves."

"I have often witnessed these rude sports in vessels of the
King, but I do not remember to have known any more serious result than the settlement of some ancient quarrel, or
some odd freak of nautical humour, which has commonly
proved as harmless as it has been quaint."

"Ay; but the ship which often runs the hazards of the
shoals gets wrecked at last!" muttered the Rover. "I rarely
give the quarter deck up to the people without keeping a
vigilant watch on their humours—but—to day—"

"You were speaking of to day?—"

"Neptune, with his coarse devices is no stranger to you,
Madam?"

"I have seen the God in time past."

" 'Twas thus I understood it—under the line—?"

"And elsewhere."

"Elsewhere!" repeated the other, in a tone of disappointment. "Ay, the sturdy despot is to be found in every ocean
and hundreds of ships, and ships of size too, are to be seen
scorching in the calms of the equator. It was idle to give the
subject a second thought."

"You have been pleased to observe something that has escaped my ear?"

The Rover started, for he had again rather muttered, than
spoken the preceding sentence aloud. Casting a searching
glance around him, as it might be to assure himself, that
no impertinent listener had found means to pry into the

mysteries of a mind he seldom saw fit to lay open to the examination of his associates, he regained his self-possession,
and resumed the discourse with a manner as undisturbed as if
it had received no interruption.

"I had forgotten that your sex is timorous as it is fair,"
he added with a smile so insinuating and gentle, that the
Governess cast an involuntary and uneasy glance towards her
charge, "or I might have been earlier with my assurances of
safety."

"They are welcome even now."

"And your young and gentle friend," he continued, inclining towards Gertrude, though he still addressed his words to
the Governess, "her slumbers will be none the heavier for
what has passed."

"The innocent seldom find an uneasy pillow."

"There is a holy and an unsearchable mystery in that truth!
The innocent pillow their heads in quiet! Would to God, the
guilty might find some refuge too against the sting of
thought! But we live in a world, and in a time, when men
cannot be sure even of themselves."

He then paused and looked about him with a smile so haggard, that the anxious Governess unconsciously drew nigher
her pupil, like one who was ready to yield protection against
the uncertain designs of a maniac. Her visiter, however,
remained in a silence so long and deep, that she felt the
necessity of removing the awkward embarrassment of their
situation, by speaking herself.

"Do you find Mr Wilder as much inclined to mercy as
yourself?" she asked. "There would be merit in his forbearance, since he appeared to be the particular object of the
anger of the mutineers."

"And yet you saw he was not without friends. You witnessed the devotion of the men who stood forth so bravely in
his behalf?"

"I did, and find it remarkable that he should have been
able, in so short a time, to have conquered thus completely,
two so stubborn natures."

"Four-and-twenty years are not an acquaintance of a
day!"

"And does their friendship bear so old a date?"

"I have heard that time counted between them. It is very certain the youth is bound to those uncouth companions of his, by some extraordinary tie. Perhaps this is not the first of their services."

Mrs Wyllys looked grieved. Although prepared to believe that Wilder was a secret agent of the Rover, she had endeavored to hope his connexion with the freebooters was susceptible of some explanation more favorable to his character. However he might be implicated in the common guilt of those who pursued the reckless fortunes of that proscribed and hunted ship, it was evident he bore a heart too generous to wish to see her and her young and guileless charge the victims of the licentiousness of his associates. His repeated and mysterious warnings no longer needed explanation. Indeed all that had been dark and inexplicable, both in the previous, and unaccountable glimmerings of her own mind, and in the extraordinary conduct of the inmates of the ship, was at each instant, becoming capable of solution. She now remembered, in the person and countenance of the Rover, the form and features of the individual who had spoken the passing Bristol trader from the rigging of the slaver, a form which had unaccountably haunted her imagination, during her residence in his ship, like an image recalled from some dim and distant period. Then she saw at once the difficulty that Wilder might prove in laying open a secret in which not only his life was involved, but which to a mind that was not hardened in vice, involved a penalty not less severe; that of the loss of their esteem. In short a good deal of that which the reader has found no difficulty in comprehending, was also becoming clear to the faculties of the Governess, though much still remained obscured in doubts that she could neither solve, nor yet entirely banish from her thoughts. On all these points she had leisure to reflect, for her guest, or host whichever he might be called, seemed in nowise disposed to interrupt her reverie.

"It is wonderful," Mrs Wyllys at length, resumed, "that beings so uncouth should be influenced by the same attachments as those which unite the educated and the refined."

"It is wonderful, as you say," returned the other, like one awakening from a dream. "I would give a thousand of the brightest guineas that ever came from the mint of George IId, to know the private history of that youth!"

"Is he then a stranger to you?" demanded Gertrude, with the quickness of thought.

The Rover turned an eye on her that was vacant for the moment, but into which consciousness and expression began to steal, as he gazed, until the foot of the Governess was trembling with the nervous excitement that pervaded her frame.

"Who shall pretend to know the heart of man!" he answered, again inclining his head, as it might be in acknowledgement of her perfect right to his homage. "All are strangers till we can read their thoughts."

"To pry into the mysteries of the human mind is a privilege which few possess," coldly remarked the Governess. "The world must be often tried and thoroughly known before we can pretend to judge of the motives of those around us."

"And yet is it a pleasant world to those who have the heart to make it merry," cried the Rover, with one of those startling transitions which marked his manner. "To him, who is stout enough to follow the bent of his humour, all is easy. Do you know, that the true secret of the Philosopher is not in living forever, but in living while he can? He who dies at fifty after his fill of pleasure, has had more of life, than he who drags his feet through a century, bearing the burden of the world's caprices, and afraid to speak above his breath, lest, forsooth, his neighbor should find that his words were evil."

"And yet there are some who find their greatest pleasure in pursuing the practices of virtue."

" 'Tis lovely, at least, in your sex to say it," he answered, with an air, that the sensitive Governess fancied was gleaming with the growing licentiousness of a freebooter. She would now gladly have dismissed her visiter, but a certain flashing of the eye, and a manner that was becoming gay by a species of unnatural effort, admonished her of the danger of offending one, who acknowledged no law but his own will. Assuming a tone and a manner that were kind, while they upheld the dignity of her sex, and pointing to sundry instruments of music, that formed part of the heterogeneous furniture of the cabin, she adroitly turned the discourse by saying—

"One whose mind can be softened by harmony and whose

feelings are so evidently alive to the influence of sweet sounds should not decry the pleasures of innocence. This flute and yon guitar, both call you master?"

"And finding these flimsy evidences about my person, you are willing to give me credit for the accomplishments you mention! Here is another mistake of miserable mortality! Seeming is the every day robe of honesty. Why not give me credit for kneeling, morning and night, before that glittering bauble?" pointing to the diamond crucifix which hung, as usual, near the door of his own apartment.

"I hope, at least, that the being whose memory is intended to be revived by that image, is not without your homage. In the pride of his strength and prosperity, man may think lightly of the consolations that can flow from a power superior to humanity, but those who have oftenest proved their value, feel deepest the reverence which is their due."

The look of the Governess was averted; but profoundly filled with the feeling she expressed, her reflecting eye turned to him again, as she uttered the simple sentiment. The gaze she met was earnest and thoughtful as her own. Lifting a finger, he laid it on her arm with a motion so light as to be scarcely perceptible while he asked—

"Think you we are to blame, if our temperaments incline more to evil than power is given to resist?"

"It is only those, who attempt to walk the path of life alone that stumble. I shall not offend your manhood if I ask, do you never commune with God?"

"It is long since that name has been heard in this vessel, lady, except to aid in that miserable scoffing and profanity, which simpler language made too dull. But what is he, this unknown deity, more than what man, in his ingenuity, has seen fit to make him!"

"The fool hath said in his heart, there is no God," she answered in a voice so firm, that it startled even the ears of one so long accustomed to the turbulence and grandeur of his wild profession. "Gird up now thy loins like a man; for I will demand of thee, and answer thou me. Where wast thou when I laid the foundations of the earth? Declare, if thou hast understanding."

The Rover gazed wildly on the flushed countenance of the

speaker. Bending his face aside, he said aloud, evidently giving utterance to his wandering thoughts rather than pursuing the discourse—

"There is nothing more in this, than what I have often heard, and yet it comes over my feelings with the freshness of native air! Lady, repeat thy words. Change not a syllable, nor vary the slightest intonation of the voice, I pray thee."

Though much amazed and even alarmed at the request, Mrs Wyllys complied, delivering the holy language of the inspired writers with a fervor that found its support in the strength of her own faith. Her auditor listened, like a being enthralled. For near a minute neither eye nor attitude was changed, but he stood at the feet of her who had so simply but so powerfully asserted the majesty of God, motionless as the mast against which he leaned. It was long after her accents had ceased, that he drew a deep respiration, and again spoke.

"This is retreading the whole path of life at a single stride!" he said. "I know not why my pulses, which in common are like iron beat so irregularly now! Lady, this little hand of thine might check a temper, which has so often braved—"

He ceased, for his eye following his own hand, which had unconsciously touched that of Mrs. Wyllys, was fastened on the member he had named, which he appeared to study as if examining a relic. Drawing a sigh, like one who awakened from an agreeable illusion, he turned away, leaving the sentence unfinished.

"You would have music!" he recklessly exclaimed. "Then music there shall be, though its symphony be rung upon a gong!"

As he spoke, the wayward and vacillating being we have been attempting to describe, struck the instrument so quick and powerfully as to drown all reply in the din. Though deeply mortified that he had so quickly escaped from the influence she had partially acquired, and secretly displeased at the unceremonious manner in which he had seen fit to announce his independence again, the Governess was aware of the necessity of concealing her disappointment.

"This is certainly not the harmony I invited," she said, when the overwhelming sounds had ceased to fill the ship;

"nor do I think it of a quality to favor the slumbers of those who are less dangerous in their hammocks than when awake."

"Fear nothing for them. The seaman will sleep soundly with his ear near the port at which the cannon bellows, and he awakes at the call of the boatswain's whistle. He is too deeply trained in habit, to think he has heard more, than a note of the flute, stronger and fuller than common, if you will, but still a sound that has no interest for him. Another tap would have sounded the alarm of fire; these three touches say no more than music. It was the signal for the band. The night is still and favorable for their art, and we will listen to sweet sounds awhile."

His words were scarcely uttered before the low chords of wind instruments were heard without, where the men had probably stationed themselves by some previous order of their captain. The Rover smiled, as if he exulted in this prompt proof of the sort of despotic, or rather magical, power he wielded, and throwing his form on the divan, he sat listening to the sounds which followed.

The strains which now rose upon the night, and which spread themselves, soft and melodiously, abroad upon the water, would have done credit to more regular artists. The air was wild and melancholy, and perhaps it was the more in accordance with the present humour of the man for whose ear it was created. Then losing the former character, the whole power of the music was concentrated in softer and still gentler sounds, as if the genius who had given birth to the melody were pouring out the feelings of his soul in pathos. The temper of the Rover's mind answered to the changing expression of the music, and when the strains were sweetest and most touching, he bowed his head like one who wept.

Though secretly under the influence of the harmony themselves, Mrs Wyllys and her pupil could but gaze on the singularly constituted being, into whose hands, they had been cast by their evil fortune. The former was filled with admiration at the fearful contrariety of passions which could reveal themselves in the same individual, under so very different and so dangerous forms, while the latter, judging with the indulgence of her years, was willing to believe that a man whose emotions could be thus easily and kindly excited was rather the victim of circumstances, than the creator of his own habits.

"There is Italy in those strains," said the Rover, when the last chord died upon his ear—"sweet, indolent, luxurious, forgetful Italy. It has never been your chance, Madam, to visit that land, so mighty in its recollections and so impotent in its actual condition?"

The Governess made no reply, but bowing her head, in turn, her companions believed she was submitting also to the influence of the music. At length, impelled by another changeful impulse, the Rover, advanced towards Gertrude, and, addressing her with a courtesy that would have done credit to a different scene, he said,—

"One who in common speaks music should not have neglected the gifts of nature. You sing?"

Had Gertrude possessed the power he affected to believe, her voice would have denied its services at his call. Bending to his compliment, she murmured her apologies, in words that were barely audible. He listened intently, but without pressing a point that it was easy to see was unwelcome, he turned away, and gave the gong a light quick tap.

"Roderick," he continued, when the light footstep of the lad was heard upon the stairs that led into the cabin below, "do you sleep?"

The answer was slow and smothered; of course it was in the negative.

"Apollo was not absent at the birth of Roderick, Madam. The lad can raise such sounds as have been known to melt the stubborn feelings of a seaman. Go; place yourself by the cabin door, good Roderick, and bid the music, run a low accompaniment to your words."

The boy obeyed, stationing his slight form so much in shadow, that his countenance was not visible to those who sat within the stronger light of the lamp. The instruments then commenced a gentle symphony, which was soon ended, and twice did they begin the air, but no voice was heard.

"Words—Roderick, words—" exclaimed the Rover—"we are but dull interpreters of the meaning of the flutes."

The boy then began in a full rich contralto voice, which betrayed a tremor, however, that threatened more than once to interrupt his song. The words so far as they might be distinguished ran as follows.

> "The land was lying broad and fair,
>     Behind the Western sea
> And holy solitude was there,
>     And sweetest liberty.
>
> The lingering sun, at evening hung,
>     A glorious orb, divinely beaming,
> On silent lake and tree,
>     And ruddy light was o'er all streaming
>     Mark, man, for thee,
>     O'er valley, lake and tree!
>
> And now a thousand maidens stray,
>     Or range the echoing groves,
> While fluttering near, on pinions gay,
>     Fan twice ten thousand loves.
> In that soft clime, at even time,
>     Hope says—"

"Enough of this, good Roderick," impatiently interrupted his master. "There is too much of the Corydon in that song for the humor of a mariner. Sing us of the sea, and its pleasures, boy; and roll out thy strains in a fashion that will suit a sailor's fancy."

The lad was mute, perhaps in disinclination to the task, perhaps from inability to comply.

"What, Roderick, does the muse desert thee, or is thy memory getting dull? You see, the child is wilful in his melody; he must sing of loves and sunshine, or he fails. Now touch us a stronger chord, my men, and put life into your cadences, while I troll a sea air, for the honor of the ship."

The band caught the humor of their master, for he well deserved the name, sounding a powerful and gayer symphony to prepare the listeners for the song of the Rover. Those treacherous and beguiling tones which so often stole into his voice when speaking, did not mislead expectation as to its powers. It proved to be equally rich, full, deep and melodious. Favored by these natural advantages and aided by an exquisite ear, he rolled out the following stanzas in a manner which was singularly divided between that of the reveller and the man of sentiment. The words were probably original for they smacked strongly of his own profession and were not entirely without a touch of the peculiar taste of the individual.

> All hands, unmoor! unmoor!
> Hark! to the hoarse, but welcome sound,
>   Startling the seaman's sweetest slumbers;
> The groaning capstern's laboring round,
>   The cheerful fife's enlivening numbers;
> And lingering idlers join the brawl,
> And merry ship-boys swell the call;
>   All hands, unmoor! unmoor!
>
> The cry's, 'A sail! a sail!'
> Brace high each nerve to dare the fight,
>   And boldly steer to seek the forman;
> One secret prayer to aid the right,
>   And many a secret thought to woman!
> Now spread the flutt'ring canvass wide,
> And dash the foaming sea aside;
>   The cry's, 'A sail! a sail!'
>
> Three cheers for victory!
> Hush'd be each plaint o'er fallen brave;
>   Still ev'ry sigh to messmate given;
> The seaman's tomb is in the wave;
>   The hero's latest hope is heaven!
> High lift the voice in revelry!
> Gay raise the song, the shout, the glee;
>   Three cheers for victory!

When he had ended the song, and without waiting to listen if any words of compliment were to succeed an effort, that might lay claim to great excellence both in tones and execution, he arose, and desiring his guests to command the services of his band at pleasure, he wished them "soft repose and pleasant dreams," and coolly descended into the lower apartments, apparently for the night. Mrs Wyllys and Ger-

trude, notwithstanding they had been amused, or rather se-
duced, by the interest thrown around a manner that was so
wayward while it was never gross, felt a sensation as he disappeared like that produced by breathing a freer air, after having
been too long compelled to respire the pent atmosphere of a
dungeon. The former regarded her pupil, with eyes in which
open affection struggled with inward solicitude, but neither
spoke, since a slight movement near the door of the cabin
reminded them that they were not yet alone.

"Would you hear further music, Madam?" asked Roderick,
stealing timidly out of the shadow as he spoke. "I will sing
you to sleep, if you will, but I am choked when he bids me to
be merry against my feelings."

The brow of the Governess contracted, and she was evidently preparing herself to give a stern and repulsive answer.
But the plaintive tones, and shrinking, submissive form of the
other pleaded so strongly to her heart, that the frown passed
away, leaving in its place, the reproving look which chastens
the frown of maternal concern.

"Roderick," she said, "I thought we should have seen thee
no more to-night!"

"You heard the gong. Although he can be so gay, and can
raise such thrilling sounds in his pleasanter moments, you
have never yet listened to him in anger!"

"Is his anger so very fearful?"

"Perhaps to me, it is more frightful than to others—but I
find nothing so terrible as a word of his, when his mind is
moody."

"Is he then harsh to thee?"

"Never."

"You contradict yourself, Roderick. He is and he is not.
Have you not said how terrible you find his moody language?"

"Yes; for I find it changed. Once he was never thoughtful
or out of humour, but latterly he is not himself."

Mrs Wyllys did not answer. The language of the boy was
certainly much more intelligible to her than to her attentive
but unsuspecting companion: for while she motioned to the
lad to retire, Gertrude manifested a desire to gratify the curious interest she felt in the life and manners of the freebooter.

The signal, however, was authoritatively repeated and the lad slowly and with reluctance withdrew.

The Governess and her pupil then retired into their own state-room, and after devoting many minutes to those nightly offerings and petitions which neither ever suffered any circumstances to cause them to neglect, they slept in the consciousness of innocence, and in the hope of an all powerful protection. Though the bell of the ship regularly sounded the hours throughout the watches of the night, scarcely another sound arose during the darkness to disturb the calm which seemed to have settled equally on the ocean and on all that floated in its bosom.

# Chapter XXIV

——"But, for the miracle,
I mean our preservation, few in millions
Can speak like us."

*The Tempest*, II.i.6–8.

---

D URING THESE MOMENTS of treacherous calm, the Dolphin might have been likened to a slumbering beast of prey. But as nature limits the period of repose to the creatures of the animal world, so it would seem that the inactivity of the freebooters was not doomed to any long continuance. With the morning sun a breeze came across the water breathing the flavor of the land, and setting the sluggish ship again in motion. Throughout all that day, with a wide reach of canvass spreading along her booms her course was held towards the South. Watch succeeded watch and night came after day and still no change was made in her direction. Then the blue islands were seen heaving up, one after another out of the sea. The Prisoners of the Rover, for thus the females were now constrained to consider themselves, silently watched each hillock of green that the vessel glided past, each naked and sandy key or each mountain side, until, by the calculations of the Governess, they were already steering amid the Western archipelago.

During all this time no question was asked, which in the smallest manner betrayed to the Rover the consciousness of his guests that he was not conducting them towards the promised port of the continent. Gertrude wept for the sorrow of her father; but her tears flowed in private, or were poured upon the bosom of her Governess. Wilder she avoided with an intuitive consciousness that he was no longer the character she had wished to believe, but to all in the ship she struggled to maintain an equal air and a serene eye. In this fortitude, safer than any deprecating entreaties might have proved, she was strongly supported by her Governess, whose knowledge of mankind had early taught her, that virtue was never so imposing as when it knew best how to maintain its equanimity. On the other hand, both the commander of the ship and his Lieutenant sought no other communication with the inmates of the cabin, than courtesy appeared absolutely to require.

The former, as if repenting already of having laid so bare the capricious humours of his mind, drew gradually into himself, neither seeking nor permitting familiarity with any; while the latter appeared perfectly conscious of the constrained mien of the Governess and of the altered, though still pitying eye of her pupil. Little explanation was necessary to acquaint Wilder with the reasons of this change. Instead of seeking the means to vindicate his character, however, he rather imitated their reserve. Little else was wanting to assure his former friends of the nature of his pursuits; for even Mrs Wyllys admitted to her charge that he acted like one in whom depravity had not yet made such progress as to have destroyed that consciousness, which is ever the surest test of innocence. We shall not detain the narrative to dwell upon the natural regrets in which Gertrude indulged as this sad conviction forced itself upon her understanding, nor to relate the gentle wishes, in which she did not think it wrong to indulge, that one who certainly was master of so many manly and generous qualities, might be made to see the error of his life, and to return to a course for which even her cold and nicely judging Governess allowed, nature had eminently endowed him. The kind emotions that had been awakened in her bosom, by the events of the last fortnight, were not content to exhibit themselves in wishes alone, and petitions more personal and even more fervent than common, mingled in her prayers. But this is a veil which it is not our province to raise; the heart of one so pure and so ingenuous being the best repository for its own gentle feelings.

For several days the ship had been contending with the unvarying winds of those regions. Instead of struggling, however, like a cumbered trader, to gain some given port, the rover suddenly altered her course, gliding through one of the many passages that intersect the islands, with the ease of a bird that is settling to its nest. A hundred different sails were seen, but all were avoided alike, the policy of the freebooters teaching them the necessity of moderation in a sea so crowded with vessels of war. After the vessel had shot through one of the straights, which divide the chain of the Antilles, it issued in safety on the more open sea which separates them from the Spanish Main. The moment the passage was effected, and a broad and clear horizon was seen stretching on every side of them, a manifest alteration occurred in the mien of every individual of the crew. The brow of the Rover himself lost the look of care and his reserve disappeared, leaving him the reckless wayward being we have described. Even the men, whose vigilance had needed no quickening in running the gauntlet of the cruisers, which were known to swarm in the narrower seas, appeared to breathe a freer air, and sounds of merriment and thoughtless gaiety were once more heard, in a place over which the gloom of distrust had been so long and so heavily cast.

On the other hand the Governess saw new ground for uneasiness in the course the vessel was taking. While the islands were in view, she had hoped that their captor only awaited a suitable occasion to place them, in safety, within the influence of the laws of some of the colonial governments. Her own observation told her there was so much of what was once good, if not noble, mingled with the lawlessness of the two principal individuals in the vessel, that she saw nothing that was visionary in such an expectation. Even those tales of the time, which recounted the desperate acts of the freebooter, with wild and fanciful exaggerations, did not forget to include numberless instances of even chivalrous generosity. In short he bore the character of one, who, while he declared himself the enemy of all, knew how to distinguish between the weak and the strong, and who often found as much gratification in repairing the wrongs of the former, as in humbling the pride of the latter.

But all her agreeable anticipations from this quarter were forgotten when the last island of the groupe sunk into the sea behind them, and the ship lay alone on an empty ocean. As if ready to throw aside his mask, the Rover ordered the sails to be reduced, and, neglecting the favourable breeze, the vessel was brought to the wind. No object calling for the immediate attention of her crew, the Dolphin came to a stand in the midst of the waters, her officers and people abandoning themselves to their pleasures or to idleness, as whim or inclination dictated.

"I had hoped that your convenience would have permitted us to land in some one of his Majesty's Islands," said Mrs Wyllys, speaking for the first time, since her suspicions had been awakened, on the subject of her quitting the ship, and addressing her words to the self-styled Capt. Heidegger, just after the order to heave-to the vessel had issued from his lips. "I fear you find it irksome to be so long dispossessed of your cabin."

"It cannot be better occupied," he rather evasively replied, though the observant and anxious Governess fancied his eye was bolder and his air under less restraint than when she had before dwelt on the same topic. "If custom did not require that a ship should wear the colours of some people, mine should always sport those of the fair."

"And as it is?"—

"As it is, I hoist the emblems that belong to the service I am in."

"In fifteen days, that you have been troubled with my presence, it has never been my good fortune to see those colours set."

"No!" exclaimed the Rover, glancing his eye quickly at her, as if to penetrate her thoughts, "then shall the uncertainty cease on the sixteenth—Who's there, abaft?"

"No one better nor worse than Richard Fid," returned the individual in question, lifting his head from a locker into which it had been thrust, while its owner searched for some mislaid implement, and who added, a little quickly, when he ascertained by whom he was addressed, "always at your honour's orders."

"Ah! 'Tis the friend of *our* friend," the Rover observed to Mrs Wyllys, with an emphasis which the other understood. "He shall be my interpreter. Come hither, lad, I have a word to exchange with you."

"A thousand at your service, Sir," returned Richard, complying; "for though no great talker, I have always something uppermost in my mind, which can be laid hold of at need."

"I hope you find that your hammoc swings easily in my ship?"

"I'll not deny it, your honour; an easier craft, especially upon a bowline, might be hard to find."

"And the cruise—I hope you also find the cruise such as a seaman loves?"

Fid rolled over the portion of the weed which his mouth contained and look'd a little queerly at his companions before he answered—

"D'ye see, Sir, I was sent from home with little schooling, and so I seldom make so free as to pretend to read the captain's orders."

"But still you have your inclinations," said Mrs Wyllys, firmly, determined to push the investigation even further than her companion had intended.

"I can't say that I'm wanting in natural feeling, your ladyship," returned Fid, endeavoring to manifest his admiration of the sex, by the awkward bow he made to the Governess as its representative, "thof crosses and mishaps have come athwart me as well as better men. I thought as strong a splice was laid between Kate Whiffle and me, as was ever turned into a sheet-cable; but then came the law, with its regulations and shipping articles, luffing short athwart my happiness, and making a wreck at once of all the poor girl's hopes, and giving but a Flemish account of my comfort."

"It was proved that she had another husband!" dryly remarked the Rover.

"Four, your honor. The girl had a love of company, and it grieved her to the heart to see an empty house. But then, as it was seldom more than one of us could be in port at a time, there was no such need to make the noise they did about the trifle; but envy did it all, Sir; envy, and the greediness of the land sharks. Had every woman in the parish as many husbands as Kate, the devil a bit would they have taken up the precious time of judge and jury in looking into the manner in which a wench like her kept a quiet household."

"And since that unfortunate repulse, you have kept yourself altogether out of the hands of matrimony?"

"Ay, ay; *since*, your honor," returned Fid, giving his commander another of those droll looks in which a peculiar cunning struggled with a more direct and straight going honesty, "*since*, as you say rightly, Sir. Though they talked of a small matter of a bargain, that I had made with another woman, myself, but in overhauling the affair, they found, that as the shipping articles with poor Kate wouldn't hold together, why they could make nothing at all of me. So I was white-washed like a queen's parlor and sent adrift."

"And all this occurred after your acquaintance with Mr Wilder—"

"Afore, your honour, afore—I was but a yonker in the time of it, seeing that it is four and twenty years, come May next since I have been towing at the stern of Master Harry. But then as I have had a sort of family of my own, since that day, why the less need you know to be berthing myself, again, in any other man's hammock."

"You were saying it is four and twenty years," interrupted Mrs Wyllys, "since you made the acquaintance of Mr Wilder?"

"Acquaintance! Lord, my lady, little did he know of acquaintances at that time, though, bless him, the lad has had occasion to remember it often enough since."

"The meeting of two men of so singular merit must have been somewhat remarkable," observed the Rover.

"It was, for that matter, remarkable enough, your honor, though as to the merit, notwithstanding Master Harry is often for overhauling that part of the account I've set it down for just nothing at all."

"I confess, that in a case where two men, both of whom are so well qualified to judge, are of different opinions I feel at a loss to know which can have the right. Perhaps by the aid of the facts, I might form a truer judgement."

"Your honour forgets the Guinea, who is altogether of my mind in the matter, seeing no great merit in the thing either. But as you are saying, Sir, reading the log is the only true way to know how fast a ship can go, and so, if this lady and your honour, have a mind to come at the truth of the affair, why, you have only to say as much, and I will put it all before you in creditable language."

"There is reason in this proposition," returned the Rover, motioning to his companion to follow to a part of the poop where they were less exposed to the observations of inquisitive eyes. "Now place the whole clearly before us, and then, you may consider the merits of the question disposed of definitively."

Fid was far from discovering the smallest reluctance to enter on the required detail, and by the time he had cleared his throat, freshened his supply of the weed and otherwise disposed himself to proceed, Mrs Wyllys had so far conquered her reluctance to pry clandestinely into the secrets of others, as to yield to a curiosity she found unconquerable, and to take the seat to which her companion invited her by a gesture of his hand.

"I was sent early to sea, your honour, by my father," commenced Fid, after these little preliminaries had been observed, "who was, like myself, a man that passed more of his time on the water than on dry ground, though as he was nothing more than a fisherman, he generally kept the land aboard, which is after all, little better than living on it altogether. Howsomever when I went, I made a broad offing at once, fetching up on the other side of the Horn, the very first passage I made; which was no small journey for a new beginner; but then as I was only eight years old—"

"Eight! you are speaking of yourself!" interrupted the disappointed Governess.

"Certain, Madam, and though genteeler people might be talked of, it would be hard to turn the conversation on any man who knows better how to rig or how to strip a ship. I was beginning at the right end of my story, but as I fancied your ladyship might not choose to waste time in hearing concerning my father and mother, I cut the matter short, by striking in at eight years old, overlooking all about my birth and name and such other matters, as are usually logged, in your every day narratives."

"Proceed," she rejoined, resorting to a compelled resignation.

"My mind is pretty much like a ship that is about to slip off its ways," resumed Fid. "If she makes a fair start and there is neither jam nor dry rub, smack she goes into the water, like a sail let run in a calm, but if she once brings up, a good deal of labor is to be gone through to set her in motion, again. Now in order to wedge up my ideas, and to get the story slushed so that I can slip through it with ease, it is needful to overrun the part which I have just let go: Which is, how my father was a fisherman, and how I doubled the Horn—Ah! here I have it again, clear of kinks, fake above fake like a well coiled cable, so that I can pay it out, as easily as the Boatswain's yeoman can lay his hand on a bit of ratling stuff. Well, I doubled the Horn, as I was saying, and might have been the matter of four years cruising about among the islands and seas of those parts, which were none of the best known then, or for that matter, now. After this I served in his Majesty's fleet a whole war and got three wounds and as much honour as I could stow beneath hatches. Well, then I fell in with the Guinea, the black, my lady, that you see turning in a new clue-garnet-block for the starboard clue of the fore course—"

"Ay, then you fell in with the African," said the Rover.

"Then we made our acquaintance, and, although his colour is no whiter than the back of a whale, I care not who knows it, after Master Harry there is no man living who has an honester way with him, or in whose company I take greater satisfaction. To be sure, your honour, the fellow is something contradictory, and has a great opinion of his strength, and thinks his equal is not to be found at a weather earing, or in the bunt of a topsail, but then he is no better than a black, and one is not to be too particular in looking into the faults of such as are not actually his fellow creatures."

"That would be uncharitable in the extreme."

"The very words the chaplain used to let fly aboard the 'Brunswick!' It's a great thing to have schooling, your honor, since, if it does nothing else, it fits a man for a boatswain, and puts him in the track of steering the shortest course to heaven. But as I was saying, there were I and Guinea, shipmates, and in a reasonable way friends, for five years more, and then the time arrived when we met with the mishap of the wreck in the West-Indies."

"What wreck?"

"I beg your honor's pardon, I never swing my head yards till I'm sure the ship won't luff back into the wind, and before I tell the particulars of that wreck, I will overrun my ideas to see that nothing is forgotten, that should of right be first mentioned."

The Rover, who saw, by the expression of her countenance,

how impatient his companion was becoming for a sequel that approached so tardily, and how much she dreaded an interruption, made a significant sign to her to permit the straight going tar to take his own course, as the best means of coming at the facts they both longed so much to hear. Left to himself, Fid soon took the necessary review of the transactions in his own quaint manner, and having happily found that nothing, which he considered as germain to the narrative was omitted, he proceeded at once to the more material, and, what was to his auditors by far, the most interesting portion of his narrative.

"Well, as I was telling your honor," he continued, "Guinea was then a maintopman and I was stationed in the same place aboard the 'Proserpine,' a quick-going two and thirty, when we fell in with a bit of a smuggler between the islands and the Spanish Main. And so the Captain made a prize of her, and ordered her into port, for which I have always supposed, as he was a sensible man, he had his orders. But this is neither here nor there, seeing that the craft had got to the end of her rope, and foundered in a heavy hurricane that came over us, mayhap a couple of days' run to leeward of our haven. Well, she was a small boat, and as she took it into her mind to roll over on her side before she went to sleep, the master's mate in charge, and three others slid off her decks to the bottom of the sea, as I have always had reason to believe, never having heard any thing of them since. It was here that Guinea first served me the good turn, for though we had often before shared hunger and thirst together, this was the first time, he ever jumped overboard to keep me from taking in salt water like a fish—"

"He kept you from drowning with the rest?"

"I'll not say just that much, your honor, for there is no knowing what lucky accident might have done the same good turn for me. Howsomever, seeing that I can swim no better nor worse than a double-headed shot, I have always been willing to give the black credit for as much, though little has ever been said between us on the subject, for no other reason as I can see, than that settling day has not yet come. Well, we contrived to get the boat afloat, and enough into it to keep soul and body together, and made the best of our way for the land, seeing that the cruise was to all useful purposes over in that smuggler. I needn't be particular in telling this lady of the nature of boat duty, as she has lately had some experience, in that way herself, but I can tell her this much: Had it not been for that boat in which the black and myself spent the better part of ten days, she would have fared but badly in her own navigation."

"Explain your meaning."

"My meaning is plain enough, your honor, which is that little else than the handy way of Master Harry in a boat could have kept the Bristol trader's launch above water, the day we fell in with it."

"But in what manner was your own ship-wreck connected with the safety of Mr Wilder?" demanded the Governess, unable any longer to await the dilatory explanation of the prolix seaman.

"In a very plain and natural fashion, my lady, as you will say yourself when you come to hear the pitiful part of my tale. Well, there were I and Guinea rowing about in the ocean, on short allowance of all things but work, for two nights and a day, heading in for the islands, for though no great navigators we could smell the land, and so we pull'd away lustily, for you consider it was a race in which life was the wager, until we made, in the pride of the morning, as it might be here, at east and by south, a ship under bare poles, if a vessel can be called bare that had nothing better than the stumps of her three masts standing, and they without rope or rag to tell one her rig or nation. Howsomever, as there were three naked sticks left, I have always put her down for a full rigged ship, and when we got nigh enough to take a look at the hull, I made bold to say she was of English build."

"You boarded her—" observed the Rover.

"A small task that, your honor, since a starved dog was the whole crew she could muster to keep us off. It was a solemn sight when we got on her decks, and one that bears hard on my manhood," continued Fid, with an air that grew more serious as he proceeded, "whenever I have occasion to overhaul the log-book of memory."

"You found her people suffering of want!"

"We found a noble ship as helpless, as a hallibut in a tub.

There she lay, a craft of some four hundred tons, water-logged and motionless as a church. It always gives me great reflection, Sir, when I see a noble vessel brought to such a strait, for one may liken her to a man who has been docked of his fins, and who is getting to be good for little else than to be set upon a cat-head to look out for squalls."

"The ship was then deserted."

"Ay, the people had left her, Sir, or had been washed away in the gust that laid her over, I never could come at the truth of the particulars. The dog had been mischievous I conclude, about the decks, and so he had been lashed to a timber-head, the which saved his life, since, happily for him, he found himself on the weather side, when the hull righted a little, after her spars gave way. Well, Sir, there was the dog and not much else, as we could see, though we spent half a day in rummaging round in order to pick up any small matter that might be useful: But then, as the entrances to the hold and cabin were full of water, why we made no great affair of the salvage after all."

"And then you left the wreck."

"Not yet, your honor. While knocking about among the bits of rigging and lumber above board, says Guinea, says he, 'Mister Dick, I hear some one making their plaints below.' Now I had heard the same noises, myself, Sir, but had set them down as the spirits of the people moaning over their losses, and had said nothing of the same for fear of stirring up the superstition of the black, for the best of them are no better than superstitious niggers, my lady; so I said nothing of what I had heard, until he saw fit to broach the subject himself. Then we both turned-to to listening with a will, and sure enough the groans began to take a human sound. It was a good while, howsomever, before I could make up my mind as to the truth, whether it was any thing more than the complaining of the hulk itself, for you know, my lady, that a ship which is about to sink, makes her lamentations just like any other living thing."

"I do—I do—" returned the Governess shuddering. "I have heard them, and never will memory lose the recollection of the sounds!"

"Ay, I thought you might know something of the same;

and solemn groans they are! But as the hulk kept rolling on the top of the sea, and no further signs of her going down, I began to think it best to cut into her abaft, in order to make sure that some miserable wretch had not been caught in his hammock, at the time she went over. Well, good will and an axe soon let us into the secret of the moans—"

"You found a child!"

"And its mother, my lady. As good luck would have it, they were in a berth on the weather side, and as yet the water had not reach'd them. But pent air and hunger had nearly proved as bad as the brine. The lady was in the agony, when we got her out, and as to the boy, proud and strong as you now see him there on yonder gun, my lady, he was just so miserable that it was no small matter to make him swallow the drop of wine and water that the Lord had left us, in order, as I have often thought since, to bring him up to be as he at this moment is, the pride of the ocean!"

"But the mother!"

"The mother had given the only morsel of biscuit she had to the child, and was dying, in order that the urchin might live. I never could get rightly into the meaning of the thing, my lady, why a woman, who is no better than a Lascar in matters of strength, nor any better than a booby in respect of courage, should be able to let go her hold of life in this quiet fashion, when many a stout mariner would be fighting for each mouthful of air the Lord might see fit to give. But there she was, white as the sail on which the storm has long beaten, and limber as a pennant in a calm, with her poor skinny arm around the lad, holding in her hand the very mouthful that might have kept her own soul in the body a little longer."

"What did she, when you brought her to the light?"

"What did she," repeated Fid, whose voice was getting thick and husky—"why she did a d——d honest thing. She gave the boy the crumb, and motioned, as well as a dying woman could motion, that we should have an eye over him till the cruise of life was up."

"And was that all?"

"I have always thought she prayed, for something passed between her and one who was not to be seen, if a man might judge by the fashion in which her eyes were turned aloft and her lips moved. I hope among others she put in a good word for Richard Fid, for certain she had as little need to be asking for herself, as any body. But no man will ever know what she said, seeing that her mouth was shut from that time forever after."

"She died!"

"Sorry am I to say it. But the poor lady was past swallowing when she came into our hands, and then it was but little that we had to offer her. A quart of water, with mayhap a gill of wine, a biscuit, and a handful of rice was no great allowance for two hearty men to pull a boat some seventy leagues within the tropics. Howsomever, when we found no more was to be got from the wreck, and that since the air had escaped by the hole we had cut, she was settling fast, we thought it best to get out of her, and sure enough we were none too soon, seeing that she went under, just as we had twitched the jolly boat clear of the suction."

"And the boy, the deserted child!" exclaimed the Governess, whose eyes had now filled to overflowing.

"There you are all aback, my lady. Instead of deserting him, we brought him away with us, as we did the only other living creature to be found about the wreck. But we had still a long journey before us, and to make the matter worse, we were out of the track of the traders. So, I put it down as a case for a council of all hands, which was no more than I and the black, since the lad was too weak to talk, and little could he have said otherwise in our situation. So I begun myself, saying, says I, 'Guinea, we must eat either this here dog or this here boy. If we eat the boy, we shall be no better than the people in your own country, who you know, my lady, are cannibals, but if we eat the dog, poor as he is, we may make out to keep soul and body together, and to give the child, the other matters.' So Guinea, he says, says he, 'I've no occasion for food, at all; give 'em to the boy,' says he, 'seeing that he is little and has need of strength.' Howsomever, Master Harry took no great fancy to the dog, which we soon finished between us, for the plain reason that he was so thin. After that we had a hungry time of it ourselves, for had we not kept up the life in the lad, you know, there was so little of it that it would soon have slipt through our fingers."

"And you fed the child, though fasting yourselves!"

"No, we wer'n't altogether idle, my lady, seeing that we kept our teeth pretty busy on the skin of the dog, though I will not say that the food was over savory. And then as we had no occasion to lose time in eating we kept the oars going so much the livelier. Well, we got in at one of the islands after a time, though neither I nor the nigger had much to boast of as to strength or weight when we made the first kitchen we fell in with."

"And the child?"

"Oh, he was doing well enough, for, as the doctors afterwards told us, the short allowance on which we put him did him no harm."

"You sought his friends?"

"Why as for that matter, my lady, so far as I have been able to discover, he was with his best friends already. We had neither chart nor bearings by which we knew how to steer in search of his family. His name he called Master Harry, by which it is clear he was a gentleman born, as indeed any one may see by looking at him, but not another word could I learn of his relations or country, even, except that as he spoke the English language and was found in an English ship there is a natural reason to believe he is of English build himself."

"Did you not learn the name of the ship?" demanded the attentive Rover, in whose countenance the traces of a lively interest were quite discernible.

"Why as to that matter, your honor, schools were scarce in my part of the country, and in Africa, you know, there is no great matter of learning; so that, had her name been out of water, which it was not, we might have been bothered to read it. Howsomever, there was a horse-bucket kicking about her decks, and which as luck would have it, got jammed in with the pumps in such a fashion that it did not go overboard, until we took it with us. Well, this bucket had a name painted on it, and after we had leisure for the thing, I got Guinea, who has a natural turn at tatooing, to rub it into my arm in gunpowder, as the handiest way of logging these small particulars. Your honor, shall see what the black has made of it."

So saying, Fid very coolly doffed his jacket, and laid bare, to the elbow, one of his brawny arms, on which the blue impression was still very plainly visible. Although the letters were rudely imitated, it was not difficult to read in the skin, the words, "Ark of Lynnhaven."

"Here then you had a clue at once, to find the relatives of the boy," observed the Rover, after he had deciphered the letters.

"It seems not, your honor, for we took the child with us aboard the Proserpine, and our worthy captain, carried sail hard after the people. But no one could give any tidings of such a craft as the 'Ark of Lynnhaven,' and after a twelve-month or more we were obliged to give up the chase."

"Could the child give no account of his friends?" demanded the Governess.

"But little, my lady, for the reason that he knew but little about himself. So we gave the matter over, altogether, I and Guinea and the Captain, and all of us turning-to to educate the boy. He got his seamanship of the black and myself, and mayhap some little of his manners also; and his navigation and Latin of the Captain, who proved his friend 'till such a time, as he was able to take care of himself and, for that matter some years afterwards."

"And how long did Mr Wilder continue in a King's ship?" asked the Rover, in a careless and, apparently, an indifferent manner.

"Long enough to learn all that is taught there, your honor," was the evasive reply—

"He came to be an officer I suppose."

"If he didn't, the King had the worst of the bargain. But what is this I see, hereaway, atween the backstay and the vang? It looks like a sail, or is it only a gull flapping his wings before he rises?"

"Sail, ho!" called the lookout from the mast-head. "Sail, ho!" was echoed from top and deck, the glittering, though distant, object having struck a dozen vigilant eyes, nearly at the same instant. The Rover was compelled to lend his attention to a summons so often repeated, and Fid profited by the circumstance to quit the poop, with the hurry of one who was not sorry for the interruption. Then the Governess arose, too, and thoughtful and melancholy she sought the privacy of her cabin.

"SAIL HO!" in the little frequented sea in which the rover lay, was a cry that quickened every pulsation in the bosoms of her crew. Many weeks had now, according to their method of calculation, been entirely lost in the visionary and profitless plans of their chief. They were not of a temper to reason on the fatality which had forced the Bristol trader from their toils. It was enough for their rough natures that the rich spoil had escaped them. Without examining into the causes of this loss, they were disposed to visit their disappointment on the head of the innocent officer who had been charged with the care of a vessel that they already considered a prize. Here then was at length an opportunity to repair their loss. The stranger was about to encounter them in a part of the ocean where succour was nearly hopeless, and where time might be afforded, to profit to the utmost, by any success that the freebooters should obtain. Every man in the ship seemed sensible of these advantages, and as the words sounded from mast to yard, and from yard to deck, they were taken up in cheerful echoes from fifty mouths, which repeated the cry until it was heard issuing from the inmost recesses of the vessel.

The Rover himself manifested unusual satisfaction at this new prospect of a capture. He was quite aware of the necessity of some brilliant or of some profitable exploit to curb the rising tempers of his men, and long experience had taught him that he could draw the cords of discipline the tightest in moments that appeared the most to require the exercise of his own high courage and consummate skill. He walked forward therefore among his people with a countenance that was no longer buried in reserve, speaking to several, whom he addressed by name, and of whom he did not even disdain to ask opinions concerning the character of the distant sail. When a sort of implied assurance that their recent offences were overlooked, had thus been given, he summoned Wilder, the General and one or two others of the superior officers to the poop, where they all disposed themselves to make more particular and more certain observations by the aid of a half-dozen excellent glasses.

Many minutes were now passed in intense scrutiny. The day was cloudless; the wind fresh without being heavy; the sea long, even and far from high, and in short all things combined, as far as is ever seen on the restless ocean, not only to aid their examination, but to favor those subsequent evolutions which each instant rendered more probable would become necessary.

"It is a ship!" said the Rover, lowering his glass, the first to proclaim the result of the long inspection.

"It is a ship!" echoed the general, across whose weather-worn features a ray of something like satisfaction was making an effort to shine.

"A full rigged ship!" continued a third, relieving his eye in turn, and answering the grim smile of the soldier.

"There must be something to hold up all those lofty spars," resumed their commander. "A hull of price is beneath. But you say nothing, Mr Wilder! You make her out—?"

"A ship of size," returned our adventurer, who, though silent had been far from the least interested and occupied in his investigations. "Does my glass deceive me—or—"

"Or what, Sir?"

"I see her to the heads of her courses."

"You see her as I do. It is a tall ship on an easy bowline, with every thing set that will draw. And she is standing hitherward. Her lower sails have lifted within five minutes."

"I thought as much. But—"

"But what, Sir? There can be little doubt but she is heading north-and-by-east. Since she is so kind as to spare us the pains of a chase we will not hurry our movements. Let her come on. How like you the manner of the stranger's advance, General?"

"Unmilitary, but enticing! There is a look of the mines about her very royals!"

"And you, gentlemen—do you also see the fashion of a Galleon in her upper sails?"

" 'Tis not unreasonable to believe it," answered one of the inferiors. "The Dons are said to run this passage often in order to escape speaking us gentlemen who cruise with roving commissions!"

"Ah! your Don is a Prince of the earth! There is charity in lightening his golden burthen, or the man would sink under it, as did the Roman matron under the pressure of the Sabine shields. I think, by your eye, you see no such gilded beauty in the stranger, Mr Wilder."

"It is a heavy ship."

"The more likely to bear a noble freight. You are new, Sir, to this merry trade of ours, or you would know that size is a quality we greatly esteem. If they carry pennants, we leave them to meditate on the many 'slips which exist between the cup and the lip;' if stored with metal no more dangerous than that of Potosi, they generally sail the faster after passing a few hours in our company."

"Is not the stranger making signals?" demanded Wilder, quickly.

"Is he so alert? A good look-out must be had, when a vessel that is merely steadied by her staysails can be seen so far. Vigilance is a never failing sign of value!"

There was a pause, during which all the glasses, in imitation of Wilder's, were again raised in the direction of the stranger. Different opinions were given; some affirming and some doubting the fact of the signals. The Rover himself was silent, though his observation was keen and long continued.

"We have wearied our eyes till sight is getting dim," he said. "I have found the use of trying fresh organs when my own have refused to serve me. Come hither, lad," he continued, addressing a man who was executing some delicate job in seamanship on the poop, at no great distance from the spot where the groupe of officers had placed themselves. "Come hither, lad. Tell me what you make of the sail in the south-western board."

The man proved to be Scipio, who had been chosen for his expertness to perform the task in question. Placing his cap on the deck, in a reverence far deeper even than that which the seaman usually manifests toward his superior, he lifted the glass in one hand, while with the other he covered the eye for which at that moment he had no particular use. No sooner did the wandering instrument fall on the distant object than he dropped it again, and fastened his look, in a sort of stupid admiration on Wilder.

"Did you see the sail?" demanded the Rover.

"Masser can see him, wid he naked eye."

"Ay, but what do you make of him with the glass?"

"He'm a ship, Sir."

"True. On what course?"

"He got he starboard tacks aboard, Sir."

"Still true. Has he signals abroad?"

"He'm got t'ree new cloths in he main-top-gallant royal, Sir."

"His vessel is all the better for the repairs. Did you see his flags?"

"He'm show no flag, Masser."

"I thought as much myself. Go forward, lad—stay—one often gets a true idea by seeking it where it is not thought to exist. Of what size do you take the stranger to be?"

"He'm just seven hundred and fifty tons, Masser."

"How's this! The tongue of your negro, Mr Wilder, is as exact as a carpenter's rule. The fellow speaks of the size of a vessel that is hull-down, with an air as authoritative as a runner of the King's customs could pronounce on the same, after she had been submitted to the Office admeasurement."

"You will have consideration for the ignorance of the black; men of his unfortunate state are seldom skilful in answering interrogatories."

"Ignorance!" repeated the Rover, glancing his eye, uneasily and with a rapidity peculiar to himself from one to the other, and from both to the rising object in the horizon. "Skilful! I know not. The man has no air of doubt—You think her tonnage precisely that which you have said?"

The large dark eyes of Scipio rolled, in turn, from his new commander to his ancient master, while, for a moment, his faculties appeared to be lost in confusion. But the uncertainty continued only for a moment. He no sooner read the frown that was gathering darkly over the brow of the latter, than the air of confidence with which he had pronounced his former opinion vanished in a look of obstinacy so settled, that one might well have despaired of ever driving or enticing him again to seem to think.

"I ask you, if the stranger may not be a dozen tons larger or smaller than what you just have named?" continued the Rover when he found his former question was not likely to be soon answered.

"He'm just as Masser wish 'em," returned Scipio.

"I wish him a thousand; he will then prove the richer prize."

"I s'pose he'm quite a t'ousand, Sir."

"Or a snug ship of three hundred, if lined with gold might do."

"He look berry just like t'ree hundred."

"To me it seems a brig."

"I t'ink he'm a brig, too, Masser."

"Or possibly, after all, the stranger may prove a schooner, with many lofty and light sails."

"A schooner often carry a royal," returned the black, resolute to acquiesce in all the other said.

"Who knows it is a sail at all! Forward, there! it may be well to have more opinions than one on so weighty a matter. Forward, there! Send the foretop-man that is called Fid upon the poop. Your companions are so intelligent and so faithful, Mr Wilder, that you are not to be surprised, if I show an undue desire for their opinions."

Wilder compressed his lips, and the rest of the groupe manifested a good deal of amazement, but the latter had been too long accustomed to the caprice of their commander, and the former was too wise to speak at a moment when his humour seemed at the highest. The top-man, however, was not long in making his appearance, and then the chief saw fit to pursue his purpose.

"And you think it questionable whether it be a sail at all?" he continued.

"He'm sartain not'ing but a fly-away," returned the obstinate black.

"You hear what your friend the negro says, Master Fid; he thinks that yonder object which is lifting so fast to leeward is not a sail."

As the top-man saw no sufficient reason for concealing his astonishment at this wild opinion, it was manifested with all the embellishments with which the individual in question usually delivered his sentiments. After casting a short glance in the direction of the sail, in order to assure himself there had been no deception, he turned his eyes, in great disgust on Scipio, to vindicate the credit of the association at the expense of some little contempt for the ignorance of his companion.

"What the devil do you take it for, Guinea; a church?"

"I t'ink he'm church, too," responded the acquiescent black.

"Lord help the dark-skinn'd fool! Your honor knows that conscience is d——nably overlooked in Africa, and will not judge the nigger hardly for any little blunder he may make on account of religion. But the fellow is a thorough seaman, and should know a top-gallant-sail from a weathercock. Now look you, S'ip, for the credit of your friends, if you have no great pride on your own behalf just tell his—"

"It is of no account," interrupted the Rover. "Take the glass yourself, and pass an opinion on the sail in sight."

Fid scraped his foot, made a low bow in acknowledgement of the compliment, and then deposing his little tarpauling on the deck of the poop, he very composedly, and as he flattered himself, very understandingly, disposed of his person to take the desired view. The gaze of the topman was far longer than that of his black companion, and it is to be presumed, in consequence much more accurate. Instead, however, of venturing any sudden opinion, when his eye was wearied he lowered the glass, and with it his head, standing long in the attitude of one whose thoughts had received some subject for deep cogitation. During the process of thinking, the weed was rolled diligently over his tongue, and one hand was stuck a-kimbo into his side, as if he would brace all his faculties to support some extraordinary mental effort.

"I wait your opinion," resumed his attentive commander, when he thought sufficient time had been allowed to mature the opinion even of Richard Fid.

"Will your honor just tell me, what day of the month this here may be, and mayhap, at the same time, the day of the week too, if it shouldn't be giving too much trouble?"

His two questions were answered.

"We had the wind at East with Southing, the first day out, and then it chopped in the night, and blew great guns at

North West where it held for the matter of a week. After which there was an Irishman's hurricane, right up and down, for a day. Then we got into these here trades, which have stood as steady as a ship's chaplain over a punch bowl, ever since."

Here the topman closed his soliloquy in order to agitate the tobacco again, it being impossible to conduct the process of chewing and talking at one and the same time.

"What of the stranger?" demanded the Rover, a little impatiently.

"It's no church, that's certain, your Honour," said Fid, very decidedly.

"Has he signals flying?"

"He may be speaking with his flags, but it needs a better scholar than Richard Fid to know what he would say. To my eye there are three new cloths in his main-top-gallant-royal,* but no bunting abroad."

"The man is happy in having so good a sail! Mr Wilder, do *you* too see, the clothes in question?"

"There is certainly something which might be taken for new canvass. I believe I first mistook it, as the sun fell brightest on the sail, for the signals I named."

"Then we are not seen, and may lie quiet for a while, though we enjoy the advantage of measuring the stranger foot by foot, even to the new cloths in his royal!"

The Rover spoke in a manner that was strangely divided between sarcasm and suspicion. He made an impatient gesture to the two seamen to quit the poop. When they were alone, he turned to his silent and respectful officers, continuing in a manner that was grave, while it was conciliatory.

"Gentleman," he said, "our idle time is past, and fortune has at length brought us active service. Whether the ship in sight be of just seven hundred and fifty tons is more than I can pretend to pronounce, but something there is which any

---

*It has been objected to this term, that the sail is called the main-royal. The writer is old enough to remember when seamen always inserted the other word, when they wished to speak with a "full mouth." Main-sail; main-top-sail; main-top-gallant-sail, main-top-gallant-royal, were, and indeed are still, the proper appellations of these sails. "Main-royal" is, beyond dispute, the familiar name now most in use.

seaman may know. By the squareness of her upper yards, the symmetry with which they are trimmed and the press of canvass she bears on the wind, I pronounce her to be a vessel of war. Do any differ from my opinion? Mr Wilder, speak."

"I feel the truth of all your reasons, and think with you."

The shade of distrust, which had gathered over the brow of the Rover during the foregoing scene, lighted a little, as he listened to the direct and frank avowal of his Lieutenant.

"You believe she bears a pennant! I like this manliness of reply. Then comes another question. Shall we fight her?"

To this interrogatory it was not so easy to give a decisive answer. Each Officer consulted the opinions of his comrades, in their eyes, until their leader saw fit to make his application still more personal.

"Now, General, this is a question peculiarly fitted for your wisdom," he resumed; "shall we give battle to a pennant, or shall we spread our wings and fly?"

"My bullies are not drilled to the retreat. Give them any other work to do, and I will answer for their steadiness."

"But shall we adventure without a reason?"

"The Spaniard often sends his bullion home, under cover of a cruiser's guns," observed one of the inferiors who rarely found pleasure in any risk that did not infer its correspondent benefit. "We may feel the stranger; if he carries more than his guns he will betray it, by his reluctance to speak; if poor, we shall find him fierce as a half-fed tiger."

"There is sense in your counsel, Brace, and it shall be regarded. Go then, gentlemen, to your several duties. We'll occupy the half-hour that must pass, before his hull shall rise, in looking to our gear, and overhauling the guns. As it is not decided to fight let what is done be done without display. The people must see no receding from a resolution that is once taken."

They separated, each man preparing to undertake the task that more especially belong'd to the situation he fill'd in the ship. Wilder was retiring with the rest, when a sign kept him on the poop alone with his new confederate.

"The monotony of our lives, is now likely to be interrupted, Mr Wilder," commenced the latter, first glancing his eyes around to make sure they were alone. "I have seen enough of your spirit and steadiness to be sure, that, should accident disable me to conduct the fortunes of these people, my authority will fall into firm and able hands."

"Should such a calamity befall us, I hope it will be found that your expectations are not to be deceived."

"I have confidence, Sir; and where a brave man reposes his confidence, he has a right to hope it will not be abused. Do I speak in reason?"

"I acknowledge the justice of what you say."

"I would, Wilder, that we had known each other earlier— but what matter vain regrets! Those fellows of yours are keen of sight, to note those new cloths so soon!"

" 'Tis just the observation of people of their class. The nicer distinctions, which marked the cruiser came first from yourself."

"And then the seven hundred and fifty tons of the black! It was giving an opinion to a foot."

"It is the quality of ignorance to be positive."

"Very true. Cast an eye at the stranger, and tell me how he comes on."

Wilder obeyed, glad to be relieved from a discourse that he found embarrassing. Many moments were passed before he dropped the glass, during which time not a syllable fell from the lips of his companion. When he turned, however, to deliver the result of his observation, he met an eye, that seem'd to pierce his soul, fastened on his countenance. Coloring high, as if he resented the suspicion betrayed by the act, Wilder closed his half opened lips and continued silent.

"And the ship?" deeply demanded the Rover.

"The ship has already raised her courses; in a few more minutes we shall see the hull."

"It is a swift vessel! She is standing directly for us?"

"I think not. Her head is lying more to the eastward."

"It may be well to make certain of that fact. You are right," he continued after taking a look himself at the approaching cloud of canvass. "You are very right. As yet we are not seen. Forward there! haul down that head stay-sail; we will steady the ship, by her yards. Now let him look with all his eyes; they must be good to see these naked spars at such a distance."

Our adventurer made no reply, assenting to the truth of
what the other had said, by a simple inclination of his head.
They then resumed the walk, to and fro, in their narrow
limits, neither manifesting however any disposition to renew the discourse.

"We are in good condition for the alternative of flight or
combat," the Rover at length, observed, while he cast a rapid
look over the preparations which had been unostentatiously
in progress, from the moment when the officers dispersed.
"Now will I confess, Wilder, a secret pleasure in the belief
that yonder audacious fool carries the boasted commission of
the German who wears the Crown of Britain! Should he
prove more than man may dare attempt, I will flout him,
though prudence shall check any further attempts, and should
he prove an equal—would it not gladden your eyes, to see St.
George come drooping to the water?"

"I thought that men in our pursuit left honor to silly heads,
and that we seldom struck a blow that was not intended to
ring on a metal more precious than iron."

" 'Tis the character the world gives us; but I for one, would
rather lower the pride of the minions of King George, than
possess the power of unlocking his treasury. Said I well, General?" he added, as the individual he named approached. "Said
I well, in asserting there was glorious pleasure in making a
pennant trail upon the sea?"

"We fight for victory," returned the martinet. "I am ready
to engage, at a minute's notice."

"Prompt and decided as a soldier. Now tell me, General, if
Fortune, or chance, or Providence, whichever of the powers
you may acknowledge for a leader, were to give you the
option of enjoyments, in what would you find your deepest
satisfaction?"

The soldier seemed to ruminate.

"I have often thought that were I commander of things on
Earth, I should, backed by a dozen of my stoutest bullies,
charge at the door of that cave which was entered by the
tailor's boy, him they call Aladdin."

"The genuine aspirations of a freebooter! In such a case the
magic trees would soon be disburthened of their fruit. Still it
might prove an inglorious victory, since incantations and

charms are the weapons of the combatants. Call you honor nothing?"

"Hum. I fought for honor half of a reasonably long life, and found myself as light at the close of all my dangers as at the beginning. Honor and I have shaken hands, unless it be the honor of coming off conqueror. I have a strong disgust of defeat, but am always ready to sell the mere honor of the victory cheap."

"Well, let it pass. The quality of the service is much the same find the motive where you will. How now! who has dared to let yonder top-gallant-sail fly?"

The startling change in the voice of the Rover caused all within hearing of his words to tremble. Deep, anxious and threatening displeasure was in its tones, and each man cast his eyes upwards, to see on whose devoted head the weight of the dreaded indignation of their chief was likely to fall. As there was little but naked spars and tightened ropes to obstruct the view, all became, at the same instant apprised of the truth. Fid was standing on the head of that top-mast which belonged to the particular portion of the vessel where he was stationed, and the sail in question was fluttering, with all its gear loosened, far and high in the wind. His hearing had probably been drowned by the heavy flapping of the canvass, for instead of lending his ears to the powerful call just mentioned, he rather stood contemplating his work, than exhibiting any anxiety as to the effect it might produce on the minds of those beneath him. But a second warning came in tones too terrible to be any longer disregarded by ears even as dull as those of the offender.

"By whose order have you dared to loosen the sail?" demanded the Rover.

"By the order of King Wind, your honor. The best seaman, must give in, when a squall gets the upper hand."

"Furl it! away aloft and furl it!" shouted the excited leader. "Roll it up, and send the fellow down who has been so bold as to own any authority but my own in this ship, though it were that of a hurricane."

A dozen nimble top-men ascended to the assistance of Fid. In another minute the unruly canvass was secured, and Richard himself was on his way to the poop. During this brief interval the brow of the Rover was dark and angry as the surface of the element on which he lived, when blackened by the tempest. Wilder, who had never before seen his new commander thus excited, began to tremble for the fate of his old comrade, and drew nigher, as the latter approached, to intercede in his favor, should the circumstances seem to require such an interposition.

"And why is this?" the still stern and angry captain demanded of the offender. "Why is it that you, whom I have had such recent reason to applaud should dare to let fall a sail, at a moment when it is important to keep the ship naked?"

"Your Honour will admit that his rations sometimes slips through the best man's fingers, and why not a bit of canvass?" deliberately returned the delinquent. "If I took a turn too many of the gasket off the yard, it is a fault I am ready to answer for."

"You say true, and dearly shall you pay the forfeit. Take him to the gangway and let him make acquaintance with the cat."

"No new acquaintance, your Honor, seeing that we have met before, and that too for matters which I had reason to hide my head for; whereas here will be many blows but little shame."

"May I intercede in behalf of the offender?" interrupted Wilder with earnestness and haste. "He is often blundering, but rarely would he err, had he as much knowledge as good will."

"Say nothing about it, Master Harry," returned the topman, with a peculiar glance of his eye. "The sail has been flying finely, and it is now too late to deny it, and so I suppose the fact must be scored on the back of Richard Fid, as you would put any other misfortune into the log."

"I would he might be pardoned. I can venture to promise in his name, 'twill be the last offence."

"Let it be forgotten," returned the Rover, struggling to conquer his passion. "I will not disturb our harmony at such a moment, Mr Wilder, by refusing so small a boon, but you need not be told to what evil such negligence might lead. Give me the glass again. I will see if the fluttering canvass has escaped the eye of the stranger."

The topman bestowed a stolen but exulting glance on Wilder, when the latter motioned the other hastily away, turning himself to join his Commander in the examination.

# Chapter XXVI

"As I am an honest man, he looks pale: Art thou sick, or angry?"
*Much Ado About Nothing*, V.i.130−31.

THE APPROACH of the strange sail was now becoming rapidly more and more visible to the naked eye. The little speck of white, which had first been seen on the margin of the sea, resembling some gull floating on the summit of a wave, had gradually arisen during the last half-hour, until a tall pyramid of canvass was reared on the water. As Wilder bent his looks again on this growing object, the Rover put a glass into his hands, with an expression which the other understood to say, "You may perceive that the carelessness of your dependant has betrayed us!" Still the look was one rather of regret than of reproach, nor did a single syllable of the tongue confirm the language of the eye. On the contrary, it would seem that his commander was anxious to preserve their recent amicable compact inviolate. For when the young mariner, attempted an awkward explanation of the probable causes of the blunder of Fid, he was met by a quiet gesture, which said in a sufficiently intelligible language, that the offence was pardoned.

"Our neighbor keeps a keen look out, as you may see," observed the other. "He has tacked, and is laying boldly up across our fore-foot. Well, let him come on, we shall soon get a look at his battery, and then may we come to our conclusion as to the nature of the intercourse we are to hold."

"If you permit the stranger to near us, it might be difficult to throw him out of the chase, when we should be glad to get rid of him."

"It must be a fast going vessel to which the Dolphin cannot spare a top-gallant sail."

"I know not, Sir. The sail in sight is swift on the wind, and it is to be believed that she is no duller off. I have rarely known a vessel rise so rapidly, as she has done, since we first made her."

The youth spoke with such earnestness as to draw the

attention of his companion from the object he was studying to the countenance of the speaker.

"Mr Wilder," he said, quickly and with an air of decision, "you know the ship."

"I'll not deny it. If my opinion be true, she will be found too heavy for the Dolphin, and a vessel that offers little inducement for us to attempt to carry."

"Her size?—"

"You heard it from the black."

"Your followers know her also?"

"It would be difficult to deceive a top man in the cut and trim of sails, among which he has passed months, nay, years."

"Ha! I understand the new cloths in her top-gallant-royal! Mr Wilder, your departure from that vessel has been recent."

"As my arrival in this."

The Rover continued silent for several minutes. His companion made no offer to disturb his meditations, though the furtive glances he often cast in the direction of the other betrayed some little anxiety for the result of his own frank avowal.

"And her guns?" his commander at length abruptly demanded.

"She numbers four more than the Dolphin."

"The metal?—"

"Is still heavier. In every particular she is a ship a size above your own."

"Doubtless she is the property of the King?"

"She is."

"She shall change masters. By heaven, she shall be mine."

Wilder shook his head, answering only with an incredulous smile.

"You doubt it. Come hither and look upon that deck. Tell me, can he, whom you so lately quitted muster fellows like these?"

The crew of the Dolphin had been chosen by one who thoroughly understood the character of a seaman, from among all the different people of the Christian world. There was not a maritime nation in Europe which had not its representative among that band of turbulent and desperate spirits. Even the descendant of the aboriginal possessors of America had been made to abandon the habits and opinions of his progenitors, to become a wanderer on that element which had laved the shores of his native land for ages without exciting a wish to penetrate its mysteries in the bosoms of his simple minded ancestry. All had been suited by lives of wild adventure on the two elements for their present lawless pursuits, and directed by the mind which had known how to obtain and to continue its despotic ascendancy over their efforts they truly formed a most dangerous and, considering their numbers, a resistless crew. Their commander smiled, in exultation, as he watched the evident reflection with which his companion contemplated the indifference or fierce joy, which different individuals among them exhibited at the appearance of an approaching conflict. Even the rawest of their numbers, the luckless waisters and after-guard, were as confident of victory as those whose audacity might plead the apology of uniform and often-repeated success.

"Count you these for nothing?" asked the Rover, at the elbow of his Lieutenant after allowing him time to embrace the whole of the grim band with his eye. "See, here is a Dane, ponderous and steady as the gun, at which I shall shortly place him—you may cut him limb from limb, and yet he will stand like a tower until the last stone of the foundation has been sapped. And here we have his neighbors the Swede and the Russ, fit companions for managing the same piece, which I'll answer shall not be silent, while a man of them all is left to apply a match or handle a spunge. Yonder is a square built athletic mariner from one of the free towns; he prefers our liberty to that of his native city; and you shall find that the venerable Hanseatic institutions shall give way, sooner than he be known to quit the spot I give him to defend. Here you see a brace of Englishmen, and though they come from the island that I love so little, better men at need, will not be often found. Feed them and flog them, and I pledge myself to their swaggering and their courage. D'ye see, that thoughtful looking, bony miscreant, that has a look of godliness in the midst of his villany? That fellow fished for herring till he got a taste of beef, when his stomach revolted at its ancient fare, and then the ambition of becoming rich got uppermost. He is a Scot, from one of the lochs of the north."

"Will he fight?"

"For money, the honor of the Macs, and his religion. He is a reasoning animal, after all, and one I like to have on my own side in a quarrel. Ah! yonder is the boy, for a charge. I once told him to cut a rope in a hurry, and he severed it above his head instead of beneath his feet, taking a flight from a lower yard into the sea, in reward of the exploit. But then he always extols his presence of mind in not drowning! Now are his ideas in a hot ferment, and if the truth could be known, I would wager a handsome venture, that the sail in sight, is by some mysterious process, magnified to six in his fertile fancy."

"He must be thinking then of escape."

"Far from it: he is rather plotting the means of surrounding them with the Dolphin. To your true Hibernian, escape is the last idea that gives him an uneasy moment. You see that pensive looking, sallow fellow at his elbow. That is a man who will fight with a sort of sentiment. There is a touch of chivalry in him, which might be worked into heroism, if one had but the opportunity and the inclination. As it is, he will not fail to show a spark of the true Castilian. His companion has come from the rock of Lisbon; I should trust him unwillingly, did I not know, that little opportunity of taking pay from the enemy is given here. Ah! here is a lad for a dance of a Sunday! You see him, at this moment, with feet and tongue going together. That's a creature of contradictions. He wants for neither wit nor good-nature, but still he might cut your throat on an occasion. There is a strange medley of ferocity and bonhommie, about the animal. I shall put him among the boarders, for we shall not be at blows a minute, before his impatience will be for carrying every thing by a coup de main."

"And who is the seaman at his elbow that is apparently occupied in divesting his person of some superfluous garments?" demanded Wilder, irresistibly attracted by the manner of the Rover to pursue the subject.

"An economical Dutchman. He calculates that it is just as wise to be killed in an old jacket as in a new one, and has probably said as much to his Gascon neighbor who is however, resolved to die decently, if die he must. The former has

happily commenced his preparations for the combat in good
season, or the enemy might defeat us before he would be in
readiness. Did it rest between these two worthies to decide
this quarrel, the mercurial Frenchman would defeat his neighbor of Zeeland before the latter believed the battle had commenced, but should he let the happy moment pass, rely on it
the Dutchman would give him trouble. Forget you, Wilder,
that the day has been, when the countrymen of that slow-
moving and heavy moulded fellow swept the narrow seas
with a broom at their mast-heads!"

The Rover smiled wildly as he spoke, and what he said, he
uttered bitterly. To his companion, however, there appeared
no such grounds of unnatural exultation in recalling the success of a foreign enemy, and he was content to assent to the
truth of the historical fact with a simple inclination of his
head. As if he even found pain in this tacit confession, and
would gladly be rid of the mortifying reflection altogether, he
rejoined in some apparent haste —

"You have overlooked the two tall seamen, who are making
out the rig of the stranger with so much gravity of observation."

"Ay, those are men who come from a land in which we
both feel some interest. The sea is not more unstable than are
those rogues in their knavery. Their minds are but half made
up to piracy—'tis a coarse word, Mr Wilder, but I fear we
earn it. But these rascals make a reservation of grace in the
midst of all their villainy."

"They regard the stranger as if they saw reason to distrust
the wisdom of letting him approach so near."

"Ah! they are renowned calculators. I fear they have detected the four supernumerary guns you mentioned, for their
vision seems supernatural in affairs which touch their interests. But you see there is brawn and sinew in the fellows, and
what is better there are heads which teach them to turn these
advantages to account."

"You think they fail in spirit."

"Hum—it might be dangerous to try it, on any point they
deem material. They are no quarrellers about words, and seldom lose sight of certain musty maxims which they pretend
come from a volume that I fear you and I, do not study too

intently. It is not often that they strike a blow for mere chivalry; and were they so inclined, the rogues are too much disposed to logic to mistake, like your black, the Dolphin for a church. Still if they see reason, in their puissant judgements to engage, mark me, should they see reason—the two guns they command will do better service than all the rest of the battery. Should they think otherwise, it would occasion no surprise were I to receive a proposition to spare the powder for some more profitable adventure. Honor, forsooth! The miscreants are too well practised in polemics to mistake the point of honor in a pursuit like ours! But we chatter of trifles when it is time to think of serious things. Mr Wilder, we will now shew our canvass."

The manner of the Rover changed as suddenly as his language. Losing the air of sarcastic levity in which he had been indulging in a mien better suited to maintain the authority he wielded, he walked aside, while his subordinate proceeded to issue the orders necessary to enforce his commands. Nightingale sounded the usual summons, lifting his hoarse voice in the cry of "All hands make sail, ahoy!"

Until now the people of the Dolphin had made their observations on the sail, that was growing so rapidly above the waters, according to their several humours. Some had exulted in the prospect of a capture; others, more practised in the ways of their commander had deemed the probability of their coming in collision at all with the stranger as a point far from settled, while a few, more accustomed to reflection, shook their heads as the stranger drew nigher, as if they believed he was already within a distance that might be attended with too much hazard. Still, as they were ignorant alike of those secret sources of information which their chief had so frequently proved he possessed to an extent that often seemed miraculous, the whole were content patiently to await his decision. But when the cry above mentioned was heard, it was answered by an activity so general and so cheerful as to prove it was entirely welcome. Order now followed order from the mouth of Wilder, in quick succession, he being, in virtue of his station, the proper executive officer for the moment.

As both Lieutenant and crew appeared animated by the same spirit, it was not long before the naked spars of the

Dolphin were clothed in vast volumes of snow-white canvass. Sail had fallen after sail, and yard after yard had been raised to the summit of its mast, until the vessel bow'd before the breeze, rolling to and fro, but still held stationary by the position of her yards. When all was in readiness to proceed on whichever course might be deemed necessary, Wilder ascended, again to the poop, in order to announce the fact to his superior. He found the Rover attentively considering the stranger, whose hull had, by this time, risen out of the sea, exhibiting a long, dotted yellow line, which the eye of every man in the ship, well knew to contain the ports where the guns that marked her particular force were to be sought. Mrs Wyllys, unaccompanied by Gertrude stood nigh, thoughtful, as usual, but permitting no occurrence of the slightest moment to escape her vigilance.

"We are ready to gather way on the ship," said Wilder. "We wait merely for the course."

The Rover started, and drew closer to his subordinate. Looking him full and intently in the eye, he said, —

"You are certain that you know that vessel, Mr Wilder."

"Certain."

"It is a Royal cruiser?" said the Governess, with the swiftness of thought.

"It is. I have already pronounced her to be so."

"Mr Wilder," resumed the Rover, "we will try her speed. Let the courses fall, and fill your forward sails."

The young mariner made an acknowledgement of obedience and proceeded with alacrity to execute the wishes of his commander. There was an eagerness, and perhaps a trepidation, in the voice of Wilder as he issued the necessary orders, that was in remarkable contrast to the deep toned calmness which characterised the utterance of the Rover. The unusual intonations did not entirely escape the ears of some of the elder seamen, and looks of peculiar meaning, were exchanged among them, as they paused to catch his words. But obedience followed these unwonted sounds, as it had been accustomed to succeed the more imposing utterance of their own long-dreaded chief. The head yards were swung; the sails were distended with the breeze, and the mass which had so long been inert, began to divide the waters, as it heavily overcame the state of rest in which it had reposed. The ship soon attained its velocity, and then the contest between the two rival vessels became of engrossing interest.

By this time the stranger was within a half league, directly under the lee of the Dolphin. Closer and more accurate observation had satisfied every eye in the latter ship, of the force and character of their neighbor. The rays of a bright sun fell clear upon her broadside, while the shadow of her sails was thrown across the waters, in a direction opposite to their own. There were moments when the eye, aided by the glass, could penetrate through the open ports, into the interior of the hull, catching fleeting and delusory glimpses of the movements within. A few human forms were distinctly visible in different parts of her rigging, but in all other respects the repose of high order and perfect discipline was discernible on all about her.

When the Rover heard the sounds of the parted waters, and saw the little jets of spray that the bows of his own gallant ship cast before her, he signed to his Lieutenant to ascend to the place, which he still occupied on the poop. For many minutes his eye was on the strange sail, in close and intelligent contemplation of her powers.

"Mr Wilder," he at length said, speaking like one whose doubts on some perplexing point were finally removed, "I have seen that cruiser before."

"It is probable; she has roamed over most of the waters of the Atlantic."

"Ay, this is not the first of our meetings! A little paint has changed her exterior, but I think I know the manner in which they have stepped her masts."

"They are thought to rake more than is usual."

"They are thought to do it, with reason. Did you serve long aboard her?"

"Years."

"And you left her—"

"To join you."

"Tell me, Wilder, did they treat you too as one of an inferior order! Ha! Was your merit called Provincial; did they read America in all you did?"

"I left her, Capt. Heidegger."

"Ay, they gave you reason. For once they have done me an act of kindness—but you were in her, during the equinox of March?"

Wilder made a slight bow of assent.

"I thought as much—and you fought a stranger in the gale? Winds, ocean and man were all at work together!"

"It is true. We knew you, and thought for a time, that your hour had come."

"I like your frankness. We have sought each other's lives, like men, and we shall prove the truer friends, now that amity is established between us. I will not ask you further of that adventure, Wilder, for favor in my service, is not to be bought by treachery to that you have quitted. It is sufficient that you now sail under my flag."

"What is that flag?" demanded a mild firm voice at his elbow.

The Rover turned suddenly, and met the rivetted, calm and searching eye of the Governess. The gleamings of some strangely contradictory passions crossed his features, and then his countenance changed to that look of bland courtesy which he most affected, when addressing his captives.

"Here is a female reminding two old mariners of their duty!" he exclaimed. "We have forgotten the civility of showing the stranger our bunting. Let it be set, Mr Wilder, that we omit none of the observances of nautical etiquette."

"The ship in sight carries a naked gaft—"

"No matter. We shall be foremost in courtesy. Let the colours be shown."

Wilder opened the little locker which contained the flags most in use, but hesitated which to select, out of a dozen that lay in large rolls within the different compartments.

"I hardly know which of these ensigns it is your pleasure to show," he said, in a manner that appeared sufficiently like putting a question.

"Try him with the heavy moulded Dutchman. The Commander of so noble a ship should understand all Christian tongues."

The Lieutenant made a sign to the quarter master on duty, and in another minute the flag of the United Provinces was waving at the peak of the Dolphin. The two Officers narrowly watched its effect on the stranger, who refused however to make any answering sign to the false signal they had just exhibited.

"The stranger sees we have a hull that was never made for the shoals of Holland. Perhaps he knows us?" said the Rover, glancing at the same time a look of inquiry at his companion.

"I think not. Paint is too freely used in the Dolphin for even her friends to be certain of her countenance."

"She is a coquettish ship, we will allow. Try him with the Portuguese; let us see if Brazil diamonds have favor in his eyes."

The colours, already set, were lowered and, in their place the emblem of the house of Braganza was loosened to the breeze. Still the stranger pursued his course in sullen inattention, eating closer and closer into the wind, as it is termed in nautical language, in order to lessen the distance between him and his chase as much as possible.

"An ally cannot move him," said the Rover. "Now let him see the taunting drapeau blanc!"

Wilder complied in silence. The flag of Portugal was hauled to the deck, and, in its place, the white field of France was given to the air. The ensign had hardly fluttered in its elevated position, before a broad, glossy blazonry rose like some enormous bird taking wing, from the deck of the stranger, and opened its folds, in graceful waves at his gaft. At the same instant a column of smoke issued from his bows, and had sailed backward through his rigging, ere the report of the gun of defiance found its way against the fresh breeze of the trades to the ears of the Dolphin's crew.

"So much for national amity!" dryly observed the Rover. "He is mute to the Dutchman, and to the crown of Braganza, but the very bile is stirred within him at the sight of a table cloth! Let him contemplate the colours he loves so little, Mr. Wilder; when we are tired of showing them, our lockers will furnish another."

It would seem however that the sight of the flag which the Rover now chose to bear, produced some such effect on his neighbour as the muleta of the nimble banderillero is known to excite in the enraged bull. Sundry smaller sails which could do but little good, but which answered the purpose of appearing to wish to quicken his speed, were instantly set aboard the stranger, and not a brace, or a bowline, was suffered to escape without an additional pull. In short he wore the air of the courser who receives the useless blows of the jockey, when already at the top of his speed, and when any further excitement is as fruitless as his own additional exertions. Still there seemed but little use in these efforts. By this time the two vessels were fairly trying their powers of sailing and with no visible advantage in favor of either. Although the Dolphin was renowned for her speed, the stranger manifested no inferiority that the keenest scrutiny might detect. The ship of the freebooter was already bending to the breeze, and the jets of spray before her were cast still higher and further in advance; but each impulse of the wind was equally felt by the stranger and her movement over the heaving waters seemed to be as rapid and as graceful as that of her rival.

"Yonder ship parts the water as a swallow cuts the air," observed the chief of the freebooters to the youth, who still kept at his elbow, endeavouring to conceal an uneasiness which was increasing at each instant. "Has she a name for speed?"

"The curlew is scarcely faster. Are we not already nigh enough, for men who cruise with commissions no better than our own pleasure?"

The Rover glanced a look of impatient suspicion at the countenance of his companion, but its expression changed to a smile of haughty audacity, as he answered—

"Let him equal the eagle in his highest and swiftest flight, he shall find us no laggards on the wing. Why this reluctance to be within a mile of a vessel of the crown?"

"Because I know her force and the hopeless character of a contest with an enemy so superior," returned Wilder, firmly. "Capt. Heidegger, you cannot fight yonder ship with success and unless instant use be made of the distance which still exists between us, you cannot escape her. Indeed I know not but it is already too late to attempt the latter."

"Such, Sir, is the opinion of one who overrates the powers of his enemy because use and much talking have taught him to reverence them as something more than human. Mr Wilder, none are so daring, or so modest, as those who have long been accustomed to place their dependance on their own exertions. I have been nigher to a flag even, and yet you see I continue to keep on 'this mortal coil.' "

"Hark! 'tis a drum. The stranger is going to his guns."

The Rover listened a moment, and was able to catch the well known beat, which calls the people of a vessel of war to their quarters. First casting a glance upward at his sails, and then throwing a general and critical look on all and every thing which came within the influence of his command, he calmly answered—

"We will imitate his example. Mr Wilder, let the order be given."

Until now the crew of the Dolphin had either been occupied in such necessary duties as precede an action, or were gazing at the strange ship. The low, but continued hum of voices, sounds such as discipline permitted, had afforded the only evidence of the interest they took in the scene, but, the instant the first tap on the drum was heard, each groupe severed, and every man repaired with bustling activity to his well known post. The stir among the crew was but of a moment's continuance; it was succeeded by the breathing stillness, which has already been noticed in our pages, on a similar occasion. The officers, however, were seen making hasty but strict inquiries into the conditions of their several commands, while the munitions of war, that were drawn from their places of deposit announced a preparation more serious than ordinary. The Rover himself, had disappeared, but it was not long before he was again seen, at his elevated look-out, accoutred for the conflict that appeared to approach, and employed as ever in studying the properties, the force and the evolutions of his advancing antagonist. Those who knew him best, however, saw that the question of combat was not yet decided in his mind, and many eager glances were thrown in the direction of his eye, as if to penetrate the mystery in which he chose to conceal his purpose. He had thrown aside the sea-cap, and stood with his fair hair blowing about a brow that seem'd formed to give birth to thoughts far nobler than those which apparently had occupied his life, while a species of leathern helmet lay at his feet, the garniture of which, was of a nature to lend an unnatural fierceness to the countenance of its wearer. Whenever this boarding-cap was worn, all in the ship were given to understand that the moment of serious strife was at hand. But as yet that never failing evidence of the hostile intention of their leader was unnoticed.

In the mean time each Officer had examined into, and reported the state of his division, and then, by a sort of implied permission on the part of their superiors, the death-like calm which had hitherto reigned among the people was allowed to be broken, by suppressed but earnest discourse; the calculating chief permitting this departure from the usual rules of more regular cruisers, in order to come at the temper of the crew on which so much of the success of his desperate enterprises so frequently depended.

# Chapter XXVII

—"For he made me mad,
To see him shine so brisk, and smell so sweet,
And talk so like a waiting gentlewoman."—
*I Henry IV*, I.iii.53–55.

THE MOMENT was one of high and earnest excitement. Each individual charged with a portion of the subordinate authority of the ship, had examined into the state of his command with the care which always deepens as responsibility draws nigher to the proofs of having been worthily bestowed. The voice of the harsh master had ceased to inquire into the state of those several ropes and chains that were deemed vital to the safety of the vessel; each chief of a battery had assured and re-assured himself that his artillery was ready for the most effective service, extra ammunition had already issued from its dark and secret repository and even the hum of dialogue had ceased in the all absorbing interest of the scene. Still the quick and ever-changing glance of the Rover could detect no reason to distrust the firmness of his people. They were grave as are ever the bravest and steadiest in the hour of trial, but their gravity was mingled with no signs of concern. It seemed rather like the effect of desperate and concentrated resolution such as braces the human mind to efforts which exceed the ordinary daring of martial enterprise. To this satisfactory exhibition of the humour of his crew the wary and sagacious leader saw but three exceptions. They were found in the persons of his Lieutenant and his two remarkable associates.

It has been seen that the bearing of Wilder was not altogether such as became one of his rank in a moment of great trial. The keen, jealous glances of the Rover studied and re-studied his manner, without arriving at any conclusion as to its cause. The colour was as fresh on the cheeks of the youth and his limbs were as firm as in the hours of entire security but the unsettled wandering of his eye, and an air of doubt and indecision which pervaded a mien that ought to display qualities so opposite, gave his commander concern. As if to find an explanation of the enigma in the deportment of the associates of Wilder, his look turned to the persons of Fid and the negro. They were both stationed at the piece nearest to the place he himself occupied, the former filling the station of captain of the gun.

The ribs of the ship itself were not firmer in their places than was the attitude of the topman, as he occasionally squinted along the massive iron tube over which he was placed in command, nor was that familiar and paternal care which distinguishes the seaman's interest in his particular trust wanting in his manner. Still an air of broad and inexplicable surprise had possession of his rugged lineaments and as his look wandered from the countenance of Wilder to their adversary, it was not difficult to discover that he marvelled to find the two in opposition. He neither commented on, nor complained however of an occurrence he evidently found so extraordinary, but appeared perfectly disposed to pursue the spirit of that well known maxim of the mariner which teaches the obedient tar "to obey orders though he break owners." Every portion of the athletic form of the negro was motionless except his eyes. These large, jet-black orbs, however, rolled incessantly like the more dogmatic organs of the top man, from Wilder to the strange sail, seeming to drink in fresh draughts of astonishment at each new look.

Struck by these evident manifestations of some extraordinary and yet common sentiment between the two, the Rover profited by his own position, and the distance of the Lieutenant, to address them. Leaning over the slight rail that separated the break of the poop from the quarter deck, he said in that familiar manner which the commander is most wont to use to his inferiors when their services are becoming of the greatest importance,—

"I hope, Master Fid, they have put you at a gun to your liking?"

"There is not a smoother bore, nor a wider mouth in the ship, your honor, than these of 'Blazing Billy's,'" returned the top-man, giving the subject of his commendations an affectionate slap. "All I ask is, a clean sponge and a tight wad. Guinea, score a foul anchor, in your own fashion on a half dozen of the shot, and after the matter is over, they who live through it, may go aboard the enemy and see in what manner Richard Fid has planted his seed."

"You are not new in action, Master Fid?"

"Lord bless your honor, gun powder is no more than dry tobacco in my nostrils! Thof I will say"—

"You were going to add"—

"That sometimes I find myself shifted over in these here affairs," returned the top-man, glancing his eye first at the flag of France and then at the distant emblem of England, "like a jib-boom rigged abaft for a jury to the spanker. I suppose Master Harry has it all in his pocket, in black and white, but this much I will say, that if I must throw stones I should rather see them break a neighbour's crockery than that of my own mother. I say, Guinea, score a couple more of the shot since if the play is to be acted, I've a mind the Blazing Billy should do something creditable for the honor of her good name."

The Rover drew back thoughtful and silent. He caught a look from Wilder, whom he again beckoned to approach.

"Mr Wilder," he said, in a tone of kindness, "I comprehend your feelings. All have not offended alike in yonder vessel, and you would rather your service against that haughty flag should commence with some other ship. There is little else but empty honor to be gained in the conflict—in tenderness to your feelings I will avoid it."

"It is too late," said Wilder with a melancholy shake of the head.

"You shall see your error. The experiment may cost us a broadside, but it shall succeed. Go; descend with our guests to a place of safety; by the time you return, the scene will have undergone a change."

Wilder eagerly disappeared in the cabin, whither Mrs. Wyllys had already withdrawn and after communicating the intentions of his commander to avoid an action, he conducted them into the depths of the vessel in order that no casualty might arrive to embitter his recollections of the hour. This grateful duty promptly and solicitously performed, our adventurer again sought the deck with the velocity of thought.

Notwithstanding his absence had seemed but a moment the scene had indeed changed in all its hostile images. In place of the flag of France, he found the ensign of England floating at the peak of the Dolphin, and a quick and intelligible exchange of signals in active operation between the two vessels. Of all that cloud of canvass which had so lately borne down the vessel of the Rover, her topsails alone remained distended to the yards; the remainder was hanging in festoons, and fluttering loosely before a favorable breeze. The ship itself was running directly for the stranger, who in turn was sullenly securing his lofty sails, like one who was disappointed in a high prized and expected object.

"Now is yon fellow sorry to believe him a friend whom he had lately supposed an enemy," said the Rover, directing the attention of his Lieutenant to the confiding manner with which their neighbour suffered himself to be deceived by his surreptitiously obtained signals. "It is a tempting offer but I pass it, Wilder, for your sake."

The gaze of the Lieutenant seemed bewildered, but he made no reply. Indeed little time was given for deliberation, or discourse. The Dolphin rolled swiftly along her briny path, and each moment dissipated the mist in which distance had enveloped the lesser objects on board the stranger. Guns, blocks, ropes, bolts, men and even features became visible, in rapid succession, as the water that divided them was parted by the bows of the lawless ship. In a few minutes, the stranger, having secured most of his lighter canvass, came sweeping up to the wind and then as his after-sails, squared for the purpose, took the breeze on their outer surface, the mass of his hull became stationary.

The people of the Dolphin had so far imitated the confiding credulity of the deceived cruiser of the Crown, as to furl all their lofty duck, each man employed in the service trusting implicitly to the discretion and daring of the singular being whose pleasure it was to bring their ship into so hazardous a proximity to a powerful enemy; qualities that had been known to avail them in circumstances of even greater delicacy than those in which they were now placed. With this air of audacious confidence the dreaded rover came gliding down upon her unsuspecting neighbour, until within a few hundred feet of her weather beam, when she too, with a graceful curve in her course, bore up against the breeze and came to a state of rest. But Wilder, who regarded all the movements of his superior in silent amazement, was not slow in observing that the head of the Dolphin was laid a different way from that of the other, and that her progress had been arrested by the counteracting position of her head yards, a circumstance that afforded the advantage of a quicker command of the ship should there be need to require a sudden recourse to the guns.

The Dolphin was still drifting slowly under the influence of her recent motion, when the customary hoarse and nearly unintelligible summons, came over the water demanding her appellation and character. The Rover applied his trumpet to his lips with a glance directed towards his Lieutenant, and returned the name of a ship, in the service of the King, that was known to be of the size and force of his own vessel.

"Ay, ay," returned a voice from the other ship, " 'twas so I made out your signals."

The hail was then reciprocated, and the name of the Royal cruiser given in return, followed by an invitation from her commander to visit his superior.

Thus far no more had occurred than was usual between seamen in the same service but the affair was rapidly arriving at a point that most men would have found too embarrassing for further deception. Still the observant eye of Wilder detected no hesitation or doubt in the manner of his chief. The beat of the drum was heard from the cruiser, announcing the "retreat from quarters;" and with perfect composure he directed the same signal to be given for his own people to retire from their guns. In short, five minutes established every appearance of entire confidence and amity between two vessels which would have soon been at deadly strife had the true character of one been known to the other. In this state of the doubtful game he played, and with the invitation still ringing in the ears of Wilder, the Rover motioned his Lieutenant to his side.

"You hear that I am desired to visit my senior in the service of his majesty," he said, smiling ironically. "Is it your pleasure to be of the party?"

The start with which Wilder received this hardy proposal was far too natural to proceed from any counterfeited emotion.

"You are not so mad as to run the risk!" he exclaimed when words were at command.

"If you fear for yourself, I can go alone."

"Fear!" echoed the youth, a bright flush giving an additional glow to the flashing of his kindling eyes. "It is not fear, Capt. Heidegger, but prudence that tells me to keep concealed. My presence would betray the character of this ship. You forget that I am known to all in yonder cruiser."

"I had indeed forgotten that portion of the plot. Then remain, while I go to play upon the credulity of his Majesty's captain."

Without waiting for an answer, the Rover led the way below, signing for his companion to follow. A few moments sufficed to arrange the fair golden locks that imparted such a look of youth and vivacity to the countenance of the former. The undress, fanciful frock, he wore in common, was exchanged for the attire of one of his assumed rank and service, which had been made to fit his person with the nicest care and with a coxcombical attention to the proportions of his really fine person; and in all other things was he speedily equipped for the disguise he chose to affect. No sooner were these alterations completed, and they were effected with a brevity and readiness that manifested much practice in similar artifices, than he disposed himself to proceed on the intended experiment.

"Truer and quicker eyes have been deceived," he coolly observed, turning his glance from a mirror to the countenance of his lieutenant, "than those which embellish the rugged countenance of Captain Bignall."

"You know him then?"

"Mr Wilder, my business imposes the necessity of knowing much that other men overlook. Now is this adventure, which by your features I perceive you deem so forlorn, in its hopes of success, one of easy atchievement. I am convinced that not an officer or man on board the Dart has ever seen the ship whose name I have chosen to usurp. She is too fresh from the stocks to incur that risk. Then there is little probability that I, in my other self, shall be compelled to acknowledge acquaintance with any of her officers, for you well know that years have passed since your late ship has been in Europe, and, by running your eye over these books, you will perceive I am that favoured mortal the son of a Lord, and have not only grown into command, but into manhood, since her departure from home."

"These are certainly favouring circumstances, and such as I had not the sagacity to detect; but why incur the risk at all?"

"Why! Perhaps there is a deep laid scheme to learn if the prize would repay the loss of her capture, perhaps it is only my humour. There is fearful excitement in the adventure."

"And there is fearful danger."

"I never count the price of these enjoyments. Wilder," he added, turning to him with a look of frank and courteous confidence, "I place life and honour in your keeping; for to me it would be dishonor to desert the interests of my crew."

"The trust shall be respected," repeated our adventurer in a tone so deep and choaked as to be nearly unintelligible.

Regarding the countenance of his companion intently for an instant, the Rover smiled as if he approved of the pledge, waved his hand in adieu, and turning, was about to leave the cabin. But a third form at that moment caught his wandering glance. Laying a hand lightly on the shoulder of the boy, whose form was placed somewhat obtrusively in his way, he demanded a little sternly—

"Roderick, what means this preparation?"

"To follow my master, to the boat."

"Boy, thy service is not needed."

"It is rarely wanted, of late."

"Why should I add unnecessarily to the risk of lives, when no good can attend the hazard?"

"In risking your own, you risk all to me."

The answer was given in a tone so resigned and yet so faltering, that the tremulous and nearly smothered sounds caught no ears but those for whom they were intended.

The Rover for a time replied not. His hand still kept its place on the shoulder of the boy, whose working features he read, as the eye is sometimes wont to penetrate the mysteries of the heart.

"Roderick," he said, in a milder, and a kinder voice, "your lot shall be mine. We will go together."

Dashing his hand hastily across his brow, the wayward

chief, ascended the ladder, attended by the lad, and followed
by the individual in whose faith he reposed so great a trust.
The step with which the Rover trod the deck was firm and
the bearing of his form as steady as if he felt no hazard in his
undertaking. His look passed, with a seaman's care, from sail
to sail; not a brace, yard or bowline escaped the quick glances
he cast about him, before he proceeded to the side. At length
he entered a boat which he had ordered to be in waiting. A
glimmering of distrust and hesitation was now, for the first
time discoverable through the decision of his features. For a
moment, his foot lingered on the ladder. "Davis," he said
sternly, speaking to the individual whom, by experience, he
knew to be well practised in treachery, "leave the boat. Send
me the gruff captain of the forecastle in his place. So bold a
talker, in common, should know how to be silent at need."

The exchange was instantly made, for no one there was
ever known to dispute a mandate that was uttered with the air
of authority that he then wore. A deeply intent attitude of
thought succeeded; then every shadow of care vanished from
his brow. A look of high and generous confidence was seated
in its place, as he added—

"Wilder, adieu. I leave you Captain of my people and
master of my fate; I am certain that both trusts are reposed in
worthy hands."

Without waiting for reply, as if scorning the vain ceremony
of idle assurances, he descended swiftly to the boat, which, at
the next instant, was pulling boldly towards the King's
cruiser. The brief interval between the departure of the adventurers and their arrival at the hostile ship, was one of intense
and absorbing suspense on the part of all whom they had left
behind. The individual most interested in the event, however,
betrayed none of the anxiety which so intensely beset the
minds of his followers. He mounted the side of his enemy,
amid the honours due to his imaginary rank, with a self-
possession and ease that might readily have been mistaken, by
those who believe these fancied qualities have a real existence,
for the grace and dignity of lofty recollections and high birth.
His reception, by the honest veteran, whose long and hard
services had received but a meagre reward in the vessel he
commanded, was frank, manly and seamanlike. The usual

greetings had no sooner passed, than the latter conducted his guest into his own apartments.

"Find such a berth, Capt. Howard, as suits your inclination," said the unceremonious old seaman, seating himself as frankly as he invited his companion to imitate his example. "A gentleman of your extraordinary merit must be reluctant to lose time in useless words, though you are so young—young for the pretty command, it is your good fortune to enjoy!"

"On the contrary, I do assure you, I begin to feel myself quite an antediluvian," returned the Rover, coolly posting himself at the opposite side of the table, where he might from time to time deliberately look his half disgusted companion in the eye. "Would you imagine it, Sir, I shall have reached the age of three and twenty, if I live through the day."

"I had given you a few more years, young gentleman; but London can ripen the human face, as speedily as the equator."

"You never said truer word, Sir. Of all cruising grounds, Heaven defend me, from that of St. James's! I do assure you, Bignall, the service is quite sufficient to wear out the strongest constitution. There were moments that I thought I should have really died that humble, disagreeable mortal a Lieutenant!"

"Your disease would then have been a galloping consumption!" muttered the old seaman, between his teeth. "They have sent you out in a pretty boat at last, Capt. Howard."

"She's bearable, Bignall, but frightfully small. I told my father, that if the First Lord didn't speedily regenerate the service by building more comfortable vessels, the Navy would get altogether into vulgar hands. Don't you find the motion excessively annoying in these single deck ships, Bignall?"

"When a man has been tossing up and down for five and forty years, Capt. Howard," returned his host, stroking his gray locks, for want of some other manner of suppressing his ire, "he gets to be indifferent whether his ship pitches, a foot more, or a foot less."

"Ah! that, I dare say, is what one calls philosophical equanimity, though it is little to my humour. But after this cruise, I am to be posted, and then I shall make interest for a guardship in the Thames; every thing goes by interest, now a days, you know, Bignall."

The honest old tar swallowed his displeasure as well as he could, and as the most effectual means of keeping himself in a condition to do credit to his own hospitality, he hastened to change the subject.

"I hope among other new fashions, Capt. Howard," he said, "the Flag of old England continues to fly over the Admiralty. You wore the colours of Louis so long, this morning, that another half hour might have brought us to loggerheads."

"Oh! that was an excellent military ruse! I shall certainly write the particulars of that deception home."

"Do so. Do so, Sir. You may get Knighthood for the exploit."

"Horrible, Bignall! My lady mother, would faint at the suggestion. Nothing so low has ever been in the family, I do assure you, since the time when chivalry was genteel."

"Well, well, Capt. Howard, it was happy for us both, that you got rid of your Gallic humour so soon, for a little more time would have drawn a broad-side from me. By Heavens, Sir, the guns of this ship would have gone off of themselves, in another five minutes."

"It is quite happy as it is. What do you find to amuse you (yawning) in this dull quarter of the world, Bignall?"

"Why, Sir, what between his Majesty's enemies, the care of my ship and the company of my Officers, I find few heavy moments."

"Ah! Your Officers. True, you *must* have officers on board; though I suppose they are a little oldish, in order to be agreeable to *you*. Will you favor me with a sight of the list?"

The commander of the Dart, did as he was requested, putting the quarter bill of his ship into the hands of his unknown enemy, with an eye that was far too honest to condescend to bestow even a look on a being so despised.

"What a list of thorough 'Mouthers! All Yarmouth, and Plymouth, and Portsmouth and Exmouth names, I do affirm. Here are Smiths enough to do the iron work of the whole ship. Ha! here is a fellow who might do good service in a deluge. Who may this Henry Ark be, that I find rated as your first Lieutenant?"

"A youth who wants but a few drops of your blood, Capt. Howard, to be one day at the head of His Majesty's fleet!"

"If he be then so extraordinary for his merit, Capt. Bignall, may I presume on your politeness to ask him to favor us with his society. I always give my first Lieutenant half an hour of a morning; if he happen to be bearable."

"Poor boy! God knows where he is to be found at this moment! The noble fellow has embarked, of his own accord, on a most dangerous service, and I am as ignorant as yourself of his success. Remonstrance and, even entreaties were of no avail. The Admiral had great need of a suitable agent, and the good of the nation demanded the risk; then, you know men of humble birth must earn their preferment in cruising elsewhere than at St. James's; for the brave lad is indebted to a wreck in which he was found an infant, for the very name you find so singular."

"He is, however, still borne upon your books as first lieutenant, I see?"

"And I hope ever will be, until he shall get the ship he so well merits. Good Heaven, are you ill, Capt Howard—boy, a tumbler of grog, here."

"I thank you, Sir," returned the Rover, smiling calmly, and rejecting the offered beverage, as the blood returned into his features with a violence that threatened to break through the ordinary boundaries of its currents. "It is no more than an ailing I inherit from my mother. We call it in our family, the De Vere ivory, for no other reason that I could ever learn, than that one of my female ancestors was particularly startled, in a delicate situation you know, by an elephant's tooth. I am told it has rather an amiable look, while it lasts."

"It has the look of a man who is fitter for his mother's nursery than a gale of wind. But I am glad it is so soon over."

"No one wears the same face long now a days, Bignall. And so this Mr Ark is not any body after all."

"I know not what you call any body, Sir, but if sterling courage, great professional merit, and stern loyalty count for any thing in your estimation, Capt. Howard, Henry Ark will soon be in command of a frigate."

"Perhaps if one only knew exactly on what to found his claims," continued the Rover, with a smile so kind, and a voice so insinuating that they half counteracted the effect of his assumed manner, "a word might be dropp'd in a letter home, that should do the youth no harm."

"I would to Heaven I dared but reveal the nature of the service he is on," eagerly returned the warm-hearted old sea-man, who was as quick to forget as he was sudden to feel disgust. "You may however safely say, from his general char-acter, that it is honorable, hazardous, and has the entire good of his Majesty's subjects in view. Indeed, an hour has scarcely gone by, since I thought that it was completely successful. Do you often set your lofty sails, Capt. Howard, while the heavier canvass is rolled upon the yards? To me, a ship clothed in that style, looks something like a man with his coat on, before he has cased his legs in the lower garment."

"You allude to the accident of my main-top-gallant-sail get-ting loose, when you first made me."

"I mean no other. We had caught a glimpse of your spars with the glass, but had lost you altogether when the flying duck met the eye of a look-out. To say the least it was remark-able, and it might have proved an awkward circumstance!"

"Oh! I often do things in that way in order to be odd. It is a sign of cleverness to be odd. But I too am sent into these seas on a special errand."

"Such as what?" bluntly demanded his companion, with an uneasiness about his frowning eye, that he was far too simple minded to conceal.

"To look for a ship, that will certainly give me a famous lift should I have the good luck to fall in with her. For some time, I took you to be the very gentleman I was in search of, and I do assure you, too, if your signals had not been so very unexceptionable, something serious might have happened be-tween us."

"And pray, Sir, for whom did you take me?"

"For no other than that notorious knave, the Red Rover."

"The devil you did! And do you suppose, Capt. Howard, there is a pirate afloat who carries such hamper above his head, as is to be found aboard the Dart! Such a set to her sails, such a step to her masts, and such a trim to her hull! I hope for the honour of your vessel, Sir, that the mistake went no further than the Captain."

"Until we got within reading distance of the signals, at least a moiety of the better opinions in my ship was dead against you, Bignall, I give you my declaration. You've really been so long from home, that the Dart is getting quite a roving look. You may not be sensible of it, but I assure you of the fact merely as a friend."

"And perhaps since you did me the honour to mistake my vessel for a freebooter," returned the old tar, smothering his ire, in a look of facetious irony that changed the expression of his mouth to a grim grin, "you might have conceited this honest gentleman here to have been no other than Beelzebub."

As he spoke the commander of the ship which had borne so odious an imputation, directed the eyes of his companion to the form of a third individual, who entered the cabin with the freedom of a privileged person, but with a tread so light as to be inaudible. As this unexpected form met the quick, impatient glance of the pretended officer of the Crown, he arose involuntarily, and for half a minute, that admirable command of muscle and nerve which had served him so well in maintaining his masquerade, appeared entirely to desert him. The loss of self-possession, however, was but for a time so short, as to attract no notice, and he coolly returned the salutations of an aged man of a meek and subdued look, with that air of blandness and courtesy which he so well knew how to assume.

"This Gentleman is your chaplain, Sir, I presume by his clerical attire," he said, after he had exchanged bows with the stranger.

"He is, Sir. A worthy and an honest man whom I am not ashamed to call my friend. After a separation of thirty years, the Admiral has been good enough to lend him to me for the cruise, and though my ship is none of the largest, I believe he finds himself as comfortable in her, as he would aboard the flag. This gentleman, Doctor, is the *honorable* Capt. Howard, of his Majesty's ship Antelope; I need not expatiate on his remarkable merit, Sir, since the command he bears at his years is a sufficient testimony on that important particular."

There was a look of bewildered surprise in the gaze of the divine, when his glance first fell upon the features of the pretended scion of nobility, but it was far less striking than had

been that of the subject of his gaze, and of much shorter continuance. He bowed meekly, and with the respect which long
use begets in those who are accustomed to pay deference to
hereditary rank, but he did not appear to consider that the
occasion required more than the customary words of salutation. The Rover turned calmly to his veteran companion and
continued the discourse.

"Capt. Bignall," he said, again wearing that grace of manner which became him so well, "it is my duty to follow your
motions in this interview. I will now return to my ship, and
if, as I begin to suspect we are in these seas on a similar
errand, we can concert at our leisure a system of cooperation,
which properly matured by your experience, may serve to
bring about the common end we have in view."

Greatly mollified by this concession to his years and to his
rank, the commander of the Dart pressed his hospitalities
more warmly on his guest, winding up his civilities by an
invitation to join in a marine feast at an hour somewhat later
in the day. All the former offers were politely declined, while
the latter was accepted, the invited making the invitation itself
an excuse that he should return to his own vessel, in order
that he might select such of his officers as he should deem
most worthy of participating in the promised banquet. The
veteran, and really meritorious Bignall, notwithstanding the
ordinarily sturdy blustering of his character, had served too
long in indigence and comparative obscurity not to feel some
of the longings of human nature for his hard earned and protracted preferment. He consequently kept, in the midst of all
his native and manly honesty, a saving eye on the means of
accomplishing this material object. It is to occasion no surprise, therefore, that his parting from the supposed son of a
powerful champion at Court was more amicable, than the
meeting. The Rover was bowed from the cabin to the deck,
with at least an appearance of returning good will. On reaching the latter, a hurried, suspicious and perhaps an uneasy
glance was thrown from his restless eyes on the many faces
that were grouped around the gangway; but their expression
became calm again, and a little supercilious withal, in order to
do no discredit to the part in the comedy it was his present
humour to enact. Then shaking the worthy, and thoroughly

deceived old seaman heartily by the hand, he touched his hat with an air half haughty, half condescending, to his inferiors. He was in the act of descending into the boat when the chaplain was seen to whisper something, with great earnestness, in the ear of his captain. The commander hastened to recall his departing guest, desiring him, with startling gravity, to lend him his private attention for another moment. Suffering himself to be led apart, by the two, the Rover stood awaiting their pleasure with a coolness of demeanor that, under the peculiar circumstances of his case, did signal credit to his nerves.

"Capt. Howard," resumed the warm-hearted Bignall, "have you a gentleman of the cloth in your vessel?"

"Two, Sir," was the answer.

"Two! It is rare to find a supernumerary priest in a man of war, but I suppose court influence could give the fellow a Bishop!" muttered the other. "You are fortunate in this particular, young gentleman, since I am indebted to inclination rather than to custom, for the society of my worthy friend here. He has, however, made a point that I should include the reverend gentleman—I should say gentle*men*—in the invitation."

"You shall have all the divinity of my ship, Bignall, on my faith."

"I believe I was particular in naming your first Lieutenant—"

"Oh! dead or alive he shall surely be of your party," returned the Rover with a suddenness and vehemence of utterance that occasioned both his auditors to start with surprise. "You may not find him an Ark to rest your weary foot on, but such as he is, he is entirely at your service. And, now, once more, I salute you."

Bowing again, he proceeded with his former deliberate air over the gangway—keeping his eyes rivetted on the lofty gear of the Dart as he descended her side, with the sort of expression with which a petit maitre is apt to regard the fashion of the garments of one new arrived from the provinces. His superior repeated his invitation with warmth, and waved his hand in a frank, but temporary adieu, thus unconsciously suffering the man to escape him whose capture would have purchased the long postponed and still distant advantages, for whose possession he secretly pined with the withering longings of a hope cruelly deferred.

# Chapter XXVIII

—"Let them accuse me by invention; I will answer in mine honour."
*Coriolanus*, III.ii.143–44.

"YES!" muttered the Rover, as his boat rowed under the stern of the royal cruiser; "yes! I and my officers will taste of your banquet, but the viands shall be such as these hirelings of the King shall little relish. Pull with a will, my men, pull; in an hour you shall rummage the store rooms of that fool for your reward!"

The greedy freebooters could scarcely restrain their shouts, in order to maintain the air of moderation which policy still imposed; but they gave vent to their excitement by redoubling their efforts to regain their own ship. In another minute the adventurers were all in safety again, under the sheltering guns of the Dolphin.

His people gathered from the haughty eye of the Rover, as his foot once more touched the deck of his own ship, that the period of action was at hand. For an instant he lingered on the quarter deck, surveying, with stern joy, the sturdy materials of his command; then he abruptly entered his cabin, forgetful that he had conceded it to others, or, in the excited state of his mind, indifferent to the circumstance. A sudden and tremendous blow on the gong announced not only his presence but his humour.

"Let the first Lieutenant be told I await him," was the order that followed the appearance of the attendant he had summoned.

During the short period which elapsed before his mandate could be obeyed, the Rover seemed struggling with a passion that choked him. But when the door of the cabin was opened, and Wilder stood before him, the most suspicious and closest observer might have sought in vain any evidence of the fierce feelings which agitated the inward man. With the recovery of his self command returned a recollection of the manner of his intrusion into a place which he had himself ordained should be privileged. It was then that he first sought the shrinking females, and hastened to relieve the terror that was too plainly to be seen in their countenances, by words of apology and explanation.

"In the hurry of an interview with a friend," he said, "I may have forgotten that I am host to even such guests, as it is my happiness to entertain, though I discharge my duties so indifferently."

"Spare your civilities, Sir," said Mrs Wyllys, with dignity; "in order to make us less sensible of intrusion, be pleased to act the master, here."

The Rover first saw the ladies seated, and then, like one who appeared to think the occasion might excuse any little departure from customary forms, he signed, with a smile of high courtesy, to his Lieutenant to imitate their example.

"His Majesty's artisans have sent worse ships than the Dart upon the ocean, Wilder," he commenced, significantly, as if he intended that the other should supply all the meaning that his words did not express, "but his ministers might have selected a more observant individual for the command."

"Capt. Bignall has the reputation of a brave and an honest man."

"He should deserve it; strip him of these two qualities and little would remain. He gives me to understand that he is especially sent into this latitude in quest of a ship that we have all heard of, either in good or in evil report; I speak of the Red Rover!"

The involuntary start of Mrs Wyllys, and the sudden manner in which Gertrude grasped the arm of her Governess were certainly seen by the speaker, but in no degree did his manner betray the consciousness of such an observation. His self possession was admirably emulated by Wilder, who answered with a composure that no jealousy could have seen was assumed —

"His cruise will be hazardous, not to say without success."

"It may prove both. And yet he has lofty expectations of the results."

"He probably labors under the common error as to the character of the man he seeks."

"In what does he mistake?"

"In supposing that he will encounter an ordinary freebooter—one coarse, rapacious, ignorant and inexorable like others of—"

"Of what, Sir?"

"I would have said of his class: but a mariner like him, we speak of, forms the head of his own order."

"We will call him, then, by his popular name, Mr Wilder, a rover. But is it not remarkable that so experienced a seaman, should come to this little frequented sea, in quest of a ship whose pursuits ought to call her into more bustling scenes?"

"He may have traced her through the narrow passages of the islands, and followed on the course she has last been seen steering."

"He may indeed," returned the Rover, musing. "Your thorough mariner knows how to calculate the chances of winds and currents, as the bird finds its way in air. Still a description of the ship would at least be needed as a clue."

Wilder, notwithstanding an effort to the contrary, suffered his eyes to sink before the piercing gaze they encountered.

"Perhaps he is not without that knowledge too," he answered.

"Perhaps not. Indeed he gave me reason to believe he has an agent in the secrets of his enemy. Nay, he expressly avowed the same, and acknowledged that his prospects of success depended on the skill and information of that individual, who no doubt has his private means of communicating what he learns of the movements of those with whom he serves."

"Did he name him?"

"He did."

"It was—"

"Henry Ark, alias—Wilder."

"It is vain to attempt denial," said our adventurer, rising with an air of pride, that he intended should conceal the uneasy sensation that in truth beset him, "I find you know me—"

"For a false traitor, Sir."

"Capt. Heidegger, you are safe, here, in using these reproachful terms."

The Rover struggled, and struggled successfully, to keep

down the risings of his temper, but the effort lent to his countenance gleamings of fierce scorn.

"You will communicate that fact also to your superiors," he
said with taunting irony. "The monster of the seas, he who
plunders defenceless fishermen, ravages unprotected coasts
and eludes the flag of King George as other serpents steal into
their caves at the footstep of man, is safe in speaking his
mind, backed by a hundred and fifty freebooters, and in the
security of his own cabin. Perhaps he knows, too that he is
breathing in the atmosphere of peaceful and peace-making
woman."

But the first surprise of the subject of his scorn had passed,
and he was neither to be goaded into retort, nor terrified into
entreaties. Folding his arms with calmness, Wilder simply
replied—

"I have incurred this risk in order to drive a scourge from
the ocean, which had baffled all other attempts at its exter-
mination. I knew the hazard, and shall not shrink from its
penalty."

"You shall not, Sir," returned the Rover, striking the gong
again, with a finger that appeared to carry in its touch the
weight of a giant. "Let the negro and the top-man his companion be secured in irons; on no account permit them to
communicate by word or signal with the other ship." When
the agent of his punishments, who entered at the well known
summons, had retired, he again turned to the firm but
motionless form that stood before him. "Mr Wilder," he continued, "there is a law which binds together this community,
into which you have so treacherously stolen, that would con-
sign you and your miserable confederates to the yard arm the
instant your true character should be known to my people. I
have but to open that door, and to pronounce the nature of
your treason, and to yield you to the tender mercies of the
crew!"

"You will not—no—you will not!" cried a voice at his
elbow, which thrilled on even his iron nerves. "You have
forgotten the ties which bind man to his fellows, but cruelty
is not natural to your heart. By all the recollections of your
earliest and happiest days, by the tenderness and pity which
watched your childhood, by that Holy and omniscient Being

who suffers not a hair of the innocent to go unrevenged, I conjure you to pause before you forget your own awful responsibility. No—you will not—you cannot—dare not be so merciless."

"What fate did he contemplate for me and my followers, when he entered on this insidious design?" hoarsely demanded the Rover.

"The laws of God and man are with him," continued Mrs. Wyllys, for it was she; " 'tis reason that speaks in my voice, 'tis mercy which I know is pleading at your heart. The cause, the motive sanctify his acts, while your career can find justification in the laws neither of Heaven nor earth."

"This is bold language to sound in the ears of a blood-seeking, lawless, remorseless pirate," said the other, looking about him with a smile so proud that it seemed to proclaim how plainly he saw that the speaker relied on the very reverse of the qualities he named.

"It is the language of truth, and ears like yours cannot be deaf to the sounds. If—"

"Lady, cease," interrupted the Rover, stretching his arm towards her with calmness. "My resolution was formed on the instant, and no remonstrance nor apprehension of the consequence can change it. Mr Wilder, you are free. If you have not served me as faithfully as I once expected, you have taught me a lesson in the art of physiognomy which shall leave me a wiser man for the rest of my days."

The conscious Wilder stood self-condemned and humbled. The strugglings which stirred his inmost soul were to be read in the workings of a countenance that was no longer masked in artifice, but which expressed both shame and sorrow. The conflict lasted but a moment.

"Perhaps, you know not the extent of my object, Capt. Heidegger," he said. "It embraced the forfeit of your life, and the destruction or dispersion of your crew."

"According to the established usages of that portion of the world, which, having the powers, oppresses the remainder, it did. Go, Sir, rejoin your proper ship: I repeat, you are free."

"I cannot leave you, Capt. Heidegger, without one word of justification—"

"What, can the hunted, denounced and condemned free-booter, command an explanation! Is even his good opinion necessary to a virtuous servant of the Crown!"

"Use such terms of triumph and reproach as suit your plea-sure, Sir; to me, your language can convey no offence; still I would not leave you, without removing part of the odium which you think I merit."

"Speak, freely, Sir. You are my guest."

The most cutting revilings could not have wounded the re-pentant Wilder so deeply, as this generous conduct, but he subdued his feelings, and continued,—

"You are not now to learn," he said, "that vulgar rumour has given a colour to your conduct and character which is not of a quality to command esteem."

"You may find leisure to deepen the tints," hastily inter-rupted his listener, though the tremor in his voice denoted how deeply he felt the wound given by a world that he af-fected to despise.

"If called upon to speak at all, my words shall be those of truth, Capt. Heidegger. Is it surprising that filled with the ardor of a service you once thought honorable yourself, I should be found willing to risk life, and, if you will, even to play the hypocrite in order to achieve an object that the world would have not only rewarded, but approved, had it been successful! With such sentiments I embarked on the enter-prise, but as Heaven is my judge, your manly confidence had half disarmed me, before my foot had scarcely crossed the threshold of my enterprise."

"You turned not back!"

"There might have been irresistible reasons to the contrary," resumed the defendant, glancing his eyes at the females. "I kept my faith at Newport, and had my two followers then been released from your ship, my foot should never have entered her again."

"Young man, I am willing to believe you; I think I pene-trate your motives. You have played a delicate game; instead of repining, you will one day rejoice that it has been fruitless. Go, Sir. A boat shall attend you to the Dart."

"Deceive not yourself, Capt. Heidegger, in believing that any generosity of yours can shut my eyes to my proper duty.

The instant I am seen by the commander of the ship you name, your character will be betrayed."

"I expect it."

"Nor will my hand be idle in the struggle that must follow. I may die here, a victim to my mistake, if you please, but the moment I am released, I unavoidably become your enemy."

"Wilder!" exclaimed the Rover, grasping his hand with a smile that partook of the wild energy of his manner, "we should have been acquainted earlier! But regret is idle. Go— should my people learn the truth any remonstrances of mine would be like whispers in a whirlwind."

"When I joined the Dolphin last, I did not come alone."

"Is it not enough," rejoined the Rover, recoiling a step, "that I offer you liberty and life?"

"Of what service can a being, fair, helpless and unfortunate as this, be in a ship devoted to pursuits like those of the Dolphin?"

"Am I to be cut off forever from communication with the best of my kind? Go, Sir, leave me the image of virtue, at least, though I may be wanting in its substance."

"Capt Heidegger, once in the warmth of your better feelings, you pronounced a pledge in favor of these females, which I hope came from the heart."

"I understand you, Sir. What I then said is not, nor shall it be, forgotten. But whither would you lead your companions? Is not one vessel on the high seas safe as another!—Am I to be deprived of every means of making friends unto myself— Leave me, Sir. Go, you may linger until my permission to depart cannot avail you."

"I will never desert my charge," said Wilder, firmly.

"Mr Wilder, or I should rather call you, Lieutenant Ark, I believe," returned the Rover, "you may trifle with my good nature 'till the moment of your own security shall be passed!"

"Act your will on me: I die at my post, or go accompanied by those with whom I came."

"Sir, the acquaintance of which you boast, is not older than my own. How know you that they prefer you for their protector? I have deceived myself and done poor justice to my own intentions if they have found cause for complaints since their happiness or comfort has been in my keeping. Speak, fair one; which of us do you choose for a protector?"

"Leave me! Leave me!" exclaimed Gertrude, veiling her eyes, from the insidious smile, with which he approached her, as she would have avoided the glance of a basilisk. "Oh! If you have pity in your heart, let us quit your ship."

Notwithstanding the vast self-command which the being she so ungovernably and spontaneously repelled had, in common, over his feelings, no effort could repress the look of deep and humiliating mortification with which he heard her. A cold and haggard smile gleamed over his features, as he murmured in a voice which he, in vain, endeavored to smother.

"I have purchased this disgust from all of my species, and dearly must the penalty be paid!—Lady, you and your lovely ward, are the mistresses of your own acts. This ship and this cabin are at your command, or, if you elect to quit both, others will receive you."

"Safety for our sex, is only to be found beneath the fostering protection of the laws," said Mrs Wyllys. "Would to God—"

"Enough," he interrupted, "you shall accompany your friend. The ship will not be emptier than my heart, when all have left me."

"Did you call?" asked a low voice at his elbow, in tones so plaintive and mild, that they could not fail to catch his ear.

"Roderick," he hurriedly, replied—"you will find occupation below. Leave us, good Roderick. For a while, leave me."

Then as if anxious to close the scene as speedily as possible, he gave another of his signals on the gong. An order was given to convey Fid and the black into a boat, whither he also immediately sent the scanty baggage of his female guests. So soon as these brief arrangements were completed, he handed the Governess with studied courtesy through his wondering people, to the side, and saw her safely seated, with her ward, and Wilder, in the Pinnace. The oars were manned by the two seamen, and a silent adieu was given, by a wave of his hand, after which he disappeared from those, to whom their present release seemed as imaginary and unreal as most of the other events of the few preceding weeks.

The threat of the interference of the crew of the Dolphin was, however, still ringing in the ears of Wilder. He made an impatient gesture to his attendants to ply their oars, cautiously steering the boat on such a course, as would soonest lead her from beneath the guns of the freebooters. While passing under the stern of the Dolphin, a hoarse hail was sent across the waters, and the voice of the Rover was heard, speaking to the commander of the Dart.

"I send you a party of your guests," he said, "and among them all the Divinity of my ship."

The passage was short, nor was time given for the liberated to arrange their thoughts, before it became necessary to ascend the side of the cruiser of the crown.

"Heaven help us!" exclaimed Bignall, catching a glimpse of the character of some of his visiters through a port. "Heaven help us both, Parson. That young hair-brained fellow has sent us a brace of petticoats aboard, and these the profane reprobate calls his divinities. One may easily guess where he has picked up such quality; but cheer up, Doctor, we may honestly forget the cloth in five fathom water, you know."

The facetious laugh of the old Commander of the Dart, betrayed that he was more than half disposed to overlook the fancied presumption of his audacious inferior, furnishing a sort of pledge that no undue scruples should defeat the hilarity of the moment. But when Gertrude, flushed with the excitement of the scene through which she had just passed, and beaming with a loveliness that derived so much of its character from its innocence, appeared on his deck, the veteran rubbed his eyes in an amazement which could not have been greatly surpassed had one of that species of beings the Rover had named, actually fallen at his feet from the skies.

"The heartless scoundrel!" cried the worthy tar, "to lead astray one so young, and so lovely—ha! as I live, my own Lieutenant! How's this, Mr Ark! Have we fallen on the days of miracles?"

An exclamation, which came from the heart of the Governess, and a low and mournful echo from the lips of the Divine, interrupted the further expression of his indignation and his wonder.

"Capt. Bignall," observed the former, pointing to the

tottering form, which was leaning on Wilder for support, "on my life, you are mistaken in the character of this lady. It is more than twenty years since we last met, but I pledge my own character, for the purity and truth of hers—"

"Lead me to the cabin," murmured Mrs Wyllys. "Gertrude, my love, where are we? lead me to some secret place!"

Her request was complied with, the whole party retiring in a body, from the sight of the spectators who thronged the deck. Here the agitated governess regained a portion of her self-command, and then her wandering gaze sought the meek countenance of the chaplain.

"This is a tardy and heart-rending meeting," she said, pressing the hand he gave her to her lips. "Gertrude, in this gentleman, you see the divine that united me to the man who once formed the pride and happiness of my existence."

"Mourn not his loss," whispered the reverend priest, bending over her chair with the interest of a parent. "He was taken from you at an early hour, but he died as all who loved him might have wished."

"And none was left to bear, in remembrance of his qualities, his name to posterity! Tell me, good Merton, is not the hand of Providence visible in this dispensation? Ought I not to humble myself before it, as a just punishment of my disobedience to an affectionate, though too obdurate parent?"

"None may presume to pry into the mysteries of the righteous government that orders all things. Enough for us, that we learn to submit to the will of him who rules, without questioning his justice."

"But," continued the Governess in tones so husky as to betray how powerfully she felt the temptation to forget his admonition—"would not one life have sufficed! Was I to be deprived of all—"

"Madam, reflect. What has been done, was done in wisdom, as I trust, it was, in mercy."

"You say truly. I will forget all of the sad events, but their application to myself. And you—worthy and benevolent Merton, where and how have been passed your days since the time of which we speak?"

"I am but a low and humble shepherd of a truant flock," returned the meek chaplain, with a sigh. "Many distant seas have I visited, and many strange faces, and stranger natures, has it been my lot to encounter in my pilgrimage. I am but lately returned from the East into the Hemisphere where I first drew breath, and by permission of our superiors, have I come to pass a month in the vessel of a companion, whose friendship bears even an older date than yours."

"Ay, ay, Madam," returned the worthy Bignall, whose feelings had been a little disturbed by the previous scene, "it is near half a century since the Parson and I were boys together, and we have been rubbing up old recollections on the cruise. Happy am I, that a lady of so commendable qualities has come to make one of our party."

"In this lady you see the daughter of the late Captain ——, and the relict of the son of our ancient commander, Rear-Admiral de Lacey," hastily resumed the divine, as if he knew the well meaning honesty of his friend was more to be trusted than his discretion.

"I knew the both—I knew them both; brave men and thorough seamen were the pair! The lady was welcome as your friend, Merton, but she is doubly so, as the widow and child of the gentlemen you name."

"De Lacey!" murmured a voice in the ear of the Governess.

"The law gives me a title to bear that name," returned she whom we shall still continue to call by her assumed appellation, folding her weeping pupil, long and affectionately to her bosom. "The veil is unexpectedly withdrawn, my love, and concealment would now be worse than useless. My father was the captain of the flag-ship: Necessity compelled him to leave me more in the society of your young relative than he would have done, could he have foreseen the consequences. But I knew both his pride and his poverty too well to dare to make him arbiter of my fate, after the alternative became to my inexperienced imagination worse even than his anger. We were privately united by this gentleman, and neither of our parents knew of the connexion—Death—"

The voice of the widow became choked, and she made a sign to the chaplain as if she would have him continue the tale.

"Mr de Lacey and his father-in-law fell in the same battle, within a short month of the ceremony," added the subdued voice of Merton. "Even you, dearest Madam, never knew the melancholy particulars of their end. I was a solitary witness of their deaths, for to me were they both consigned amid the confusion of the battle. Their blood was mingled, and your parent, in blessing the young hero, unconsciously blessed his son."

"Oh! I deceived his noble nature, and dearly have I paid the penalty!" exclaimed the self debased widow. "Tell me, Merton, did he ever know of my marriage?"

"He did not. Mr de Lacey died first, and upon his bosom, for he loved him, ever, as a child; but other thoughts than useless explanations were uppermost in their minds."

"Gertrude!" said the Governess in hollow, repentant tones, "there is no peace for our feeble sex but in submission, no happiness but in obedience."

"It is over now," whispered the weeping girl, "all over and forgotten. I am your child, your own Gertrude, the creature of your formation."

"Harry Ark!" exclaimed Bignall, clearing his throat, with a hem so vigorous as to carry the sound to the outer deck, seizing the arm of his entranced Lieutenant and dragging him from the scene while he spoke. "What the devil besets the boy! You forget that, all this time, I am as ignorant of your own adventures, as his Majesty's Prime Minister is of navigation. Why do I see you here, a visiter from a Royal cruiser, when I thought you were playing the mock pirate, and how came that harum scarum twig of nobility in possession of so goodly a company, as well as of so brave a ship?"

Wilder drew a long breath, like one that awakes from a pleasing dream, reluctantly suffering himself to be forced from a spot, where he fondly felt that he could have continued, without weariness, forever.

# Chapter XXIX

"Let them achieve me, and then sell my bones."
*Henry V*, IV.iii.91.

THE COMMANDER of the Dart and his bewildered lieutenant had gained the quarter deck, before either spoke
again. The direction first taken by the eyes of the latter was in
quest of the neighboring ship, nor was the look entirely without that unsettled and vague expression which seems to announce a momentary aberration of the faculties. But the vessel
of the Rover was in view, in all the palpable and beautiful
proportions of her admirable construction. Instead of lying in
a state of rest, as when he left her, her head yards had been
swung, and as the sails filled with the breeze, the stately fabric
had begun to move gracefully, though with no great velocity
along the water. There was not the slightest appearance in the
evolution, however, of any attempt at escape. On the contrary
the loftier and lighter sails were all furled, and men were, at
the moment, actively employed in sending to the deck, those
smaller spars, which were absolutely requisite in spreading the
canvass that would be needed in facilitating her flight. Wilder
turned from the sight with a sickening apprehension, for he
well knew that these were the preparations that skilful mariners are wont to make when bent on desperate combat.

"Ay, yonder goes your St. James's seaman with his three
topsails full, and his mizzen out, as if he had already forgotten
he is to dine with me, and that his name is to be found at one
end of the list of commanders and mine at the other!" grumbled the displeased Bignall. "But we shall have him coming
round, I suppose, when his appetite tells him the dinner hour.
He might wear his colours in presence of a senior, too, and
no disgrace to his nobility—by the Lord, Harry Ark, he
handles his yards beautifully! I warrant you, now, some
honest man's son is sent aboard his ship for a dry nurse, in the
shape of a first Lieutenant, and we shall have him vaporing
all dinner time about how, 'my ship does this, and I never
suffer that.' Ha! is it not so, Sir—he has a thorough seaman
for his first?"

"Few men understand the profession better than the captain of yonder vessel, himself," returned Wilder.

"The devil he does! You have been talking with him, Mr Ark, about these matters, and he has got some of the fashions of the Dart. I can see into a mystery as quick as another!"

"I do assure you, Capt. Bignall, there is no safety in confiding in the ignorance of yonder extraordinary man."

"Ay, ay, I begin to overhaul his character. The young dog, is a quiz, and has been amusing himself with a sailor of what he calls the old school. Am I right, Sir? He has seen salt water before this cruise."

"He is almost a native of the seas; for more than thirty years he has passed his time on them."

"There, Harry Ark, he has done you handsomely. Now I have his own assertion for it, that he will not be three and twenty until to-morrow."

"On my word he has deceived you, Sir."

"I don't know, Mr Ark; that is a task much easier attempted than performed. Threescore and four years, add as much weight to a man's head as to his heels! I may have undervalued the skill of the younker, but as to his years, there can be no great mistake. But where the devil is the fellow steering to! Has he need of a pinafore from his lady mother, to come on board a man of war to dine?"

"See; he is indeed standing from us!" exclaimed Wilder, with a rapidity and delight that would have excited the suspicions of one more observant than his commander.

"If I know the stern from the bows of a ship, what you say is truth," returned the other with some austerity. "Harkee, Mr Ark, I've a mind to furnish the coxcomb a lesson in respect for his seniors, and give him a row to whet his appetite. By the Lord, I will, and he may write home an account of this manœuvre too, in his next dispatches. Fill away the after-yards, Sir; fill away. Since this *honorable* youth is disposed to amuse himself with a sailing match, he can take no offence that others are in the same humour."

The Lieutenant of the watch, to whom the order was addressed, complied, and in another minute, the Dart was also beginning to move ahead, though in a direction directly opposite to that taken by the Dolphin. The old seaman highly enjoyed his own decision, manifesting his satisfaction by the infinite glee and deep chuckling of his manner. He was too much occupied with the step he had just taken to revert immediately to the subject, that had so recently been uppermost in his mind, nor did the thought of pursuing the discourse occur to him, until the two ships had left a broad field of water between them, as each moved with ease and steadiness on its proper course.

"Let him note that, in his log book, Mr Ark," the irritable old seaman then resumed, returning to the spot which Wilder had not left during the intervening time. "Though my cook has no great relish for a frog, they who would taste of his skill must seek him. By the Lord, boy, he will have a pull of it, if he undertake to come-to on that tack. But how happens it, that you got into his ship—all that part of the cruise remains untold."

"I have been wrecked, Sir, since you received my last letter."

"What, has Davy Jones got possession of the red gentleman at last!"

"The misfortune occurred in a ship from Bristol aboard which I was placed, as a sort of prize-master—he certainly continues to stand slowly to the northward!"

"Let the young coxcomb go! He will have all the better appetite for his supper. And so you were picked up by his Majesty's ship the Antelope—ay, I see into the whole affair. Give an old sea-dog his course and compass, and he will find his way to port in the darkest night. But how happened it that this Mr Howard affected to be ignorant of your name, Sir, when he saw it on the list of my officers?"

"Ignorant—did he seem ignorant?—perhaps—"

"Say no more, my brave fellow, say no more," interrupted Wilder's considerate but choleric commander. "I have met with such rebuffs myself, in my day; but we are above them, Sir, far above them and their impertinences together. No man need be ashamed of having earned his commission as you and I have done, in fair weather and in foul. Zounds, boy, I have fed one of the upstarts for a week, and then had him stare at a church across the way, when I have fallen in with him in the streets of London, in a manner to make a simple man believe the puppy knew for what it had been built. Think no more of it, Harry, worse things have happened to myself, I do assure you."

"I went by my assumed name, while in his ship," Wilder forced himself to add. "Even the ladies, who were the companions of my wreck, knew me by no other."

"Ah! that was prudent, and after all, the young sprig was not pretending genteel ignorance. How now, Master Fid; you are welcome back to the Dart."

"I've taken the liberty to say as much already to myself, your honour," returned the top-man, who was busying himself near his two officers, in a manner that seemed to invite their attention. "A wholesome craft is yonder, and boldly is she commanded, and stoutly is she manned, but for my part, having a character to lose, it is more to my taste to sail in a ship that can show her commission, when properly called on for the same."

The colour on Wilder's cheeks went and came, like the flushings of the evening sky, and his eyes were turned in every direction but that which would have encountered the astonished gaze of his veteran friend.

"I am not quite sure that I understand the meaning of the lad, Mr Ark. Every officer from the captain to the Boatswain in the King's fleet, that is, every man of common discretion, carries his authority to act as such with him to sea, or he might find himself in a situation as awkward as that of a Pirate."

"That is just what I said, Sir, but schooling and long use have given your honour a better out-fit in words. Guinea, and I, have often talked the matter over together, and serious thoughts has it given to us both, more than once, Capt. Bignall. 'Suppose,' says I to the black, 'suppose one of his Majesty's boats should happen to fall in with this here craft, and we should come to loggerheads and matches,' says I, 'what would the like of us two do, in such a god-send?'— 'Why,' says the black, 'we would stand to our guns, on the side of Master Harry,' says he, nor did I gainsay the same, but saving his presence, and your honor's, I just took the liberty to add, that in my poor opinion it would be much more comfortable to be killed in an honest ship, than on the deck of a buccaneer."

"A buccaneer!" exclaimed his commander, with eyes distended and an open mouth.

"Capt. Bignall," said Wilder, "I may have offended past forgiveness in remaining so long silent, but when you hear my tale, there may be found some passages that shall plead my apology. The vessel in sight, is the ship of the renowned Red Rover—nay listen, I conjure you, by all that kindness you have so long shown me, and then censure as you will."

The words of Wilder, aided as they were by an earnest and manly manner, laid a restraint on the mounting indignation of the choleric old seaman. He listened gravely and intently to the rapid but clear tale, which his lieutenant hastened to recount, and ere the latter had done, he had more than half entered into those grateful and certainly generous feelings, which had made the youth so reluctant to betray the obnoxious character of a man who had dealt so liberally by himself. A few strong, and what might be termed professional exclamations of surprise and admiration, occasionally interrupted the narrative, but on the whole he curbed his impatience and his feelings, in a manner that was sufficiently remarkable, when the temperament of the individual is duly considered.

"This is wonderful indeed!" he exclaimed, as the other ended—"and a thousand pities is it that so honest a fellow should be so arrant a knave. But, Harry, we can never let him go at large after all; our loyalty and our religion forbid it. We must tack ship, and stand after him; if fair words won't bring him to reason, I see no other remedy than blows."

"I fear it is no more than our duty, Sir," returned the young man, with a sigh.

"It is a matter of morals. And then the prating puppy that he sent on board me, is no captain after all! Still it was impossible to deceive me as to the air and manner of a gentleman! I warrant me some young reprobate of a good family, or he could never have acted the sprig so well. We must try to keep his name a secret, Mr Ark, in order that no discredit should fall upon his friends. Our aristocratic columns, though they get a little cracked and defaced, are after all the pillars of the throne, and it does not become us to let vulgar eyes look too closely into their unsoundness."

"The individual who visited the Dart, was the Rover himself."

"He! the Red Rover in my ship, nay, in my very presence," exclaimed the old tar, in honest horror. "You are now pleased, Sir, to trifle with my good nature."

"I should forget a thousand obligations ere I could be so bold. On my solemn asseveration, Sir, it was no other."

"This is unaccountable! extraordinary to a miracle! His disguise was very complete I will confess to deceive one so skilled in the human countenance. I saw nothing, Sir, of his shaggy whiskers, heard nothing of his brutal voice, nor perceived any of those monstrous deformities which are universally acknowledged to distinguish the man."

"All of which are no more than the embellishments of vulgar rumour. I fear, Sir, that the boldest and most dangerous of all our vices, are often found under the most pleasing exteriors."

"But this is not even a man of inches, Sir!"

"His body is not large, but it contains the spirit of a giant."

"And do you believe yonder ship, Mr Ark, to be the vessel, that fought us in the equinox of March?"

"I know it to be no other."

"Harkee, Harry, for your sake, I will deal generously by the rogue. He once escaped me by the loss of a top-mast and stress of weather; but we have here a good working breeze, that a man may safely count on, and a fine regular sea. He is therefore mine, so soon as I choose to make him so, for, after all, I do not think he has any serious intention to run—"

"I fear not," returned Wilder, unconsciously betraying his wishes in the words.

"Fight he cannot, with any hopes of success, and, as he seems to be altogether a different sort of personage from what I had supposed, we will try the merits of negociation. Will you undertake to be the bearer of my propositions—or perhaps he might repent of his moderation—"

"I pledge myself for his faith!" eagerly exclaimed Wilder. "Let a gun be fired to leeward—mind, Sir, all the tokens must be amicable—a flag of truce set at our main, and I will risk every hazard to lead him back into the bosom of society."

"By George, it would at least be acting a christian part,"

returned the Commander, after a moment's thought. "It shall be so, and though we miss knighthood below for our success, there will be better berths cleared for us aloft, lad."

No sooner had the warm hearted and perhaps a little visionary Captain of the Dart and his Lieutenant determined on this measure, than they both eagerly set about the means of insuring its success. The helm of the ship was put a-lee, and as her head came sweeping up into the wind, a sheet of flame flashed from her leeward bow-port, sending the customary amicable intimation across the water, that those who governed her movements would communicate with the possessors of the vessel in sight. At the same instant a small flag, with a spotless field, was seen floating at the topmost elevation of all her spars, while the flag of England was lowered from the gaft. A half minute of deep inquietude succeeded these signals. Their suspense was, however, speedily terminated. A cloud of smoke issued from the vessel of the Rover, and then the smothered explosion of the answering gun came dull upon their ears. A flag similar to their own was seen fluttering, as it might be like a dove fanning its wings, far above her tops; but no emblem of any sort was borne at the spar where the colours which distinguish the national character of a cruiser are usually seen.

"The fellow has the modesty to carry a naked gaft in our presence," said Bignall, pointing out the circumstance to his companion as an augury favorable to their success. "We will stand for him, until within a reasonable distance, and then you shall take to the boat."

In conformity with this determination the Dart was brought on the other tack, and several sails were set to quicken her speed. When at the distance of half-cannon shot, Wilder suggested to his superior the propriety of arresting their further progress in order to avoid the appearance of hostilities. The boat was immediately lowered into the sea and manned, a flag of truce set in her bows, and the whole was reported in readiness to receive the bearer of the message.

"You may hand him this statement of our force, Mr Ark, for as he is a reasonable man, he will see the advantage it gives us," said the Captain, after having exhausted his manifold and often repeated instructions. "I think you may promise him

indemnity for the past, provided he comply with all my conditions; at all events you will say, that no influence shall be
spared to get a complete white-washing for himself at least.
God bless you, boy; take care to say nothing of the damages
we received in the affair of March last, for—ay, for the Equinox, was blowing heavy at the time, you know. Adieu, and
success attend you."

The boat shoved off from the side of the vessel as he ended,
and in a few moments the listening Wilder was borne beyond
the sound of further counsel. Our adventurer had sufficient
time to reflect on the extraordinary situation in which he now
found himself, during the row to the still distant ship. Once
or twice, slight and uneasy glimmerings of distrust concerning the prudence of the step he was taking beset him; though
a recollection of the lofty feeling of the man in whom he confided, ever presented itself in sufficient season to prevent the
apprehension from gaining any undue ascendency. Notwithstanding the delicacy of his situation that characteristic interest in his profession which is rarely dormant in the bosom of
a thorough-bred seaman, was strongly stimulated as he approached the vessel of the Rover. The perfect symmetry of
her spars, the graceful heavings and settings of the whole fabric, as it rode like a marine bird, on the long regular swells of
the trades, and the graceful inclinations of the tapering masts
as they waved across the blue canopy, which was interlaced by
all the tracery of her complicated tackle, was not lost on an
eye, that knew no less how to prize the order of the whole,
than to admire the beauty of the object itself. There is a high
and exquisite taste which the seaman alone attains in the
study of a machine that all have united to commend, which
may be likened to the sensibilities that the artist acquires, by
close and long contemplation of the noblest monuments of
antiquity. It teaches him to detect those imperfections which
would escape a less instructed eye, and it heightens the pleasure with which a ship at sea is gazed at, by enabling the
mind to keep even pace with the enjoyment of the senses. It is
this powerful, and to a landsman, incomprehensible charm,
that forms the secret tie which binds the mariner so closely to
his vessel, and which often leads him to prize her qualities as
one would esteem the virtues of a friend, and almost to be

equally enamoured of the fair proportions of his ship and of those of his mistress. Other men may have their different inanimate subjects of admiration, but none of their feelings so thoroughly enters into the composition of the being as the affection which the mariner comes in time to feel for his vessel. It is his home, his theme of constant and frequently of painful interest, his tabernacle, and often his source of pride and exultation. As she gratifies or disappoints his high wrought expectations, in her speed or in the fight, mid shoals and hurricanes, a character for good or luckless qualities is earned, which are as often in reality due to the skill or ignorance of those who guide her, as to any inherent properties of the fabric. Still does the ship itself in the eyes of the seaman, bear away the laurel of success or suffer the ignominy of defeat and misfortune, and when the reverse arrives the result is merely regarded as some extraordinary departure from the ordinary character of the vessel, as if the construction possessed the powers of self-command and volition.

Though not so deeply embued with that superstitious credulity on this subject, as the inferiors of his profession, Wilder was keenly awake to most of the sensibilities of a mariner. So strongly indeed, was he on the present occasion, alive to this feeling, that for a moment he forgot the critical nature of his errand, as he drew within plainer view of a vessel that might with justice lay claim to be a jewel of the ocean.

"Lay on your oars, lads," he said, signing to his people to arrest the progress of the boat. "Lay on your oars—did you ever see masts more beautifully in line, than those, Master Fid; or sails that had a fairer fit?"

The top-man, who rowed the stroke-oar of the pinnace, cast a look over his shoulder, and first stowing into one of his cheeks a lump that resembled a wad laid by the side of its gun, he was not slow to answer.

"I care not who knows it," he said, "for, done by honest men or done by knaves, I told the people on the forecastle of the Dart, in the first five minutes after I got among them again, that they might lie at Spithead a month, and not see hamper so light and yet so handy, as is seen aboard that hooker. Her lower-rigging is harpened-in like the waist of Nell Dale, after she has had a fresh pull upon her staylanyards, and there isn't a block among them all, that seems bigger in its place, than the eyes of the girl in her own good-looking countenance. That bit of a set that you see to her fore-brace-block was given by the hand of one Richard Fid, and the heart on her mainstay was turned-in by Guinea, here, and considering he is a nigger, I call it ship-shape."

"She is beautiful in every part!" said Wilder, drawing a long breath. "Give way, my men; give way. Do you think I have come here to take the soundings of the ocean!"

The crew started at the hurried tones of their lieutenant, and in another minute the boat was at the side of the vessel. The stern and threatening glances that Wilder encountered as his foot touched the planks, caused him to pause an instant, ere he advanced further amid the crew. But the presence of the Rover, himself, who stood with his peculiar air of high and imposing authority on the quarter deck, encouraged him to proceed, after permitting a delay that was too slight to attract attention. His lips were in the act of parting, when a sign from the other, induced him to remain silent, until both were in the privacy of the cabin.

"Suspicion is awake among my people, Mr Ark," commenced the Rover, when they had retired, laying a marked emphasis on the name he used. "Suspicion is stirring, though as yet, they hardly know what to credit. The manœuvres of the two ships have not been such as they are wont to see, and voices are not wanting to whisper, in their ears, matter that is somewhat injurious to your interests. You have not done well, Sir, in returning among us."

"I come by the order of my superior, and under the sanction of a flag."

"We are small reasoners in the legal distinctions of the World, and may mistake your rights in so novel a character; but if you bear a message, I may presume it is intended for my ears."

"For no other. We are not alone, Capt. Heidegger."

"Heed not the boy; he is deaf at my will."

"I could wish to communicate to you only, the offers that I bear."

"That mast is not more senseless than Roderick," said the other calmly but with decision.

"Then I must speak at every hazard. The commander of yonder ship, who bears the Commission of our Royal master, George IId, has ordered me to say thus much for your consideration. On condition that you will surrender this vessel, with her stores, armament and warlike munitions uninjured, he will content himself with taking ten hostages from your crew to be decided by lot, yourself, and one other of your officers, and either to receive the remainder into the service of the King, or to suffer them to disperse in pursuit of a calling more creditable and, as it would now appear, more safe."

"This is the liberality of a Prince! I should kneel and kiss the deck, before one whose lips utter such sounds of mercy!"

"I repeat but the words of my superior," Wilder resumed, colouring. "For yourself he further promises that his interest shall be exerted to procure a pardon, on condition that you quit the seas and renounce the name of Englishman forever."

"The latter is done to his hands—but may I know the reason, that such lenity is shown to one, whose name has been so long proscribed of men?"

"Capt. Bignall has heard of your generous treatment of his officer, and the delicacy that the daughter and widow of two ancient brethren in arms have received at your hands. He confesses that rumour has not done entire justice to your character."

A mighty effort kept down the gleam of exultation that flashed across the features of the Rover, who however succeeded in continuing utterly calm and immoveable.

"He has been deceived, Sir—" he remarked, as if to encourage the other to proceed.

"That much is he willing to acknowledge. A representation of this common error to the proper authorities will have weight in procuring the promised amnesty for the past and as he hopes, brighter prospects for the future."

"And does he urge no other motive than his pleasure, why I should make this violent change in all my habits, why I should renounce an element that has become as necessary to me as the one I breathe, and why, in particular, I am to disclaim the vaunted privilege of calling myself a Briton!"

"He does. This statement of a force, which you may freely

examine with your own eyes, if so disposed, must convince you of the hopelessness of resistance, and will, he thinks, induce you to accept his offers."

"And what is *your* opinion?" the other demanded with a peculiar emphasis, as he extended a hand to receive the written statement. "But I beg pardon," he hastily added, taking the look of gravity from the countenance of his companion, "I trifle, when the moment requires seriousness."

The eye of the Rover ran rapidly over the paper, arresting itself, once or twice, with a slight exhibition of interest, on particular points that seemed most to merit his attention.

"You find the superiority such as I had already given you reason to believe?" demanded Wilder, when the look of the other wandered from the paper.

"I do."

"And may I now ask your decision on the offer?"

"First tell me what does your own heart advise. This is but the language of another."

"Capt Heidegger," said Wilder, earnestly, "I will not attempt to conceal that, had this message depended solely on myself, it might have been couched in different terms, but as one who deeply retains the recollection of your generosity, as a man who would not willingly induce even an enemy to an act of dishonor, I urge their acceptance. You will excuse me if I say that, in our recent intercourse, I have had reason to believe you already perceive that neither the character you could wish to earn, nor the content that all men crave is to be found in your present career."

"I had not thought I entertained so close a casuist in Mr Henry Wilder! Have you more to urge, Sir?"

"Nothing," returned the disappointed and grieved messenger.

"Yes, yes, he has," said a low but eager voice, at the elbow of the Rover, which rather seemed to breathe out the syllables than dare to utter them aloud. "He has—he has. He has not yet delivered the half of his commission, or sadly has he forgotten the sacred trust!"

"This boy is often a dreamer," interrupted the Rover, smiling with a wild and haggard look. "He sometimes gives form to his unmeaning thoughts, by clothing them in words."

"My thoughts are not unmeaning," continued Roderick in a louder and bolder strain. "If his peace or happiness be dear to you do not yet leave him. Tell him of his high and honorable name, of his youth, ay, and of that gentle and virtuous being that he once so fondly loved, and whose memory, even now, he worships. Speak to him of these, as you know how to speak, and on my life, his ear will not be deaf—his heart cannot be callous to your word."

"The urchin is mad—!"

"I am not mad, or if maddened it is by the crimes—the dangers—of those I love. Oh! Mr Wilder, do not leave him. Since you have been among us, he is nearer to what I know he once was, than formerly. Take away that mistaken statement of your force; threats do but harden him. As a friend admonish, but hope for nothing as a minister of vengeance. You know not the fearful nature of the man, or you would not attempt to stop a torrent. Now—now speak to him, for his eye is already growing kinder."

"It is in pity, boy, at witnessing how thy reason wavers."

"Had it never swerved more than at this moment, Walter, another need not be called upon to speak between thee and me! My words would then have been regarded, my voice would then have been loud enough to be heard. Why are you dumb—a single happy syllable might now, save him."

"Wilder, the child is frightened by this counting of guns and numbering of people. He fears the anger of your anointed Master. Go: give him a place in your boat, and recommend him to the mercy of your superior."

"Away, away!" cried Roderick, "I shall not, will not, cannot leave you! Who is there left for me in this world but you!"

"Yes," continued the Rover, whose forced calmness of expression changed to one of melancholy musing; "it will indeed be better that he should go. See, here is much gold; you will commend him to the care of that admirable woman, who already watches one scarcely less helpless, though possibly less—"

"Guilty. Speak the word, boldly, Walter; I have earned the epithet and shall not shrink to hear it spoken. Look," he said, taking the ponderous bag, which had been extended towards Wilder, and holding it above his head in scorn, "this can I cast from me, but the tie which binds me to thee shall never be broken."

As he spoke the lad approached an open window of the cabin; a plash upon the water was heard, and then a treasure that might have furnished a competence to moderate wishes, was lost forever to the uses of man. The Lieutenant of the Dart turned in haste to deprecate the anger of the Rover, but he could trace in the features of the lawless chief no other emotion than a pity, which was discoverable even through his unmoved smile.

"Roderick would make but a faithless treasurer," he said. "Still is it not too late to restore him to his friends. The loss of the gold can be repaired, but should any serious calamity befall the boy, I might never regain a perfect peace of mind."

"Then keep him near yourself," murmured the lad, whose vehemence seemingly had expended itself. "Go—Mr Wilder—go. Your boat is waiting; your longer stay will be without an object."

"I fear it will!" returned our adventurer, who had not ceased during the previous dialogue to keep his look fastened, in manly commiseration, on the countenance of the boy. "I greatly fear it will. Since I have come the messenger of another, Capt. Heidegger, it is your province to supply the answer to my proposition."

The Rover took him by the arm, and led him to a position, whence they might look upon the outer scene. Pointing upward at his spars, and making his companion observe the small quantity of sail he carried, he simply said—"Sir, you are a seaman, and may judge of my intentions by this. I shall neither seek nor avoid your boasted cruiser."

# Chapter XXX

——"Front to front,
Bring thou this fiend——
Within my sword's length set him; if he 'scape,
Heaven forgive him too!"

*Macbeth*, IV.iii.232-35.

---

"You HAVE BROUGHT the grateful submission of the
pirate!" exclaimed the sanguine commander of the Dart,
as the feet of his messenger touched his deck.

"I bring nothing but defiance!"

"Did you exhibit my statement? Surely, Mr Ark, so material
a document was not forgotten!"

"Nothing was forgotten that the warmest interest in his
safety could suggest, Capt. Bignall. Still he refuses to hearken
to your conditions."

"Perhaps, Sir, he imagines that we are defective in some of
our spars? He may hope to escape by pressing the canvass on
his own light-heeled ship—"

"Does that look like flight?" demanded Wilder, extending
an arm towards the nearly naked spars, and motionless hull of
their neighbor. "The utmost I can obtain is an assurance that
he will not be the assailant."

"Fore George he is a merciful youth! and one that should
be commended for moderation. He will not run his disor-
derly, picarooning company under the guns of a British man
of war, because he owes a little reverence to the flag of his
Master—Harkee, Mr Ark, we will remember the circumstance when questioned at the Old Bailey. Send the people to
their guns, Sir, and ware the ship round, to put an end, at
once, to this foolery, or we shall have him sending a boat
aboard to examine our commissions!"

"Capt. Bignall," said Wilder, leading his commander still
further from the ears of their inferiors, "I may lay some little
claim to merit for services done under your own eyes, and in
obedience to your orders. If my former conduct gives me any
title to presume to counsel one of your great experience,
suffer me to urge a short delay."

"Delay! does Henry Ark hesitate, when the enemies of his King, nay, more, the enemies of man, are daring him to his duty?"

"Sir, you mistake me. I hesitate in order that the flag under which we sail may be free from stain, and not with any intent of avoiding the combat. Our enemy—*my* enemy, knows that he has nothing now to expect for his former generosity, but kindness should he become our captive. Still, Capt. Bignall, I ask for time to prepare the Dart, for a conflict that will try all her powers, and to insure a victory that will not be bought without a price."

"But should he escape?—"

"On my life he will not attempt it. I not only know the man, but his formidable means of resistance. A half hour will put us in the necessary condition, and do no discredit either to our spirit or to our prudence."

The veteran yielded a reluctant consent, which was not, however, accorded, without much muttering concerning the disgrace a British man of war incurred in not running along side the boldest pirate that floated, and blowing him out of water with a single watch. Wilder, who was accustomed to the honest professional bravado that often formed a peculiar embellishment to the really firm and manly resolution of the seamen of that age, permitted him to complain at will, while he busied himself in a manner that he knew was now of the last importance, and in a duty that properly came under his more immediate inspection.

The order for "all hands to clear ship, for action" was again given, and received in the cheerful temper, with which mariners are wont to welcome any of the more important changes of their exciting profession. Little remained, however, to be done, for most of the previous preparations had still been left, as at the original meeting of the two vessels. Then came the beat to quarters, and the more serious and fearful-looking preparations for certain combat. After these arrangements were completed, the crew at their guns, the sail trimmers at the braces, and the officers in their several batteries, the after yards were swung and the ship was once more put in motion.

During all this time, the vessel of the Rover lay, at the distance of half a mile, in a state of entire rest, without betraying the smallest interest in the obvious movements of her hostile neighbor. When, however, the Dart was seen yielding to the breeze, and gradually increasing her velocity, until the water was gathering under her fore-foot in a little rolling wave of foam, the bows of the other fell off from the direction of the wind, the topsail was filled, and, in her turn, the hull was held in command, by giving to it the impetus of motion. The Dart, now set again, at her gaft, that broad field, which had been lowered during the conference, and which had floated in triumph, through the hazards and struggles of a thousand combats. No answering emblem was however exhibited from the peak of her adversary.

In this manner the two ships "gathered way," as it is expressed in nautical language, watching each other with eyes as jealous, as if they had been rival monsters of the great deep, each endeavoring to conceal from his antagonist the evolution he contemplated next. The earnest manner of Wilder had not failed to produce its influence on the straight minded seaman who commanded the Dart and by this time he was as much disposed as his Lieutenant to approach the conflict leisurely and with proper caution.

The day had hitherto been cloudless, and a vault of purer blue never canopied a waste of water, than the arch which had stretched for hours above the heads of our marine adventurers. But, as if nature frowned on their present bloody designs, a dark, threatening mass of vapour was blending the ocean with the sky in a direction opposed to the currents of the air. These well known and ominous signs did not escape the vigilance of those who manned the hostile ships, but the danger was deemed too remote to interrupt the higher interest of the approaching combat.

"We have a squall brewing in the west," said the experienced and wary Bignall, pointing to the frowning symptoms as he spoke, "but we can handle the pirate, and get all snug again, before it works its way up against this breeze."

Wilder assented, for by this time, professional pride was swelling in his bosom also, and a generous rivalry was getting the mastery of feelings that were possibly foreign to his duty, however natural they might have proved in one as open to kindness as himself.

"The Rover is even sending down all his lighter masts!" exclaimed the youth. "It would seem that he distrusts the weather."

"We will not follow his example, for he will wish they were aloft again, the moment we get him fairly under the play of our batteries. By George our King, but he has a pretty moving boat under him! Let fall the main-course, Sir; down with it, or we shall have it night before we get the rogue abeam."

The order was obeyed, when the Dart, feeling the powerful impulse, quickened her speed, like an animate being that is freshly impelled by its apprehensions, or its wishes. By this time she had gained a position on the weather quarter of her adversary, who had not manifested the smallest desire to prevent her attaining so material an advantage. On the contrary, while the Dolphin kept the same canvass spread, she continued to lighten her top-hamper, bringing as much of the weight as possible, from the towering height of her tall masts, within the greater security of the hull. Still the distance between them, was too great, in the opinion of Bignall to commence the contest, while the facility with which his adversary moved ahead, threatened to protract the important moment to an unreasonable extent or to reduce him to a croud of sail that might prove embarrassing, while enveloped in the smoke, and pressed by the urgencies of the combat.

"We will touch his pride, Sir, since you think him a man of spirit," said the veteran. "Give him a weather gun, and show him another of his Master's ensigns."

The roar of the piece, and the display of three more of the fields of England, in quick succession, from different parts of the Dart, failed to produce the slightest evidence even of observation, aboard their seemingly insensible neighbor. The Dolphin still kept on her way, occasionally swooping up to touch the wind, and then deviating from her course again to leeward, as the porpoise is seen to turn aside from his direction to snuff the breeze, while he lazily sports along his briny path.

"He will not be moved by any of the devices of lawful and ordinary warfare," said Wilder, when he witnessed the indifference with which their challenges had been received.

"Try him with a shot."

A gun was now discharged from the side next the still receding Dolphin. The iron messenger was seen bounding along the surface of the sea, skipping lightly from wave to wave, until it cast a little cloud of spray upon the deck of their enemy, as it boomed harmlessly past her hull. Another and yet another followed without in any manner extracting signal or notice from their adversary.

"How's this!" exclaimed the disappointed Bignall. "Has he a charm for his ship, that all our shot sweep over him in vain! Master Fid, can you do nothing for the credit of honest people, and the honour of a pennant? Let us hear from your old favorite. In times past she used to speak to better purpose."

"Ay, ay, Sir," returned the accommodating Richard, who in the sudden turns of his fortune found himself in authority over a much-loved and long cherished piece. "I christened the gun after Mistress Whiffle, your Honor, for the same reason that they both can do their own talking. Now, stand aside, my lads, and let clattering Kate, have a word in the discourse."

Richard, who had coolly taken his sight, while speaking, deliberately applied the match with his own hand, and with a philosophy that was sufficiently to be commended in a mercenary sent what he boldly pronounced to be "a thorough straight goer" in the direction of his recent associates. The usual moments of suspense succeeded, and then the torn fragments which were scattered in the air, announced that the shot had passed through the nettings of the Dolphin. The effect on the vessel of the Rover was nearly magical. A long stripe of cream coloured canvass, which had been artfully extended, from stem to stern, in a line with her guns, disappeared, as suddenly as a bird would shut his wings, leaving in its place a broad blood-red belt, that was bristling with the armament of the ship. At the same time, an ensign of a similar ominous colour rose from her poop, and fluttering darkly and fiercely for a moment, it became fixed at the end of her gaft.

"Now I know him for the knave that he is!" cried the excited Bignall, "and see, he has thrown away his false paint, and shows the well-known bloody side, from which he gets his name. Stand to your guns, my men; the pirate is getting to be in earnest."

He was still speaking, when a sheet of bright flame glanced from out that streak of red, which was so well adapted to work upon the superstitious awe of the common mariners, and was followed by the simultaneous explosion of a dozen wide-mouthed pieces of artillery. The startling change from inattention and indifference to this act of bold and decided hostility, produced a strong effect on the boldest heart on board the King's cruiser. The momentary interval of suspense was passed, in unchanged attitudes, and looks of breathless attention; and then the rushing of the iron storm was heard hurtling through the air, as it came fearfully on. The crash that followed, mingled as it was with human groans, and succeeded by the tearing of riven plank and the scattering of splinters, ropes, blocks and the implements of war, proclaimed the fatal accuracy of the broad-side. But the surprise, and the brief confusion, endured but for an instant. The English shouted, sending back a return to the deadly assault they had just received, recovering manfully and promptly from the shock it had assuredly given.

The ordinary and more regular cannonading of a naval combat succeeded. Anxious to precipitate the issue both ships pressed nigher to each other the while, until in a few moments the two white canopies of smoke, that were wreathing about their respective masts were blended in one, marking a solitary spot of strife, in the midst of a scene of broad and bright tranquility. The discharges of the cannon were hot, close and incessant. While the hostile parties, however, closely imitated each other in their zeal in dealing out destruction, a peculiar difference marked the distinction in character of the two crews. Loud, cheering shouts accompanied each discharge from the lawful cruiser, while the people of the rover did their murderous work in the silence of desperation.

The spirit and uproar of the scene soon quickened that blood in the veins of the veteran Bignall, which had begun to circulate a little slowly by time.

"The fellow has not forgotten his art!" he exclaimed, as the effects of his enemy's skill were getting to be but too manifest in the rent sails, shivered spars and tottering masts of his own ship. "Had he but the commission of the King in his pocket, one might call him a hero!"

But the emergency was too urgent to throw away the time in words. Wilder answered only, by cheering his own people to their fierce and laborious task. The ships had now fallen off before the wind and were running parallel to each other, emitting sheets of flame that were incessantly glancing through immense volumes of smoke. The spars of the respective vessels were alone visible at brief and uncertain intervals. Many minutes had thus passed, seeming to those engaged but a moment of time, when the mariners of the Dart found that they no longer held their vessel in the quick command so necessary to their situation. The important circumstance was instantly conveyed from the master to Wilder, and from Wilder to his superior. A hasty consultation on the cause and consequences of this unexpected event was the immediate and natural result.

"See!" cried Wilder. "The sails are already hanging against the masts like rags; the explosions of the artillery have stilled the wind."

"Hark!" answered the more experienced Bignall. "There goes the artillery of heaven among our own guns. The squall is already upon us. Port the helm, Sir, and sheer the ship out of the smoke—Hard a-port with the helm, Sir, at once!—hard with it a-port, I say."

But the lazy motion of the vessel did not answer to the impatience of those who directed her movements, nor did it meet the pressing exigencies of the moment. In the mean time, while Bignall and the officers whose duties kept them near his person, assisted by the sail-trimmers, were thus occupied, the people in the batteries continued their murderous employment. The roar of cannon was incessant, and nearly overwhelming, though there were instants, when the ominous mutterings of the atmosphere were too distinctly audible to be mistaken. Still the eye could lend no assistance to the hearing, in determining the judgement of the mariners. Hulls, spars and sails were alike enveloped in the curling wreaths which wrapped heaven, air, vessels, and ocean alike, in one white, obscure, foggy mantle. Even the persons of the crew were merely seen at instants labouring at the guns through brief and varying openings.

"I never knew the smoke pack so heavy on the deck of a

ship before," said Bignall, with a concern, that even his caution could not entirely repress. "Keep the helm a-port—jam it hard, Sir! By heaven, Mr Wilder, these knaves well know they are struggling for their lives."

"The fight is all our own!" shouted the second lieutenant, from among the guns, staunching, as he spoke, the blood of a severe splinter wound in the face, and far too intent on his own immediate occupation to notice the signs of the weather. "He has not answered with a single gun for near a minute."

"Fore George, the rogues have enough!" exclaimed the delighted Bignall. "Three cheers for vic—"

"Hold, Sir," interrupted Wilder with sufficient decision to check his Commander's premature exultation. "On my life, our work is not so soon ended. I think, indeed, his guns are silent—But see the smoke is beginning to lift. In a few more moments if our own fire should cease, the view will be clear."

A shout from the men in the batteries interrupted his words, and then came a general cry that the pirates, were sheering off. The exultation at this fancied evidence of their superiority, was however soon and fearfully interrupted. A bright vivid flash penetrated through the dense vapour, which still hung about them, in a most extraordinary manner, and was followed by a crash from the heavens, to which the simultaneous explosion of fifty pieces of artillery would have sounded feeble.

"Call the people from the guns," said Bignall, in those suppressed tones, that are only more portentous from their forced and unnatural calmness. "Call them away, at once, Sir, and get the canvass in."

Wilder, startled more at the proximity and apparent weight of the squall than at words to which he had been long accustomed, delayed not to give an order that was so urgent. The men left their batteries, like athletæ retiring from the arena, some bleeding and faint, some fierce and angry, and all more or less excited by the furious scene in which they had just been actors. Many sprung to the well known ropes, while others, as they ascended into the cloud which still hung on the vessel, became lost to the eye in her rigging.

"Shall I reef or furl?" demanded Wilder, standing with the trumpet at his lips, ready to issue the necessary order.

"Hold, Sir. Another minute will give us an opening."

The Lieutenant paused, for he was not slow to see that now, indeed, the veil was about to be drawn from their real situation. The smoke which had lain upon their very decks, pressed down by the superincumbent weight of the atmosphere, first began to stir, was then seen eddying among the masts, and, finally, whirled wildly away before a strong current of air. The view was, indeed, now all before them.

In place of the glorious sun, and that bright blue canopy, which had lain above them, a short half-hour before, the heavens were clothed in one immense black veil. The sea reflected the portentous colour, looking dark and angrily. The waves had already lost their regular rise and fall, and were tossing, to and fro, awaiting the power which was to give them direction and force. The flashes from the heavens were not in quick succession, but the few that did break upon the gloominess of the scene, came in Majesty, and with dazzling brightness. They were accompanied by the terrific thunder of the tropics, in which it is scarcely profanation to fancy that the voice of one who made the universe is actually speaking to the creatures of his hand. On every side was the appearance of a fierce and dangerous struggle in the elements. The vessel of the Rover was running lightly before a breeze, which had already come fresh and fitful from the cloud, with her sails reduced, and her people coolly but actively employed in repairing the damages of the fight.

Not a moment was to be lost in imitating the example of the wary freebooters. The head of the Dart was hastily and happily got in a direction contrary to the breeze, and as she began to follow the course taken by the Dolphin, an attempt was made to gather her torn and nearly useless canvass to the yards. But precious minutes had been lost in the smoky canopy that might never be regained. The sea, changed its colour from a dark green to a glittering white, and then the fury of the gust was heard rushing fearfully along the water, and with a violence that could not be resisted.

"Be lively, men," shouted Bignall, himself, in the exigency in which his vessel was placed. "Roll up the cloth; in with it all—leave not a rag to the squall. Fore George, Mr Wilder, but this wind is not playing with us. Cheer the men to their work, speak to them cheerily, Sir."

"Furl away!" shouted Wilder. "Cut, if too late: work away with knives and teeth—down, every man of you down—down for your lives all!"

There was an energy in the voice of the Lieutenant which sounded supernatural in the ears of his people. He had so recently witnessed a calamity similar to that which again threatened him, that his feelings lent horror to the tones. A score of forms descended swiftly through an atmosphere that appeared sensible to the touch. Nor was their escape, which might be likened to the stooping of birds that dart into their nests, too earnestly pressed. Stripped of half its rigging, and already tottering under numerous wounds, the lofty and over-loaded spars, yielded to the mighty force of the squall, tumbling in succession towards the hull, untill nothing stood, but the three firmer, but shorn and nearly useless, lower masts. By far the greater number of those aloft reached the deck in time to ensure their safety, though some there were, too stubborn and still too much under the sullen influence of the combat to hearken to the words of warning. These victims of their own obstinacy, were seen clinging to the broken fragments of the spars, as the Dart, in a cloud of foam, drove away from the spot where they floated, until their persons and their misery were alike swallowed in the distance.

"It is the hand of God!" hoarsely exclaimed the veteran Bignall, while his eye drunk in the destruction of the wreck. "Mark me, Henry Ark, I will forever testify that the guns of the pirate have not brought us to this condition."

Little disposed to seek the same miserable consolation as his Commander, Wilder exerted himself in counteracting as far as circumstances would allow, an injury that he felt, how-ever, to be, at such a moment, irreparable. Amid the howling of the gust, and the fearful crashing of thunder, with an atmosphere now lurid with the glare of lightning, and now nearly obscured by the dark overhanging canopy of vapor, and with all the frightful evidences of the fight still reeking and ghastly before their eyes, did the crew of the British cruiser prove true to themselves and to their ancient reputa-tion. The voices of Bignall and his subordinates were heard in the tempest, uttering those mandates which long experience had rendered familiar, or encouraging the people to their duty. Happily the strife of the elements was of short continuance. The squall soon swept over the spot, leaving the currents of the trade returning into their former channels, and a sea that was rather stilled than agitated by the counteracting influence of the winds.

But as one danger passed away from before the eyes of the mariners of the Dart, another scarcely less to be apprehended forced itself upon their attention. All recollection of the favors of the past, and every feeling of gratitude was banished from the mind of Wilder, by the mountings of professional pride, and that love of glory which becomes inherent in the warrior, as he gazed on the untouched and beautiful symmetry of the Dolphin's spars, and all the perfect and beautiful order of her tackle. It seemed as if she bore a charmed fate or that some supernatural agency had been instrumental in preserving her unharmed amid the violence of a second hurricane. But cooler thought and more impartial reflection compelled the internal acknowledgement that the vigilance and wise precautions of the remarkable individual who appeared not only to govern her movements, but to control her fortunes, had their proper influence in producing the result.

Little leisure, however, was allowed to ruminate on these changes, or to deprecate the advantage of their adversary. The vessel of the Rover, had already opened many broad sheets of canvass, and, as the return of the regular breeze gave her the wind, her approach was rapid and unavoidable.

"Fore George, Mr Ark, luck is all on the dishonest side to-day," said the veteran, when he perceived, by the direction which the Dolphin took, that the encounter was likely to be renewed. "Send the people to quarters, again, and clear away the guns; we are likely to have another bout with the rogues."

"I would advise a moment's delay," Wilder earnestly observed, when he heard his Commander issuing an order to his people to prepare to deliver their fire the instant their enemy should come within a favorable position. "Let me entreat you to delay; we know not what may be his present intentions."

"None shall put foot on the deck of the Dart, without

submitting to the authority of her royal master," returned the stern old tar. "Give it to him, my men; scatter the rogues from their guns! Let them know the danger of approaching a lion, though he should be crippled."

Wilder saw that remonstrance was too late, for a fresh broadside was hurled from the Dart, to defeat any generous intentions that the Rover might entertain. The ship of the latter received the iron storm, while advancing, and immediately deviated from her course in such a way as to prevent its repetition. Then she was seen sweeping towards the bows of the nearly helpless cruiser of the King, and a hoarse summons was heard ordering her ensign to be lowered.

"Come on, ye villains!" shouted the excited Bignall. "Come, and perform the office with your own hands."

The graceful ship, as if sensible herself to the taunts of her enemy, sprung nigher to the wind, and shooting across the forefoot of the Dart, delivered her fire, gun after gun with deliberate and deadly accuracy, full into that defenceless portion of her antagonist. A crush like that of meeting bodies followed, when fifty grim visages, were seen entering the scene of carnage, armed with the deadly weapons of personal conflict. The shock of so close and so fatal a discharge, had, for the moment, paralyzed the efforts of the assailed, but no sooner did Bignall and his lieutenant see the dark forms that issued from the smoke on their own decks, than with voices that had not even then lost their authority, each summoned a band of followers, backed by whom they bravely dash'd into opposite gangways of their ship to stay the torrent. The first encounter was fierce and fatal, both parties receding a little to wait for succor and recover breath.

"Come on, ye murderous thieves!" cried the dauntless veteran, who stood foremost in his own band, conspicuous by the gray locks that floated around his naked head; "well do ye know that heaven is with the right!"

The grim freebooters in his front recoiled and opened; then came a sheet of flame from the side of the Dolphin through an empty port of her foe, bearing in its centre a hundred deadly missiles. The sword of Bignall, was flourished furiously and wildly above his head, and his voice was still heard shouting, till utterance failed him,—

"Come on, ye knaves! come on!" he cried.—"Harry—Harry Ark—oh! God—Hurrah!"

He fell like a log, and died the unwitting owner of that very commission for which he had toiled throughout a life of hardship, and danger. Until now, Wilder had made good his quarter of the deck, though pressed by a band fierce and daring as his own. But at this fearful crisis in the combat a voice was heard in the melée, that thrilled on all his own nerves, seeming even to carry its fearful influence over the minds of his men.

"Make way, there, make way—" it said, clear, deep, and breathing with authority. "Make way, and follow; no hand but mine shall lower that vaunting flag."

"Stand to your faith, men," shouted Wilder, in reply—"on—on, and sweep the miscreants from our decks."

This second shock was much more fatal than the first. Shouts, oaths, imprecations and groans formed a fearful accompaniment of the rude encounter, which was, however, too violent to continue long. Wilder saw with agony that numbers and impetuosity were sweeping his supporters from around him. Again and again he called them to the succour with his voice, or stimulated them to daring by his example.

Friend after friend fell at his feet, until he was driven to the utmost extremity of the deck. Here he again rallied a little band, against which, several furious charges were made in vain.

"Ha!" exclaimed a voice he well knew; "death to all traitors! Spit the spy as you would a dog. Charge through them, my bullies; a halberd to the hero, who shall reach his heart!"

"Avast, ye lubbers," returned the staunch Richard. "Here are a white man and a nigger at your service, if you've need of a spit."

"Two more of the gang!" continued the general, aiming a blow that threatened to immolate the topman, as he spoke.

A dark, half-naked form was interposed to receive the descending blade, which fell on the staff of a half-pike, severing it as if it were a reed. Nothing daunted by the defenceless state in which he found himself, Scipio, made his way to the front of Wilder, where, with a body divested to the waist of every garment, and empty handed he fought with his brawny arms, like one who despised the cuts, thrusts, and assaults, of which his athletic frame became the helpless subject.

"Give it to 'em, right and left, Guinea," cried Fid, "here is one who will come in as a backer as soon as he has stopped the grog of the marine."

The parries and science of the unfortunate General were at this moment set at naught, by a blow from Richard, which broke down all his defences, descending through cap and skull to the jaw.

"Hold, murderers—" cried Wilder, who saw the number-less blows that were falling on the defenceless body of the still undaunted black—"Strike here but spare an unarmed man."

The sight of our adventurer became confused for he saw the negro fall, dragging with him to the deck two of his assailants, and then a voice, deep as the emotion which such a scene might create, uttered in the very portals of his ear—

"Our work is done. He that strikes another blow, makes an enemy of me."

# Chapter XXXI

——"Take him hence;
The whole world shall not save him."
*Cymbeline*, V.v.320—21.

THE RECENT GUST had not passed more fearfully and suddenly over the ship than the scene just related. But the
smiling aspect of the tranquil sky and the bright sun of a
Caribbean sea, found no parallel in the horrors that succeeded
the combat. The momentary confusion which accompanied
the fall of Scipio, soon disappeared, and Wilder was left to
gaze on the wreck of all the boasted powers of his cruiser, and
on that waste of human life, which had been the attendants of
the struggle. The former has already been sufficiently described, but a short account of the present state of the actors
may serve to elucidate the events that are to follow.

Within a few yards of the place he was permitted to occupy
himself, stood the motionless form of the Rover. A second
glance was necessary however to recognize, in the grim visage, to which the boarding cap, already mentioned, lent a
look of artificial ferocity, the usually bland countenance of the
man. As the eye of Wilder roamed over the swelling, erect,
and triumphant figure, it was difficult not to fancy that even
the stature had been suddenly and unaccountably increased.
One hand rested on the hilt of a yattagan, which, by the crimson drops that flowed along its curved blade, had evidently
done fatal service, in the fray, and one foot was placed, seemingly with supernatural weight, on that national emblem,
which it had been his pride to lower. His eye was wandering
sternly but with perfect understanding over the scene, though
he spoke not, nor, in any other manner betrayed the deep
interest he felt in the past. At his side, and nearly within the
circle of his arm, stood the cowering form of the boy, Roderick, unprovided with weapon, his garments sprinkled with
blood, his eye, contracted, wild and fearful, and his face pallid
as those in whom the tide of life had just ceased to circulate.

Here and there were to be seen the wounded captives, still
sullen and unconquered in spirit, while many of their scarcely

more fortunate enemies, lay in their blood around the deck, with such gleamings of ferocity on their countenances, as plainly denoted, that the current of their meditations was still running on vengeance. The uninjured and the slightly wounded of both hands, were already pursuing their different objects of plunder or of secretion.

But so thorough was the discipline established by the leader of the freebooters, so absolute his power, that a blow had not been struck or blood drawn, since the moment his prohibitory mandate was heard. There had been enough of destruction, however, to satisfy the most gluttonous longings, had human life been the sole object of the assault. Wilder felt many a pang, as the marble-like features of some humble friend, or faithful servitor, came, one after another, under his recognition; but the shock was greatest when his eye fell upon the rigid and still frowning countenance of his veteran Commander.

"Capt. Heidegger," he said, struggling to maintain the fortitude which became the moment, "the fortune of the day is yours. I ask mercy and kindness for the survivors."

"They shall be granted to those who of right may claim them; I hope it may be found that all are included in this promise."

The voice of the Rover was solemn and full of meaning: it appeared to convey more than the simple import of the words. Wilder might have mused long and vainly, however, on the equivocal manner in which he had been answered, had not the approach of a body of the hostile crew, among whom he instantly recognised the most prominent of the late mutineers of the Dolphin, speedily supplied a clue to the hidden meaning of their leader.

"We claim the execution of our ancient laws!" commenced the foremost of the gang, addressing his chief, with a brevity and fierceness which the late combat might have generated, if not excused.

"What would you have?"

"The lives of traitors," was the sullen answer.

"You know the conditions of our service. If any such are in our power, let them meet their fate."

Had any doubt remained in the mind of Wilder, as to the

meaning of these terrible claimants of justice, it would have vanished at the manner with which he and his two companions were immediately dragged before the lawless chief. Though the love of life was strong and active in his breast, it was not, even in that fearful moment, exhibited in a deprecating or unmanly form. Not for an instant did his mind waver, or his thoughts wander to any subterfuge that might prove unworthy of his profession or of his former character. One, anxious, enquiring look was fastened on the eye of him, whose power alone could save him. He witnessed the short, severe struggle that softened the rigid muscles of the Rover's countenance, and then he saw the instant, cold and calm composure which settled on every one of its disciplined lineaments. He knew, at once, that the feelings of the man were smothered, in the duty of the chief, and more was unnecessary to teach him the hopelessness of his condition. Scorning to render his state degrading by useless remonstrance, the youth remained where his accusers had seen fit to place him, firm, motionless and silent.

"What would ye have?" the Rover at length asked, in a voice that even his iron nerves scarce rendered deep and full toned as common. "What ask ye?"

"Their lives!"

"I understand you—go—they are at your mercy."

Notwithstanding the horrors of the scene through which he had just past, and that high excitement which had sustained him through the fight, the deliberate, solemn tones with which his judge delivered a sentence that he knew consigned him to a hasty and ignominious death, shook the frame of our adventurer nearly to insensibility. The blood recoiled backward to his heart, and the sickening sensation that beset his brain, threatened to upset his reason. But the shock passed, on the instant, leaving him erect, and seemingly firm as ever, and certainly with no evidence of mortal weakness that human eye could discover.

"For myself nothing is demanded," he said with admirable steadiness. "I know your self-enacted laws, condemn me to a miserable fate. But for these ignorant, confiding, faithful followers, I claim—nay beg—intreat—implore your mercy. They knew not what they did, and—"

"Speak to these," said the Rover, pointing with an averted eye to the fierce knot by which he was surrounded. "There are your judges, and the sole minister of mercy."

Strong and nearly unconquerable disgust was apparent in the manner of the youth; with a mighty effort he subdued it and turning to the crew, continued—

"Then even to those will I humble myself in petitions. Ye are men, and ye are mariners—"

"Away with him!" exclaimed the croaking Nightingale. "He preaches! away with him, to the yard arm, away!"

The shrill, long-drawn winding of the call which the callous boatswain sounded in mockery, was answered by an echo from twenty voices, in which the accents of nearly as many different people mingled in hoarse discordancy, each shouting in turn,—

"To the yard arm! away with the three! Away!"

Wilder made a last appeal to the Rover with his eye, but he met no look in return, the face of the other being intentionally averted. With a burning brain, he felt himself rudely transferred from the quarter-deck into the centre and less privileged portion of the ship. The violence of the passage, the hurried reaving of cords, and all the fearful preparations of a nautical execution, appeared but the business of a moment, to one who stood so near the verge of time.

"A yellow flag for punishment!" bawled the revengeful captain of the forecastle. "Let the gentleman sail on his last cruise under the rogue's ensign!"

"A yellow flag! A yellow flag!" echoed twenty brawling throats. "Down with the Rover's ensign, and up with the colours of the provost marshall! A yellow flag! a yellow flag!"

The hoarse laughter, and mocking merriment with which this coarse device was received stirred the ire of Fid, who had submitted in silence, so far, to the rude treatment he received, for no other reason than that he thought his superior was the best qualified to utter the little which it might be necessary to say.

"Avast, ye villains!" he hotly exclaimed, prudence and moderation losing their influence under the excitement of anger. "Ye cut-throat, lubberly villains! That ye are villains, is to be proved in your teeth, by your getting your sailing orders from the devil, and that ye are lubbers, any man may see, by the fashion in which ye have rove this cord about my throat. A fine jam will ye make with a turn in your whip! But ye'll all come to know how a man is to be decently hanged, ye rogues, ye will—ye'll all come honestly by the knowledge in your day, ye will!"

"Clear the turn, and run him up!" shouted one, two, three voices in hurried succession. "A clear whip! and a swift run to heaven!"

Happily, a fresh burst of riotous clamour from one of the hatchways interrupted the intention, and then was heard the cry of—

"A priest! a priest! pipe the rogues to prayers before they take their dance on nothing."

The ferocious laughter with which the freebooters received this sneering proposal, was hushed, as suddenly as if one answered to their mockery from that mercy seat whose power they so sacrilegiously braved. A deep, menacing voice was heard in their midst, saying—

"By heaven, if touch or look be laid too boldly on prisoner in this ship, he who offends had better beg the fate ye give these miserable men, than meet my anger. Stand off, I bid you, and let the chaplain approach!"

Every bold hand was instantly withdrawn, and each profane lip was closed in trembling silence, giving the terrified and horror-stricken subject of their liberties room and opportunity to advance to the scene of punishment.

"See," said the Rover, calmly, but still with authority, "you are a minister of God, and your office is sacred charity: If you have aught to smooth the dying moment to fellow mortal, haste to impart it."

"In what have these offended?" demanded the divine, when power was given to speak.

"No matter. It is enough that their hour is near. If you would lift your voice in prayer, fear nothing. The unusual sounds shall be welcome even here. Ay—and these miscreants who so boldly surround you, shall kneel and be mute, as beings whose souls are touched by the holy rite. Scoffing shall be dumb, and unbelieving respectful at my beck. Speak freely."

"Scourge of the seas!" commenced the chaplain, across whose pallid features a flush of holy excitement cast its glow—"remorseless violator of the laws of man; audacious contemner of the mandates of your God, a fearful retribution shall avenge this crime! Is it not enough that ye have this day consigned so many to a sudden end, but your vengeance must be glutted with more blood! Beware the hour when these things shall be visited in Almighty power on your own devoted head."

"Look!" said the Rover, smiling wildly, but with an expression that was haggard, in spite of the unnatural exultation that struggled about his quivering lip. "Here are the evidences of the manner in which heaven protects the right!"

"Though its awful justice be hidden in the inscrutable wisdom, for a time, deceive not thyself; the hour is at hand when it shall be seen and felt in Majesty." The voice of the chaplain became suddenly choked for his wandering eye, had fallen on the frowning countenance of Bignall, which, set in death, lay but half concealed beneath a flag, which the Rover himself had cast upon the body. Then summoning his energies, he continued, in the clear and admonishing strain that befitted his sacred calling. "They tell me you are but half lost to feeling for your kind, and though the seeds of better principles, of better days, are smothered in your heart, that they still exist, and might be quickened into goodly—"

"Peace. You speak in vain. To your duty, with these men, or be silent."

"Is their doom then sealed?"

"It is."

"Who says it?" demanded a low voice at the elbow of the Rover, which coming upon his ear at that moment, thrilled upon his most latent nerve, chasing the blood from his cheek to the secret recesses of his frame. But, the weakness passed away with the surprise, as he calmly, and almost instantly, answered—

"The law."

"The law!" repeated the Governess. "Can they who set all order at defiance, who despise each human regulation, talk of law! Say it is heartless, vindictive vengeance, if you will, but call it not, by the sacred name of law. I wander from my object! They have told me of this frightful scene, and I have come to offer ransom for the offenders. Name your price; and let it be worthy of the subject we redeem; a grateful parent shall freely give it all for the preserver of his child—"

"If gold will purchase the lives you wish," the other interrupted, with the swiftness of thought, "it is here, in hoards, and ready on the moment. What say my people? Will they take ransom?"

A brooding pause succeeded, and then a low, ominous murmur was raised in the throng, announcing their reluctance to dispense with vengeance. The glowing eye of the Rover scanned the fierce countenances, by which he was environed; his lips moved with vehemence, but disdaining further intercession, nothing was uttered for the ear. Turning to the divine, he added with the forced composure of his wonderful manner—

"Forget not your sacred office. Time is leaving us." He was then moving slowly aside, in imitation of the Governess, who had already veiled her features to exclude the shocking spectacle, when Wilder addressed him.

"For the service you would have done me from my soul I thank you," he said. "If you would know that I leave you in peace, give me yet one solemn assurance before I die."

"To what?"

"Promise that they who came with me into your ship, shall leave it, unharmed and speedily."

"Promise, Walter!" said a solemn, smothered voice in the throng.

"I do."

"I ask no more. Now, reverend Minister of God, perform thy holy office, near my companions. Their ignorance may profit by your service. If I quit this bright and glorious scene, without thought of, and gratitude to that being who, I humbly trust, has made me an heritor of still greater things, I offend wittingly and without hope. But these may find consolation in your prayers."

Amid an awful silence the chaplain approached the devoted companions of Wilder. Their comparative insignificance had left them unobserved during most of the foregoing scene, and material changes had occurred unheeded in their situation.

Fid was seated on the deck, his collar unbuttoned, his neck encircled with the cord, sustaining the head of the nearly helpless black, which he had placed with singular tenderness and care in his lap.

"This man at least will disappoint the malice of his enemies," said the divine, taking the hard hand of the negro into his own. "The termination of his wrongs and his degradation approaches. He will soon be far beyond the reach of human injustice. Friend, by what name is your companion known?"

"It is little matter how you hail a dying man," returned Richard, with a melancholy shake of the head. "He has commonly been entered on the ship's books as Scipio Africa, coming as he did from the coast of Guinea; but if you call him S'ip, he will not be slow to understand you."

"Has he known baptism? Is he a christian?"

"If he be not, I don't know who the devil is!" responded Richard with an asperity that might be deemed a little unseasonable. "A man who serves his country, is true to his messmate, and has no skulk about him, I call a saint, so far as mere religion goes. I say, Guinea, my hearty, give the chaplain a gripe of the fist, if you call yourself a christian. A Spanish windlass would not give a stronger screw than the knuckles of that nigger an hour ago, and now you see, to what a giant may be brought!"

"His latter moment is indeed near! Shall I offer a prayer for the health of the departing spirit?"

"I don't know! I don't know!" answered Fid, gulping his words, and uttering a hem, that was still deep and powerful, as in the brightest and happiest of his days. "When there is so little time given to a poor fellow to speak his mind in, it may be well to let him have a chance to do most of the talking. Something may come uppermost, which he would like to send to his friends in Africa; in which case we may as well be looking out for a proper messenger. Ho! what is it, boy? You see he is already trying to rowse something up out of his ideas."

"Misser Fid, he'm take a collar," said the black, struggling for utterance.

"Ay—ay—" returned Richard, again clearing his throat, and looking to his right and left fiercely, seeking some object on which to wreak his vengeance. "Ay—ay—Guinea; put your mind at ease on that point, my hearty, and for that matter on all others. You shall have a grave as deep as the sea, and christian burial, boy, if this here parson will stand by his work. Any small message you may have for your friends, shall be logg'd, and put in the way of coming to their ears. You have had much foul weather in your time, Guinea, and some squalls have whistled about your head that might have been spared, mayhap, had your colour been a shade or two lighter. For that matter, it may be that I have rode you down a little too close myself, boy, when overheated with the conceit of skin, for all which, may the Lord forgive me, as freely as I hope you will do the same thing."

The negro made a fruitless effort to rise, endeavoring to grasp the hand of the other, saying as he did so,

"Misser Fid beg a pardon of a black man! Masser aloft, forget he'm all, Misser Richard—he t'ink 'em no more."

"It will be what I call a d——d generous thing if he does," returned Richard, whose sorrow and whose conscience had stirred up his uncouth feelings to an extraordinary degree. "There's the affair of slipping off the wreck of the smuggler has never been properly settled atween us, neither, and many other small services of like nature, for which d'ye see, I'll just thank you while there is opportunity, for no one can say, whether we shall ever be borne again on the same ship's books."

A menacing sign from his companion caused the topman to pause, while he endeavored to construe its meaning as well as he was able. With a facility that was in some degree owing to the character of the individual, his construction of the other's meaning was favorable to himself, as was quite evident by the manner in which he resumed—

"Well, well, mayhap we may. I suppose they berth the people there, in some such order as is done here below, in which case we may be put within hailing distance after all. Our sailing orders are both signed, though as you seem likely to slip your cable before these thieves are ready to run me up, you will be getting the best of the wind. I shall not say much concerning any signals it may be necessary to show, in order to make one another out, aloft, Guinea, taking it for granted that you will not overlook Master Harry, on account of the small advantage you may have in being the first to shove off, intending myself to keep as close as possible in his wake, which will give me the twofold advantage of knowing I am on the right tack, and of falling in with you"—

"These are evil words, and fatal alike to your own future peace, and to that of your unfortunate friend," interrupted the divine. "His reliance must be placed on one different in all his attributes from your officer, to follow whom or to consult whose frail conduct would be the height of madness. Place your faith on another—"

"If I do may I be—"

"Peace," said Wilder. "The black would speak to me."

Scipio had turned his looks in the direction of his officer, and was making feeble efforts towards extending his hand. As Wilder placed his own within the grasp of that of the dying negro, the latter succeeded in laying it on his lips, and then flourishing with a convulsive movement that herculean arm which he had so lately and so successfully brandished in defence of his master, the limb stiffened and fell, though the eyes still continued their affectionate and glaring gaze on that countenance he had so long loved, and which, in the midst of all his long endured wrongs, had never refused to meet his look of love in kindness. A low murmur followed this scene, and then complaints succeeded, in a louder strain, till more than one voice was heard openly muttering its discontent that vengeance should be so long delayed.

"Away with them!" shouted an ill omened voice from the throng. "Into the sea with the carcass, and up with the living!"

"Avast!" burst out of the chest of Fid, with an awfulness and depth, that stayed even the daring movements of that lawless moment. "Who dare to cast a seaman into the brine, with the dying look standing in his lights, and his last words still in his messmate's ears! Ha! Would ye stopper the fins of a man, as ye would pin a lobster's claw! That for your fastenings and your lubberly knots together!" The excited topman snapped the lines by which his elbows had been imperfectly secured, while speaking, and immediately lashed the body of the black to his own, though his words received no interruption from a process that was executed with a seaman's dexterity. "Where was the man in your lubberly crew that could lay upon a yard with this here black, or haul upon even a lee earing, while he held the weather line! Could any one of ye all give up his rations in order that a sick messmate might fare the better, or work a double tide to spare the weak arm of a friend! Show me one who had as little dodge under fire as a sound main mast, and I will show you all that is left of his better. And now sway upon your whip, and thank God that the honest end goes up, while the rogues are suffered to keep their footing for a time."

"Sway away!" echoed Nightingale, seconding his hoarse cry by the winding of his call. "Away with them to Heaven."

"Hold!" exclaimed the chaplain, happily arresting the cord, before it had yet done its fatal office. "For his sake, whose mercy may one day be needed by the most hardened of ye all, give but another moment of time. What mean these words— Do I read aright—Ark of Lynnhaven."

"Ay, ay," said Richard, loosening the rope a little in order to speak with greater freedom, and transferring the last morsel of the weed from his box to his mouth, as he answered— "seeing you are an apt scholar, no wonder you make it out so easily, though written by a hand that was always better with a marlingspike than a quill."

"But whence came the words? Why do you bear those names thus written indelibly in the skin—Patience, men, monsters, demons, would ye deprive the dying man of even a minute of that precious time which becomes so dear to all, as life is leaving us?"

"Give yet another minute!" said a deep voice from behind.

"Whence come these words, I ask?" again the chaplain demanded.

"They are neither more nor less than the manner in which a circumstance was logged, which is now of no consequence, seeing that the cruise is nearly up with all, who are chiefly concerned. The black spoke of the collar, but then he thought I might be staying in port, while he was drifting between heaven and earth in search of his last moorings."

"Is there aught here, that I should know!" interrupted the eager, tremulous voice of Mrs Wyllys. "Oh! Merton, why these questions! Has my yearning been prophetic—does nature give so mysterious a warning of its claim!"

"Hush! dearest Madam, your thoughts wander from probabilities, and my faculties become confused. 'The Ark of Lynnhaven' was the name of an estate in the islands belonging to a near and dear friend, and it was the place where I received, and whence I sent to the Main, the precious trust you confided to my care—but—"

"Say on!" she exclaimed, rushing madly in front of Wilder, and seizing the cord which a moment before had been tightened nearly to his destruction, stripping it from his throat, with a sort of supernatural dexterity: "It was not then the name of a ship?"

"A ship! surely not—but what mean these hopes—these fears—"

"The collar—the collar—speak; what of that collar?"

"It means no great things now, my lady," returned Fid, very coolly placing himself in the same condition as Wilder, by profiting by the liberty of his arms, and loosening his own neck from the halter, notwithstanding a movement made by some of the people to prevent it, which was, however, stayed by a look from their leader's eyes. "I will first cast loose this here rope, seeing that it is neither decent nor safe for an ignorant man like me to enter into such unknown navigation ahead of his officer. The collar was just the necklace of the dog, which is here to be seen on the arm of poor Guinea, who was, in most respects, a man for whose equal one might long look in vain—"

"Read it—" said the Governess, a film passing before her own eyes—"read it—" she added, motioning with a quivering hand to the divine to peruse the inscription that was distinctly legible on the plate of brass.

"Holy dispenser of Good, what is this I see! 'Neptune, the property of Paul de Lacey!' "

A loud cry burst from the lips of the Governess, her hands were clasped one single instant upward in that thanksgiving which oppressed her soul, and then, as recollection returned, Wilder was pressed fondly, frantically to her bosom, while her voice was heard to say, in the piercing tones of all powerful nature—

"My child! My child! you will not, cannot, dare not rob a long stricken and bereaved mother of her offspring. Give me back my son—my noble son, and I will weary heaven with prayers in your behalf. Ye are brave and cannot be deaf to mercy. Ye are men who have lived in constant view of God's Majesty, and will not refuse to listen to this evidence of his pleasure. Give me my child, and I yield all else. He is of a race long honoured upon the seas, and no mariner will be deaf to his claims. The widow of de Lacey, the daughter of ——, cries for mercy. Their united blood is in his veins, and it will not be spilt by you! A mother bows herself to the dust before you to ask mercy for her offspring. Oh! give me my child—my child!"

As the words of the petitioner died upon the ear, a stillness settled on the place, that might have been likened to the holy calm which the entrance of better feelings leaves upon the soul of the sinner. The grim freebooters regarded each other in doubt, the workings of nature manifesting themselves even in their stern and hardened visages. Still, the desire for vengeance had got too firm a hold of their minds to be dispossessed at a word. The result would have been doubtful had not one suddenly re-appeared in their midst, who never ordered in vain, and who knew how to guide, to quell, or to mount and trample on their humours, as his own pleasure dictated. For half a minute he looked around him, his eye still following the circle which receded as he gazed, until even those longest accustomed to yield to his will began to wonder at the extraordinary aspect in which it was now exhibited. The gaze was wild and bewildered; and the face pallid as that of the petitioning mother. Three times did the lips sever, before sound issued from the caverns of his chest. Then arose, on the attentive ears of the breathless and listening crowd, a voice that seemed equally charged with inward emotion and high authority. With a haughty gesture of the hand and a manner that was too well understood to be mistaken, he said,—

"Disperse! Ye know my justice; but ye know I will be obeyed. My pleasure shall be known to-morrow."

# Chapter XXXII

—"This is he;
Who hath upon him still that natural stamp:
It was wise Nature's end in the donation,
To be his evidence now."
*Cymbeline*, V.v.365–68.

---

THAT MORROW came, and with it an entire change in the scene and character of our tale. The Dolphin and the Dart were sailing in amity, side by side, the latter again bearing the ensign of England, and the former carrying a naked gaft. The injuries of the gust and the combat had so far been repaired, that to a common eye each gallant vessel was again prepared equally to encounter the hazards of the ocean or of warfare. A long, blue, hazy streak to the north, proclaimed the proximity of the land, and some three or four light coasters of that region, which were sailing nigh, announced how little of hostility existed in the present purposes of the freebooters.

What those designs were, however, still remained a secret, buried in the bosom of the Rover alone. Doubt, wonder, and distrust were each in its turn, to be traced in the features of his captives, and in those of his own crew. Throughout the whole of the long night which had succeeded the events of the important day just passed, he had been pacing the poop in brooding silence. The little he had uttered was merely to direct the movements of the vessels; and when any ventured with other design to approach his person, a sign that none there dared disregard, secured him the solitude he wished. Once or twice indeed, the boy Roderick was seen hovering at his elbow, but it was as a guardian spirit would be fancied to linger near the object of its care, unobtrusively, and, it might almost be added, invisible. When however the sun came burnished and glorious out of the waters of the East, a gun was fired to bring a coaster to the side of the Dolphin, and then it seemed that the curtain was to be raised on the closing scene of the drama. With his crew assembled on the deck beneath, and the principal personages among his captives beside him on the poop, the Rover addressed the former.

"Years have united us by a common fortune," he said: "we have long been submissive to the same laws. If I have been prompt to punish, I have been ready to obey. You cannot charge me with injustice. But the covenant is now ended. I take back my pledge, and I return you your faiths—Nay, frown not—hesitate not—murmur not. The compact ceases, and our laws are ended. Such were the conditions of the service. I give you your liberty, and little do I claim in return. That you need have no grounds of reproach, I bestow my treasure. See—" he added, raising that bloody ensign with which he had so often braved the power of the nations, and exhibiting beneath it sacks of that metal which has so long governed the world, "see, this was mine; it is now yours. It shall be put in yonder coaster; there I leave you to bestow it yourselves, on those you may deem most worthy. Go: The land is near—Disperse for your own sakes, nor hesitate, for without me, well do ye know, that vessel of the King, would be your Master. The ship is already mine; of all the rest, I claim these prisoners alone for my portion—Farewell."

Silent amazement succeeded this unlooked for address. There was, indeed, for a moment, some disposition to rebel, but the measures of the Rover had been too well taken for resistance. The Dart lay, on their beam, with her people at their guns, matches lighted, and a heavy battery. Unprepared, without a leader, and surprized, opposition would have been madness. The first astonishment had scarce abated, before each freebooter rushed to secure his individual effects, and to transfer them to the deck of the coaster. When all but the crew of a single boat had left the Dolphin, the promised gold was sent, and then the loaded craft was seen hastily seeking the shelter of some secret creek. During this scene, the Rover had been silent as death. He next turned to Wilder, and making a mighty, but successful effort to still his feelings, he added,—

"Now must we, too, part. I commend my wounded to your care. They are necessarily with your surgeons. I know the trust I give you will not be abused."

"My word is the pledge of their safety," returned the young de Lacey.

"I believe you. Lady," he added, approaching the elder of the females, with an air in which earnestness and hesitation strongly contended, "if a proscribed and guilty man, may still address you, grant yet a favor."

"Name it—a mother's ear can never be deaf to him who has spared her child."

"When you petition heaven for that child, forget not there is another being who may still profit by your prayers—No more—and now," he continued, looking about him like one who was determined to be equal to the pang of the moment, however difficult it might prove, and surveying, with an eye of painful regret, those naked decks which were so lately teeming with scenes of life and revelry, "and, now—ay—now we part. The boat awaits you."

Wilder soon saw his mother and Gertrude into the pinnace; but he still lingered himself.

"And you," he said, "what will become of you?"

"I shall shortly be—forgotten—Adieu."

The manner in which the Rover spoke forbade delay. The young man hesitated, squeezed his hand and left him.

When Wilder found himself restored to his proper vessel, of which the death of Bignall had left him in command, he immediately issued the order to fill her sails, and to steer for the nearest haven of his country. So long as sight could read the movements of the man who remained on the decks of the Dolphin, not a look was averted from the motionless object. She lay, with her maintopsail to the mast, stationary as some beautiful fabric placed there by fairy power, still lovely in her proportions and perfect in all her parts. A human form was seen swiftly pacing her poop, and by its side glided one, who looked like a lessened shadow of that restless figure. At length distance swallowed these indistinct images, and then the eye was wearied in vain, to trace the internal movements of the distant ship. But doubt was soon ended. Suddenly a streak of flame flashed from her decks, springing fiercely from sail to sail. A vast cloud of smoke broke out of the hull, and the deadened roar of artillery followed. To this succeeded, for a time, the awful and yet attractive spectacle of a burning ship.

The whole was terminated by an immense canopy of smoke and an explosion, that caused the sails of the distant Dart to waver, as if the winds of the trades were deserting their eternal direction. When the cloud had lifted from the ocean, an empty waste of water was seen beneath, and none might mark the spot, where that beautiful specimen of human ingenuity had so lately floated. Some of those who ascended to the upper masts of the cruiser, and were aided by glasses believed, indeed, that they could discern a solitary speck upon the sea, but whether it was a boat or some fragment of the wreck was never known.

From that time, the history of the dreaded Red Rover became gradually lost in the fresher incidents of those eventful seas. But the mariner long after was known to shorten the watches of the night, by recounting scenes of mad enterprise, that were thought to have occurred under his auspices. Rumour did not fail to embellish and pervert them, until the real character and even the name of the individual were confounded with the actors of other atrocities. Scenes of higher and more ennobling interest, too, were occurring on the Western Continent, to efface the circumstances of a legend that many deemed wild and improbable. The British Colonies of North America had revolted against the Government of the Crown, and a weary war was bringing the contest to a successful issue. Newport, the opening scene of this tale, had been successively occupied by the arms of the King, and by those of that Monarch who had sent the chivalry of his nation to aid in stripping his rival of her vast possessions.

The beautiful haven had sheltered hostile fleets, and the peaceful villas had often rung with the merriment of youthful soldiers. More than twenty years after the events just related had been added to the long record of time, when the island-town witnessed the rejoicings of another festival. The allied forces had compelled the most enterprising leader of the British troops to yield himself and army, captives to their numbers and skill. The struggle was believed to be over, and the worthy townsmen had, as usual, been loud in the manifestations of their pleasure. The rejoicings, however, ceased with the day, and as night gathered over the place, the little city was resuming its customary provincial tranquility. A gallant frigate which lay in the very spot, where the vessel of the Rover had first been seen, had already lowered the gay assemblage of friendly ensigns, which had been spread in the usual order of a gala day. A flag of intermingled colours, and bearing a constellation of bright and rising stars, alone was floating at her gaff.

Just at this moment another cruiser, but one of less magnitude was seen entering the roadstead, bearing also the friendly ensign of the new States. Headed by the tide, and deserted by the breeze, she soon dropped an anchor, in the pass between Conanicut and Rhode, when a boat was seen making for the inner-harbor, impelled by the arms of six powerful rowers. As the barge approached a retired and lonely wharf, a solitary observer of its movements was enabled to see that it contained a curtained litter, and a single female form. Before the curiosity which such a sight would be apt to create, in the breast of one like the spectator mentioned, had time to exercise itself in conjectures, the oars were tossed, the boat had touched the piles, and borne by the seamen, the litter, attended by the woman, stood before him.

"Tell me, I pray you," said a voice, in whose tones grief and resignation were singularly combined, "if Capt Henry de Lacey of the Continental marine has a residence in this Town of Newport?"

"That has he—" answered the aged man addressed by the female, "that has he; or, as one might say, two; since yonder frigate is no less his than the dwelling on the hill, just by."

"Thou art too old to point us out the way, but if grandchild or idler of any sort be near, here is silver to reward him."

"Lord help you, lady!" returned the other, casting an oblique glance at her appearance as a sort of salvo for the term, and pocketing the trifling piece she offered, with singular care, "Lord help you, Madam, old though I am, and something worn down by hardships and marvellous adventures, both by sea and land, yet will I gladly do so small an office for one of your condition. Follow, and you shall see, that your pilot is not altogether unused to the path."

The old man turned and was leading the way off the wharf even before he had completed the assurance of his boasted ability. The seamen and the female followed, the latter walking sorrowfully and in silence by the side of the litter.

"If you have need of refreshment," said their guide, pointing over his shoulder, "yonder is a well known inn, and one much frequented in its time by mariners. Neighbor Joram and the Foul Anchor have had a reputation, in their day, as well as the greatest warrior in the land, and though honest Joe, is gathered in for the general harvest, the house stands as firm as the day he first entered it. A goodly end he made, and profitable is it, to the weak-minded sinner to keep such an example before his eyes."

A smothered sound issued from the litter, but though the guide stopped to listen it was succeeded by no other evidence of the character of its tenant.

"The sick man is in suffering," he resumed, "but bodily pain, and all afflictions which we suffer in the flesh must have their allotted time. I have lived to see seven bloody and cruel wars, of which this which now rages is I humbly trust to be the last. Of the wonders which I witnessed, and the bodily dangers which I compassed in the sixth, eye hath never beheld nor can tongue utter their equal!"

"Time hath dealt hardly by you, friend," meekly interrupted the female. "This gold may add a few more comfortable days to those that are already past."

The cripple, for their conductor was lame as well as aged, received the offering with gratitude, apparently too much occupied in estimating its amount to give any more of his immediate attention to the discourse. In the deep silence that succeeded, the party reached the door of the villa they sought.

It was now night, the short twilight of the season having disappeared while the bearers of the litter were ascending the hill. A loud rap was given by the guide, and then he was told that his services were no longer needed.

"I have seen much and hard service," he replied, "and well do I know, that the prudent mariner does not dismiss the pilot, until the ship is safely moored. Perhaps old Madam de Lacey is abroad, or the Captain himself may not—"

"Enough. Here is one who will answer all our questions—"

The portal was opened, and a man appeared on its threshold, holding a light. The appearance of the porter was not, however, of the most encouraging aspect. A certain air, which can neither be assumed nor gotten rid of, proclaimed him a son of the ocean, while a wooden limb which served to prop a portion of his still square and athletic body, sufficiently proved he was one who had not attained the experience of his hardy calling without some bodily risk. His countenance as he held the light above his head to scan the persons of those without, was dogmatic, scowling and a little fierce. He was not long, however, in recognizing the cripple, of whom he unceremoniously demanded the object, of what he was pleased to term "such a night squall."

"Here is a wounded mariner," returned the female with tones so tremulous that they instantly softened the heart of the nautical Cerberus, "who is come to claim hospitality of a brother in the service, and shelter for the night. We would speak with Capt. Henry de Lacey."

"Then you have struck soundings on the right coast, Madam," returned the tar, "as Master Paul, here, will say in the name of his Father, no less than in that of the sweet lady his mother, not forgetting old Madam his grandam, who is no fresh water fish herself for that matter."

"That he will," said a fine, manly youth of some seventeen years, who wore the attire of one who was already in training for the seas, and who was looking curiously over the shoulder of the elderly seaman. "I will acquaint my father of the visit, and Richard—do you seek out a proper berth for our guests, without delay."

This order, which was given with the air of one who had been accustomed to act for himself and to speak with authority, was instantly obeyed. The apartment selected by Richard, was the ordinary parlour of the dwelling. Here in a few moments, the litter was deposited. The bearers were then dismissed, and the female only was left, with its tenant, and the rude attendant who had not hesitated to give them so frank a reception. The latter busied himself in trimming the lights, and in replenishing a bright wood fire, taking care at the same time that no unnecessary vacuum should occur in the discourse to render the brief interval, necessary for the appearance of his superiors, tedious. During this state of things, an inner door was opened, the youth already named leading the way for the three principal personages of the mansion.

First came a middle aged, athletic man, in the naval undress of a captain of the new States. His look was calm, and his step still firm, though time and exposure were beginning to sprinkle his head with gray. He wore one arm in a sling, a proof that his service was still recent; on the other leaned a lady, in whose matronly mien, but still blooming cheek and bright eyes were to be traced most of the ripened beauties of her sex. Behind them followed a third, a female also, whose step was less elastic but whose person continued to exhibit the evidences of a peaceful evening to the troubled day of life. The three courteously saluted the stranger, delicately refraining from making any precipitate allusion to the motive of her visit. Their reserve seemed necessary, for by the agitation which shook the shattered frame of one who appeared as much sinking with grief as infirmity, it was too apparent that the unknown lady needed a little time to collect her energies and to arrange her thoughts.

She wept long and bitterly, as if alone, nor did she essay to speak until further silence would have become suspicious. Then drying her eyes, and with cheeks on which a bright hectic spot was seated, her voice was heard for the first time by her wondering hosts.

"You may deem this visit an intrusion," she said, "but one whose will is my law, would be brought hither—"

"Wherefore—" mildly asked the officer, observing that her voice was already choaked—

"To die!" was the whispered, husky answer.

A common start manifested the surprise of her auditors, and then the gentleman arose and approaching the litter, he gently drew aside a curtain, exposing its hitherto unseen tenant to the examination of all in the room. There was understanding in the look that met his gaze, though death was too plainly stamped on the lineaments of the wounded man. His eye alone, seemed still to belong to earth, for while all around it appeared already to be sunk into the helplessness of the last stage of human debility, that was still bright, intelligent and glowing—it might almost have been described as glaring.

"Is there aught, in which we can contribute to your

comfort, or, to your wishes?" asked Capt. de Lacey, after a long and solemn pause, during which all around the litter had mournfully contemplated the sad spectacle of sinking mortality.

The smile of the dying man was ghastly, though tenderness and sorrow were singularly and fearfully combined in its expression. He answered not, but his eyes wandered from face to face until they became riveted by a species of charm on the countenance of the oldest of the two females. His gaze was met by a look as settled as his own; so evident was the sympathy which existed between the two, that it could not escape the observation of the spectators.

"Mother!" said the officer, with affectionate concern; "my mother! what troubles you?"

"Henry—Gertrude," answered the venerable parent, extending her arms to her offspring, as if she asked support; "my children, your doors have been opened to one who has a claim to enter them. Oh! it is in these terrible moments, when passion is asleep and our weakness most apparent, in these moments of debility and disease, that Nature so strongly manifests its impression! I see it all in that fading countenance, in those sunken features, where so little is left but the last lingering look of family and kindred!"

"Kindred!" exclaimed Captain de Lacey: "Of what affinity is our guest?"

"A brother!" answered the lady, dropping her head on her bosom, as if she had proclaimed a degree of consanguinity which gave pain as well as pleasure.

The stranger, too much overcome himself to speak, made a joyful gesture of assent, but he never averted a gaze that seemed destined to maintain its direction so long as life should lend it intelligence.

"A brother!" repeated her son, in unfeigned astonishment. "I knew you had a brother; but I had thought him dead a boy."

" 'Twas so I long believed, myself; though frightful glimpses of the contrary have often beset me; but now the truth is too plain, in that fading visage and those fallen features, to be misunderstood. Poverty and misfortune divided us. I suppose we thought each other dead."

Another feeble gesture proclaimed the assent of the wounded man.

"There is no further mystery. Henry, the stranger is thy uncle—my brother—once, my pupil!"

"I could wish to see him under happier circumstances," returned the officer, with a seaman's frankness; "but, as a kinsman, he is welcome. Poverty, at least, shall no longer divide you."

"Look, Henry—Gertrude!" added the mother, veiling her own eyes as she spoke, "that face is no stranger to you. See ye not the sad ruins of one ye both fear and love?"

Wonder kept her children mute, though they looked until sight became confused, so long and intense was their examination. Then a hollow sound, which came from the chest of the stranger, caused them to start, and, when his low, but distinct enunciation reached their ears, doubt and perplexity vanished.

"Wilder," he said, with an effort in which his utmost strength appeared exerted, "I have come to ask the last office at your hands."

"Captain Heidegger!" exclaimed the officer.

"The Red Rover!" murmured the younger Mrs de Lacey, involuntarily recoiling a pace from the litter.

"The Red Rover!" repeated her son, pressing nigher with ungovernable curiosity.

"Laid by the heels at last!" bluntly observed Fid, stumping up towards the groupe, without relinquishing the tongs, which he had kept in constant use, as an apology for remaining in the room.

"I had long hid my repentance, and my shame, together," continued the dying man, when the momentary surprise had a little abated; "but this war drew me from my concealment. Our country needed us both, and both has she had! You have served as one who never offended might serve; but a cause so holy was not to be tarnished by a name like mine. May the little I have done for good be remembered, when the world speaks of the evil of my hands! Sister—mother—pardon!"

"May that God, who forms his creatures with such fearful natures, look mercifully on all our weaknesses!" exclaimed the weeping Mrs de Lacey, bowing to her knees, and lifting her hands and eyes to heaven. "O brother, brother! you have been trained in the holy mystery of your redemption, and need not now be told on what Rock to place your hopes of pardon!"

"Had I never forgotten those precepts, my name would still be known with honour. But, Wilder!" he added with startling energy, "Wilder!—"

All eyes were eagerly bent on the speaker. His hand was holding a roll on which he had been reposing, as on a pillow. With a supernatural effort, his form arose on the litter; and, with both hands elevated above his head, he let fall before him that blazonry of intermingled stripes, with its blue field of rising stars, a glow of high exultation illumining every feature of his face, as in his day of pride.

"Wilder!" he repeated, laughing hysterically, "we have triumphed!"—He fell backward, without motion, the exulting lineaments settling in the gloom of death, as shadows obscure the smiling brightness of the sun.

# Chronology

1789  Born James Cooper to William Cooper and Elizabeth Fenimore Cooper, both of Quaker ancestry, September 15 in Burlington, N.J., the twelfth of thirteen children. Four brothers (Richard, b. 1775, Isaac, b. 1781, William, b. 1785, and Samuel, b. 1787) and two sisters (Hannah, b. 1777, and Anne, b. 1784) survive childhood.

1790–91 Family moves to Lake Otsego, in upper New York State, where father has acquired a large tract of land formerly owned by Col. George Croghan and has established the wilderness settlement to be known as Cooperstown.

1791–1800 Otsego is made a county, and Cooper's father, a Federalist squire with firm convictions about the relationship between property and political power, begins term as first judge of the Court of Common Pleas for Otsego County, and is elected to Congress in 1795 and 1799. Cooper attends public school in Cooperstown (except for the winters of 1796–97 and 1798–99, when he is enrolled in school in Burlington, N.J.). Reported to have been venturesome, athletic, and an enthusiastic reader. Sister Hannah says her brothers are "very wild" and "show plainly that they have been bred in the Woods." Hannah dies when she falls from a horse September 10, 1800. (Cooper later wrote that she was "a sort of second mother to me. From her I received many of my earliest lessons. . . . A lapse of forty years has not removed the pain with which I allude to the subject at all.")

1801–02 Becomes a boarding student in the home of father's friend, Rev. Thomas Ellison, rector of St. Peter's Church, Albany, N.Y., where he is drilled in Latin and forced to memorize long passages of Virgil. After Ellison dies in April 1802, goes to New Haven to be tutored for Yale College.

1803  Matriculates at Yale in February. (One of his professors, Benjamin Silliman, recalled twenty-five years later that the young Cooper was a "fine sparkling beautiful boy of alluring person and interesting manners.") Career at Yale marred by inattention to studies and a series of pranks (family tradition says that he tied a donkey in a professor's chair and stuffed a rag impregnated with gunpowder into the keyhole of another student's door and set it afire). Dismissed from Yale in junior year, returns to Cooperstown, and continues education with tutor, the Reverend William Neill, who regards him as rather wayward, disinclined to study, and addicted to novel-reading.

1806–07    To prepare for a naval career, serves as sailor-before-the-mast on the merchant vessel *Stirling*. Sails October 1806 to the Isle of Wight, London, Spain, then London again before returning home September 1807. On this voyage meets Edward R. Meyers, an apprentice seaman (whose biography he would write in 1843).

1808–09    Receives midshipman's warrant January 1, 1808. Serves in the bomb ketch *Vesuvius* from March to July. Stationed at Fort Oswego, a frontier outpost on Lake Ontario, August 22, 1808, to October 1809 to apprehend smugglers during the 1808 embargo. In November, requests transfer to the sloop *Wasp 18*, anchored in New York City, under Lieut. James Lawrence, and is assigned task of recruiting sailors. Meets fellow recruiter William Branford Shubrick (later rear admiral), who becomes his most intimate friend. Judge Cooper dies December 22 of pneumonia (contracted after being struck from behind by a political opponent). Cooper willed $50,000 as his share of the legacy and a remainder interest with his brothers and sister in the $750,000 estate.

1810       Meets Susan Augusta De Lancey, eighteen, daughter of a prominent Westchester County family that had supported the Loyalist cause during the war. "I loved her like a man," Cooper writes to his brother Richard, "and told her of it like a sailor." Requests a year's furlough to settle affairs following father's death, and a year later resigns from the navy.

1811–13    On New Year's Day, 1811, marries Susan De Lancey at her home in Mamaroneck, N.Y.; in April begins farming in a small way in New Rochelle. First child, Elizabeth, born September 27. Buys a farm, which he names Fenimore, on the western shore of Lake Otsego about a mile from Cooperstown, hoping to establish residence there permanently. Oldest brother, Richard, dies March 6, 1813. Second daughter, Susan Augusta, born April 17, 1813. Elizabeth dies July 13, 1813, soon after the move to Fenimore.

1814    Family lives in small frame house while permanent stone manor house is built. Cooper, a gentleman farmer and one of the founders of the county agricultural society, is active in the militia and the local Episcopal church.

1815–17    Two more daughters are born: Caroline Martha, June 26, 1815, and Anne Charlotte, May 14, 1817. Family moves back to Westchester County, autumn, 1817, because Mrs. Cooper wishes to be near her family and also because Cooper faces increasing financial difficulties caused by the depression following the War of 1812, claims against estate, and personal debts.

1818    Builds home on De Lancey land, Scarsdale, N.Y., and names farm Angevine. Attempts to retrieve family fortune in speculative ventures. Becomes active in local Clintonian Republican politics. Two brothers die: William, to whom he was most attached, and Isaac, who had been most like his father. Mother, who has been living in the family residence, Otsego Hall, dies in December.

1819    With associate Charles Thomas Dering, invests in Sag Harbor whaler *The Union*, April 15 (Cooper owns the ship and two-thirds of the outfit); frequently sails on it. June 15, daughter Maria Frances is born. Appointed quartermaster, with rank of colonel, in New York State militia, July. Last remaining brother, Samuel, dies.

1820    Writes first novel, *Precaution*, an imitation of a class of popular British novels, reportedly on challenge from wife. Its publication in November brings him into New York City literary and artistic circles. Begins to frequent the bookshop of Charles Wiley, meeting friends, among them Fitz-Greene Halleck and William Dunlap, in a back room he later christens "The Den," and to write reviews for Wiley's *Literary and Scientific Repository*.

1821          First son, Fenimore, born October 23. Second novel, *The Spy*, published December 22, is an immediate and resounding success. Translated into French and published in Paris.

1822          Quarrels with De Lancey family, and moves with wife and children from Westchester County to New York City, to be near publishers and to improve daughters' opportunities for schooling. Founds the Bread and Cheese, a lunch club often referred to as "the Cooper Club," whose informal membership includes merchants, painters, poets, journalists, and army and navy officers. Though his earnings are improved, Cooper's financial difficulties are not fully resolved.

1823          *The Pioneers* sells 3500 copies on the morning of publication, February 1. English edition published by Murray is the first of Cooper's works not to be pirated. Becomes interested in journalism; writes account of a horse race for the New York *Patriot*. April, becomes a member of the American Philosophical Society. Moves to 3 Beach Street, New York City, in May. In July, the house at Fenimore burns to the ground. Son Fenimore dies August 5. In autumn, household goods inventoried (but not sold) by Sheriff of New York. Has "bilious attack" from which he continues to suffer for several years.

1824          Publishes first sea romance, *The Pilot*, in January, an attempt in part to show admirers of Sir Walter Scott's *The Pirate* what a book written by a seaman would be like. Paul Fenimore Cooper born February 5. Writes account of the celebration at Castle Garden in honor of General Lafayette for the New York *American*. Moves family in May to 345 Greenwich Street, New York City. In August, receives honorary M.A. from Columbia College. Accompanies four English noblemen (including Edward Stanley, Earl of Derby and future prime minister of England) on a sight-seeing trip to Saratoga, Ballston, Lake George, Ticonderoga, and Lake Champlain. In a cavern in Glen Falls with Stanley, decides to write *The Last of the Mohicans*. ("I must place one of my old Indians here.")

1825          Publishes *Lionel Lincoln*, the first of his commercial failures. Forms close friendship with Samuel F. B. Morse, artist (and future inventor of the telegraph).

1826    *The Last of the Mohicans*, published in February, receives enthusiastic press and becomes the best known of his novels on both sides of the Atlantic. Formally adds Fenimore to his name in fulfillment of pledge to his mother. Receives silver medal in May from the Corporation of the City of New York. Attends a farewell banquet in his honor given by the Bread and Cheese. In June, the family (including sixteen-year-old nephew William) sails for Europe for Cooper's health, the children's education, and, as Cooper confesses, "perhaps . . . a little pleasure concealed in the bottom of the cup"; European residence will extend to seven years. Carries with him unfinished manuscript of *The Prairie* and a nominal commission as U.S. Consul for Lyons, France. Following a brief visit to England, family settles in Paris, July 22, and after a few weeks in the Hotel Montmorency, moves to the Hotel Jumilhac, 12 Rue St. Maur, in the Faubourg St. Germain, where Cooper is courted by Parisian society. "The people," he writes to a friend, "seem to think it marvelous that an American can write." Visits Lafayette, who becomes his closest European friend, at his home, La Grange. November, Sir Walter Scott visits to enlist his help to change the American copyright laws and secure revenue from his American imprints.

1827    Publishes *The Prairie* (April, London; May, Philadelphia). Works on *The Red Rover* and, at Lafayette's suggestion, begins work on *Notions of the Americans*, intended to describe American institutions and the American character and to correct misconceptions about the United States current in England. Translations of works into French are paid for and published by Goddelin. June 1 to November 16, family lives in a thirty-room walled-in villa in St. Ouèn, on the Seine, four miles from Paris. Health improves in the country air. *The Red Rover* published November in Paris and London, and January in Philadelphia.

1828–29 February, visits London with wife, son Paul, and nephew William to finish *Notions* and see it through the press, and is astonished by the warmth of his reception in literary and political, mainly Whig, circles. Finishes the book May 17. Returns to Paris June 9, via Holland and Belgium. July 28, family settles in Berne, Switzerland, where Cooper works on *The Wept of Wish-ton-Wish* and makes notes on his Swiss travels. Takes excursions to many parts of the country. Resigns as Consul of Lyons September 8, and leaves for Italy in October. Resides at Palazzo Ricasoli in Florence, November 25 to May 11, 1829. (Later writes of Italy: ". . . it is the only region of the earth that I truly love.") Mingles widely in Florentine society and comes to know members of the Bonaparte family. Among American expatriates, is especially attracted to young American sculptor Horatio Greenough, from whom he commissions a work. (". . . of all the arts that of statuary is perhaps the one we most want, since it is more openly and visibly connected with the taste of the people.") February, sets out alone to Paris to arrange for the printing of *The Wept of Wish-ton-Wish*, but after negotiations in Marseilles, the work is set and printed in Florence. *Notions of the Americans* published in England June 1828, and in America two months later. In July 1829, family travels from Leghorn to Naples in a chartered felucca, and in August settles in a chateau called "Tasso's house" in Sorrento, where Cooper writes most of *The Water-Witch*. December, family settles in Rome for a stay of several months. Goes riding on the campagna. ("Rome is only to be seen at leisure, and I think, it is only to be seen well, on horseback.")

1830    Reads Jefferson's letters and writes to a friend: "Have we not had a false idea of that man? I own he begins to appear to me, to be the greatest man, we ever had." Coopers leave Rome in mid-April, travel slowly north, pausing ten days in Venice, and arrive late in May in Dresden, where Cooper supervises the printing of *The Water-Witch*. August, returns to Paris (". . . the revolution which was consummated in Paris . . . induced me to come post haste . . ."). Through Lafayette, a prime mover in the events of the July revolution, follows closely the course of the new monarchy of Louis Philippe, to whom he is presented. Interests himself also in revolutionary movements in Belgium, Italy, and particularly Poland, whose struggle with Russia he actively supports.

1831    Decides to stay at least another year in Europe so daughters can finish their education, and in April takes large, unfurnished flat at 59 St. Dominique in the Faubourg St. Germain. Undertakes to revise and write new prefaces to his previously published works for Colburn and Bentley, who pay him £50 per title. Receives additional money from European translations of his works. No longer encumbered by debts, expects to earn $20,000 during the year. September, tours Belgium and the Rhine with wife, Paul, and Frances. Sends nephew William, who has been ill, to Le Havre in the hope that sea air may cure him. William dies of consumption October 1. *The Bravo*, first novel in a European trilogy chronicling the decline of feudalism and the rise of popular institutions, published October 15. At Lafayette's urging, enters the "Finance Controversy" (provoked by an article in the *Revue Brittanique* on the French national budget that claimed monarchy is less expensive than the American republic) by writing a "Letter to General Lafayette," dated November 25 (published in English by Baudry in December, and in French translation in the *Revue des Deux Mondes* in January), citing official records to prove the republic is less expensive.

1832    Letter becomes focus of debate in the January session of the Chamber of Deputies, and further exchanges of letters are published. Cooper suspects, incorrectly, that the American minister to France, William C. Rives, has taken a view contrary to his. Goes less into society; spends much time with Samuel Morse after he comes to Paris in September, visiting galleries, viewing and discussing art. Writes to William Dunlap: "I have cut all Kings & Princes, go to no great Officers and jog on this way from the beginning to the end of the month." Considers visiting America to decide whether family should ever return permanently. Feels "heart-sick" about unfavorable American criticism of his political actions in Europe and of *The Bravo*. Cholera epidemic breaks out in Paris in April. Morse returns to America in July. *The Heidenmauer*, second volume in European trilogy, published (London, July; Philadelphia, Sept.). Between July and October the Coopers travel in Belgium, the Rhineland, and Switzerland for Mrs. Cooper's health and a long-deferred vacation. On return to Paris, works on *The Headsman*. Arranges for Bentley's publication of William Dunlap's *History of the American Theatre*. Becomes increasingly restive as European attacks on his republicanism are published in America together with adverse reviews of his books. Resents what he calls "this slavish dependence on foreign opinion" and determines to abandon writing after *The Headsman*.

1833   June 15, goes to London to supervise the printing of *The Headsman*, last volume of the European trilogy (published London, Sept.; Philadelphia, Oct.). Soon after returning to Paris at the end of July, family leaves for America, stopping en route for a few weeks in England. Arrives in New York November 5, and moves family temporarily into a house on Bleecker Street rented for them by Samuel Morse. Sensing a chill in homecoming reception, Cooper declines testimonial dinner in his honor proposed by the Bread and Cheese. Enters speculative cotton market with James de Peyster Ogden and makes tour of Washington, Baltimore, and Philadelphia in December for business reasons and to observe firsthand the effects of five years of Jacksonian democracy. Concludes that country has changed but not improved and that there is "a vast expansion of mediocrity." Writes a friend that "were it not for my family, I should return to Europe, and pass the remainder of my life there."

1834   Spring, family moves to townhouse at 4 St. Marks Place. Publication, in June, of *A Letter to His Countrymen* (arguing that American "practice of deferring to foreign opinion is dangerous to the institutions of the country") increases unpopularity and provokes widespread attacks in the Whig press. After seventeen years' absence, revisits Cooperstown in June; October, purchases the family seat, Otsego Hall, and sets about renovating it for possible permanent occupancy. "My pen is used up—or rather it is thrown away," he writes a correspondent. "This is not a country for literature, at least not yet." Resumes the writing of *The Monikins*, allegorical satire on England, France, and America begun in Paris in 1832. Writes the first of a series of political articles in December—dealing mainly with the payment of the French debt, the differences between American constitutional government and the French system, and the functions of the three branches of government in America—for the New York *Evening Post* under the pseudonym "A.B.C."

1835   Sends manuscript chapter of *The Bravo* to Princess Victoria (later Queen of England) when asked for autograph.

*The Monikins*, published July, fails with critics and public. Family spends summer in Cooperstown, winter in New York City.

1836     Family leaves house at St. Marks Place in May and moves the remainder of their furniture to Cooperstown. Cooper goes to Philadelphia in July to see *Sketches of Switzerland* through the press (a practice he will continue with many of his future works). Part I published May, Part II, October.

1837     Becomes involved in a misunderstanding with towns-people over public use of Three Mile Point, a picnic ground on Lake Otsego owned by the Cooper family for which Cooper is trustee. After users damage the property, Cooper publishes No Trespass Notice, offending those who assumed the Point was public property. Local excitement subsides after Cooper sends two letters to the *Freeman's Journal* explaining the situation. Some county newspaper editors disregard explanation and publish articles attacking him. When offending newspapers refuse to retract statements, Cooper sues for libel. (Before these suits come to trial, publishes *Home as Found*, a novel of social criticism, in which a fictionalized version of the incident caricatures a newspaper editor. Major New York Whig editors now join in the quarrel against Cooper, justifying their attacks by maintaining that he put himself into the book and has thus made himself a legitimate target. Cooper begins suits against them. Though eventually winning most of these suits, it is at the cost of much time, energy, and popularity. Awarded $400 in damages in May 1839, writes to a correspondent, "We shall bring the press, again, under the subjection of the law. When one considers the characters, talents, motives and consistency of those who control it, as a body, he is lost in wonder that any community should have so long submitted to a tyranny so low and vulgar. When it is rebuked thoroughly, it may again become useful.") Travel books drawn from his European letters and journals are published under the general title *Gleanings in Europe*. (*France*: London, Jan., Phila., Mar.; *England*: London, May, Phila., Sept.; and *Italy*, published as *Excursions in Italy* in London, Feb. 28, 1838, Phila., May 1838.)

1838        Publishes *The American Democrat* (Cooperstown, Apr.),
            *Chronicles of Cooperstown*, *Homeward Bound* (London,
            May; Phila., August) and its sequel *Home as Found*
            (Nov.). Attacked in Whig press for his condescending
            portrayal of American manners. Meanwhile, works on
            *History of the Navy of the United States of America*, a project
            contemplated for more than a decade. December, goes
            with wife and four daughters to Philadelphia to research
            and see the work through the press. Stays until May 1839.

1839        Begins friendship with historian George Bancroft. *History
            of the Navy*, published May, sells well until it is attacked in
            the press by partisans of Commodore Oliver Hazard Perry
            for its account of the controversial Battle of Lake Erie.
            Defends account in letters to the *Freeman's Journal* and
            sues his critics (particularly William A. Duer). Suits for
            libel continue to occupy much of his time for the next
            several years. Writes *The Pathfinder* and goes to Philadel-
            phia in December to see it through the press.

1840        *The Pathfinder* published (London, Feb.; Phila., March).
            It is well received, and Balzac writes an admiring tribute
            to Cooper's work. Goes again to Philadelphia to see
            *Mercedes of Castile* (his "Columbus book") through the
            press in October, taking a cruise during this time with old
            friend Commodore Shubrick on the *Macedonian*. The
            work is published November in Philadelphia, and a month
            later in London.

1841        Continues to purchase old family property. June, tries
            once again, unsuccessfully, to interest publishers in a "sea
            story all ships and no men." August, delivers the com-
            mencement address at Geneva College, where son Paul is
            a student, on the thesis "Public Opinion is a Despot in a
            Democracy." Travels to Philadelphia in June, and again in
            August to see works through the press. *The Deerslayer* and
            a short version of *The History of the Navy* published in
            September.

1842        Addresses a series of letters to "Brother Jonathan" (begun
            Dec. 1841), defending *Homeward Bound* and *Home as
            Found* as fictions. ("When a work *professes* to be fiction,
            the reader is bound to consider all those parts fiction,
            which cannot be proved otherwise.") Wins judgments in

court in libel suits against William Leete Stone of the *Commercial Advertiser* (for the William A. Duer articles on the Battle of Lake Erie) and against Thurlow Weed and Horace Greeley (for articles on Three Mile Point). Large audience attends the Duer-Stone trial and Cooper speaks eloquently for himself. Publishes *The Two Admirals* (May) and *Wing-and-Wing* (*Jack O'Lantern* in England, Nov.). Persuaded by editor Rufus Wilmot Griswold to write for *Graham's Magazine*, agrees to do a series of brief biographies of naval officers, for the first time receiving pay for serial publication (sketches appear between 1842–45, beginning with "Richard Somers," October).

1843    Becomes engrossed with the *Somers* mutiny case and the proceedings against Capt. Alexander Slidell Mackenzie, on whose orders one midshipman and two crew members, presumed mutineers, had been executed at sea, the midshipman being the son of the Secretary of War in Tyler's cabinet. Writes eighty-page review of the case (published as an annex to the *Proceedings* of the naval court martial in 1844). *Autobiography of a Pocket Handkerchief* (or *Le Mouchoir*) serialized in *Graham's* January through April. After thirty-six years hears from old shipmate, Edward (Ned) Meyers, and brings him for five-month stay in Cooperstown. Writes Ned's biography, using his own words as much as possible. Journeys with John Pendleton Kennedy and William Gilmore Simms to Philadelphia. Publishes *The Battle of Lake Erie* (June), *Wyandotté* (London, Aug.; Phila., Sept.), *Ned Myers, or a Life Before the Mast* (Nov.). Income from writings begins to diminish seriously because of cheap reprints from abroad and difficult economic conditions at home.

1844    Writes in January to William Gilmore Simms, "We serve a hard master, my dear Sir, in writing for America." *Afloat and Ashore* published by Cooper himself in America and by Bentley in London, June. Second part, entitled *Miles Wallingford*, published October (Sept. in England, with title *Lucy Hardinge*). Begins work on the anti-rent (or Littlepage) trilogy, tracing the history of four generations of a landed New York family which culminates in conflict between tenants and landlords.

1845        First two volumes of the trilogy, *Satanstoe* (June) and *The Chainbearer* (Nov.), published and criticized on the grounds that Cooper is too partial to the interests of landed proprietors. John Pendleton Kennedy family visits Otsego in August. Attends Annual Diocesan Convention of the Protestant Episcopal Church in September, to consider the charge against Bishop Benjamin Tredwell Onderdonk of "immorality and impurity." Convinced of the truth of the charges, speaks at the convention, offering a solution to the tangled procedural system, but without success.

1846        Final volume of the anti-rent trilogy, *The Redskins* (*Ravensnest* in England), published July. *The Lives of Distinguished Naval Officers*, originally serialized in *Graham's*, published in two volumes in Philadelphia, March and May. *Jack Tier* serialized in *Graham's* and Bentley's *Miscellany*, November 1846–March 1848, under title "The Islets of the Gulf" (published March 1848; English title, *Captain Spike*).

1847        Begins a series of trips in June to Michigan in connection with unfortunate land investments and is impressed with the unspoiled country. August, publishes *The Crater*. ("It is a remarkable book, and ought to make a noise.") October, goes again to Detroit on business.

1848        Enters debate concerning the circumstances of General Nathaniel Woodhull's death during the American Revolution, writing several letters to the *Home Journal*, February–June. Writes letters on the new French republic in March and April for the Albany *Argus*. June and October, travels to Michigan. Publishes *The Oak Openings; or the Bee Hunter*, set in frontier Michigan, in August.

1849        Writes a long appreciative letter to Louis Legrand Nobel about Thomas Cole: "As an artist, I consider Mr. Cole one of the very first geniuses of the age." Daughter Caroline Martha marries Henry Frederick Phinney in Cooperstown, February 8. Though Cooper has quarreled with members of the groom's family and is unhappy about the match, he writes his daughter: ". . . your happiness will be the first consideration . . . Under no circumstances must there be coldness, alienation, or indifference. You are my dearly beloved child . . ." Publishes *The Sea Lions*, April, which does well in America but fails in England. The success of the collected edition of Washington Irving's writings encourages G. P. Putnam to begin issuing a uniform edition of Cooper, extending only to eleven volumes. Spends most of the time from October through April at the Globe Hotel, New York City, mainly to be close to the publishing center. Works on *The Ways of the Hour* and renews old acquaintances.

1850    Last novel, *The Ways of the Hour*, published in April. Cooper's only play, *Upside Down, or, Philosophy in Petticoats*, a satire on socialism, is performed June 18–21 at Burton's Chambers Street Theatre, New York, featuring actor-producer William E. Burton. Works on a projected third volume of his *History of the Navy*. July, travels to Niagara and Michigan with wife and daughter Charlotte. Goes to New York City in November to consult Dr. John Wakefield Francis about health problems: sharp pains in heels, with other symptoms, such as numbness of hands and feet. Daughter Maria Frances marries cousin Richard Cooper, December 10, in Cooperstown.

1851    Works on a history of greater New York, *The Towns of Manhattan* (unfinished, though he dictates a chapter in August after he is too ill to hold a pen). Writes to friend that he has lost twenty-two pounds. Continues to suffer from ailments, and in March goes to New York on business, and also to consult doctor. Consents to receive sacraments of the Protestant Episcopal Church. With great effort, travels the short distance to Christ Church, July 27, to be confirmed by Bishop De Lancey (his wife's brother). Sends introduction and eight chapters of *The Towns of Manhattan* to Putnam in July. Handwriting fails, and he dictates letters and work in progress to wife and daughters. Condition worsens, though he feels little pain. Dies at 1:30 P.M., September 14, 1851, in Otsego Hall. Buried in the family plot in Cooperstown.

# Note on the Texts

This volume contains the first two of James Fenimore Cooper's sea tales: *The Pilot* (1824) and *The Red Rover* (1827 in England and France, 1828 in the United States). The texts printed here are those established for *The Writings of James Fenimore Cooper* under the general editorship of James Franklin Beard and Kay Seymour House, with James P. Elliott as textual editor, and published by the State University of New York (SUNY) Press, Albany. The SUNY edition of *The Pilot* was published in 1986, and *The Red Rover* is now in page proofs. These texts were prepared according to the standards established by—and they have received the official approval of—the Center for Scholarly Editions of the Modern Language Association of America (as set forth in *The Center for Scholarly Editions: An Introductory Statement*, 1977). In selecting their copy-texts, the editors of the SUNY edition give priority to the holograph manuscripts, in whole or in part, when they exist; when they are not known to survive, preference goes next to amanuensis copy and then to proofs corrected in the author's hand, or, if these are missing, to the editions Cooper is known to have supervised or revised. Though circumstances beyond his control frequently defeated his intentions, Cooper was a painstaking reviser who corrected compositorial errors, rewrote sentences and phrases, altered punctuation and spelling (though his own punctuation and spelling were not always consistent), sharpened diction, and resisted the attempts of editors, compositors, and amanuenses to normalize dialect expression.

Cooper wrote the first half of *The Pilot* in the spring of 1823, but the second half was delayed by a series of disasters: the loss of the Coopers' house by fire in July, the death of their son in August, and debts so great that their household goods were inventoried by the sheriff in the autumn. Cooper finally completed *The Pilot* late in 1823. The novel was published in two volumes by Charles Wiley in New York on January 7, 1824, and in three volumes by John Miller in London later in the same month.

In the absence of a manuscript (except for a fragment) or proofs, the copy-text of the SUNY edition of *The Pilot* is the text of the Wiley first edition. Cooper made corrections on some thirty pages of the Wiley first-edition proofs that he sent to Miller to use as printer's copy. These changes were not made in the American edition, nor were they made in any later editions. Soon after the publication of the novel, Cooper visited his old friend William Shubrick, a naval captain, and what Cooper described as their "*joint* efforts" led to revisions in the second edition published by Wiley on February 11, 1824. After Wiley's death in 1826, Cooper sold the rights to print *The Pilot* to Carey, Lea and Carey of Philadelphia, and this firm published a stereotyped edition (the third American) in 1827. Cooper took no part in preparing this edition, or the one-volume edition set from the Carey, Lea and Carey version and published in 1831 by Colburn & Bentley in London as the first novel in Bentley's Standard Novels series. In 1849, however, when G. P. Putnam undertook to publish a uniform revised edition of his works, Cooper made some last revisions in the text and wrote a new preface, using the 1831 Bentley edition as printer's copy. *The Pilot* was published in 1849 as the second volume in Putnam's edition of Cooper's works.

In preparing the SUNY edition of *The Pilot*, Kay Seymour House, the editor, collated the relevant editions in order to assess which of the many variants among them reflected Cooper's intentions and which were caused by outside editorial intervention or typographical error. Once this judgment had been made, she inserted into the copy-text what appeared to be Cooper's intended readings, and this emended text is printed in the SUNY edition of *The Pilot*.

*The Red Rover* was written by Cooper during his stay in Paris. He began work on it almost immediately after he had seen *The Prairie* through the press in late February 1827, and he completed it by October of that year. For convenience in correcting proofs, Cooper had earlier arranged to have the Parisian publisher, Hector Bossange, print English editions of the works he wrote during his stay in France. Corrected and revised proofs of *The Red Rover* were sent in installments to Carey, Lea and Carey in Philadelphia, and Henry Colburn in London. *The Red Rover* was published in three volumes by

Bossange in Paris on November 27 and by Colburn in London on November 30, 1827. Carey, Lea and Carey published the American edition in two volumes on January 9, 1828.

In 1833, when he was preparing *The Red Rover* for inclusion in Bentley's Standard Novels series, Cooper extensively revised the text, using a copy of the Colburn edition in which to make his changes. At this time, according to Marianne and Thomas Philbrick, the SUNY editors, he eliminated modifiers, altered archaicisms, added eight footnotes, and wrote a new preface. The Bentley edition was published in 1834. The last time Cooper reviewed *The Red Rover* was in 1850 when he was preparing it for G. P. Putnam's uniform edition of his works. The Bentley's Standard Novels edition was used as printer's copy, but Cooper does not seem to have revised the text at this time. He did write a new preface, of which half exists in Cooper's holograph manuscript. *The Red Rover* was published as the third volume in the Putnam edition in February or March 1850.

Unlike the case of *The Pilot*, prepublication materials of *The Red Rover* still survive. Cooper's holograph manuscript is available for over 85 percent of the text, and it was used by the SUNY editors as copy-text. For the bulk of the remainder, they used the fair copy made by Cooper's nephew William Yeardley Cooper, which served as printer's copy for the first edition (97 percent of this fair copy is known to exist). The Bossange edition served as copy-text for the few remaining pages that are missing from both these manuscripts.

To establish the text of *The Red Rover* for the SUNY edition, the editors sifted through all the variants among the multiple versions of the work. The amanuensis copy was collated with the holograph, and Cooper's corrections of that text were examined to see if they were emendations intended by Cooper or were simply made to repair misreadings by his nephew in the copying. This same process of collation and evaluation of variants was done in the later editions of the work. Variants determined to be caused by outside editorial intervention or typographical error were discarded, but revisions apparently intended by Cooper were entered into the copy-text and appear in the SUNY edition of *The Red Rover*.

This volume presents the texts of the SUNY editions of *The*

*Pilot* and *The Red Rover* but does not attempt to reproduce features of their typographic design, such as the display capitalization of chapter openings. The texts are printed without change, except for the correction of typographical errors. As the SUNY editors recognized, spelling, punctuation, and capitalization are often expressive features, and they are not altered, even when inconsistent or irregular. The following is a list of typographical errors corrected, cited by page and line number (these errors will also be corrected in future SUNY printings): 1.4, 1.2; 26.2, as a great; 109.4, of veriest; 138.1, colonel; 139.24, deserve,and; 142.39, goaler; 169.17, with ——th.; 172.1, hoipe; 221.5, V.iv.138–140.; 275.12, sparking; 283.1, I"; 335.34, wtihout; 341.33, neglected.,; 404.16, of the the.

# Notes

In the notes below, the reference numbers denote page and line of this volume (the line count includes chapter headings). No note is made for material found in standard desk-reference books such as *Webster's Collegiate* and *Webster's Biographical* dictionaries. Epigraphs from Shakespeare are identified by the play and are keyed, as are noted quotations, to *The Riverside Shakespeare*, ed. G. Blakemore Evans (Boston: Houghton Mifflin, 1974). Footnotes in the text are Cooper's own. For additional textual and explanatory information see *The Pilot*, ed. Kay Seymour House, and *The Red Rover*, eds. Thomas and Marianne Philbrick, in *The Writings of James Fenimore Cooper* (Albany: State University of New York Press, 1986, 1991). For further biographical background than is included in the Chronology, see *The Letters and Journals of James Fenimore Cooper*, James Franklin Beard, ed. (6 vols., Cambridge: The Belknap Press of Harvard University Press, 1960–68).

## THE PILOT

1.4    G. A. Stevens]  English author and dramatist George Alexander Stevens (1710–84).

2.2    WILLIAM BRANFORD SHUBRICK]  William Branford Shubrick (1790–1874), to whom *The Red Rover* as well as *The Pilot* is dedicated, was the novelist's closest friend. Cooper and he had served together aboard the *Wasp 18* in 1809–10, and the two remained in contact over the ensuing forty years. Shubrick's distinguished naval career ended with his retirement in 1861.

4.3–7  Bon-Homme . . . Triumph]  John Paul Jones was given command of a French ship, *Bonhomme Richard* (rebuilt and so-named by Jones in honor of Benjamin Franklin and his *Poor Richard's Almanack*), in 1779. It sank off Flamborough Head September 22, 1779, after Jones and his men had defeated and boarded the British *Serapis*, a larger and heavier vessel, following a more than three-hour engagement. The *Milford* and the *Solebay* were British frigates eluded by the *Providence*, which Jones commanded in 1776. The *Drake* was a British ship captured by Jones on the *Ranger* April 24, 1778, off Carickfergus, northern Ireland. The *Triumph*, an English Letter of Marque ship, was captured by Jones, but then escaped, in 1780.

4.8    desperate projects]  In 1778, Jones attempted to burn the ships at Whitehaven after spiking the guns of its forts, then went to the Scottish coast to seize the Earl of Selkirk and hold him hostage for the proper treatment of

American prisoners (Selkirk, however, was away from home). He had also planned to seize British ships in the port city of Leith, now part of Edinburgh, and hold them for payment of Scottish currency.

4.14    One . . . officers]  Commodore Alexander Murray (1754–1821).

5.13    authorship . . . novels]  Scott, whose novels were being published anonymously, did not acknowledge authorship until 1827.

5.23    *vraisemblance*]  Verisimilitude.

6.9    *maladie de mer*]  Sea-sickness.

6.19    Englishman]  Charles Wilkes (1764–1833).

9.2–3    rolling, . . . sides."]  In the work (1797) by Charles Dibdin (1745–1814), "rolling" reads "flowing" and "her sides" reads "its sides."

10.6    Nagurs]  Nathaniel Fanning, one of Cooper's sources, wrote in his *Narrative of the Adventures of an American Naval Officer* (1806) that "the country people" outside of Portsmouth, England, would often remark, " 'Why, Lard, neighbour, there be white paple; they taulk jest as us do,' " when viewing American prisoners during the Revolutionary War.

11.8    German ocean]  The North Sea.

17.6    Prior]  Matthew Prior (1664–1721).

17.29–30    cockswain]  In a man-of-war, the captain's coxswain has charge of his boat and attends his person.

19.3    chebacco-man]  A two-masted, narrow-sterned boat built at Chebacco (now Essex) in Massachusetts.

23.18    wind-galls]  A fragment of a rainbow or of a prismatically fragmented halo, supposed to presage windy weather.

27.3–4    its comment . . . *Julius Caesar*]  In *The Riverside Shakespeare* and some other editions, "his comment."

27.13    timber-man]  A ship carrying timber as cargo.

27.35    deep-sea]  A lead and line used for soundings in deep water.

31.14    leading strings]  Strings that guided and supported children learning to walk.

31.20    half-two]  A ship having a draught of two-and-a-half fathoms.

32.33    capstern]  Variant spelling for capstan, a vertical drum-shaped mechanism that is rotated to raise the anchor.

33.19    tafferel]  Variant spelling for taffrail, the rail around the stern.

38.28    pall]   To prevent the capstan from recoiling by using short, stout bars (pawls) to arrest it.

41.4    jackall]   The jackal was at one time believed to go before the lion and hunt up his prey for him.

46.2    ware]   Ancient corruption of veer.

48.31    chains]   Contrivances used to carry the heavy shrouds, i.e., supporting ropes, of a mast outside the ship's side by means of a chain-wale, a strong projecting timber; a leadsman standing upon the chain-wale between two shrouds was said to be "in the chains."

48.37    hammock-cloths]   Cloths covering hammocks to protect them from wet when stowed in nettings on top of the bulwarks.

51.16    mainchains]   The chains supporting the main mast.

51.22    cun]   Or con, the commanding post from which nearby objects can be seen and directions given to the ship's helmsman.

52.16    Clear . . . best-bower]   To clear away is to let out a line or cable free from entanglement. Best-bower is the name for one of the anchors (the other is the small-bower) carried at the bow of the ship, and for its cable.

54.30    hom-moc]   An American word for a hummock, a small eminence of conical form sometimes covered with trees.

55.27    springs her luff]   Brings her head closer to the wind.

55.34    bolt-ropes]   Ropes sewn around the edge of a sail to keep the canvas from tearing.

59.29    lying-to]   Nearly at a standstill, accomplished by arranging the sails in such a way as to counteract one another.

66.24    Lady Selkirk under contribution]   On April 23, 1778, after a failed attempt to seize Lord Selkirk, some of John Paul Jones's officers and men took the Selkirk silver. Jones later bought it from them and returned it with a note of apology to Lady Selkirk. See note 4.8.

78.33–34    haul . . . aboard]   Put the ship on a course for land.

82.31    dog-vane]   A small vane of thread, cork, feathers, or bunting placed on the weather gunwale to show the direction of the wind.

88.29–30    'vox . . . nihil,' ]   "A voice, and beyond that nothing," which was a Spartan's description of a nightingale plucked of its feathers, according to Plutarch.

88.35    cannister]   Shot consisting of bullets packed in a tin case or canister.

95.9–11     siege . . . Braddock]   Important battles during the French and Indian War (1754–63). Quebec, then the capital of New France, surrendered September 18, 1759, after General James Wolfe defeated Louis-Joseph de Montcalm on the Plains of Abraham. In 1760 a numerically superior force under François-Gaston de Lévis tried to retake Quebec, but after an indecisive battle outside the city was forced to retreat when British naval reinforcements arrived. Fort Ticonderoga in New York, garrisoned by a force under Montcalm, was successfully defended against an attack by General James Abercrombie in 1758, but was finally taken by General Jeffrey Amherst in 1759. In 1755, General Edward Braddock's army was ambushed and routed near Fort Duquesne in Pennsylvania. Braddock was mortally wounded and many of his men were killed.

95.38–39     queen . . . princes]   Charlotte Sophia, who married George III in 1761, was to be the mother of nine sons and six daughters. Her eighth son was born in 1779, and her ninth in 1780, but neither of them lived to adulthood.

99.30–32     pirate . . . Whitehaven]   Jones gained the reputation of a pirate, or corsair, among the English after his cruise in British waters aboard the *Ranger*, April 10–May 8, 1778, when he took seven prizes and alarmed the British. See also notes 4.3–7 and 4.8.

127.12     fairy . . . Nights,]   "The Adventures of Prince Ahmed and the Fairy Peri-Banou."

157.5     incognitus, incognitii, 'torum]   Declension of the Latin: unknown person, unknown people, of the unknown people.

162.1–2     'seniors . . . reverend?' ]   Cf. Shakespeare, *Othello*, I.iii.76: "Most potent, grave, and reverend signiors."

172.24–27     The immortal . . . Cacique]   In the "Fundamental Constitutions" of the Carolinas (1669), written at the request of his friend Anthony Ashley Cooper (later Lord Shaftesbury), John Locke provided a series of titles to be used by a hereditary landed gentry. *Cacique*, the West Indian word for prince, or chief, indicated the lowest rank of this proposed nobility. The settlers refused to ratify the constitution.

196.14     start . . . end]   Rouse him, as though by flicking him with the end of a rope.

196.25     no-man's-land]   A part of the deck used for the storage of gear occasionally needed on the forecastle.

198.11     ridge ropes]   Several ropes were so named, including safety lines going from gun to gun, which would be the lowest down.

202.15     better-end]   Nathaniel Fanning, one of Cooper's sources, used better-end for bitter-end in his *Narrative of the Adventures of an American Naval Officer* (1806). The bitter-end of a cable is the part that is around a bitt and remains inboard. Fanning (1755–1805), a privateer, served as midshipman on the *Bonhomme Richard* in 1779, and fought in the engagement with the *Serapis*. He then served under Jones on the *Ariel* until December 1780.

205.7    Munny-Moy]  Monomoy Point, a narrow peninsula extending south from Chatham on Cape Cod, at times becoming an island.

205.10    rolling-tackle]  Devices used to limit the movement of the yards and prevent chafing produced by the rolling of the vessel.

205.17    song . . . Kidd]  "Ye Lamentable Ballard of Captain Kidd" (1707), which runs to twenty-five stanzas.

205.18    Cape Poge]  The northeast point of Chappaquiddick Island, East Martha's Vineyard, Massachusetts.

207.3–4    Frenchman, Thurot . . . business of '56]  In 1756, François Thurot (1727–60) planned to burn Portsmouth and its dockyards. Spies working as clerks in the French embassy warned the English in time to thwart the scheme.

207.9    honest Paul]  John Paul, a Scotsman, adopted the name Jones when he came to America.

208.32    cable-tiers]  The places where cables are coiled away.

216.39    half-pike]  A short pike used in repelling boarders.

222.35    Poictiers]  Variant spelling for Poitiers, France, where in 1356 Edward the Black Prince, son of Edward III of England, defeated and captured John II of France.

223.22    battle of Blenheim]  During the War of the Spanish Succession, John Churchill (Corporal John was the common soldiers' name for him), first duke of Marlborough, marched his forces from the Netherlands to Bavaria at the request of Vienna, which was under threat of attack. At Blenheim he joined forces with the Austrian general Prince Eugène of Savoy, and on August 13, 1704, overwhelmed French and Bavarian forces under Marshall Tallard and the electoral prince of Bavaria, Joseph Ferdinand.

223.24    Culloden]  Culloden Moor at Inverness-shire, Scotland, where the English under the Duke of Cumberland defeated the Highlanders under Prince Charles Edward Stuart, ending the Jacobite uprising of 1745.

223.40    Mr. Eugene]  Prince Eugène of Savoy (1663–1736).

233.32    Le Maire]  Le Maire Strait of Tierra del Fuego Island and Isla de los Estados, off the southeast tip of Argentina.

239.36    rullocks]  Variant of rowlocks, or oarlocks.

239.37    night-glass]   A short refracting telescope specially constructed for use at night.

242.10    banyan]   Banyan-day, one of the days on which sailors were not served meat; derived from banyans, or banians, Hindu traders. Hindus do not eat meat.

246.37–38    goule . . . bodkin.]   In the *Arabian Nights* tale "The History of Sidi Nouman," Sidi wonders how his beautiful wife, Amine, can subsist only on the grains of rice she eats with her bodkin. He soon discovers that she is really a ghoul and secretly feeds on human corpses.

249.31    Manly's time]   In the autumn of 1775, John Manly (c. 1734–93) became the first commissioned American naval officer to fire a gun in the Revolution.

270.20    fencibles]   Soldiers liable only for defensive service at home.

271.20–21    fowling-piece . . . gun]   A fowling-piece is a light gun used for shooting wild fowl. A ducking gun carries a heavy charge a long distance, killing many ducks in a flock with one shot.

271.31–32    Queen Anne's pocket-piece]   A large gun at Dover.

277.12    sheet-cable]   A cable fastened to the sheet anchor, which was used only in emergencies.

279.27    "gripes,"]   Lashings that secure a boat on deck.

288.9    run . . . entrance]   A "run" is the aftermost, an "entrance" the foremost, part of a ship's bottom.

296.24    statu . . . bellum]   Pre-war conditions.

343.37    shore-draft]   Sailors selected for shore duty.

346.18    choused]   Cheated, tricked, or defrauded.

355.2–4    plot . . . Thomson]   "Plot" reads "blot" in the tragedy (1749) by Scottish poet James Thomson (1700–48).

372.31    nip to a rope]   To nip a rope is to fasten a nipper, a piece of braided cord used to keep a cable from slipping, around it.

372.31    mats]   Thick webs of yarn used to protect the standing rigging from the friction of other ropes.

372.32    crowning a cable]   Forming the strands of a cable into a sort of knot to prevent untwisting.

373.7    scraper]   A cocked hat.

374.33    "Flag,"]   The answer returned to a sentry's challenge by an admiral's boat.

374.39    weather helm]   A tendency of a sailing ship to come too near the wind.

376.16    leach]   Variant of leech, the edge of a sail.

376.17    settle away]   Ease off.

376.20    gibs]   Variant of jibs, triangular sails set forward of the foremast.

383.6    Percy . . . River,"]   Thomas Percy's translation of "Rio Verde, Rio Verde," from Ginés Pérez de Hita's *Historia de los bandos de los zegríes y abencerrajes* (1595–1614), better known as *Las guerras civiles de Granada* (*History of the Civil Wars of Granada*). The translation appeared in *Reliques of Ancient English Poetry* (1765), edited by Percy.

384.15    Helder]   Den Helder, a city in the northwestern part of the Netherlands.

384.16    weather tide]   A tide whose current carries a vessel to windward.

388.17    pack on]   To carry all possible sail.

388.39    ninety's]   Ninety-gun ships.

391.13    spread . . . clue]   Positioned the lower corners of a square sail wide apart.

399.4    sheet home]   Extend the sails to the outer extremities of the yards or booms.

401.2    double their tail]   Turn back on their course.

408.22    shifting-boards]   Wooden partitions put up in a ship's hold to prevent the shifting of cargo.

411.33    a-taunt-o]   With all light upper spars fully rigged, hence in order or shipshape.

412.6    fasts]   Ropes or other contrivances by which a ship is fastened to a wharf.

414.9–10    Liverpool . . . Edinburgh]   Jones had planned to attack Liverpool in the spring of 1779, burn ships at Whitehaven, and seize ships in port at Leith. All these schemes were thwarted, some by political intrigues against him.


## THE RED ROVER

424.2    W. B. SHUBRICK]   See note 2.2.

425.1    *Preface*]   Written for the first edition.

425.3    former occasion]   See the 1823 Preface to *The Pilot*, pages 3–4 in this volume.

425.23    "watch-bill."]   The roster of enlisted men aboard a naval vessel, indicating the station and watch to which each man is assigned.

427.5–6    "The Standard Novels"]   An inexpensive series published in England by Richard Bentley (1794–1871), and later by his son, George Bentley (1825–95).

427.19–20    the name . . . book]   Walter Scott in *The Fair Maid of Perth* (1828) mentions the early 14th-century pirate Thomas de Longueville, known as the Red Rover for his use of a blood-red flag.

429.1    *Preface*]   Written for the Putnam edition.

429.31–37    Those . . . hemisphere]   In 1839, Thomas H. Webb, sometime secretary of the Rhode Island Historical Society, informed the Danish historian Charles Christian Rafn of the Newport tower, raising doubts about its English origin. On the basis of Webb's information, Rafn, the leading authority on Norse activity in the New World, attributed the tower to Eric Gnupsson, a 12th-century Vinland bishop. Rafn's connection of the tower to the Norsemen was popularized by a number of writers, among them Henry Wadsworth Longfellow in "The Skeleton in Armor" (1841). Two Newport residents, William H. Cranston and Henry Tisdale, wrote a series of hoaxing letters that appeared in Rhode Island newspapers in 1847 and were widely reprinted, denouncing disbelievers like Cooper and inventing a Danish archeological expedition to Newport in 1832 that was supposed to have established the Viking construction of the tower beyond all question. The ruins are presently thought to be of a windmill built by Benedict Arnold, a 17th-century governor of Rhode Island (and ancestor of the traitor).

430.29–34    Rhode Island . . . displeasure]   Cooper's defense of the conduct of Commodore Jesse Elliott (1782–1845) at the battle of Lake Erie (*History of the Navy of the United States of America*, 1839, Volume II, chapter XXVI) was strongly disputed by the Rhode Island Historical Society. By defending Elliott, second in command to Oliver Hazard Perry (1785–1819) of Rhode Island, he supposedly diminished the achievement of the deceased hero. In 1845, the Society manifested its displeasure by refusing the gift of a medal struck in honor of Cooper by Elliott.

431.3    triumphantly vindicated]   In 1842, Cooper successfully defended his treatment of the battle of Lake Erie in his libel suit against William Leete Stone, editor of the *New-York Commercial Advertiser*, for publishing William A. Duer's defamatory review of *History of the Navy*.

431.11–15    the necessity . . . New York."]   The reference is to a lecture on the battle of Lake Erie that Tristram Burges delivered before the Rhode Island Historical Society in 1836. In 1839, soon after the publication of

*History of the Navy,* Burges printed the lecture with supplemental notes, diagrams, and testimony to dispute Cooper's version of the battle. Cooper gleefully pounced on the absurdity of Burges' positioning of the American squadron in his published reply to his critics, *The Battle of Lake Erie* (1843).

433.18    successful rival]   Providence, at the head of Narragansett Bay, became the leading seaport of Rhode Island after the British occupation of Newport during the Revolution.

433.21–22    "the wisdom . . . foolishness."]   Cf. 1 Corinthians 3:19: "For the wisdom of this world is foolishness with God."

435.11    Loudon]   John Campbell (1705–82), fourth earl of Loudon, was appointed commander-in-chief of British forces in America in 1756 but was recalled in 1757 for his failure to move against the French fortress of Louisbourg.

435.36    soldier of the carpet]   A carpet knight, i.e., a soldier better suited to the drawing room or the boudoir than to the battlefield; one knighted by kneeling on a carpet before the throne instead of on the battlefield.

435.37–436.1    Burgoyne gave . . . captives]   In early 1777, Burgoyne proposed to march from Canada to Albany (not Boston) with a force of 12,000 regulars, 2,000 Canadians, and 1,000 Indians. In May 1777, he set out from Trois-Rivières (Three Rivers) with an actual force of 6,400 soldiers and 649 Indians. Burgoyne planned to advance along Lake Champlain to Albany, where he would be joined by Sir William Howe coming up the Hudson from New York City and by Barry St. Leger advancing east from the Mohawk River, splitting the American colonies along the Hudson. Neither Howe nor St. Leger reached Burgoyne, and he was defeated at Saratoga, New York, on October 17, 1777. His defeat led to the signing of the Franco-American alliance in February 1778, and is considered the turning point of the war.

439.5–6    "animalculæ, . . . genius,"]   In *Gleanings in Europe: France* (1837), Cooper attributes this saying to Samuel Taylor Coleridge.

439.16    dogmatic German]   George II of the House of Hanover, king of Great Britain and Ireland, 1727–60.

440.13    shop-board]   A table or raised platform on which tailors sit while sewing.

441.29    ossenbricks!]   Osnaburgs, coarse linen fabrics originally made in Osnabrück in northern Germany.

442.16–17    the business . . . coasts]   During the War of the Austrian Succession (1740–48), Sir Peter Warren commanded a British squadron off the coast of North America that captured many lucrative French prizes and took part in the successful expedition against the French fortress of Louisbourg on the eastern shore of Cape Breton Island.

442.19    business in Garmany] British troops fought the French in Germany in 1743, the year before the War of the Austrian Succession spread to North America.

442.24    rebellion of '15] The Jacobite uprising in Scotland and northern England following the accession of the Hanoverian George I to the British throne after the death of Queen Anne in 1714.

442.34–35    a great . . . throne] Nader Kuli Beg (1688–1747), a robber chieftain, became a general under Tahmasp Mirza in 1726 and won a series of major victories against Ghilzai Afghan and Turkish invaders. He deposed Tahmasp in 1732 after the Shah made an unfavorable peace with the Turks, and placed himself on the throne in 1736, ruling as Nader Shah until his assassination.

442.36    laws . . . Persians] Daniel 6:8, 12: "the law of the Medes and the Persians, which altereth not."

442.40–443.1    Porteous Mob] On April 14, 1736, the Edinburgh town guard commanded by Captain John Porteous fired on a sympathetic crowd that rioted at the execution of the smuggler Andrew Wilson. Eight or nine persons were killed and about twenty injured. Porteous, accused of giving the order to fire and of firing himself, was sentenced to death. When the execution was stayed, an armed mob wearing disguises took Porteous from Tollbooth Prison and hanged him. No one was ever convicted of the murder.

445.29    fifty] A ship that mounts fifty guns.

454.27    under-foot] Under the ship's bottom.

454.39    a stream] A stream-anchor, which could be more quickly weighed or more cheaply abandoned than the heavy bower usually used for mooring.

462.31–32    Colony . . . Oglethorpe] Massachusetts to Georgia.

468.22    lee-swifter] The foremost shroud (supporting rope) on the leeward side of a lower mast.

472.18–22    More than . . . antiquarian.] For example, an unsigned letter published in the Providence *Gazette* for April 12, 1823, indicates that a group of New Yorkers had become interested in the origins of the Newport tower. The group seems to have included the polymath Dr. Samuel Latham Mitchell (1764–1831) and Andrew Thompson Goodrich (1789–1845), Cooper's first publisher.

480.15    'bone] A breaking bow wave.

480.36–37    a rose . . . as sweet?"]  Cf. Shakespeare, *Romeo and Juliet*, II.ii.43–44.

482.32    'Land . . . water rats?' ]   Cf. Shakespeare, *The Merchant of Venice*, I.iii.22–24: "there be land-rats and water-rats, water-thieves and land-thieves."

490.27    "The night . . . a-reconnoitring,"]   Louisbourg, returned to the French in exchange for Madras, India, by the Treaty of Aix-la-Chapelle in 1748, fell to General Jeffrey Amherst and Admiral Edward Boscawen in 1758. See also note 442.16–17.

491.21    iron]  The grappling iron, or grapnel.

493.12    nettings]  A network of stout ropes extended above the gunwales by attachment to the rigging to prevent an enemy from boarding.

496.16    stream]  The channel where the tidal current runs most strongly.

500.2–4    "The good . . . can."]  In Wordsworth, the stanza reads: "For why?—because the good old rule / Sufficeth them, the simple plan, / That they should take, who have the power, / And they should keep who can."

503.31–32    true . . . bush."]  The proverb is from the Roman vintners' custom of decorating their booths at fairs with ivy, which was sacred to Bacchus, to advertise their wares.

505.36    white flag]  *Le drapeau blanc* of the kings of France.

506.29–30    satellites . . . Africa]  The Barbary States of North Africa which, with the exception of Morocco, were then autonomous provinces of the Ottoman Empire.

507.22    double-headed monsters]  The double-headed eagle of czarist Russia or of the Holy Roman Empire.

508.19    field . . . blue]  The ensigns flown by ships of the Royal Navy in the 18th century had fields of red, white, or blue, depending upon the rank of the flag officer commanding the part of the fleet to which they were assigned.

519.14    'laborer . . . hire,' ]   Cf. Luke 10:7.

525.22    his most Faithful Majesty]  The king of Portugal.

526.11–12    our valour . . . discretion]  Cf. Shakespeare, *1 Henry IV*, V.iv.119–20: "The better part of valor is discretion."

528.2–5    yon . . . "Marry,]  In *The Riverside Shakespeare* and other editions of the play, "yon" reads "yond" and "there" reads "here." "Marry" does not occur in line 133. Lines 130–31 read: "*Juliet.* What's he that now is going out the door? / *Nurse.* Marry, that, I think, be young Petruchio."

528.33–34    'all . . . heir,' ]  Cf. Shakespeare, *Hamlet*, III.i.61–62: "the thousand natural shocks / That flesh is heir to."

529.32    last treaty of amity]  The Treaty of Ghent, signed December 24, 1814, concluding the War of 1812.

531.11    put their . . . bushel]  Matthew 5:15: "Neither do men light a candle, and put it under a bushel, but on a candlestick." See also Mark 4:21 and Luke 11:33.

538.39    harpen]  The harpens, or harpings, are horizontal timbers at the bow of a vessel that define the shape of the forward part of the hull; thus a vessel that was lean in the harpen and full in the counter (the curved part of the stern of the ship) would steer easily, not badly.

540.25    well-known proverb]  "So many men, so many minds" (Terence, *Phormio*, l. 454).

542.39    gipsy hat]  A straw hat with a ribbon passing over the brim on either side and tied beneath the chin, introduced to America in 1745.

546.34    'Mudian . . . full]  A Bermudian, a sloop with a jib-headed mainsail, on a close reach, the fastest point of sailing for such a rig.

557.2    ears]  Supports for the bolt of the pump handle.

557.24    breaking ground]  Beginning to lift the anchor from the bottom.

559.35–36    the unceremonious . . . knot]  Under colonial Rhode Island law, divorce was to be granted "upon due proof" that a spouse had "wickedly and wilfully broken and violated the Marriage Covenant, either by an Act done or committed, or by a continual Absence from his or her Wife or Husband, without any just Cause, by the Space of Seven Years."

586.30    cast]  Turned from the direction of the wind.

589.38    light sails]  Any sails set above the topgallant sails, in this case, the royals.

589.38    lift]  A term applied to a square sail when the wind catches it on the leading edge and causes it to ruffle slightly.

593.10    palm]  A sailmaker's device of leather or canvas with a round iron plate in the palm. It is strapped around the hand and used in place of a thimble.

593.14    in irons]  The condition of a vessel that stalls between tacks and, having no headway, fails to respond to her rudder.

593.18    full, and by]  As close to the wind as possible without letting the sails shiver.

594.12    spring]  A light hawser running from the stern of a vessel to an anchor, planted so that the vessel pivots when the hawser is drawn taut.

594.38    half-board]  Half a tack.

596.24    aft gib sheet]  Pull the corner of the jib more toward the stern.

596.24    Board main tack]  Draw the lower corner on the windward side of the mainsail forward and down.

601.13–14    the solitary . . . transformed]  In the *Arabian Nights* tale "Julnar the Sea-Born and Her Son King Badr Basim of Persia," Badr comes upon a city inhabited only by an old grocer, who tells him that all previous visitors have been transformed into animals by the enchantress Queen Láb.

607.8    Knighthead]  In nautical usage, a knighthead is a heavy timber that rises obliquely, one on either side of the stem of a vessel, to form the support for the bowsprit.

607.34    chains]  Stout iron links or plates to which the lower ends of the shrouds are attached. The chains are bolted through the ship's side and then led upward over notches cut on the outer edge of the channels, or chain-wales, broad and thick planks projecting from either side of the vessel. The man "seated in the chains" is thus perched on a channel among the chains and overhangs the water, a position from which he could readily aid in the recovery of a small boat.

610.7    taught bowline]  A course as close as possible to the direction from which the wind is blowing.

619.25    night-glass]  A short refracting telescope made for use at night.

624.25    pack]  Set all possible sail.

626.2    driver]  A sail set at the aftermost part of a vessel.

629.22    fly-block]  A traveling block used in hoisting the upper yards.

629.27    bright cloud]  The Magellanic Cloud, either of two cloudlike star clusters visible only from the southern hemisphere, both of which can be seen with the unaided eye.

629.34    knee]  A heavy timber, naturally bent in an angular form, used to secure the main parts of a ship's frame together.

629.34    bomb-ketch]  A small but massively built vessel armed with one or two large mortars.

632.7    chops of the Channel]  The entrance into the English Channel from the Atlantic.

641.15    cheerily]   Heartily, quickly.

649.20    Lie down]   Come down.

660.30    sheer-hulk]   A vessel no longer fit for sea service that has been equipped with shears, a hoisting apparatus used for stepping, i.e., setting up or taking down, masts in port.

666.25    gripes]   A system of ropes and hooks used to secure a ship's boat to ring bolts fastened to the deck.

682.3–4    Take then . . . *Julius Cæsar*]   "Take thou" in *The Riverside Shakespeare* and some other editions.

688.26    'roar . . . dove,']   Shakespeare, *A Midsummer-Night's Dream*, I.ii.82–83.

690.17    quarter-gunners]   Subordinates to the ship's gunnery officer, numbering one to every four guns.

690.18    waisters]   Men who work in the ship's waist, or midsection, usually chosen for their strength rather than their skill.

690.19    after-guard]   Men who work the after sails of the man-of-war, generally drawn from the least experienced members of the crew.

693.8    stropping]   Ropework encircling the body of a block by which the block is attached to the spars or rigging.

693.24    combings]   Coamings, raised borders around a hatchway to prevent water from entering the hatch.

694.12    handicraft]   Craftsman.

701.2    perruquier]   Wig-maker.

704.20    at the fore]   At the head of the fore-royal mast.

710.40    shot-plugs and stoppers]   Wooden cones used to plug holes made by cannon balls, and rope devices used to strengthen or replace rigging damaged in action.

711.4    "Let . . . slung,]   Reinforce the attachment of the yards to their masts by means of ropes or chains to lessen the chance of their being shot away in combat.

711.31–32    "set . . . extenuate,"]   Cf. Shakespeare, *Othello*, V.ii.342–43: "Nothing extenuate, / Nor set down aught in malice."

711.37–38    'Execution . . . flag']   Execution Dock at Wapping in London where condemned sailors were executed. The yellow flag was run up to signal capital punishment aboard ship.

712.2–3    'that . . . last.' ]   Cf. Luke 13:30, Matthew 19:30, 20:16, Mark 10:31.

712.3–4    round-abouts]   Sailors, so called for their short jackets known as round-abouts.

714.9    heart]   A triangular block of wood, pierced with one large hole and attached to the end of a stay; by means of a lanyard passed through the hole, the tension of the stay can be adjusted.

715.9    clapp'd a stopper]   Literally, applied a restraining line to the anchor cable in order to prevent it from running out.

716.7    white line]   Untarred rope.

722.33    boat service]   The hazardous duty of attacking a hostile vessel or shore position by means of the ship's boats.

727.3    That sure,]   Cooper quotes the version of the text printed in the Second Folio (1632) of Shakespeare's plays. The authoritative First Folio (1623) lacks the word "sure."

740.33    "The fool . . . no God,"]   Psalms 14:1, 53:1.

740.36–39    "Gird . . . understanding."]   Job 38:3–4.

744.20    Corydon]   Traditional shepherd's name in pastoral poetry.

752.20    sheet-cable]   The hempen cable attached to the sheet-anchor, a large anchor used only in emergencies.

752.23    Flemish account]   An account that shows a deficit; in nautical usage, ship books that will not balance.

754.15    kept the land aboard]   Kept within sight of land.

756.14    two and thirty]   A ship that mounts thirty-two guns.

756.35    double-headed shot]   A projectile formed of two balls joined by a bar, used for destroying spars and rigging.

762.30    vang]   One of two ropes used to steady the mizzen gaff, extending from the peak to the aftmost part of the ship's quarters.

764.28    lifted]   Risen above the horizon.

765.5    Roman matron]   Not a matron, but the maiden Tarpeia, who, as a payment for her betrayal of Rome to the Sabines, asked them to give her what they had on their arms, meaning their golden bracelets. Instead, the Sabine warriors heaped their shields upon her, crushing her to death.

767.33    fly-away]   A mirage.

769.2    Irishman's hurricane]   A dead calm.

772.36–37    that cave . . . Aladdin]   In the tale "Aladdin; or, The Wonderful Lamp" in *The Arabian Nights*, Aladdin enters a cave and comes upon a grove of magical trees that bear as fruit large precious stones. Although the boy gathers some, he is ignorant of their value.

776.24    across our fore-foot.] On a course that will pass directly in front of us.

777.24    "The metal?—"] The aggregate weight of the shot thrown by the guns of a ship of war.

778.28    free towns] Lübeck, Hamburg, and Bremen, all of which had been leading members of the Hanseatic League.

780.10    broom . . . mast-heads!] The symbol of control of the English Channel, said to have been displayed by the Dutch admiral Maarten Harpertszoon Tromp (1598–1653) after his victory over the British fleet off Dungeness in 1652.

789.11    master] A commissioned officer ranking under the lieutenants of a ship of war and charged with the navigation and working of the vessel.

790.38    spunge] An instrument for cleaning out the bore of a cannon and extinguishing any lingering sparks there after each firing, usually made of a block of wood covered with sheepskin and attached to a length of stiffened rope.

797.27    First Lord] The head of the Board of Admiralty, the branch of government that superintends the Royal Navy.

797.38    posted] Promoted to the rank of full-grade captain.

797.38–39    guard-ship] A ship of war assigned to protect a harbor and oversee its maritime affairs.

798.30    quarter bill] The list of the battle stations of a ship of war together with the names of the officers and men assigned to those stations.

817.2    Let] "Bid" in *The Riverside Shakespeare* and some other editions of the play.

819.13    pull] A passage in a rowing-boat.

825.39    hooker] An affectionate name for a ship.

825.39    harpened-in] Drawn in toward the center of the ship by catharpings, ropes used to girt in the shrouds of the lower masts in order to tighten them and to give the lower yards more room to swing.

831.3    this fiend——] In Shakespeare, "this fiend of Scotland and myself."

831.28    Old Bailey] The criminal court of London.

843.29    a halberd] A promotion to the rank of sergeant.

844.4–5    stopped the grog of] Killed.

852.21–22   Spanish windlass]   A hand tool for tightening rope.

861.27   that Monarch]   Louis XVI, king of France 1774–92.

861.34–35   compelled . . . army]   Besieged at Yorktown by French and American armies, Lord Cornwallis capitulated on October 19, 1781.

862.18   tossed]   Thrown upward out of the oarlocks and raised perpendicularly on end.

CATALOGING INFORMATION

Cooper, James Fenimore, 1789–1851.
    Sea tales: the Pilot, the Red Rover.
    Edited by Kay Seymour House and Thomas L. Philbrick.

    (The Library of America ; 54)
    1. Sea stories, American. I. Title: The Pilot.
II. Title: The Red Rover. III Series.
PS1402      1991        813'.2—dc20        90–52923
ISBN 0–940450–70–4 (alk. paper)

*This book is set in 10 point Linotron Galliard,*
*a face designed for photocomposition by Matthew Carter*
*and based on the sixteenth-century face Granjon. The paper*
*is acid-free Ecusta Nyalite and meets the requirements for perma-*
*nence of the American National Standards Institute. The binding*
*material is Brillianta, a 100% woven rayon cloth made by*
*Van Heek-Scholco Textielfabrieken, Holland. The com-*
*position is by Haddon Craftsmen, Inc., and The*
*Clarinda Company. Printing and binding*
*by R. R. Donnelley & Sons Company.*
*Designed by Bruce Campbell.*

# THE LIBRARY OF AMERICA SERIES

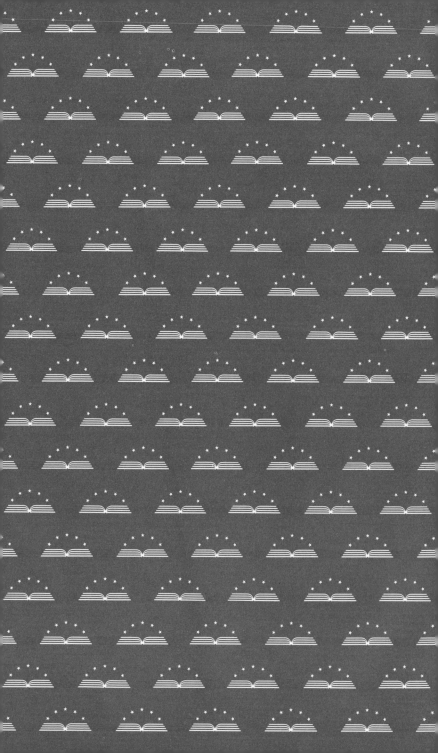